"If you loo

I dug at Ebon's fla

Wind tore at my j

master had taught.

"For Rodrigo!" Rus

"For Caledon!"

No time for more

Rust spurred Santr

sailed over the fallen

tore through his chest

Fostrow thundered

Form a line!"

I tugged gently on

for him to close. In a

the line.

Behind the fallen t

charge them head on

But Verein hadn't fin

men, and to our righ

I waved my javeli

width of the field, a

many of us . . .

"Feintuch is the real deal as a storyteller."

— *Internet Book Information Center*

ALSO BY DAVID FEINTUCH

THE SEAFORT SAGA

Midshipman's Hope
Challenger's Hope
Prisoner's Hope
Fisherman's Hope
Voices of Hope

DAVID FEINTUCH

THE STILL

WARNER BOOKS

A Time Warner Company

This is a work of fiction. Names, characters, places, and incidents are either the product of the author's imagination or are used fictitiously, and any resemblance to actual persons, living or dead, events, or locales is entirely coincidental.

Copyright © 1997 by David Feintuch
All rights reserved.

Aspect® name and logo are registered trademarks of Warner Books, Inc.

Warner Books, Inc., 1271 Avenue of the Americas, New York, NY 10020
Visit our Web site at
http://pathfinder.com/twep

W A Time Warner Company

Printed in the United States of America
First Printing: July 1997
10 9 8 7 6 5 4 3 2 1

Library of Congress Cataloging-in-Publication Data

Feintuch, David.
    The still / David Feintuch.
      p.   cm.
    ISBN 0-446-67285-8
    I. Title
PS3556.E436S75   1997
813'.54—dc21   97-7059
                                                      CIP

Book design by H. Roberts
Cover design by Don Puckey
Cover illustration by Keith Birdsong

THE STILL

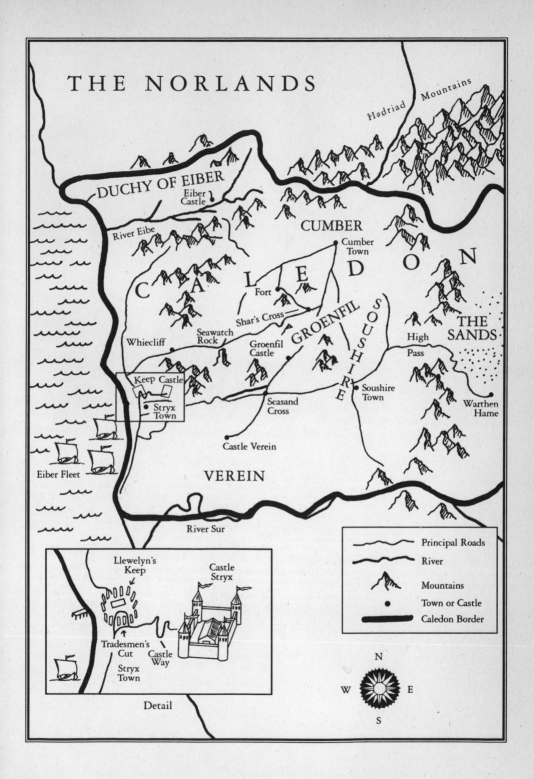

THE NORLANDS

DUCHY OF EIBER

Eiber
Castle

River Eibe

CUMBER

Cumber
Town

Hodriad Mountains

C A L E D O N

Fort

Shar's Cross

GROENFIL

SOUSHIRE

THE
SANDS

Seawatch
Rock

Whiecliff

Groenfil
Castle

High
Pass

Keep Castle

Seasand
Cross

Soushire
Town

Stryx
Town

Warthen
Hame

Castle Verein

Eiber Fleet

VEREIN

River Sur

Llewelyn's
Keep

Castle
Stryx

Tradesmen's
Cut

Castle
Way

Stryx
Town

Detail

Principal Roads

River

Mountains

Town or Castle

Caledon Border

N

W   E

S

Prologue

WHEN I WAS YOUNG, BEFORE A WASTING ILLNESS gripped her, Elena Queen of Caledon took me to the secluded vault that held the Vessels. I was barely twelve, and in the dank windowless corridor a nameless dread prickled my spine. I didn't want to think about our Power, or behold its implements.

Deep in the bowels of Castle Stryx, at the corridor's end, a smoky torch hissed and sputtered in a sconce. Brusquely, Mother dismissed Chamberlain Willem and the ever-present sentries.

The Queen withdrew a chain with two keys from her bosom. Facing the massive bronze door that barred the vault, she inserted each key into a recess so deep it swallowed her whole arm.

She paused, and a fleeting smile warmed her eyes. "Don't worry, Roddy. The locks won't eat my fingers."

"I didn't—I wasn't . . ."

"You hadn't heard? Perhaps it's best for now."

The second tumbler clicked; the door swung open. She ushered me into the vault.

Dusty oaken chests filled much of the chamber. I picked at the hasp of the nearest. "What's inside?"

"Leave it. We've not come to muse over keepsakes."

"How about this one?" I bounded across the cell. "What's that ewer? Why are these swords—"

She stamped her foot. "Stop racing about. Must you finger everything in reach?"

Sullenly, I threw myself on a trunk, but Mother settled on a dark walnut bench, patted the seat beside. "Rodrigo, never speak of what I show you."

I sat at her side. "I won't, not even to Rustin. By the True I swear."

Her hand shot out to cover my mouth. "Hush. You're too young for such vows."

"But Hester says . . ."

"I say." Abruptly she was Queen.

"Aye, madam." I made the short bow of assent. Still, pride coursed within. "I only meant to assure you—"

"And you have. But I include family, not just your playmates. Even Uncle Mar."

I shifted, impatient at her caution. "You said you'd show me the Vessels." Somewhere beyond the light, water dripped.

"Then pay attention. We ride this afternoon to Warthen's Gate, so I haven't much time. What do you see?"

My eyes darted to an ornate marble stand, on which a crimson pillow rested. Atop sat a gleaming pitcher. I recalled her whispered stories in the night. "Is that the Chalice?"

"Well said."

I jumped to my feet, peered at its luminous surface. "May I hold it?"

"No you'd better—"

"Please?"

She sighed. "For a moment. But carefully."

I took the ewer from its pillow, sat to examine it. "This pours the stillsilver."

"Yes." Her fingers brushed the damp hair at the nape of my neck. The tenderness startled me. Since my father died, she'd seemed ever more distant, and our quarrels had grown more fierce. Perhaps she was hardening me for the isolation of the throne. Perhaps she preferred my brothers. I never knew.

"Go on, Roddy."

I tried to concentrate. "You pour into the bowl. The Receiver."

"Receptor."

"Then it happens." I regarded the empty Chalice. "Show me."

Her laugh was brittle. "I can't." Her hand fluttered to the golden clasp in her hair.

"Please, Mother."

"What did I tell you about my Power?"

"That it's gone. But not for me. Show me how to use it."

"When the time nears."

"Later, always later." I stamped my foot. "Always you treat me as a child."

"As you are." Her tone cooled.

"Or perhaps you fear my betrayal!"

"Don't be a fool."

"I'll bet you showed Elryc, and he's just eight."

"Roddy, didn't I tell you the Power won't manifest until I die?"

"You love him more! You're planning to renounce me!"

Her slap stung. "That does it." She was on her feet. "Out!"

"But I only—"

"Now you'll go to Willem." Her voice was low, an omen I should have heeded earlier. "If your father saw you he'd knot his fists in shame. Renounce you? Don't remind me of it while you try my patience!" She shoved me from the vault, locked the bronze doors behind us. The tumblers clicked loudly as they fell into place.

"Madam, I pray thee . . ."

She strode down the corridor, a firm grip on my sleeve. Her guards fell in alongside. "It's too late for courtesy and high speech, Rodrigo. *When* will you learn to hold your tongue?" She swept me along. "To the Chamberlain, this very moment!"

Afterward, my rump smarting, I yearned for the solace of my comrade Rustin, in his family's keep that bestrode the harbor, but I was sent in haste to make ready for our journey through the hills to the Warthen of the Sands, Mother's distant vassal.

Uncle Margenthar, Mother's spokesman in matters of state, came along, as did his son Bayard and half our court. Were the Duke of Eiber to sweep down from the north, Castle Stryx would be ill-tended. But no mishap befell the realm.

The very day we returned I raced to tell Rustin the wonders I'd beheld. He presented me with a magnificent young stallion he'd trained, the best horse I'd ever seen, and I dissolved in tears.

Summer storms swept the granite battlements, Mother's peasants scythed wheat in the baking sun, and riding my glorious new mount through fields and town and rutted roads, I began to grow out of my childhood.

It was then I knew the torment.

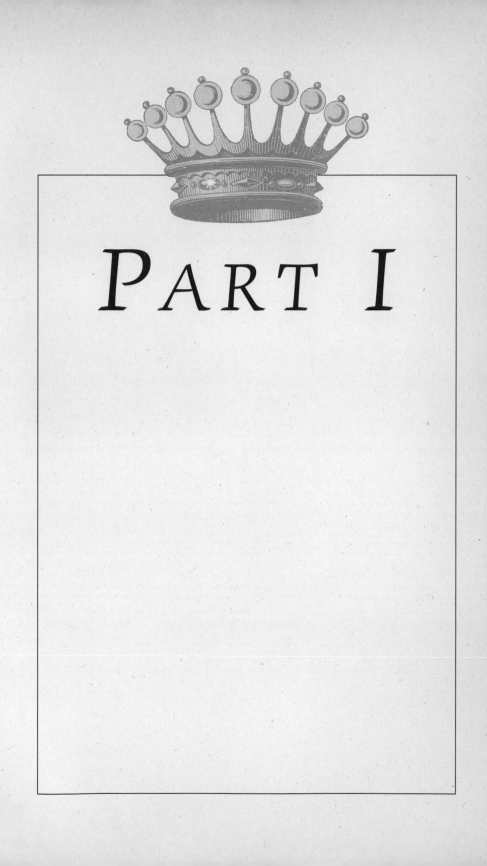

PART I

Chapter 1

THUNDER RUMBLED ACROSS THE RAMPARTS AND COBBLES of the keep. Gray sheets of summer rain reduced the courtyard of the donjon to an inland sea of mud that lapped at the battlements.

Safe within, I smoothed my damp hair and knocked at Mother's chamber, exhilarated from a long gallop to outrun the sudden summer storm. Below, Stryx harbor whipped into a froth and hurled whitecaps across the low shore road. Perhaps when the Still of Caledon was mine at last, I would choose my own weather, and ride free of care.

At Mother's iron-belted door, Nurse Hester met me with her customary scowl. "She's resting well. Say nothing to rile her, or I'll—" She subsided, wrinkling her nose at Ebon's sweat redolent on my leather jerkin. As always, Hester's speech was too free. She'd nursed me from infancy, as she had Mother before, and our rank held no awe for her.

"Hold your tongue, old woman." Then, quickly, before she could shrivel me with a fierce reply, "How is she?"

Her gnarled hand whipped round. I flinched, but she only waved a swollen knuckle under my nose. "Think you that lanky and long makes you a man, Rodrigo?" Her voice scratched like a blade on glass. "Courtesy marks a true nobleman, and grace!" With that, she hobbled to Mother's bedside, dabbed her dozing lady's forehead with a damp towel.

"My lady, the *boy* Rodrigo"—I reddened at Hester's emphasis—"answers your summons." As if in emphasis, thunder rumbled the windowpane.

Mother blinked, focused her troubled blue eyes on mine.

I bowed to Elena, Queen of Caledon. Mine was the informal bow, the house bow, scarce more than a nod, but required of me nonetheless. I blurted, "How do you feel?"

"Roddy." A smile eased creases worn by long months of pain. "Sit." She patted her plump featherbed.

"Madam, he'll soil the linens; he's come from that great stinking horse."

"Then have them changed; it's past time you let me sit by the window." Mother tapped the teal coverlet. Obediently, I perched at her side. Her brow wrinkled at the sway of the bed on its ropes. Hester muttered disapproval, but retired to the scarred plank table across the bedchamber.

I asked, "Do the herbs help?"

"I'm long beyond that." Mother's tone was cross. "As well you know."

"Lord Tannel said—"

"Elwyn Tannel is a fool, like all surgeons and physickers. If I didn't chew his dreadful lozenges he'd nag me to my grave faster than this disease of wasting." She grimaced. "Lord knows of what the tablets are made. Stable droppings and frog's bowels, or whatever Estland vogue holds sway this season."

I kneaded my knuckles, waiting.

She asked, "You rode with Rustin?"

"He was attending Llewelyn. Ebon and I raced almost to Whiecliff before the clouds gathered."

"With Elryc and Pytor?"

"No!" I grimaced. "I see enough of my brothers." If I let them, they'd follow me everywhere. Elryc, eleven, sniffed constantly, and Pytor whined more than any boy of eight should be allowed. They trailed me about the castle grounds, sometimes urging me to join their games, but often merely to see what I was about. Perhaps they even reported to some inquisitive noble of Stryx. We were none of us free from schemes, liaisons, intrigues of state.

Trust was for commoners, who had naught to forfeit.

"I met our outguard patrol, Mother. Tantroth remains in his hills; no sign that his folk approach." Not that we really expected him to lunge, yet.

Her voice gentled. "I'll try to give you time, Roddy."

She had so little time to give. I kept my expression hard, lest she and Hester think me a weak mewling youngsire.

Mother said, "Tantroth will wait, at least 'til I fall into unwakeable sleep and the family gathers to glean my last breath. The Norduke may covet our crown, but he's not fool enough to risk his head."

Our crown. I thrilled. As eldest son of Elena Queen, mine would be the inheritance, but I must ever be cautious. Until her death Mother had power to renounce me, and in that case, I were nothing. Despite our frequent harsh words, I'd never truly had reason to think she'd cast me down, but one treads lightly in the halls of kings.

Mother's voice dropped. I strained to hear over the steady drumbeat of rain on the ledge. "Roddy, concern yourself with more than Tantroth. On my death he'll strike for city and crown, but other hands crave the realm. With luck they'll thrust him back before turning on each other. Then, you—"

"Which lords would seize the throne?"

"Margenthar, Groenfil, half the earls of the realm. They—"

My tone dripped disdain. "What petty Powers have they to threaten Stryx? The bark of dogs?"

"Scorn not what you don't ken. Groenfil's gales topple oaks on his peasants' cribs, and Cumber could set our keep ablaze if the mood came upon him. Any of them would seize the kingdom, given—"

"But Uncle Mar is my godfather."

"Interrupt again, boy, and I'll send you to Willem!"

On the bedcover, out of Mother's view, my fist tightened. She kept me a child, or tried to, when I'd become a man.

Mother seized my wrist. Off balance, I nearly fell across her bosom. "Mar is your uncle by birth, and your godfather by maneuver." Her voice grated in wrath, whether at me or Uncle Mar, I knew not. "Yet first and always, he's Duke of Stryx, with sons of his own and ambition that burns. That's why his pledged troops are barred from Stryx. If you think his pledge of loyalty weighs against his aspiration, you're a fool!" She panted for breath.

Time to regain her respect. I raised an eyebrow. "Madam, do you mistake my inexperience for idiocy?"

It brought a pleased smile, as I knew my calm assurance would.

Her voice softened. "No, else I wouldn't waste my dying hours plotting with you." She patted my hand.

"Are you . . ." My voice shot into the upper register; I fought it down to a tenor. "Is it near that time?" It was all I could manage to hold her gaze.

"Not quite yet." She attempted a smile, but pain stabbed and turned it to a frown. "Perhaps I'll rally again. When you're eighteen, you'll be safe. Well, no one is ever truly safe, but with the Still . . ."

"I'm sixteen. What if—"

"Fifteen."

Two months weren't enough to matter. "What if I'm not yet eighteen when you . . ." I couldn't say it to her face.

"Rodrigo, we die. Your father Josip did, I'm working at it. You will too, in your own time. It's no disgrace. Say it!"

I sighed. "If I'm not eighteen when you die." Mother had her ways. I had to submit; else I might find myself slung across Chamberlain Willem's table, gasping from the blows of his strap.

She nodded her satisfaction. "Was that so hard? Now, once you gain the crown you'll have your wits to protect you. And hopefully, the Still." Her eyes darted to me. "Have you—?"

I shook my head, unwilling to trust my voice.

"Control yourself, at any cost."

"Mother!" I sought another topic, but not before my ears flamed and my humiliation was complete.

"Did you hear?"

I snarled, "How could I not?"

"To wield the Power, you must—"

"I know!" Could I for a moment forget, with her constant harping? I bounded to my feet. "Mother, I've appointments to keep. Good day. I hope you feel better."

Her voice snapped like a whip. "You have no leave!"

Fuming, I sat again.

"Immature child! Insolent whelp! Is it any wonder I fret?"

I swallowed. "I'm sorry, Mother." She could be pushed just so far, and without intent, I'd overstepped the line.

She regathered her breath. Then, "If I don't recover, even with the Still, the risk is great."

"Will they go for my life?"

"Yes."

My stomach churned, but I let nothing show in my face.

She added, "Not at first, I judge. A regency, so they'll have time to set their men in place. Later, a sudden accident, a flux of the intestines. Perhaps a stray arrow. The kingdom will pass into their hands."

"What should we do?"

A sigh. She lay back, her face gray and pained.

Old Hester, disregarding rank and propriety, tottered across the bedchamber, hauled me from the bed. "Say your farewells and begone to your stables. She needs rest."

I shook off the old crone's arm, but even I could see Mother was played out. "Good-bye, Mother." My tone was stiff, as befit a prince to his Queen.

Weary, drifting, she nodded, murmured something I could not hear. I made my bow, turned to leave. As the door creaked open her words came more clearly. "The Power. It is key to all. Be True and it will not fail."

Before I could respond, Hester shooed me from the room like an irate hen.

I strode past the rooms of Mother's maids in waiting to the iron-studded door that segregated the Queen's quarters from the body of the donjon. Slamming it behind me, I stalked to the great stone central stairs of Castle Stryx. No one was about. I perched sidesaddle on the wide walnut banister, slid down to the ground level of the keep.

In the lower hall a servant on a stool dug wax from a sconce; as I hurtled past he gave a startled yelp. Nonchalantly, I hopped off the rail, paused to look about as if to survey our citadel for the first time.

Here at the foot of the stairwell, one passed into a wide vaulted chamber that served as Castle Stryx's banquet hall and assembly place.

To the right of the massive stair, an entryway led to the vaulted offices where Mother's chamberlain, Willem of Alcazar, managed the business of the household and oversaw Griswold's stables, the cooks, and the various servants. In the opposite wing, Margenthar, Duke of Stryx, maintained his sumptuous quarters.

Uncle Mar. Mother's only brother. He had his own castle at Verein, but lived much of the year with us. From his apartments in Castle Stryx he conducted affairs of state, as Mother's surrogate.

I glanced back to the silent stairwell. Upstairs, the north wing housed our favored courtiers and staff such as Willem and Griswold. The south hall held the Queen's own chambers and above them, my own, my brother Elryc's, and the nursery where Pytor still dwelt.

The servant finished polishing the sconce. With a familiar slight bow of acknowledgment, he went about his business. I trotted down the half flight to the massive, carved outer door. The guard swung it open with proper deference. Ignoring him, I snatched a cloak from the cupboard to shield me from the downpour.

"Your brother asked for you, youngsire."

I glared. "Which one?" Why did the guard still call me "youngsire"? If I corrected him I'd only look petulant. Reluctantly I let it pass.

"Lord Elryc. He wanted—"

"I care not." I skipped down the stone stairs and crossed the rocky courtyard. At the outer wall, where the horsepath turned sharply to break the charge of an invader, a gatesman opened the small daily door set in the huge weathered portal of state. Holding my cloak tight, I left the grounds.

Castle Stryx. Set against the high cliffs of the Estreach, it was accessible in force only by Castle Way, or above from the rocky foothills that sloped from cliffs to our ramparts.

I strode down the hill toward the city. The rain was abating, but not soon enough. I'd be soaked ere long.

Thinking of Mother's admonishments, I snorted with disgust. Of course the Still wouldn't fail, were I True. That was its nature. So I'd been taught for as long as I could remember.

Great kingdoms possessed great Powers, small realms only minor encant.

Each Power had its own properties. When carried into battle, the Rood of Norland lent our northern neighbors ominous strength. The White Fruit of Chorr was said to make whoever ingested it forever a servant, and secured for the King of the Chorr the loyalty of his intimates. In Parrad, the very trees could be made to speak. The Powers followed crown and land, inseparably. Within every kingdom it was so. Our vassal earls themselves had some small Powers; Lady Soushire's ire spoke to dogs, and drove them to rage.

Our own endowment was the Still. Of little use at war, it nonetheless had its merit. Carefully wielded, it was said to bestow some degree of foresight. And Mother said it embodied the age-old wisdom of the rulers of Caledon. Just how, she'd not made clear.

How would I feel, when at last it was mine to wield? I shivered. I couldn't know until Elena Queen was gone, and despite the Powers I'd gain, I dreaded that day.

Perhaps even after Mother's death I'd not know the Still. The Power was conferred with the crown, and it wasn't certain I'd live to wear it.

I bent, picked up a small stone, and flung it up the hill. A slim figure in cloak and hood ducked behind a tree. I snarled, "Walk with me, lout, or run to your nurse, but don't skulk behind me, sniffling!"

Sheepish, my brother Elryc came forth, a forearm raised lest I concealed another stone. "Let me go with you." At eleven, his voice still piped. His limp brown hair was cut as if a bowl had been laid over his head.

My voice was sharp. "I suppose Pytor's just past the bend?"

"He's at fencing." We all had our lessons. Even I, who no longer needed them.

I grunted. One shadow was less bothersome than two, and Mother would be annoyed if Elryc complained again. "Come, if you must." I set forth down the hill.

"Where to?"

"Rustin." My tone was curt.

"Why not send for him?" My friend Rustin, son of Llewelyn, Householder of Stryx, was a nobleman in his own right. His House was autonomous and no fief. But nonetheless Rust would still have eagerly answered my call.

"Too many eyes watch, near the castle."

Elryc sniffed. "As if there were fewer in the city."

I glanced at him with new respect. "Well said. You learn."

"What are you and Rustin up to, that you don't want watched?"

"Talk. Whatever." Sometimes a young lord wanted to be by himself, or with his own kind. Elryc nodded as if he understood. We trudged along the muddy path.

The City of Stryx nestled at the foot of the winding supply road, called Castle Way, that twisted upward from the wharfs toward the castle gate. Tradesmen who struggled with loaded carts and sweating oxen cursed Castle Way's narrow turns and steep banks. No matter; our concern wasn't their convenience, but our security. The Norland was but two days sail from our harbor, and Hriskil's hostile ships had more than once scudded into the bay, bristling with pikemen and shieldbearers.

The midsummer sun battled with the persistent drizzle. I considered abandoning the road, crashing through the underbrush, sliding down the steep hillside. Less distance, but more work, and I'd muddy my breeks. On a drier day, without Elryc, I'd walk by way of Besiegers' Pond. A shallow pool, hidden by brush, it lay but a few dozen paces off the road. Oft I lounged on its banks beside the inviting still waters, and thought private thoughts.

"What did Mother tell you?" Elryc plodded beside me.

"That I'm to have you thrown in the cells, the moment I'm King."

He started with alarm, but realized I couldn't be telling truth. Sullen, he muttered, "I hope you lose the Power!"

I jerked him to the side of the road, flung him against the rocky shoulder. "So says my brother?" I raised my arm.

"Don't, Roddy!"

I punched him in the chest; he squealed his pain. He hadn't much flesh between skin and bone.

"The brother who begged me to hide him from Uncle Mar, the day you poured wine into his boot?" I jabbed him again. "Lose the Power? What would come of you, little one? Would you be heir, or a corpse thrown in the gutter alongside mine?"

"Stop or—I'll tell!"

I cuffed him again for good measure, let him slide sobbing to the soggy ground, knowing it wasn't a good day for the Queen to hear I'd lost my temper.

I crouched, waiting while he wiped his tears. "Did I say you'd learned, Elryc? I was wrong. Hold your feelings tight. What when I'm King? How, if I remember this day, and hold it against you?"

His breath came in a shudder. "You won't." I glared, but his reddened eyes rose and held mine. "You bully me and make me cry, but you won't really hurt me. You never have."

"Fool." I scuffed at his knee with my toe. "Come along, or I'll leave you bawling in the dirt."

He got to his feet. "About the Power—"

"Don't start again." I moved on, and he scurried to follow.

"I don't really want you to lose it. But what of the True? You lied to me, Roddy."

"That doesn't count." A moment's doubt, which I resolutely quenched. "Not between us."

"You're sure?"

"Mother told me." Another lie. I fell silent, before I ruined myself utterly.

Chapter 2

THE WEEK PASSED QUIETLY. I VISITED MOTHER, ONCE with my brothers, then alone. She seemed less ill.

Meanwhile, preparations were under way for the meet of our Council of State. Duchess Larissa rode in from Soushire; the other members were expected anon. To escape the hubbub I waited until Elryc was at lessons, sternly bade little Pytor stay behind, and crossed the stony courtyard to the stables.

Kerwyn the groomsman bent into the half bow, that of a household servant to his masters. "An hour, my lord. Ebon's at his oats, and Genard is combing him."

The afternoon was young and I had no errands, but I stamped my foot with irritation at the delay. "I'm ready now."

"Ebon is not." Kerwyn gave an apologetic shrug. "Truly, my lord, Griswold is most insistent that the horses be fed."

"Bring my mount!" At times, servants were impossible.

"If my master heard, it would cost me a day's wage—"

"Imps take your wages!" I unknotted my pursestring, fished out a silver pence, flicked it onto the straw. "I'm your master. Bring Ebon!"

Kerwyn bit his lip, bent for the coin, nodding. "A moment, my lord." He disappeared through the tall double doors to the inner stable.

I paced, fuming. Palace freemen recited petty rules and instructions, forgetting whom they were supposed to serve. In reality, we, the House of Caledon, served them. Vast sums from our treasury supported fools like the lazy, argumentative stablehand I'd sent away.

Muttering, I reknotted my purse, tied it to my fraying belt rope. In a gesture of munificence I'd thrown to the floor a half month of my stipend for sundries, and the Chamberlain would merely laugh were I to ask for more.

The door opened. I glanced over my shoulder, expecting the stableboy, leading Ebon. Instead, I met the stern eyes and graying beard of Griswold, Master of the Stables. "How may we serve you, youngsire?"

I flushed at the rebuke. Were he pleased with me, it would have been, "my lord."

"I came for Ebon."

"So Kerwyn said. He isn't ready."

"He's mine to ride when I wish!"

Griswold pursed his lips, considering. Then, "After you take a horse, there's none to stop your killing him. Here in stables, they're mine to protect. You can't feed him a bag of oats and then—"

"That's for me to say!" What these folk needed was a firm hand.

He sighed. "Very well. I'll tell Queen Elena you overruled me."

I stopped short. "Griswold, there's no need—"

"She's my mistress. I must."

I swallowed. "She's ill. I don't want her disturbed." His stern visage didn't waver. "Very well, I'll wait."

"Good." He opened his hand. The silver glinted. "Stablehands are paid well enough; no need to spoil them. This is a month's wages."

I reached for my coin. "That was only for—"

His hand snapped shut. "Kerwyn didn't earn it, so he won't keep it. But you gave it away, so it's no longer yours."

I held fast the shreds of my temper. "Neither did you earn it, sir."

"True. It'll go to the Chamberlain, with an explanation."

"Imps take you, Griswold!" Chamberlain Willem would tell Mother, and she'd have him close his purse to me for a month if not more.

"Yes, youngsire, you've always had a temper."

"Don't do this!" My cheeks flamed.

"You do it to yourself. If you'd be our King, learn the art of persuasion. At least pretend to have patience. Exhibit grace."

I forced the words through unwilling lips. "I'm sorry, Griswold." The gall of a servant, to lecture me.

"Too easily said." The old man turned, passed through the door, swung it half closed behind him. "Unless . . . you'd like time to consider the fix you've put me in?"

I knew that he knew he had me. In despair I asked, "How?"

"Comb Ebon yourself." That wasn't so bad. As we passed through the gate he added gently, "And a few stalls need cleaning. Time for an energetic lad to reflect, while he busies himself."

I cursed long and fluently, but without voice. Petulantly, I followed. A day of revenge would come.

Late in the afternoon, in foul temper, I rode Ebon down the trail as fast as was safe. Rust would no doubt be within his father's stronghold that guarded the harbor. If not, Stryx was not so large I couldn't find him.

At the foot of Castle Way the road passed through a formidable gate in the walls of Llewelyn's keep. Another gate, near the shore, released traffic to a seaside road that passed through town.

The arrangement of road and keep would force an invading army to subdue Llewelyn's stronghold before attacking the hill to the castle. Over time, tradesmen's wagons had bypassed the keep by driving through an adjoining field, but even the awkward Tradesmen's Cut was well within arrow reach of the keep's high walls.

I had word sent to Rustin. Of course, the gatekeepers dared not hold me waiting like a commoner. Within the sprawling keep, I paced Ebon slowly along the garden path.

Rustin loped to meet me. "Rodrigo!" His smile was framed by a mop of curly red hair.

"Rust!" I was almost giddy with relief. Rustin's moods changed like the summer breeze. At times, we'd be giggling over some trivial incident, when his face would darken abruptly, and all joy would vanish from his voice. It was best then to leave until his good humor returned. When I'd sought him with Elryc, a few days past, I'd given up after an hour and trudged back up the hill.

Still, at seventeen, two years older than I, Rust was my closest comrade. I hesitated to say "friend." A Prince of Caledon dared have no friend.

In the presence of his family we adopted semi-formal manners. In their company he was accustomed to give me the bow of intimacy, that nod of the head and the so-slight movement of the back. But, secluded in the orchard, we'd sprawl easily in the soft cool grass, and he would hear out my confidences, and offer his own.

He knew how I felt about my uncles, about the earls of the realm. He'd heard which lessons I liked and which I could barely abide. Heraldry, for example. Why in Lord of Nature's name should a young royal have to study the marks on shields and banners? We had clerks for that folderol.

Today, we settled ourselves in his bedchamber on the third floor of the keep. He threw himself across a billowy divan; I crossed my legs in a thick, rough-carved cherrywood chair. I told him of my encounter with obstinate old Griswold. Rust said little, but snickered when I told how I'd been made to clean the stables.

I glared. "Great consolation you give." Still, I felt better for the telling.

"Prince Rodrigo the stableboy!" Rust's chest shook with a silent spasm.

"You mock me?" I scrambled to my feet, hand momentarily brushing my dagger.

"Oh, sit, dunce. Laugh at yourself before others do. Then they'll have no need!"

Nonsense, of course. But, grumbling, I bore it, and let him coax me back to my seat. Rust was the only one I could talk with about Tantroth, Duke of Eiber. There was no doubt of our family's position in that regard; everyone, including the uncles, expected Rust's father Llewelyn to defend his keep and the city or die in the attempt, and there'd be no forgiveness should Llewelyn falter.

I led the talk in a roundabout manner, so Rust wouldn't know my concern. We spoke first of clothing, and after a time I mentioned the bright dyes for which Eiber was famous. "They're fitting me for a cloak of Eiber orange," I said. Then, casually, "I suppose I should bid them hurry, lest the supply is interrupted."

"How? By war?"

"It's always possible."

Rust pondered. "They say Eiber bristles with war implements, and Tantroth seeks an excuse to use them. Just a year ago he seized the Isle of Malth under some silly pretext."

"And started a blood-feud with the Norlanders, who claim it."

"He keeps a full-time army, you know. Imagine armed men who never return to their crops. A wonder his whole earldom doesn't starve. Of course with such a horde he's in no danger of falling. The dye trade should be safe."

"Unless he wars on a second front."

Rust leaned back, crossed his arms behind his head. "Ah, why didn't you say so?" A gentle amusement was in his eyes. "Yes, he'll attack us, when the time is right. At least, that's what Father says."

I listened.

"He'll try for what he's always wanted, Roddy. You'll have to face it."

"Imps take his grandfather, anyway." I kicked at a pillow.

It was ancient history. First came Varon of the Steppe, who wrested Caledon and Eiber from Cayil of the Surk, and held them as fiefdoms. The son of his second marriage was Rouel, grandfather of Tantroth, the Duke of Eiber. But Varon's son by his first marriage was Tryon, my mother's father.

On Varon's death the Steppe collapsed, overrun by the fierce Norlanders. Tryon seized Caledon, the most prosperous province, and was able to hold it even without benefit of the Still. His half brother Rouel, who seized Eiber, claimed Caledon was his by will of their father.

Over a generation's time the Seven Wars decided the issue in our favor. After Tryon died, Mother was able to wield the Still, which balanced Eiber's Cleave that sundered friends and allies. Now, the descendants of Rouel were the Nordukes, who held Eiber, in theory, as a vassalage of Caledon.

"Curse them all you wish," said Rust. "It won't help Elena hold the realm."

"If only she had the . . ." My voice trailed off.

We almost never spoke of the Power.

"Yes, it would help." A quick grin. "But then you wouldn't be among us."

A soft knock at the door forestalled my reply. "It's me, Sir Rustin. I had time before supper." The door opened; a pretty little wench with russet hair peered in, hands twisting at her apron. "I'm so sorry! I—I mean—forgive me!" She glanced round in confusion, curtsied, and fled.

I growled, "What was *that* all about?"

Rustin shrugged. "Chela. She helps in the kitchen." Under my gaze his cheeks reddened.

"Why would she—oh!"

His words came in a rush. "She's just—we're not particularly . . ."

"It's nothing to me," I said, fighting for composure. "You're grown." Casually, I stood. "Well, I have business to attend. See you another day." I escaped to the stairs, rushed out to the stable.

By the time I'd unknotted Ebon's bridle, Rust had caught up to me. "I'm sorry she burst in." His hand fell on my arm. "Wait."

I shook him off. My voice was tight. "Another time." I flung up a leg.

He caught me before I could mount. Ebon whinnied in alarm. "I'm sorry, Rodrigo. It must be hard for you, never having—"

I swung a knotted fist, and knocked him to the straw-scattered floor.

Rust lay on the planking, half-dazed.

"Don't speak of it," I said. "Ever."

Hard for me? He couldn't possibly imagine.

I was near sixteen, sported a faint moustache, tall almost as a man. The castle servants, young visiting cousins, my town companions, and, for all I knew, my little brother, rutted like stallions, while I writhed alone in the damp sheets of my chamber.

I could not lie with a woman.

"Roddy, I—"

I howled, "Shut thy mouth!" I clutched at Ebon.

Not that I was physically unable. Were I impotent, I'd be spared the frenzies of desire, the sticky sheets, the unbearable humiliation. But I must withhold my yearning.

Prince Rodrigo, heir presumptive to the throne of Caledon, must remain a virgin.

Else he could not wield the Still.

My vision blurred, I clawed blindly for the saddle. A sob. My own. I swung up my leg to mount.

A lithe form hurtled across the floor, hauled me from my steed, toppled me to the dung-specked straw. We rolled and thrashed. I pummeled Rustin's arms, his chest, his face, until at last he pinned me helpless under his legs. "You'll listen," he grated. "As we are friends, by the Lord you will listen!"

"Get off! I'll have your life!" I bucked and kicked. "Mother will—"

"Oh, stop your nonsense!" His palm lashed out in a slap that spun my head and rang against the rafters.

I squawked. "It's treason to lay hand on—" I faltered, as he raised his hand again.

"Stop your foolery! Think you Elena Queen of Caledon cares if two youngsires tussle in the hay, as we have for years? Fah!" He flung a loose tuft of straw at my face. I blinked, unhurt. Rustin rolled to one side, releasing me. "Roddy, I've known for years how miserable your need makes you. Never do you speak of—"

I aimed a kick at his side, which he avoided by a dexterous twist. Again, he swarmed atop me, pinning my shoulders. His strong fingers seized my jaw, held it still. "You'll listen, or I'll stuff this hay down your throat!" He snatched up a handful, waved it in my face. "By the Lord of Nature, I will have my say!" His eyes blazed.

I sobbed in frustration, but knew better than to try to break free. When Rustin's temper was well and truly ignited, he was a formidable adversary. After a time, I lay quiet. "Have your way."

"Your word, that we will not fight, and you will hear me."

I had no choice. I nodded. He rolled aside, helped me to my feet.

"We've horse dung all over us." He wiped his knees. "Let's wash and change. Then we'll talk."

I followed him to the well, where we poured icy water on our leggings and shirts, until the worst of the mess was rinsed. Then, soggy and shivering, we ran up the stairs to his chamber and shucked off our soaking clothes outside his door for a servant to gather.

Inside, naked as I, he tossed me a towel and pawed through a trunk while I dried myself. He found clothes for himself, and dug to the bottom of the chest for his discarded, smaller garments. "These will do for now."

I stole a glance at his parts while we dressed. Rustin had always been bigger than I. Hair adorned his chest, while I had none.

He sat me in a chair, pulled up another across. "I was four, when first I remember my father taking me to the castle. Even from the safety of his shoulder, it seemed immense, except for you, on your stool at

Elena's skirts. Then, you were barely two. We've been friends ever since. Why hide your grief from me?"

"Rustin, I beg you, don't." A wave of shame.

"Aye, I'll do the talking; you promised to listen, not to speak. You think I haven't seen how hard it was for you? When you were twelve, and your cousin Bayard began to moon over Lady Agora, speaking of her without cease until we wanted to plug our ears, I saw your expression for the first time. You stopped playing with Bayard then, and haven't spoken to him since."

I shifted, tried to look as if he talked of things that mattered not.

He studied me, gauged his words. "As each of our friends found a girl's company, you withdrew from him because you couldn't do likewise. I was the only one you didn't abandon."

I yearned to shut my ears, but I could not. I'd given my word.

"Surely you know Chela wasn't my first. I'm sorry she came to my room. I've tried not to rub it in your face that I could satisfy myself, while you are barred."

"I beg you, Rustin—"

"Speak of it! Before it destroys you!"

Frightened, I drew back. Rustin hunched forward in his oaken chair, eyes locked to mine. The silence lengthened. I waited for him to urge me further, but he did not.

An eon passed.

Abruptly my words gushed forth in a torrent, as if spring floods had broken a decrepit dam. "I'm more than a boy, though everyone treats me as one. Mother threatens a strapping, and even old Griswold considers me a child. But I have a man's feelings, and a man's"—my voice quavered—"needs. Even horses do it in the pasture. Why should I, of all the kingdom, be the only one denied?"

"For the—"

"I know. The Still. The precious force of Caledon. Someday I'll wield our Power, if I haven't sullied myself first." I hesitated; this was as much as ever we'd spoken of things sacred and arcane. "And from all I hear, I'll need the Power. Our line is not so secure after two generations that rivals won't rise."

"You have many. Some closer than you think."

"Uncle Mar? He's loyal." Rust, friend or no, was not family, and I couldn't speak to him of betrayal from within. "Someday, I'll mount the throne. The longer Mother lives the greater my chance. But—" My voice cut short.

He waited. Then, "Yes, Rodrigo?"

I hadn't known I would say it. I hadn't ever been aware I'd had the thought. "The longer Mother lives, the heavier my burden. Can you imagine how that makes me feel? I love Mother, and ought to, but she's been ill for years, everyone knows even if no one admits so. When she's gone, I'll have the kingdom, and for a while I'll be able to wield the Power, until I judge it safe to put it aside for my heirs."

Rustin was silent, his gaze like a confessional urn into which I poured the libation of my soul.

"But while she lives, I can't bear the lust! I wait, loving her truly, unable to stand the nights, resenting her life that locks me ever longer into chastity." I could not meet his eye.

"Roddy." The words came soft. "My friend."

He unmanned me, but the cup of my despair was not yet emptied. I said, "Chastity, Rustin. But not abstinence." I spun my chair to face the empty hearth, my face scarlet. "I make love with myself, as a child."

Blessedly, Rustin left me time to compose myself, to make my breath again steady, to dry my face. Then he approached. His hand fell gently on my shoulder. "Tell me of the Power."

Gratefully, I turned my chair to face the setting sun, cleared my throat. "The Still of Caledon. The Receptor's a sort of bowl, made of white gold, set with emeralds. There's a Chalice, with a stopper, kept full of stillsilver. One pours the liquid into the Receptor. Almost instantly, it becomes Still."

For a moment I debated whether to reveal the rest, but Rustin already held my soul; all he could steal was the crown. "You put your hands over the Still, say the words of encant. Mother says it's as if a great peace comes over you, and the world slides away. Then you know the Power." I shivered.

"Who may use it?"

"The King. He who has been crowned. No one else. And perhaps, not even he." I tried to make light of the oppression. "I have to be True, you see. Sometimes that's even harder than the other."

Rust crouched on his bed. "No one can live free of lies, Roddy. It doesn't seem possible. Can you never tell an untruth to anyone, about anything?"

"I hope not, or it's too late." My smile was unsteady. "I'm not sure it has to do with lies. It may be about keeping my word. Mother simply says the wielder must be True, and she'll speak no more of it. The other, she reminds me of incessantly. It's a miracle she doesn't have me put in—" On my lips was a jest about a chastity belt, but my dread of it was too real to mention.

Rustin nodded, his eyes sorrowful. "The wielder must be virgin."

"As was Mother when she was crowned. Only when she vanquished our enemies and held Stryx secure in her hand did she send for Father. The marriage was prearranged." I'd loved him with all my soul, until one night he lay down to sleep and did not wake. I was nine.

Rust stirred awkwardly. "Roddy, are there ways you can—I mean, you can do things with a girl aside from . . ."

"Not even those." My tone was firm.

"But if it's all right by yourself . . . that seems unfair."

I snorted. "It's not a constraint I'd have asked."

"What about . . ." He blushed. "Other than girls?"

"You'd have me take a lover? Perhaps a cook's boy, wriggling in my sheets until I satisfied myself, sniggering afterward to his kitchenmates? Or a stablehand? Leave me *some* pride."

"So you're alone."

"Always." It came as a whisper.

A silence, in which I heard the cry of gulls from the harbor.

"You see . . ." I peered out the narrow window, past the iron arrowguard. "One by one you drop away, to take the life of a man. It's hard to bear, when those we grew up with are already giggling behind my back. When—"

"No one giggles beh—"

"Castor did, to Michel, when he thought I couldn't hear. We were playing roundfield ball, in the pasture. 'Think he'd even know where to put it?' Aurrgh!" I sat, astonished that I'd spoken aloud the words with which Castor had mortified me, a year past.

"So that was why." He sighed.

"May I be struck dead if I ever consort with either of them again!"

I stared at the stone tiles. "Each day it's worse. Bayard is married, and Kronin. They've made babies, and they're no older than I. What when I'm seventeen, or twenty? My whole court will have the laugh of me! 'Virgin King Roddy, who's never known a woman's embrace.' Jeers like Castor's, only twentyfold."

Rustin sighed, rose from the bed. "Come, let's find dinner. You'll stay the night, and tomorrow I'll ride home with you."

"Better I go now."

"Please. For my sake." Without waiting for answer, he crossed to the door. "We'll send word to the castle. By morning your clothes will be dry, and the Queen need never learn you attacked me like a common ruffian."

I'd have thrown a boot, but he was already gone. Meekly, I followed.

Downstairs, Rustin poked his head into the kitchen, bussed the fat perspiring cook, wheedled her out of some meat still warm from the gatekeepers' dinner. The woman bade Chela throw a few ears of corn into a pot, and a few minutes later Rustin and I bore our bronze trays into the garden for a secluded supper.

Our chat came more easily, away from the bedchamber. We talked of Tantroth, of the crown, then of boyish things. Afterward, we paid our respects to Rustin's parents Joenne and Llewelyn, went outside to kick his sewn leather ball back and forth until the light was gone. Then we made ourselves ready for bed.

Rustin's room was big enough for us both. The servants had made up a divan, the same one on which I'd slept often enough over the years, while we'd grown from childhood to youth.

I lay quietly, in the light of the guttering candle. In this chamber where my shame had been revealed, my earlier vexation was rekindled. I tossed and turned, until at last I raised myself on my elbow.

I saw Rustin was awake.

"Those matters I spoke of, when I was upset." My voice was low and cold. "If you repeat them to a living soul, I'll kill you. This I so swear." I blew out the candle, turned away onto my side.

Silence, then a long sigh. "Rodrigo, at times you're an ass."

An hour passed, minute by excruciating minute, while I pretended to sleep. The effort to hold myself still was nearly intolerable.

At last, the sound of a striking flint. The candle flickered. "Stand."
His voice was a command.

I lay still, but my covers were snatched away. For a moment I lay
curled in nothing but my breechcloth.

"Out of bed." Rustin's tone bore no refusal. I complied, wondering
if he'd strike me. At the very least I'd let myself in for one of his prolonged sulks.

But I saw no anger in his gaze. He glided closer until we were face-
to-face.

Rust was inches taller. His fair unclothed skin shone in the candlelight. For a moment I was near panic, thinking he intended an amorous
advance, out of charity. Then, truly, I'd have to kill him. Not for the
advance, but for the pity.

"My prince."

I met his eyes, startled.

"I am Rustin, son of Llewelyn, Householder of Stryx. Our rank is by
ancient right and from time immemorial, and I am vassal to no man."

I nodded, my lips dry. I knew this, as who did not?

"Rodrigo, I acknowledge you as lawful and rightful heir of the
House of Caledon. I shall accept no other while you live, save that your
mother the Queen renounce you."

I gaped, incapable of a word.

He dropped to a knee. "I pledge myself to thee as vassal, from this
moment unto our deaths or my release. I shall serve and protect thee
with honor. I do swear my loyalty, and vow I shall take no other as my
liege save thee." In the age-old gesture, he touched his palm to my
chest, and bowed his head.

For a moment I stood transfixed, almost in dread. He'd proffered
me his life, his independence. Then, slowly, my hand dropped to his
forehead. "Rustin, son of Llewelyn, I accept thee as vassal, and pledge
by my honor that I shall do thee and our House no shame."

I released him. Dazed, I fell back on my bed. He sat alongside me,
fluffed my quilt as tenderly as a nursemaid, covered me.

I caught his arm. "Rust, I know I'm not—that is . . ." I forced myself
to meet his eyes. "Am I worth so much?"

"You're foolish at times." His smile was gentle. "More often than I'd
wish. And selfish. Thoughtless. Yet you're more. That day the drunken

guard came at me in the tavern, and you leaped to defend me, with nothing but a tankard. And the day I gave you Ebon . . ."

"Yes?" I recalled the foolish tears I'd shed.

"I saw a boy who could be King." His hand flicked out, stroked my brow.

"But by swearing fealty . . . you gave me everything."

"I saw you need it."

My scorn dripped. "This afternoon, by my shame?"

"No, my lord. Tonight, by your fear." He sighed. "Now, perhaps, you can allow yourself a friend."

He settled in his bed.

Much later, I said into the night, "Rustin, I'm so sorry." There was no reply. I snuggled into my pillow and, swallowing a sob mixed with joy, slept like a child.

At daybreak Rustin made clear by his silence that he preferred to be left alone. Dressed and combed, I trotted downstairs to the airy hall, chatted with his mother Joenne while a servant brought breakfast. I downed eggs and soft cheese, and the weak wine mixed with water that made a common day-drink among the nobility.

"Hallo, Mother." Rustin crossed the flagstoned hall, his sandals clicking against the tiles.

She beckoned him for a quick kiss, held his face for swift scrutiny. "You kept each other up again?"

"I slept well." His tone was cool. He poured apple-wine, downed the draught in one swallow. "I'm going with Roddy to the smithy."

I said, "No, I'll ride home." He seemed to take me for granted, and I couldn't allow that.

He turned on me. "Your clothes haven't dried yet, you lout. Would you ride in rags, like a nomad?"

Even his mother was taken aback.

He sighed, his brow clearing in an instant. "Oh, come along, Roddy. We'll see about my new sword, and if the sun lasts you'll have your clothes dry."

Still irritated, I plucked at my tunic. "In these rags?"

He crossed the hall, tugged gently at my forearm. "Sorry for my temper. Please come. I want your advice."

It was why I could seldom refuse him. I nodded to Lady Joenne, followed him meekly to the gate. At times, I understood why my young brother Elryc followed me about.

The keep that Llewelyn guarded lay athwart the harbor, a forbidding stone stronghold that served as the first barrier to invasion by sea. A stone seawall jutted into the bay, cleaving the harbor in twain. This was to make more difficult the task of an invading army intent on siege. They'd have to struggle neck deep or worse, to encamp north of the keep's walls.

Because Llewelyn's keep occupied the northern end of the harbor, the town of Stryx had no choice but to spread southward. We ambled along the sunny road that ran along the lapping sea.

Along much of the coast, waves met only unyielding cliffs, but at Stryx the cliffs fell back a thousand paces to where our castle sat high over the town. From my room, I had view of a rocky shoreline that wound along a wide inviting bay.

We ambled along the shore road. Rust squinted in the bright morning light. "Until you're eighteen, you need your uncle Mar's favor to be crowned. If you go about like an unwashed ragamuffin—"

"You're not my father!"

"No, my prince. Your vassal, and sworn to protect you. Even from yourself."

"Such service I don't need." But I said it lightly. I really ought to take more time choosing an unstained cloak, and make sure my breeches matched my blouse.

Even were we blind, we'd have located the smithy from the clanking within, or the sooty breath of coal in the air.

The swordsmith was a runty fellow, not at all the giant one might expect. Beside him, working the bellows with a grin, stood a huge muscled boy who served as prentice.

"Ah, Rustin of the keep. Your sword's on the rack. Not done yet. Two more dippings, I imagine, perhaps three."

"That long?" Rustin sounded forlorn. He plucked the weapon from its rack, hefted it, handed it to me with eyebrow raised. I made a few passes, as if testing.

"Take it now, if you want dross. A work of beauty wants time."

"You've had weeks."

"And I have other orders. Margenthar refitted half his cavalry this year. Those dangling iron stirrups your guards catch their foot in when they ride." He snorted. "As if mounted spearmen decide a battle. Newfangled nonsense, like all the Norberk fashions, but who am I to argue? I'm just a poor, simple—"

The bellows boy winked. Haughtily, I put him in his place by ignoring his effrontery.

Rust growled, "You're the best swordsmith in Stryx, but you charge as if you're the finest in the Estreach." Rustin's tone was polite, but had an edge. "I've already laid out the expense. When may I have my sword?"

"Um . . . three days hence?" The smith took up a hammer, donned his glove to pull a bar from the fire.

I scowled at a hayroll, chopped at a haystalk that towered above the rest.

Rust turned to me. "What think you, Rodrigo?"

"A few days don't seem too—"

"Of the sword, dolt."

"Oh." How in blazes should I know? A sword was a sword, in my hand. Falla of Toth, our master of swordplay, droned about the merits of the long blade versus the epee, the weight, the haft, the grip, the—

"Well?"

"It seems a touch out of balance," I said, guessing wildly. "Perhaps too heavy in the—"

"Precisely!" The smith dropped his bar on the anvil, took the sword from my hand. "Fine discrimination, my lord. The blade is a touch overbalanced as yet for the haft." He fussed at the sword, flung open the window to hold it in the light. "You see there, where the jewels will be set? And here, the silver? Gold would be better, but the expense . . . It takes a fine hand to discern such a trifling imbalance."

I nodded politely, saying nothing. I'd meant to say the haft was too heavy for the blade, not the reverse.

"Three days, then. I can't wait." Rustin's eyes shone. "Thank you." He bid the smith good day, and we made our way out of the sweltering shop. "You see why I wanted your advice? I'd have never noticed in a million—"

A clatter of horses. We stepped aside, pressed against the wall of the smithy.

A troop of Llewelyn's guard flashed past. Someone pointed: "There he is!" They reined in so abruptly that one mount reared, pawing the air. Rustin, vigilant, thrust himself in front of me.

The captain dismounted, hurried toward me, his hand well clear of his sword, and my tension eased. "My lord, you're to return to the castle at once."

So Mother had noticed my absence. Although Rustin had sent word that I was spending the night, actually it was I who was supposed to inform her. Well, she demanded I ask, not merely inform, but . . .

Above, the distant call of a trumpet. I ignored it, aware of the smith's boy who'd come out from his bellows, of windows thrown open and faces peering from above. I strove for dignity. "We'll be along presently. Leave us, now."

Mother would be all the more furious if I spurned her summons, but she'd humiliated me in public. How could I submit, under the eyes of mere tradesmen?

"Sir, Llewelyn himself said I was to see you home, and Lord Rustin to the keep. I dare not disobey."

"Llewelyn isn't my master," I said coolly. "We have business at the wineshop for an hour or so." To Rustin, "It won't hurt Mother to wait a few—"

"*The Queen your mother is dying!*"

For a fleeting instant the street swam. Rustin touched my arm.

The guard stammered, "I wasn't to tell you! She fell into sleep that will not wake. Your uncle Margenthar ordered you summoned at once."

Again the mournful peal of trumpets from the high ramparts.

I shuddered. It was a dirge I'd last heard six years past, on my father's death.

Mother was gone.

My voice was dull. "Had I not fought with you and stayed the night, I'd be at her bedside."

Rustin snapped, "Captain, a horse for Rodrigo. We'll return it later."

I clutched his arm, wishing I didn't feel a stupid young boy. "Rust, I'm frightened. Come with me."

"All right. Two horses, then."

The guard said, "Lord Rustin, your father wants you—"

"I must attend my lord the King. I'll be home after."

I gulped. *My lord the King*. What had befallen me? Dazed, I swung myself into the proffered saddle, spurred the perspiring bay into a canter toward the familiarity of the castle. Perhaps I could stay with Rustin a few days, during the rituals. But I also had need to guard Mother's body, lest . . . I knew not what.

Ahead were the iron-belted doors of the keep. I veered to the Tradesmen's Cut, to save time. Rust galloped behind. "Rodrigo!"

"King?" I repeated.

"Well, not yet." His face was set. "Not crowned."

"Will I be?" I clutched the pommel as if to keep from falling.

"Am I a Ritemaster?" Then Rustin's eyes softened. "Now, your troubles begin."

"Aye," I said. Then, under my breath. "King." I felt a chill, and there was no wind.

Chapter 3

MY BORROWED MOUNT WAS WHEEZING BY THE TIME WE took sight of the outer wall, and it was all I could do not to leap from the saddle and lead him on foot. I missed Ebon, left in our haste at the keep. To my right, Rustin paced his gelding. The captain of Llewelyn's guard led the way. The rest of the troop straggled behind.

The winding hill of Stryx was not made for processionals.

As we neared, I studied the outer wall. Within, drums pounded a solemn beat. Trumpeters manned the ramparts, resplendent in the formal livery Mother had designed for state occasion, and which had so impressed Hriskil of the Norland that he'd had it copied in his own colors.

At the conclusion of each dirge the trumpets fell silent. For minutes, there could be heard only the thump of the kettle and the roll of the toms, until the trumpeters began again. Lanford, officer of the gate, who'd chased me in play through the orchard when I was but a sprig, commanded the hornsmen standing atop the wall.

As the horns fell silent once more I made for the low daily door, dreading that it would not open, that I'd have to dismount and knock, a supplicant in my own house.

No movement.

Rustin took a deep breath. "Make way for Rodri—"

Not the daily door, but the high portal of state swung wide in all its splendor, the bolt-studded iron straps creaking shrill.

I caught my breath. At the head of a gathering in the courtyard stood Uncle Mar, Duke of Stryx, in full dress and cloak, attended by the stout Lady of Soushire, Lord Groenfil, and their retinues. They'd journeyed here for a council meet that Mother would never hold. Now they'd stay for a funeral.

We passed through the portal, and I realized for the first time how thick was our outer wall at its base. I muttered to Rustin, "Were they waiting for us all the while?"

"No, you blockhead, the guards alerted them when we neared. We've been visible for ten furlongs." Rust snorted. "Do you know nothing of ceremonies?"

Mother had enjoyed the planning of them, but she brushed aside my idle curiosity and sent me out to play. No, I knew not what I should. I had better learn, for Uncle Mar's arrangements had the desired effect, and my knees trembled against my stallion's flanks.

A groom darted forward, cupped his bridle. I waited, unsure whether I was expected to dismount.

"Rodrigo of Caledon." Uncle Mar stepped forward, his cloak flowing. A tall man, broad-chested, with a neatly cropped gray-streaked beard, he dominated the courtyard. "I bear tidings of sorrow. Thy mother the Queen has passed from life. All here, nobles and men, mourn with thee." His hand closed around the hem of his cloak, and he gave it a wrench. The material tore and hung loose.

A moment passed. Lady Soushire shifted in vexation before I realized they awaited a reply. I glanced at Rustin, but found no aid. "Thank you." It seemed inadequate for the occasion. "I— We thank thee, my lord, and all those who grieve with us." I tugged furiously at my jerkin, but it wouldn't rip. Blushing, I gave it up. "We will don mourning clothes in our chamber. Elena Queen was a good lady, and true. She will be missed."

"Aye, that and more." In three measured strides Margenthar was at my side, extending his hand. "I'll escort you."

I swung down nimbly. "I know the way, Uncle." Could he forget I lived in this castle, as did he?

"Protocol," he muttered under his breath. "Behave yourself." Louder, "Those kinsmen who would see the body of Elena may step forth."

My words came fast on his, and equally loud. "Yes, as soon as I have my time to bid her farewell. Gather the kinsmen, that they may follow my visit."

His arm twined with mine as we walked at stately pace toward the entry of the donjon. Softly, "I've made the arrangements, and you're not to befoul them. Open viewing is part of the ritual." His fingers dug into my forearm.

We proceeded past the banister down which I'd so recently slid. Would I ever be free to act the child again in Castle Stryx? I looked for Rustin, but he was caught somewhere behind the nobles, in the long slow procession.

At the entry to the hall wherein lay Mother's chambers I whirled to face the stairs. "Elena Queen is dead," I sang out. Larissa of Soushire looked startled; Uncle Mar glided purposefully toward the open door.

"Now do we, Rodrigo King and heir, commune with her remains—"

"King?" A snarl, half whisper, that only I heard. Uncle Mar's eyes blazed. "You overstep yourself. The Council of State hasn't yet—"

"—in the ancient and secret rite of our House. We shall be alone with her for that purpose."

He hissed, "Secret rite? What nonsense is this?"

I slipped between him and the door, gripped the brass handle with sweaty hand. I flashed a tight smile full of malice, as I murmured, "We're in public, Uncle." I clapped my hands. "Where is my liegeman? Rustin, come forth!"

A muttered oath, as Rust thrust his way through the astonished ranks. "Here, my lord."

"Out of the way, boy." Uncle Mar reached for the door.

I stepped back, barring Uncle's way, scowled at Rustin. "Your place was at our side. Heed what you were told, worthless vassal!"

While Uncle Mar gaped I slipped through the doorway, hauled Rustin after. I swung the door closed, blotting out the staring faces, Mar's rage, the nobles and their minions. I slid tight the bar.

Rust shook his head. "Rodrigo! Even Father never spoke to me so, before nobility." Something in my face stilled his jest. "Oh, my liege!" He caught my head in the crook of his arm, pressed me tight. "Don't cry, Roddy. I can't abide it."

I wiped my eyes. "I was scared witless."

"Mar couldn't tell. Nor I. All we saw was that you defied him in front of them all. And then to dress down a noble, in full view of the court. No man would dare provoke an inevitable duel, save the King."

I tugged him along the corridor toward Mother's chamber. "You're not angry, then?"

"Mortified." He tried to glower, but his approval broke through like a sunbeam in a scattering storm. "Unless you're acknowledged King. What shame could there then be, in accepting rebuke from the King himself?"

"Then I must be proclaimed."

At Mother's chamber, from habit, I knocked.

Within, half a dozen of Mother's ladies clustered about the bed. Nurse Hester, her acid voice for once stilled, her eyes bleak, trudged wearily to her plank table.

Lady Rowena of Halle bowed deep, the formal bow of state. "I'm so sorry, Rodrigo." I thanked her, and shooed the ladies from the chamber as graciously as I could. Only Hester refused to budge.

As they departed, fluttering, a small form shot across the room, buried itself wailing in my arms. I staggered from the force of his assault. "Easy, Elryc."

"Mother's gone!"

"Be a man." I tried to pry loose his fingers. "Don't disgrace yourself."

Rustin opened his mouth to speak, decided on silence. Before he turned away, I saw his reproach.

I clawed at Elryc's fingers that locked round my waist stifling my breath. I shifted the boy to a safer position, cuddled his head under mine. How could I forget he was but eleven? "I'm sorry." Awkwardly, unused to giving kindness, I patted his head. "Cry, Elryc. As much as you have need."

I thought he would never stop. Even when his breath slowed, his head remained buried on my breast, as if joined to my flesh in one of those occasional caprices of nature.

I made my way to the bed.

They had done washing the corpse, and had Mother laid out in white. Her form was wasted, but seemed more at peace than ere I'd known. She was one with Lord of Nature, and the peace was fitting.

"Let go, Elryc." I tried unsuccessfully to lower myself on the edge of the bed. I worked to loosen his grip, knowing it was unfitting to fling him to the floor, as I would on another day. "Sit on that footstool. I won't leave you. Here, take my hand." I looked to Nurse Hester. "When did she die, and how?"

"My lady slept the night and did not wake. I thought to bring her the sweet Francan cheese that she so liked. So I left her a few moments. When I'd returned, she'd slid into the deep sleep from which few return, while her foolish ladies babbled among themselves. It was then we called you."

I looked at the Queen's still form, and swallowed. "Leave us, Hester. I would be alone with my mother."

The old woman fixed me with a disapproving eye. "What concerns have you with my lady's remains, eh? It isn't fitting—"

I jumped to my feet, almost knocking Elryc from his perch. My authority wavered; it was barely six months since Hester herself had hauled me by an ear to the door and expelled me from Mother's chambers, fuming at some impudence in my tone.

"I must be alone. Can't you understand?" No answer. I hissed, "Get out, else I'll fling you from the window!"

Her eyes widened; she studied my face. Then, with a look of contempt, she made as if to spit on the floor, went instead to Mother, kissed her softly on the brow. With dignity she hobbled to the door.

"You too, Rust. Wait outside." I snapped my fingers. "Go, Elryc."

"No." My brother folded his arms. "I stay." He caught at a sob. "She was my mother too!" A determined look settled on his features.

"Very well." I closed my eyes, my melancholy broken only by Elryc's sniffles. "Shut up, brother, or I'll—I'll warm your rump!"

"You haven't the right."

"We're orphans. Someone has to look after you. If not me, then who? Uncle Mar?"

"At least *he* doesn't throw stones at me." Elryc's sulky expression wavered as I crossed back to the bed. "Why'd you chase them away?"

"I don't know. So I could get to know her." It made no sense, even to me. I knelt, took Mother's hand. To my shock, it was cold. "Madam, I'm—" My voice seized; I could but kneel, stroke the lifeless fingers, knead the rings that once I'd kissed. I stifled a sound.

A small palm, on my shoulder; from it, a gentle squeeze. A sniffle.

Then, to my infinite astonishment, a shy kiss, on the top of my head. Unable to speak, I buried my face in the bedclothes, cuddling the cold hand that responded not.

In the mournful distance, Elryc wept.

When I felt able, I got to my feet, gave Elryc a gruff embrace, pushed him away. "We're in for it."

"How do you mean?"

"I'm not crowned, and the best we can hope for is a regency."

"The best?"

"Others covet the throne. Perhaps even you." I threw him a crooked smile.

"Yes, me." He sniffled, took a deep breath. "I've thought of it, Roddy. I'd make a good king. I'd set aside all the boring ceremonies and rituals, and spend our gold where it would serve better." He rested his head on my arm. "But not by killing you. I don't want a crown that badly."

I shook him off. "Hold your tongue, simpleton. Never let it be known what you want. What if someone hears, and puts me aside, because you're younger and more tractable?"

As was his habit, Elryc looked wise beyond his years. "More likely they'll kill us both, and raise Pytor to do what he's told. His mind isn't yet made." He peered out the window, at the trumpeters below. "I don't want to die, Roddy. Protect me."

"I can't protect myself." I sat again at the silent bed. "Mother, what do we do?"

No reply.

"Will the Power be mine, if I am King under a regent?"

The silent form waited for eternity.

I blurted, "If only I'd listened!" Always I'd been prone to interrupt her, impatient at the careful organization of her thoughts. "Forgive me, Madam." I knelt, caressed once more the cold hand.

"Does Uncle Mar have the Power?" For a moment I imagined Elryc's high voice was Mother's.

"No, only a King can—" My eyes darted. "The Chalice and Receptor. Where did she keep them?" I ran past the trunk room into Mother's dressing chamber, threw open the wardrobe, pushed aside the hanging clothes. Nothing. Once they'd been in the vault, but I recalled the day I'd been—what—thirteen? Mother had demonstrated the rite that summoned the Still, and like a foolish boy I'd been disappointed that no candles had dimmed, no thunder crashed, no velvet curtains swayed. Yet it couldn't have been otherwise; Mother's Power had long been extinguished.

That day, the Vessels had been set on the marble table. Mother took my hand and placed it in the proper place. Excited, still a child, I'd had no curiosity as to where the emerald-studded Receptor had been stored. I'd seen no clue, and had not asked.

"In a chest?" Elryc sounded hopeful.

I cursed; Mother had at least a dozen trunks and a vast collection of garments. The Vessels could be anywhere. I flung open the first, pawed among carefully folded clothing, slammed down the lid. "Check that one with the brass straps." I crossed to the door, undid the bar, pulled him in. "Rustin! Help us find the Receptor and Chalice." I waved to the trunk room.

"This is her chamber? I've never been admitted before." When visiting the castle Rustin had the run of my quarters, and we roamed the ramparts without hindrance. But though Mother might receive family or intimates in her rooms, no others ever saw them, even my companions.

He opened a trunk, blushed at the undergarments within, resolutely plunged his hands to the bottom. "Not here." He moved to another. "Where'd you see them last?"

"There." I pointed to the pleasant salon under the high windows.

We searched on. A soft knock at the door, which we ignored. After a few moments, another, more insistent.

With a curse for which Mother would have boxed my ears, I flung open the door. Rowena and Hester not far behind. "Roddy, you left Duke Margenthar and the nobles at the stairs! He demands I open the outer door, and really there's no reason I shouldn't."

"The reason," spat Hester, "stands in front of you."

I snarled. "Five minutes, tell him."

"But you can't—"

The old woman closed in on Rowena, murder in her eyes. I blurted, "Hester, we need you inside. Please."

To the Nurse, mother took precedence over vengeance. She hobbled in and I slammed the door.

"Where's Mother's Power?"

She gaped. "In her soul, her essence. It's—"

"The Receptor!"

She peered past me to the trunk room. "What do you louts meddle with, that's none of your—*her clothes?* Elryc! Shut that lid or I'll take a stick to you!" My brother leaped from the trunk. Hester brushed me aside, darted to the wardrobe, almost stumbling in her haste. "Have you no respect, no decency? Are you Llewelyn's boy?" She snatched Rustin's ear, led him yelping to the wall. "Your filthy hands touched my lady's garments?" A cuff. "Out!" She herded him to the door.

Rustin's eyes fastened on me in silent plea; it roused me from stupor. I said, "Hester, he's helping—"

"Oaf!" The old woman stamped her foot. "What would Lady Elena think of these carryings on? Were she alive, she'd—" Again she stamped her foot, but no words came. Eyes brimming, she threw her hands to her face. Rustin rubbed furiously at his ear.

I motioned to Rustin, to Elryc. "In the salon, and shut the door." They rushed out to escape her rage.

My voice was hesitant. "Please, Nurse . . ."

Her hands came down. "Desecrator!" She slapped my face.

I chopped off my words, fought the humiliation and the sting. Then, quietly, "Thinkest that thou loved her more than I?"

Her finger stabbed at the garments strewn about by our negligence. "Is that love, or greed? Oh, you great coarse boy!"

"If you loved Mother, I beg you, help me. For Elryc's sake and mine. We must have the Vessels."

Her eyes studied my face a long while. Then she nodded, and spoke in my ear.

After a few moments I opened the door to the salon. "It's well now. Hester says Mother sent the Vessels back to the vault."

Elryc looked to Hester. She nodded. "Guarded night and day, by two men of my lady's own choosing."

Again, the demanding knock, at the door. I ignored it. "Will they open the vault for me?"

Hester shook her head. "Even if they had the will, they could not. The vault's locked and wants two keys, held separately by your mother and the Chamberlain."

That didn't sound like the Queen I knew. "She wouldn't put possessions so valuable beyond her own reach. What if the Chamberlain—"

"Don't be a fool. Willem of Alcazar was raised in the castle. Your mother and he played together until they grew to the age where it was not seemly. He was her closest friend, and would no more betray her than—than would I!"

The knock, ever louder.

"We'll have to let them in." I ran to the bed. "Where's the key to the vault?"

"She kept it always on a golden chain around her neck."

I reached out, pulled back my hand as if burned. I couldn't explore my mother's body as if it were some dead bird I'd found in the field. "Could you—would . . ." I gritted my teeth. This was my responsibility. Forcing down bile, I forced my hand to her neck, felt inside her garment.

"Don't waste your time." The Nurse scowled. "She's already been washed and laid out. Think you they'd have left it on her?"

"Where is it?"

"In Margenthar's hands, if Rowena had her way."

We were lost. Dully, I sank upon the bed.

"But she did not." Hester fished within the hem of her garment. Her wrinkled hand came forth, closed. Her eyes bore into mine. Then, in an instant, her fingers opened, bright metal flashed.

"*YOU?* You had it, all along?"

"Aye." She tossed the chain, and I snatched it from the air. "I knew not whom those ladies serve, and took it when their eyes were elsewhere."

"To do what with?"

"Ere day's end, to give to you, or Margenthar. I'd not made up my mind. You're not much, but you're better than he."

I thrust the chain in my shirt, responded with the curtness she'd shown. "I thank thee. Rust, we'll have somehow to get the other key. Let them in, and let's try to slip out in the rush."

Two doors to unlock; the inner, and the main door at the end of the corridor, by the stairs. I opened the inner door, slipped past the diminished flock of ladies, got no more than halfway along the corridor before Duke Margenthar and his entourage swept down on me. Had looks the power to kill, I were extinct.

"Let the kinsmen come forth!" My tones were regal, but this time Uncle Mar would have none of it. I scuttled aside before he ran me down.

"We'll settle this later, boy!"

Toward the rear of the throng came Lady Rowena, her face triumphant.

I said, "You couldn't wait five minutes?"

"You'd have asked five more, and ten beyond that." She swept past. Then, over her shoulder, "He who would be King need show a king's grace! Like your uncle!"

When the last of the household had passed I waited, until Rustin peered out, found me. He trotted down the corridor, Elryc in tow. "Now what?"

"We visit Willem." I loped down the great stairs, Elryc clutching my hand with unfamiliar intimacy. Below, servants and hirelings had gathered, muttering among themselves and staring toward the Queen's chambers.

I clapped sharply. "Have you no business? Is dinner ready, are the week's chores done? Get about your work!"

Sullen murmurs. Grudgingly they made way, but they did not disperse. By the time we three had circled the stairs to the Chamberlain's entry, they'd resumed their uneasy places at the staircase.

Rustin raised an eyebrow. "You'll just walk in and ask? 'Willem, may I have Mother's key?' "

"Well, I . . . um." I hadn't thought that far. "We'll follow the quarry where it runs."

At the Chamberlain's door, I debated whether to walk in as if I were master of the place, decided I'd best knock.

A clerk opened. "Yes? Oh, Rodrigo. I'll tell him you're here." He disappeared into an inner chamber, leaving me frowning through a side doorway at a room full of clerks on high stools, bent over their papers and accounts.

I paced the anteroom, fists knotted, feeling the boy who'd so often come to collect his stipend, preparing to endure the admonitions and censure that were part of its dispense.

Elryc, also accustomed to the place, took a chair meekly, hands folded in his lap.

Rustin studied the wall hangings. "We have a tapestry much like that at home. Do you recall?"

I nodded, having not the slightest idea what he was talking about. "I want you with me, when we confront him."

"As you wish." He took a book from a shelf, examined the gold-leafed adornment in the leaves. "Love Poems of Milibar?" A sly grin flitted across his features. "Ever read them? They'd make a gelding rise—"

"Rodrigo." The stocky Chamberlain was framed in the doorway. In his velvet-trimmed robes he looked prepared for a meeting of state. "A terrible day. Come in."

I passed through the doorway, Rustin at my heels. We settled ourselves in the stiff high-backed chairs set around Willem's ornate desk.

He studied Rust. "I recognize you. You're . . . the envoy's son, from Eiber?"

Rustin flushed. "No, Sir Willem. My father is Llewelyn."

The man's eyes rose. "Time races. Forgive me; the last time we spoke, you were so high." He patted the desk, and dismissed Rustin from his mind. "I'm sorry, Rodrigo. She was a wonderful soul, and I'll miss her more than you can know." His eyes teared. Perhaps he even meant it. I waited, while his commiseration played out. "So, Prince Rodrigo, how may I be of service?"

I licked my lips, risked a glance to Rustin. He sat straight, eyes on the Chamberlain. "I want to enter the vault."

His jaw dropped, then a chuckle. "So do many folk. Whatever for?"

I took the bit between my teeth. "To see if the Vessels are in their place."

"Do you think she kept them there?"

"Did she not?"

"That's not mine to disclose, Prince Rodrigo. If the Queen wanted you to know, surely she'd have told you."

"They'll be mine to wield!"

He nodded. "When you are King, yes. Soon, I hope."

"I'm King now." I wished I didn't sound petulant. "Mother didn't renounce me, and now she's dead. I am King, crowned or not. I want to open our vault."

"But why come to me?"

Rustin intervened. "How else would one gain entry, Sir Willem?"

The Chamberlain looked astonished. "You think the Queen let clerks such as myself wander freely among her treasures? I have no access."

"You don't?" Could Hester have made up the whole story, to divert me? Did she gloat over the Vessels, even now?

"No one entered the vault, save in your mother's presence. She herself carried a key."

I said, "And you—"

"Oh, Lord of Nature and his minions!" Rustin jumped to his feet. "The fitting! Roddy, we're late. Did you forget your appointment for the mourning robes? Hurry; if the earls get fitted first you'll have to wear that ridiculous sable that you've outgrown. Do you want to look a country lout?"

"What nonsense—"

"Make notes, like I do, and you won't forget. When will you learn!" He hustled me protesting from my chair. "I'm sorry, Sir Willem, may we see you after the fitting?"

"It's going to be a frightful day, youngsire. The funeral wreaths, the cortege to organize—"

"But you'll find a moment for us, won't you? Roddy, hurry!" He propelled me to the antechamber. Elryc gaped at our quick retreat, but followed.

Dumbstruck, I let Rustin drag me clear of the Chamberlain's wing before I dug in my heels. "Let go, you lunatic! Have demons taken you? I was about to ask—"

His hand shot across my mouth. I swatted it away. "How dare you!"

A courtier strode past, on his way to see the Chamberlain. Rustin leered. "Outside, then, if you want to see who's the stronger!"

Elryc rammed him with a bony shoulder. "Leave Roddy alone!"

Rust shoved me into the wall, aimed a kick at Elryc, dashed for the door. Cursing like one possessed, I gave chase.

Rustin charged up the rampart steps two at a time, just ahead of my grasp. He veered for the high towers manned only in time of war. I flew after, Elryc bringing up the rear. At the watchtower Rust made his mistake; he dashed up the stairs that had no exit, and I knew I had him. Grimly, I climbed the three flights. At the landing I shoved aside an empty barrel, swung open the door to the open deck, girded myself for the battle to come.

I rushed out into sunlight. Panting, Rust leaned against the battlement. "We should be safe here."

"Betrayer! False vassal!"

"What? Didn't you realize I was—"

I circled. "Fight, you bastard son of a serf!"

He rolled his eyes. "For the love of . . . you dimwit, I had to get you alone before you ruined everything. Elryc, make him understand."

My brother stepped between us. "Listen."

I raised my fist to strike him down.

Elryc's eyes fastened on mine, unafraid. "Roddy, who'll protect me, once you're dead?"

My hand stayed.

"Hear him out. You can always fight after." Elryc sat against the parapet, drew up his knees.

Rustin examined me with wonder. "How would you be King, with such a temper?"

"Have your say!"

"We went to Willem to get his key. Would he have given it?"

"How would I know? I had no chance to ask before—"

"Think, dunce!"

His scorn penetrated my fury. "Willem said Mother had her key, and allowed no one access without her presence. So?"

"He was helpful?"

"He told truth in what—oh!"

"What, Roddy?" Elryc.

"Willem didn't admit he had a key. He was waiting to see if I knew."

"Brilliant." Rustin's tone dripped irony.

I asked, "So why not tell him?"

"Whose man is he?"

"Mother's. Now she's gone—" My shoulders slumped. Wearily, I sat alongside Elryc. "If he denied he had the key, I'd be powerless to prove it."

Elryc asked, "Why should he lie?"

"He need not. Say he admits he has a key. 'But my lady the Queen had the other key, and without it, mine is useless.' Then I must admit I have Mother's."

"And?" Rustin.

"And if he's Uncle Mar's man, they'll have me, and both keys, and the Vessels." My voice turned bitter. "Shall we put *you* on the throne, Rust? You have a head for these matters."

He dropped to one knee. "You are my liege lord, and I will have no other King while you live."

I had to look away. "Forgive me."

"Never mind that. What now?"

We crouched together like three boys scheming to evade their tutor. Rust and Elryc waited for my lead.

I pulled the cast brass key from my shirt, examined it. "Should I give this to you, for safekeeping?"

Elryc asked, "Who'd search you, Roddy? The Chamberlain? Only Mother could order that. If he tries, refuse."

I snorted. "Brother, you're a babe in arms." He colored. "The crown's at stake; Uncle Mar wouldn't hesitate to lay a hand on me. He never has. Remember last year when he caught us at his hawks?" My uncle had boxed my ears, and sent me wailing on my way with a contemptuous kick in the rear.

I took the key from round my neck, and felt unclothed. Reluctantly, I extended it to Rust, pulled back my hand. What if he sold the key and my kingdom to Margenthar? Rustin's moods were legendary.

"Keep it." His tone was curt, as if he'd read my mind.

"A day ago you knocked me from my horse, shoved my face in the mud. Now I'm to rely on your loyalty?"

Rustin's voice was thin. "Is there anything else you want of me this day?"

I drew a breath. "I'm going to see the Chamberlain."

Elryc asked, "Isn't all you said about Willem still true?"

"Of course. But I'll know to guard my speech. And I won't carry the key." I hesitated again. Without faith in Rust, life seemed too bleak. I stood, opened my hand, tucked Mother's golden chain into Rustin's brown tunic. "Keep it safe, my vassal."

"You're sure?"

"I have to trust someone. Besides, they'd never imagine you carried it."

"Your grace inspires me." His tone was acid.

I sighed. I might as well accommodate myself to Rustin's moods. As much sense to complain as about the weather.

Chapter 4

WE PERCHED ON A BENCH IN THE CHAMBERLAIN'S anteroom. He was engaged, his clerk told us, and would see us when he was able. I'd begun to drum the bench with impatient fingers, when Earl Cumber, my great-uncle, hobbled in, accompanied by his valet. "What are *you* boys doing here? Clerk, announce me."

I gaped. "Uncle Cumber?" I made the bow of courtesy. "How did you get here so fast? Cumber Town is nearly to the Norland passes—"

He turned to his valet. "Hah. The boy teaches me the lay of my lands." He favored me with a scowl. "We were en route to Council when word came of the misfortune."

Paying me no further notice, Great-uncle Cumber tapped his staff on the flagstones. Within a moment, he was ushered in to Willem.

We waited.

After some moments the Earl left, and the Chamberlain's door shut again. Over an hour passed, while we fidgeted like tykes at Ritehouse.

"Might as well give it up, Roddy. He won't see us."

Furious, I crossed to the Chamberlain's private door, thrust it open without a knock.

Behind me, the scurrying clerk. "My lord! You can't—"

I strode in. Willem of Alcazar sat at his carved desk, quill in hand. "What's this?"

I said, "We've waited half the afternoon. I'm sure you weren't told." Coolly, I took my seat.

"I was—these accounts must be paid."

"We won't be long, will we, Rust?" I crossed my legs. The

His expression tight, the Chamberlain waved away his clerk. The door slammed shut. "Very well. Proceed, my prince."

"We were discussing the vault."

His eyes met mine. "Can I offer you some wine? Cheese, perhaps?"

"No, thank you." I realized I was famished, and my stomach began to churn at his offer.

"Sorry if I seemed abrupt. It's just that . . . a terrible day."

I said nothing.

Willem took the bit in his teeth. "Rodrigo, I can't get you into the vault. Only your mother had access."

"By her key alone?"

"Please, Roddy, this is a very awkward matter. My duty is to the crown, and there's no declared—"

I leaned forward. "It took two keys to open the vault, and you have one. Give it here." I held out my hand.

His hand shot to his neck, returned almost instantly to the table. "What use would it be without the Queen's key? Have you that?"

"In its time. I'll start with yours."

Willem offered a placating smile. "The Duke has pledged to guard the assets of the realm until there's a proper accounting by the regent. Don't make that face, my lord, you know you're too young to rule."

"Uncle Mar is not regent."

"The Council will appoint him after the burial. It's for the regent to give you the key, but certainly you should ask. You'll find your uncle—"

I growled, "Are you his man or mine, Willem? You must choose."

A time passed, while Willem's thick fingers drummed on the massive desk. Then he sighed. "Young Rustin of Stryx, be so kind as to open the door and see my clerk isn't crouching at the keyhole."

Swiftly Rustin complied, flinging open the heavy door, peering both directions. "No one."

The Chamberlain's voice dropped. "I'm caught between two hooks, Roddy. May I call you that still, for the nonce? Yes, you'll be King, if your mother's wishes are followed."

I shivered. He'd said it so baldly, it somehow made my peril more real.

"And I assure you, it's my desire as well." His tone turned pious. "Not that I, a mere clerk, have any say in the matter."

"You're of the Council."

"Well, yes, but I'm one voice among seven, and not much heeded. It was your mother's edict set me among the great nobles, on her Council of State." He might be speaking truth, though I couldn't know, never having been allowed to attend a Council meet. Mar, Grand-uncle Cumber, Lady Soushire and Lord Groenfil, Vessa as Speaker of the City, and Lord Warthen of the Sands were the other Council members. Imposing figures all.

"Go on." I waved aside the distraction.

"Roddy, I have no dominion of my own, no benefice. I serve at the whim of the throne. If I go against you and you're crowned, you won't forget. But if I go against Margenthar and he's regent—Roddy, he's almost sure to be appointed, he's made promises and has the pledges— why, he'll throw me into the cells without a moment's thought."

He looked away. "I loved Elena. Would that I'd had noble blood and could have been her consort." Abruptly he stood, went to the window. After a time, a melancholy sigh. "Ah, well. That water's long since flowed to the sea." He sat again. "I want you crowned king. Do you understand that? Had your mother had her wish"—his voice dropped to a whisper—"I could have been your father."

"Well, then—"

"But I am a realist. Were you to walk in here with your mother's key around your neck"—he peered at my open shirt, and it was all I could do to keep from glancing at Rustin—"still, I could not give you mine. Not unless I were sure you were crowned, and Margenthar's power broken."

Rustin. "Who guards the vault?"

"Don't think of it, youngsire. They'd strike you dead."

"Who?"

"Usually, two men from the household troop. But this morning Margenthar had them replaced by five from his own regiment."

I said in awe, "So soon?"

For the first time the Chamberlain's tone was gentle. "Roddy, your mother's death was not . . . unforeseen."

I swallowed. "Thank you, sir, for forthright speech." I got to my feet. "Is there any way you could—I mean . . ." I blushed.

He waited, eyebrow raised.

"Funds. I mean, my usual stipend doesn't seem enough."

"Of course." He went to a closet, slipped a chain from round his neck, unlocked the door. Inside, a chest. He smiled. "Petty cash." He counted out twenty gold pieces, tinkled them into a small purse, handed it across.

A full year's stipend. "Thank you."

He closed the chest, replaced it in the closet, fished again for his chain. Something glinted, gold. Abruptly he turned his back to us, moved his bulk between me and the lock. When the closet was secure he thrust his hand in his garment.

I fingered the purse. "Will Uncle Mar know of this?"

"Lord of Nature, please don't tell him!" The Chamberlain smiled, weakly. "The accounts will be, um, smoothed."

"Now, sir." I leaned over his desk, my face close to his. "Will you vote in Council to crown me?"

"No. I cannot." He raised his hands, as if to shrug. "I won't sacrifice myself in a hopeless gesture."

I hesitated. "Sir Willem, if I have three other votes, will you cast the fourth?"

"It depends on the circumstances, whether it's sure—"

"Answer!" My tone snapped like a whip.

He looked away, waited, but eventually his gaze found its way back to mine. At last, "Prince Rodrigo, if thou hast three votes in Council, I will vote to crown thee King. I so swear."

"Done." I offered my hand, and he took it.

I strode to the outer door, followed the corridor to the nearest turn before I sagged against the wall.

Rustin threw his arm across my shoulder, squeezed.

I shrugged off his hand. "Don't. We failed; all I got was coin and a useless promise."

"Outside."

We found a secluded spot, under the courtyard wall. He said, "Now you have coin, should we need to flee. And you know where Willem stands. Not only that: his key. Did you notice?"

"He keeps it round his neck, with his others."

"And his promise is far more than you had before."

"Bah." I kicked at the earth. "Without the Still—"

"And of most import . . ." Rustin, eyes dancing, waited for my full attention. "He saw you act the King. That's worth more than the rest put together."

Uncle Mar summoned me as the sun set, before the Rite of Mourning. My inclination was to ignore his call, but Rustin persuaded me to respond. I found Mar in his opulent quarters on the first floor of the castle. The door was ajar; servitors and henchmen bustled about the outer halls.

"Ah, there you are. Giles, leave us while I have a word with my nephew." In a few moments we were alone in the sumptuous anteroom to his sleeping chamber. It was a well-aired room, his favorite place of business. Handsome murals adorned the vaulted ceiling, and colorful tapestries softened the walls.

The Duke surveyed me affably. "This afternoon we got off on the wrong foot, lad. You must be reeling with shock. I could have been more gentle."

"Thank you." It was all I could do not to snarl.

"Would you forgive me?" He clapped my shoulder. "We'll have to get along, you and I."

I ached to throw off his hand. "Why, Uncle?"

A look of surprise. "Well, perhaps not me, you're right. The Council's made no appointment yet. But someone will be regent until you're of age."

"Why?"

"Think, Roddy. Tantroth prowls his frontier, and beyond Eiber lurks Hriskil and his Norlanders. Think you they'd linger a moment outside our borders, knowing a stripling held the throne?"

"Our guards are—"

"For that matter, do you imagine our yeomanry would rally to a standard set to earth by a beardless boy? No, we need the confidence of the common folk to defend the realm." He paused for breath.

"Uncle, Mother is dead. I'm to be King."

"Undoubtedly. We all want that. But, Roddy . . ." The Duke threw open a tall window, breathed deeply of the dusk. "Will you have a kingdom to rule, or no? Would you rather be a half king, an exile, like poor Freisart of Kant?"

"Is that a threat, sir?"

"Confound it, boy." He strode across the chamber to shake me like a puppy. "Don't fight us on this, we're doing it for your own—"

"Us?"

"The Council. It's arranged. Your poor mother's been dying for years. We've talked—"

"Plotted behind her back!" I stood on tiptoe; we were nose to nose.

"Nonsense! We're the Council of State; could we risk going unprepared?"

"To thwart her wish?"

He bellowed, "To save your throne!" With an effort, he lowered his voice. "Roddy, always you unravel my temper. You lost your mother today; I must make allowances. But look you: I also lost my sister!" His eyes glistened.

I said nothing.

"Children we were together, Elena and I, so little time past. She was elder; the land would be hers to rule. I had no quarrel with that, and have none still. Our father Tryon's old duchy, the City of Stryx, was mine after his death, and gladly the Queen and I shared a home. Even our old playmate Willem of Alcazar found refuge with us. We raised our families together; you and your brothers, my sons Bayard and Chayne, Willem's Kronin. Can we not still live in peace?"

I hugged myself, in want of response.

"Please, Rodrigo. Let us sort this out together." His hand came forth, entreating.

"Uncle, crown me now, and give me the Vessels with which to practice my Power. Then I'll not fight your regency. You'll lead our armies if we're attacked, and I'll strengthen us with the Still."

Margenthar's hands went to his hips, and he stood staring at me, biting his lip. Then, "I don't see why not."

My joy knew no bounds. "How soon—"

"I'll need the Council's approval, of course. And we certainly can't stage a coronation on the heels of a funeral. A month or so, perhaps three. Time to invite foreign nobles, make a splendid affair of it."

"The Vessels are mine. I want them now."

"Do they not need the crown, to be potent?"

"You know that as well as I." I watched his face for deception.

"If you can't wield the Power, best the Vessels remain in safekeeping."

"I'll look after them. Uncle, don't look so disgusted. Would you rather I went to Council and objected to having you as regent? Surely I have *some* friend in the meet."

Mar gauged the shadows on the window ledge. "We'll be late for the Rite, boy. You don't want me as regent? Well, Soushire is eager for it, and she's gathered two votes. Would you have Larissa speak for Caledon?"

"Lord, no!" The Lady of Soushire was obese, smelled of garlic, and boasted a foul temper.

"I admit, if you go to Council, you might shake one vote loose from me; I won't tell you whose. I guarantee you, a Soushire regency will be the result." He threw his cloak over his arm. "Come along, we'll walk to the Rite together."

"And the Vessels?"

"Are under guard."

"On second thought, I rather admire the Lady of Soushire."

"You're so foolish as to do that? Well, on your own head be it."

He'd called my bluff. I took breath to concede defeat.

He spoke first, and his tone was cross. "Very well, I'll see you get your Vessels." I did my best to hide my elation. "I'll have to clear it with the Council, and that must wait until I'm regent. May Lord of Nature help you if they're stolen."

I nodded.

"Hurry now. Your mother waits; we must show her respect."

"Yes, Uncle."

Elryc bounced on his feather mattress. "We won! We won!"

"Uncle Mar gets his regency, brother."

"But you'll have the crown and the Power. Can Uncle Mar hurt us, then?" He sniffled.

Rustin stirred from his cushion. "Elryc, stop that confounded prancing. My head aches."

Elryc slowed, but did not stop. "Can he, Roddy?"

"Well . . . we're safer." I'd bearded the lion in—literally—his den. I smiled at the thought of it.

Rustin swarmed to his feet, caught Elryc's wrist, flopped the boy onto his stomach, dropped alongside him, a firm grasp on his arm.

"Let go!" Elryc.

"I told you to be still, and you weren't." Rust's eyes rose. "What worries me is—"

"Roddy, you're King! Tell him to let me loose!"

"—the three months until coronation. Much could happen in—"

"Roddy!"

I growled, "Let go the Prince's arm, Rust. That's right. Now, sit on his back." Elryc squawked. "And box his ears if he utters another sound. I never agreed to three months. I'll talk to the Seven, and we'll see."

"Nearly all of them were at the Rite."

"It wasn't the moment." Despite my best efforts to be a man, I'd wept like a child while the Ritemaster carried the flickering tapers three times round my mother's draped form. To make things worse, Rustin had put his arm around me, in comfort, and seemed oblivious to my rage when I threw him off. Lord knew what the nobles must think of me, after I'd carried on, and suffered a boy's embrace.

Rust asked, "When do the Seven meet?"

"Tomorrow, at the third hour."

"Where?"

"I'm not sure. In the great hall, I think."

"Odd your uncle didn't tell you."

"Roddy?" Elryc. "Ow! Let me up, I'll be quiet. Stop, Rust!"

Rustin cuffed him again, inquired of me by a raised eyebrow. I nodded. Released, Elryc curled in a corner of his bed, knees drawn tight, his mien sullen.

We sat in silence, until I drew a sharp breath. "Rust . . . How is Uncle Mar to give me the Vessels, if we have the key to the vault?"

"He doesn't know you have it."

"He certainly knows he doesn't have it."

Rust pondered. "They'd have searched the Queen's chamber."

I nodded. "Hester told them nothing, I'm sure of it. A team of horses couldn't draw tidings from her when she's in a mood to be obstinate."

"Which means he knew he couldn't keep his promise to you."

I stood. "Let's go."

"Where?" Elryc.

"The strongroom, of course."

"At this hour?" He yawned. "Why?"

"I want . . ." I wasn't sure what.

Rust said, "It's unwise. They ought not see you're interested—"

"Come." I was out the door, and Rust had little choice but to follow.

"What about me?" Elryc's wail pursued us.

"To your bed, brat!" We raced down the stairs.

The strongroom was reached through winding passageways from the kitchens and winery. Perhaps the builders thought such design would make the chambers less tempting to invaders, but the builders were tasting earth these many generations, and couldn't be asked.

Rust and I wandered casually into the kitchen, as was our custom, and Rustin helped himself to an apple from the cold bins. Out to the hall, with no one in sight. We raced giggling down the stairs, through the tunnels.

When I was a toddler my father scared me with old tales of brave men imprisoned in the cellars, but now I knew better. We rushed past the chamber that held our casks of aging wine, supposedly a torture room in the days of my great-grandfather Varon of the Steppe. We turned past the armory, silent at this hour of night, found the double doors of the passageway leading to the strongcellar. From the far end, a murmur of low voices.

I slowed, tiptoed my way along the musty corridor lit at either side by a smoking torch. Something chill ran down my back; I'd been here before, but only by day. Though day and night were indistinguishable in the dank cellars, somehow one knew the hour.

"It's around the corner." My whisper echoed.

"What do we do?"

Stroll into the anteroom of the vault, as if we boys always skulked the cellars at night? Creep along, cheek pressed to the wall, and peer carefully round the corner? That didn't suit my royal station.

"This is my castle. I want a look at the chamber door." Boldly, I strode like a prince to the intersecting corridor, stopped just short of the corner. With an apologetic shrug I dropped to my knees, then my stomach, inched forward until my forehead was at the turn. I peered out.

A handful of guards. Two dozed outside the closed wrought-iron gate some paces from the vault, while the others inside played at dice. A peaceful scene.

A hot breath on the back of my neck. I jerked, sucked in air.

"Quiet, dunce." Rustin pressed his palm into my back, his face just above mine as he knelt at my side. "Where are the locks?"

"Past the gate, see the two square holes?" The vault's thick bronze door was pierced by handholes at either end. The locks themselves were recessed an arm's length within the door; it was said a false key triggered a blade that slashed down, severing the offender's hand. When I'd asked Mother, she merely smiled, and said it would have to wait until I was older.

"We've seen it. Now what?"

I was wondering the same myself. I studied the guards, and the anteroom. The vault could be reached only through the corridor we'd just traversed. The doors behind us at the far end of the corridor were left open for convenience, but in an emergency they could be sealed from within.

Within that vault lay my crown, and my Power. The crown was little good without the ceremony of coronation; Mother had made sure I understood at least that much. One couldn't gain the Still of Caledon, even in a state of sexual innocence, merely by propping a gold diadem on one's head. The Rites must be followed, but if they were, and the crown was possessed, even a usurper might wield the Power.

A strong force could seize the anteroom. Swords or spears would quell the outside guards; arrows would slaughter those behind the gate.

But there'd still be the great bronze door, and it wanted two keys. Softly, we crept away.

At the safety of the winery, Rustin said only, "We can't storm the vault, Roddy."

I nodded and, despite myself, yawned.

"Yes, it's late." He clapped my arm. "I'd best be home."

"Stay, Rust!" It was a plea, without thought.

"I'll be back on the morrow." Despite my entreaties, he left for the stable.

When I woke, I found Elryc had crawled into my bed during the night. I left him asleep, and descended bleary and tousled to the kitchen. Cook broke three eggs into a butter-rinsed skillet, and served them with a slab of goat cheese and a hunk of steaming bread torn from a loaf just out of the oven. I sat next to Kerwyn, the stablehand, and took a huge bite.

Mother was wise, but in some things she plainly erred. My brothers and I were royalty, not mere nobility, and a certain distance from the house servants was suitable. How could commoners respect me if we rubbed shoulders at a kitchen table amid the droning flies? But ever since I'd been freed from Hester's care I'd been consigned to this kitchen, except for dinner.

I loped up the narrow steps to the third floor, wherein lay the nursery. Out of courtesy, I knocked, waited for Hester's grunt of admission.

"Hello, Pytor." I felt a pang of remorse. My towheaded brother's eyes were red from weeping, his voice muffled.

"Roddy." He abandoned Hester, threw his puny arms around my neck. I picked him up, rocked him gently.

"He lay awake until the moon was high," said the old Nurse. "Neither song nor sweets could bring him peace."

Pytor was but eight, and now had none but an ill-tempered crone to look after him. I resolved to be kinder than in the past. "Will you walk with me today, to the burial?"

"May I?" For once, the whine was gone from my brother's voice.

"You on one side, Elryc on the other."

"I get your hand."

I tousled Pytor's locks. "Whichever you want."

Hester grunted her approval. "He needs that." She glanced at my apparel. "You won't wear those rags to your mother's rest."

I looked down at my jerkin and breeks. "And why not?"

"They're torn, they're stained with raspberry jam, they're a size too small."

"I can look after—"

She snorted. "When pigs fly. I'll find something suitable."

I let it be, secretly relieved. Let her act the servant that she was; how else was a king's mind to be on affairs of state?

The gentry, the nobility, and the royalty of the surrounding boroughs of Stryx had gathered for the procession and burial. Uncle Mar had sent couriers with Mother's last breath. It was fitting, else many could not have arrived in time. Especially in summer, funerals must be held quickly, and one grew used to dropping the day's tasks to answer a distant summons.

I walked in the front row, Pytor's hand in mine, alongside to Uncle Mar. To my disgust, Elryc was nowhere to be seen. No matter how upset he was, missing the burial was a vile act he'd regret the rest of his life. One I'd make him regret.

"Ow, you're hurting me!"

"Sorry, Pytor." I loosened my grip.

Behind us, within the second rank, walked Llewelyn and Joenne. I was amazed that Rustin chose to be absent. When I'd paid my respects, Llewelyn inclined his head with a stony stare that forbade any inquiry.

I tried to suppress my hurt. Rust and I could have quietly weighed our plans during the long, slow processional, though Uncle Mar wouldn't have been pleased to see him at my side in the front rank.

The windswept hill was strewn with faded markers. The realm of Caledon had been knit for many generations before Varon of the Steppe seized it, and rulers with names ancient beyond ken were here laid to rest. From hand to hand, crown to crown, the Still had been passed.

Pytor sobbed into my waist while the words of descent were chanted, and the ropes slowly loosed. Old Hester worked her way past nobles and gentry, rested her twisted fingers on his shoulder.

Slowly, the coffin settled into the grave. Despite myself, I shivered. "See, Pytor? They've brought marigolds, her favorites. Send one to her, with me."

Unable to speak, he nodded, pressed tight against me while I made my way to the floral urns, picked out two stems to pluck. I gave him one, knelt in the damp earth beside the pit. "Throw yours in first, then I."

"Together." His voice was a quavering reed.

I held his hand and my flower, guided his forward. "Now." We dropped the blossoms on the casket. Uncle Mar waited, his eyebrow raised.

I nodded. Uncle Mar took the spade, poured a shovelful of earth onto the lowered coffin. I restrained a wild urge to leap in and brush it off. When he handed me the spade I'd have thrust it away, but that all eyes were on me.

For an endless moment I stood motionless atop the pit. Then I dug into the earth, hurled a huge spadeful into the grave. Mar reached to take the shovel. Ignoring him, I ground the blade into the dirt, tore out another clod, flung it onto my mother.

"Rodrigo." Mar's hand grasped at the haft. I shoved him in the chest with the flat of my palm, nearly sent him sprawling. I slashed at the ground, hurling chunks of dirt and stone into the pit.

Murmurs of disbelief; voices calling. Pytor tugged frantically at my sleeve. I shrugged him off, dug anew.

A gnarled, wrinkled hand on my neck. Sharp-nailed fingers pulled my face against a black garment, a familiar hand rubbed the small of my back. "There, boy. It's done." Insistent fingers pried the spade from my grip. "Leave him! Think ye that I know not still the soothing of him?"

"Hester, let me—"

"Not yet." Firmly, she held me close, while around us the assembly dispersed.

Finally, mortified, I pulled my nose from her garment, blinked in the sudden light. "I'm sorry. I shouldn't have done that."

She shrugged. "You did as you must. Take my arm. If I fall it's the end of me." Gingerly, we made our way through the rock-strewn field.

She freed me at the safety of the path. I looked about; nearly all had gone ahead. "Where's Pytor?"

"Run back on his own, I expect. He never would abide my pace."

A figure detached itself from the bystanders, approached casually. "Rodrigo—" The groomsman, Kerwyn. He inserted himself between me and the Nurse, dropped his voice to a whisper. "Elryc sent me. Danger."

"Tell my gutless brother he can—what?"

"Danger." His words were almost soundless. "He said to meet him where you met him and Rustin last, and to bring Pytor."

"What's happened?"

"I don't know. Elryc's a strange child, and I'd have paid no heed but for the odd look he bore. Griswold said—well, no matter. You'd best find out what he wants."

I swallowed. Rust would know what to do, but where was he? "If this is a trick, some peasant jest, I'll cut out your heart!" Without waiting for answer, I started down the trail.

Hester caught at my arm. "You're off? To where?"

"Later, Nurse." I loped down the hill.

She called after. "Tell Pytor there's no use to hide from me; I'll only switch him the worse!"

I left the trail to pick my way to the rear wall, and the servants' entrance. Brushing past startled washmaids, beyond the kitchen and the guards' barracks, along the stairs to the courtyard, I flew up the steps to the ramparts, ran past the ceremonial guard, made for the tower in which we three had conferred.

The tower stairs were steep, and I paused for breath halfway. If Elryc had mounted some prank, by the Lord of Nature, I'd have his ears. My pace more sober, I climbed the last steps, squeezed past the stack of barrels, strode out onto the deck.

Elryc was nowhere in sight. Imps take the boy. Brother or not, I'd—

"Roddy!" A hoarse murmur.

I whirled. "Where are you? End your games!"

"Here." A whisper.

I peered through the tower door. At first, in the dim light, I saw nothing. Then, behind the row of barrels, a figure. I bounded over the pile of staves, grasped Elryc's shirt, hauled him to his feet. "What are you playing at?"

"Where's Pytor? Did they follow you?"

"Leave him. Speak, ungrateful son of a buried Queen!" I shook him so his teeth rattled.

"Stop it, you ass!" He tore loose. He peered down the circular flights to the entry door. "Someone may hear us. Listen for steps." He perched on a barrel. "This morning, I was asleep in your bed."

"Like a log. You—"

"They knocked, but I didn't want anyone to know I'd needed company last night, so I lay quiet in my cave."

"Under my quilt. Get on with it; I've a Council meet to attend."

"They walked in without leave, can you imagine? 'He's not here,' one said. 'Obvious enough,' growled the other."

"So, servants came looking for me. Uncle Mar probably wanted—"

"Shut up, you big lout! Will you never listen?"

I filed his insolence in my list of revenges, lapsed into grudging silence. "Finish."

"The raspy voice said, 'He wasn't in his own room, wasn't at breakfast; where the devil could he have gone?' I lay very still. 'Don't blame me,' the other said. 'It was your idea to wait until day. You be the one to tell the Duke we didn't grab the little ones.'"

I stared dumbly at the rampart deck.

"The first voice answered, 'No, we'd best find them before we report. You know his lordship's moods.' When I was sure they were gone, I sneaked to the stables, gave Kerwyn a message for you. Then I hid. I've had no food since yesterday. Did you bring a bite? Anything?"

I was as one drugged. What was this about?

"Roddy, don't you see? We were to be seized, Pytor and I!"

"But Pytor trotted right past Uncle Mar to climb the hill with me. Mar didn't lift a finger. You're making a—"

"Imbecile! Think you Uncle Mar would take a child, in front of all his guests?"

"Mind your tongue." My voice was cold. "Even from you, I won't—"

"Fool! Dunce! Dimwit! Why didn't you bring Pytor?" Elryc danced with frustration. "Care you as little for him as for me? Why didn't you protect him!"

I slammed my brother against the stone, knocking the breath from him. "Never call me such names; I'm King! Pytor ran off before Kerwyn brought me your cursed message."

Elryc wheezed, his face purple. "Not King yet. Won't be, unless you rouse yourself." He gasped for air. "You won't even let us help you!" His shoulders shook. "Go seek your throne! I'll worry for Pytor."

Dazed, I sat on a barrel. What would Uncle Mar want with Pytor and Elryc? Why not me? I was his danger. He could have taken me in the privacy of his chambers. "Elryc, I'm sorry. Did I hurt you? Here, sit with me."

Sobbing, reluctant at first, he let me comfort him.

"You're sure you got it right? They said, 'Grab the little ones'?"

He nodded.

I struggled to pull myself together. "Wait here while I find Pytor, and send for Rustin." I strode to the steps. "I'll bring you apples."

"Anything." His voice was small. I started down the winding steps at a moderate pace, found myself leaping the last few treads. I dashed along the rampart, raced around the corner to the courtyard steps, cannoned into an armored figure, and sprawled with him in the dust.

"Clumsy buffoon!" The guard snatched up his scattered gear. "Why don't you watch where you're going?" Then he caught a look at my face, and his jaw dropped.

I staggered to my feet, my ribs afire. "Forgive me, Lanford. I was in a hurry." Clutching my side, I staggered off.

Fool. Ass. Imbecile. If my little brother Pytor was in danger, I deserved every name I'd been called, and more. I loped up the steps, through the great oaken doors to the donjon. Three flights to the nursery; I took them as fast as I could.

It was vacant.

The first room I'd try would be Elryc's, then my own. Pytor would be in one of his usual hiding—I hurtled down the steps.

"Aiee!" I averted a collision with the climbing figure, but slipped and rolled down half a flight, bumping ribs and buttocks on each cold stone step. From above Nurse Hester watched, incredulous.

"That's how you mourn your mother, eh? Galloping about the palace like a maddened—"

"Where's Pytor?"

"He's where Pytor goes when he would not be found. Why the sudden interest? For a year you've consigned him to—"

"Have you seen him since the hill?"

"Think you my legs take me faster than yours? I'm just returned. Why do you search for your brother?"

"Hester . . ." I hobbled up the steps. "Put aside our rancor for the moment." I put my lips close to her ear. "Pytor's in peril. When he returns, hide him, and send for me at once." I turned to go. Her hand lashed out, grabbed my ear, twisted. I yelped, clawing at her iron grip.

"Not so fast, Prince of Caledon."

"Let go my—"

"What about my boy? Peril? How?" Her eyes held a glint I'd never seen.

"Keep your voice dow—hargh!" My neck was cocked at an impossible angle. "Please, Nurse." My words tumbled, lest she wrench off my ear. "Elryc says Uncle Mar sent soldiers to take him and Pytor. I don't know what it means."

Her grip unlocked, and I was freed. She growled, "Where? And is Elryc safe?"

"He's in hiding. I was supposed to bring Pytor, but by the time I heard—"

"He'd already run down the hill. It's not your fault, Roddy." Her wrinkled hand flicked out to pat my throbbing ear. "We'll find him. You check the grounds; I'll search the castle."

"Three stories, and cellars? That's beyond you."

"I'm slow, but not crippled." She sighed. "Still, you might be faster, once you get the knack of stairways. I'll watch the nursery, your room and Elryc's, and the Queen's chambers. No one's thought to bar me from them." She sniffed. "My lady's been gone only a day."

"Right." I took her hand, squeezed it to cement the truce, limped off with what dignity I could muster.

I prowled wine cellars and holds, kitchen and storerooms, all the places a small boy might dawdle, all the places I'd known as a child, a few seasons past.

No Pytor.

In the courtyard I spotted Genard, the stableboy. Not much older than Elryc, he sprouted new inches like a weed gone wild. I fished out a coin. "You. Run down the hill to Llewelyn's keep. Ask for Rustin, tell him to come at once; I need him."

He eyed the copper dolefully. "Aye, but it's an hour's climb back up—"

"Or I could have Griswold lash your rump; it's all the same to me. Oh, don't pout like that." I sighed. "Here." I handed him a second copper, and a third.

Genard's face brightened; he flicked a knuckle to his forehead. "Thank ye, youngsi— m'lord."

When he dashed off I roamed casually through stables, smithy, orchards, the myriad of alcoves and lean-tos outlying any castle fort, but secure within its thick walls. Most folk let me pass unmolested, but a few were bold enough to offer kind words to a disconsolate heir wandering the grounds to no apparent purpose.

Hours passed, and I grew weary. My ribs ached from my tumble, and repeated tours up three flights of stairs to see if Hester had found my brother didn't help. Impatient, but glad of the rest, I sat on a ledge overlooking the courtyard to await Rustin. Even if he'd been at some chore when my message arrived, he'd have had time to be done and answer my call.

Shadows lengthened. Where in the demons' vale was Rust? I knew I ought to confront Uncle Mar, but first Rustin and I should—

I leaped to my feat cursing. The Council meet.

I dashed up the front steps into the frescoed hall, made for the vaulted meeting room to the rear, where armed sentinels stood post.

A graying guard thrust himself between me and the door, halberd poised across his chest.

"Out of my way. Are the Seven still within?" I squinted. "Who are you?"

"Fostrow, my lord. No one may pass. Council is at session."

"That's why I've come. Let me through."

A second guardsman stepped forth. "It's forbidden, Prince Rodrigo."

I felt myself grow red. "It's *my* Council now! Stand aside!"

"No one may enter." His mates took stations on each side of me, uncomfortably close.

I stamped my foot. "Whose men are you? You're not of the household."

One said proudly, "I'm Baron Stire, of the Duke's troop, from Castle Verein."

My jaw dropped. "What? Soldiers of Verein are forbidden the city, by long-standing treaty."

He shrugged. "We go where my lord the Duke sends us."

Infuriated, I pushed past. "Take your hands off—let me go!"

I found myself pinned to the opposite wall by half a dozen strong arms. One hand gripped a dagger.

I snarled, "Pierce me, would you? They'd hang the lot of you! Faugh!"

"Easy, lads." The guard Fostrow. To me, "No one spoke of killing—"

"Why the knife, churl? To mince your dinner?" My voice grew even louder. "I won't have it! Send for the Duke! Let me loose!"

The blade slipped into its scabbard, but despite my struggles I was firmly held. In a moment I would begin to cry, and in their sight that was intolerable. I shouted, "Margenthar! Duke of Stryx!"

Hands reached for my mouth, but I evaded them. "Treason! False Council! Disloyal villains, come forth from your nest and face your King! Margenthar!"

The doors were hurled open. Uncle Mar stood framed in the entry. "What lunacy is this?"

I struggled, nearly maddened with frustration. *"I WON'T BE HELD!"*

He snapped his fingers. "Let him loose." The hands fell away. "Whatever is the matter with you, lad?"

"Nothing." I wiped my face, brushing aside a perfidious tear. "These treacherous louts stopped me from joining you." I crossed to the entry, but Uncle Mar himself barred my way. Peering past, I saw old Earl Cumber, his rheumy eyes blinking, seated among the other councilors.

"Council meets unobserved. Such is the law."

"The Queen attended."

"Of course."

"Then shall I."

"No." Mar turned away.

"I'm heir!"

"I'm appointed regent and attend in your place." I tried to shoulder past; he thrust me back.

"When will I be crowned?"

"If you'd leave us to our meet I could tell you. Roddy, what's come over you? Look at yourself: sweaty, your hair awry, hollering like a field hand's whore! And you would instruct Council to make you King? Brush the dust from your clothes, and go to your chamber!"

Had I my blade I'd have slashed his throat. I said, "What mischief do you work? Why are your troops—"

"Business you're not man enough to attempt." His contempt was unsheathed.

Not man enough? My voice betrayed my rage. "Where's Pytor?"

"Unharmed. Where is Elryc?"

"How should I know? Try his room." I made sure my face showed nothing. "Let me talk to Pytor."

"Of course. As soon as the rituals are done."

"Where is he, damn you?"

Mar's eyes were drawn daggers. "Sent to Verein. We decided it was best he be raised quietly, away from commotion."

"You imprisoned a—a little boy?"

"Nonsense. He's free as you or I. The funeral has only upset him; he needs a time away—"

"He needs Hester!"

"We have our nurse, who's raised my sons. Your Hester's too old and feeble."

"She is not!" How did I come to be defending Mother's vengeful crone? "She's all he has!"

"No longer. Elryc too will find a home with us."

"How dare you take the princes of Caledon!"

"Enough." He addressed Fostrow. "Don't harm him, but keep him out of earshot; I won't have the meet disrupted. Roddy, you're overwrought. Go to the well, rinse your head in cold water, sit until you calm yourself."

"If I ride to Verein, will they let me in?"

"You're not to leave the castle grounds. I've informed the guard."

"I am King!"

"You are heir. The crown comes when you're of age. No, hear me out! Elena let you run wild like a peasant's runt, but I won't have it. You'll find your own discipline, boy, or by Lord of Nature you'll know mine! Baron Stire, take him out!'

Stern fingers closed round my arm. Uncle Mar strode into Council without a backward glance.

Chapter 5

 TWISTING FREE OF THE UBIQUITOUS HANDS, I STOMPED
outside to the chill sunset, snatched up a handful of
gravel, flung it at the great oaken doors.

"M'lord?"

I whirled, wiping my eyes. Genard, the stableboy.

"I been lookin' for you."

"Where's Rustin?"

"He said, tell Prince Rodrigo I can't come today."

"He what?" My world reeled.

"I hadda talk through the small window; the gate 'cross the road
was closed. Isn't it left open most of the time?"

"What else did he say?"

"Nothin', m'lord. He had a guard give me a coi—well, he tol' me be
sure you got the message at once. 'Sorry, I can't come today.' That's all."

"Hurl him into the seventh lake of fire!"

The stableboy made a hex, for protection. "May I go now, m'lord?
Griswold says I'm to—"

"Go."

Still, he hesitated. "Sire, please, don' send me on your errands,
down hill an' all. I look after horses, and wheel dung carts to the fields.
What's between lords isn't my ken."

I shook him. "You'll do what a noble of this House commands!
Begone!" He scurried off.

Uncle Mar would treat me as a child, and I couldn't prevent it.

Now, even a stableboy defied me. In as foul a temper as I could recall I climbed the ramparts, made sure no one was looking, ascended the high tower. "Elryc?"

Behind the barrels, no one.

"Where are you, brat of Caledon?" I peered out the door to the empty deck. "If you've run off to play, I'll throw you off the cursed wall!"

"Here." I whirled; saw nothing until the lid of a barrel moved. "Help me out."

"What in blazes are you doing?"

"It was safer, in case they made you tell." He rolled onto the floor, brushed himself clean as he stood. A glance at my empty hands. "Roddy, I haven't had a bite since—" His eyes darted to the bench, to my empty hands. "You *forgot?*" His voice rose to a piercing squeak.

"I'm sorry."

"You gorged yourself, and didn't even bring me an apple?"

"I couldn't. Since I left I've been—" No use; a tear rolled down his cheek. "Oh, stop, Elryc, I'll get you a meal."

He slumped on the bench, crestfallen. "How could you? Do I mean nothing?"

"They took Pytor to Verein."

He gulped. "Uncle Mar's castle?"

"I asked to ride to him, and was forbidden."

"What will they do to him?"

"You're to be sent also, as soon as they find you."

"Roddy, protect me." He sidled close, sniffling, and rubbed his cheek softly on my shoulder. "I'm sorry I snarled about the food, I'm so afraid, I didn't mean it."

Before thought intervened, my arms snaked round, wrapped him tight. "Of course I will."

"They'll kill me! I'll be good, Roddy, I won't ever make fun of—"

Lord of Nature. What was I, that made even my own brother cower? "Stop!" I covered his mouth. "I won't let them take you."

"We'll have to hide." He shivered. "The nights get cold; I'll need blankets. Water, and . . ." He looked apologetic. "Food."

I forced my brain to a canter. "We can't keep you here; sooner or later they'll search."

"If I show myself . . ."

"I know. Very well, stay here the night. I'll be back with dinner and blankets. By morning I'll know where to hide you. Rust can—" I bit off my words.

He buried his face in my arm. "How would they kill me, Roddy? A knife in the heart? Poison?"

My chest tightened. "Nobody will hurt you."

"Aggh, what if they cut my throat?" He retched, brought up naught but bile. When he turned back, his eyes were wild. "Mother warned us he might—Roddy, help me escape! Can we get our horses before— Do you think Pytor's already dead? Will they throw me in a ditch?"

I cuffed him, lightly, but enough so his words ceased to tumble. "Get hold of yourself! I'll protect you."

"But you'll be angry with me; I can't help saying what—"

"Elryc." I managed to keep my voice steady. "Look at me. No, stop darting; look into my eyes."

I waited until he complied.

"Elryc of Caledon, Prince and brother. I shall protect thee from this evil. Nor Uncle Mar nor his minions shall harm thee while I draw breath. By the Power I would wield, by the crown I would don, I tell thee so in Truth!"

"Roddy." He fell into my arms, trembling.

Later, making ready for bed, I considered what I'd done. In a moment of weakness, of foolish pity, I'd committed myself to the cause of my brother. Were I to betray him now, virgin or no, I could not ever take up my Power. And given my enemies and rivals for the crown, without the Still, I could not hold Caledon.

I felt sick.

I'd sworn utter loyalty to this boy, and hadn't thought to demand he swear the same to me.

By the time I woke, the candle had burned below the ninth hour. I threw on my clothes, hopped to the door while fastening my boot, and loped down the stairs. In the kitchen, I managed to swipe half a loaf of bread soaked in bacon fat, and stuffed my eggs within. Shortly after, I climbed the tower.

"First light, hah!" Elryc rubbed his eyes. "For hours I've been worrying you were seized." He snatched the rough cloth napkin in which I'd wrapped the food. "Eggs within bread? Are you crazed? And no water to wash with, or even to drink? Is dilute wine all you brought?"

"I'll do better next meal." My tone was sour.

"I hope so." He tore off a huge chunk of bread, and silenced himself with it.

When he'd wolfed the last of his food we sat together behind the stacked barrels.

"Roddy, I can't stay here another night."

"I know. It's a nuisance bringing you—"

"I'm cold and miserable, and they'll search the walls sooner or later."

"That too. Right now I'm going to the keep, to see why Rust abandoned us. I'll try to be back by midday, but you've apples left." I left him grumbling, and went to the stables.

I could have had the boy summon the stablemaster, but chose instead to wander through the fly-infested stalls to the leather shop behind, where the old man was examining harness. I spoke with care, anxious not to provoke a new confrontation. "Griswold, I need a horse, if one is ready."

A glint of what might have been humor. "Well said, my lord. But where do you ride?"

I bristled. "Is that concern of yours?"

He spoke softly. "They say the gate's closed to you unless you've gained Mar's leave." The old man's face hid his thoughts.

So, Uncle Mar had been serious about confining me to the castle grounds. Imps take me, I would not beg for leave like a mere child. I gave Griswold a curt nod. Then, thinking better, I leaned over the pommel, put my mouth close to his ear. "Thank you for the counsel."

I stalked off. Rustin would arrive this morning. Surely he must.

But he did not.

As the day lengthened, my rage grew sharper. How dare Rustin abandon his liege lord? How was I to take Elryc his meals, clothes, a chamber pot? How could I move him to safety? Everyone knew his face, as they did mine.

Dinner hour neared, and I grew more frantic. My calves ached from walking about. Needing a place to think, I slipped into the stables.

Within, all was dust, as Genard wielded a tall straw broom with manic haste. "Hey, boy!" I coughed. "Set it down, before you choke us both!"

"Sorry, m'lord." He grinned. "There's always dirt and dust in a stable. You wouldn't know, living up high."

Intimacy, from an urchin in torn soiled shirt and outgrown breeches? How dare he speak to me? His station was as far below mine as— as his filthy jerkin was to my cloak.

I turned on my heel, strode two paces, stopped as if I'd run into a wall. Would it work? Just possibly. "You. Garror."

"Genard."

"Whatever. Come close." I looked him over. "How many shirts have you?"

"I can't help it, Griswold made me clean it new-moon-day last, and I haven't had time since—"

"Have you another?" I made my voice stern.

"Aye, but it's small, and besides I save it for the Rites, when—"

"And breeches?"

He looked down, fingered a ragged hole. "The other pair's worse than these. I'm sorry."

I opened my tiepurse, fished out half a dozen coppers. "I want the loan of your worse breeks, and the shirt you wear. Be quick, before I— be quick."

The unexpected treasure disappeared into his shirt. "Aye, sir." In one lithe motion he stripped off his rank shirt, thrust it into my hand, dropped the broom. "It won't take me long!" He vanished, half-bare.

He returned a moment later, redressed, bearing breeches I would have tossed out the window rather than don. I took them between two fingers.

"What do you need them for, sir?"

I glowered. "For matters beyond you."

" 'Cause everyone's short-tempered now, what with their search for Elryc. Master Griswold might ask why I wear my best shirt, and if he gives me the stick, five more coppers would keep me silent."

I fixed him with a steely eye. "Shall I turn you into a toad, after I'm crowned? I'll have the Power then. No, I have a better idea. A dung beetle!"

His look was one of awe. "Can the Still do that?" No, of course not. But, searching my face, he found something that subdued him. "Forget it, m'lord." He backed away. "Not a word. I won't . . ." He was at the door.

"Stop." Never had I sounded so imperious. "Finish your sweeping. Where's Griswold? If I come back and find you not here, you'll live henceforth as a beetle!"

Moments later I was in the shoeing room, waiting politely for Griswold to finish his words with the smith. When I got him aside I said casually, "I told one of Llewelyn's stableboys he might stay here for a while."

Griswold's eyebrow raised, and I could see what he supposed. I flushed. Were I not constrained by need of the Still, no one would think me unmanly, and in need of the solace of boys.

Doggedly, I went on. "Your lad sleeps in the loft, I suppose? Would you let this other stay with him, and no need to mention him to the household?"

Griswold's tone was carefully flat. "Very well. I'll put your, uh, friend to work, of course."

"As you wish. The thing is, Uncle—the Duke Margenthar—is rather put out with me of late, and—"

"I won't go out of my way to call his attention."

Thanking him, I rounded up the stableboy, bade him follow me to the battlement, and wait at the foot of the winding stone steps. Before I left I took pains to discuss with him the short life and limited menu of a dung beetle.

Above, Elryc was aghast at the garb I tendered him. "Me? That?"

It took some persuasion before I had his good garments off him, and the others on. He held his arms away from his sides, as if afraid of his own touch. He said only, "Laugh at me and you'll rue it!"

I doubt he knew the effort it took to keep a straight face. I ruffled his hair to make it unkempt, bent to the deck, rubbed my hand in dust, wiped it on his face. "Come along. No, you idiot, don't walk like you own the place. Shamble. And stop limping!"

"The gravel hurts! I need my boots."

"Boys of your station have no boots." I led him down the stairs. The stableboy's eyes widened. "Garron, this is, um, Rendall, from Llewelyn's house. Griswold said he's to sleep in the loft."

"Him? But he's—"

"Shall I feed you some horse droppings, to introduce you to a beetle's life?"

"Urk." He shook his head vehemently.

"Rendall, go directly to the stable, stay inside. Garror here will find some dinner."

"Genard, m'lord!"

I eyed the long open walk to the stable. "I'll go ahead; you two follow, making fun of my walk and jabbing each other in the ribs. Carry on like the idiots you are."

"M'lord, I'm not—"

"Bottle it." I strode off, trying to keep my pace slow enough so as not to attract undue notice.

When dark fell, I dropped with weary relief into my bed, but barely had off my shirt when a sharp knock rattled the door. A servant summoned me to my uncle. Furious, I struggled back into my jerkin.

Uncle Mar paced his spacious anteroom, in the flickering candlelight. "Roddy, a serious matter."

"I hope so. I was just getting to sleep."

"Where is your brother?"

My lip curled. "You should know. Crying his heart out, in your imp-cursed castle of Verein."

"I speak of Elryc!"

"Ask Hester. It's a struggle to rid myself of his company." I held Uncle's eyes. So far, I'd told no untruth. "Why should I bother myself where he plays?"

"A night and day he's been gone. Has someone taken him? My responsibility as regent—"

"You look after the crown. I'll worry about my brother." I could have bitten out my tongue, for the saying of it. I had no choice but to brazen it out. "If he's gone, so much the better. Think ye that I want a rival so near at hand, that those who dislike my inheritance may think to alter it in his favor?"

"You had no such fears about Pytor, when you came charging into Council."

"Pytor's our pet, and not cunning. Elryc is too smart, and cold. If you find him dead, be not too sure that my hand didn't grasp the blade!"

"Nonsense. You two have been close."

"While Mother lived." I chose my words with care. "Hers was the power to Renounce."

"Ah, a schemer." His tone was sardonic. "And you call Elryc cold."

I shrugged. "Right now, I'm tired. I'd like to go to bed."

"In a moment. Answer me True, Prince Rodrigo. By the Power you would wield, do you know where Elryc is?"

I'd left him in the stables. But crossing the courtyard, he and Genard had danced after me like fools at a festival, and seemed friends when I'd left. After working hours, the stableboy was free to go where he wished. Perhaps Elryc was with him.

I looked Margenthar straight in the eye. "I do not know where Elryc my brother is. I tell you True." I tried to breathe normally.

He seemed disappointed. "Very well, you may go."

What colossal gall; dismissing me so. Did he think I was some cringing menial?

"We thank our gracious regent." My tone was at its most formal. I tried an airy wave, but it didn't quite come off. I'd have to practice.

Back in my chamber I peeled off my damp clothes, crawled gratefully into bed. I'd gotten away with it, as far as my uncle was concerned, but had I squandered the Still by prevarication? I closed my eyes, laid my palms flat against my stomach, pretending my body was the stillsilver of the Still. How would it respond, when came the time?

If Elryc was in the stable, had I lied? What if he was with Garmond, on some boyish prank? Had I told True, in that case? On the other hand, was Elryc so stupid, as to risk all for a lark? If he were caught and forced to tell how he'd been hidden, I was undone.

Elryc's danger, the problems of my coronation, could wait until morning. I thought briefly of Mother, wished I'd listened more closely to her warnings, and fell into sleep.

In the middle of the black night there came a hammering and caterwauling at my door such as I'd never heard. "Open, in the name of the Duke! At once, Rodrigo!"

Trembling, I leaped out of bed, dashed to the window. Below, the courtyard flickered with soldiers bearing torches.

"Open, or we'll break in the door!"

I scrambled into my breeches, snatched up my dagger, wishing Mother had let me store my sword in my room, instead of at the fencing master's.

"Now!" A terrific thud at the door.

I glanced under the bed, thought of hiding, realized it would not do. I unbarred, braced myself for attack.

Soldiers swept me aside. "Search the trunks! Pull off the mattress, look under."

I gaped.

"Behind the curtains!"

"This is my personal chamber! By what right—"

"By order of the regent." Stire, the Duke's baron. "Where's Elryc?"

"At Council, you told me he'd be sent to Verein with Pytor."

"You know well he's not— Do you have him?"

With dismay, I watched clothes, knickknacks and playthings strewn about. "How dare you! I'm Prince of Caledon!"

His face grew red. "Where in the demons' lake is he?"

"I don't know!"

We glared at each other, until he turned to a guard. "Any sign?"

"No, my lord."

"He's sure to be somewhere in the castle. Help them search the servants' quarters."

"What about this mess?" My voice was too high-pitched.

I jumped, as he spat at my bare feet. "Why, clean it up, youngsire." A slam, and they were gone.

To my utter disgust, I sat amid the chaos of my belongings and sobbed. My rage finally spent, I threw water on my face, paced until just before dawn, when at last I was calm enough to rest.

The noise of the household woke me in early morn. Thoroughly short of sleep, I picked my way across the mess on the floor. My mood wasn't improved when I slopped water from the washbasin onto my bare toes.

Last night, while the furious wind of soldiers had torn through my chamber, I'd thought with some worry of Hester. Certainly they'd search the nursery, and her temper might well provoke the Duke's men to violence.

Now, yawning over the breakfast table, I realized that though I'd pounded up and down the steps to the third floor of the castle while searching for Pytor night before last, I'd never gone back to tell Hester where I'd hidden Elryc. After a quick breakfast, I looked into the stables, found Genard, who'd made no secret that he'd recognized my brother. Now, when I threatened him anew, he shrugged. "Elryc—Rendall says you're not like that, m'lord."

"Who have you told?"

The boy's eyes had shifted. "No one, m'lord—don't make that sign at me!" Quickly he threw up the hex of protection. "Master Griswold, was all. None else!"

"Griswold? Lord of Nature!" I rushed past the stalls, through the hayloft into the tack room, and found him there, knotting a harness.

"Ah, Prince Rodrigo."

I slipped shut the door, as if a waist-high barrier would muffle our words. "You—Genard said he told—I mean, the new stableboy . . ."

"The new lad hasn't worked out badly." Griswold's tone was placid. "Though he's been rather hungry. Doesn't Llewelyn feed his help?"

I whispered, "Please. Don't toy with me."

A look of surprise. "Why, my lord! Humility, at last?" He seemed pleased.

"He's my . . ." I couldn't say it aloud. "You know who he is."

"Me?" He seemed shocked. "Some lout from the town, I suppose. Kerwyn hired him; I've nothing to do with it. As long as he's gentle with the horses." He eyed me sternly, as if to make his point.

"They searched my room."

"I heard the commotion. They came here twice, the day of my lady's funeral." Was the burial already two days past? I thought of Mother, below the earth, and shivered.

He waited. "Was there else?"

"I, uh, no . . ." I thought to demonstrate my gratitude. "No, sir."

This time he positively smiled. "There's hope for you yet, Lord Rodrigo. Just one thing . . ."

"Yes?"

"Don't loiter about the stable. You never did it before, and you'll attract attention."

He was right. Disconsolate, I climbed wearily to the nursery.

The door was ajar; with trepidation I walked in, unbidden.

The old lady was at her table, her cheese and bread untouched. Her eyes seemed even more sunken than before. I lowered myself to the squat bench, ran my fingers along the splintered plank on which I'd been fed, spoon by spoon, by the crone who now sat dazed.

"Pytor would be done with his meal."

I jumped at the cracked voice.

She eyed the sun. "He'd be chafing to go out and play."

"I'm sure he's well. Soon, we'll ride to visit him."

"Oh, my Pytor." She rocked, clutching her knees. "Lord of Nature be kind." Her eyes were closed.

"I, uh, have news."

"From Verein?" Rheumy eyes found mine.

My lips moved, but no sound emerged. "Of Elryc."

Her gaze fastened on my face, but she said not a word.

"He's nearby." I waited for a reply, but had only her fixed stare. I had to make sounds, to break the awful silence. "In the castle."

She stood. "Take me to him."

"Are you mad? They're searching. The moment they see you—"

"They've been here, and gone." Her fingers drummed the table. "Has he food?"

"Yes." Whatever stableboys eat. I hadn't thought to inquire.

She glared. "Who else knows?"

I hemmed and hawed, not quite willing to trust her with my secrets. "Nobody—well, one man. And a boy, but he's too frightened to—they're to be trusted." I yawned.

She spat. "No one's to be trusted. Get Elryc clear of them, or kill them both!"

"Hester!"

"Don't Hester me, you foolish whelp. If Margenthar takes him, it's his life. Doubt you not!"

"I can't go about murdering—"

"Then I will. Tell me the names."

"It's not come to that." I eyed her with new wariness. I'd never realized how protected we boys had been, under her vigilance.

"You've always been the stupid one. Now you'll be the death of your brothers!"

"As will you, unless you keep your voice low!" We glowered in mutual hostility. Stupid? Had I not saved Elryc's life, daringly marched him across the courtyard to safety in full view of all?

"Good day, Nurse." My tone was sulky.

"Keep me appraised, day by day." She pointed a crooked finger. "Or I'll seek you out."

I made my escape, wandered disconsolately through the castle. Perhaps Rustin would come today. If he didn't appear by the noon meal, I'd walk down the hill and fetch him and Ebon both. I'd—no, I couldn't get out the gate, now it was manned by Uncle Mar's men.

What a nightmare life had become: Mother gone, Pytor taken, Elryc in hiding, and I myself restrained like a hawk on a strap.

I must be crowned. Only then could I turn events.

No one had told me what date the Council had fixed for my coronation. I braced myself, put on an affable face, sought out Uncle Mar in his chambers.

He was gone to Verein, expected back the day after the morrow. No, he hadn't left a message. I stalked out, barely able to keep from slamming doors in my wake.

He hadn't even bothered to inform me.

I retreated to my room, bolted my door, cursed the fates that had placed me in his hands, and hating Rustin for his disinterest.

The Council had met, and scattered to the winds. Lord Warthen of the Sands, his bleak expression one of constant pain, had returned to his desert domain. Even to enlist his help, I had no desire to set forth on that long journey.

Grand-uncle Cumber had bid a curt good-bye, and returned to his hills. I knew Cumber disapproved of me, and probably wouldn't help my cause. Worse, he'd tell Uncle Mar.

Still, if I could get through the gate I could ride to inquire of other Council members. Earl Groenfil's castle was three days to the east, Soushire more southeast. I'd slept in the open before, without harm.

Abruptly I cursed myself for the dolt I was. No need to leave Elryc and journey so far to learn the plans for my coronation. I smoothed my hair, loped down the stairs to the Chamberlain's offices. In the anteroom sat his supercilious clerk.

I debated whether to ask an audience, decided not to humiliate myself. Still, no need to go out of my way to alienate the Chamberlain. I crossed to Willem's office, knocked politely, opened the door, and looked in.

A sigh. "Well, what now, Roddy? More coin?" He turned his paper on its face.

"Uncle Mar left."

"Of course. What of it?"

"What with the funeral and the Rites, I didn't get a chance to sit at the meet."

"No, it's closed to outsiders."

I snarled, "You call me outsider?"

Willem raised a placating palm. "A figure of speech."

"What did they decide?"

"I can't discuss it."

"Of course you may. You met in my name."

"I'm sworn by oath not to—"

"Sir Willem, this is me. Rodrigo."

It had the opposite effect from what I'd intended. His eyes drifted to the wardrobe, in which he kept the strap Mother had from time to time bade him apply. I flushed. "Those times are past." Lord will that it be so. If Mar bade him beat me, I supposed I'd kill one of them, or myself, whichever were possible.

I changed the subject as casually as I could. "Why was Pytor taken?"

"He'll come to no harm; we have Margenthar's unequivocal word on that. It was felt that the three of you made too tempting a target, should enemies consider a strike."

"Rubbish."

"Oh, not really. At Verein they've other lads Pytor's age; he'll be happy. And it's not as if he'll be gone forever."

"Pray he's not." I was surprised at the menace in my tone.

"Is there else?" Willem was curt.

"What more did they—"

"I will *not* discuss Council matters!" He rang his bell.

"When will I be crowned?"

The door opened.

"Hallor, show the youngsire to the door."

"What did Uncle Mar arrange? A month?" I ignored the clerk's beckoning hand.

"Roddy, that's quite enough."

"Two months? Three?"

The clerk beckoned. "My lord, you must come with me."

"Not until I have answer!" My scream tore at my throat. "Tell me, Willem! How long did he say I must wait? A year?" I leaned over his desk. *"TELL ME!"*

He gestured; the clerk scurried out. Willem said hesitantly, "Roddy, we never discussed it."

At my dumbfounded silence, he added, "Didn't Mar tell you? The matter was put off 'til the next meet. Six months."

Speechless, I stared at nothing. After a while I realized my gaze had never left Willem.

He licked his lips. "Prince, I told you before, I must tread with care. I'm but a hireling, and the quarrels of lords . . ."

"You sound like a stableboy I know."

"What?"

"No matter." I crossed to the door, paused. "If Mar hears you've told me, he'll be annoyed." I held his eyes. "So we won't tell him."

Willem studied my face, and, at last, nodded.

Chapter 6

 FOR TWO DAYS I WAITED FOR RUSTIN, RAGE BATTLING resignation.

Uncle Mar returned from Verein in full retinue. Alerted with the rest of the household by the hornsmen, I hurriedly donned formal garments and was poised on the steps to receive him, much as he'd greeted me.

I nodded my head in a gesture of courtesy; he did likewise, not even offering the trifling incline of the house bow. I pretended not to notice. He responded affably to my words of welcome; we played out the charade until we were within the keep, and went our separate ways.

By evening of the second day, Rustin had still not come. Nearly deranged from dallying in wait, I had a horse saddled, rode to the gate, where unfamiliar faces stood guard. They wouldn't let me through. Stymied, I sought out Uncle Mar to ask his leave, but I couldn't get past the anteroom. I had to beg my uncle's leave secondhand, through the guardsman Fostrow on duty outside his door.

The man returned in moments. "No, he says. It's too late of the evening."

"But it's only to ride down the hill. To Rustin."

"Don't whine at me, Prince; it's the Duke's word."

"Let me speak to him!"

"He's occupied. Try tomorrow."

I couldn't bandy words with this—this hireling; I dreaded his contempt, though he might not show it openly. With what dignity I could summon, I left. In my room, I threw myself on my bed.

Our Power wasn't worth the cost. I'd renounced my manhood for a crown that might never be mine, for a Still I'd never wield against dangers I might never face. Chela would lie with me, or some house-girl of our own. It was time my imaginings were supplanted by the intimacy my friend Rustin, Mar's son Bayard, perhaps even Elryc had already savored.

Moreover, if I gave up the Still, Uncle Mar wouldn't see me as a threat. Perhaps then he'd allow me my crown. Soon or late, he'd go the way of all flesh, and I could reign in earnest. The only part I couldn't fathom was how to assure him I'd become a man. Even if he provided the girl, Mar wouldn't take my word for it; in our family we were realists. But I couldn't very well let him watch. That was unthinkable.

What if I got him to supply a virgin? One of the household churls, or a field hand's whelp. After, he could have her examined. Surely, that would satisfy even a suspicious man like Uncle.

I wondered what she'd look like. After a time, my thoughts became less coherent. I fought the urge, found myself outmatched, chose surrender. At the end, lying inert, covers thrown back to evaporate my sweat, I fought back tears.

Then, at last, I slept.

In the sweltering morn I lay drowsing beyond my usual hour, until roused by a persistent knock. I covered myself with a sheet before I unbarred.

Rustin waited, wearing only a light, loose-fitting robe.

My breath hissed. "Where have you been?"

"I couldn't come."

"Rutting with your kitchen girl, were you? She means more than our friendship." I kicked at a chair.

For answer, he untied his loose belt, shrugged off his robe.

"Lord of Nature!" My breath hissed. His back and rump were a mass of fading red welts. "Who did that?"

"My father." His voice was almost inaudible.

"Couldn't you free yourself? You're bigger than he. Didn't you call for help, take away the stick—"

"I let him." Rust's misery extinguished the embers of my rage. He picked up the robe, wincing.

I laid it carefully across his bare shoulders. "Why, Rust?"

"Because I rode with you up the hill."

"Didn't you explain? I couldn't have faced the lords without you."

"That, he understood. But I'd defied him before his—no, don't shake your head, it *does* matter. I was too impetuous to go back to the keep and explain; I spurned his order in sight of his guards. That, he couldn't forgive."

"Still, how could you let him beat you so?"

His tone sharpened. "Would you I challenged him twice in two days, and be known through Caledon as unruly and willful? Whose gate would open to me then?"

"Better that than have the skin flayed from your back!"

"His hurt had to be assuaged, and the welts will fade. Next time I'll be more cautious." He grinned, with little mirth.

I found clothes, threw them on. "Uncle Mar is back."

"We saw his procession." The road from Verein intersected the descent from our hill, at Llewelyn's keep. "He must have emptied his castle. Fully two hundred horse."

"They're posted everywhere. I couldn't slip out last night. How'd you get in?"

"The gate's open for tradesmen. I went round to the kitchen, where everyone knows me." He perched on my bed. "Throw open your window; the room's musty."

It wasn't his place to tell me so, but I did as bidden. Then, beckoning him close, I told him of Pytor, and how I hid Elryc.

"Where is he?"

I splashed water on my face, wiped it dry. It would do for ablutions. "A good day to talk outside."

We strolled out to the dusty courtyard, round the foundation walls of the keep, to the orchard that, along with outbuildings, stables, smithies and fruit cellars, surrounded Stryx Castle. All were enclosed by the stronghold's massive outer walls. On three sides, jagged rock and plunging ravines made assault hopeless. The battlements on the fourth wall, facing the road from Stryx, were bristling with round stones, spears, arrows. Guardhouses every hundred paces overlooked the winding Castle Way.

Now, the ramparts were guarded as if for war. Torches pierced the night shadows; sentries patrolled each catwalk. Even the high tower was manned. Thank Lord of Nature we'd moved Elryc in time.

We went to the orchard, where under welcome shade and safe from prying ears, I finished my story. "The only ones who know are old Griswold and Garmond, the stableboy."

"A dung beetle." He laughed softly.

"It was all I could think of."

"Might we smuggle Elryc to your room?"

"Stire may search again." I shifted out of the advancing sun. "What about your father's keep?"

"No." A tone of finality.

"Not for Elryc's sake, for mine."

"I won't ask it." He leaned forward, spoke to my frown. "Roddy, it would mean Father's death. Mother's too."

"Uncle Mar may be spiteful, but he doesn't go about slaughtering—"

"He's not had need. Would you he set an example?"

I had no answer. I recalled Uncle Mar's glance of hatred as I'd barred him from Mother's door.

From the courtyard, trumpets.

Rustin glanced about. "Now what?"

I shrugged. Perhaps Uncle Mar was leaving again for Verein. Good riddance. "Rust, I've been thinking about giving up the Power."

He sucked in a breath, then busied himself with a blade of grass. Finally he said, "Not yet." He licked his lips, as if nervous. "When it's time, you'll know."

He got carefully to his feet, favoring his welts.

We roamed the grounds of Castle Stryx. Tents had been set up near the scullery for the extra men from Verein. Boys of the town and castle jostled to watch the soldiers clean and arrange their gear; I tugged Rustin's arm and made him come away, lest we appeared to be mixing with such riffraff.

In the kitchen, Kerwyn looked up from his meal. "The Duke's men seek you."

"Why?"

He snorted. "Lord Mar doesn't consult me, sire."

I retreated with Rustin to the sultry daylight. "Should I go?"

"Three days ago you were anxious enough to see him."

True, but Uncle Mar had taken on aspects of Mother at her most imperious. He wasn't my parent, nor my liege lord; I owed him nothing. Reluctantly, I trudged along the massive inner wall of the keep itself, toward the front entrance.

I ran my hand across the rough stones as we approached the corner. "How does it look, that I come crawling to his summons?"

"Stuff and nonsense. If I called, wouldn't you come?"

"That's diff—"

A figure cannoned round the corner, knocked me to the turf. I lay stunned, breathless.

With a roar Rustin hurled the intruder off my chest, flung him aside. His dagger unsheathed, he whirled, searching for more attackers.

I croaked, "It's only Garrand."

The stableboy scrambled to his feet, rubbing his forehead. He circled me warily, keeping my supine form between himself and Rustin. "It's Genard, m'lord. Did you hear the crier?"

I struggled to draw breath. My sore rib, recovering from my fall down the steps, gave notice of misery to come. "Hear what, you misbegotten oaf?" I stumbled to my feet, braced myself against the rock wall. "Rust, I think he broke—"

"They've proclaimed Elryc!"

My mouth worked like a goldfish in the pond. It could not be so.

"You lie!" Rustin cornered the urchin stableboy against the stones.

"It's true! The crier was on the very steps of the castle. He said—"

"They proclaimed Elryc King." I slid to the ground, clutching my aches. I'd never trusted the scheming foul-minded little goblin. Here I'd risked life and station to protect him, and behind my back he'd made treaty with the Duke.

"Not King, outlaw!" Genard was beside himself. "The crier called him traitor, said that you were rightful heir, that your brother plotted against you. Twenty gold pieces to any man who found him."

"Rust, what's Uncle up to?"

The stableboy danced from toe to toe. "Twenty goldens!"

I cuffed him across the mouth. "Villein, I'll wear your skin for a jerkin, if you but breathe a word . . ."

"I won't!"

"I heard your greed." I twisted his hair, flung him to the ground. "Don't let the thought cross your pea brain!"

"Easy, Roddy."

"You too, Rust? Would you betray us for twenty goldens? Or perhaps you'd bargain for— Ow!"

Rustin stood over me, fists ready. "You call *me* traitor?"

From the turf, the stableboy watched, jaw agape, a tear drying on his cheek.

I rubbed my chin, half-dazed from Rustin's blow, wondered if I was in position to kick his legs from under him. Then, despite my fury, a smile twitched. My head lay no more than a foot from Genard's. As I had done, Rustin had done to me.

"Oh, stop!" Grumbling, I got to my feet, waving away the threat of his blow. "I didn't mean it."

Rustin's passion was aflame. "You're a lout and a bully!"

"And your liege."

"True. My liege lord, you're a lout and a bully!"

"Some vassal you." I winced, offered a hand to the stableboy. "Up. My temper got the better of me."

"Should he think that an apology?" Rust's tone was acid.

"Need I apologize to a churl?" Preposterous. I pulled the urchin to his feet.

The boy's lip quivered, much as Elryc's had, in his terror atop the tower. Well, I could have regrets, and speak them, with honor. "I wish I hadn't lost my temper."

The boy nodded, eyes downcast. Somehow, it didn't seem enough.

I hoped I wouldn't ruin him for service. "I hope you're not much hurt, Garmond."

"Genard." His eyes rose shyly. "I'm all right, m'lord."

Rustin thrust a warning finger at me, spoke to the urchin. "His brother's life is in your hands, stableboy. Only a fool would betray it for a mere twenty goldens. When Rodrigo's King, your loyalty will reap a fortune." Genard's eyes grew round.

Now Rust was raiding my treasury before I'd secured it. After a moment my frown relaxed. It was he who'd made the promise. Let *him* pay the stableboy his ransom.

"Satisfied, Rust? Or must I apologize to you, for knocking me down?"

"A lout and a bully." But his anger was fading.

"What's Uncle Mar up to?"

"You're the one to be King. Think."

Sometimes he was beyond bearing. I sighed. "Mar hopes to unearth Elryc. But a reward would do that by itself. Why talk of treason?" I leaned against the wall, dabbed again at my lip.

Uncle Mar wanted all three of us under his control. Elryc loose was a danger, however ill-defined. By proclaiming him traitor, he would separate my adherents from Elryc's, and neutralize them as players in the game of state. And also . . .

My eyes went up. "He's raising the stakes."

Rust asked quietly, "How so?"

The stableboy swiveled between us.

"Mar suspects I've helped hide my brother, despite my denial. Condemning Elryc is a warning to me, not to cross him further."

"But if they find him—" Genard.

"Did we ask you?" The boy wilted under my glare.

"No, sire. I'll go now." He sidled away.

"Hold! Where are you off to?" Hester was right; the only safe mouth was one closed by death.

"To warn him, m'lord! The stable's not safe, with everyone looking. If someone from kitchen or the smith's boy recognizes him . . ." He seemed about to bolt.

"Rustin, he's right. We have to move him."

"Where?"

"The winery? A toolshed?"

Genard blurted, "He isn't safe at the castle. Outside."

I glowered. "*You're* not safe. Begone, and we'll stir our stew without your nose in the pot."

"No, stay," said Rustin. "Roddy, we have few enough allies."

"Him? A simpering fool who knows not who his father is? A peasant?"

"As always, your grace is inspiring." Rust's tone turned colder. "Roddy, I do think I'm about to feed you grass, until you come to your senses."

Hastily I backed away, desperate to avoid humiliation in the sight of a stableboy. "Don't you dare—"

Rustin rolled up his sleeves. "You can't treat folk like—"

"All right, I'm sorry!" I flushed crimson. "Both of you! Garmand, I didn't mean any insult."

"My father was a singer of lays!" The boy's face was red. "He sang his tales for your mother the Queen. My ma told me ofttimes!"

"I said I'm—"

He squalled, "And my name is Genard! Not Garmand, or Garron, or any of the stupid things you call me!"

I looked with disgust to Rustin. "See what you made of him?" How dare a churl shout at a prince? Even if my temper was undone, I'd been gracious enough to apologize. As soon as we got to the stable, I'd have Griswold lay a stick to the young lout's back.

Rust seemed less put out than I. "Lower your voice, Genard. I accept your apology, Prince Rodrigo." He bowed.

"Arghh." I should have stayed under my covers, and ignored Rustin's knock. "It's too hot to fight." I sat, leaned against the wall, waited until the throbbing of my ribs subsided. "Genard of the stables, sit over here." I patted the grass. "Rust, we'd better think quickly. Where can we move Elryc?"

"Have you coin for a bed at the Thorn and Briar?"

"He couldn't sit to eat in the public—"

Rust said, "I could bring him food, in his room. If not me, Chela."

"The inn's too crowded." Someone would spot him, soon or late. "Nowhere in the city. Too many greedy folk prowl the streets." Once, when I'd been nine, my purse had been cut from my belt, and I'd never known 'til I dug for a copper.

"What, then?"

"Hester." The word thrust from my throat, unbidden. "She'll know."

"Can we trust her?"

"Don't ask it to her face, Rust. Pytor was her life. Second to him, Elryc."

"Let's go, then."

"Genard, tell my brother to hide as deep in the stables as he might. In the loft, behind the hay. It'll be hot." I fumbled for a coin. "Bring him mulled wine, dilute and cold. We'll decide our course."

After all I'd done for him, the stableboy seemed sullen. "You'd trust me, then? What if I run to the Duke?"

"Well, there's always life as a dung beetle. Besides, have I choice but to trust you?" I frowned; it hadn't come out the way I'd wished. "Garm—Genard, will you pledge to serve me, for the House of Caledon? Serve me personally, that is?"

"As your sworn man?"

I pondered. Only the well-born might take an oath of loyalty to a particular noble. Rustin had done so, on my behalf. But an unwashed bumpkin such as Genard? Ridiculous, but I had little choice.

"Yes. My sworn man."

He hesitated a long moment. Then, "No, m'lord."

As I turned molten he blurted, "I'll serve Elryc, if he'll have me."

"You—what?"

"I'd be *his* liegeman." He drew himself up to his small stature. To my stunned silence he said, "I'll tell him."

Genard stalked toward the stable. I watched with grudging eye. His bearing had, for the first time, dignity.

Rustin and I hurried round the foundation wall of the castle. "I imagine she'll be in the nursery." We passed through the entry to the great stone stairs. The vaulted ceiling of the hall offered cool relief from the relentless sun.

"Ah, there you are!" Stire, the Duke's man. "Where go you?"

My shirt hung damp, my lip had begun to swell; I'd narrowly avoided a mouthful of grass from my lunatic vassal, and I'd had altogether enough. "I don't answer to you!"

An elaborate bow, suffused with sarcasm. "Perhaps not, my prince. But Margenthar of Stryx, Duke and Regent, my master, asks you to remain in your chambers until he speaks with you."

"I'll consider it." I started up the stairs, Rustin in tow.

"Consider it well. I'll post guards if you don't cooperate."

I stopped short. "You'd make me prisoner, Stire?"

"I'd do worse were it up to me." His face made clear his inclination. "Be in your rooms, youngsire, when your uncle comes to visit. Your playmate"—a contemptuous gesture at Rustin—"may keep you company."

I nodded, too enraged to speak. We disappeared from his sight; I stalked past the entry to my chambers, galloped up to the third-floor nursery.

I knocked. "Hester?" Last time I'd visited, she'd sat despondent at her table. "Are you in?" No answer; I opened the unlocked door and went in. "Rust, if she's out, go— *Lord of Nature!*" An apparition lunged across the chamber, jagged blade clenched tight in hand.

"Come you again, demons of the lake?"

I cowered against the wall opposite. Her eyes half-mad, Hester bore an ancient notch-edged knife she used to slice our bread and cheese. A whirl sent Rustin dancing to safety. A jab in my direction; I sucked in my stomach, avoided by a whisker the spill of my guts. "Lord's love, Hester! It's me, Roddy!"

A snarl, to Rustin. "Get away, you!" Her lip curled. "Where's my boy?"

I tensed at each flick of her blade. "Hester, don't you know me?"

"Think ye I'm daft, arrogant Princeling? You were to inform me day by day: I had your word! Where's my Elryc?"

"That's what we—"

"Tell me this moment, or I'll gut you like a trout!" The point of her blade pressed at my navel. Rustin, dagger drawn, circled behind. "This instant!"

A pinprick, on my tensed belly. I yelped. "In the stables!"

She swung to Rustin. "Is it true, whelp?"

"Put down the knife, grandmother. If you harm my prince—"

"Faugh. Call off your watchpuppy, Roddy." Blade still in hand, she brushed past Rustin as if he didn't exist. Rust's jaw dropped.

"Sit, both of you. I'll bar the door."

I rolled up my shirt, peered, wiped a droplet of blood from my navel. I took a long, slow breath to slow my heart's pounding. "See what I've put up with?" I shoved Rustin to a bench.

"She tried to kill us!"

"No, I'd be gawping my life out, if she so intended. Think ye Mother trusted just anyone, with her cubs?"

"But she's so old, so bent. How can she . . ."

"Sit." I pushed him down. "She's a tad irate." Not to say deranged. On the other hand, she was firmly on our side.

"Why the stables?" With a sigh, Hester lowered herself to the bench opposite, absently fingering the point of her blade.

"He's made friends with the stableboy. The boy brings him food and drink."

"Elryc's had nothing but that slop? Arr." She lay aside the blade, flexed her withered fingers. "You, Llewelyn's boy, see if the tea on the hearth is warm." A moment's reflection. "Griswold's a good man, I judge. The reward won't bend him." Her eyes shot up. "Your precious uncle put a bounty on Elryc's head. Called him a traitor."

"I heard, Nurse." My tone was meek.

"That shrew Rowena came running, delighted with the news. A goodly while you took, before you came to me." She brooded while Rustin poured steaming tea into her well-used cup. I wondered how she could stand the heat of it. She sighed. "Where shall we take him?"

"We?"

"I might need your help, to fetch and carry. My bones are old. Lord of Nature knows you can't be trusted alone to watch a foal in a stall, lest some butterfly float past and you—"

"Please!" Perhaps some hint of my anguish reached her, for she fell silent.

I swallowed a lump in my throat. Mother had kept me at heel in matters that concerned her, but otherwise I'd done as I pleased. I thought nothing of roaming off to see Rustin, or galloping through the fields with Griswold. As long as I appeared at my lessons, and promptly answered Mother's summons, my days had been my own. Now I was fenced on all sides, by Mar's scheming, the Chamberlain's uncertainty, Stire's contempt.

"Faugh." Hester sipped at her tea. "Feeling sorry for yourself? A habit you'd best outgrow if you'd be King. Think instead of poor Elryc, alone and terrified." Another sip. "I have a sister, Tarana. Had. Three years now she's gone. But her cottage remains, and it's mine. The mill-keeper tends it for me."

"Where?"

"In the hills south of Cumber."

Almost two days hard ride. For us younger ones, that was. Even if Hester could still sit a horse, she couldn't possibly ride at such a pace. She'd either dash her bones to splinters at her mount's first shy, or drop from exhaustion before the day was out.

"Rust and I will take him. Just tell us the way."

"Goatbabble. Think you I'd leave a helpless child to your notion of—"

"Nurse, would you risk his life by slowing us?"

"Bah." She eyed her tea with distaste. "Time was when you and that brute stallion of yours couldn't catch me on my mare, if your life itself lay in balance." A sigh. "I'll ride, if I must, though my saddlebags will be packed with liniment." She gestured to the pot. "Heat it well, this time."

Obediently, Rustin tossed the dregs of her cup in the slop bucket, put the kettle back on the embers.

"Besides, lad, there's not such haste. Margenthar has no need of a nurse; I'll tell him I've retired to my demesne. My gear will fill a wagon, and its pace will befit an old lady."

"That's ridiculous. Once they know you've sneaked Elryc away, mounted soldiers could ride in an hour what you'd manage in a day."

"Why would they?"

"And you can't drive out the gate with my brother sitting at your side. No matter where you hide him, knowing your feelings they'll search every inch—"

Her hand cracked down on the table, and made me jump. "He'll leave Stryx unharmed, if I have to turn him into a sparrow and fly him over the wall. Leave you that to me."

Rustin coughed. "Think, Roddy. Nurse can get a day's start; we can ride after, to meet her. Else we'd all troop through the gate like—"

"Oh!" I'd forgotten. I couldn't troop through the gate, with Elryc or alone. Uncle Mar had restricted my movement. Somehow, I'd have to break my chains. "We can't separate; what if out paths fail to cross? I won't leave Elryc."

Hester's fingers made a mysterious sign at my eyes. I snapped shut my mouth, ice chilling my spine. When I'd been small she'd shushed me so, warning me she had the Black Way. I'd never dared test her of it. "Elryc and I leave together, my young Prince Roddy. We'll wait for you outside the town. If you break free, you may ride with us."

"How kind of you." But my sarcasm seemed lost on her.

"And one other matter. Pytor."

I swallowed. In our concern for Elryc, I'd almost forgotten.

"When you pry him from Margenthar's grip, I will raise him, to finish the work your mother set me. If you are King, then here at the castle. Else, in my cottage."

"Hester, you're getting on in years . . ."

"Your word, prince. Or I'll stay to find Pytor, and let Elryc look after himself."

Protecting Elryc was my immediate task; I'd deal later with the complication of Pytor. I nodded. "My word."

"Then go about your business, you two. I'll demand my wages, tell the Duke I'm done with the House of Caledon. We'll leave on the morrow."

My lips were dry. "What of Elryc, tonight?"

"I'll see to him."

I protested, but she gave no ground. Eventually, tiring of my urging, she shooed us from the room, slammed the door in our faces.

We walked slowly down the stairs. I asked, "Can she—"

"Not another word about your imp-ridden housegirl!"

I gaped, but, finally understanding, kept shut until we'd reached my chamber. No guards were posted; at least I'd been spared that humiliation. Inside, I barred the door. I led him to my oaken wardrobe, stepped inside, slid shut the curtain. We'd be hot, but if we whispered, safe.

He asked, "Can Hester accomplish all that? Is her mind well?"

I shrugged; realized he couldn't see me in the dark. "I'm not sure. What choice have we?"

"How will we get you out of Stryx?"

I wiped my damp forehead. "I'm not sure. We'll figure a way."

"And what when you return?"

Abruptly my voice was unsteady. "I face Uncle Mar." He asked all the wrong questions.

Fingers felt for my shoulder, squeezed. "Have courage, my liege."

I knocked away his hand. "I'll be all right." From somewhere, a scent of cinnamon mixed with the acrid aroma of my fear. "It's an oven in here." I threw open the curtain, climbed out into the welcome air. Curiously, I flicked a row of cloaks. "What was that spice? Did someone put a sachet in my clothes?"

Rustin blushed. "Chela gave me scented soap from the market. Is it too strong?"

"No." Just unmanly. I took some comfort in that. Rustin was older, bigger, stronger; if it weren't for his flaws I'd loathe him.

After the wardrobe, even my room had seemed cool, but the heat of the day rapidly asserted itself. Eventually we settled on the floor, cross-legged, and played listlessly at dice.

It was two hours before a knock came, during which I'd managed to lose three silver pence to my supposed friend.

Uncle Mar, with an armed henchman. "Fostrow, retire to the bench by the stairs; I'll speak with my nephew alone."

"Aye, sire." The guard gave Rustin a dubious eye, departed.

Rust came to his feet, with courtesy. "Shall I leave you, my lord?"

"No need." Mar sauntered into my room, glanced about, wrinkled his nose, but said nothing. "He toyed with my slate, plucked it from its hook near the window.

I composed myself, waited.

"This matter of Elryc." His glance flickered to mine, back to the slate. "If he's been taken by some foe, my proclamation will neutralize his value to them. If he's hiding for some boyish motive beyond our ken, this will flush him out."

"By branding him traitor, you risk his life."

"My prince, consider whether in fact he is not precisely such." He set down the slate. "You are firstborn, therefore heir. Think how that makes him feel. But for the fluke of birth, he would enjoy the fruits of office, the riches, the honors, the majesty that will be yours."

I shivered. Of whom was he speaking? Elryc . . . or himself?

"Remember what you said yourself. Elryc's a calculating little soul, isn't he? He may have left the castle entirely, to make union with an enemy, that they might secure your throne."

"Uncle, you could put a stop to that, by having me crowned."

"Which will be done. Didn't I give you my word?" No, he had not, but he left me no time to answer. "Think you that a coronation guarantees a kingdom? The crown is more than that bauble that sits in the vault. A diadem won't maintain a state."

"If it's so worthless, then give it—"

"Your crowning must be an affair of splendor, held when Caledon stands secure. Else it will seem—and be—a sham." He took up the slate, licked his fingers, drew idly in the dust. "Tantroth comes."

"What?" My voice came hoarse.

"Uncle Cumber sent scouts to probe the high passes. Tantroth of Eiber gathers his troops, and they take boats toward the bay."

"He's always holding maneuvers, of one sort or another." I swallowed, nonetheless. The castle of Eiber stood secure in the Hadriad Mountains, but from the foothills, streams poured into the River Eibe, a wide road that chuckled its way to the sea. In a following wind, tall ships from Tantroth's port could dash from Inlet Eibe down to Stryx in little more than a day.

"Tantroth's always wanted our lands, Roddy. Now, it's pressing that we know Elryc's whereabouts. For the sake of Caledon, will you help?"

I shook my head. "I wish I could."

Rustin stirred. "You have my oath, my lord, that Roddy had no idea where Elryc is headed. We spent the morning worrying over him, and gave it up."

"So I see." The Duke eyed our dice, smiled, again turned serious. "Roddy, I must ask you to stay close, until Tantroth's intentions are known. You're too valuable to risk, running about."

"Even down the hill? There's no danger in the market, or the inn, if—"

"Even so. Remain in the castle, where we can guard you. This must be." To Rustin, "Help him pass the time. You're welcome in Stryx Castle, son of Llewelyn."

"Why, thank you, sire." Rustin's courtesy was such that even I couldn't detect a hint of irony. "If my father permits, I'll be happy to come. Perhaps I can shop at the docks for Roddy, bring him what trifles he would buy."

"You see?" said Uncle Mar. "It all works out." He crossed to the door. "You'll know, the moment we find Elryc. In the meantime, be at ease." A friendly nod, and he was gone.

I paced the room, while Rustin tossed dice to no purpose. "I shouldn't have let that old witch take care of, um, the bundle for the night. If she fails, Uncle will have an unexpected gift."

"The same as if you failed."

"At least I can trust my judgment." He snorted; I flicked him an annoyed glance. "Besides, it's *my* promise."

"Calm yourself."

"How am I supposed to do that?" I paced anew.

"Try a bath. I'm serious; it will do you good in other respects." Languidly, he got to his feet. "Who draws your water?"

"A footman, but I don't have time. We have to plan."

"Is there a bellpull?"

"Rustin, leave it be!" My face was hot with embarrassment. "I'm not a baby, to—"

"But you've had a lot of worry, you've been running about under that blazing sun, and I had to climb in the closet with you."

To end the mortification, I let him persuade me. The water, I had to admit, was pleasantly cool. I began slowly to relax.

"What will happen to us, Rust?"

"We'll settle Elr—the bundle with its, uh, keeper, and come back to Stryx."

"What will Uncle do?" I was sure our absence would send him into paroxysms of rage.

"He won't be happy."

A stab of fear chilled me. "I want to dress." I climbed to my knees.

"I'll be with you, my prince."

Why did I gulp back tears? I took slow, deep breaths, willed away my panic as I groped for a robe. "Will Llewelyn beat you again, if you leave with me?"

"I think not." He turned me around, fastened my sash. Then, unexpectedly, he drew my face close, kissed me softly on the forehead.

I froze. He gave sort of an embarrassed cough, turned to the window, hands clasped behind him.

I dressed quickly, wishing Rust would leave, answering his queries with little more than grunts, hoping he'd sense my unease. But his conversation was so casual, so natural, that slowly I began to relax.

At any rate, we had pressing business. In low tones we planned our journey. Rustin would go home for the night, satisfy his father as to his forthcoming absence. He'd pack saddlebags with gear for the two of us, leave them at Llewelyn's keep, come back to the castle to be with me when Hester took Elryc. I knew I could never face that spectacle alone; my nerves were already at the point of breaking.

We'd wait, until that evening or the next day, so as not to throw suspicion on Hester by our sudden absence. Then we'd gallop after.

On our trip I'd have to wear Rust's hand-me-downs; I wasn't sure whether I'd gain permission to ride a horse down the hill, or have somehow to jump the wall under the noses of the guards, and either way, I couldn't carry about conspicuous changes of clothing.

As evening approached I grew ever more nervous. "Must you go?"

"It would be best." His calm licked me like a mother cat her kitten.

"What if your father doesn't let you return?"

"He will. I'll explain in private, and humor his needs."

Reluctantly, I let him leave. As an afterthought, I gave him my purse, with most of the year's stipend Willem had given me. Best Rust should have it, lest I lose it to Mar's guards.

"You trust me with your coin?"

I grimaced. "You already have the key—"

He clapped his hand over my mouth. I gulped, nodded. Instead of releasing me, he squeezed my lips into a fish's gawp. "Do demons have your mind? *Think* before you speak!"

I pushed his hand away, without rancor. "Yes, Father." It was an odd thing to say. My father, Josip, had died when I was nine, and I'd been raised without. Until now, I'd not felt the lack.

"Hah. Were I your father, I'd set you across . . ." He shook his head. "Until tomorrow, my prince." Impulsively, I squeezed his hand, brought it to my cheek. To my astonishment, his eyes teared, but he turned away before I could ask the matter.

Chapter 7

DURING THE NIGHT IT STORMED. WHAT WITH THUNDER, worry about Elryc, and an odd discomfort whenever I thought about Rustin, I barely slept. At first light I stumbled groggy out of bed, splashed water on my face, climbed into the nearest clothes. The day had a chill, welcome relief from the oppressive heat just past. I flung open my door.

On the bench a few steps down the corridor, a soldier dozed; I hurried past.

"Hold. Where go you, my lord?" Bleary, but alert, he got to his feet.

I frowned. It was Fostrow, the man who'd barred my way to Council, and later to my uncle's chamber. "Breakfast. Upstairs. About the castle." Who was he to question me?

Fostrow shook his head. "Let them bring your meal."

"And seal my door, while they're about it! Have you tested the bars on my window?" My voice seethed.

"Easy, my lord; I but do the Duke's bidding."

"Did he tell you to hold me within?" The man had heft, but I knew I could outrun him. Yet it would burn a bridge that later I might have need to cross.

"No, but I must come with you, where you go." He took his shield from its resting place.

"Oh, for—nonsense. Look, I'll run to the kitchen and visit Hester. It won't take—"

"I can't let you, alone. Particularly outside."

I sighed, blinked away the last remnants of sleep. It was important to hold back my ire. "I'm the heir, and I depend on my Power. You've heard of the True? Good. I tell you True, I'll go only about the castle. Breakfast first, and then upstairs; my old nurse is leaving service, and I would say good-bye. You have my word I won't go out, until I've come back to get you. My True word."

He hesitated.

"Fostrow, weren't you ever young? Don't make me go to breakfast with a nanny."

As I'd hoped, it brought a smile. "My lord, I'll trust you in this. Please, don't do us both a wrong." Gratefully, he sat, laid aside his shield.

"I'll bring you fresh bread." Before he could change his mind I loped down the stairs, wondering how I would manage a trip to the stables, to see what had become of Elryc. Obviously, I couldn't visit with Uncle's watcher in tow. At least I'd freed myself to find what Hester was up to. The Still had its uses, I realized, even before having the wield of it. Even a simpleton like Fostrow realized I wouldn't risk its loss by being untrue.

Light rain beat a tattoo on the roof of the kitchen, and occasional drops sizzled in the hearth. I wolfed down a breakfast, hardly aware of its nature. What if Hester had already slipped out, telling no one her destination? The High Road through the mountains to Cumber had bypasses and trails aplenty; what if we lost her in its windings?

What if she meant to take Elryc for her own ends, or even meant him harm? Without Elryc, I'd have to face Uncle Mar alone, except for what little help Rust could provide.

A knot congealing in my stomach, I dashed up flight after flight to the nursery.

A housemaid slopped water in the corridor, mop in hand. "Watch your step, my lord!" Her tone was irked.

"Where's Nurse gone?"

She rested her palm atop the mop handle. "No, it's 'When's Nurse finally going?' if you ask me. 'Magret, bring me this. Have footmen bring my trunks from the second storeroom. Watch how you fold that robe, it's older than you are.' Fah!" An angry wipe. "She can't be gone soon enough for me."

"Magret!" The voice inside the door held a sharp edge. "Where's the packet of dried foods Cook was to make ready?" The door whipped open. "Leave that confounded mopping and see to, it! What do *you* want, you lout?" A glare, in my direction.

I peered past her shoulder. "Are you alone? Have you packed—"

"Get away from us!" She snatched the mop from the startled Magret, slapped water over my breeks. "Leave me be!"

A sympathetic eye from the housemaid was hardly of help. "I just came to say good-bye." Now I sounded a supplicant.

"Good-bye, then. Think you I have time for such folderol, if I'm to be at Whiecliff Hamlet tonight, and past Seawatch Rock by morrow? Take your foolishness elsewhere!"

"Imps take your uncivil tongue, and addled head!" I stalked away, wet breeches swishing. "The sooner you're gone, the happier we'll all be."

Her grating voice chased me to the steps. "I'll miss my Pytor, and Elryc. Proper children were they!"

I stomped down the stairs, startling a houseman with my muttered curses. To think I'd trusted Elryc's safety to that demented old crone. As soon as Rustin returned, we'd wrest my brother from her clutches.

I hadn't even been allowed entry to her chambers, to say nothing of private speech. Did she expect me to ask our arrangements while a sullen servant girl took in every word?

I flung open the corridor gate, rousing the guard Fostrow. She'd booted me out like a child, with no hint where she'd concealed my brother, and worse, without agreement on where we were to meet, after. All I knew was that she would leave during light, and . . . I stopped dead in my tracks."

"Is something amiss, Lord Rodrigo?"

"No. Sorry, I forgot the bread." I fumbled for my chamber door, barred it behind me.

All I knew was that Hester would spend the night at Whiecliff Hamlet, and the morrow night at Seawatch Rock. Before the housemaid's very ears she'd given me our meet, making it seem of no consequence, and bustling me away before I could make a hash of it.

"Damn you, Nurse," I said to the empty room. "Clever, but why make me a fool in the process?" I'd long known that Hester never cared a whit for me. Her parting dart, that Elryc and Pytor were her favorites, had the ring of truth.

I peeled off my wet breeches, fell on my bed. Within a moment I bounded to my feet. If Hester wouldn't hint at Elryc's hiding place, perhaps the stableboy knew. I thrust on fresh breeks, grabbed a cloak against the rising wind, threw open my door. "I'll be back in a few moments."

Fostrow looked sorrowful. "Then so will I." He stood.

"Again, I give you my word—"

"Margenthar will clap me in gaol if he sees you larking outside without a keeper. You seem a nice laddie, would you want that?"

"Gladly."

He seemed unaware of my sullenness while we strode down the steps. I managed to look busy as we traversed the entry hall; Lord willing, no one would notice I was leashed to a watchguard like a toddler on his first outing.

Outside, I blinked in the unexpected wind, threw the hood of my cloak over my hair. The soldiers on guard at the doors wore hemp raincovers over their gear; those at the closed entry gates had a rude lean-to under which they lolled, but Fostrow, I was pleased to note, had no protection from the weather.

"Where do you go, my lord?"

"To take air."

The front steps ended in a sort of flagstone terrace, one side of which gave way to the clay courtyard I would have to cross, to the stables. On the terrace the ceremonial guard of the door chatted idly with Lanford, chief officer of the gate sentinels.

A scarred, grimy wagon barred our way, parked almost on the flagstone itself.

"What's that?"

Lanford snickered. "That shrew from the nursery had it hauled here last night. Said she'd claw the eyes out of any man who moved it."

I eyed the conveyance with doubt. High flat sides of rough-cut timbers; thick wheels on aged axles that cried for grease. The wagon itself was so heavy that once loaded, a team of eight oxen would barely manage to pull it. Worst, the high closed box seat was set gracelessly athwart the frame, and no padding at all; the rump that sat on it would ache almost from the start. And that only if the driver weren't knocked off his high perch by overhanging branches.

"Where'd she get that monstrosity?"

"It was abandoned behind the stable. I'd feel sorry for her if . . ." His words trailed off.

"Yes?"

"Pardon, my lord. I know she was your nurse."

I kicked the wheel. "Would it weren't so. Go on."

"She's rather a . . . harridan, isn't she? No need to plant that wreckage here so early as last eve, but no, she said, she'd have the maids lugging trunks and whatnot downstairs through the night, and unless she set the cart in front of the guards' noses, none of her gear would be left by morning, amid the thieves and knaves of Castle Stryx." He spat. "Look, noon nigh upon us, and the wagon empty as the day it was made."

Nothing he told me was much reassurance as to Hester's good sense, or even sanity. On top of all, parking her hulking wagon in the middle of the courtyard gave her almost no chance to smuggle Elryc aboard.

As I stood morose, Hester herself hobbled down the steps behind us. A band of onlookers exchanged grins of derision as she puttered about her wagon, cloak and shawl drawn tight against the rain. She issued an incessant stream of complaints to the struggling footmen and flustered housemaids.

"Careful with that trunk, dolt! Would you break the straps before it's seen the wagon? Oh, clever, putting it next to the barrel. At the first rut the cask will—Magret, who told you to bring that drapery? It belonged to my lady; think you I'm a thief like yourself? Put it back—no fold it first; damask will wrinkle like the very demon. Has no one taught you a thing? Faugh!"

No Elryc in sight. Not that I'd expected it.

She banged her stick. "You soldiers, stop gawking and help lift that chest over the rail. Steady! By first light I should have been gone, and look at this mess! Were a single soul in Castle Stryx not lazy as a pregnant sow I'd be long on my way!"

Someone muttered, "And none too soon."

"I heard that, you gapemouth churl!" She squinted. "Isn't your mother fat Etha of the laundry? Hold your tongue, or I'll give her a piece of my mind for misraising her whelps!"

A nudge in my ribs, from Fostrow. "She hasn't a piece to spare." Despite myself, I grinned.

"Aye, laugh, all of you. It's little enough I bring away from the years I served Caledon!" She fussed at a set of leather boxes, making sure they were covered by canvas against the wet.

"There you are." A hand on my shoulder, Rustin's. "I've been looking everywhere."

At his voice, I sighed with relief. "She has them in a dither. Been packing all night." I glanced at Fostrow, dropped my voice to a whisper. "No sign of the bundle." Rust nodded.

We sauntered around the cart. Two of the barrels were large enough to hide Elryc, though he'd be sore cramped. Three trunks were possibilities as well, though if Hester were demented enough to stuff him into any of them, he'd be long smothered and gone. They had no airholes.

Under the cart, then. Across the way, I spotted Genard gawping amid the crowd, and nudged Rustin. The stableboy had been enlisted. What more natural than two urchins, nosing about the wagon? One would slip under, hoist himself into ropes or straps readied for the purpose.

I yearned to bend and look, and thought of fussing with my boot, but didn't dare risk it. "Rust, go ask that dung beetle about, um, you know." I whispered to him my suspicions. Rust nodded, drifted off.

Someone sent word to the stables; in a few minutes Kerwyn and another groom led six sturdy dray horses to the thick-hewed wagon.

"Put that star-faced mare in front. Team her with the bay, you simpleton!" Hester, to my surprise, took avid interest in the harnessing, and showed sense in the pairings. Had she truly been a horsewoman, in her long-vanished youth?

The steady soak began to work a chill through my bones, but I couldn't go inside until I'd seen the cart safely out the gate. At my side, Fostrow shivered, and I felt a moment's compassion, before remembering he was the Duke's man.

Rustin poked me in the back.

"Well?"

He shook his head. "Says he knows nothing."

"He must." I eyed my neighbors; Hester's devilments held them in thrall. I whispered into Rustin's ear the plans Hester had snarled at me, across a wet mop. He nodded.

I returned my attention to the wagon, mystified at my brother's whereabouts. Finally the last cinch was pulled tight, the reins were in the old woman's hand. Hester climbed aboard the high box seat. A boot braced against the footboard, the other on the brake, she took one last look about.

"A loathsome place," she said in her disagreeable scratched voice. "And not one of you fit to hold the hem of my lady's gown." She clicked to the horses, flicked the reins, began a slow laborious turn round the courtyard.

I pressed my knees together, wishing I'd visited the privy.

"Come, let's get out of the chill." Fostrow.

"Not yet." The wagon rumbled over the cobbles toward the gate.

Not two steps from where the front wheel splashed in a puddle, Elryc had once slipped and cut his knee, and I'd had to help him inside to wash off the sting. He was a mangy brat, an ill-tempered know-it-all, who harbored Lord knew what designs on my throne. And he sniffled.

Where in the demons' lake was he?

The huge wagon approached, but the gate didn't open. Instead, Lanford, the chief gate guard, detached himself from his fellows at the lean-to. "Hold, old woman."

She spat, catching him neatly on the tip of his boot. "Dame Hester, to the likes of you!"

"Not so fast, crone." He caught the lead mare's bridle.

"Get away from my team, and do your work at the gate!" She gestured with the whip.

"Oh, we'll open soon enough. You'll hear our cheers long before we've seen the last of you. But get off, while we search."

"Hah! Think you I'd take one pence of my lady's—"

"Not for coin, for the traitor you raised, brother to the true Prince." An eye in my direction, a nod.

Hester fixed him with an eye gone iron. "Lanford of the gate, thank Lord of Nature that your face shows your witlessness, else I'd take offense and I'd set the dark word at your throat." Her hand twitched, as if to make a sign.

Lanford stepped back so fast he almost fell. "Enough of that!" He made the protective sign. "Down off your wagon. You louts, what are you gawking at? Open the barrels!" Two soldiers jumped aboard.

Instead of climbing down Hester scaled the box seat, stood with arms akimbo, let loose a cry I thought was anguish, until I realized it was a shriek of mirth. "Aye, poke through an old woman's undergarments; you'll have much to dream about tonight!"

I moved closer, with the rest of the crowd. Evidently, Elryc wasn't in the barrel; after a perfunctory search the crimson-faced young soldier pressed the lid in place.

"The trunk has a key, simpleton. Try the one under your loincloth; it's small enough to fit." The crowd roared with laughter. She fished through a ring, tossed a key at his feet.

He swung open the trunk.

"Carvings from the Sands. One of them is your precious Elryc." A shrill cackle. "I turned him into that oaken bird."

"Enough, old woman."

"*Dame*. The title is mine by right. *Don't touch that box!*"

A sudden hush.

Lanford snapped, "Get it open, quick! Use that pry strapped to the siding."

From Hester, a smirk. "Don't open it, I warn you."

Five feet long, a proper width to conceal a child. I held my breath.

A creak, then another. As one, we surged forward. Hester, on her high perch, kicked at a hand that trespassed.

Furs, old and worn. A woman's hat. A bed quilt, well made, neatly tended. Two work gowns. No more.

"Try them on, guardsman. Well you'd look in them." The old woman's voice was shrill with spite. "They belonged to my sister."

In silent fury, the two soldiers hammered shut the lid.

She hissed, "Who died of the plague."

Sudden silence. The one soldier stared in horror at his hands, glanced about helplessly for something on which to wipe them. Hester did a little dance on her box seat, humming to herself. I hoped she'd stop before she pitched headlong to the courtyard.

"Get on with it, you dolts. I have leagues to ride by nightfall!"

Reluctantly, the guards fell to work. Hester aided them with constant commentary, of a virulence such that I began to fear for her life. Fortunately, few boxes left were Elryc's size.

"On your way, witch!" The rattled young soldier jumped down from the cart.

Hester clambered off her promontory to the bed of the wagon, snatched up a blanket. "Shake it out, my darling; a boy might be inside!"

Over the years I'd seen Nurse in foul temper, but never had she so baited misfortune. I leaned close to Rustin. "Her wits are gone."

His face drawn, he shook his locks in disapproval of the spectacle. "She brings shame on herself and your House."

Grumbling, Hester settled herself on the high seat. A flick of the reins. "Hsk, my loves. Now that my lady's under the earth, no reason to stay." The gate swung open.

In a few moments she'd rumble down the hill, and with her, the dregs of my childhood. This weathered, half-mad old biddy had tended my hurts, rocked me to sleep, fed me mush until my milk teeth came. Though we'd soon rejoin her on the road, no longer would she be the dragon of my nursery.

I swallowed an odd lump in my throat.

"Hold!" Lanford, at the gate. "You, crawl under, and look."

Elryc was done for. I clutched at my side, but I wore only a dagger. My sword was still at the fencing master's, where Mother had bade me store it. If, after they dragged Elryc out, I lunged for the one holding him, perhaps we could race down the hillside, dodging the guards' arrows. I drifted toward the gate.

"Nothing." The soldier brushed mud from his breeks.

My breath rushed out in a hiss. Dazed, I watched the ancient cart rumble through the portal.

After, we went to Uncle's quarters. In whispers, Rust and I had decided Pytor was to be my excuse; I sought leave to visit him at Verein. Once outside the walls, we would find a way to evade our escort.

Mar's tone was dry. "I don't recall you cared so much for his company."

"He *is* my brother, despite all. And I'm restless. I'll admit that."

"It's a bad time, my boy. Storm clouds gather."

"It's been raining all morn—"

"Roddy, please. I spoke metaphorically."

I shrugged. Mother had never made me study metaphysics.

"Oaf! It's too dangerous now to let you go riding. Have I made it plain enough?"

"Uncle, Verein is but a night and a day; I rode it with old Griswold, not a year ago." With an effort, I kept my voice pleasant.

"Aye, when you weren't heir to a vacant throne." His fingers drummed an alabaster stand, on which sat a bowl of fresh grapes. "In a few days we'll be sending a troop across the hills. Wait until then."

"But—"

"Roddy, I do wish you'd be more sensitive to risk. Your bones are of great value, while you surround them. Others would prefer you separated from them."

"In which category do you fall?" My temper smoldered and caught flame. "Both, perhaps. While I live, my treasury is yours to loot as regent. After you dispose of me—of us—there's the crown itself."

He swept away the bowl of grapes with a crash, leaped to his feet. "What grounds have you to accuse me?"

"None but the obvious. You've separated me from my brothers, denied me word with the Seven. Bayard sits waiting at Verein, while I—"

His hand shot out, slapped me hard. My hand flew to my stinging cheek.

"Elena was my sister. Think you I'd kill a son of hers?"

My tone was like ice. "Only if a silver pence were to be gained."

He rushed across the room, flung open the door, caught me in an iron grip. One hand on my jerkin, the other on the rope of my breeks, he propelled me across the chamber and out to the hall where Rust sat. "Out, until you learn manners! Out, before I have you strapped like the royal brat you are! Begone!" The door hurled shut with a tremendous crash.

Fostrow shook his head sadly as I picked myself up. "You shouldn't rile him so. Your uncle has a fearsome temper."

"Guard me, but don't presume to lecture me!" I set out for the courtyard, my stride so brisk my companions had to scurry to keep up.

Rustin panted, "Roddy, what did he—"

"Bottle it, and shove the cork . . ." I bit off the rest.

Fostrow a few steps behind us, we prowled the battlements. Torches were mounted, ready to light, and the walls fully manned as if for siege. Ignoring the steady rain I climbed to the secluded spot where it had been my wont to throw over a rope and disappear into the night, until Mother caught me and put a stop to it. Now, the place was within ten paces of a guard's post.

After a time I slowed my pace. I said softly, "Rust, I feel like a badger in a trap."

He glanced back to where Fostrow lurked, just out of earshot. "That rampart isn't the only way out."

"But this west wall of the castle is. You know how much steeper are the other walls. Why do you smile? From here to that tower are the only places we can safely—"

"We need not scale walls. No, let it wait; later we'll be alone."

Upstairs once again, Fostrow trudged along the hall, shivering. "Catch a death of cold, I could. All afternoon in pouring rain, and no chance to change clothes. It's a long day my master's set me; early morn 'til Vanire comes at midnight. No warm fire, no dinner, either."

I snarled, "You have my pity. Better yet, my leave to go."

He stood hands on hips, glaring. "Be thankful you're not behind a barred door. From what I hear, Lord Mar would as soon brick you in your chamber!"

"I—we . . ."

"And I'd volunteer to set the mortar!" His eyes had a dangerous light as he shook the wet from his grizzled hair. "Royalty you may be, but a more brazen young charge I've never seen. All day you run me about the castle, upstairs and down, in and out, and delight in my discomfort."

I paused at the entry to my chamber. "Oh, for Lord's sake, Fostrow, I only want the freedom I've known."

Fostrow muttered something, shook his head. "And for your sake, Prince, don't mock Vanire as you do me. Stay your roaming, and your complaint."

For answer, I slammed my door.

In my room, I relived my conversation with Uncle Mar, pacing with reignited fury, while Rustin sat comfortably on the rug. After a time my diatribe slowed to a muttered string of oaths. I marched from window to door, my fists knotted.

Rust cast his dice. "Tell me when you're calm enough to hear."

"Now."

"Hah." Another cast. "Why do twos come up so often?"

I thought to launch myself at him, reined myself in. "You're no friend, Rustin son of Llewelyn, and a wretched vassal to boot."

"Yes, it's all my fault."

"Would you care to eat those dice?"

He gathered them in. "If you can feed me." Another cast. "Royal brat, eh? An interesting phrase, and apt."

I threw myself at him while he was still rising to his feet; in one graceful motion Rust caught me round the waist, swung me to the floor, climbed on my chest. His powerful hands pinned my wrists to the flagstone.

"How often have I said you lack patience?" His look was one of sorrow. I bucked, almost heaving him off, but he held his position. "A word of refusal from Mar, a gibe from me, and you froth at the mouth."

I tried to bite his wrist.

"Oh, Roddy." He grasped my hair, raised his hand for a blow, instead dropped my head with a thump. "No, you've already been slapped today. It does no good." A lithe spring, and he was on his feet. "I'll go, if you wish."

"Yes, and never come back! Leave me to my fate!" I flung open the door. "Better yet, join that oaf in keeping guard on me." I wiped a damp cheek. "Leave!"

He made a house bow, courteous and correct. I tried to catch him with the slam of the door, missed by an inch.

Buried in my bed, I muffled my sobs so Fostrow wouldn't hear; that would have been the ultimate indignity. When at last I was spent I lay dazed, overcome by the magnitude of my calamity. Rust, my only friend, my sworn ally, was lost forever, through—I hated to admit it— my fit of temper.

Now what would I do? I could resign myself to Uncle's rule, and the risk of murder. Might I still flee the castle, without Rust's help? If so, was there any point to it?

Even if I found Hester, I could be of no help to my brother; I'd end up following her to her cottage, to be raised alongside Elryc by a mad old crone. I snorted with derision. Me, a bucolic peasant boy? Better Uncle's knife in the night.

Still, I was better off outside Stryx than penned here a prisoner. The day was wasting; better I go about my escape. Without Rust's help, I'd emerge with nothing but the clothes I wore, and perhaps not even a horse.

On the other hand, if I could reach the outer wall, perhaps I could throw over a bundle to retrieve later. Best I scout the terrain below, but for that I'd have to devise a way past my jailer. That depended on his mood. I took a deep breath, unbarred the door.

Rustin perched on the bench, chatting amicably with Fostrow. I gaped; he waved. "Good day, my prince." Idly, he rose to his feet. "Are you ready now?"

I nodded dumbly. He sauntered back into my room, closed my door. "Ready to listen, I hope." He sat me in a stiff carved chair. "You act the fool, Roddy. Your innermost thoughts flicker on your face or roll off your tongue. Where's the guile that once you displayed?"

My tone was sullen. "Why do you berate—"

"Answer, or I'll leave in earnest."

I flared, "You're my sworn vassal, and I call you to my standard! You can't leave!"

"Ah, that's another case." He sat. "I will do your bidding."

"Tell me what to do."

"It's for you to tell me. And, know thou that I would not serve thee, were it not for my oath."

I recoiled, as if stabbed. "You'd leave me here?"

"Until I see again the one I would gladly serve." He waited out my silence.

My voice was small. "Rustin, please help."

"As vassal, or friend?"

"Vassal. Friend. Both." I wanted to hurl the chair at him, or Uncle, or the window. "Friend. Please."

"Wash your face."

I did as bidden, too shaken to protest. After, he pulled up a second chair, sat close, arms folded over his knees. "If fear clouds your judgment and loosens your tongue, we must know it. Tell me True, Roddy. Are you afraid?"

So much he asked of me, I thought I could not give. We of the House of Caledon could have no friend, no confidant. But I was desperate beyond any need I had ever known.

To the floor, I mumbled, "Every waking minute of each day since Mother died." I shifted under the shame of my confession. "It isn't seemly, for one of royal blood."

"Perhaps." He walked behind my chair, enveloped my shoulders in his strong arms. "Yet I hardly blame you."

"I'm so alone." The words came of their own volition.

"Then I will be with you, my prince, and we'll face fear together." His hug was like Father's, of dim memory.

"Rust, take me from this place!" The cry of a supplicant.

His hands tightened on my shoulder blades. "As I live, Rodrigo. Tonight."

Chapter 8

CASUALLY, RUST BID ME FAREWELL, MOUNTED SANTREE, his favorite bay, and trotted through the main gate with a friendly wave to the guard, while I peered down from my window high above. In his saddlebags was enough of my clothing for several days change.

Uncle Mar had no need to monitor the traffic in goods to and from the castle. His concern was that Elryc or I should escape his control, or some unknown enemy enter. To that end, he'd doubled the guard, but Rust was as well known as the alemaster whose cart was mired in the still-soggy courtyard, where sweating helpers rolled barrels round to the servitors' entrance.

Scarce two hours later, Rust was back, and passed through the guards' scrutiny at the gate without incident. Shortly after, he was in my room. "Done."

"You're sure you—"

"Everything." He glanced at the walls, put a finger to his lips. "Think you the night will be cloudy?" A full moon would inhibit a climb down a rope from the battlements.

"Who knows." I couldn't abide the wait until dark.

Somehow, in our planning, it had become clear that my absence might be a protracted one. Uncle's attitude toward princes and crown became ever more proprietary, and his physical custody of me, as opposed to the formality of a regency, was intolerable. Still, I hesitated at casting myself adrift. Events would tell.

I paced anew. When Rustin settled himself at dice, it was too much. "Let's walk outside." In good humor, he followed. "Sleep on, Fostrow. No need to stalk us." The yawning guard struggled to his feet, assembled his gear.

Outside, all was as to be expected, except for the manned battlements. During my whole lifetime, and before, Mother had ruled with her foes subdued and no need to cower behind armed ramparts.

We sauntered along the walls, Fostrow bringing up the rear. As I'd feared, the only wall low enough to lower myself down was rife with soldiers from Verein. Our household troop would hesitate before firing on me; these louts of the Duke would skewer me with an arrow with nary a thought.

I hummed, barely loud enough for Rust to hear. "It looks a bit awkward."

"Perhaps." Rustin guided me down the stairs. "Let's sit outside the kitchen." We traipsed around the side of the keep, along the foundation wall. I glanced back at Fostrow, increased my pace, trying to make him sweat.

Cook gave us meat and bread, shooed us out into the damp afternoon. I settled on an overturned barrel, took a bite.

Rustin let me ruminate in peace. Fostrow made a few stabs at conversation, but I ignored him with lofty condescension until he lapsed silent.

A stir, in the kitchen. Voices raised, men running about. A squad of soldiers left off their raillery with the washermaids, loped around the corner of the keep. I looked inside. "Cook, did someone piss in the stew?"

The rotund woman wiped her face on an apron. "They're coming! Lord of Nature!" Leaving me gaping, she rushed away.

I spotted Kerwyn, the groom. "What's afoot?"

"The trumpets gave alarm." His voice was uneasy. "The guards are gone to the ramparts."

Fostrow's rough hand grasped my arm. "To your chambers, this very moment, or I'll bind and carry you! Move!" He shoved me along. "The Duke would have the hide off me, if anything happened to—where do you think you're going?"

"Let's have a look. Come on!" My pace was barely short of a run.

Perhaps it was because I was young, and could move faster. Or perhaps the old soldier's itch to know was as great as mine. Fostrow hurried after, without protest. Rust loped past him to stride with me.

I led them around the foundation wall of the keep, past the stables, to the main gate and the west ramparts.

In the courtyard, red-faced brewer's men struggled to free their cart from the muck. Empty return barrels, ill-tied, rolled in the wagon bed. Men and boys dashed about. I spotted Genard, leading a horse to gate-keeper Lanford. The battlements were a frenzy of activity.

The gates were open. A stream of folk were making their way up the hill from town. Townsmen trickled into the courtyard, bearing what supplies they could carry, while above on the ramparts, troops passed rocks from hand to hand to augment stacks, arranged kindling in the firepits under the cauldrons, rolled barrels of oil.

Rustin gave way to a soldier with an armful of pikes.

I raced up the steps, peered over the rampart into the setting sun. "What is it, Roddy?"

Dozens of black sails were silhouetted against the sun-flecked water. A chill stabbed at my spine. "Tantroth's fleet is athwart the bay!"

Fostrow's face puckered with dismay. "Tantroth of Eiber? We're in for a siege now, let me tell you."

Slowly, inexorably, the laden ships glided on the gentle breeze, toward the beach south of the docks, far from Llewelyn's keep.

"You've seen, my lord. Now, to your chambers!" Fostrow, with a firm grip on my upper arm, hauled me to the steps. "Young Rustin, go home; your father will have need—"

"I stay with my prince."

"Then you'll stay in his rooms for the duration. It's a lock and bolt I'll warrant Margenthar will want for the guarding. Hurry, laddie." With a flick of my dagger I could have sliced the tendons of his wrist and left him screaming in helpless rage, but this was not the time or the place.

I let Fostrow lead me into the castle and deposit us in my rooms. The moment the door was shut I ran to the window, peered past the walls to the warming harbor below.

"What now, Rust? Quick, before Uncle Mar locks us in!"

He said, "Confusion reigns, and will for hours. How can we dispose of Fostrow?" I pulled my dagger; Rust looked shocked. "Imps and demons, Roddy. I didn't mean it literally."

A few moments later he looked out the door. "Fostrow, help us with the trunk, would you? Roddy's leather jerkin and shield are inside, and the hasp's stuck." Rust strode to the trunk room.

Fostrow bent over the trunk, grumbling. "What need have you of shields? You're well guarded, and high in—"

I emerged from behind the cupboard, clubbed him with my upraised chair. With a cry, he sank to his knees.

Rust kicked shut the door, threw himself onto the fallen guard. "His blade!" With effort, he held the man's hand clear long enough for me to snatch the sword from its sheath.

"The dagger also."

"I know." I clawed for the blade, tossed it across the room out of reach.

Fostrow arched his back, threw Rustin half off. He took breath, let out a shout. Rust elbowed him in the stomach; Fostrow oofed silent. I swarmed onto the guard's back, helped Rust subdue him.

With belt ropes and curtain ties, we soon had Fostrow bound. I asked, "What about a gag?"

"Use a shirt."

I grabbed one from the floor.

"Not an unwashed one; you'll smother him!" I glared, but Rust paid no heed. He peered at the soldier's scalp. "Water, and a cloth."

"Are you serious? He's our enemy!"

"Water!" Rust's tone was peremptory. Sighing, I brought it; he dabbed at Fostrow's forehead. "The Duke is our enemy, my prince. This man is a guard, doing his duty."

"Which is to gaol me."

"His duty." Rust finished his ministrations.

Fostrow chewed at the gag. His voice was muffled, but distinct. "Let me go. Mnpff. What are you boys about? There's no place for you to hide." He tried to twist free of his ropes. "The castle's secure, Prince; we're all trapped together. Untie me and I'll say nothing of—"

"Some gag." I joined Rust in dragging the protesting guardsman across the tiles.

"Into the wardrobe."

I helped him bundle Fostrow into the closet. "We can't leave him alive. Listen to his caterwauling! If you tied his knots like you stuffed his mouth, he'll be free in minutes."

"They'll hold long enough. Or would you slit his throat?"

Fostrow was abruptly still.

"Where's my dagger?" I looked about, found it on my belt, its accustomed place. A tug, and it was unsheathed.

Rustin stood aside, his eyes on my face.

I brought the dagger to my gaoler's throat. Fostrow whinnied. "Lord of Nature, laddie! What did I do that—"

"Shut thy mouth." I took a deep breath, steeled myself for my slash, waited for Rustin's inevitable objection.

Silence. Very well, then, I'd do it. Yet my arm seemed paralyzed. I looked past Fostrow's terror, concentrated on the blade.

At last, I sighed, sheathed the knife.

Rustin sagged in relief.

I said sourly, "I stopped only for you, vassal. You'd have nagged and badgered until—"

His hand flew to my lips. "Shh. I feared for you, but you passed the ordeal." Without waiting for answer he strode to my door, opened, peered both ways. "Hurry."

"Sometimes I can't begin to figure you. Where to?"

"Below." We raced down the stairs.

Just above the landing, I caught Rust's arm. "What if Uncle sees us?"

"He'll be directing our defenses, not pacing the hall." Nonetheless, Rust peeked over the rail. I joined him. In the entry, sentries stood watch, with greater vigilance than usual. We tiptoed back upstairs.

"Now what?" Dazed by the press of events, I was content to let him lead.

For a long moment, he thought. Then, "Roddy, what welcome, when you return?"

We'd planned on my jumping the wall and making a brief journey to Hester's cottage. Instead, we'd clubbed and bound a guard. Uncle's wrath would be formidable. I'd be lucky to be sent to the Chamberlain; more likely, I'd be cast into a cell.

My eyes were bleak. "Shall I never come home?"

Staring at the rush-covered flooring, he shrugged. Then, his gaze met mine. "As King."

I swallowed. "I'll need the Still."

"The vault? There's no way to . . ."

"The castle is in an uproar. If ever we could, now." I felt a tingle of fear, and with it, welcome excitement. I would risk all, on a throw of the dice. "We'll need to break the lock."

"What you need is Willem's key."

"I don't dare be seen in the Chamberlain's wing. Everyone knows by now I'm supposed to be guarded." I felt an unaccountable exultation. I commanded, and Rustin but followed. "Mother's key opens one lock. All we must force is the second."

"A spear, perhaps? But the guards . . ."

"The armory is nearby. We'll manage one, somehow. For the guards, a distraction."

He paused. "Tell them we're under siege?"

"Yes! No, too unlikely. They'll know Tantroth can't have landed yet." I took a deep breath. "Fire."

"Roddy!"

My expression was grim; I knew, well as he, that fire was the bane of every stronghold. Woven floor covers, timber supports, and cotton and damask curtains would burn like pitch. Worse, the keep was full of vents and cubbyholes; it would draw like a chimney. If our blaze got out of hand, we'd destroy Castle Stryx.

On the other hand, the vault was at the end of a long corridor with no other exit save the passage we'd use. The guards would realize that if they remained at their posts they'd be roasted like autumn chestnuts. Fire was our best, if not our only way to get to the strongroom.

"We'll make smoke, so it looks like a bigger fire than it is. A barrel." My mind cast about. "One from the winery. A wet blanket, soaked in oil."

"Where?"

"The kitchen. Run." My speed was urgent, lest my courage falter. I ran headlong into the kitchen, bustling to provide food to our defenders. "Cooking oil! Where do you keep it?"

Cook gaped. "What are you—"

"Quick, tell me!"

"The scullery."

I dashed past the tables where Genard sat lapping a bowl of stew, ran out onto the grounds, made for the scullery. A kitchenmaid loomed in the doorway. I thrust her aside, looked about for a bowl, such as Cook used.

"Not there; it'd be in a cask. Aha!" Rust seized one, wrenched out the cork, sniffed. "Fresh-pressed olives."

"That's plenty. Can you carry it?" The cask was but a tenthweight of a barrel. I grabbed the biggest jug I could find, filled it with water from the barrel by the door.

"Roddy, are you sure you'd risk burning—"

"For the Still itself? Do you jest?" I trotted back to the kitchen, leaving Rustin to shoulder the cask.

Beyond the kitchen, steps to the cellars. I seized a doused torch from its place on the wall, lit it from a taper in a niche. I glanced behind, waited impatiently for Rust to catch up.

The tunnel to the winery was deserted, the winery's gate securely locked. Outside, empty wine barrels waited to be cleaned. I stood atop one, smashed at it with my boot until the lid splintered.

"What do you here?" A harsh voice echoed.

I whirled. Stire, the Duke's man, in full battle gear. His half-sword was drawn.

Rust giggled, swayed. "It's hard to get the dregs, m'lord." He gestured. "Have to open the barrel; it's too heavy to tip and suck at the bung." He staggered toward me, recoiled as if I'd pushed him away. P'haps you can help us with the nexsht?"

"You're drunk, lout?" Stire's lip curled.

My voice came in a squeak, not from mummery, but real fear. "He is not!" I stumbled, in Stire's direction. "No more'n I. We came down to—"

He sheathed his sword. "I see what you came—"

As one, Rust and I tackled him. Uncle's henchman went down, cursing and struggling. Rust's eyes were wild. "Roddy, the sword!"

I let go Stire's legs, dived for the hilt of the half-sword, pulled it loose. Rust's hand shot out, beckoning.

I dropped the sword into his fingers. "Run him through!"

Stire's knee came up; Rust grimaced. His arm shot out. Using the jeweled hilt like a club, he smashed the sword into Stire's temple. The man went limp.

"Oww." Rustin rolled off, crouched with knees pressed together, his face red. A deep breath, then another. "Why are you gawking? There's your cloth for burning."

"Huh?"

"His clothes!"

Unconscious, Stire was almost too heavy to move. But, grunting and panting, I rolled him over and about until I'd stripped off his garments. "Loincloth too?"

Rustin leaned against the wall, recovering. "As you wish."

"He mocked me." With a flick of the sword I parted his loincloth, dropped it in the barrel. Rustin emptied the water jug into it. I poured in a measure of oil. "Now for a spear."

"Stire leaned his against the doorsill." He gestured. "Roddy, if this doesn't work, they'll hang us."

"I suppose." No time for that now. I rolled the barrel into the corridor. It made a ghastly clattering.

We stopped short of the armory gate. I tiptoed along the corridor, peered in. The armorer, his apprentice, and two soldiers were gathered, tying sheaves of arrows.

There was no way to roll the cask past them without discovery.

Rustin's hand fell on my shoulder; I stifled a shriek. He tugged me back to the winery passage. "Wait here a moment." He handed me Stire's sword. "Use it, if needs be." He loped along the corridor toward the safety of the kitchen.

I fumed, my valor ebbing with each breath. Ours was the most harebrained, unthought, foolhardly scheme ever to—

"Come." Rustin dragged me from the dank barrel on which I sat. We made our way back to the armory and peeked in. None watched us. Rust flitted across the entryway to the safety of the other side. After a moment, I followed.

"What good does this do?"

"Shh." He waited. Of necessity, I waited too, every nerve strained. A clatter. Banging, a scrape. A flickering torch, beyond the bend.

"We're found!" I hefted my sword.

A barrel advanced down the corridor, on its side. Behind it, a castle workboy, torch raised against the gloom, head bent to his onerous task.

I peered toward the armory. A soldier glanced up, went back to his selections.

The boy rolled his barrel past the armory, found the alcove in which we huddled. "Now what, m'lord?"

"Garrond!" I saw the curl of his lip, corrected hastily. "Genard. You'd better run along."

"Is this about Lord Elryc?" He searched my face. "You'd best tell me."

I cast prudence to the winds. "Yes."

"I'll help."

I nodded. "From here, we'll have to carry it."

Thank Lord of Nature, the iron gates in the strongroom corridor were open. We lugged the barrel as close to the far end as we dared, set it down. I glanced at the torch. The flame wavered, as if pulled both directions.

It would have to do. I poked the torch into the barrel, waved it about until the contents caught. An acrid aroma. Sputtering. I prodded the soggy clothing, until at last I was rewarded with a few wisps of smoke.

Genard frowned at our efforts. "You need straw, and lots of water." He scampered off, before I could grasp his arm.

"Rustin, this is madness."

His voice was calm. "A trifle disorganized, I'll admit." He leaned against the wall, arms folded. "Wait upstairs, if you'd rather. The boy and I will—"

"Arghh." I fanned the barrel.

In a surprisingly short time Genard trotted back, staggering under a load of straw. I thrust a handful into the barrel; he slapped my hand away. "Not yet! Would you have smoke, or the castle in flames?"

"Sorry."

He ran off. Rustin shook his head.

A few agonizing moments, and Genard was back with two buckets of water. "Cook is boiling mad," he advised us. "We'd better get on our way."

He poured half a bucket onto the mound of straw, felt it, considering. "All right." He gathered armfuls and tossed them into the barrel. "Just wait. There. Now, *that's* smoke."

Billows of black smoke rose from the barrel. Obligingly, Genard added another armful of wet straw.

The ceiling was barely above our heads; the smoke had to dissipate outward. More went toward the kitchen than inward.

"Well?" Genard glanced between us.

"It's not . . . they need more—"

"Nobles." He spat his contempt. In one quick motion he stripped off his shirt, began fanning the smoke toward the vault. "All they need is a sniff, m'lord."

"He's right." Rustin. "I'll go first, shouting. Duck into that alcove, out of sight. Hopefully they'll flee."

Genard stared in dismay. "You? An outsider, and a friend of Prince Roddy?" He panted from the exertion of fanning. "Here, do this." He handed me the grimy shirt, darted bare-chested toward the strongroom.

"Fire! Save us!" His child's voice came shrill. "The castle's ablaze! Fire! Help, before we burn! We need buckets!"

Beyond the black curtain of smoke, the boy capered. A moment, then the thud of footsteps.

Eyes tearing, I cowered back in the alcove, stifling coughs. The steps receded.

Silence.

"Hurry, Lord Rust!" The voice came near the ground. "They'll figure out something's not right."

A hand tugged at my ankle. "Stay low, m'lord."

Anything, for relief. I got to my knees, found the air more bearable. I sucked in a breath. "To the vault."

"Shouldn't we put out—"

"Let it burn; we need more time." I scuttled along the floor, until the smoke lessened, and we found ourselves outside the great bronze doors.

"Mother's key!"

Rust peeled it from his neck, thrust it into my hands. "But which lock?" I stared at the deep entry holes.

I swallowed. A false key, and the offending hand would be severed. Or so the whispers had said.

"Genard, open it." I handed him the key.

"Hah." He tossed it back. "Your Powers, your fingers."

I lifted the point of my sword to his throat. "Open!"

He swiveled to Rustin. "Is he that wicked, my lord? Would he?"

"He thinks he would." Rust took the key from him, placed it in my hand. "Roddy, you'd best hurry."

I kept my arm rock-steady as I extended it toward the lock, into the gaping hole. They would have been persuaded I was fearless, had I not moaned and kept my eyes glued shut.

I felt for the keyhole. Nothing. I probed farther, yelped as something sharp pricked my fingertip. I yanked out my arm, sucked my fingers. "Give me the torch!" Trying not to singe my ear, I peered in the hole. "Demons of the lake!"

"What, Roddy?"

"It's been forced!" The iron of the lock was bent and broken. I pressed on the door; it didn't budge.

In the distance, shouts.

I ran to the second lock, squinted. It was whole. I thrust in my key.

It didn't turn. With all my strength I twisted. It moved not an iota. I withdrew the key, stared. "What means this?"

Rustin waved away a puff of smoke. "That your key fit the forced lock."

"But if they didn't force both . . ."

"We'll know when we get in." He took Stire's spear, thrust it into the hole, twisted. Outside, the cries grew nearer.

Rustin strained, to no avail. In fury, he withdrew the spear, rammed it into the lock, over and again.

"Here, let me." I slammed the spear into the long keyhole, smashed it against the lock. Something caught. I twisted hard. Rust seized the shaft, added his own weight.

A snap.

I pulled out the spear, pressed tentatively on the door.

The top of the door glided away from us, as the bottom rose and whacked my shins. I cursed, stepped aside, raised it the rest of the way.

A few chests were overturned in the corner; I ran to one, flung it open. Moldering scrolls of state. In the others, trinkets and gifts. I stood, perused the shelves.

A cushion. My breath hissed. I remembered that bolster. I hurried to it.

Still impressed in it were the hollows where long the Chalice had lain, and near it the Receptor.

They were gone, and with them, my Power.

A groan escaped my lips.

"Look, m'lord!" Genard's eyes were wide. He pointed.

The crown of Caledon, Mother's formal diadem. It lay carelessly on a cedar stand, as if discarded, and without value.

After all I'd risked, the agonies I'd endured, my nights of shame, the Still was gone.

"Take it!" Rustin.

I stood as if made of stone.

Genard snatched up the crown, wrapped it in his grimy jerkin.

Rust poked among the chests. "Roddy, there's no coin here."

"I know. Mother had Willem keep most . . ." My voice trailed off. Not only had I lost the Receptor and Chalice, the most valued objects in Caledon, but now they could be wielded against me. If, in all the realm, another virgin could be found to mount the throne.

"Hurry." Rustin tugged. When I resisted, he wrapped his arm around me, guided me down the hall toward the smoke. "Genard, guard the crown and meet us outside."

"Aye, sir." The stableboy took a handful of deep breaths, plunged into the swirl.

"He'll steal it!"

"No." Rust pressed me into a kneel. "Keep your head low, for the air."

"Fire! Save us! Hakkk!" Genard coughed and wheezed. "The castle burns!" His voice faded.

Rust pushed and prodded, forcing me through the smoke. Rivulets of water, in the passage. Voices shouting, near.

I'd lost the Still.

Amid bellows and frenzy, we thrust through a milling crowd, fought our way clear to beyond the scullery.

Rust seemed a madman, his hair awry, blue eyes shining from a filthy mask. "Do I look as awful as you?" He led me to a well. "Rinse— no, perhaps not." He stayed my hand.

"They have my Power." I couldn't focus my thoughts.

With what might have been compassion, Rust took my hand, steered me along the foundation wall. Moments later we were in the cool of the stables. A flickering taper was wedged in its sconce.

He swung shut the doors. "Sit. No, there by the water pail, out of sight." He disappeared.

Outside, in the dusk, excited shouts faded to unheard whispers.

Tantroth sought Caledon, and might yet have it, but the Still was beyond him. And so was the crown. The demon's imp who served as stableboy would sell it for a song, if he wasn't gutted and tossed in the offal by a thief larger than he.

Something rough jabbed at my lap. I pushed it aside, my eyes on the beams above, my thoughts awhirl. A fly buzzed at the bucket of water, rippling it.

My fingers toyed with the tight-bound hay on which I sat. What now, Mother? I've lost the Vessels, a guttersnipe has your crown, Elryc and Hester are gone, Pytor's imprisoned, and we're under Tantroth's siege. Uncle Mar has me at his mercy.

All is lost.

A figure crossed the anteroom. Rustin.

I asked, "Did you find the brat?"

"He sits at your feet, my prince."

I looked down. "Where's my crown, thief?"

Genard flushed at my epithet. "Where you dropped it."

I stared past him, at the gold bauble in the dust.

"Genard, we need horses." Rustin seemed strangely impatient. I no longer cared.

"Aye, m'lord. How many?"

"Can you ride? Of course, you work the stables. Where can we find soldiers' garb?"

Genard bit his lip. "Each day the washerwomen take garments to boil, and dry them on the rocks by the well."

"Do the soldiers haul back their own clothes?"

"No, m'lord. The women bring them the next—"

"Come along, I'll need help. Roddy, stay here." They went.

Perched on my hay, I dangled the crown, from time to time twirling it on my finger. No coronation. No Power.

If Tantroth my cousin, Duke of Eiber, had his way, no realm either.

Time would soon tell; by now he'd have landed at least his first force, and would be racing to secure the Castle Way.

I stared at the bucket. No need any longer to hide my face; I could wash off the grime, meet my fate like a king. Placing the crown on my head, I reached toward the still water, half-mesmerized.

"Who goes?" A familiar voice, which I couldn't place.

My voice came from far away. "Rodrigo of Caledon, Prince and heir." Again the fly buzzed at the bucket, and I shivered. I thrust out my hands, palms down, to guard the water.

"What do you in my stable?" The old man. Griswold.

"I hide, from the Duke."

"Why?"

"He is my enemy."

"What makes him so?"

"He would have my birthright, and my realm."

The old man's voice wavered in and out of earshot. "Where go you, now?"

"I flee."

"Whence?"

"To my brother, and the witch who raised me."

"For what purpose?"

My arms ached from the effort of keeping them still, but the fly must not have at my pail, before I washed. "To gain their alliance, and my strength." The words might be mine, or might not.

"And then?"

I came slowly to my feet, and spoke in a tone of resolve. "I shall claim my kingdom, and seek my Power."

The door swung open. "Roddy, we found— Oh!"

Griswold scowled. "He's in a muddle. Where do you take him?"

"To safety." Rustin dumped his pile of clothing; the stableboy added an armful of helmets. Rust snapped, "Genard, saddle our horses."

"Who rides?"

"You, me, Rodrigo." Seeing the crown on my head, Rust frowned, removed it. He plunged his hands into the bucket, splashed my face, wiped it on his sleeve. "We need more riders. Who?"

I stirred.

Griswold snapped, "Fetch Kerwyn."

"Aye, sir." The boy ran.

Rustin helped me dress in soldiers' garb still damp from scrubbing. When he had my clothes arranged he wrapped the crown in my old shirt.

"How will we get out?" My mind began to work, as if awakening from long disuse.

"Through the gate." He shucked his own garments, donned the guards' clothing.

A time passed, moments or hours. Kerwyn, ridiculous in a trooper's jerkin, led two horses. Behind him came Genard with two others.

Rustin adjusted his own helmet, mounted his chestnut mare. "We'll need to show swords and shields; all we have is that half-sword of yours. I'm going to the armory."

"You'll be recognized."

"Your household troops and the men of Verein still don't know each other." He clattered to the door in soldier's garb and boots, reached down to the catch. "Besides, no one looks at a soldier's face. I grew up in a soldier's house." He was gone.

Genard fussed at his uniform. "It overflows on me. How will I keep the arms from—"

"Quiet." Griswold rolled the boy's sleeves and leggings so they seemed less outlandish. "You'll be a small young soldier. Kerwyn, keep your faceplate down; everyone knows that nose of yours. I want you both back, soon as it's safe."

The door swung open. Guards with torches, their swords drawn. "Stableman, have you seen the boy Prince?"

Griswold's eyes never strayed to mine. "Not of late."

I blinked, coming at last into the remainder of my senses. My fingers played at my guardsman's knife. I said, "We've already searched, trooper."

"Captain Stire was attacked. He's livid." The man's eyes flickered to Kerwyn, and the stableboy in man's clothing. Then past the shirt thrown casually on the hay. "I'll try the kitchens."

After they left I eased myself back on the hayroll, hoping the others wouldn't see the tremble of my knees. I gathered my wrapped crown to my chest, hugged it. We waited in silence, until steps approached. Rustin.

He grinned. "Three swords and scabbards. And shields." He distributed them. "I used Stire's name."

"They're looking for me. Fostrow must be loose."

"No matter, now." He handed me the reins to a snorting gelding. "Up, my prince. Stay close, and let me speak. I'm the captain."

He wheeled his mount out the door, clattered toward the gate. We spurred to follow. "Lanford!" A bellow. "The aleman's cart! Where is it?"

The gatekeeper frowned. "Left an hour ago, guardsman. They finally got the wheel high enough to repair—"

"And you let them through? The Duke will have your ears, if not worse!" Rustin's horse pranced with conveyed excitement. "You fool!"

"What—why shouldn't I let—they were desperate to get down the hill and away, before Tantroth's troops blocked the road."

"The boy Rodrigo was on the cart!"

"We checked every barrel. And looked under—"

"He was the helper in brown, perched on the backboard! Open the cursed gate. Hurry, they can't be far down the hill."

Swearing, Lanford swung open the gate, and we charged through. Behind us the doors thudded shut.

The wind tore at Rustin's exultant cry. "He'll have your ears!"

Chapter 9

"NOW WHAT?" RUST SLOWED HIS MOUNT, SIDESLIPPING to avoid a cart full of sacks and squalling babies, pulled up toward the castle by a gasping townsman.

"Down the hill like the demons themselves were after us." I sounded as sure as I felt. "From the towers they can watch us almost to Llewelyn's keep. If we dawdle, they'll wonder why we were in such an all-fired hurry to get out." I spurred.

The hill was crowded with refugees. As we rode I peered below to the harbor whenever shrubbery was sparse enough to permit.

Castle Stryx faced west. In the last rays of daylight, Tantroth's black-sailed fleet lay silhouetted against the pale pink sky of the inlet. Sensibly, the Duke of Eiber had made no attempt to land at the wharves along the waterfront near Llewelyn's stronghold. Instead, their ships were beached a league south, where their foreguard could get a foothold before Llewelyn's men fell on them.

I was appalled at the number of townsmen struggling toward the gates. There was ample room within the castle's outer walls, but if Tantroth succeeded in mounting siege, how long could our stores sustain such a quantity of folk?

"Make way for the guard!" Rustin, sword raised, cleared a path by gesture and voice.

"Look, Ma, it's the Prince!" A youngster tugged at her mother's hand; the woman shook her head. "No, not that one, Ma! The one behind!" Her voice pierced, and other faces swiveled to peer at us.

I thrust down my helmet, did my best to look inconspicuous, but word of my passage leaped down the hill.

"Sire, do you join the guard below?" An old man clutched at my bridle. "Will you save the town?"

Never mind the flimsy hovels of the city; how could I save myself? Not if I stopped to parlay with fools. I threw an airy salute, cantered past.

The most difficult stretches were the sharp bends where our road nearly doubled back on itself. There the path was choked with wagons, bullocks, handcarts, mulesters, crying babies, anxious women, sweating peasants. At least we need not fear scrutiny from the ramparts; the road must look like a disturbed anthill.

"Roddy, look!" Rust pointed. For a few paces we had a clear view of the sea road from Llewelyn's keep past the swordsmith's, into the town of Stryx. A small troop of cavalry clattered south toward the invaders; one lonely scarlet banner drooped on a standard.

"Are they all we can muster?"

"Those aren't the first, I'm sure. And my father has to hold the keep, as well." Rustin sounded defensive. "The stronghold guards this very road to the castle."

Thanks to the congestion, we were barely halfway down the hill. "Rust, let's rest at Besiegers' Pond." The turnoff was near, and my mind reeled from the crowd of events. Scarce an hour before, we'd broken into the vault, after setting fire to Castle Stryx.

"We haven't time."

Ignoring him, I spurred off the road to the familiar path. For lack of choice, my companions followed.

After the mad fear of the townsmen, the wood seemed a peaceful refuge. I picked my way toward the brackish pond, an eagerness arising.

Kerwyn pressed his mount forward. "Sire, if there's no further need, I'll turn back."

"Very well." I dismounted. "I need a moment to think." I knelt by the still water. A thirsting mosquito buzzed, settled on my hand; I flicked it off.

Rust frowned. "This is no time to—"

"Do as I say." In this familiar place of solitude, I felt a strange confidence.

Perhaps, hours or day hence, Tantroth's soldiers would settle on these banks, while awaiting the fall of my ancestral home. Had I a duty to climb the hill, join my people for what awaited them? How could I be King, and abandon my realm?

"Am I not traitor, that I flee in time of battle?" I'd scarce formed the thought before I realized I'd spoken it aloud.

Rustin sat cross-legged at my side. "No, my lord. Preserve thyself, to succor thy kingdom." The intimacy of his high speech warmed my courage.

An avid blue-winged dragonfly, flicking in the day's last grudging rays, drew intricate designs in the humid air.

"Easy to say, to justify my escape. How then shall I be King, and succor my people?"

Rust had no answer.

I raised my hands, brought them palm down to the waters. "Would that I had my Power, and the wisdom it brings." I closed my eyes, seeking calm.

Rustin snorted. "Modesty, at last."

Returning to the castle was not the solution; Uncle Mar held Pytor, sought Elryc, and had reduced me to the status of a child. Despite honeyed words, Duke Margenthar had seized power in Caledon.

Behind my shoulder, Genard coughed. "How long will you sit and stare at a lake like an addled Ritemaster?"

I opened one eye. "I could throw you in, and contemplate the ripples."

"Aye, that'd be like you, m'lord." But he settled, stirring only to slap an occasional mosquito.

After a time I sighed. My vigil had brought no peace, only the sense of more pressing urgency.

We made our way through the undergrowth to the cut of the road. The folk laboring up the hill moved with heightened anxiety. Perhaps it was that dark was nigh, and terrors swelled with the receding light. Cries and warnings floated up the hillside, from below.

We descended the few remaining bends to the keep that straddled the road. With the last turn, its high outer wall came into view. Soldiers at the battlements brandished long-tipped spears. Below us, beyond the Tradesmen's Cut, Castle Way ran through a high gate, passed between the inner and outer walls of the keep, and emerged again at the turn just above the seafront.

To save asking entry at the keep, what had started as a cut across a muddy field had over the years become an awkward bypass, used by tradesmen and riders alike. The cut now streamed with townsmen.

A blare of trumpets; sweating villeins turned their carts aside lest they be run over by a returning troop of Llewelyn's horse. One townsman cursed roundly, raising his fist at the ruckus as the guardsmen shot past. He stood thus a moment, then froze, staring down the road toward Stryx.

My grip tightened on the pommel.

The man whirled to his cart. He tugged at it, glanced over his shoulder, abandoned it to dash toward the sandy shore. Others, on the shortcut, made desperate haste with their loads.

"Rustin, what's—"

A clatter of hooves.

On the beach, the cartsman threw himself down, as if to bury himself in the sand.

Trumpets sounded. A few foot soldiers scrambled toward the gate of the keep. Some tossed away their weapons as they ran.

Cries of exultation. Shouted commands.

A troop of black-clad horsemen swung into view, slashing at all in their path.

My voice was hoarse. "They're not ours."

They made for the gate, hurling spears upward at the defenders as they shut themselves in. Others of their band veered toward the Tradesmen's Cut, barely fifty paces beyond us.

"Tantroth comes!" Rust gauged the distance to his keep. "Make for the gate!"

I spurred, but reined in on the instant, driving my horse half-mad. "No time, and they can't open!"

An enemy captain pointed to our party. I glanced about. "To the pond!" I wheeled about, raced up the slope. Genard led our retreat, heels stabbing at his mount's sides. I shouted, "Past the pond, to the keep's north gate!"

"In the dark?" Rustin spurred to keep pace. I stroked my gelding's mane. If the cutoff to the pond wasn't so near, I wouldn't dare run him upward so.

An arrow flicked through the brush, buried itself in a tree. My back prickled. I bent forward to cut the wind, hoping I wouldn't receive a shaft in the rear. Passing frantic townsmen, I gained steadily on Genard.

"Hold, Roddy!" Rustin's mount foamed at the bit. "My mare's played out."

I slowed my pace a trifle. It was a mistake. A panting churl seized my leg, jerked me out of the saddle. We landed together in a heap. My mount neighed, reared.

The peasant seized the bridle. He'd have swung himself up but for the lash of Rustin's whip. He staggered, and fell. I swarmed into the saddle so fast I nearly went off the far side, kicked madly onto the pond trail. At full gallop I plunged into the concealing brush.

Behind, a shriek of dismay.

Rust swung off his foaming mare. "Genard's down!"

"Too bad. Hurry."

"Go for him! My mare's done!"

I swallowed. Rustin always expected too much. I cantered back to Castle Way.

Genard lay in a pool of blood, his leg pinned under a feebly kicking horse. A dozen black-clad troopers panted up the hill, a handful of terrified townsmen scrambling for safety a few paces before them.

I looked about. The stableboy was dead, so—

"Help, m'lord!" Genard struggled to free himself.

Cursing, I jumped down, grasped his saddle, hauled upward until my head swam. The horse was dead weight, immovable. I strained harder.

Genard slithered out.

The peasants were upon us, clawing for my horse. I hauled my half-sword from the scabbard, slashed at arms, managed somehow to remount. In one desperate motion I scooped the weeping boy over the saddle, wheeled, galvanized my steed with a mighty kick. We crashed into the underbrush. "Ride, Rust! To the keep!"

Llewelyn sipped his wine, while his wife, Joenne, watched in unhappy silence. "The keep is our main defense, not the sea road."

"Still, we must leave before first light." I finished the last of my beef, a headache throbbing.

Rustin said, "The keep's seawall splits the beach in twain. Tantroth's men have to swim around, or climb a steep wall. They'll do it, or land upcoast, but not while they're still off-loading their main force."

Llewelyn nodded agreement. "We're well stocked, and the walls are thick. We've birds to send messages to the castle, and they to us. If worse comes to worse, Margenthar will sortie to our defense."

I yearned for sleep, but Lord of Nature knew where Hester would roam with my brother. "We must go," I said again. With Rust's help, I'd make my way to Hester and find what she'd done with Elryc.

Rust stirred. "What *will* break the siege, Father?"

"Time, and Nature willing, the weather. Fall is nigh upon us. It's damp and aguey, especially for men in tents or huddled round camp-fires. And come winter, their supply ships will be harbor-bound." Llewelyn warmed his hands at the crackling fire, as if in anticipation of the chill to come.

I squinted through the open portal into a night lit by the blaze of torches. From time to time an unsettling thump rolled across the garden, and a grinding, dragging noise occasionally made itself heard. The unfamiliar sounds grated against my headache, and it was all I could do to be civil.

As if reading my mind, Llewelyn said, "They bring up their siege engines. By morning they'll invest the north wall. The tide is lowest at the fifth hour, and then they'll struggle across the seawall."

I sighed, resisting the folly of rest. "We'd best go soon." Thank heaven Ebon was waiting in Llewelyn's stables. Without him I'd feel even more lost.

Rust rose to his feet. "I'll ready my gear." He left.

Llewelyn paced. "My son says your relations with the Duke are not cordial." Llewelyn paused. "But for that, you'd be safest within the Castle walls."

"What of yourself?"

"Oh, I'd rather be there too, but duty prevents." He swung to glow-er at his wife. "And when the sails were sighted, Joenne refused to go, leaving me with more worry. But my loyalty"—his gaze bore into mine—"is to the crown. For the moment, that means the regent."

I stifled any show of resentment. "Then why do you aid us?"

"Ah. You're Elena's child, and she wanted you King. I'm not entire-ly sure . . . Margenthar's intent is not always clear. Just a moment." Abruptly he strode to the door, looked outside, had a word with the guard.

When he returned to settle himself by the fire I asked, "Think you Uncle Mar is a traitor?"

"A word too easily bandied." His eyes held mine until I flushed.

"I apologize, Lord Llewelyn."

A grunt. "Well, you're excitable, and don't mean half of what tum-bles out your mouth. As to Mar, I have no cause to know he means you ill." Delicately said; he might guess, or suspect my uncle's intentions, but because he had no sure knowledge, he need not choose a side.

"Then why not hold us for his custody?" I knew not why I baited him.

"After Tantroth decamps, Mar will have enough on his mind with-out naming me enemy for aiding you." He stood to pace. "Still, I'd rather see you gone. The cortege that escorted Pytor to Verein passed within our walls. The little lad wailed for his nanny, and none gave him comfort. If Mar meant him well, I can't see why he didn't send old Hester along. Elryc needed her no longer."

"Thank you." My voice was soft.

He faced me. "Between you and Margenthar, I'd have you as King, Lord Rodrigo. Especially when you're grown. But I can't commit against the Duke, living close under his walls. I wish you well, but won't take part in your quarrel."

"I understand, sir. I'd better find Rust."

"Tell him, Llewelyn." Joenne's soft voice.

"Wife, stay out—"

"He'll know soon or late, and be your enemy. Soften the blow with truth!"

Llewelyn paced anew. "To be candid, boy, I don't want Rustin going with you. Not that I wish you ill, but the kingdom's unsettled, and he's too young to gallop off and enrage the Duke of Stryx in the bargain. I'd order him to forego his journey, but unfortunately, he swore fealty . . ." A shrug. "By honor he cannot gainsay his word."

"So you'll let him go?"

"I'm not bound by his honor. Rust went to his chamber for clothes, but will stay there. Two men guard his door."

"Sons of demons!" White-faced, I could say no more.

"Rodrigo, I bear you no ill will. Gladly I'll give you horses, weapons, even two of my men as outriders, as far as you would take them. But Rustin is my son whom I love, so I will protect him." Though his face was stony, his words were unsteady. "Hate me if you must."

"Gladly!" I snatched up the bundle that held my crown and stalked into the night.

Did Llewelyn think he could pick and choose among the aids he proffered—giving me steeds but locking away Rustin—and keep my goodwill? He would see me King, but only after I matured to his liking? Hah! When I was King, his head would roll.

Yet, how was I to become King, if none save Rust would stand with me, and his way was barred?

Fuming, I crossed to the stable. Inside, I searched for Ebon's stall. I hadn't seen him since the trumpets sounded Mother's death. Gladly, I fed him an apple, wiped his slobber on my breeks.

In the next stall, Genard, on tiptoe, stroked the muzzle of a strong young stallion as he adjusted the cinches. I couldn't see how he'd climb the beast, to say nothing of riding him.

I said, "I'll have Llewelyn send you back to Griswold when the siege lifts."

"No, I ride with you."

"Servants do as they're told."

The stableboy shouted, "I'm liegeman to Lord Elryc! I go with him!"

I was exhausted, and in no mood for nonsense. "Will you *ever* shut your mouth? No one gives a plowman's hoe whether you're bondsman or churl!"

Before aught could stop him, the boy jumped the gate, pawed through my gear, seized my crown from its dirty wrap. "Deserve you this, lying Prince? Hah!" He pitched the crown across the stall; it bounced off a rough-hewn beam. "I should have given it to the Duke!"

I scrambled to my feet.

My head ached. Outside, the hated troops of Eiber made ready for siege. My brothers were gone, Uncle Mar despised me, Llewelyn betrayed me. And now, a jeering stableboy flung my crown at a wall.

Oblivious to my white rage, Genard babbled on. "You knew I was Elryc's man when you took me! Think you I'll rot in Stryx, when Elryc—when he—" Genard's lip trembled. He blinked, for once without words.

I glanced about. In the aisle, a coil of rope hung on a hook. It would do.

I seized Genard by the neck, hauled him to the door. "Guard!" No one was about. I dragged the unresisting stableboy into the night. On the battlements, torches flickered. "Guardsmen!" Very well, if none would help, I'd hang him myself. I dragged the boy to a tree with a low-hanging limb.

From behind, a soft familiar voice. "Let him go; you choke him."

"This piece of dung bent the crown of Caledon!"

Rust sighed, gripped my forearm. "Let him be." He worked at loosening my grip on Genard.

My free hand shot to my waist, in an instant my dagger glinted in the firelight. "Stay back!"

"You'd slash me?" Slowly, deliberately, Rust placed his hand atop mine. "Do it, then." I made a threatening gesture; his grip loosened. He shut his eyes. "Best I not see it, lest I flinch."

I hurled Genard into the dust, kicked him, spun to Rustin. "Villein! Coward knave! You're all against me, sworn or no! Imps take you, your house, your lickspittle father, your mother! Demons drink your peasant blood and—"

Not gently, but with less fury than I expected, he caught my knife hand, twisted my arm, threw me to the ground. Instead of a blow, he rolled me onto my belly, sat athwart my back, pinning me to the grass while I raged weeping and cursing, trying to grasp the fallen knife.

After a time I lay still, helpless. Rustin stroked the back of my neck. "It's no shame to cry, my prince. Nor to rage at events. But you have friends, Genard and I among them, who risk their lives for you."

"Get off, you toad!"

"Not yet." His strong hands massaged my shoulders. "It's but the eye of the storm."

"Damn you!" I couldn't gain purchase to free myself. I kicked, tore grass, pounded the earth in frustration, until at last I lay spent and sobbing in the dirt. Only then did Rustin climb off my back, gather me into a rough sort of hug.

I sniffled. "Why did you stop me?"

"For the guilt you'd bear, if I did not."

For a moment I sat quietly, welcome of the embrace. "Rust, what do you think of me?"

He sighed. "That you're ill raised, and not yet fit to be King."

The words slashed like a razor. I recoiled, realized I'd asked for truth. "Why do you stay with me?"

A silence that stretched interminably. At last he flashed a curious smile, got to his feet, looked down at me where I lay sprawled. "Why should I not?"

"That's no answer."

"It's late, and we must ride before light."

I tried to shake off my daze. "You were locked in your room."

"Lower your voice, lest they hear. Go wash off the dust, change your clothes. I've made arrangements; Chela will tell you." He squeezed the back of my neck. "I stay with you because I wish, and because I'm your vassal." He loped toward the house. Before disappearing behind a wall he called over his shoulder, "And because I like you."

For some reason, despite his ruthless and unprovoked assault, a burden lifted. With a long shuddering breath I picked myself up, dusted my jerkin. I became aware of a pair of eyes watching, intent. "What do *you* want?"

Genard rubbed his throat. "M'lord, may I . . ." He approached with caution. He saw my scowl, blurted, "Elryc told me—was it an oath you gave, when you said you'd save him?"

"What business of yours, crown breaker?"

He moved closer, perhaps sensing from my listless tone that I had no energy to renew my assault. "Please, m'lord?"

The easiest way to get rid of him was to answer. "I said Uncle Mar and his minions—helpers—shall not harm him while I draw breath."

"You swore?"

"I told him in Truth. It's the same. My Power depends on keeping True."

"Well, then." Genard nodded, as if he'd made a point. "He told me the words. 'Elryc, Lord of Caledon, I pledge myself to thee as vassal.'

Somethin' like that. Until our deaths, and I'll serve him with honor and shall have no other liege." His eyes shone. "I'm Elryc's man. That's why I have to go along."

"He was playing with you."

Genard shook his head.

"Or being kind. Elryc wouldn't take a stableboy as vassal; it's absurd." I made a gesture of dismissal. "Don't worry yourself. Go home."

"That's for him to say!" His head came up proudly. "Could Duke Mar dismiss Lord Rustin as your vassal?"

"Of course not, but . . ." I sighed. Chivalry had its rules. Though Elryc was eleven and a fool, it was a profound breach of etiquette to interfere in his relations with a vassal.

I tried another tack. "Even if you're sworn, that's no reason to tag along. Lord knows when we'll see the castle again—" The argument supported Genard's position instead of my own, so I dropped it. "You'll only slow us. Besides, you have no mount."

"Me, slow you?" Withering scorn. "I can ride any horse in the stable, and with my little weight, I'll be watching over my shoulder for you!" His tone changed. "Please, m'lord! I'm sorry about—I won't be any trouble, I swear!"

I yawned. Had I had a decent night's sleep since Mother died? Genard was persistent, and we needed a servant. "Very well, you may fetch and carry for us. I'll have Llewelyn provide you a horse."

"Yes, m'lord." His mission accomplished, he retreated. "Did I break the crown? I'm sorry."

"I'd have hanged you, if not for Rust. Touch my crown again and I'll gut you; by the Truth I so swear!"

"Aye, m'lord!" He fled.

I turned back toward the house, got no more than a few paces before a figure approached from the darkness.

I peered. "Who's—oh!" Chela, the servant girl.

She beckoned urgently, drew me into the shadows. "Lord Rustin says he'll ride with you!"

"I know. How did he escape?"

"Out the window, the moment his door closed from inside. In room, out window, bang, just like that!" She giggled. "Then he found me to give you word."

"What's his plan?"

"He says don't alien—don't make his father mad. Say good-bye, leave as you would have."

"And?"

"We'll wait for him at the two-trunked tree, just past the curve in the road."

My mind whirled. "Where?"

She giggled. "I'll show you. Just say you want a servant to help with the cooking."

"You're the last one I'd . . ." I stopped myself. "Chela, we'll ride hard, and I know not where. Stay behind."

"Rust wants me to show you the waiting place." She shrugged. "Then we see.'"

"How will he get out?"

"Through the small door in north wall. Same as you."

"It's guarded."

"Remember when Llewelyn beat Lord Rust?" She sniffed. "He keeps family quarrels private. He thinks Rust safe in his room, so he won't mention it to the guards outside. Rust will ride up to the north gate and order it opened."

It might work, but . . . "Imps take Llewelyn!"

Her eyes widened. "Shh, not in Llewelyn's house. Bad luck."

Foolish peasant superstitions. Everyone knew demons went where they chose, and no ill speech could summon them. I sighed. "This had better work. If the guards hold him for his father . . ."

Her eyes flashed. "No one stops Lord Rustin, if he doesn't want to stay. And if they do"—she drew an imaginary sword—"he's still going with you!"

"How soon can we leave?" I yearned to leave the keep that had seemed a refuge, and now was sour with intrigue.

"Get your horse ready."

When I returned to the hall Llewelyn and Joenne showed no sign that anything untoward had passed. I bowed, the stiff, short bow that a guest might give to his host regardless of lower rank. "I would leave now."

Llewelyn paced, by the fire. "Alone?"

I shrugged. "Genard will come along. And if I could borrow a servant girl? She'll need a horse."

"One less to feed." It was of no consequence to him.

A few moments later, at the north gate, I shifted on my saddle, anxious to get our stratagem under way. Genard patted his mount, whispering soothing words.

Llewelyn had insisted on providing us with an extra nag, loaded with blankets and cookware for camping in the hills. "As I said, Lord Prince, I mean you no ill." I nodded my thanks, my feelings firmly in check. The beast would do for Chela to ride back to the keep. I hadn't told her, but I'd no intention of letting her tag along.

The mare's cookware clanked like a tinner's cart, and Llewelyn fussed with her strappings until I was ready to burst. Finally he tied the reins to Genard's saddle, gave the signal. "Is the north road still clear?"

"Aye, sire." A guardsman.

"Archers on the wall, stand ready in case foes lurk in the darkness. Open! Hail and farewell, Prince of Caledon. May the Lord of Nature keep you safe."

Genard, the girl, and I galloped into the night.

Behind us, the gate swung closed before we'd gone a dozen paces.

Chapter 10

GENARD STIRRED. "MAYBE HE WON'T COME."

"Shut thy mouth." Half-concealed in low bushes, I squinted into the night, but could see naught but dim shadows under the half moon.

"What if Tantroth comes? We shouldn't be near—"

"Wait with the horses!"

The boy muttered something under his breath, and retreated. I stifled an urge to give chase; I'd distinctly heard the words "better company" in his reply.

A shadow flickered in the moonlight. I peered eagerly, detected nothing. Then a dark form, cantering across the field. I recognized Rustin's familiar features, atop a wide-nosed bay.

"Here," I called, from the bush.

Rust whirled with dagger drawn. "Who's that?"

I tried to stifle a laugh, but only half succeeded; what emerged was more a moan.

He squawked, threw up the sign of protection. "Demons, begone!"

I giggled, pushed through protesting branches. "Don't carry on so. It's just me."

He jumped down from the saddle, sagged as if his legs wouldn't support him. "You scared me out of two years!"

"Good." I clapped his shoulder. "Send the girl back, and let's be on our way."

"It's night. They wouldn't open for her."

"Let her wait 'til light."

"After she helped me escape? Father would lash her to ribbons!"

"What matter whether a . . ." To him she was more than just a servant. I sighed. "Let's move on. Who knows how long Hester will tarry at Whiecliff, now Tantroth's attacked." I brooded. "You were right. Eiber's come for his lost realm."

"Between Father and Margenthar, he won't get far."

We rejoined Genard and Chela, at the split tree.

The girl jumped down from her mount, wrapped herself round Rust in an eager hug. Only when he'd returned her embrace with sufficient ardor did she release him, look to his steed. "Oh, it's Santree!"

Rust's delight was obvious. "You thought I'd abandon my horse? Does not Roddy ride Ebon?"

We galloped northward along the coast road, past fishermen's shelters and open pasture. The seawall lancing into the bay had discouraged commerce along the north road; Llewelyn's keep had no public way through its north wall as through the south. Still, Hester must have guided her wagon past the soldiers on the battlements, through the very gate we used. The northern settlements were rude hamlets, cut off from the town of Stryx.

The road to Whiecliff was perhaps a league distant. It followed a meandering stream through the foothills of the Caleds, until it met the coastal way on which we rode, some hours north of the keep.

As we paced our mounts alongside the ocean in the lightening dawn, I glanced to the hills. Along the ridge, the King's forest clothed the slopes in rich umber. Accompanied by Griswold and a party of retainers, I'd hunted boar and deer in its depths, as I'd lengthened to manhood.

At the junction of the two trails a few houses clustered as if for mutual protection, though the borough had been peaceable for as long as I could remember. Ebon plodded past a foundering hut. Two peasant boys stopped their hoeing to gawk. I paid them no notice, but Genard, oaf that he was, sat proudly in his saddle, and deigned to look neither left nor right.

The road climbed swiftly. A twist brought us a view of the shore.

Rustin drew a sharp breath. "Look!" Glittering below us was the sparkling sapphire sea, Llewelyn's keep but a faint smudge on the horizon.

Lying off the beach, twixt Searoad Meet and the keep, where but three hours before we'd ridden, black sails fluttered in the morning breeze.

"Tantroth won't have to swim the seawall," I muttered. He'd mounted a second incursion, north of the keep.

Time pressed. Somberly, we resumed our quest, alternately trotting and walking to conserve the horses.

Whiecliff was still two hours ride, and Hester surely long gone to Seawatch Rock. Would I ever see Elryc? Some part of me whispered it was best if not; I'd be free of responsibility for him, and the risk of betrayal. Manfully I thrust down the thought, mindful of my oath. I could not risk the Still.

The gait of a well-trained horse is steady, even if one's attention drifts from the reins. Ebon plodded on through the warm sun, and I couldn't help but doze. Behind me, Genard was all but asleep; only Rustin was alert. It was in near stupor that I lurched into the outskirts of Whiecliff.

"Demons and imps!" Ebon pricked up his ears at my exclamation. What a miserable collection of hovels. Grass grew in the roadway—pathway, more like—that traversed the center of the town. Abutting the road was what claimed to be an inn, but it seemed more a pig-farmer's dwelling, with a sign propped against the stairs, that I suspected few in the hamlet could decipher.

Still, the morning was well advanced. I was thirsty, and Ebon would welcome a rest. We dismounted, and I had Genard water the horses.

The innkeeper threw open the windows to dispel the fetid air, made grand gestures of welcome as he ushered us to a grimy oaken table, which he ostentatiously wiped with his apron.

Genard would have sat with us, but I bade him sit with Chela. Circumstances forced me to break bread in a dirty country inn, but I wasn't about to dine with servants. No matter that at the castle I took breakfast every day in the kitchen; that was Mother's fiat, not a sign of my station.

There was nothing like a bill of fare, but the landlord promised us breakfast fit for a king. I snorted, but Rust put a finger to his lips.

While we waited, I made conversation. Rustin seemed preoccupied and sulky. I put it down to his moodiness, until at last his silences began to rankle. "Does my talk disturb you?" My voice was laden with sarcasm.

He grunted, and I fixed him with an angry glare. At last, he noticed. "Do you ever think beyond yourself?" He leaned forward, searched my eyes. "I've defied Father, my home is under siege and my family's lives at risk. So I beg pardon if I don't clap with glee at your tale of Ebon's last shoeing."

How unfair, that he lash at me. "If my company's so distasteful, why don't you sit with the servants?"

He considered. "It hadn't occurred to me." He picked up his cloth and glass, moved to the lesser table.

When the food came I tore at it in sullen fury, not deigning to spare Rustin a glance. While he and the servants mopped their plates, I snapped my fingers for the landlord. "Did an old crone pass through, driving a wagon?"

The proprietor's eye flicked to my purse. "I could inquire, your worship. If I hadn't so much else to—"

I fished in the purse, found a few coppers. "There can't be so much traffic that it wouldn't cause a stir." Especially considering the drover.

Instantly the coins disappeared into the folds of his apron. "I'll ask." He hurried to the kitchen, was inside barely long enough to close and reopen the door. "Yesterday, my lord. A penniless old woman with her grandson."

"That doesn't sound—was the cart a great ugly affair pulled by a team of six drays?"

"Aye, and they should have been fed my fresh hay." He licked his lips at the lost profit, but added mournfully, "She looked at my lodging, decided they couldn't afford a bed. I heard they slept in Jorath's barn."

"Do they tarry?"

He shook his jowls. "They left early of the morn."

"Very well. We'd best be going." To my disgust, my party looked to me to pay the bill for all. Rustin was a noble, and should have thought to bring coin of his own. I knew Genard had none to speak of, but then, he'd insisted on coming along. By rights he should do without, unless he could pay his way. As for Chela, she was Rust's responsibility. But I knew he'd take offense if I suggested it, and the few pence weren't worth the trouble. I had coin for food and lodging for a month or more.

We asked directions to Seawatch Rock, and rode on in silence. Rust plodded alongside, while Genard and Chela rode behind. "We make good time."

I grunted, my mood sour.

His tone was light. "Will you be angry long, my prince?"

"When I wanted your company, you chose a churl. Now you'd be in my good graces?"

"Only if you want it so." Always, Rust seemed to laugh at my moods.

Still, the road was long, and the boredom considerable. "As you wish." I guided Ebon past a downed limb, that would have knocked a man from his horse as it fell. Gnats swarmed.

Seawatch Rock was a famed landmark, one I'd never seen. It jutted from a range of the Caleds between the coast and my great-uncle's domain of Cumber. At its base three roads met: Nordukes' Trek, which threaded through the high passes to Eiber; Cumber Trail, to my great-uncle's domain; and the Sea Road Track, up which we had toiled.

Were the track less neglected, two hours brisk ride would see us to the rock.

I nursed my resentment against Rustin, Elryc, the witch who led us on this foolish chase. Were the world just, I'd be lazing in the castle, waiting for Mar to arrange my coronation.

Ahead, the road wound round the base of a great granite monolith towering over the surrounding terrain. From the drawings I'd seen, it must be Seawatch. Though five leagues from the sea, it offered a spectacular view of the bay, and for the sharp-sighted, the town of Stryx itself.

Because the imp-cursed road wound back nearly on itself, the afternoon was near spent before we arrived. I'd expected nothing but the rock, but we found farms nestled about its base, and a small town where the roads crossed.

An inn of respectable proportions stood along the roadside, and even a smithy advertised itself on the edge of town. Its proprietor amused himself between shoeings by turning out crude replicas of the rock, which he sat on a plank in front of his door. We stopped for a stretch.

Genard examined his gewgaws openmouthed, but I paid scarce heed; I was sore of saddle, weary, and of a great appetite. "What of the inn, smith?"

The burly fellow laid down a hammer, poked at his fire. "Aye, what of it?" His tone was surly.

"Is the food good?"

He spat. "So it's said. Though with Eiber's men in the bay, Lord knows how long before they loot our farms."

"Genard, leave that toy. Have you seen an old woman in a wagon, coming from the sea road?"

"What if I have?" An angry swipe of the hammer, at some rod on the anvil.

"Then you might tell us. Genard, put that down unless you have coin for it."

"And you might get on your mounts and begone."

Reluctantly, Genard sat down the artifact, his eyes fixed on mine as if in dimming hope of a miracle. I slammed the door as we left, but it wedged against the porch with an unsatisfying thunk.

"What demon trod on his soul?"

"Who knows." Rustin. "Maybe Hester's at the tavern."

We had no need to inquire; the door to the livery was ajar, and our drays were nowhere in sight. Nor was there a great lumbering wagon in the yard. We found a table. Chela sat before I could object. Dejectedly, Genard made to sit alone, but Rustin caught his arm, beckoned to a seat.

I glared, but Rust said, "We travel as a party, whether you like it or not. Why make him an outcast?"

"He has no right to eat with—"

Rust's hand shot to my mouth; I flinched, thinking at first he meant to strike me. "Do you truly want it known, Roddy?"

The innkeeper approached, and I held my peace. After we ordered, it seemed too much trouble to make the boy remove himself.

Rust pointed out the window. "Shall we climb it?"

"We haven't the time."

Pungent soup in steaming bowls was set before us. I took a spoonful, gulped at tepid beer to soothe my burning tongue.

Rust regarded me quizzically. "Where's you sense of adventure?"

I gave it thought. "I don't like the countryside. I'll be glad to leave it."

The innkeeper approached with a pitcher, refilled our mugs.

Rustin nodded his thanks. "Innkeeper, why is your smith so peevish?"

"Ertha's son? Coutil's spent too many nights in the forest, camped off the road. It's soured him."

I raised an eyebrow. "Oh, really."

"Who doesn't know that abandoned earth bears a grudge?" He glanced at the stairs, widened his smile in a grotesque attempt at grace. "We've good rooms, if you'd stay the night."

"No, thanks."

"I'll make up a bed with fresh straw, enough for all. The woods are too cranky, these days."

I smiled at his peasant prattle. "The old woman driving the wagon. Which way did she go?"

"Estra, her boy called her." Absently, he wiped his hands on his apron, eyeing a pair of travelers at the door, whose walking sticks suggested they'd just been to the peak. "Nordukes' Trek, she said. Directions she asked."

"Thank you."

"But not the way she went this morn. Hanto, here"—he indicated the perspiring barman—"met her near the brewhouse, on the old abandoned Cumber Way. She got turned around, or is too addled to know that rutpath from the new Cumber Trail. On her own head be it, as but five farms rest along the foul stretch to the Gap. Sirs, a fine table, by the door!" He hurried off to his customers.

"This morning." I drummed the table while we ate.

"In that huge sow of a wagon. She can't be more than a league—"

"Suppose it was a ruse."

Rustin said, "Her ruse was asking the way to Eiber."

"Or being seen on old Cumber Way instead of the proper trail. We speak of mad old Hester. What if she turned around and took the trail?"

Rust slapped the table. "I have it! She took neither. She's on Sea Road Track!"

Yes, that would be just what the old—"No, that's the road *we* were on. How could she have passed—" I looked up, saw his grin. "Demons take you!" I stood, threw coin on the plank. "Genard, get the horses. Rust, ask the innkeeper if he has a place for Chela."

His eyes beseeched me. "Couldn't she . . ." My face was stony. He sighed.

Rust took the innkeeper out of hearing. He beckoned to Chela; she joined them. Afterward, Rustin disappeared for a suspiciously long while, and when he returned, straw was stuck to his shirt.

"Come along!" I stalked out, and was astride Ebon by the time he emerged.

We chose the old abandoned road to Cumber. Hester had been seen on it, and she'd said her sister's cottage was near Cumber.

The rustic village at the rock was soon swallowed in leafy curtains. I rode alone, behind Genard. Rust, moody and silent, brought up the rear.

Our path took us through thickets and groves, ever upward. For long stretches, stands of sycamores and maples supplanted the bright-lit meadows. Only the occasional wagon or rider had kept vegetation from overrunning the road.

At intervals we passed terrain once cultivated but now abandoned. Decaying shelters were reclaimed by relentless vines and shoots.

At least, as we rose, the air was cooler. But a canopy of drooping leaves blocked the sun, and the afternoon bled away in sullen mist.

Rustin fell in alongside. "Hester can't make much speed on such a road. We'll soon be upon her."

"If she isn't bound for the Eiber passes." Who could know Hester's mind. She was a law unto herself.

We plodded along. "Desolate country," Rust muttered.

"Mother spoke of settling the land, to hold it against Cumber's ambitions." I'd played at her feet, while she conversed with Uncle Mar. "Nothing came of it."

"When you're King, think of it again." He looked to the brooding forest canopy. "It could be made good grange, I warrant."

"I wonder if once it had a Power of its own. It seems . . . sullen."

"How can a land have Power, without a people?"

I shrugged. "I'm no Ritemaster."

Above the thick blanket of trees, the sky was darkening, as if to storm. It was impossible to get dry if one set up shelter after the rain started. If we were in for a tempest, best we unroll our canvas tarpaulins, hang them from suitable branches, and shield ourselves from the worst of it.

I said hesitantly, "I hate to waste the time."

Rustin wrinkled his brow, laboriously worked through my unspoken thoughts. "It's too early to stop."

We toiled on. Once, we came to a rivulet, not deep enough to warrant a bridge. I got down, examined the ruts. "I think she's been this way. These look recent."

As I remounted, the first raindrops hit. Quickly we put on our cloaks. Genard, to my disgust, had none. When the downpour intensified I had to lend him a spare jerkin as an overshirt, lest he sneeze and whine and complain all the way to Cumber. He swam inside it, wet and forlorn.

Heads bowed against the driving rain that lashed us regardless of the twists of the road, we made our way deeper into the hills. Hours passed in dreary monotony. Ebon trudged along a track grown muddy, on which water gurgled in the roadbed. Surely Hester, if she had indeed come before us, was forced to stop and wait out the squall.

As suddenly as the torrent had started, it stopped. But instead of the cool that oft followed a summer shower, a sultry mist rose from the earth. The leafy canopy dripped persistently on my neck, but I couldn't wrap myself in my cloak, lest I broil.

"Demons take this weather!" I stood in my saddle, massaged my aching rump. Ebon chose that moment to slip on a stone, almost catapulting me over his head. I clung precariously to his mane, adding wet horse to the effluvia of our journey.

Another hour, and I'd had enough; Elryc wasn't worth the misery. I needed sleep, food, dry clothes. Brusquely, I ordered Rustin to look for a suitable place to camp. For once, he made no objection, either because he shared my weariness, or had at last learned to heed his liege.

We stumbled on under darkening sky for what seemed a good hour. At a clearing, I veered off the road, found an isolated glade where a quiet brook flowed.

"Here!" I swung myself off Ebon, stamped the ground to see if it was marshy.

Rustin glanced about. "We need to be under trees to tie the canvas."

"Bother the tarpaulins, the rain's come and gone. We'll sleep in the open."

"Boars may roam the forest, and—"

"A canvas won't stop a razor tusk. Genard, lay the tarps on the ground, put our blankets on top." I stretched, groaning.

"Aye, m'lord." As if resigned, he began unlacing our bedrolls.

Rustin unknotted a saddlebag. "I'll loosen the cinches but leave the horses saddled in case a patrol comes on us."

"And gather firewood after. We'll brew strong hot tea, to wash down our jerky."

"Aye, master. And what about you?"

"Me?" I kicked at a rotting log. "I suppose I'll start the fire." Did he expect a prince to labor alongside a stableboy?

We made do with dried fruits and crackers, and torn chunks of dried meat washed down with the tea I'd promised. Not the finest meal I'd known, but it appeased my hunger, and the tea revived me.

I threw another stick onto the blaze, watched sparks shoot skyward. Genard leaned close to the fire.

I said, "You'll roast, boy."

"Gotta dry my clothes."

"Wear others, and hang them to dry, as we did." I flicked a thumb at my wet clothes, on a branch.

His glance asked if I could be serious. "I have but one other jerkin, and Lord Elryc wears that."

I shrugged. If peasants weren't so lazy they could afford proper attire.

Rust said, "Hang your clothes from branches, lad, and wrap yourself in my second blanket." He grimaced at his dried meat, said to me, "A pity we didn't bring a roast fowl from the inn."

My mouth watered. "Why didn't you think of it at the time?"

"You gave me other to think about."

"Bah." If he took that road, we soon wouldn't be speaking. "The light's gone. I'll match you stories."

Behind us, Genard peeled off his garments, draped them over a limb. He wore no underclothes; Lord knew how he survived our snow-blest winters. He unpacked Rustin's blanket, padded back to the fire in it, stumbling over its tail. "Thank you, m'lord."

"Sit." Rustin made a place. "Stories? Made up, or truth?"

"Truth. Tell me what you know, that I don't." I made myself as comfortable as I could in the oppressive heat.

Genard said eagerly, "Tell of the Furies. Or the Settling."

Rust pondered. "No, I'll speak of Powers."

I stirred uneasily. We ought not discuss the Still, or its requirements.

"My father Llewelyn is initiate in the Rite of the Seven Nations."

"Seven?"

"Not the nations you know, Genard." He patted the boy's blanketed leg, held up a warning hand. "Though perhaps . . . the Steppe. In old days, Varon came to rule there, but we speak of times when he was not yet seed in his mother's belly, nor his grandfather yet born."

He tossed a berry into the fire; it sizzled and vanished.

"In those times, they say, the Steppe was a vast forsaken land, and its Power was strong."

Genard piped, "Strong enough to—"

"Hush. The Steppe was one nation. Soushire was another."

I said, "Soushire's a mere fiefdom of—"

"The name remains, as a great man will hand down his name to his son, and he to his, until a once-proud title is worn by an idiot of the village, who remembers not."

An owl hooted.

"Soushire is today such a place, forgotten of the glory of old. The Lady Larissa is but an echo of the Lord who ruled a dominion that stretched west from Farreach Ocean to lands unknown. And the Lady's Power to make dogs fierce is but a remnant of the land's ancient Power."

"Impossible. No king can master so great a—"

"Not kings of our day." Rustin waved away an inquiring insect. "There were the lands of Cambod, and the Russ, and the Hills of Evalon, a place of such beauty that it is remembered still, though it's long sunk under the waves."

"How, m'lord?" Genard couldn't help himself.

"No man knows. Perhaps Lord of Nature was jealous of its grace."

For a time we were silent.

Genard counted on his fingers. "That's six."

"Aye, and I'll speak of Erre."

High above, a bird of night screamed. Ice shivered my spine, despite the stultifying heat. Genard giggled. "Erre is what you say when you forget someone's name."

Rustin smiled, but his eyes were solemn. "Fitting then, for Erre is forgotten. Long before Evalon, and the Russ, Erre held sway over lands so vast that Soushire, the Steppe, and even the Norlands are but pebbles on the beach of them."

I contented myself with throwing twigs at the fire, to watch them glow into nothingness. After a time I said, "Great Powers such a people must have plied."

"Aye, and there's the mystery." Rustin brooded. "There's one thing on which the legends agree."

I waited, but Genard blurted, "Yes?"

"Erre had no Power."

I knew Rustin well. If I spoke my mind he'd stalk off in a fury, and the next days would be dreary until again he came round. But I knew full well no land could subsist without its Power.

True, some talents were more useful than others. The Rood of Norland, carried into battle, brought fear and consternation on the enemy, which was often enough to weaken them and turn the tide. As a result, the Norlanders were enemies to be reckoned with. On the other hand, I couldn't see what a tree in Cambod might say of interest, when the moon was full upon it. And the Warthen's Power of Return was a dreadful gift.

The point was, what was a land without its particular Power? How could it be distinguished from its neighbors, hold its character? Caledon was of the Still, and the Still was Caledon. The Power ran with the crown, and the land. Before Elena, long before Varon, there had been the Still.

I grumbled, "How can I know about mysteries and Rites I've never been told? It seems to me—" Recalling my good intentions, I restrained myself from saying more. "Let's go to sleep." I unrolled my blanket on the canvas carpet. "Bank the fire."

In faintly hostile silence we got ready for bed. I stepped out of my breeks and shirt lest I smother from the heat, wrapped half the blanket under me for a pillow, threw the other half loosely on top, slapped at a mosquito.

It had been a night and a day since I'd slept, and that poorly. I drift-ed almost immediately into an exhausted stupor, not quite the blessing of sleep.

Time passed, in the glow of the embers. Lying on my back, I could see few stars; the clouds of evening had not dispersed. I sighed, rolled over onto my stomach, and drowsed.

I woke in the dim night, a persistent insect buzzing round my ear. I chased him off, scratched my back, drifted into torpor.

Again a buzz, and I fanned the darkness. A pin pricked my leg; I spread the blanket to cover me more fully. A moment later I swatted two mosquitoes on my arm. With a muttered curse, I made a tent of the blanket, crawled completely inside. Gnats swarmed about my head.

Rustin yelped, cursed under his breath. Across the firepit I listened to his scratching.

I buried myself under my cover, ears and all. At last I was left in peace, though between breaths I heard the swarm buzzing outside the blanket. I drew up my legs, made sure my toes were covered, drifted into a doze.

I woke moments later, drenched with sweat. I threw off the cover, gasped for breath, batted away a hundred insects, dived back under the covers.

Something was wrong. The ground on which we camped wasn't marshy. The day's heat had evaporated what was left of the rain. Why were we plagued with—

"Demons' lake!" I slapped something on my leg whose bite burned like a coal.

The buzz was incessant. Genard and Rustin too were kicking at the blankets, slapping at invisible tormentors.

I rubbed my face, found swellings where I hadn't known I was bit-ten. Desperate, I dived back under my covers, sucked in breaths through the stifling heat.

"Roddy!"

I grunted an unheard answer.

"Dress! Now!"

I moved the cover an inch. "Are you giving up sleep?"

"Aiyee! Hurry, for Lord's sake!"

I risked a view, waving away an avid swarm of pests. Rustin had kicked the last of our pile of twigs onto the embers. He danced, slapping himself, trying to get into his breeks, staggering like a souse. "Now, Roddy! A woods Power is aroused!"

I took a deep breath, flung off the cover, felt for my discarded clothes. Mosquitoes attacked with a vengeance. I batted at my upper arms, my chest. My back prickled as if I'd stumbled into a briar. Where in the demons' lake were my breeches?

"M'lord, are we leaving?"

"Yes!" I tripped on the blanket, went down cursing. I rose, shaking off ants. "Quick!"

Genard stopped thrashing under his covers, jumped to his feet, made no effort to dress. Instead, he ran, blanket and all, for the road.

Ebon reared and neighed, his eyes white with terror. Santree bucked in frenzy, as if mites bored under his saddle.

I couldn't find my clothes.

Rustin was half-dressed, his bare chest swarming. "Free the horses!"

"I can't find my breeks!"

"Leave them!" Easy to say, when he had his. Rust stumbled across the firepit, grabbed my arm, hauled me toward the road. "Run! There's evil loose!"

"Where did I leave—aich!" I slapped at my loincloth, squashing whatever had darted underneath.

"Now!" He half dragged me toward safety, shutting his eyes to a squint against a horde of probing mites.

"Grab Ebon's reins!"

With a swipe, he pulled the reins free of the bush on which they'd been tied, but Ebon reared in a frenzy. Rust threw his hands in front of his face, dropped the reins. "No time!" He dragged me to the trail.

On the roadway, Genard did a mad dance, pounding at his wrap, kicking at nothing. "They itch! It hurts!"

I staggered to the miserable excuse for a road, stopped for breath. The swarm had definitely thinned; here only a dozen mosquitoes landed on my chest. I crushed them with frantic blows, leaving spots of blood. "Ebon, here!"

My stallion bucked and kicked, too frantic to heed. Rustin scratched himself, swiveled his head constantly as if expecting ambush. I waved away gnats.

"They'll kill the horses!"

"We've got to—" He braced himself. "Now!" We charged into the treacherous meadow. He raced toward Santree; I veered to Ebon. A thousand pinpricks. Rustin slipped a foot in Santree's stirrup, but the desperate bay bucked too hard for him to mount. Rust slapped his rump and the bay clattered to the road, turned back toward Seawatch, galloped off.

Ebon wouldn't let me mount. I got behind the frantic whinnying horse, shooed him out toward the road, eyes near-shut against the angry swarm. Huge mosquitoes, fat with blood, landed on my exposed parts. Flailing, I dashed after the horse, hoping to overtake and mount him.

Ebon cantered along the trail. I tripped on a log, fell hard enough so the breath was knocked out of me. While I struggled to my feet, an ominous buzz grew louder.

Tiny shapes flitted past my head.

"Wasps! Run!" Genard, on the roadway, lifted the skirt of his blanket, raced toward Cumber. I sprinted to the trail, batting aside angry drones that attacked as if in concert. From Rustin, a cry of dismay.

For an instant I paused, thinking to help him, but I wore nothing but my loincloth; a horde of wasps might sting me unto death.

Even as the thought came, the menacing swarm swooped, flitted, danced toward me. "Run, Rust! Save yourself!" I dashed headlong down the road, praying to Lord of Nature that I not trip again.

My eyes were nearly shut from bites. Genard, screaming as he ran, was well ahead, chasing Ebon. Behind me, silence. I hoped it meant Rust had escaped; were he attacked, I could do naught.

As I ran, the meadow alongside gave way to a dark brooding canopy that made a tunnel of the road. Hearing or imagining the whine of wasps I panted into darkness, feeling more than seeing the roadway, knowing from Genard's panicked cries that I followed him.

I blundered into something large and wooden, squawked with pain, staggered on. I'd gone no more than three steps when a lash cracked onto my bare back, sounding the clap of doom. I shrieked, fell to my knees. The whip cracked again. I convulsed in torment.

"Begone, scoundrels of the night!" A high-pitched voice, from above, that creaked and grated. "Rob us, would you?" Another lash of the whip, which missed my face by a whisker. "Willem, Verstad, to arms! Wake the others!"

Hands behind me to protect my bleeding back, I lurched away, collided with something hard, went down. I clutched it as I fell; it was a wheel.

"Begone, assassins!"

I gibbered, eyes squeezed shut.

"Don't hurt the Prince!" Genard scampered toward me, arms spread wide, his blanket gone. "Hold, Dame Hester!" He threw his arms round me, tried to haul me to safety. "Help! Lor' Rustin! Help!"

Another crack of the whip. Genard howled.

From above, silence. Then, "Roddy? Rustin?"

I wailed, "Please, no more, Hester, I'll be good!"

The clearing reeled. I tumbled, and knew no more.

Chapter 11

I WOKE TO A COOL COMPRESS ON MY FOREHEAD, AND forced open my swollen eyes.

Elryc, framed against sunlit canvas, grinned down at me. "You look a fright."

I blinked, tried to orient myself. "Where . . ."

"In the wagon." As I frowned he added, "Hester's thrown up a tarp. It makes the cart into a tent." He looked small, in a worn peasant shirt.

"Hester." Scratching an itch, I shuddered, recalled the horror of the night. "How did you escape? I know you weren't in the wagon."

He smirked. "Turned me into a bird, she did, and I flew over the—"

I snatched at his arm, but he easily dodged me. Dizzy, I fell onto my back.

"Be careful, you'll—"

"Aiyee!" I spun back onto my side, teeth clenched against the searing pain between my shoulder blades.

"Take care. Aside from the lashes, you're covered with bites."

I groaned, threw back the cover to inspect my body. From ankles to shoulders, I was a mass of tiny welts. The sight of them drove me to a fit of scratching and rubbing.

Elryc tried to restrain me. "Hester, he's at it again!"

A muttered imprecation, and the weight of the cart shifted. The curtain parted. She came into view. "Stop, boy; scratching makes it worse."

I groaned. "I can't help it." I rubbed vigorously at an inflamed bite. "Where's Rustin?"

"There's no Rustin. Just Elryc's boy." She moved a cask, sat at my side. "He's tending the horses. It's about time you woke."

"Where are we?" I couldn't see past the canvas, but from the heat I knew it was full day.

"Where we've been. By the side of the road."

I tried to rise. "Move us! When night falls, they'll swarm!"

"Bah. We had a peaceful night until you crazed brigands came whooping into camp and startled me out of a year I can't afford."

I looked about. "How did Willem get here? And who's Verstad?'"

"Who? Oh, those were the first names I could think of. When you attacked us—"

"Hester!"

"Well, you came shrieking in the night, with horses galloping. What was I to think? I had naught but my whip and a dagger good only for close labor, with Elryc to protect." She threw an arm across his shoulders.

I squirmed, rubbing my knees together to soothe a bite. With the motion, my back smarted anew. I tried to peer over my shoulder. "How bad is it?"

Her tone was gruff. "I've seen worse. Try to lie still awhile, and you may not scar."

I groaned. "Do you have some balm that would ease the itch?"

She considered. "Brandy. A rub with alcohol will help. You'll smell like an alehouse, but that befits you." She got laboriously to her feet, fished in a box. "Elryc, unstopper this." She leaned over, threw back my sheet.

My loincloth was gone. I clutched my private parts, trying to shield myself. "Get away!"

Hester snorted. "I diapered you. There's no part of you I haven't wiped oft enough. Besides, many's the man with more to hide." She upended the flask into a cloth.

Scarlet, I groped for the blanket, did my best to cover myself.

Elryc snickered.

I seized his wrist, squeezed until he grimaced. "I almost died to find you, little brother. Laugh again and you'll pay."

Hester gave my hand a sharp cuff, pried loose my fingers. "Leave him be. It wasn't he who ran about naked as a jay, chasing a screaming stableboy."

I groaned in humiliation, clamped shut my eyes. I thought of throwing her bodily from the wagon, but her brandied cloth brought almost instant relief. Slowly, my fists began to unclench, and despite a resolve to hoard my anger, my muscles began to relax. Reluctantly I submitted myself to her ministrations.

I must have dozed anew. Later I awoke, hot, but much refreshed, to the bumping and jogging of the cart. Someone had left fresh clothes from my saddlebags; I dressed and emerged into the afternoon light.

Legs dangling over the tailgate, Genard sat munching an apple. " 'Allo, m'lord." He wore an outfit I recognized as the one he'd lent Elryc, when my brother was hidden. Behind him, their reins tied to the gate, paced Ebon and Santree.

Steadying himself on the siderail, Genard knocked loose the center pole holding the canvas. He twice folded the sagging tarpaulin, rolled it into a bundle.

The obstruction cleared, I gazed at the backs of the nurse and my brother, sitting together on the high box set. Elryc glanced back over his shoulder, nudged Hester.

She fixed me with a craggy eye. "Show him the apples, Genard. No time to stop for his lazy lordship's breakfast, or we'll never reach home."

"I never asked—" I stopped. It was hopeless; nothing I could say would win Hester's respect. Remembering the covers she'd snatched from my body, I blushed. Sulkily, I took a proffered apple. "Where's Rustin?"

The stableboy shrugged. "Dunno, m'lord. Dame Hester made me go back an' look. I told her to go herself, if she wanted to be stung to death. She said she'd take a stick to me." He took a bite of his apple like the snap of a predator's jaws. "Nasty old hag. No bugs, though, she was right about that. And no sign of Rustin."

I'd feared he'd find Rustin a bloated corpse, crawling with feeding mites. Thank Lord of Nature that wasn't so. On the other hand, Rust had deserted me and fled to the safety of Seawatch; so much for my loyal vassal. More than once, I'd spat out mouthfuls of grass and hay, when he'd lost his temper over some careless remark. I saw now the advantage of Eiber's paid and full-time soldiery; at least they played at no hypocrisy of oaths and pretended allegiance.

I sighed, knowing Rustin wouldn't leave me if he had a choice. Perhaps another evil of the woods had snared him. Morose, I clumped to the front of the wagon. "Where are we headed?"

"To Tarana's cottage."

"Where's that?"

"Where I've always said. South of Cumber, outside Fort hamlet."

"You never told—Hester, why are we on this imp-infested path, instead of the Cumber Trail?"

She nudged Elryc aside, knuckled the seat between us. As I squeezed between them she said, "A faster road, and shorter, that. But I like solitude."

"For no better reason, you led us on a wild chase through savage—"

"Enough." A warning glint, as of old. Like a boy, I hushed. She went on, "*You* may be brainless as a hare, but I at least think of Elryc. Cumber Trail is well traveled, especially now that Tantroth's camped on the coast road. Would you that word went back to Margenthar that Elryc was seen with me?"

My brother's lips formed, "Brainless as a hare." Casually, so as not to attract Hester's attention, I elbowed his ribs, hard enough to narrow his eyes in momentary pain.

I ducked, as we neared a low branch. "You could have hid him when folk approached. This road is a travesty."

"When you're King, repair it."

"And it has evil. Hester, those insects attacked us."

"They're what you deserved, you dolt, camping off the roadbed!" She flicked her switch, as if to expend her ire on the horses.

"I don't . . ." I hated to admit ignorance, but we'd blundered into disaster, and I needed to know. "Please, tell me."

"Have you not heard of the Settling? Think you the land is reconciled to the House of Caledon, while trees still live that knew days before Varon?"

"But there are no folk to wield—"

"Untended, Powers go sour with native cunning. Your mother tamed the roadway, by great effort, while the Still waxed great within her. But think you one Lady could work her will on the whole countryside? The Power of Caled Forest sustains itself, and no one in his right mind not born to this place sets foot off the roadway!"

I swallowed. "No one told me. I mean, I heard about the Settling, yes, but those was just old tales, legends . . ."

"We'll have a fool for a king." Her face was set, and stony.

I kneaded my knuckles, wondering if ever I'd be free of boyhood. Though I knew myself a man, in her eyes I was nothing.

"Besides," she added, "had you met me at Whiecliff as you promised, we'd have conferred about our path. As it was, I knew not whether to wait for you."

"I couldn't help it." All my life, whatever I'd done, I had to ward off her rebukes. Oft, they were unstated, but made themselves felt in her tone or glance. My voice was sullen. "Uncle Mar tried to impound me in the castle, and then we barely got past Tantroth. Genard's horse was shot from under him."

"Yes, he told me how gallantly you rode back for him." Suspicious, I searched her face, but found nothing. I changed the subject. "How far are we past the rock?"

"By horse, three hours at most. But the cart is slow."

"And noticeable. We had but to ask, and it was remembered." As was the spectacle of Hester herself. I thought better of saying so. "An old woman and a boy, they said. How did you get Elryc out from—"

"M'lord! Dame Hester!" Genard scrambled forward. "Someone follows!"

I jumped to my feet, almost fell from the wagon's high seat. Could it be Rustin?

A tired nag stumbled over the small rise, doggedly followed our track. It could barely keep pace with the drays.

My heart fell. Rust had no horse; his Santree followed our wagon.

In the distance the rider, bare-chested, waved menacingly.

And he had two heads.

I chilled at this new evil wrought by the forest. Tighter I gripped my sword. If one head were lopped, would the demon die?

As if to reveal the answer, he rose in the saddle, shouted words lost to the wind, windmilled his arms.

I groped for my dagger, found none. Like most of my gear, it had been lost in the clearing. Thank Lord of Nature my crown was wrapped safe and in Ebon's saddlebag, else I'd have had to return for it, even if it cost my life.

"Elryc, crawl beneath the canvas!" Hester's rheumy old eyes peered. "I can't see so far." She hurried the horses. "Roddy, you hide too. Now that you're fugitive from the Duke, you mustn't be—"

"Cower under a blanket? Bah. Give me a weapon!"

She sighed. "Well, if you're ever to reach manhood, I suppose you must defend yourself. There's a half-sword in the green-painted trunk."

I leaped for the blade.

"Don't show the sword yet," Hester growled. "Sharp steel sets a tone, and he may be a simple—"

"Yes, Nurse. Genard, untie Ebon and Santree. Mount one and lead the other. Ride ahead of the cart, to safety."

"I'm not afraid, m'lord. Let me—"

"Who cares about you? I won't have Ebon injured. Be quick!"

His eyes bleak, the boy jumped directly from the cart to Ebon's saddle. He unhitched the reins, sped off, Santree in tow. I recalled Rustin's good sword was still tied to Santree's saddle, but there was no time to call Genard back. He reined in a hundred paces beyond the cart, turned to watch.

The wagon jounced down the road, Hester muttering grim imprecations to her horses.

From ahead, the gallop of hooves. I whirled to meet the new threat, saw Genard streak past on Ebon. "Lor' Rustin! Hi aiyee! Lor' Rustin!"

I squinted. Had Rustin been taken by the forest, transformed into some unspeakable two-headed—

My grip on the sword relaxed. Two riders. No wonder the nag could barely keep pace.

Their elderly horse looked ready to lay itself down. As our wagon rolled to a standstill, Rustin jumped from the saddle, led the nag and rider the remaining fifty paces.

Panting, Rustin drew near. I dropped the sword, leaped down, the better to berate him for his perfidy in abandoning us. I drew breath as he rushed close. "Where have you been, you ungrate—"

He enveloped me in his arms, squeezed the breath from me. "Thank Lord you're safe! I was worried sick!" My feet dangled as he danced me across the roadway. The reopened cuts on my back stung like fireants.

"Ow! Put me down, you oaf!"

"Couldn't you hear us shout? Why wouldn't you stop?"

I managed to free myself, but not before he planted a kiss on my nape. Angrily, I wiped it off. My gaze fell again on his companion. "You!" I whirled back to Rust. "With all the misery we endure, you had to fetch that . . . harlot?"

His mouth tightened. "Speak softly, Roddy. She—"

Chela jumped down from the wheezing mare. "Call me that, who risked my life to join you and Lord Rustin? Prince or no, I'll scratch—" She lunged at my eyes.

Rustin dived between us, held us apart. "Don't. You're both my friends. Chela, behave; he's my liege lord! Ow! Roddy, why do you hit me?"

The whip cracked sharply over our heads, and brought us to our senses. Hester's glare was enough to wilt a lily. She clambered down from her high perch. "Lunatics, the lot of you."

Rustin looked abashed; Genard stared at Chela with undisguised admiration. Only the girl appeared unready to give up her quarrel. I moved casually to put Rust again between us.

"May I come out now?" Perspiring, Elryc poked his head from under the canvas. "They don't sound very dangerous." He giggled. "Except to you, Roddy."

I filed it with my long list of reprisals. "Tie yourself in a sack and throw yourself in the river." I eyed Rustin's bare chest. "You lost your clothes too?"

He blushed. "Chela offered a chemise, but I couldn't . . ." He peered into the distance, and his eyes lit. "Santree!"

"Never mind him. What's this—*woman* doing here?"

She hissed, "Looking after Lor' Rustin, more than his liege cared to!" A flick of her head, to toss back her hair.

"You were to work at the inn!"

"Why? What if Tantroth's soldiers came? Or Llewelyn's, who knew me?"

"You could say you knew nothing. They wouldn't hurt you. More likely, they'd . . ." I colored.

"I won't be a soldiers' whore!"

"Go elsewhere, then. We have errands of—"

"You stole my Rustin, where should I go, but to him?" Her face dissolved as she threw herself into his arms. "An' thank Lor' of Nature I came. He was racing along the road swatting bees, stung half to death!"

Rustin met my eyes, offered an embarrassed shrug.

With a growl I turned away. I glanced up the road, and froze. A horseman, in the colors of Margenthar. "It's not over." I scrambled onto the wagon, snatched up the sword. "Your lying whore led the enemy to us!"

The soldier waved and shouted as his charger cantered down the roadway. He was garbed for war, sword bouncing at his side, arm in shield. A helmet shadowed his eyes from the midday sun.

Rustin's good sword was still strapped to Santree, where Genard had tied him. Rust snatched a dagger from his belt.

"Elryc, Genard, behind the cart!" I had time to mount Ebon, but our attacker bore a shield, and I had none; that would give him advantage to drive me off. On foot, I was at more risk of injury, but with luck I could slash his horse's legs, bring him down.

"Hold, Rodrigo!" The soldier gestured anew.

My jaw went tight at the hated colors of the Duke. "He's mine, Rust. Stay back!"

"You can't bring down a mounted man with—"

"Watch me!" As the man neared I lunged at his steed, sword extended.

Though caught by surprise, the soldier had quick reactions; he bent over the pommel, got his shield between my blade and his mount's legs. In a flash, his sword was drawn. "No, Prince!"

I aimed a dismembering blow at his midsection; he parried. Again I struck, and again he countered. Despite my orders, Rustin quietly circled, waiting for an opening. From the cart Hester watched, her eyes grim, a protective arm around Elryc. Chela had disappeared behind the wagon.

Rust feinted. The soldier's steed reared. The man drove his mount in a circle, fending off us both. "Wait, Roddy!"

Rustin lunged, almost managing to drive his dagger into the man's thigh. For an instant the soldier had opportunity to run Rustin through. He was too dull-witted to take advantage. Instead, he batted Rust with his shield. Rust reeled, his legs unsteady.

While the man's attention was diverted I slashed viciously at his right arm. The shy of his horse threw off my blow; I succeeded merely in parting the reins. The edge of my blade buried itself in his pommel, wrenched itself from my grip.

At the impact, the soldier whirled, raising his shield for a blow. In desperation I leaped, clung to his forearm, gave a mighty tug. With a cry of despair he flew from the saddle, fell atop me, sword clattering. Half-stunned, I managed to twist myself free, climb atop his chest. I snatched up the sword.

"Kill him, m'lord!" Genard pranced in a frenzy of excitement. "Kill him!"

The man bucked, flinging me into the air. I raised both hands, gripped the blade for the plunge into his chest.

He shrieked, "Mercy, Lord!" It stayed my hand just long enough for him to draw breath. "Always you want to kill me!"

The voice seemed familiar. I hesitated.

"Vicious boy, not a moment did you grant me to plead my case! Go ahead then, end it!"

"Fah! Nothing you say could excuse Margenthar's—"

"I speak not for the Duke! Please, Lord Prince!"

With an oath I twisted his helmet, nearly cracking his neck in my haste to have it off.

Fostrow, my gaoler.

I gaped. "What do you here?"

"I've chased you through hill and dale for two imp-laden nights!"

"To drag me back!"

"To join you!"

That doused the embers of my rage. While they still sizzled and smoked I held his shoulders, uncertain. "Have you lost your wits?"

"What choice had I?" He groaned. "Let me up; my spine is on a rock."

"Good." I jounced his stomach; he gasped with pain. "Explain, churl!"

"Know you not your uncle's ways? Think you I could knock at his chamber, say I let you dump me in a clothing chest? Oww! If you'd break my back, have done with it!"

Reluctantly, I shifted.

"He'd have hanged me on the spot. He warned as much, when he set me to guard you. Even while I was suffocating in that cursed wardrobe I knew better than to cry for help." Fostrow glowered, as if his dilemma were my fault. "By the time I worked myself loose, the castle was in an uproar. Smoke in the cellars, Tantroth's troops charging toward Llewelyn's keep." He shook his head. "Easy enough it was to mount, and slip out in the confusion."

My grip tightened on the sword. "You left earlier, by the Duke's order. Else, you couldn't have gained entry to Llewelyn's keep to follow us."

Fostrow's face grew red. "Think you I don't know the path through Besiegers' Pond? Was I not raised under the castle walls?"

I caught Rustin's eye, exchanged glances. He shrugged.

"Youngsire, why are you so suspicious?" Fostrow loosed a hand enough to pat my leg. "A townsman saw you and the two boys slip onto the pond trail. The dead mare with an arrow through its throat was marker; I recognized the charger from our stable."

I growled, "*My* stable. You come from Verein."

He said with dignity, "I was *sent* to Verein. I *come* from Stryx."

"And you're here to drag me back." I raised Rustin's dagger.

"Stay, Roddy." Elryc, his tone urgent.

I glared at his interference. "He'd carry you off to Pytor's cell!"

"I would not!" Fostrow was indignant.

"Hear him out."

"His tales get wilder and—"

"I climbed down the ravine, but you'd disappeared into the keep. I couldn't go to the gate, lest you'd have them shoot me before I could explain. So I waited half a league up the road you must surely take. All night I paced, cursing the imps and demons of the dark. It was full dawn before I risked going off the road to piss, and while I was behind a bush your party galloped past in a flash. I mounted and followed, but . . ." His face puckered. For a moment I thought he was going to cry.

The danger seemed past, and he was unarmed. I slipped off his stomach, helped him to a sitting position.

"Ill luck rode my shoulder. My horse caught a stone in her foot, and I was an hour dislodging it. At Whiecliff they said you were but two hours ahead, so I had no chance to eat. Then Nell lost her shoe, and I had to walk her the rest of the way into Seawatch. I found the smith, but I was hours persuading the scoundrel to reshoe her. His mind has a warp, like a mishammered sword."

Rustin leaned over, brushed dirt from the man's back. "How did you find us?"

"How not, youngsire? Folk at Whiecliff said you'd inquired about an old lady's wagon and followed her path; think you such a procession would go unnoticed? Wherever I went I had merely to ask for a cart followed by three boys."

"I'm no boy." Reluctantly, I sheathed the sword. "Go back whence you came. I'll have none of you."

"Back to what, Prince Rodrigo?" Fostrow's tone was injured. "The Duke won't have me, and Tantroth holds the coast. All I know is to soldier."

"Then serve my uncle at Cumber. Begone."

"Think you I serve for coin, like Eiber's black-clad troops?" He drew himself up. "I'm of Caledon!"

"Fah! You swore fealty to my uncle, and abandon him without remorse."

"It's a sore point," he admitted. "But I've pondered it. Does my oath require me to go meekly to my own hanging? Would you expect such of me, my lord?"

"A vow is a vow."

"Easy to say, for one who demands fealty and need not give it." His tone was a rebuke. He rubbed his back, winced. "My lord, if Margenthar isn't Caledon, then you are. I offer my service. I ask only that you feed and clothe me, and provide me arms."

I glanced from Rustin to Elryc. "Can you imagine such gall? Not two days ago, he held me prisoner."

Elryc overrode me, with unexpected eagerness. "Fostrow, I'm the Prince's brother, and heir in the event of his mishap. If he'll not have you, gladly I offer you vass—"

"Hold! I didn't refuse! Fostrow, how can I know you won't betray me?"

His tongue roved his cheek, as if searching for a lost crumb. "Why, I guess you can't, my lord. Who can look inside another's soul? But I'll swear an oath on whatever Rite you ask."

I hesitated, half-certain I was committing folly. But Elryc waited, to snatch any morsel I disdained. "Very well, then."

Chela came out of hiding to watch the solemn oath I administered a few moments later, and Fostrow became my man. Though Rustin seemed glad of his presence, I made note not to let him ride close behind me, armed. Genard introduced himself, with ludicrous dignity, as Elryc's liegeman. Fostrow gravely gave his hand.

With acid realism, Hester prodded us onward. "We haven't food for so large a party; you boys eat like horses. Even when we reach a village, we'll be pressed for coin to support ourselves." She glared at me, as if in blame.

I paced Ebon to match the roll of the cart. "I have enough." With another sworn vassal, I felt magnanimous. "A year's stipend will buy—" I patted the remaining saddlebag, jerked the reins so hard Ebon reared. "Rust! It's gone!"

"What is?"

"My coin was in the bag we left in the clearing!" I slammed my forehead with the edge of a fist. "Hester, we have to go back."

She made no move to brake the cart. "Go, then. Catch up to us, if you survive."

"Hester!"

She wheeled on me, her face set in stone. "*You* were fool enough to leave the road, it was *you* who loosed your saddlebags when you camped. Flaunt the forest once more, if you dare."

"But it's day." I appealed to her frown.

"Was there gold in your purse?"

"Twenty pieces." Also silver, and coppers.

"Powers mingle with land, and gold, and the folk who rule. Now the forest has the gold, and would keep it. The insects were but a growl. Do you want to face white-hot rage?"

"Genard, ride back, would you? The bags are next to the bush with the pink flowers. While you're there, pick up our cloth—"

Rustin leaned over, gripped my arm. "Help me be proud of you, Roddy."

Genard rode on as if he hadn't heard.

"Let go." I massaged my arm. We rode in sullen silence.

We camped the night at the edge of the road. I gnawed at dried beef, resentful that Rustin had insisted I share our precious stores. I didn't begrudge feeding him; after all, he was my friend. Besides, he'd brought food of his own to share. But our supplies would hardly last another day, with Chela, the soldier, and Genard devouring them.

Hester and Elryc slept in the wagon under the tent. Genard stretched across a bed of boxes in the back of the cart. Stolidly, Fostrow unpacked his gear, made a bed of a worn cloth.

To my disgust, Rustin and Chela shared a blanket. I twisted and turned on the dewy grass, trying to make myself comfortable, listening for the inevitable sounds of their intertwining. Though there were none, my imagination was inflamed, and I grappled with indecent passions. I brooded on the misfortune of Chela's presence, until finally I was able to sleep.

The day began in sultry mist, under a steady drip from the canopy above. It was not so wet as to force us to seek shelter, but clammy and dank enough so our clothes hung uncomfortably on us. Elryc arose sullen and restless, his face flushed.

The road climbed steadily. By midday, in the hills, the oppressive heat had dissipated. Even Hester's dark mutterings took on a less irritated tone. "From the last ford, this was old Cumber land, and bears no ill will to our House."

Our House? The old nurse spoke as if she too bore the blood of Varon and his heirs. I snorted with contempt.

When we stopped to make a meal and rest the horses, Rustin noticed my blotched jerkin, made a great fuss over the scabs given by Hester's whip. He led me to a small stream, gently patted my lacerated back with a cold cloth. I forbore to remind him his own bear hug had reopened my wound.

"Have faith, my prince. This must be a great trial."

"The cuts? They'll heal in a couple of days."

"The whole affair. Abandoning your home, your worry lest Tantroth prevail, finding yourself without weapon or coin."

I stopped to consider. Actually, I hadn't thought of it so; freeing myself from Uncle's surveillance was a joy, regardless of the consequences. And I hadn't thought much about Tantroth, once I was beyond reach of his arrows. But I gave a great sigh. "Yes."

He embraced me, careful of my back. "I'm with you."

I loosed myself. "Elryc too, and Hester. Between you, enough will find work so I don't starve."

The look he gave was unfathomable. "Is that your concern, my prince?"

"That and lack of a weapon. All I have is that paltry half-sword on the cart. Could I have the use of yours?"

He seemed aghast. "The blade Fallon made, that I had to await so long?"

"Good heft on it, no?" I reached for his waist, withdrew it carefully from its scabbard.

"What weapon would be mine, Roddy?"

"The half-sword, until we find you a better. I'm head of our House, and should have a decent blade. Besides, we have Fostrow to defend us. You won't need one." I decapitated a few stalks of hay. "Yes, Fallon did good work. Please, Rust. After all, what's a vassal for?"

"I truly love that sword. It's the first I chose myself."

"Oh, come on, I won't nick it." I waved it, lunged against a pretended foe. "Is it fitting that I go without?"

His voice was toneless. "As you desire, my lord." Slowly, his fingers unlaced the scabbard. "Guard it well."

I buckled it onto the rope of my belt. "Shall we walk, while they set our meal? Hester says the forest's safe here."

"No." Rustin stalked up the knoll to the wagon. He'd undergone one of the mysterious lightning changes that despoiled his moods.

He shared a plate with Chela, to spite me. I tore at meat that ached my teeth, chomped viciously at an apple. Rustin seemed oblivious. Elryc squatted alongside me with his meal.

I kept my voice low. "How did you get out of the castle?"

"I told you Hester turned me into a bird. She has great Power."

I raised a fist to club him, decided not to demean myself in front of the others. "The truth."

He sniffled. "Ask Nurse, if you don't believe me."

Later, as we rode, I took occasion to draw alongside the cart. Elryc dozed at Hester's side, his head lolling against her shoulder. My voice low so he wouldn't wake, I strove to sound casual. "How did you bring Elryc out of the castle?"

Her eyes swiveled to mine, expressionless. Then, like a snake, her hand shot out at me, made a sign. I shied so violently I almost fell from my saddle. She hissed, "Ask not, Princeling!"

I muttered a curse, spurred Ebon several paces ahead, rode with head down, clutching the pommel, until I ceased to shake. Lucky we were to have survived her. I wondered if Mother knew our nurse was a witch. Had I submitted my brother to more peril than he faced from Duke Margenthar?

At evening, grumbling, Hester called a halt near a bubbling brook. "I hoped to reach Fort by tonight, or at least Shar's Cross. But we need to rest the drays. Rustin, Roddy, unhitch them, hobble them to pasture."

Dutifully, Rust obeyed. It wasn't my place to do the work of a stableboy, but Genard had taken charge of Ebon, Santree, and Nell, so without making an issue of it I held the team's reins while Rust tended to their needs.

I couldn't tolerate another night near Rustin and his whore. The tent in the wagon was rightfully mine, as the whole purpose of our voyage was to preserve our House. Yet I didn't feel up to requisitioning the canvas from Hester. I made a place near Genard in the back of the wagon, slept again in the open.

At first light Hester shook me awake, demanded I hitch the drays. I rolled over back to sleep, but she snatched my blanket, leaving me shivering in the morning mist. "Elryc runs a fever. We'll hurry to the village."

Elryc always ran a fever of one sort or another; his eternal sniffle was sentinel to his erratic health. Grumbling, I prodded Genard awake, made him do the more wearisome tasks. I thought of kicking Rustin out of the soft blanket he shared with his whore, but that wasn't safe; at times he could turn on me with violence. Still, the work should have been his. After all, it was he who'd unhitched the team.

When we were under way Fostrow rode alongside me. "I don't know this country, laddie. Between Stryx and Verein, I could tell you every rock, yet northward . . ."

I grunted, but he seemed unaware I wasn't enjoying his chatter.

"Where, exactly, do we ride?"

I shrugged, turned it into a scratch. It wouldn't do for him to know

I was as ignorant as he. "To Fort. A village near the Cumber hills." I made my tone condescending. "You know of Cumber?"

"Aye, who doesn't? The land rests uneasy between Caledon and the Norland, with only great hills and steep passes to keep the barbarians at bay. That old fart held it as fiefdom of the Queen."

My voice was cold. "That old fart is my great-uncle Raeth, Earl of Cumber." The guardsman's view was accurate, but he was but a minion.

"Sorry, my lord. The way he doddered around Stryx Castle, peering at everything, with that silly valet hovering . . ." He cleared his throat. "Sorry."

A time passed. I drowsed, lulled by Ebon's steady plod, and the squeak of the wheels.

"When Elryc—excuse me, Lord Elryc—is escorted safely to Fort, what will you do after?"

"Do?"

"About the crown. About Tantroth."

"What concern is it of yours?"

His brow wrinkled. "Why, I've sworn to you, Rodrigo. I should like to know—"

"You'll go where you're told." I spurred Ebon, caught up to Rustin, who rode Santree alongside Chela's nag. "Ride ahead with me, Rust."

"Hester won't like—"

"Demons take her. Come." I galloped down the path, and after a moment Rust followed. We were soon lost from the others amid leafy turnings.

"Not so far, Roddy." Rustin slowed.

"Afraid? Hester says the wood is benign."

"And what of Elryc, if marauders overtake the cart?"

Reluctantly, I reined in. "You think too much. It spoils the fun." I slipped out of the saddle, held the straps loosely while Ebon nuzzled the grass.

The wood was silent, except for the rustle of trees and the gentle buzz of insects. Rustin studied my face.

I blurted, "Rust, will you marry Chela?" Aghast, I waited for his anger at my intrusion. Until the words had flown from my mouth, I had no idea that I would ask.

"Of course not!" He seemed shocked at the very thought.

"Good. She isn't suitable." I giggled. "And Llewelyn would have fits."

"Aye." His face darkened. "May all go well for them at the keep."

"The walls are stout."

"You've never seen siege engines at work, Roddy."

"Neither have you." Sometimes his assumed superiority was nettlesome. To divert him, I changed the subject. "Tell me truth. Did you arrange for Chela to ride after us?"

"Lord of Nature, no!" He reddened. "I had no idea, when things began between us, that it would carry this far." He shifted uncomfortably. "Besides, I'm—not ready to marry." He prodded the turf with the toe of a boot, as if testing. "Not . . . for a long while."

I nodded wisely. "You'll want your title first, when Llewelyn's time is past. With that you'll make a better marriage."

He said nothing. I sat, to lean against a tree. "Rust, how is it we wander down an abandoned goat track, so far from home? What plans should I make?"

He leaned back, shoulder to shoulder with me, closed his eyes. "It's for you to decide. You're Prince of Caledon."

"What *can* I do?"

He ticked off options. "Stay with Hester, at Fort. Or go on to Cumber, where surely the Earl will take you in."

"Not Cumber. I won't exchange one keeper for another." I brooded. "Hester is a madwoman, and I shouldn't leave Elryc in her charge. But if I stay she'll make a madman of me too. Is there nothing else?"

"Aye, my lord. Set your standard, and try to raise an army to free Caledon."

Tents unfurled, hooves galloped, swords rang amid the flutter of pennants. Slowly, my glorious vision faded. "I haven't funds to support an army, even if they'll come at my call. I'm not yet crowned." I chewed at a knuckle. "Though, I have the crown in my saddlebag. What if I don it, and call myself King?"

"Self-crowned, would you wield the Still?"

"No, but Uncle Mar stole the Vessels; I'll never find them. The Still's useless." I thought again of Rustin, rolling with Chela in the sultry night, felt an unexpected stir. "Rust, it doesn't matter. My body won't let me wait much longer."

"Oh, my prince." His eyes opened, turned to mine. His knuckles stroked my cheek.

The tenderness startled me; I reached to thrust him away, found my eyes brimming. He gathered my head onto his chest, sat quite still, had the sense to say nothing while I stifled my sobs. Only the gentle stroke of his fingers revealed he was awake.

Chapter 12

THE INN AT SHAR'S CROSS WAS A STOUT-RIBBED structure, whose great oaken beams buried themselves in fly-specked walls. I slurped at fragrant lentil soup, glad of its warmth, greedy for the nourishment after days on end of tough jerky, dried peas, apples, tea.

The town of Shar was more substantial than I'd expected. From their stalls hugging the roadway, drayer, carter, cooper, clothier, bootmaker, scribe, coinchanger, candler, smith, and leatherer all cast hopeful eye on the passing traveler.

The inn had but half a dozen rooms, and two of those taken when we'd arrived.

Hester had disappeared with Elryc into the chamber the two would share. Rustin, the stableboy, Chela, Fostrow, and I would have to sort ourselves into two other chambers, which were all she'd pay for, and that only for the one night, "So my Elryc may sleep with walls about him."

It wasn't fitting, but I was helpless in the matter. My own coin was lost to the wasps and mosquitoes. Genard lived on our charity, and Fostrow claimed likewise, though I suspected he lied. Chela flounced her hips and dared me to search, when I asked what she had.

As to Rust, I knew he had sense to bring what he owned, but I dared not ask. Borrowing his sword had called forth a reaction totally unwarranted in its intensity. Despite our interlude under the tree, his eyes hardened and his lips went grim every time his eyes chanced to fall on my blade. Almost, I considered doing without, to end the unpleasantness.

It wasn't meet, that a king should share a bed with two, even three of his vassals. Camping under the stars was one thing; we all shared Lord of Nature's hard earth. While I sat brooding, Rustin's hand strayed to Chela's leg.

I fidgeted. There was no combination of sleepers I found tolerable, save that I have my own chamber, as befit my station. Before I could devise a way to suggest it, Rust overthrew my plans. "Genard can sleep with me, my liege. As can Chela. You and Fostrow will have more room, two to a bed."

I slammed down my mug, beer sloshing on my hand. "How if I proclaim myself, and ask lodging in the name of my House, since you're too stingy to buy it?"

Rustin's voice went quiet, as the forest before a fearsome storm. "I have few coins, my prince. You'd have me toss them to an innkeeper, instead of providing food?"

I tossed my head. "Do as you wish, vassal."

He tore viciously at his bread, attacked it. Then, "Innkeeper!" He waited until the man appeared. "You have one room unused, yes? Set the bed for my companion, here. The soldier and the boy will share, and the girl and I will have the other."

He pulled his purse from inside his breeches, held it below the edge of the table, counted out the pence. I couldn't tell what remained. "Good night!" Taking Chela by the hand, he stalked off. She ran along, docile, turning only to flash me a grin of malice.

Tossing and turning on my straw during the night, I heard every creak of the joists, the windows, perhaps of the straw in the next room. I knew to a certainty that Rust would sport with his housegirl.

I willed myself to fall asleep, fidgeted until the straw was matted and stony. Finally, I slipped on my breeks, padded shirtless down the stairs to the silent eating room, sat alone in front of the embers at the hearth, rocking, hugging myself. I smelled of dried sweat; my hair was awry, my eyes glued half-shut. And I had a thirst.

Someone had left a wide-mouthed mug, nearly full of beer or water. I licked my lips, reached for it, hesitated not knowing why.

Slowly, as if of their own volition, my fingers opened, and I placed my palm atop the mouth of the mug. Were the liquid an inch higher, I could stroke it with the palm of my hand, caress it with my fingertips.

I rested my left hand atop my right, pressed as if trying to meld my palm with the rim of the glass. Why, Mother, couldn't you trust me with the Vessels? Now, while Rustin rutted with Chela, I suffered humiliation and agonies of self-denial, and for . . . what? I'd lost the kingdom to Uncle Mar, if not Tantroth. I had but a haphazard crew of ragged followers who cared not one whit for me.

Slowly, I rocked my torso, head bowed, holding my hands still over the glass. Forward, back. Ah, Mother. Would that you were not under the cold earth.

After a time, I woke with a start. Slowly, I peeled my aching wrist from the mug, rubbed the indent left by its rim. Wearily, I stood, looked down into the still liquid of the glass. Then, I crept up the cold rough steps to my solitary room, closed the door.

"I won't put Elryc into a cart; he'd be cold when we took him out!" Hester glared as if it were my fault. "There's nothing for it but to stay, 'til he's himself."

A light rain tapped on the windowpane. "He can't be *that* ill. Just yesterday—"

"Your brother burns like the demons' lake." Her swollen knuckles tightened, over the rough plank table. "I can't be away from him. See for yourself." She stood, grimaced, hobbled toward the stair.

"Come along," I said to Rust. It was more order than request. Somberly, he followed.

Elryc lay dozing atop a straw mattress. My nose wrinkled; the chamber held the dank odor of sickness. "Give me to drink, Nurse." His voice was the high pipe of a child, with a thready weakness that startled me.

"How are you, brother?" I took the glass from Hester, raised his head from the pillow.

He slurped. Water ran down his chin, across his puny chest. "Roddy, did you hear them last night? Demons, on the windowsill!"

"Nonsense." My tone was gruff. "A fever vision."

"Two of them, with black horns." He coughed, from deep in his chest, cried out in anguish. "Oh, it hurts."

"Good." Hester prodded his leg. "Cough more, boy. It keeps you alive."

I waved it away. "What foolishness is this? Let him rest in peace."

"Cough!"

"Hester, take some air, regain your sense. I'll—"

Her fingers clawed at my hair, wrenched me from the bedside. "What know you, ignorant lout? Let him cough out the demons, lest they seize his lungs! Begone." She swept me to the door. "And take your overgrown shadow along!" She hurried Rustin along in front of her, slammed the door in our faces.

Rust shrugged, a smile flickering. "Did she ever marry? I pity the man whose wife has such a tongue."

"If so, he killed himself." I trotted down the stairs, out into the cool rain. "Come, let's see what delights the town has to offer."

"You jest." He hunched down his head, walked alongside. "Where's Genard?"

"With the horses, I suppose. Who cares?"

Just off the main road was a small market square, but only one stall was set up for the day. At the edge of town, an ambitious House of Rites was constructed of quarried stone, with a tile roof. Set in the outer walls were niches and alcoves designed for decoration, but vacant. "Looks like their coin ran low."

Rust pondered. "I wonder if there's a Ritemaster."

I scurried after. "You need to cleanse your soul?"

"Don't we all?" He took the steps two at a time, tried the door. It was unbarred.

Inside all was dark and gloom, until our eyes grew accustomed. Then, the tall narrow windows served well enough. Rust advanced toward the Circle of Rites.

"How may I help you?"

I jumped. The voice from the shadows was deep and strong, the face bearded.

"Hail, Master." Rustin put on his best face. "Is the place open to travelers?"

"For most Rites. There is that of initiates, but you need not concern yourself with intruding."

Rust bowed. "Thank thee for thy welcome, Ritemaster."

"Onter, I am called. What would you, here?"

"The Rite of Cleansing."

I stirred, not overjoyed at the prospect of a dreary hour mumbling the expected responses. "Rust, I don't need . . ."

"Wait at the inn, if you prefer. I won't be long."

I sighed. Outside was a bleak drizzle, and we'd be stuck in this forsaken hamlet another night at least. I had no hurry. "All right." I took my place at the Circle.

The Ritemaster looked us over. "Who are you?"

Rust spoke before I could. "I am Rustin son of Llewelyn, of Stryx Keep. My friend Roddy's mother worked at the castle."

A lie, and to a Ritemaster. I hoped it wouldn't annul the peace Rust hoped to find.

The Ritemaster seemed to accept his words. "We won't see many more of your kind, until Tantroth is decamped."

"Pray that it's soon." Rust.

"Aye, but little chance of that. He'll dig at the walls of the keep 'til winter, I warrant."

Rust pursed his lips, but said nothing.

"And then, who knows. They say the boy Prince turned coward and fled, and Duke Mar is beside himself with worry."

I recoiled from Rustin's sharp jab, to nurse my ribs. My mouth snapped shut.

The Ritemaster sighed. "Ah, well, who can blame the child, with fair Elena but recently laid into the ground? He must be greatly hurt."

My unspoken rebuke melted like spring snow. I settled on my haunches, awaiting the Rite.

The aim of the ritual was to rid the soul of worries and fears, of the self-contempt engendered by unspoken sins. Confession was made to the Vessel of Rite, not to the Ritemaster, but at home I'd oft suspected the Master listened too carefully to one's whispered words, and so I usually withheld that confession which wasn't seemly.

Today, I felt grubby and unclean, both of body and soul. Chela's arrival had driven a wedge between Rustin and me, and I resented that he didn't have sense to send her packing. The moment she appeared, I should have put my foot down. But I'd been distracted by Fostrow, and now it was too late.

As a result, at night I writhed in torment, imagining the pleasure that was denied me, and could take only the feeble substitute of my hand. Though Rustin did his best to hide his scorn at my virginity, Chela did not. Her saucy grin, wriggling hips and provocative stare were deliberate incitements. Try as I might to ignore them, my mind went ever to the enchantments of her body.

Like anyone, I knew the ritual almost by heart. I muttered the responses at the proper times, waited until the clay vessel was passed. When it came to me, I found myself whispering the dark and petty jealousies, the resentments, the lust that consumed me. After, the Ritemaster smashed the vessel, bowed to end the Rite.

We got up from the cold floor and stretched. I felt surprisingly better. Rust put a copper in the offering bowl, thanked the Ritemaster once more. "By the way, does the town perchance have a steamhouse?"

"On the edge of town." He pointed. "A few minutes walk."

"Is there a charge?" Rust colored. "Our journey was in some haste, and we haven't much coin."

The Ritemaster smiled gently. "No. It's open to all."

We emerged into a drizzle. "Satisfied, now?" My voice was caustic.

"I feel better. Don't you?"

I shrugged, reluctant to admit the truth. I glanced both directions, wondering what else we could do to pass the day.

"Come." As if he were Prince and I vassal, Rust strode back toward the inn.

I hurried to keep up. "Now what?"

"Fresh clothes. You don't want to wear those filthy things again, do you?"

"If you think I'm about to roast myself in a steaming—"

"There's cool water too, and tepid, if you're fearful."

"Of what?" I was indignant.

"A hot bath." I swiped at his arm, but he evaded me, raced up the stairs. "I'll get your clothes, if you like."

I followed him to the room, dug my saddlebag out from under the straw where I'd hidden it. My crown, wrapped in a shirt, filled one bag. Reluctantly, I pawed for a garment. "This is a waste of time."

"But you'll be clean."

Before I could object, he clapped my back, ushered me toward the stairs. I made up my mind to resist. "Rust, go on ahead, I'll—"

"No, you come too." He propelled me along the hall, dropped his voice. "I find your reek offensive."

In a white rage, I stalked across the road, tromped through the mud toward the edge of the wood, debating whether to seize a stone and bash in his head. By the time we reached the brick steamhouse my rage had ebbed only slightly.

Rustin struck flint, lit the taper, used it to ignite the kindling that waited in the hearth, while I gathered more wood for the next user, as was the universal custom.

The steamhouse was a crude affair, with little adornment, but had tubs for washing, stones to make the steam, an adequate supply of water. Built around a well, it featured two clammy tubs that one filled with buckets, an arduous task Rustin left to me. I was too cross to object, and after a while the hard work soothed my fury. The water was cool but not unpleasantly so, and when the tubs were full, I stripped off my clothes, sank in with a sigh.

I wiggled my toes, resting my neck against the headboard, my nose barely above water. "It's nice, but rather pointless without soap." In the next tub, Rust splashed.

"Lucky that one of us remembered. I'll toss you mine, when I'm done." He lathered. I suppressed a pang of envy as his muscles rippled. He had the body and the bearing of a king. I was clumsy as a house-boy, unless I set my mind to maintain a regal manner. Authority came naturally to Rust, while I had to strain to achieve what I deserved.

A splash, that woke me from my musings. I wiped my eyes, groped for the rough soap.

After, soaking in the cool tub, girding for the steam to follow, I felt almost forgiving of his crudity, his brutality of expression. "Rust?"

"Aye, my prince?"

"What are our stations, yours and mine? Are you vassal or friend?"

"Why, I—" He swallowed. It surprised me to see him disconcerted. "Can I not be both?"

"Are you truly my vassal?"

This time he didn't hesitate. "To the very life, my lord."

"Then why do you bully and insult me? Does that show respect?"

He climbed out of his tub, sat nude and dripping on the edge of mine. Our eyes locked.

"And why do I allow it?"

He essayed a smile. "Perhaps because you enjoy it?"

"I hate you when you're vile, or haul me about like a baby or a dimwit." My tone held a petulance I wasn't sure I felt. "Why can't you be courteous and respectful?"

"I'm vassal, not servant. There's a difference." He scooped a handful of water, ran it through my hair. "My blood is noble, as is—"

"And that!" I slapped away his hand. "Always you're playing with me, as if I'm a stuffed doll."

His voice grew taut. "What would you have me, my lord? Shall I be vassal, and no other?"

"Yes!" I heaved myself out of the tub, took the shovel from the wall, padded barefoot to the hearth, prodded the stones baking on the red embers. "Let's get on with it, before I'm too cold."

"Aye, my lord." Rust's voice was without inflection. First closing the windows, he took the shovel from my hands, carried the rocks carefully, one at a time, to the pit. I sat on the bench, one knee curled under my chin, while he drew two buckets of water, set them aside, took the clay pot, filled it, splashed water on the white-hot rocks.

He sat, on the bench opposite, breathed deep.

In the flickering candlelight I waited for steam to fill the room. Outside a bird chirped hopefully. Rust sat patiently.

After a time, I found the silence oppressive. "I didn't say you couldn't speak."

"Yes, my lord. What shall we talk about?"

"Stop it, Rust!"

"Aye, my lord." He said no more.

Pulse throbbing, I stalked around the pit, stood in front of him, raised my fist. He gripped the bench as his eyes met mine.

Slowly, I lowered my hand. "Demons take you!"

"I'll be what you want of me, Roddy, but I can't cleave myself in twain. Would you have servant, or friend?"

"Vassal!"

"Aye, my lord. I am that."

I wanted to throttle him, but again he'd defeated me. The more humiliation in it, as he'd had no need even to raise a finger. "Be what you wish," I muttered, and went back to my corner to sulk.

Rustin threw more water on the rocks, until the air was thick. My sweat coated me like a chill blanket, but the soap had cleansed me and the feeling wasn't unpleasant. Despite myself, I began to relax.

"We should do this more often." Rust's tone was peaceable.

"Aye." I knew I sounded curt, and, sighing inwardly, chose to soften it. "I'll have Hester load a steamhouse onto her cart."

He giggled. Then, abruptly, "I'm sorry my manner troubles you, Roddy."

It was why I couldn't hate him for long. "It's all right, Rust." I stood, indicating I'd had as much of the steam as I could manage. He doused the rocks, overwhelming their heat with the rest of the water. I shivered.

"I *do* want you to be a great king," he said.

Basking in his transparent sincerity, I stood hugging myself while he poured a cold clean bucket of water over my head. I gasped, rubbed water out of my eyes, groped for my towel.

"You're handsome, Roddy, when you care for yourself."

"Hah." I was half a head shorter than he, and nowhere as muscled. In my silver mirror, I sometimes glimpsed a calculating expression I didn't much care for. What would he say, if he knew I'd oft practiced his smile, alone in my chamber?

We dressed, tidied the bathhouse for the next user, went out into the day. In companionable silence, we started back to the inn. My bundle of old clothes seemed soggy and distasteful, and I held them with reluctance. Nonetheless, I thought, Rustin carried his washing fetish too far. I stepped over a mud puddle. Even when you'd been riding on a hot day—

"Look." Rust sounded amused.

Genard churned down the road, arms windmilling. Halfway to us, he sprawled headfirst in the muck, bounded again to his feet, resumed his run. I watched with amusement.

"Come quick!" He sucked in breath. "Elryc's dying!"

"Lord of Nature!" A stab of fear wrenched my gut. Not Elryc, so soon after Mother. I'd be truly alone.

"Hester sent Fostrow one way, me the other. She says to hurry!"

We raced back to the inn. I scrambled up the stairs, flung open the door to their room.

Hester's eyes were bleak. "Hear his lungs gurgle. He can't draw breath." She bent over the small form that lay listless on the straw.

Elryc's chest rose, fell again. The movement seemed so slight.

I cried, "Do something!"

"I know not what!" With an effort she tottered to her feet, moved toward the door. "The crisis came so fast, I had no idea . . ." She pulled herself together. "I'll seek an herbsman. Perhaps he'll know a remedy." She brushed Rustin aside. "You boys stay with him, at all cost. If he goes, it mustn't be alone." She vanished.

I stroked Elryc's head, snatched away my hand. "He burns!"

"He's been hot since the morn." Genard moved close.

"Get away, you're covered in mud."

"This room's stifling." Rustin crossed to the window, threw it open. "How can he breathe, without air?"

Obstinately, Genard kept his place by the bedside. I gritted my teeth. In a moment, I'd fling him from the window.

Elryc muttered, opened his eyes. His breath rasped. "Roddy. You're all staring. What's wrong?"

I sat. "We're worried for you, brother." I kept my voice light. "You slept long."

"Aye." He drifted off. After a few moments he was back. "It's more, isn't it?" He studied us. "Do I die?"

Rustin shook his head in negation.

"No, m'lord." Genard.

"Tell me." A long hacking cough, which left him exhausted.

I took his hand. "We fear we may lose you, but . . . We'll stay at your bed."

He nodded, as if agreeing. Again, the awful cough. It shook me to the soul. I blurted, "Forgive me!"

A look of puzzlement.

"For not letting you go down the hill with me. For the times I punched you, and told Mother lies."

A tear glistened. "Now I know I die. Else you wouldn't . . ." A gasp for breath. ". . . I wanted to see Fort. Be nice to Genard for me."

The door hurled open. "Let me see him." The Ritemaster, Hester panting at his side.

I blocked the way. "His soul is clean; he needs none of your mumblings! Leave him in peace."

"Fool!" The old man pushed me aside. He put his had to Elryc's chest. "Breathe." Feebly, my brother complied.

The Master pursed his lips. "The drowning fever, and we may be too late. He'll need strong tea, lots of it. Send to the kitchen for hot water." He strode to the door. "Stay with us, boy, I have a balm that will help you piss away the fever. Breathe hard." He bolted down the stairs.

Elryc's hand crept out from under the covers, squeezed mine. "I'm scared."

"Breathe. Take in air." I twisted, found Hester slumped over the table. "Why'd you wait, you old fool? He's practically gone!"

Her eyes flashed. "It came fast upon us. If a fever killed by itself, he'd be long dead, and you with him. While I slept—"

"Silence, the both of you!"

I gaped. Never had I heard Rustin so.

He crossed to the bed, grasped my brother's shoulders. "Live, Elryc. Roddy needs you, more than he knows."

"I want to." It was no more than a whisper.

I found my cheeks damp. "Live, that we may take the throne!" I fell to my knees. "Uncle Mar is a knave. I'll make you Duke of Stryx, and you'll rule at my side."

Even in his current state, that caught his attention. "Really?"

It seemed vital that we not lower him into the earth. "You'll have horses and servants and—you'll sit at my right hand. I won't set a plan in motion without you. I swear, Elryc!"

He coughed deep, spat a gob of yellow that oozed down his chin. He wheezed, "Didn't you hate me?"

"Never." I considered. "Only a little, as brothers who quarrel. Mostly, I—" My voice caught.

"What?"

"I love—"

The door slammed against the wall. "Is the water here yet? Boy, make haste!" The Ritemaster shoved Genard to the passage. "Prop him up."

In moments Elryc was in Hester's arms, half sitting, shivering as if from cold, his face flushed. Genard, tongue between his teeth, stirred industriously at a foul-smelling brew. I watched from the corner to which I was banished, Rustin's arm around my shoulder.

Sip by sip Elryc consumed the tea, gagging, fighting for breath. "Let me lie."

Hester shook him. "Later. Drink."

When he was done the Ritemaster brewed another batch. "Enough of this, and you'll piss like a horse. Your breath will clear."

I waited for a miracle, saw none. Elryc lay gasping, his face a sickly white. I snarled, "The man's a fraud."

"Give it time." Rustin.

"Put more tea in him." The Ritemaster

I growled, "You've only made him worse. He barely breathes."

"Nurse—" Rust guided me to the door. "Call us if—if there's need."

Downstairs, we waited at a table near the hearth. Rustin stared at the table. My mouth watered for a midday meal, but we ordered only wine. Mostly we sat in silence, sometimes we spoke.

From time to time Genard brought down a report. Elryc passed water, slept. He took more tea. His fever rose. I steadily drank my wine. Rustin seemed disgusted when I ordered more, and said he wouldn't pay for it. Again Elryc slept. I absorbed the bulletins until my own breath came short, and the room drifted to and fro. Elryc woke, took more of the tea.

A hand on my shoulder roused me. I lifted my head from the table. Genard, in a clean well-made shirt that could not have been his. "He lives! The fever's broke!"

"Good." I lay down my head, fell back to sleep.

Late in the afternoon, I roused myself to a general air of disfavor. Chela sniffed, turned away with head high. Genard's glance held active hostility; Fostrow merely looked sad and shook his head.

I begged a flagon of water, finished it in one breath, and trudged to Hester's room. The old lady was sound asleep at the table. I tiptoed to the bed.

Elryc woke at my step. His face was wan, but his breath came more easily. "Roddy."

"Shhh." I sat, shifted the straw under the coarse blanket.

"I feel better." He cuddled my hand. "Never will I forget how you sat with me, told me truth while others lied."

I puzzled, tried to remember. "I said we feared for your life."

"I needed to know." He yawned. "Roddy, I've been thinking. We must raise a force. We won't be treated seriously without men-at-arms."

"We?" My eyebrow raised. "Are you to be King too?"

A silence, while he studied me. "You didn't mean you'd share the kingdom, that I was to be Duke of Stryx?"

Careful, now. He could be made a potent enemy, forever. I said, "Of course I meant it, but you're only eleven. That's all in future. For now, you'll go with Hester."

His look was one of wonder rather than hurt. "You lie, and risk the True?"

"It wasn't a lie when I— No! Besides, the True can't apply to idle— I mean, of course I meant—"

"Let me sleep." He turned his back to me.

"Elryc, listen."

"Go away!" His voice was louder, and would wake Hester, and the madwoman would rage at me. I beat a sullen retreat.

I sought the privacy of my room, found the door barred. Rustin? I banged. Had he taken that slut Chela inside, for a bit of sport? Let him find his own chamber.

The door swung open. A swarthy fellow, with the look of a teamster. "Get thee gone!"

"This is my room!"

"Two of my pence say not, and so does the innkeeper. I've a wagon to load tonight, and would sleep!"

I twisted past. "You can't take—"

He collared me, slammed me against the wall, whirled me breathless to face the door. "My room, you sot! Out!" A mighty kick to my rump propelled me into the hall, bounced me off the wall opposite. I slid to the floor, my tailbone numb. Behind me, the door slammed.

I lay stunned, fighting tears, losing my battle. At length I limped down to the crowded dinner room. Rustin was nowhere in sight.

Fostrow sat at a side table, sopping bean soup with a great chunk of bread. "What hails, my lord?"

Cautiously, I sat, my buttocks throbbing. "What happened to my room?" My voice was small.

"Dame Hester found you snoring at the table. She remarked she had no coin to waste on extravagance."

"But Rust was the one who paid—" I blushed.

"Rustin was here, and didn't object." He eyed me as if a curious specimen. "Youngsire, it's not a good idea to guzzle jugs of strong—"

"Stuff it in your saddlebag!" After a moment I spoke more softly, to soothe the pounding of my temple. "Where are my clothes?"

"I have them. You share with me and Genard or, I suppose, Lord Rustin and his lady."

"Lady!" I snorted. I'd sleep with the stableboy and the soldier, rather than demean myself with her. On the other hand, that would leave Rustin free to fornicate the night through, after having spurned his duty to his liege. I hid a smile of triumph. "I'll stay with Rustin." I looked about. "Did Hester deny us to eat, as well?"

"No, she said a good meal might clear your addl—your head." He fished out a few pence. "Order as you will."

A good dinner—broiled trout, new potatoes, corn sopped in butter, fresh hot bread—did much to restore my spirits, even though I watered my wine well to keep my head from exploding. After, I bid Fostrow good day with something approaching civility, went upstairs to jolly Elryc out of his sulk.

Hester met me at the door. "He's asleep." Her face showed fatigue, but vast relief. "He mends visibly. Perhaps we can leave in the morn."

"Wonderful."

"Pah." In the hall, she shut the door behind her, kept her voice low. "You're that anxious to see Fort? It's long enough you'll tarry, once we've arrived."

"What does that mean?"

Her eyes narrowed, as if studying a rock. "You have elsewhere to go? War is in the land, your uncle's under siege, and you threw away your pence. Would you roam with Rustin as a pair of young tinkers? Go to bed." She slipped inside the door, shut it sharply in my face.

Who was she to order me about? Outside, there was still light. I went downstairs, strode out, nearly collided with Rust.

"Good evening, my prince." Rust made a mocking bow.

Loud voices. I looked beyond him to the road. Two horsemen, in front of the inn. Townsmen had gathered. "Something's afoot, Rust."

Under the innkeeper's watchful eye a stableboy was transferring a rider's bags from his tired mare to a fresh gray, while the newcomer paced off the stiffness of his limbs. "I'd stay for your venison stew, Jennison, by the imps' mist I would. But the news must haste to Lord Cumber."

"Are you sure, Kariok?"

The man snorted. "It's not a thing you could mistake. The keep's fallen!"

I stood dumbstruck.

Rust blanched. "Say you what?"

"Tantroth holds the keep! Tell him, Kariok!"

"Aye, it's true, and no good tidings be it."

Rust stammered. "This—it cannot be. The keep had food and arms for months, and the walls were—"

"Walls do no good, undefended. The traitor Llewelyn dines in Tantroth's tent this very day. He and his bitch—"

With a roar Rustin launched himself at the man's throat. As they tumbled in the mud I leaped just in time to wrest the dagger from Rust's hand, before he commit murder and be hanged.

"You lie! Llewelyn holds for the crown!"

"Jennison, Styrer, pull this madman off me!" Cursing, the messenger struggled free. Rustin flailed at his subduers, was dragged to his feet and pinioned, shouting his impotent fury.

Kariok's face was red. "Coward, that you attack without warning!" Before any could react he lunged, slammed his fist into Rustin's belly, and again. Panting, he drew back, while Rustin, retching, tried to double over. Vomit trickled down his shirt.

"Peasant dog!" Kariok brushed himself off. "Last day the keep was opened, while still the sky held light. I myself was among the guard Duke Mar posted on the hill! Llewelyn rode forth, acknowledged Tantroth of Eiber, went with him as his guest. Eiber mans the keep, and will have it for winter quarters. By Lord of Nature, I'll teach this lout." His hand shot to his dagger. "Hold him, Styrer. I'll have his ears for remembrance!"

I stepped between him and his prey. "Pass me first." My legs were unsteady. Why in Lord's sake hadn't I brought my sword?

"Out of my way!" He made as if to lunge.

"My friend meant no harm. He knew the keep well, and holds strong for Caledon. Forgive him." Reluctantly, my hand went to my dagger.

"I'll sew your ears to my belt next to his!" His hand came forward, and he took the fighter's crouch.

Jennison the innkeeper surged his bulk forward, words gushing to quench the flames. "Now, now, my lords, gentlemen, soldiers, youngsire, look you, Kariok, you've had your revenge, the boy can't stand unaided. No one doubts your word. Styrer, let go, there's a good fellow. Cumber will wait while you two have had a good dinner, no? Smell the slices of roast boar I'll bring . . ."

From somewhere, Genard materialized. He and the inn's boy led Rustin away, while Jennison interposed himself between them and Kariok, who still smoldered.

I backed away, never once turning my back to the messenger, or lifting my hand from my dagger. At last inside, I turned, raced up the stairs.

Rust lay groaning across our bed, clutching his midriff. "Lying son of demons! Motherless spawn of the deepest lake . . ."

"Out." I thumbed Jennison's boy to the door, lowered the bar.

"Go!" Rustin's tongue was thick. "Get their story, before they leave." He moaned. "Oh, that hurt. Please, Roddy. Find out whence this foolish tale."

"I'll stay with him, m'lord," said Genard.

I was reluctant, but Rust's need was greater for knowledge than comfort. I slipped downstairs into the public room, where all were agog with the news. Kariok's companion, Styrer, eyed me cautiously, but, palms outward, I made a gesture of peace, and he let me be.

The sordid tale unfolded. Eiber's catapults had been strung, stones gathered, siege engines readied in two days of strenuous effort. I frowned at the hearing; decent war was fought at a more leisurely pace. When Mother's army had subdued the rebellion at Soushire, a full fortnight had passed between surrounding the walls and readying the instruments of siege. It gave a gentleman time to reflect on the nobility of his doings. I sighed. One could hardly accuse old Tantroth, the black warrior, of being a gentleman.

Hardly a few arrows had flown, save those the guards on the walls and Tantroth's men had unleashed at each other for sport, when Eiber's envoys had ridden to the south gate, under flag of parlay. Instead of curt refusal, Llewelyn had allowed him entry, and they spoke into the night.

The next day, all was calm. Despite his apparent readiness, Tantroth attacked not. In afternoon, he sent another envoy. Before the sun set, Llewelyn himself had ordered the gates swung ajar.

There was no slaughter.

Llewelyn and Joenne rode at the head of an honor guard, flags flying, to Tantroth's tent. Tantroth himself greeted them publicly, and embraced them.

Uncle Mar watched brooding from the towers, and no doubt sent messengers to Verein and to Cumber. This was wise; soon Tantroth's troop would climb the hill unimpeded, and invest the castle. I supposed the two guardsmen at our inn had gone as we had, by way of Besiegers' Pond.

Upstairs, I reported as much to Rustin.

He lay curled on the bed, his face anguished. "But why, Roddy? How could he?"

"I don't know." I forbore to say more. Llewelyn's life was forfeit, of course. Perhaps Tantroth would let him live, though if he was cunning he would wait, and later, quietly, put an end to him. A man who betrays you once will do it again. Should Uncle Mar prevail, Llewelyn would lose his head as a matter of course. I hoped he'd do it before I came to power, to save me the trouble.

A long silence. "Leave me alone awhile."

"You needn't—"

"I beg you!" His voice caught. "You too, Genard."

Saddened, I went downstairs, settled at Fostrow's table, watched him placidly eat his dinner. The soldier asked, "What of your friend?" He poured me a mug of mulled wine.

"He sulks in his room."

"Ah, laddie, you're a harsh one." He gnawed at a bone.

"Llewelyn betrayed us all." I toyed with my wine. "Thanks to him I may never don my crown. I feel sorry for Rustin, but he should realize—"

Fostrow leaned forward, made an apologetic gesture. "Do you know compassion?"

"Oh, leave it." I broke off a piece of Fostrow's bread. "He'll get over it. Besides, I never told him I blamed—"

"Well, it's good you don't feel ill toward him. After all, your own father was a vile traitor."

The bread fell from my hand. My eyes widened. "How dare—damn you for a churl!" I leaped to my feet. "You'll die tonight! Come, have at me!" My dagger glinted.

"See?" he said reasonably. "It's not an easy thing to bear. When Rustin—"

"Take it back, or I'll slice you where you sit!"

"Of course I take it back, it isn't true. Sit, calm yourself."

"You call my father traitor, and think I'd sit—faugh! It's a lie!"

"Didn't I just say so? It was by way of example."

"What do you mean, example? My father betrayed no one!" My fist wavered; in frustration I slammed the dagger into the plank table. "No one!"

"I was showing how you'd feel—"

"I know how I feel to hear your lies! How could you say such a thing? He was beloved of my mother the Queen, and died respected by all." I was trembling.

"Yes, youngsire. Sit." He ushered me to my chair. The blade quivered next to my mug. "It's how Rustin feels, you see."

"What?" I worked loose the blade. "But Llewelyn *is* a traitor. There's no reason for Rust to get so—"

"Llewelyn's his father."

"I know that; think you I'm a dunce?" I found my bread, bit off a savage chunk. What had come over Fostrow, making such a claim? Llewelyn would die, by Tantroth's hand or our own. Did Fostrow think I'd show mercy, by playing tricks on my wits? Wait 'til I told Rustin how little more than a word drove me to—

Rustin already knew.

I swallowed. Fostrow's foolery aside, Rustin had no right to feel wounded. What he should feel was shame, remorse. He'd expressed no such to me. Had my father betrayed us, I'd curse his name, revile his memory, spit on his—

I'd love him.

Subdued, I swallowed my bread. If it had a taste, I knew not.

Rust was deep wounded.

Perhaps I could explain, help him in some way. I pushed back my chair. "I'm going upstairs."

"Be kind to him, laddie." Fostrow's look was almost approving.

I knocked on our door. No answer. "Rust?" I waited. "Let me in."

Could he have gone out? I hadn't noticed him come downstairs. I tried the door; it was barred. Someone had to be inside, unless he'd crawled out the window.

From inside, a scrape. Then silence.

Ah, well. If he wanted to sulk, I'd see him after. I started down to the public room. No need to make a fool of myself, begging at his door.

I slowed. What difference did it make what these rustics thought? I was Prince of Caledon, and could do as I wished. Who was Rustin, for that matter, to deny me entry? I'd had enough of his sullenness; if he was upset, he could by Lord of Nature tell me why. I went back to the door, banged hard. "Rust, open!"

No answer. Relief was what I felt, instead of anger. I'd half expected him to come charging into the hall, pummel me for disturbing his pout.

I knocked once more, felt the unyielding handle. It was unlike Rust to let me bother him so, without response. I pushed harder, got nowhere. I stepped back, gave the door a kick, then another. Harder and harder I kicked.

"Boy, leave my door be!" Jennison, below. "If he's inside, he'll be out when—"

My boot smashed against the bar, until at last the door splintered, gave way an inch. In a frenzy, I struck again. The panel sagged, fell away. I reached through, lifted the bar, rammed open the shattered door.

Rust hung in the center of the room, from a beam, eyes open, face empurpled. His feet twitched. One hand was at this side, the other clawed at the knot around his neck.

With a cry I dashed forward, stumbled over the chair he'd kicked aside, got under him, threw my arms around his waist, heaved upward. He was impossibly heavy, and did nothing to assist.

"Someone, help!" My voice was muffled by his breeks. I tossed my head, yelled louder. "Genard! Fostrow! Innkeeper!"

Thudding feet. "Oh, Lord!" We swayed, as someone put his shoulder to my burden.

Rust's foot lashed out, caught me in the stomach. "Get him down, quick!"

"A knife!"

I daren't let go. "In my belt!" A hand reached for my dagger, and suddenly Rust weighed twice as much as before. We tumbled to the floor.

Fostrow and the innkeeper sorted themselves out, attacked the knot. They couldn't cut it without slashing Rust's throat; instead they fiddled for maddening moments until it came loose.

I heaved Rust over onto his back. "Does he breathe?"

As if in answer Rustin's mouth opened wide. He took in a swallow, wheezing breath, gasped it out. His eyes bulged.

"Breathe!" Desperate, I massaged his throat. It might have helped; perhaps nature reasserted herself on her own. He gasped, coughed, wheezed, began to breathe more normally. Slowly, his face lost its unhealthy hue.

Babbling voices, over our heads. Someone wanted to throw water, others to light a fire. Someone suggested leeches. Fostrow, with genial patience, shooed them all out until the room was quieted. We helped Rust to the bed.

"You should . . . have let me . . . die." His voice was no more than a croak.

"Never." I massaged his hand, as if it were cold.

His free hand went to his throat, where rope burns would show a long while. "It hurts."

"Good, you fool, you moron! Dolt!"

He wriggled loose his hand, raised it to my cheek. "You're weeping."

Angrily I wiped my face. "I'm sweating. You made me work too hard." I stopped, lest my voice break. "How could you!"

His eyes were bleak. "How could I not? Now I'll have to . . ." I barely caught the next words, in his misery. "Try again."

"Not while I live!"

To my astonishment, Fostrow came behind me, clapped me on the shoulder as if in approval, squeezed gently, and left the room.

"How can I look anyone in the eye, with my father a traitor?"

"Llewelyn is not you. You're my Rustin, and I"—I hesitated—"admire you." I tucked the blanket over him, clothes and all. "Stay with me, Rust. Else . . . how shall I become King?"

Chapter 13

 NEXT MORNING I CAME DOWNSTAIRS YAWNING, AND wandered into the public room.

To my amazement, Elryc sat beaming, with Chela and old Hester. When he saw me his smile faltered, but he greeted me with a civil nod.

I asked, "Are you well enough to be about?"

"I haven't much strength. Hester had to catch me, or I'd have fallen down the stairs."

"You'll sleep all day, if you wish, in the cart. Eat, Roddy. We must be off."

Rust came to join us, his throat livid. His dull expression made me uneasy. I urged Hester to let us ride in the cart, on the pretext of tending Elryc.

Later, as we jounced along, Rustin gripped my wrist. "I swear, I'll avenge what Father's done. With my own hand, I'll kill hi—"

I clapped my hand over his mouth, almost too late. "Would you have demons and imps hound you the rest of your days? How could you be so foolish!" No man could swear such a horrendous thing, and remain sane.

"I meant—"

"Oh, Rust, you swore it to yourself, not to me— If to me, I release you, and gladly—promise you'll go to a Ritemaster, and expiate your oath!" The Rite of Setting Aside.

"I . . ."

"You must!"

He lay back, as if too tired to object. "All right." For one vanquished, he seemed strangely grateful. "I promise."

The road to Fort led ever upward, and the going was slow. We passed an occasional dreary hamlet, watched dull-eyed farmers' wives in peasant smocks work their fields. Summer was near past, and theirs was a constant battle to save crops from marauders and weather.

At midafternoon we stopped for a meal. Hester tucked Elryc into blankets, and brusquely bade me gather wood.

Why was I less than nothing, and my brother everything, in Hester's dim eye? As I'd grown I resisted her attentions, but that was natural for a growing boy, and surely Elryc had done the same. Would Mother have entrusted me to her care, knowing Hester would come to despise me?

Chela crossed the glade, hips swaying, deftly avoiding outstretched hands. Unbidden, she dropped into a crouch by my side. "You saved Rustin. Thank you for that."

I watched for mockery, but saw none. I grunted. She flicked her skirts with casual disdain, flounced off.

A full day we spent, alongside the cursed wagon, while Hester sat like a gargoyle on the high box seat, reins in hand. I rode Ebon, and imagined myself King, in procession among my people.

At last the dusk lengthened, and Hester found a meadow in which to pull off. Then we worked no better than churls until the horses were watered, gear set out, a fire begun, and cookpots arranged. Hester growled every time I took my ease. She expected me to labor alongside my own servants, which was mad. I was too tired to object.

I dawdled at my meal until I could hardly hold open my eyes, then went reluctantly to bed.

Inside the cart Hester had erected her usual tent, where she nestled with Elryc. Quietly I crawled beneath the wagon, and spread my blanket.

Nearby, Chela and Genard were fast asleep. I made my place on the outer side, near Rust.

He lay altogether too near Chela for me to sleep. I waited for his hand to steal to her body, but though he tossed and turned, he made no move to her.

Resolutely, I tried to ignore them. Why did Rust dally with such a slut? Had he no eyes for the finer things in life? On the other hand, why would the son of a traitor care if his reputation was—no, that wasn't fair. But she was a vile woman, mocking, throwing herself about, rubbing against . . . I felt a yearning I dared not attend. Not when I lay so near to Rust, and the girl.

Near dawn, Chela stirred, crawled from under the wagon. I watched her through barely parted eyelids. Shamelessly, she scratched herself, wandered off.

What treachery was she up to? Did she mean to have my crown from the wagon? Steal the horses?

Stealthily, I sat up, cracking my head on the unseen axle. Furiously I rubbed my scalp. When I extricated myself from the wagon, she was gone.

Wrapped in my blanket, I tiptoed about the clearing. No sign. Thirsty, irritable, I found my way down to the nearby stream.

I knelt to drink, turning my head as I brought water to it. Abruptly I froze.

Not ten paces from me, Chela threw off her shift, stood naked, nipples erect, her every gesture a taunt. "You stare, Prince?" Slowly, she fingered her bare gleaming breast. "Rust would know what to do. Even Genard, if I woke him."

I considered pretending I couldn't hear, but she was intolerable. "I warn you, be silent, or . . ."

Her laugh was harsh. "I'm frightened, Prince of Caledon."

Clutching my blanket, on my knees at the slippery bank, I fought for control. Never again would she and I share a journey, if I had to ride alone to escape her. Better yet, I'd have her sent back to—no, it didn't matter what Rustin said about it; he wouldn't be in charge any longer.

My fists curled and unclenched. If I were dressed, I'd give her the thrashing she deserved. And it wouldn't be so much trouble, to go back and slip on my breeches and boots. I wouldn't need a shirt. Nor boots, except to kick her. I knotted the blanket, gritted my teeth.

She made no sound, as if afraid. Good. Fear was what such folk understood. It was probably how Rust had tamed her in the first place. I considered that, until my imaginings made my skin prickle.

I should go back, find my clothes. There was moon enough—no, she'd seen me make ready for bed; I needn't bother to dress. I muttered a curse, bounded to my feet. Four strides and I'd crossed the clearing.

She knelt before me, hands on her breasts. When I loomed, a smile of triumph.

"It isn't as you think!" My voice was harsh. I clawed at her, but she caught my arm, pulled me down. I stubbed my toe on an unseen stone, grunted in pain, lashed at her.

She laughed softly, fighting me off. "What of your Power, Princeling? Am I worth all that?"

"Still thy tongue, you—" My head fell against her breasts; I breathed the warm animal smell of her, wanted to bite until she screamed.

I pinned her arms, decided how best to punish her. A beating, yes. But more? What of my Power, of the Still of Caledon? Would I ever wield it? Was it worth the contempt of such as she?

Was I ever to be King?

Would I ever know what Rust knew, the soft moist juices in which he reveled each night, her caresses, her enfolding warmth?

"Get off, Rodrigo." Her voice was uncertain. She snatched up her shift, hugged it to her flesh.

Pressing her into the grass with one elbow I wrestled away the shift. I held her arms, fondled her breasts, squeezed them until she cried out. I settled my groin against hers.

"Stop!" Her refusal drove me on. We'd see who was master of the House of Caledon. She shouted; I paid no heed.

I squirmed my loincloth down to my ankles, rubbed myself upon her, all the time fighting to hold her wrists. "Bitch! Whore! Demon spawn, I'll show you who—"

She relaxed all at once, smiled, and in delight and awe I kissed her breast. I nuzzled the cleave that divided her.

Like an adder, her knee struck at my testicles. The force of it drove my whole body upward. I convulsed, made a choking sound.

In the whole of my life, nothing had ever hurt so.

I rolled, thrashing and moaning, unable to draw breath. Chela began to screech.

"Rustin! Help! Someone come! RUSSTTIINN!" She snatched her shift, threw it over her head. "Genard, wake!"

I shrieked, flailing from side to side.

A pounding of feet. "Lord of Nature, oh, Rust, hold me, he tried . . . he—"

Howling, loincloth at my ankles, I clutched my ruined parts.

"How would he think I'd want him? Look at him, simpering half-man! He's a boor, won't wash, orders us about—"

"Shhhh."

She wailed, "Rust, he was nearly in me!"

Standing above, Rustin ignored me, as if I were a hound scratching fleas. He embraced Chela, comforted her. At the embankment Genard appeared, groggy. "What is it, m'lord?" Empurpled, I couldn't answer.

After a while, Rust sent Chela to the cart. He knelt by my side. "On your back. Draw your legs up tight." There was that in his eyes, which, despite my torment, I dreaded to see. "Take deep breaths. It will pass."

I grabbed his fingers, held them to my breast, squeezed as if to pass him a share of my misery. "I'm sorry. Sorry." My words were a jumble, barely audible. "I didn't mean . . . Lord, oh, oh, oh." I held him tight.

He sighed, eased himself into sitting, made no effort to free his hand. His other reached out, stroked my forehead. "Be easy, Roddy. Genard, pull up his loincloth, there's a boy. Be gentle. Breathe deep, my prince."

Wishing I were dead, I passed the night into day.

The wagon jounced, and lying on my side atop a bed of boxes, I felt each rut, each stone.

I'd made an effort to mount Ebon, and actually managed it. A few paces convinced me that it was impossible to ride this day. My genitals were swollen and tender. I let Rust help me down, hobbled to the wagon, climbed aboard with painstaking care.

I shifted position, gritting my teeth against the constant throb. As if it weren't enough, my healing back itched. Hester's was the only hurt not given with intent. Well, she'd intended to hurt someone, but not me. Perhaps she wouldn't have cared, had she known. Or perhaps she knew. Wallowing in my woe, I wasn't sure it mattered.

Chela spurred her nag, came alongside, her face full of spite. "Well, you came between us as you desired, Prince. Now he'll have none of me."

"Leave him be." Rust, his tone sharp. He clicked to Santree, guided him alongside the creaking wheel. "If you'd ride with us, remember what I said." Stone-faced, he waited until Chela had dropped away.

I pounded my bedroll into a softer pillow. "What was it you told her?"

His nose went up. "That's between us, my prince." After a moment he relented. "That I'd find her a place at an inn, and this time she'd stay." Santree snorted, waved his head at a fly.

"You'd leave Chela, after—"

"I'm bound to you, and anyone who impedes my duty I must set aside." For a moment he looked pained. "Even her."

I hated to take her side, but he spoke nonsense. "You swore service, not celibacy."

"You cannot abide my dallying with her, so it's the same."

I groaned, as the cart rocked from side to side. "May women know such pain as she gave me."

"I think they might, in childbirth."

"You'll be in her bed by the morrow."

"I will not." His tone was cold. "That much is settled."

I felt vague satisfaction, but another jounce returned me to more pressing matters. "I'll never be good for a woman again."

"Again?" He smiled, but without malice. "It will pass, Roddy. Next time—after you're done wielding the Still—wait for consent."

"With the Still, I won't need consent." I said it under my breath.

I dozed through the day in the rear of the wagon, while Ebon trotted behind the board. Elryc, Hester's favorite, was at her side. They ignored me, which left me undismayed. I didn't feel up to civil conversation.

My contretemps with Chela seemed to revive Rustin's spirits. He put aside his own sadness, at least for the time. When at last we stopped, he helped me down, brought my food, sat with me, understanding and patient.

Afternoon found us on a desolate plain, high in the hills. We stopped to ease ourselves. Gone by myself to piss, I examined myself closely. I was swollen and aching. I handled my affected parts tenderly. She might as well have gelded me, the whore. It would have hurt less, and left me no less fearful. How ever could I lie with women, if they could do such to me, without warning? How could any man?

I thought to ask Rustin, realized I could not. In the last weeks, I'd revealed far more to him than ever I'd expected, or he had right to know. Some things, a man must bear alone. Wiping my eyes, I returned to the wagon.

While I was gone Rustin had resettled my blankets, and sat alongside. I slipped wearily under the cover. A time passed. "Rust, don't laugh."

"I'll try not."

My voice was tremulous. "Does life get better? Will it always be this wretched?"

Silence. Then, "Oh, my prince." His hand groped for mine.

As the day lengthened Hester sent Elryc aft to keep me company. He went protesting, sat reluctantly across from me.

I wasn't sure how to make amends for whatever had offended him. "Do you hate me, little brother?"

"Sometimes." His candor shook me, but he went on, "Not at this moment. You are what you are. Can a crow be a lion, or a daisy a rose?"

"Such philosophy, for one not yet twelve." I reined in my scorn; it wasn't what I'd had in mind. "Elryc, help plan our course."

"We're running away. What plans would you lay?" He glanced, saw I expected more. "I know, you're for jumping on Ebon and riding off to do something bold, but let Uncle Mar and Tantroth fight it out. Gather men, and see what passes. Don't weaken Mar, or the castle may fall."

I was impressed despite myself. "Go on."

"When they're done, you'll know who your enemy is, and you'll be older. Men will follow you more readily when you're full grown."

"Bah." Disappointed, I waved away a horsefly. "Delay is the counsel of old women."

"Roddy, your voice still squeaks when you get excited. You have no beard. Will men risk their lives for you?"

"Think you they'd risk their lives for a beard?" In my disappointment I made no effort to wipe the contempt from my tone.

His voice was quiet. "No. It takes something more."

I sighed. What was it about Rustin, that all showed him respect? Rarely had he to raise his voice. Girls such as Chela, even my royal cousins, fell over him.

Was I such a mean, degraded thing? All that I'd done was justified.

Yet here I was, Prince of the blood, to whom no one gave deference. I was satisfied with myself, yet it seemed others were not. Would Elryc know why, if I asked? Could he help fashion me into what I wished?

I dared not ask. Self-doubt was a weakness, and if he learned of it, in time he'd use it against me. Such were the ways of power.

I pretended to doze.

It was well toward evening when we rolled onto a ridge overlooking a rich valley, dotted with forest and fields. A swift river bubbled down from the sheer hills across the vale, and had cut a channel through the loam. Nestled among the steep bank was a sleepy hamlet, perhaps two dozen dwellings, no more. I looked up. "What's this place?"

For the first time Hester's voice held an eager note. "Fort. We're near home."

I gawked. "It's not even a—Lord of Nature, what a desolate—" Words failed me.

"Oh, I forget." Hester's voice was laden with sarcasm. "The sophisticate from Stryx. Our world traveler."

"*This* is our destination?"

"My cottage, I said, not the town. The millkeeper's been tending it. I've sent him pay, these many years."

"And for the night? Another inn?"

"Look at the place; you expect an inn? Bah." She glanced at the sky, judging. "There's time to be home, if we hurry. Water the horses."

Grumbling, clutching myself where it hurt, I tried to help Elryc and Genard tend our mounts. "Where's Fostrow?" I asked.

"He rode ahead, to buy hens for our dinner."

"He's liegeman, and I the Prince. Why doesn't he tend the horses?" No one responded.

When we continued on our way I elbowed Elryc, made room for myself on the high seat. Even if I wasn't up to riding Ebon, I refused to be carted to our sanctuary like a piece of baggage.

Our road wound us down the hill, into the village. Though the sun shined bright, recently it had rained, and the gap between the houses that constituted the road was a mess of mud. Gaping peasant faces, devoid of intelligence and respect, peered as we passed rude hutments, a communal granary, a ramshackle mill along the rushing river.

Fostrow rode up grinning, with two live hens, feet pinioned, tied across his saddle. He tossed them into the wagon, joined Genard and Chela.

I asked Hester, "You came from this place?" It might explain her.

Her visage softened. "Once, when the world was young, Lord Tryon passed through, from a hunting trip. I was youthful, and charmed him."

My jaw dropped. "You were—were my grandfather's—"

"I don't doubt he had that intention. He bade me join his train, and I was glad to go. I bade farewell to my mother and sister, rode off to better. Barely had we got to Stryx Castle when word came the Norlanders had massed at Cumber, and off he rode again. I had naught to do, and even wondered if they'd turn me out to starve. But chance intervened."

A long silence, broken only by the clop of the horses through mud and muck. I knew enough to be patient.

"Washerwomen's children they were, a pair of ragamuffins, but crying because their ma was too busy to tend them. I played with them, upon a rock near the stream, when your grandmother Seldana found me with the brats, and she liked what she saw. When came the time, I became her nurse, and raised Elena."

"Seldana trusted her child to a peasant, a—"

Hester's chin rose. "I'm free-born, and can read far better than you. Poverty is no bar to gentility."

Rubbish. How could a nobleman hold his head high without servants, gamekeepers, a fortified place? My distant relative Freisart of Kant, who'd lost throne and castle, wandered pitied and disdained from noble to noble, living off charity. I'd throw myself from a cliff before I'd do likewise.

Rustin drew near, and my eyes fell upon his purse. I flushed, resentful of my dependence. It wasn't my fault the malevolent forest had attempted my life, seized my goods. Were it up to me, I'd be strong and secure at Stryx, not wandering with a half-mad old woman, a lecherous servant girl, and the son of a traitor.

"What ails you, my prince?"

I rubbed a hand over my scowl. "I'm tired, is all."

"From sleeping too much." Rust rode on.

The village petered out behind us. "Now what, Hester?"

"Hold your water, boy." She flicked at the drays. "A league, no more."

"That's hours, in this lumbering—"

"Then walk; you'll be faster and I'll have peace."

Glumly, I pulled a twig from a branch that brushed the cart as we passed. "What was my grandfather doing in a place like this?"

"Hunting, they said. He'd been in Cumber. It's not so far from here."

"Another world." It was years since I'd seen Cumber. I was but a boy, and Father still lived. He'd held my hand, walked with me along neat-groomed garden paths. Robins chirped, and one had landed almost at my feet.

I shifted in the seat, willing away my aches. Even without my new ills, such a journey as we'd made would inflict pains enough. I wondered how Hester's back tolerated her seat day after day, even with the cushion she favored.

The road, little more than a path, twisted down a curve, both sides curtained by a dense mass of underbrush. The fall of night lent a brooding nature to the place. I waved away gnats, for a moment alarmed. But Hester had said the forest was benign.

"It opens out, beyond this hill. Our cottage is shaded, but surrounded by our fields."

The last pinks were fading into gray as we emerged.

Alongside the road, a rotting fence sagged, down in many places. An untended field disappeared in the dark; I couldn't tell its length.

Hester shook her head, pursed her lips.

We jounced on. Brush gone wild overran the fence. I squinted; the first stars had appeared. Rust drew alongside. "Shall I ride ahead to find it?"

"We're near." A moment of doubt, while she studied the fence. Abruptly she reined in, peering at the road. A faint outline of a rutted path, gone to weeds and brambles. She muttered, "Don't say this is . . . Help me down!"

For a moment Hester steadied herself against the wheel, then lifted her skirts, picked her way through the brush. We followed.

In the last dim light of day, we came upon the cottage.

Of hewn logs it was built. A plank door sagged half-open, under a rude and rotting overhang that served as a porch. The boards below were half-gone. Even as we watched, a small creature darted from within, scurried under a bush.

"Hester, look!" Elryc pointed.

I raised my eyes to the thatched roof. Weakened by snow or neglect, it had fallen in, leaving a gaping hole from chimney to front wall, about half the width of the cottage.

Hester made a noise, which sounded like stone against stone.

I said, "*This* is home?"

Rustin caught my arm. "Leave her, Roddy. Can't you see . . ."

"Halfway across Caledon she's dragged us, for—for what?"

Fostrow said, "We'll repair it."

"How? And where do we sleep the night?"

"The field?" He looked about, dubious. "A bit overgrown. On the road."

"A mud pit!"

"In the wagon, then. Leave it, laddie!"

I was so astonished at his impudence that I gave way.

Hester emerged from the hut, her mouth grim. "It's too dark to seek the millkeeper. Drive the wagon back to that high spot, a hundred paces or so. Set the canvas, it will hold the mud away for sleep. We'll unload part of the wagon, if some of you must have better."

I'd have given her my opinion of where things stood, but Rustin grasped my arm, vehemently shook his head. Reluctantly, I subsided. We did as she asked.

Fostrow, with cheerful urging that set my teeth on edge, did the most to organize our camp. It was he who handed half our goods down to Rustin, set the blankets, traipsed into the brushland to gather kindling, dug us a firepit, set going our campfire. Resentful of his taking charge, I did as little as I could, but of the fire I was truly glad. After dark, the hills grew chill. In the days we'd dawdled at the rustic inn, summer had gone.

I went into the brush to relieve myself, apprehensive of night sounds, but neither imp nor beast molested me. It was dark enough that I examined myself more by feel than sight. The swelling had abated, to a degree. Thank Lord of Nature for that. I fingered my dagger.

Could I slit the girl's throat without Rust hearing, and blame it later on robbers? Surely she deserved no less.

When I got back, Chela was under her covers below the wagon, between Fostrow and Genard. Rustin patted the place he'd set for me, near his own. I sighed. Chela would wait.

Chapter 14

MORNING CAME, AND HESTER SET US TO CLEARING brush. Genard and Rustin pulled it with their hands; smarter than they, I hacked at weeds with the sword Rust had given me, until his glower grew so menacing I sheathed it. At times there was no talking to him. Why roughen your hands, if a blade would suffice? Nicks could be honed.

Hester and Fostrow surveyed the ruined roof. With surprising cleverness for one so stolid, the guard fashioned a stairs out of boxes leading to a half barrel and a hogshead. With clumsy gallantry he helped the old woman aboard the contrivance, steadied her while she climbed up to peer with rheumy eye at the devastation.

"The thatching's gone." Back to earth, she sat on a low box as if it were a throne. "That's bad enough, though I could teach you the art. But the beams below are rotted. For that work we'd need to fell trees, adz them flat. Or buy milled lumber."

I leaned against a pole that supported the overhang, rocking it first to make sure it wouldn't come down about me. "Buy it, then." It was her problem, not mine. As soon as Elryc was settled, Rust and I would be off, to set things right.

"With what, Rodrigo? Three men would labor a month for the cost."

"All the years you were at Stryx, did you waste everything? Have you no coin?"

"Aye, and have you no sense?" Her glare would have been withering, if I'd been in a mood to be withered. "I used what I'd saved to lay up a supply of foodstuffs. Clothes, axes, other trifles with which we'll live. Much of my pay was sent to the scoundrel Danar, whose pledge it was to keep my cottage after Tarana passed. Look at the state of things! It must have begun its ruin even before her death, while he wrote me all was well." Unexpectedly, she dabbed her skirt at her eyes. "My sister, ending her years in squalor. Had I but known . . ."

"When were you here last?" Rustin, his voice respectful.

"Eight, nine years past. Just before Pytor. I knew that after, I'd not have chance to get away. Tarana had aged; it was a shock to me, and our place was seedy. Danar agreed to look after her, if I sent wherewithal."

"Didn't she write you that he—"

Her tone was bitter. "She couldn't write. Our da never got around to teaching her; I was the clever one." I snorted, but she didn't hear me. "Surely, though, she'd have sent word. Messengers pass this way."

Fostrow said, "Through town, perhaps. But on a lonely trail, leading but to a homestead?"

"Aye." Her sigh had the weight of eons. "So I abandoned Tarana to her fate, while congratulating my love for her." She rocked. "The things I did without, that she might have. Oh." She covered her face. "Oh."

It was Elryc who crept to her side, stroked her wizened neck with his small hand. "Don't weep, Nurse, or I'll cry too."

Her hands came down from dampened eyes. "I don't cry, young fool. Can't you—all right, so I do. What of it? Will the sun stay fixed in the sky until a foolish old woman comes to her senses? I've right to weep, and mourn my folly. Go stir soup."

As if she hadn't spoken, Elryc pulled up a box, sat close. "I love you, Nurse. Glad I am that you care for me."

Her hands went again to her face. Rustin pulled me away, despite my eagerness to hear what came after. "There's brush to pull. And my neck chafes. Help me, would you?"

In the afternoon Chela and the children were set to clean the pots, and drag our gear to the dilapidated hut. Meanwhile, we held a council of war: Hester, I, Fostrow, and Rustin.

"We're four. How many men can a miller have, and armed with what—staves?"

Fostrow shrugged apologetically. "It's not that simple, my lord. We can't just take—"

"Why not? He stole a fortune from Nurse."

"Roddy, think." Rustin. "On whose authority would we act? Do we ride in like brigands, to slaughter him if he objects? They'd rouse a meet, and gather us for hanging."

"They can't lay a hand on us. I'm of blood royal, and Fostrow's my sworn man. Rust, your lineage is such—I mean, was—" I stumbled to a halt. Rustin thrust his thumbs in his belt, walked a few steps so he faced away. I'd have to remember henceforth to make no mention of Llewelyn.

When Rustin spoke his voice was controlled. "You'd slaughter the miller? When the townsmen came for us with pitchforks, then what, proclaim yourself? There's a chance they wouldn't believe you, and hang us anyhow. Or if they did, then Mar finds us and—"

A diffident cough, from Fostrow. "That's not all so likely, Lord Rustin. I imagine the castle's under siege by now, and whether or no, the good Duke has much on his mind. Would he strip his defenses by sending men to arrest the Prince?"

"More likely, send word to hold us." Rustin.

"Which these people cannot do, sire. You're nobility. At most they could apply to Earl Cumber, or if they were daring, escort you to him."

I glowered. "You know much about the law of these affairs, Fostrow."

"In the Duke's service, one must, Prince Rodrigo. It's happened that a royal cousin has gone astray, and set fire to a peasant's fields in fun."

"What befell him?"

"I know not, my lord. Your gracious mother was informed, and the young lord went elsewhere, for a while."

"So, then, the worst is that they take us to Cumber. What's wrong with that?"

Rustin waved away a gnat, or perhaps my argument. "You'd have your great-uncle see you a prisoner? Go to him on your own, if that's what—"

"I'll be damned if I'll beg charity from that pompous old . . ." I realized Fostrow was among us. "No, not Cumber. Not while we're powerless. So, rather than take a stand, you'd let Danar get away with Nurse's coin? Hester, can you conjure more?"

"Can I what?"

"Conjure it. Use your arts, the way you passed Elryc over the gate, invisible."

"Don't be daft."

"It's a proper question. Now my coin is gone, yours is all we have on which to live."

Hester looked to Rustin, then Fostrow. "Did I invite him to live on it? Was it his idea, or mine, to chase me through Caledon?" Neither gave answer. "Oh, for Elena's sake I won't turn him away, nor you, as you're his own. But I'm of Fort, and know the place. We won't begin here by shedding blood."

I ignored her gibes, focused on her answer. "What would you, then?"

"We confront Danar peaceably." Hester scowled. "That means you stay behind, as you lose your temper at the drop of—"

"I do not! I go, or no one goes!" I glared at each in turn.

Hester's voice was quiet, but not gentle. "The coin you seek is mine."

"The men you'd send are mine." I could have left it at that, but a sudden anxiety seized me. "Rust, will you go, if I forbid it?"

"Hmmmm. Should I help Hester feed you, though you insist on starving?" He withstood my fury long enough to make his point, then surrendered. "No, I cannot, if you forbid. Though our lot be reduced to this, clearly it's a matter of state."

"Fostrow?"

He grimaced. "Why do you make of it a challenge, youngsire?"

"In your dotage, do you remember swearing to me?"

He flushed. "Aye, my lord." A sigh, barely audible. "I won't go."

"There." I let her see my triumph.

"So be it." She stood painfully, sighing. "I accept your choice. No one goes." She gestured with her stick. "What food I'd eat, goes to Elryc until there's none. You, brave proud boy, fend for yourself. What say you others?"

Rust, without hesitation. "I split my rations between Elryc and my liege Prince Rodrigo."

"Rust, she's bluffing."

Hester growled, "Soldier?"

"To Prince Elryc, my lady. He's a child and needs them more. Besides, he's barely back from the dead."

Hester nodded. "Wise. The servants Genard and Chela, I'll feed. This quarrel is none of their making."

I shot to my feet. "Hester, for once in your life, act in sense! It is I who am Prince!"

She wheeled on me, threw her stick so it bounced off my boot. "Foolish boy! Arrogant, stupid boy! Stubborn boy, who risks us all because he cannot have his way. May flowers root in your mother's tears this day, for you do her not proud, nor yourself. You are not fit to be King!"

"Go easy, good dame." Rustin interposed himself. He stooped for the stick, handed it to her politely. "Let Rodrigo be, I pray you. Come, my lord, let us walk."

"I won't give an inch, not an iota, not—"

"Aye, of course not. And an evening without a meal won't kill us. Come along, we'll see what lies beyond the fence."

I sat on a barrel, glowering at Genard as he tried to hit a sapling with pebbles, waiting for Chela to make the error of speaking to me.

It had been hours; would they ever return? And why had I let Fostrow ride Ebon? Yes, Rust had Santree, and Fostrow his own mount, but that left the pitiful nag for Hester, or one of the drays. My ire was such I wouldn't consider letting the vile crone take my Ebon, but Rust, with his demon-spawned logic and calm, had made me give Fostrow the use of him.

I wouldn't have given in, but that Rustin heard me out, agreed with every word I said. I told him what I wished I could do with Hester, and he agreed with that. He heard my revised plan for dealing with the miller, and offered not a word of objection. Somehow, when it was all done, I had consented to Hester's scheme, provided she dropped her nonsense about holding her foodstuffs for those of whom she approved.

They rode off, and my jubilation turned to a certainty that I'd been gulled, either by Hester or by Rustin. I'd set myself on the barrel to think it through.

Elryc came out of the cottage, scratching a mosquito bite. "It was a cozy old place, once."

I snorted. "Show me the great hall, where the councilors meet."

"Oh, it's small, but ordinary folk live thus." He shot me a quizzical glance. "What were you shouting about, while I was scrubbing pots?"

"I demanded they go, so I could speak with you alone." I beckoned him close. A trusting fool, he came. I seized his arm, twisted it behind his back. "One thing you'll tell me, and quick."

He yelped. Genard fixed his eyes on me.

"Hester laughs, when I speak of her conjuring us coin. Has she a Power, little brother?"

"Please let him go, m'lord."

"Stay out of this, Genard. Has she?"

"How would I— Ow!" Elryc winced.

"You'd know, if truly she turned you into a bird. Tell me how she put you over the wall."

A sniffle. "I can't. Please, it hurts!"

I bent his wrist upward another inch or so. "Are you sure, little—"

Genard snatched a log from our pile of firewood. "Let go of m'lord Elryc!"

"Strike the heir, would you, stableboy?" I twisted harder; Elryc squealed. "I'll spit you like a—aiee!" I toppled from my barrel, side smarting. Genard dashed to safety.

Elryc had fallen with me, and was underfoot. I brushed him aside, made for my sword that lay in the wagon. "I'll show you, spawn of imps, motherless creature of—"

"Run, Genard!" Elryc's voice was shrill.

Instead of racing for open land like an honest churl, the urchin circled the cart, keeping its unyielding bulk between us. Three circuits of the wagon, and I'd come no closer, though I changed direction twice to catch him unawares. In a towering rage I hoisted myself onto the cart, grunted as my tender privates scraped the sideboard.

"Run, Genard! He means to kill!"

I clambered about the wagon, sword drawn, watching my chance. The boy hesitated. I leaped down, staggered to my balance.

Genard turned, raced off, cannoned into Rustin, bounced to the turf. With a cry of victory I lunged forward, sword raised.

Rust stepped in front of the fallen boy.

I cried, "Out of the way!"

"With my own sword you'd cleave me?"

"When did you get back? Leave it, 'til I finish him!"

"Hold your temper, my prin—"

I stabbed at Genard's foot, but Rust kicked aside the edge of my blade. His eyes widened. *"Elryc, put down the dagger!"*

I whirled to meet the new treachery. From behind, Rust clasped my hand. He toppled me to the ground, bent my arm, removed the sword as from a baby. I lashed out with my fist, caught only his thigh.

He dropped the blade at Elryc's feet. "Hide this!" He hauled me to my feet, shoved me so I staggered, propelled me from the cottage toward the road. "I'm ashamed of you, my prince!" Fostrow watched openmouthed. Hester's lips were set, grim.

"Let me go, I'm—"

Another shove, and I sprawled. He took me by shirt and breeches, manhandled me to the road. "Ashamed, I said!" His eyes blazed. A shake, which rattled my teeth. "Did you hear, my liege? I'm ashamed of you!" At once, he let me go, and I fell.

Slowly, I picked myself up, wary. "Rust, easy. Don't lose your . . ."

He drew breath. "Walk with me." Unwilling, I did. If I refused, no telling what he'd do. "How could you attack them, Roddy?"

He had it all wrong. I explained.

"So you would kill Genard for protecting his liege?"

"He's a stableboy, a nothing!"

Rustin's eyes were pained. "What am I, then?"

"You? My friend! Or once you were. Now you take it upon yourself to act my father, and humiliate me in front of all! I want none of you!"

"A false vassal."

"Yes!"

"Disloyal liegeman."

"The words are yours!"

"Son of a traitor."

"That too—your tongue said it, not—what are you doing?" I stepped back rapidly, staring at his unsheathed dagger.

He offered it to me, hilt first. "Strike, then, as you would Genard of Stryx. I am a nothing, no better than he."

"I don't want your life!"

"But you want his."

"He attacked me, humiliated me in front of Elryc."

"And I did not?"

"Yes, but that's—" My tone went sullen. "Always you twist me, like a piece of string. You had me hand you Ebon's reins, smiling, to stay behind with servants and children while you did my work." I glared. "Well, it's true. Now you'd have me apologize, for putting a peasant lout in his place."

"I asked no apology." Again, he proffered the dagger. "Strike, if you will. Perhaps it will satisfy your blood lust."

"You make me sound a crazed Norlander! Put that away, Rust. This is me! Roddy!"

He found a grassy spot. "Sit." He left me little choice, unless I would stare down at him. "Yes, it is you, Roddy." Then he told me things about myself that made my cheeks flush, my skin crawl with embarrassment. More than once I would have leaped to my feet and been away, but his hand stayed me, with surprising gentleness. When he was done, I followed him back to the camp, subdued.

That night, Elryc came cautiously to my place, separate from the others, farther from the fire. "Hester says it's all right to tell you."

"Leave me be."

"About the cart, and getting away from Stryx."

"I wanted to hear it from her, not you. She's the witch." I swallowed a lump in my throat. "She should have told me when first I asked."

At first he made no answer. Then, "It was noble of you to apologize to Genard tonight. I thank you for it."

I swallowed, unwilling to speak.

"He's terrified you'll come upon him in the dark. I told him that once you put aside the quarrel, your honor wouldn't let you pursue it. He's not like us, Roddy, and frets of a knife in the night. If you'd say something to reassure him . . ."

"I groveled once. It's more than enough." What was Rust to me, that his good opinion was worth such abasement? I shifted, uneasy. My mumbled words to Genard had come harder than anything I'd ever said in my life. What more could Elryc want?

He said, "Our life turns hard, brother. I love you, and that you protect me."

"Let me alone!" A cry, from the heart.

He understood, and retreated. "Sleep well."

"Elryc . . ." I didn't trust my voice. "I'll say something. To . . . to the . . . him."

He shrugged, pretending it didn't matter. "As you will."

Fostrow and Genard had strung the canvas over the gaping hole in the cottage roof, to ward off the worst of the weather, and the others had set their bedding on the thrice-swept floor. I chose to bed outside, risking rain. Perhaps I would join them, after a night or so, but for now I needed solitude.

Rustin, when he saw I meant to sleep outside, brought his bedding and settled near, his dagger close at hand. It brought from me a sour smile; first he'd made my life not worth living, and then stayed with me to protect it.

My indignity and shame were such that I hadn't asked much of the three who'd returned from their confrontation at Fort, but from scraps of their talk I gathered that the miller had first pretended ignorance, then claimed he had spent every pence sent him, in care of Tarana. In the end he vowed he'd review the matter, and decide if anything ought to be done.

Weary beyond words, still aching between my legs, I settled to sleep. During the night I dreamed that I was crying as if my heart would break, that a hand caressed my shoulder, that a soft whispered voice akin to Rustin's finally soothed me to sleep.

Chapter 15

WE DAWDLED AROUND THE HUT UNTIL MIDDAY, TO MY growing annoyance. Hester occupied herself taking stock of the cottage, Genard caring for the horses, Fostrow chatting with Chela. Rustin took Elryc on a long walk to survey the fences in need of repair. That left me, overlooked and slighted. True, Nurse had proposed that I haul the remaining boxes and stores from the cart under the canvas roof of the cottage, but the proposal was so outlandish I ignored it entirely. If she wanted laborers, let her hire louts from the village.

I sat under a tree, playing with my finely balanced sword, dreaming of the day I'd be crowned. I feared it would be long coming.

Whenever Genard passed near, hauling feed or water, I glowered, but he was too busy to notice. I wasn't sure whom to blame for last night's debacle, him or Rustin. The stableboy had struck me, but I'd drawn sword and had the situation under control when Rustin blundered in.

"Water, m'lord?" Genard proffered a cup.

"If I want, I'll ask." I scowled until he went away. My reassurance of last evening had worked all too well, it seemed. Pathetically grateful, Genard had resumed his unwelcome intimacy, and in that mode, no rebuff seemed strong enough to catch his notice.

Besides, Rustin no longer knew his place. We weren't still boys of the castle; we were young men grappling with war and privation. Yet he shoved me about, clapped his hand over my mouth, scolded worse than Nurse ever had. It was born of affection, I knew; but even those displays were unseemly. I sighed. Perhaps a subtle reference to his father would recall him to his senses. It wasn't meet that I should consort with the son of a traitor. Not that I wanted him to leave, merely to resume his proper station.

"A good day for a nap, Prince." Fostrow, his tone genial.

I opened one eye. "You have time for other than Chela? How pleasant."

His brow knitted. "What say you, youngsire?"

"Don't you notice her wiles? You moon over the strumpet as if she were goddess of—"

"She's young enough to be my—" He scratched his grizzled head. "Ah, leave it be."

I was in no mood for conciliation. "She's spoken for. Unless you'd cross swords with Rustin over the right to lift her skirts."

Fostrow shook his head, his eyes gone sad. "You've a mean streak in you, Rodrigo of Caledon, if I don't mind saying. Whatever makes you so?"

My grip on the sword tightened. "Remember to whom you're sworn."

"Let me explain." He squatted. "I'm sworn to thee, and will follow in battle. But a master doesn't hold the sentiment of men by casual contempt. Our party is small, and none will cross you. But what if you're King, and there are thousands whose grievances fester? How then will you sleep safe—"

"What know you of the rule of kings!" I waved it away. "And what about your precious Mar? You served him; can you say he won your affection?"

Fostrow said gently, "I'm here with you, Roddy. Doesn't that tell you much?" While I puzzled it out, he trudged back to the cottage.

After a meager midday meal, Hester called us together. "We mustn't let Danar think we'll let drop the matter of our coin, for lack of caring. I'll stay behind, and teach the boys the weaving of rushes, for the floor. Rustin, you might seek him out, with Fostrow." Her tone was diffident.

"As you wish, dame."

"And Roddy too, for the weight of numbers." Casually, as if it had just occurred to her. "But for Lord's sake, no violence."

Before I could react, Rust said, "Of course not. Roddy understands perfectly. We spoke of it only this morning." A bald-faced lie, if ever there was one. I nodded dutifully. Let *him* bear the untruth; he had no Power to lose, and I'd escape this forlorn wreck of a cottage, at least for a few hours. My heart quickened.

I was so glad to go along, I found myself saddling Ebon myself. I was the first ready, sat patiently in the saddle, sword at an awkward angle. Why had no one figured a proper place for a mounted man's sword? It stuck out like a—I blushed.

At last the others were ready. Rustin winked. "Let's go."

To ride was exhilarating, even at a moderate pace. Finally, I could sit the saddle without pain, and I relished every moment of it. At a canter, the town of Fort seemed much closer than it looked from the jouncing wagon. We were at the first hutments in half an hour.

Rustin said, "Roddy, when we meet the miller . . ."

"Don't give me instruction!" Time to assert myself, else his urge to mother me would grow to intolerable proportions.

"Someone must. Don't scowl. Your kingdom may depend on it."

He had my attention.

"If Elryc is to have a home and your vow be fulfilled, we need the coin Danar stole. If you do him harm, we'll be forced to reveal ourselves or flee as felons. Either would make our position more precarious. Later, we may need to approach your uncle Cumber. If we're brought to him as prisoners, we'll lose any chance of his support. Do you see?"

Sullen, I twitched the reins. "If I'm such a dolt, why do you want me along?"

He leaned over the pommel, patted my knee. "You can't succeed, if we do not risk failure. We cannot do all for you, Roddy."

Dismayed at his candor, I could but nod. How could he think so little of me, yet make himself my vassal? What bound Rust to me, if not respect and esteem?

We plodded on. A path branched off from the road, disappeared into woods. Half a hundred paces later, the way to the mill was well marked with the deep ruts of carts laden with grain.

The sluice gate was wide open, and the wheel turned with vigor. Its creaks and the rush of the river itself drowned out conversation. We hitched the horses to the rail, climbed the steps to the mill floor.

Inside, on the grinding platform, the heavyset miller and his man were hard at work, amid sacks and barrows. Summer was at its end, and the harvest was half-gathered. They fed whole grain to the great smooth stone, whose motion was fed by the impetus of the water, by a sort of Power I could scarce comprehend.

Rustin glanced at Fostrow, waited patiently for the miller's attention.

At last the man ceased his labor, wiped his brow. He lumbered down the stairs, frowning at each step. I'd thought he would somehow bring the wheel outside to a stop, but it whirled on, splashing back into the channel below, turning the rumbling millstone.

"Ah, a lad you've brought, in place of the dame." The garlic in his breath wafted close, and I grimaced. He eyed me, turned away. "It's busy I am. No chance I've had to consider."

Rust smiled, his tone courteous. "And we wouldn't press you, Danar, but our need is urgent. Come, let us settle the matter."

"How?" Again, the miller wiped his florid face.

"Return the four silvers Dame Hester sent you each year."

"Nonsense, that is. She didn't send half that amount. More than that I gave of my own charity, to poor Tarana. You've no idea how wretchedly she lived."

"I've too good an idea." Rust's voice was cold. "Do you truly care to be hauled before the justiciar? When your fraud is proved—"

"Begone. I have work." The miller turned away.

Fostrow said lightly, "The same charity you showed Tarana, you might offer good Dame Hester." With an affable smile, he clapped the miller on the shoulder. "Surely a prosperous man such as yourself can spare a few—"

"Prosperous? Are you witless?" Angrily, Danar brushed off the offending hand. "Five pence on the hundred, I'm taxed. I pay these poor folk more for their grain than I—"

"Will the Queen's justice see it so, goodman Danar? Surely, to avoid the nuisance of pleading your case . . ."

Danar's eyes flashed. "You think to frighten me? No Queen sits now at Stryx, and what's left of her justice is far from our village. Perhaps it's

Tantroth's justice we'll face, ere long." My fingers crept to my sword, but he paid no notice. "He'll care not about the ravings of a daft old woman, or the quarrel of a few pence."

With that, he grunted his way back to the platform, beckoned his perspiring man for a new barrow.

I growled to Rust, "Let's set the place afire."

"Subtle, my prince, but it won't do the trick. Danar will be ruined, and Hester will remain so." He led me outside.

"I'll bet he hasn't spent a penny," I said. "Look at the fat on him; he's a hoarder. There'll be a trunk somewhere, stuffed with coin."

"Oh, well that makes it easy. We'll just ask him its whereabouts."

"Don't jeer!" I stamped my foot, muddied my boot for my pains.

"I meant no offense. You held your temper well." Rust's smile was tight. "Well, we've had his answer. Now what?"

"Bring him to justice, as Fostrow said."

"In whose name, Hester's? Before Earl Cumber, the Lord of this place? Elryc will be long grown before the matter is resolved." He untied Santree.

Savagely, I kicked at the miller's tie rail, splintering it. I slipped loose Ebon's reins. "What a hateful place, this Fort. Mud, peasants, thieves. Would we never followed the old witch." Before any could answer, I galloped off, ignoring Rust's efforts to flag me down. To be perverse, I veered onto the path into the wood, found it led only to an ill-kept Place of Rites. Fuming, I had to retrace my steps.

When at last we were home, Hester heard our tale in grim silence, over a sparse meal. "For now, it seems we can do nothing."

"A drawn sword will teach him respect. You can't abandon all your pence to—"

"For Elryc's sake, I must. We need a refuge, do we not? While you were gone I sent Genard for the carpenter. He and his family will repair our roof, but we must pay for the wood at once, and the labor within a month."

"Is that possible?" Rust.

"Almost. I'm short two silver pence." A sigh. "Had I known, I wouldn't have bought . . . ah, well."

Rust was silent. Then, "Add this." He unstrung his purse, emptied it onto the table. With a warning finger he forestalled my angry objection. "What I do for Elryc fulfills your vow to protect him."

Hester counted the coin. "It makes enough." Her eyes studied his. "Are you sure? I may never repay it."

"I'm sure." His tone was gruff.

She gave another sigh, this time as if setting down a heavy load.

"All well and good." My tone was savage. "How do you propose to pay the carpenter's labor?"

"Why, by work." She blinked. "Labor is short, at harvesttime. There's the gathering, the smithy is always too busy, the leatherer may need a hand."

"Whose labor? You're too old for much."

"Yes?" Her gaze never wavered. "Not too old to raise three boys, and be not finished."

"So, then?" I ignored her gibe.

"The menfolk will have to hire themselves out. Roddy, don't pout, it's the only way. Fostrow says he's willing. Genard also." A pregnant pause.

Rustin. "You wish my help?"

"If you'd give it. With Roddy, that makes four. In a month, we can—"

I stumbled to my feet, threw open the door, stalked into the night. A dozen paces from the hut, a sapling was in my path; I grasped its trunk, twisted, bent, wrenched it from the earth, hurled it from my way.

A hand fell on my shoulder. "Be calm, my prince."

"Get thee gone, lickspittle!" I slapped down Rust's hand, shoved him hard enough so he stumbled. Maddened with rage, I blundered on my way.

The crash of steps, and Rustin's voice, panting. "Speak, at least. Let me know your thoughts."

"*You* work at a smithy, or scythe grain." Again, I sought to leave him behind.

Again, he followed. "You're vexed."

"Will you not leave me?" I whirled. "Vexed? You might as well speak of a spoonful of tide, or a handful of mountain!" I snatched his shoulders, propelled him backward against a tree. "Rust, I'm Prince of Caledon. Would you make me into that lout we nearly ran down today, sweating under a roll of hay? I will not work for my dinner, or Hester's. First, I'd starve!"

"A real possibility."

"Don't play at mockery! You offered your labor like—like a common churl. Shameful! You're my vassal, and it reflects on me."

"So would your starving."

"I forbid it!"

That gave him pause. He stared at me curiously, like some insect crawling on a leaf. "You what?"

"I forbid you to hire yourself out! You're nobility, of the House of Llewel—well, that explains it, you bear his blood and have no pride, and—"

"Rodrigo." The menacing note in his voice stopped me cold. "Speak not of my father."

"I—all right, it's beside the point. But I won't consider pretending we're peasants. That goes for you too, as long as you're my vassal."

Another pause. Halting, he said, "My prince, relieve me of my oath of fealty. Let me serve you as friend only."

"Demons' spawn!" My spittle sprayed his cheek. "Scum! Bastard son of a vile traitor! Never was I more than dung in your eyes!"

"Roddy I—I don't know well how to beg." He flushed. "But beg I do."

"Get thee from my sight!" I spun his shoulders, shoved him hard on the backbone. "How dare you ask, in the straits I'm in! I hate you as you must hate me!" I panted for breath, aimed a kick at his rump, caught him unawares. With a cry, he fell. "Be no vassal, then!" I aimed another kick, managed to turn aside my rage before it landed. I ran into the night. "You're nothing to me! Nothing!"

His anguished voice floated after. "Aye, my prince."

Hours later, in the faint light of the overcast moon, I sat curled in the wagon, head propped against the backboard. Soft steps. Genard, shirt flung over his shoulders, peered up at me. "Oh, there you are. I came out to piss. Why do you cry, m'lord?"

"I'm not . . ." A shudder racked me, and I gave it up.

The fool took it for an invitation, perched on the tailboard. "I cry sometimes too, m'lord. Usually over small things, like an empty plate."

I sniffled. "Don't weave tales. You were fed every day; Griswold saw to that."

"I wasn't born at the castle, m'lord. Before, I was hungry. Besides, Master Griswold gave me enough to cry over, with his strap."

"I'm sure you earned it."

"It doesn't hurt less for that." A sigh. "After a while, you get used to it. Why do you weep, m'lord?"

"Why ask so many questions, where you're unwanted?"

"Would you really have me leave? When I cry, I wish someone would come and talk me to happiness."

"I'm not you!" I wiped my nose. Then, despite myself, "Stay, if you must. I don't care."

"All right." Genard donned his shirt, knotted the strings. "Aren't you cold? I'll get us a blanket." Before I could stop him, he was off.

Moments later he was back, climbing aboard the cart to sit beside me. "Are there stars tonight? It's fun to sit outside, of a starry night. If Griswold doesn't catch you. Here, share with me." Unembarrassed, he offered me half his cover, as if I'd not object to sharing cloth with a stableboy.

I shivered, wrapped myself. He pointed. "The moon tries to break through. Rustin is very upset. And I'm sorry I hit you with the log."

I gaped.

"But Elryc was my liege, and I had no choice. I had to protect him. I think Rustin may be crying too, but he's very quiet about it." He waited for me to speak, gave up. "Should I tell him something from you?"

"To jump in the demons' lake and burn."

He drew his breath in a hiss. "Don't talk like that, m'lord. They'll hear you."

I didn't care what evil I brought on us. "Good."

He regarded me. "Truly, what ails you must ache. Let's sit quiet, then."

I struggled against my need, drew a shuddering breath.

"I understan', m'lord." His small hand sought mine. "I'll stay with you. Too bad we can't have stars."

I gave up all pretense of understanding, sat miserable and weary. After a time, the boy clasped his hands between his knees for warmth, leaned his head against my shoulder. Though I stiffened, he seemed not to notice. "You're the first lord I've ever known, to talk to."

"Do you know one to be silent to?"

My jibe escaped him. "Duke Mar came for his horse, once or twice. Usually he sent a groom. And of course I saw the Queen, but not close.

So you and Lor' Rustin are the first." His tone was marveling. "An' you're so different."

"Yes, my father was no traitor."

Genard was silent at first, then said carefully, "I know nothing of such things, m'lord."

"As little as you know of most things."

"Yes, I know little, I'm not high and wise, like your friend Rust. What sport is it to hurt me, sire? It's too easily done."

I turned, stared down at his head nestled against my shoulder. Who was he to tweak me?

"Never I dreamed I'd be more than a stablehand. I know nothing of fine words, or writing them. I have no clothes, have to bed down with horses. Is that why I offend you?"

I grunted, unsure how to respond. What had the world come to, when a groom's boy could interrogate a prince?

"I'm sorry, m'lord. I'll try to be better, now I'm Elryc's man."

I let close my eyes, dozed.

"What is it like to have a friend?"

"You anger me, boy."

"I never had one. Kerwyn, if you could call him that, but he's a man, and cares not a whit for me. Are friends what you are to Rust?"

Lord of Nature, give me strength to resist, lest I throttle him. "And what am I to Rustin?"

He gazed upward. "You know not? Ah . . ." A nod, as if he'd found an answer. "So that's why you cry."

"Tell me." I couldn't help myself.

His voice held wonder. "Everything. Sun and moon."

I snorted. "Chela is that. Not I."

"You jest." He snuggled close. "It's awfully cold. Shouldn't we go inside?"

"No!"

"All right, I'll stay too, then." He hugged himself, shivered. "Good night, Prince Rodrigo."

I frowned down at the barnacle that had attached itself to me, found the prospect of a night in the wagon less forlorn. I grunted again, let myself relax into sleep.

Chapter 16

DURING THE DAY, HESTER PRETENDED I WASN'T VISIBLE. She busied herself with Elryc or fussed over the carpenter who showed up in a wagon with three grinning half-grown louts and a wife to cook his dinner, which was seldom more than boiled potatoes or thick vegetable soup. He and his young dismembered the corpse of our roof, worked the sawn trunks with which they'd replace it into beams of the needed size. Their constant scraping and planing got on my nerves; to escape it, I saddled Ebon and rode I knew not where. Out of sheer boredom with the woods and fields, I wandered into town.

Fort wasn't much of a place, but from its open square I had a decent view of the snowy peak that towered over the valley. Careful to keep far from the mill, I wandered the dusty street, but found nothing of interest. Even the market square was virtually deserted; farmers only brought their produce on the seventh day after each new moon.

The stream frothed on the rocks as it burbled through town. In places it pooled deep; I tasted of the water. It slaked my thirst, but left my hand numb from the cold. It must descend from the high reaches of the mountain.

I'd acquired a following of peasant children, who giggled and poked each other like the village louts they were. They acted as if they'd never before seen a person of quality, with proper inlaid halter and saddle. At first I was pleased at their awe, but after a while they grew tiresome, so I spurred Ebon, and cantered off to the leafy trail that led to the Place of Rites.

A tired mule hitched to the rail flicked its ears at the flies, while an old man in a dirty dark robe swept leaves from the steps. He gave a courteous bow. "Welcome, stranger. I am Aren." Walking with some difficulty, he came closer, eyed my gear. "You're one of the lads from Stryx, youngsire?"

"Aye." The less said, the better. For a moment I wondered how he had known, but of course, Hester would have made some explanation, and in a hamlet so small, word would spread to everyone in a day.

"We conduct Rites every five-day." A flick of his broom. "Unless you have special need?"

"Thank you, I need no rituals." My disdain was more evident than I'd intended.

"Ah, a scoffer." Aren seemed not offended. "We all pass through such an age. Tell me, lad, what purpose do you think Rites serve?"

Who was he to question me? "To mark the season, to comfort the bereaved—"

"You merely recite. Tell me what you think."

His unwarranted rebuke stung me into truth. "Mumbo jumbo for old men who take comfort in the familiar, who think Lord of Nature cares what—"

"They can be that." His admission surprised me into silence, but he continued, "That's not their true purpose."

I tugged the rein, turned Ebon. "I'm sure. Good afternoon."

"Stay your fine horse a moment. In fact, get down, and let me give you a drink."

"I'm not thirsty."

"Sweet juice." He smiled. "Crushed red berries from our garden, sugared and cold."

By the imps and demons, he had me; Hester's fare sustained life, but did little else. "All right." I tied the reins. "Thank you."

Aren led me along a path that ran by the stream. A cord lay across the path. One end was tied to a tree, the other disappeared in the water. He knelt, pulled on the rope, fished out a sturdy stoneware jug.

Back at the Place of Rites, he bade me sit on the steps, went inside, emerged with two cups. The juice was icy cold, and delicious. I downed mine faster than I'd intended, and he refilled my cup. "Highborn or low, all boys like sweet, I think. Now, about the Rites."

I steeled myself for a lecture, probably about the secret cult of this place.

"Have you ever wondered about stars, or what makes mountains rise? About air turning to water, and falling on your head? Think you men haven't asked such questions through the ages?"

"I suppose you have the answers here in this—"

"The Rites are a ritual, codified attempt to express and hand down what we think we've learned. Those who make them more deceive themselves."

"Foolish learning, that must be expressed in chants and waving of tapers."

"Imagine a Ritemaster had a foolish disciple, who watched him wave his taper for emphasis, while making a point. Later, when the disciple wants to recall the point, he waves the taper in a similar manner, so as not to deviate from what his master taught him. He cannot distinguish wheat from chaff."

I smiled; it was refreshing to hear honesty from one of his calling. "But you can?"

"We try."

"Well, I've attended Rites enough, and I can't detect any hidden wisdom. Of course, I'm not as learned as you."

"You mock, youngsire. I waste my juice." He stood. "Let Elena Queen be an example. She had no such manner."

"How would you know what the Queen—"

"I could see it in her eyes!" He made as if to sweep me away with his broom. "Ah, now you look surprised. Well, I met her. And say you one word against milady and I'll throw you in the brook!"

"I wasn't about to."

"Yes, I met her." He settled himself.

I said cautiously, "That's no basis to say what's in her mind. Surely when you visited Stryx she didn't invite you to her private Rites."

"I've never in my life been to Stryx." An impatient sweep. "Didn't your father beat you properly? You have the insolence of a—bah. Wait." He disappeared into the ramshackle building.

I unhitched Ebon, in case the demented old man emerged with a stick.

The door swept open. "Here." A closed fist. He opened it, peered down, grimaced, plucked something from his hand, rubbed it vigorously on his robe. "Look, but don't touch."

"A ring." Red stones, set in gold. Aren's old eyes sparkled, as if in response to the jewel.

"If you were never in Stryx . . ."

"She was here."

"Don't be ridiculous. Why would Moth—the Queen come to such a backwoods?"

"Old Dame Hester was once high in her esteem. The Lady accompanied her here, to see where her nurse was spawned."

"In a nest of demons." But I spoke to myself. "How came you by the ring?"

"She gave it to me, from her own finger." He frowned at my expression. "You doubt? For hours she and I discussed the mysteries, and she was enthralled. So much she wanted to know, to pass on to the son she knew she'd have."

"Enough of your nonsense. No one can know whether an unborn babe—"

"She knew!" He glared. "What ken have I of the Still or the Powers it confers? She was certain, unto the russet of his hair, though he wasn't yet conceived."

I shivered, resisted an urge to brush back my locks. Could my Power do all that?

His gaze softened; he thrust the ring back inside his robe. "So much she wished she could know, to pass to her boy. Oft I've wondered how much she taught him. It's said he's haughty and ill-mannered. Of course, that may just be his time of life. We change; thank Lord of Nature for that."

"Yes." I was careful to look elsewhere.

"You're of Stryx, youngsire. Did you know milady?"

"Not really. Only in passing." I looked him in the eyes, knowing I wouldn't offend the True.

"Ah well." Again, he took up his broom. "Come again, when you have more patience. Perhaps there'll be fresh juice."

"Ritemaster . . ." I swallowed my pride. "Sir, may I see again the ring?"

Garnets, blood red, on a gold circlet. Mother had a dozen such, and

I'd thought nothing of them, but suddenly this seemed the most precious jewel ever I'd seen. Without thinking what I was doing, I stroked my lip with it, thought for a moment I felt a caress. I asked, "Would you part with it?"

"If you labored a lifetime, you'd not earn what that ring means to me. Besides, they say you folk fled destitute from Tantroth's attack. How could you pay for such a bauble, without even a roof over your head?" He held out his palm.

Reluctantly I handed back the ring. "I can't." Why, Mother, did you give such a treasure to a disheveled man of Rites, when to your own son, naught but lectures and admonitions?

"I have my work to do, but you're welcome to help."

I beat a hasty retreat, made my way back to the cottage.

Elryc waited by the trail. "Let me ride behind."

"To where?" I helped him up.

"The trees beyond the field. We need to talk." He gripped my waist.

I let Ebon have his head through the disused field. Elryc enjoyed it as much as I, despite the bouncing. We slowed our pace only where the grass was so high I feared Ebon would catch his foot in an unseen chuckhole.

"Now what?" I tied the reins to a sapling.

My brother rubbed the inside of his legs, adjusted his breeks, patted Ebon's nose. "I asked Hester to let me work with the rest of them, but she refused. It's too dangerous, she said, while Uncle Mar's looking for me. Roddy, we have to go back, or to Uncle Cumber. It's no use."

I raised an eyebrow.

"Hester sits out of the carpenters' way and weeps. I don't know how to give comfort."

"She doesn't take care of you?" My mouth tightened.

"I'm fine. Who's to care for her?" He paced. "She weeps for Pytor, and for me. Above all, she's ashamed."

"Of what?"

"That we send the others off, while you and I play. Genard bound himself to me in loyalty, not as a laborer."

"Damn Genard."

"Chela hates—"

"And damn Chela!"

"Fostrow's a soldier, not a reaper. For what he does, he gets no thanks, except from Hester. So, she's ashamed. All her life, she's made her own way. Now she's living on the work of others."

"She hates me. Why should I be bothered with her worries?"

"And Rustin?"

My tone was cautious. "What about him?"

"He demeans himself for you. How can you send a noble to work in the fields like—"

"Elryc, I forbade it. He went nonetheless."

"Think you that Hester doesn't know how you refused him, and he provides you to eat despite yourself?" He came close, eyes beseeching. "Chela will be the first to leave, I think. Then perhaps Rust, or Fostrow, and we'll be alone. We can't treat them like churls."

"So you want me to work? Did Rust put you up to this?"

He shouted, "Fool that thou art, don't you ever listen? *I* want to work! Yes, strike me, if thou will!"

Reluctantly, I lowered my fist.

"Roddy, my honor's at stake. If I can't work tomorrow, I'll forbid Genard to go. I think he'll do as I say." He took a deep breath, set his jaw. "We must do right."

I sighed. I had to admit the situation had gotten out of hand. "Give me a day. I'll deal with it."

"Lord of Nature, no. You'll assault Danar, and—"

"I won't go near him or the mill. I already promised Rust. Let it be."

"Just one more day?"

"Aye." I climbed into the stirrup. "Let's go."

I woke to bright daylight and the carpenters' saws.

"Ho, you're up at last." Hester went to the fire, poured tea, brought a crust of bread with it to my bedroll. "Eat, then." Her voice was gruff.

"Where's everyone?"

"They woke at a civilized hour to work. Elryc's following the carpenter's boy, like a pet calf." She busied herself with the contents of a trunk. "Tomorrow, I'll ask if someone wants a washerwoman. You'll watch Elryc."

I looked at my bread, ashamed. "Have you eaten?"

"Enough." Perhaps it meant she'd had nothing.

"I'm sorry for your troubles." I spoke with casual care; much sympathy and she'd douse me with scorn.

"Bah. Run off and play." She took my empty cup, hesitated. "Roddy . . ." She found a seat. "There's something I must tell you."

"What have I done now?"

"Much I haven't heard, I'll warrant, and none of it good. No." A sigh. "Some days past you spoke of my conjuring coin. Think you I would not, if I could?"

"Who knows? Perhaps our plight amuses you." I spoke with more force than I'd intended.

"Aye, you can see me holding my belly from laughing. Come outside." She led me to the wagon.

"I took Elryc out of Stryx in this."

"What did you change him to?"

"Nothing."

"I was there, and watched them search."

The grimness of her mouth relaxed into a bitter smile. "What did you see?"

"The soldiers, annoyed that you'd parked the cart to block their way. Housemaids and servants sweating with your gear, piece by piece, while you berated them. The horses hitched. Your fury when the guards insisted on searching. Then, to jeers and catcalls, you rode out."

"So now you know how I took Elryc."

"Don't mock—"

"The answer's before you."

I stared at the ugly, weather-beaten wagon, the wheel I'd slammed into while running from wasps, the awkward high box seat, the tailboard against which I'd rested. Once more I got down on my knees, peered under, looking for straps.

I sighed. "You're a witch. Would I'd known it when I was young, to protect myself."

"You're still young, and foolish as a milch cow." She reached up, rapped the seat. "Here, dolt."

I flushed, but ignored the insult. "You lie. I watched from the start, and never you had a moment to smuggle him—"

My jaw dropped.

The audacity.

"But you must have . . ." I shook my head, marveling. From the night before she left, there wasn't a moment when Hester could have smuggled Elryc into the coffin of the high box. Which meant—"You sealed him in the box prior, in the stables. Then you parked him in front of the soldiers' noses for the night. That whole show of loading the wagon—you *are* a witch!" I couldn't help but grin like a cretin.

She nodded. "It was all I could think of."

"And all that time you egged the soldiers on, you were dancing on the high seat, atop Elryc."

"Aye, and nearly tumbled to the wagon bed. But it was vital that eyes be on me, and not the cart."

"Hester, why didn't you tell when first I asked?"

Her smile faded; her shoulders slumped. "It's useful that men think you have power. But now, you had need to know. A lifetime of serving the Queen, and I'm reduced to poverty, the care of Elryc, and the company of a dim-witted heir. Ah, Roddy. How little we know of life's end, when we start the journey." She made her way back to the cottage, leaning on her stick.

I went to the stream, to think. I unlaced my boots to dangle my feet, but a moment's immersion changed my mind in a hurry. The water was just short of ice. I stared at the torrent rushing down from the hills, rubbed the blueness from my ankles, relaced my boots.

Elryc was right; our situation was intolerable. I brushed off my breeches, went to saddle Ebon.

It was near dark when I returned, near starving. A day's ride will do that. I was eager to make my announcement. The carpenters were gone, and our party was finishing a meal of bread and cheese, augmented by soup.

"Where were you?" Hester's rheumy eye was cold with disfavor.

"I had business to attend." I waited for them to ask.

"You're a fool to go off without telling us."

"I don't need your permission."

"Roddy." Rustin cleared his throat. "One of us should ride with you, for safety."

"I can take care of myself!" For a while, I sulked.

Fostrow slurped his tea. "We took grain to the mill today. I had word with Danar."

Rustin was indignant. "We agreed not to—"

"Yes, I know. I told him to make settlement with Dame Hester, or I'd slice him in twain, and let Lord Cumber judge the penalty. Don't look so aggrieved, youngsire. My back aches so, I cannot sleep. I took arms to escape such a life as this."

"It's only for a while."

"Even so." He drained his dregs. "I swore to Lord Rodrigo unto death. By my thinking, hanging is no worse than a sword in the belly. Both are more fitting than hacking at grain."

Chela spat into the fire. "You destroy yourself for him, who won't lift a finger for himself or us. Why do we this? Shush, Rustin, you know it's true. If Lord Roddy worked, we'd be done in three weeks."

I snarled, "You'd earn more on your back than ever you could scrubbing wash."

"What do you know of men lying with women?"

Rust snapped, "Both of you, stop!"

My voice cut through the babble. "There's no more need." Reveling in the moment, I stood, emptied my coinpurse, opened my hand slowly. One by one, I let the silver coins fall onto the table, all except one that I kept. "Your roof. Hens, for eggs and meat. Feed. Milk."

All was silence.

I waited.

Rustin was the first to stir. "You had your purse all the while, and let us—"

Fostrow. "How could you, Rodrigo!"

"What you'd expect of *him*." Chela. "He didn't care if—"

I sat, unable to repress my smile.

Hester stirred. "I bathed his stings when he came howling in the night, with naught but his loincloth. He had no purse."

Again, a silence. Rustin crossed to my side, bent, took my chin in his blistered hands, raised my face. "How came you by this coin, my prince?"

I glanced from one to the other. "You think I robbed your precious Danar, but I had no truck with him." From Fostrow, a sigh of relief. "I took a long ride today. Once you reach the Cumber Road it's easy going. On a good horse it's only three hours."

Rustin's hand tightened on my chin. "How came you by this silver, Rodrigo?"

"I'm telling you." I shook off his swollen hand. My moment wasn't going as expected. "I rode to Shar's Cross and sold the smith . . ." I swallowed, my triumph fading. Suddenly I feared my next words.

Hester put hands on knees, groaned to her feet. She too came close, eyed me. "What did you sell, boy?"

I shrugged. "Nothing we had need of. The sword."

"My sword!" Rust's cry was anguish.

"What use was it, if we starved? Even if we paid the carpenter, you'd still have to work—"

"How could you!"

"—to put food in our bellies. You all hated the labor."

"It wasn't yours to sell!" Rustin's face was contorted. He hugged himself.

Chela lunged at me, tore my hair, slashed at my cheek.

With a howl of rage I knocked her to the floor. "You're crazed, all of you! I saved us!"

Elryc turned away, leaned his cheek on Genard's shoulder.

I said, "Rust, I'm sorry if . . ."

His eyes glistened, but he stood as if stone.

"You gave it to me. We'll find you another sword, when times are—"

Hester opened the door, trudged into the dark.

Rustin's voice was unsteady. "I only gave you the use of it, Roddy. It was my first sword. My first ever." He wiped his face, regarded mine. "Why did you not sell Ebon?"

"My horse? Don't be ridiculous!" A nobleman was nothing, without a horse.

Or a sword.

I cleared my throat, suddenly uncomfortable. "I'm sorry if you feel—"

His face twisted. "No, it doesn't matter. What need of a fine sword has the son of Llewelyn, traitor? We've lost the keep, our place in Caledon, our name. Sell Santree, if you would. I'll have no need of him either."

"Rust—"

"I have no liege. No friend." Beside himself, he kicked off his boots. "Here, sell these too." Barefoot, he tottered into the night.

Chela scrambled to her feet, ran after.

Genard stared at the floor.

Fostrow shook his head. "It was wrong, my lord."

"Shut thy cursed mouth!"

I took my bedroll, spread it with a savage snap, lay fuming.

Chapter 17

FOR TWO DAYS, NONE WOULD SPEAK TO ME. NOT THAT they refused, if I insisted on some speech, but after a time I grew tired of curt and grudging replies, and left them to their devices. In the cool afternoons I lay near the stream, under the shade of a tree, dreaming of my kingdom. When I wore my crown, I'd show them all. Even Rustin would bow to me, and it would be the formal bow of state, at our every meeting. Elryc as well.

I'd bargained well for the sword. Now, there was no need to labor in fields or smithy. Nonetheless, each morn Rustin donned old sandals and, spurning the use of Santree, trudged off to town. Chela pleaded with him, but he refused; when she tugged at his arm he shoved her against the fence, with a force that pleased me. At night he came home weary and aching, and she rubbed his back, with sullen determination.

At last, on a cold misty evening, I grew tired of the isolation, and seeing Elryc outdoors, I drew him aside. "Brother, help me plan for when I'm King."

He seemed tired. "Not tonight." He made as if to go.

I stayed him. "Sit with me. I'm—" I hesitated, lest revealing myself give him power. "I'm lonely."

He sighed, but sat, folded his legs. "You shouldn't have done it."

"The sword? If anyone, it's Rust who should berate me."

"He won't." Elryc made a face. "He can't."

"Why? He's no longer vassal." I watched another cloud obscure the moon.

"Oh, Roddy." Silence, for a time. "How can you be so near grown, and see so little?"

"To what am I blind, wise one?" Sarcasm dripped from my tone.

"He suffers."

I waved it away. "No sword is worth that."

"Not for the sword." Elryc gave me an odd look. "Have you no thought for him?"

"He's stubborn, and a fool. Look at him, going off to slave each day, to spite me."

"He makes . . . expiation." Once again, Elryc seemed not eleven, but someone older, wiser.

"For Llewelyn? Well that he should. A shame that Rust's life is ruined, but where is he to go? After his father's treason, who would honor him?"

"Not you, certainly."

I picked at blades of grass. "Why would I? He's a nobody, a discarded playmate." I grew tired of the subject, and a chill was in the air. "What should I do, now that you're safe?"

"Whatever you wish." Elryc sounded defeated, but in a moment tried again. "Roddy, I think Rustin works as a churl—not because of Llewelyn. He does penance. For you."

"Nonsense." I wiped my hands. "I've done nothing wrong."

"Then why do you feel shame?"

"I don't." I stood. "Come, it's starting to rain."

"You won't meet my eye. You haven't met anyone's eye for days."

"Where did you dream this nonsense?" I stalked back toward the cottage.

As I neared, the conversation within lapsed. Outwardly, I ignored the snub. I got myself ready for bed, against the steady drizzle on our new thatching. Tense, I lay tossing and turning in the dark.

By invitation or on her own, Chela had crept back into Rustin's bed. I snorted. Fitting, that they pair: a churl and a housemaid. His resolve to dispose of her services had gone the way of his oath of vassalage.

I dozed, but creaks and scraping in the night kept me from sleep. I listened jealously for sound of Rustin coupling, not sure how I'd respond if I recognized it. He and Chela lay beyond Fostrow's bulk; I couldn't see them without raising myself. Doing so would be too obvious, so I refrained.

Another creak; a muttered voice. Someone spoke in his sleep.

I jerked awake. The voice, unfamiliar, had come from behind me, where there were only the slat shutters of the window.

My skin prickled. I threw off the cover, stood shivering in my loincloth.

Outside, a step.

I fumbled for my sword, realized I no longer had one. I drew breath to shout.

The door crashed open. Hooded figures swarmed. They bore clubs and sticks, and a sputtering brand.

I shouted, "Rustin! Fostrow! Arm yourselves!"

A club crashed down, on one of the sleeping figures.

I was near the table. Cursing, I picked up a chair, brandished it. A club whistled, smashed my chair to splinters. It drove me to my knees.

The hooded figure raised his cudgel to strike again. I dived under the table.

"Set the brand!" A rough, guttural voice.

From the safety of the table I watched Rust scramble to his feet. A club caught him in the midriff.

Boots, close by. The side of my table rose. I clawed at the nearby leg.

"Hurry, afore they—imps and demons!" He lurched free.

Fostrow panted, "Rustin, Genard, take arms! Put Elryc behind—ow—you'd try that, would you? Ha!" A clatter. A cry of dismay.

"Torch the roof, and let's be gone!"

"Roddy, where are you?" Fostrow.

The flickering light grew brighter. I risked a glance over the table. At the far wall Rustin was doubled over in pain, a snarl on his lips. He clutched his half-sword. Beside him stood Fostrow, legs apart, his dagger glinting red. Genard, wild-eyed, swung a chair at a burly figure.

"Get the one under the table!"

With nowhere to flee, I snatched up the table, tried to make it a shield. A club loomed high.

Fostrow's dagger whirled over my head, plunged itself into my assailant's throat.

His club fell harmlessly over my shoulder. Scrabbling fingers tore at his hood.

A swarthy man, muscled from a lifetime of labor. He swayed. Beads of sweat stood out on his knotted forehead.

I gaped.

He opened his mouth as if to speak, spewed forth a gout of blood that splattered my face, my arms, my bare chest. I screamed, careening backward. I tumbled over shattered furniture.

As the hooded figures retreated, one seized the torch, ran about the room lighting everything within reach. Fostrow charged. The attacker hurled the torch into the rafters, bolted out the door.

I touched myself, came away with gobs of blood. Frantic, I wiped my cheeks and mouth with reddened fingers, rubbed helplessly at the ooze on my chest.

My hands were crimson. I wiped them on my loincloth, on the wall, on anything I found. It wasn't enough. I bent and vomited.

When at last I could breathe, acrid smoke wafted about the room. Flames sputtered from the roof. I wiped my steaming eyes, beside myself with terror. I mustn't burn.

Fostrow lurched outside, supporting Rustin's half-limp form. I glanced about. Chela was still inside her covers. Hester, in her voluminous robe, lay on her stomach, as if dead. Of Elryc, no sign.

I crawled toward Chela, my limbs atremble. She breathed. Cursing, I seized her arms, tried to drag her toward the door. She was amazingly heavy, and I gave up as a waft of smoke blew my way. I crawled to the door, dived outside as sparks fell on my shoulder.

Genard darted past me, tugged at Chela. Not daring to display my fears, I risked all, ran inside to grab her arm. Desperate for the welcome cool of the rain, I helped him haul her to the yard.

I peered inside. Hester's body wasn't worth my cremation. I backed from the porch.

"Roddy, help!" Elryc's voice, weak.

I couldn't see him. Even he wasn't worth the flames, though the cottage hadn't yet begun to burn in earnest. "Where are you?"

"On the floor!"

Damn him. Still, I'd sworn fealty by the True. If I made no effort, I might lose my Power. Cursing, I took a tentative step into the cottage. "Do you hide, you fool?"

"Here, Roddy." Elryc's voice came from Hester. The old woman's arm moved. Elryc's own appeared below. "Help me from under!"

I glanced at the smoldering roof. Genard scrambled past, crouched, rolled the old woman aside.

Elryc coughed, eyes streaming. "She pinned me." He darted to the door, turned. "Can you get her by yourself?"

"Roddy will help, m'lord."

"Leave her, she's—oh, all right." Together Genard and I dragged the body to the door.

Elryc seized Hester's legs. In a moment we had her outside.

"Our gear!" Genard ran back to the door.

"Leave it!" Fostrow caught at his arm.

"We'll have nothing!"

"Our lives," said Fostrow.

"Look, sir, it doesn't burn so hard." Genard dashed in, emerged with a box of our stores.

Rust clutched himself, groaning. He made a motion to the cottage, nodded agreement.

Fostrow ran to the door. "Roddy, haul everything outside. Elryc, Genard, run to the stream with buckets, and mind you don't fall in. You'll drown from the cold of it." He disappeared into the cottage, emerged dragging a trunk.

I watched, openmouthed.

Rust rapped on my leg. "Help him!"

"In fire?"

"It's already half-doused." With an effort, he stumbled to his feet. "Fools they are, that pick a rainy night to torch a roof." He lurched to the door.

I thought of following, but hesitated.

Genard and Elryc raced back with slopping buckets. Fostrow grabbed one, tossed it high into the rafters. A hiss and a cloud of steam. He hurled the other bucket at something out of view, appeared a moment later to kick Hester's burning bedding out the door.

Reluctantly, I went as far as the porch, helped move the gear the rest of the way to safety.

At last all was quiet, the cottage a soggy mess.

Elryc sat on the grass, holding himself, rocking. Genard knelt by him, babbling.

Rust rubbed his stomach. The roof dripped.

Elryc spoke past Genard, to me. "Nurse threw herself on top of me, held me down." He sniffled.

I wiped at the dried blood that caked me.

"She pressed my mouth shut, before they struck her head."

A shudder, a sob, and Elryc swarmed into my arms, curled himself like a baby. Instinctively, my arms went round him. He rested his head on my chest.

At a loss, I stroked his forehead. "It's all right, brother. We live."

It made him bawl. I sat half-dazed while he cried himself out.

Rustin's face was grim. Holding his belly, he bent over Chela, patted her face. "She lives too." Rust turned his attentions to Hester. "Genard, find water, and a cloth."

The boy nodded meekly, and slipped off.

"Fostrow, you're hurt."

"Just a scratch, Lord Rustin." He glanced at his bloodied arm. "One had a butcher's knife."

"Let me bind it."

The grizzled veteran sounded weary. "As you wish." Rustin bound him. The soldier's face remained hard. "I doubt they expected much fight. Or that we'd be armed."

I tried to redeem myself. "I was the one heard them, and gave warning." Genard appeared with fresh bucket, panting.

"Yes, of course. Leave it, Rustin, and see to Hester. Put a cold cloth to her forehead."

"I was reaching for my knife when—" No use; they clustered around Hester's inert form.

Only Elryc cared that I lived or died. I sighed, rested my head against his.

My brother stirred. "Were they Uncle Mar's men? No, keep holding me."

I returned my hand to his shoulder. "Unarmed, with clubs? No, if it were Mar, we'd be mincemeat."

He shuddered. "I'm afraid of dying. I want to grow up."

My lips formed the words "So do I," but I didn't speak them.

I sat with Elryc. Rustin ignored me. To recall his attention I asked, "What of Chela?"

"I think her ribs are broken. Pray that Hester lives; she'll know what to do."

In that case, let Hester join her sister in the earth. After a time, my jealousy eased. Nurse had saved Elryc, as I should have. She deserved to live, perhaps more . . . I set Elryc down on the grass, patted him, took a few steps into the dark.

Perhaps more than I.

All night they bathed Hester's temple with cold water, but though she stirred and muttered, she didn't wake. Fostrow bade Rustin tear strips of cloth, and together, they bound Chela's ribs tight. It was what he'd seen done to soldiers, he said, and sometimes it worked.

We tried to make a fire, but the wood was damp, and it sizzled and smoked fitfully. We huddled round nonetheless, drawing comfort more from each other's nearness than its warmth.

Rustin covered Chela with blankets, squeezed beside me, tentatively put his hand on my shoulder. I flung it off. After a moment, he went to sit next to Fostrow. For a time I doubted myself, but my anxieties faded with the night, and as dawn approached I recalled that though none might acknowledge, it was I who'd given the alarm. On what I'd done after, I didn't dwell.

By the light of morning all of us, save the two unconscious women, gathered in the cottage to stare at the blood-soaked form that lay stiffening on the sooty floor.

"Who was it?" Genard.

Before I could answer Fostrow said, "They'll know in town. He was local. Sandals, not boots, and he wears homespun breeks."

I yawned, irritable, cold, and tired.

Rustin. "Dare we go into Fort, with death on our hands?"

Fostrow's mouth was grim. "This isn't an assault on the miller, lad. The dead man came to us, to do evil."

"But he's one of them. Who would disclose his name?"

"The Ritemaster." I spoke without thinking. Rust shot me a curious glance, which only annoyed me the further. I said, "I met him. he's honest."

"Fetch him, Roddy. I would, but I ache too much to ride."

"Send a servant!" I turned away. "Who are you to order me about?"

"Easy, lads." Fostrow's voice was oil. "We're all tired and hungry."

"Rustin forgets his place, as do you! I'm the Prince of Caledon. You owe me respect!"

"Ah. Yes, well. That's as may be. I'll be back presently. Genard, help me saddle, there's a boy."

While we waited Rust did his best to tend the injured. I sat against a tree, arms folded, waiting for anyone to dare oppose me. But Elryc and Genard occupied themselves elsewhere, and Rustin ignored me entirely. Churlish behavior, entirely fitting of him.

Within an hour Fostrow returned, followed by Aren Ritemaster on a mule. The old man glanced at the body, sighed. "Korell of Creek's Farm. His wife was frantic this morn."

Fostrow scratched his grizzled head. "Who were his henchmen?"

"That I can't know."

"Was he friendly with the miller?"

"Friendly? I can't say anyone is that. He had dealings with Danar, as any plowman must." Aren scratched idly, went to the door. We followed.

Outside, he turned, squinted at the women's pallets. "What's been done for your injured?"

Rust shrugged helplessly. "The girl's ribs are stove, and there's no more we can do. The old woman is knocked senseless."

"I am not." Hester stirred. "Though I'm too dizzy to sit."

"Hester!" Elryc scurried to her side.

"No sniffling. Help me up, and find me drink." She scowled at the smoke-blackened cottage. "How bad is it?"

"Not so bad as it looks," said Fostrow. "The beams are lightly scorched, and can be planed clean. You'll need new thatching."

"Who did this?"

I said, "Danar." I overrode Fostrow's objection. "You know it true, as well as I. Bring the miller here; have him look on his handiwork."

Aren's face was reproving. "It's a grave charge you'd level, youngsire. Moreover, Danar's gone to Shar; he left last noon."

"It's but a short ride." I should know; I'd made it myself, three days past.

"He has mules, but no fine stallion such as your black. And doubtless some townsmen will have seen him there, of the night."

"Doubtless." Fostrow's voice dripped scorn. "So then, Ritemaster. We're to do nothing?"

"You wish to accuse the miller. Can you be sure it was he? If not, a false charge warrants imprisonment."

I flared, "Who else would burn us out? Who has cause?"

"Why, for that matter, would Danar? The word is he refused your demands, and matters were at rest."

"Thanks to the cowardice of my companions." I didn't hide my disgust; their irresolution had brought us to this.

It brought a sudden silence, which Genard was the first to break. "*You* speak of cowardice, Prince?"

Rust nudged his ribs. "Don't."

"Who was it hid under a table while we fought for our lives? Who wouldn't go back inside to free Elryc, or bring out our gear—"

Rustin cuffed him, rather hard. "It's not your place to chide Rodrigo!" I waited for Rust to deny the boy's calumnies, but he did not.

Aren knelt by Chela. "You've bound her; that's the best you can do. After a time, though, you must make her sit, else her breath will dwindle. As for Korell's death, Lord Cumber will be informed, and we will obey his commands."

Genard rubbed his face, stuck out his tongue at Rust. When no one looked, he shot me a look of venom that shattered my restraints. I advanced on him, pulling loose my dagger.

Rustin caught my arm. "Do no violence, Roddy."

"Let me go!" I almost broke free, but failed. "He'll recant his lies or—"

"No!" Rustin twisted my hand, wrested away the knife. "Don't shed his blood for speaking truth!"

I staggered, as if from a blow. "I—how could—Rustin!"

"I was loath to say it, and Genard hadn't the right. You force me."

"Where's your loyalty, your honor?"

"To the truth." His eyes were sad, but his hand fell on my shoulder. "Roddy, I'm sorry—"

"Damn your traitor blood! Llewelyn's no worse than you!" I tore loose. "I hate you!"

Hester tried to raise herself, sank back. "Roddy, calm yourself long enough for us to—"

"I hate all of you!" I dashed across the yard, into the fallow field, along the line of trees to the brook.

I risked a glance behind.

No one followed, and I felt the more betrayed.

I spent most of the day alone by the stream, until hunger drove me back. Nobody objected when I helped myself from the stewpot. After, to assert my place, I left my bowl for Genard or another servant to clean.

That night Rustin and Fostrow took turns on guard duty. In the morning, they drew aside with Hester and conferred a long while. I grew restless, but pride prevented me from demanding admittance. Instead, I went for a long walk by the icy stream.

When I returned, they were waiting.

I took a place at the end of the table, as befit my rank. They glanced at each other; Rustin broke the silence. "We're going to Cumber."

"Oh?" I raised an eyebrow.

"For Elryc's sake, we must."

Hester added, "The Earl's disdainful, but not unkind, in the end. This is no fit place to raise Prince Elryc, if the villagers attack us. And Chela needs warmth, good food, nursing we can't give."

"You'd go to Uncle Cumber as beggars?" My gesture encompassed the table, our soiled and meager clothes. "Think you he'd entertain my claim as heir, if a bedraggled troop of—"

Rust shot back, "What choice have we? Matters go from bad to worse; would you next pawn the crown? If Cumber's generous, he'll put us up for the winter. While Tantroth roams we'll be safe behind his walls."

"He's on the Council!" My shout stirred Chela; waking, she moaned, tried to shift position. Genard, in the corner, crept to her side. "What lever have I to gain his vote, if I come to him as supplicant?"

"What of Elryc's life, if we do not?"

"This is about my life, not Elryc's! Imps take him!"

The door swung open. Elryc stood framed in the entry, pale of face. "Don't flee to Cumber, on my account. I'll stay."

"Elryc, I didn't mean—" I swallowed. "I'm sorry."

Hester slapped the table with her palm. "We go." Her glare favored us all equally. "I, at any rate, and Elryc with me."

I snarled, "I'm head of the House of Caledon."

Elryc said, "Please, Roddy. You have them at their wits' end; they know not what—"

"You betray me too, brother? So be it; I'll live well enough alone!"

"Oh, Roddy." Rust rested his head in his arms.

"Hester, I forbid your going!" There; the gauntlet was thrown.

Her crooked finger drew bead at my eye. "Enough of your selfishness. You've made our lives torment."

"How dare you!"

The old woman growled, "The boy's not born who'll forbid my rearing Elena's child! Cross me at your peril, Princeling!"

Something in her eyes recalled the hallway outside her chamber at Stryx, and the knife that pricked my belly. "Then go to Cumber, swim in the lake of fire, if you will! I hope you burn."

Fostrow. "You can't travel alone, Dame Hester. Who knows where Tantroth's patrols roam, or how venomous the miller's hatred?"

"She won't be alone." Rustin's eye was fixed on the table. "I'll go with her."

"Traitor!" My voice was hoarse.

"Come along, Roddy." Rust's tone was beseeching. "You vowed your aid to Elryc, and we shouldn't separate."

"Then stay!"

"I can't abandon them, Roddy. You have the bit between your teeth; there's no talking to you. Elryc, at least, I can protect, and Dame Hester. If you like, I'll ride directly back."

I no longer cared what I said. "Protect them? You'll run at the first sign of—no, better yet, you'll go over to Tantroth at the first sight of a patrol. Like father, like—"

Rustin shot to his feet, white-faced.

I kicked aside my chair, strode to the door. Elryc was in the way; I thrust him aside. "Demons curse the lot of you! Begone! Throw yourselves on Cumber's mercy; I'll laugh when he heaves you in his cells to await Uncle Mar."

"Roddy—Prince Rodrigo . . ." Fostrow's look was apologetic. "I'm sworn to you, and I'll return when I may."

"You're no longer my man. I won't have you. Lord of Nature curse the day I met you!"

Hester. "Roddy, don't—"

"Leave, in the morn! I'll be gone soon after; the world's a wider place than a foul hamlet under an ice-swept mount. May you all burn in the demons' lake!" I slammed the door with a satisfying crash.

I spent the night bedded under the wagon. Once, in the night, Rust came to me, but I hurled rocks at him until he fled back to the cottage. Only Ebon heard my sniffles, listened to my muttered vows of revenge.

Chapter 18

BY THE FIRST LIGHT OF DAWN I WAS UP AND ABOUT. MY limbs ached from the cold hard turf. I bridled Ebon. From the saddlebags I took the clothes Rustin had loaned me, threw them on the wagon with a grandiose gesture that, unfortunately, none were present to see. If Rust was to desert me, let him take all that was his.

I wrapped the crown in a tattered old cloth, packed it in my saddlebag. For good measure, I took also the half-sword. Hester would travel with a party large enough to protect each other; I would have nothing but dagger and sword.

Before anyone in the cottage arose, I swung atop Ebon, galloped off toward town. I would stay out of their sight until Hester's farm was again abandoned. Then I'd go back to the hut, make my plans.

For once the market square was occupied, but faces turned away as I rode into view. I fingered the silver coin in my purse, the lone remaining pence from the price of Rustin's sword. Already I was hungry, but I bided my time. The coin would have to last long.

Could the impoverished farmers in the market even make change for my silver pence? If not, would they sell me their goods without, and let me keep the coin 'til it could be exchanged?

I sighed. Life was complicated, when you had to organize it from the start.

Night would be cold, but I had my blankets, and could set a huge fire in the hearth. I had no axe, but there was enough deadwood lying about. It would be nice to send Genard to pick an armful, but he too would be gone, spiteful wretch that he was.

I realized I'd been thinking of the cottage as home. Well, for the moment, it was. Perhaps I could stay here until word came from Stryx, and I knew how went the struggle for Caledon. It would be better had I means to hire servants. Someone to cook, to gather wood, to fetch water.

What I needed was coin. Unless I sold Ebon—quite out of the question—I had no source, save the one I hoarded. I reached to my saddlebag, unwrapped the crown of Caledon, placed it on my head. No law forbade crowning myself, not waiting for the Seven to declare me. But I'd forgo the Still. Yet, would I need it? I sighed. I'd have to fight Uncle Mar as well as Tantroth. And who'd rise to follow me, against their two mighty armies?

No, I had to wait for my chance, and in the meanwhile endure poverty.

Of course, there was coin in Fort. And I knew who had it.

Danar.

I walked my stallion along the familiar trail to the mill, scheming. I decided it would be best to dismount near the road. I tied Ebon to a tree, left the sword on his saddle, sauntered the rest of the way on foot. Were anyone to ask, I was out for a morning ramble. Why I strolled here, instead of at the cottage, was another matter.

The wheel turned with its customary clatter and splash. One of the miller's men climbed the porch, went inside. Did Danar keep his treasure in the mill, or his cabin? He'd want to sleep near it, for safety. That meant I'd have to break in, put down whatever enemy arose.

A woman's face passed in front of the window. I ducked behind a tree, my heart pounding. Still, I'd have to draw near; it would be folly to attack the house without some inkling of what I'd face. I put on an innocent look, wandered a few steps closer.

The place was much larger than Hester's cottage, and sturdily built. Several rooms. From the look of it, I'd—

A mighty blow, in the small of my back. Paralyzed, I pitched headlong, gasping for breath. A leering peasant face. A shovel, raised high to strike again. Instead, the churl lowered the spade, seized me, hauled me to the mill.

"Danar, look what I found!"

The miller came out, wiping his hands. His eyes lit at the sight of me. "He came to us? What convenience, Jom. Bring him in."

"Let me go! I'm—" A fist knocked the breath out of me. They dragged me inside, held me against an oaken post, tied my hands behind it before I recovered from the blows.

Grinning, Danar whipped out a knife. He flourished the blade under my chin. "Open your mouth!" The point of the blade lurched closer.

I cried out, twisted my wrists against the rope with desperate strength. All to no avail.

"Stick out your tongue!" The knife flicked.

Frantic, I did as he bid. Instantly his fingers snatched my tongue, held it within my mouth. I gagged at the reek of garlic, and the rough fingers half down my throat.

I tried to bite, but he held my mouth too wide. "You come to our village from a far place, and call me thief? I'll cut it out at the root!" The knife wavered. I squealed.

Jom said uneasily, "Danar, take care."

"Hear, boy? Any more talk about my stealing coin from that demented old woman and—" The knife sliced at air. I screeched, staring transfixed at the nicked and scarred blade. He laughed with the pleasure of it. "You won't be telling any more lies, then, or ba, ba, ba, you'll say. Nothing else!"

His grip tightened, and he pulled my tongue half out. I screamed from the pain of it.

Danar paused, as if reflecting. "No, best if I slit your throat, and make an end to it. Jom will throw what's left of you into the river."

Blood from my lacerated wrists made my fingers slippery, but the rope would not give the merest trifle. My tongue frozen in his iron grasp, I begged and pleaded with my eyes.

Jom said, "Please, Danar. He'll heed, now. Look, he's soiled himself."

"A coward as well." Danar let go my tongue, slapped my face so hard my head whipped to the side, and ground against the post. My cheek went numb. "All right, Jom. Let him go, before the reek of him spoils my wheat."

A moment later, feet dragging like a rag doll, I felt myself half carried to the porch. A great kick sent me tumbling down the steps to the moist earth below. I lay stunned.

Behind me, the door slammed.

Holding my oozing mouth, I looked up into the wide eyes of a toddler. She picked her nose gravely. Footsteps. The mother hurried across the yard, snatched her child, disappeared into the house.

I tried to stand, couldn't manage it. Nonetheless, I had to remove myself, lest they come out and find me. I crawled along the path, mewling and whimpering, until a tree barred my way. Using it as a crutch, I staggered to my feet.

My wrists stung like fire, as did my cheek. I stumbled down the trail, eyes too full to see, blundered at last into Ebon. It took me several tries to mount, but finally, exhausted, feet dangling, I lay over his neck and urged him homeward. The familiar scent of his flesh gave me the only comfort I might have, and I clung to him weeping as if to a nurse.

After a time Ebon stopped. Dazedly, I looked about, realized we were at the cottage. I slid off his back. "Please, Rustin, be here." But the supplies were gone, and the wagon. Lord of Nature, let him change his mind, hurry back to me. I lurched into the cottage, fell on my straw.

No one was in the room, save myself. My tongue was horribly sore; each movement of my mouth brought a new throb of pain. Distracted, miserable, I rolled over onto my back, flung my arm over my eyes.

After a time I became aware of a dreadful smell. I rolled onto my side. My breeches stuck to my skin. "No. Please, no!" I staggered outside, clawed in my saddlebag, hoping I'd misremembered.

I hadn't. There was no change of clothes.

With a cry of despair I ran across the meadow to the brook, tearing off my shirt. On the bank, I hopped out of my boots, peeled off my fouled breeches, held them by two fingers, too ashamed to look. I plunged them into the stream, almost lost them to the force of the current. Gritting my teeth, I got a better grip, lay on my stomach, dunked them over and again. Then my jerkin, likewise soiled.

I lay the soaking clothes on the grass, sat back, recoiled from the sensation. My loincloth was the worst of the lot; in a frenzy I tore it off. Naked, I leaned over the bank, held the loincloth in the bubbling water, scrubbed out the mess I'd made.

I spread out the clothing. For a moment I cupped my hands under my arms, to restore feeling. Then, with nothing but water and my fingers, I did my best to wipe myself clean. When at last I was done, I washed my hand over and over.

All my clothes lay sopping in the autumn sun. Spent and freezing, I sank naked to the ground, cuddled myself for comfort.

Nothing had prepared me for such humiliation, such shame. My sword was with Ebon, at the cottage, else, I'd have used it on myself. Perhaps after a time I'd rouse myself and get it; for the moment, it seemed too much trouble.

A few inches from my nose, a puddle of water had collected in a crevice. I had a raging thirst, but my tongue ached so badly I doubted I could swallow. Still, my hand crept forth. For a moment, it hovered over the still water.

A bird called to its young. The limbs of the tree that shaded me rustled in the breeze. A beautiful day, a fine day, a lovely day to be alive. Unless you were Rodrigo of Caledon, bungler, fool, coward. Knave.

My hand lay steady over the puddle. Mother's visage floated. *I meant you to be King, Roddy.*

Ah, Mother. I know the hopes we sifted, as you lay dying. It's too late for that. Besides . . .

I pressed my palm close to the water.

Yes, Roddy?

I confess: I'm still virgin, and make love to my hand, which no doubt pleases you. But, Mother, I'm not sure I've held to the True. Well, as to Elryc, I haven't, really. So, let's say there'll be no Power in my life. It doesn't matter. Ask you why? Because I'm not fit to be King; I'm unfit even to live.

My hand trembled, touched the water. As it rippled, my revery shattered. I lay for a long while. Then, with an effort, I sat.

"No." I spoke aloud, to the breeze. "It isn't so." I stood, cupped my groin for shyness, looked about, let go myself. "It's their fault, not mine." Consider: Rust swore himself to me, led me into this mindless venture, then ran away. Elryc plots against me. It was he who convinced them to flee to Cumber.

"You hid while we fought for our lives!"

I whirled, but the stableboy's voice echoed only in my mind. "Shut thy mouth, lout!"

Coward of Caledon!

I covered my ears, but the voice was no longer Genard's; it was my own.

I cried, "I'm brave, and steady, and true!"

I fell to my knees, atop my soaking breeks. The wet on my bare knees smashed the remnants of my illusion. Am I not coward? What, then?

I put my forearm to my mouth, bit down in rage, let loose only when the toothmarks were deep in my skin.

Yes, I'd hid under the table, at the first sign of fight. And I'd been petrified when the miller seemed about to slash my tongue. When he made as if to slit my throat I'd been transported beyond terror.

Was it not understandable that I wanted life more than honor? Could I not live with that knowledge, and esteem the man I was?

No.

Not when I, Rodrigo Prince of Caledon, crouched naked and ashamed by a stream, wiping shit from my breeches.

Life itself wasn't worth that.

"I won't be coward." It didn't satisfy; I spoke again to the foaming stream. "I'll be coward no more. I swear, by all that is holy, by every Rite ever devised by man, that I will have no fear of death—well, if I have fear, it won't matter. Do you hear, river? I shall not run from fear again. If it costs my life, let it be so." My cheeks were wet.

The river babbled on, uncaring.

I picked up my soggy clothes, and my boots. "From this day forth, I am no coward." Clutching my garments, still naked as the day I was born, I picked my way across the stones to the cottage.

PART II

Chapter 19

I GATHERED ARMLOAD AFTER ARMLOAD OF BRUSH AND fallen limbs, and built a huge fire in the hearth. I draped my clothes from the mantle, holding them in place with rocks, and sat shivering, feeding sticks to the flames.

In my eagerness, I let the fire grow too hot. My jerkin began to smoke. I yanked it from the mantle, let go with a curse as it threatened to blister my hand. More cautiously, with a stick, I pulled down my breeches and loincloth. The breeks were still too wet to wear, but the loincloth was merely damp; gratefully, I put it on.

I propped the breeches farther from the fire, and examined my shirt now that it had cooled. I sighed. It wasn't my fault that sparks had burned tiny holes through the midriff. What did I know of drying clothes? That wasn't my role in life.

It didn't matter. My silver coin would be ample to buy another shirt. And food. I was now many hours without, and my stomach grew restive. A hen would be best, though I wasn't quite sure how to pluck and dress a fowl. On our hunts, Griswold or a servant handled such trifles. A fish, on the other hand, I could fry. Well, there was no pan, but I could bake it on rocks. I'd watched Rustin, once. Fish or fowl for my dinner?

I'd spin my silver pence to decide. I fished in my breeks for the coin purse.

Nothing.

Alarmed, I thrust my hand deep. No purse.

"Lord of Nature, don't do this!" I jammed my feet into my boots, dashed across the field to the stream.

I fell on my hands and knees, swept the grass with my fingers, tore at the earth, blackened and broke my fingernails.

The coin purse was gone. In my haste to wash the filth from my breeches, I'd let the brook have it. I tore off my shirt, plunged my arm deep into the searing cold stream. I could bear it only for a moment; I pulled out my arm, danced away the pain of the frigid water.

Nonetheless, I gritted my teeth, bent again to the water, tried once more to sift the bottom.

No coin.

Desolate, I trudged back to the cottage, dragging my shirt behind. I would starve.

By now my breeches were almost dry. I dressed, welcoming their warmth, not minding the sooty scent they bore. I slumped on the plank floor, stared at the crackling flames.

Nothing turned out as it should; Lord of Nature himself was against me. Was it because I'd mocked the Rites? Did they reveal arcane truth I was too dense to see?

My stomach growled. I curled myself before the fire, miserable beyond belief. Day passed into evening. At last, I raised my head.

Hard as it might be to admit, perhaps some aspect of conducting a man's life had escaped me. Though despair at his father's treason had briefly unhinged him that night at the inn, Rustin seemed far more prepared for life's vicissitudes than I.

Perhaps I could follow his ways, learn from his manner. Always, until recently, he'd been generous of his time and care. One night he'd even bathed me, soaped my hair. Would he—

No, I'd driven him away. My words had been justified, but he'd recoiled from them, and from me. Well, maybe I'd overreacted a trifle. Rust should have understood, though.

So should Hester.

And Fostrow.

And Genard.

Elryc too.

As the last flames flickered into embers, I sat appalled.

Was I so evil, that men turned their faces? Nothing else could explain their mass desertion.

Outside, an owl hooted.

Hester accused me of being selfish, making their lives a torment. Nonsense, wasn't it? Or had I really done so? My heart began to sink.

I'd ruined all. Was there still time to find them, somehow make amends?

I began to gather my few things, suddenly afraid. What if they'd turned off the Cumber road, took some bypass I knew not? What if Rust spat in my face?

What if I spent the rest of my days frightened, miserable, alone?

"Roddy, what have you done?" None answered, but the floor creaked, and my back prickled with alarm. When one was alone, imps and demons gathered near. Mother had always warned me so.

I tied my saddlebag tight, led Ebon from his grazing, mounted in the fading light. I could ride thrice as fast as the lumbering wagon could roll. With luck I'd find them. What I'd do then, I wasn't sure, but I couldn't face a night in the cabin.

"Let's go, boy." I patted Ebon's flank. The night air was cool, and I shivered. There was no help for it. I flicked the reins, and we were off.

The night was cold, and I reeled with hunger and exhaustion. My tongue still ached, but I spoke—babbled—to myself and Ebon, to stay awake, to stay sane.

I was an insufferable fool. Where Rust kept his temper, I blazed in fury. Where he stopped to ponder, I charged ahead, thoughtless. I was a hopeless dunce. No wonder they all snickered behind my back; compared to my idiocy, my virginity was but a trifle. Even before we'd left Stryx, I'd raged and ranted at Uncle Mar, like the merest child.

We climbed to the high point in the miserable road, began the long descent toward Shar's Cross, and the cutoff to Cumber Gap.

No wonder they all saw me as a youngsire; I acted the child. But that was no excuse, I was grown, or near so. Wasn't I?

Or was I . . . Unpalatable as the idea might seem, I seized on it. Did a man's feeling in my loins necessarily make me a man?

Bayard and my cousins were married, and considered adult,

though no older than I. True, Mar supervised his son's holdings, gave him to spend, collected his debts. But that was because Uncle Mar was overbearing, not because he saw Bayard as yet a youth.

A haze of doubt, nonetheless. I sucked at it greedily. If I were boy yet, and not man, I could lay down some smidgen of my burden. It would be pleasant to be cared for, if only for a while.

Slipping from the saddle, I jerked myself awake and clung to Ebon's mane. Be careful, Roddy. But hurry. You want to catch up to them before—

A bird screamed in the night, and I with him. I lashed Ebon's flank, and we thundered under the dark canopy. Did a demon lurk, waiting to seize me, eat my liver while I thrashed in helpless agony? Rustin, I'll say anything, do anything, for the comfort of your arm. Hester—even you. Feed me warm soup, tell me all will be well . . .

"Aiyee!" A smashing blow to my chest. I toppled head over heels off Ebon's rump, landed with a thud. Ebon galloped on, but the sound of his step slowed.

I lay still, too terrified to look. What imp of the night had clubbed me from my saddle? Had he fangs, rending teeth? Wicked claws? Trembling, I buried my head under my hands. So much for an end to cowardice.

No.

Cowardice was in my acts, not my fears.

I gritted my teeth, forced my glance upward. No imp. No prancing demon. Nothing, save the low-hanging branch that had knocked me from my mount.

Groaning, I got to my feet. "Ebon!" I staggered down the road. "Horse, where are you?" Ten steps, in dark. Fifty. "Cursed beast, foul hateful thing, stop hiding! You evil spawn of a mule and—oh, bless you. Hold still, boy. Wait." I clutched the pommel, rested my head against Ebon's side, waited 'til the pounding of my heart slowed.

Aching from chest to spine, head to toe, I slowly climbed upon my patient stallion. "On, boy. But not so fast." I clicked my teeth, jerked the reins. We cantered on. I bent my legs, leaned low, rested my head on Ebon's mane.

The moon floated high. At first it meant an end to my fears, but eventually the shadows took on renewed menace. Jouncing in the saddle, I squinted at shapes I couldn't make out, flinched when the breeze caused one of them to move.

From time to time I slowed Ebon to a walk, to conserve him. A cold wind pierced my every pore, and was all that kept me awake. Once, when the stream came close to the road, I got down to drink, but managed only a few mouthfuls before dread overcame my thirst. Only Hester knew which part of the forest was benign, and which swallowed adventurers in the night.

Kicking at the stirrup to remount, I clung to Ebon until a wave of giddiness passed. The ache of my empty stomach merged with my other miseries.

We cantered on down the road. I grew more fearful with each passing moment. Unless I found Hester's cart, I'd be begging on the pike, and I suspected the country folk would give me short shrift.

Why hadn't I the sense to chase after Rust and Hester the day they'd left? I'd have avoided my humiliation by Danar. Even now, the memory of washing my clothes drove me near tears. "Ebon, why didn't I realize?"

Because you're a young fool, he said in horse talk, through my grip on his mane. A child in man's garb. An insolent youth.

I tried constantly to shift my weight; I was saddle sore, and my damp breeches chafed my thighs.

Riding as if in a dream, an eerie landscape floating past, I clung to Ebon 'til at last the road joined a wider path. Dizzy, I groped for direction.

Shar's Cross lay ahead, and past it, the way back to Stryx. Cumber lay at the end of the other fork. I had but to follow the stream, the same one that chuckled past Hester's cottage.

Why was I confused? I'd been here but a few scant days past, to sell my sword—Rustin's sword. I flushed. I'd been so arrogant, and to make it worse I'd spurned his protest.

We hurried on, into the dawn. After a time I was sure I'd chosen the right road; Shar was nowhere to be seen. But where were my companions? Surely they'd stopped for the night, and in that case I should be upon them. Had they turned off the road; would I miss them entirely?

It was a chance I couldn't take, and in any event I was reeling with exhaustion. I walked Ebon awhile, dismounted, walked him some more. Then I loosened his saddle, hobbled him to graze, sank to the ground, my back against a tree. If the cart rumbled past, I'd hear it. If not, I'd ride on, after a while.

I closed my eyes.

The sun was high in the sky when I awoke, refreshed but weak. "Come, Ebon." I tightened the cinches, hanging on to him for support. For a moment I thought I'd be unable to climb into the saddle, but with a great lunge I threw myself onto my stallion, held on while the dizziness faded. I would have to find food, ere long.

I kept a steady pace, drowsing while we rode. Ebon knew enough to follow the road, so long as there wasn't a choice of paths.

What woke me, of late afternoon, was a waft of smoke. My mouth watered. Perhaps someone was cooking, and I could beg his hospitality. Perhaps I'd ride into his camp, snatch up his dinner, gallop away. I only knew that I wouldn't leave hungry.

"Who goes!"

Ebon reared. I clutched his mane and the pommel, desperate to keep my balance. My half-sword flapped uselessly at my side.

"You!" Fostrow gazed in astonishment.

"Me." I soothed Ebon while my own heart's pounding eased.

His face neutral, the soldier took a step back, gestured me past.

They'd made camp alongside the road, not far from the splash of the stream. The dray horses were unhitched and tethered, Genard sound asleep under the wagon. I dismounted, rubbed my raw thighs.

Elryc, propped against a wheel, glanced up. "Hello, Roddy. Why is your shirt scorched?" Was he glad to see me? Or even surprised? I had no way to tell.

"Where's Hester?"

"I'm here." She stepped round the cart, with an armful of firewood. "Why did you come?" She set down her load.

"Yes, tell us." Rustin poked his head over the side of the wagon. His manner seemed distant.

I shrugged. "Tantroth's men may be about, or brigands. You might need help."

"We don't." Hester's voice was flat.

"I realized I kept the half-sword, and you'd probably want another. Besides . . ." Her eyes were stony. I ground to a halt.

I turned to Rustin, searching for some sign of compassion.

"Well, I'll leave it for you." I unbuckled the scabbard, laid it on the grass. "That's all I came for." A moment's pause, while none protested my departure. Desperate, I blurted, "Rust, could you give me another chance?"

He seemed startled, and I fastened on it as a sign of hope. "I'm sorry, Rust. I don't know what to do." To me it sounded as if I'd explained all, but they merely looked puzzled.

I turned to Hester. "I'm so tired, and hungry enough to . . ." I took a tentative step her way, stopped when she made no response. "Please. I guess I've made rather a mess of things." I sat, or perhaps my legs gave way. "I'm confused. Nothing goes as it should, or as I intend." I wiped my cheek, found my hand damp.

Rustin climbed down from the cart. Hester and Elryc drifted closer.

"I'll renounce, for Elryc. I'm too clumsy to be King, and too cruel. I just want to be a man." My throat hurt, as if Danar had hold of my tongue. "But, you see, I don't . . . seem . . . to know how."

Rust knelt at my side.

"I thought I did, but . . . nothing works." My voice caught, and with an effort I brought it under control. "I say stupid things I don't mean, or perhaps I mean them, I don't know; I'm spiteful and nasty and—"

Out tumbled thoughts I hadn't known I felt, drawn by Rustin's somber gaze. "If I'm left alone I'll die, or kill myself to put an end to it. I'm lonely and tired. And scared; the fear eats at me and I—"

Rust's hand fell on my locks, in a gentle caress.

Reluctantly, as if denying I yearned for the peace he offered, I let my forehead rest on his shoulder. "Please, Rust, teach me to be a man."

He gathered me into his arms, rocked.

"Please." My arms crept round him, and I began to sob.

"Please."

The shadows lengthened. I sniffled, wiped my nose. In silence, Hester limped to the cart, conjured a loaf of bread from some hidden recess, proffered it.

I tore off a huge chunk, stuffed it in my mouth, chewed only long enough to swallow, broke off another. Pieces and crumbs fell from my lips. I was aware of Rust's bemused expression, but was too famished to care. Only when I was too dry to swallow did I slow my ravening.

Genard handed me water; I drank until the vessel was drained. With a sigh, I laid my head again on Rust's shoulder. "Thank you." I studied Hester's face. "May I stay?"

Her eyes shut briefly, as if in pain. "Not as before."

"Rust, I'm sorry I called you traitor. I won't ever—"

His voice was gentle. "Did you mean it, about teaching you to be a man?"

Less famished now, my weakness abating, I faltered. Could I not manage on my own, if I were more careful, more . . .

The sadness in his eyes pierced my very essence. With a deep breath, I plunged into unfathomed waters. "Yes, I meant it."

"You'd put yourself in my charge, for that purpose?"

Resolutely, I cast aside my doubts. "I swear it by the True, Rust."

"Then, make your peace with the others."

I turned to the old woman. "Hester, I'm sorry if I was out of sorts before you left."

Rust shook me gently. "You've been awful, Roddy. That isn't enough."

"I don't owe her—oh, all right. I apologize, Hester." I glanced at Rustin for a sign of approval. Instead he got to his feet, took my hand, led me away from the camp. When we reached a grove of beeches, far from the others, he said, "It won't do."

"I did what you—"

"I won't play games, my prince. Do as I say, or I'll turn from you and never look back."

A chill stabbed at my spine. I nodded meekly, trudged back to the glade.

Elryc regarded me solemnly, from a perch atop the wagon. Fostrow sat at the fire, eyes elsewhere.

"Nurse Hester . . ." My tone was hesitant. "What has gone wrong, between us?"

"What has not?"

"Tell me."

"You lazed about the cottage, while the others broke their backs to—"

"It was wrong." I swallowed. An apology showed weakness, yet, oddly, I felt none the worse for it. "I've been wrong about many things."

"Easy to say it, now you're starving. What of tomorrow, when your odious character asserts itself?"

My brow wrinkled. "What did I—"

"Oaf! Lout!" She skewered me with a glare. "Such a fine little boy you were. A bouquet of daisies in your chubby hands, for Nursie, oh, yes. But as you grew lanky you jeered, mocked, imitated me behind my back, thinking I was too stupid to see your reflection or your shadow."

"Dame Hester, I—"

"Aping my ways, mimicking my tone to your sniggering cousins, in that terrible shrill voice that was an echo of my own! It's an old throat I have, and sore! Do you think I've aged so by choice?"

"Nurse . . ."

"Yes, my knees are old and my back crooked. It got so from lifting small royal boys and soothing their hurts, dampening my blouse with their tears! Even my walk you mocked. Think you I didn't peer through my lady's window to watch you staggering across the garden, bent to one side, while Bayard and his ilk reeled with glee?"

Appalled, I motioned to Genard, to Elryc. "Please, leave us." They stood, wandered out of earshot. "Boys are cruel, I know, but—"

She cried, "I never deserved your hate!"

In lieu of answer, I reached to a tangled and overgrown bush, tugged on a shoot, lopped it off with my blade. I yanked off the leaves. "Over the years you've switched me many a time. Is there need again?" I thrust the stick into her hands. "Be my nurse once more, and take my woes from me."

For a moment her visage remained stern, then she wavered. "Oh, Roddy." She let fall the switch.

"It wasn't just boys' cruelty. As I grew, I hated you for doing what Mother would not: You raised me, Dame Hester, and gave me love and caring that I craved from her. Perhaps she was too busy with matters of state; I'll never know."

"She loved you." Hester limped slowly to the cart, eased herself onto the backboard. "But it was to me she admitted it. 'Twas Elryc got

the embraces, the ruffling of the hair, the daily reminders of her concern. I urged her to show you more affection, but she found it trying."

I came near. "In Mother's memory, have pity, if naught else. I'll give
Caledon to Elryc; I want no more of—"

"Don't be a fool." Her tone was gruff.

"Anyway, no one would have me King. If I'm crowned, they'll kill
me, or set me off the throne." I pondered. "I don't understand why I'm
so unliked, but I recognize it's so."

"That's a start."

"Hester, after my insults and my gibes I can't ask that you love me,
but—" I extended my hand.

She slapped away my fingers. "Of course I'm enraged with you—
who would not be?" A long pause. At last, the set of her face softened.
"But I've always loved you, from the time I dandled you on the knee
that jounced baby Elena, in her time." Her voice quavered. "A daughter she was to me, so long past. But I've had no sons, Rodrigo of
Caledon, save you and your brothers."

I looked up, hoping beyond hope. She nodded, and I fell at her
knees. She seized my face in her lap, swaying and crooning, patting my
neck with cold wrinkled fingers. "There, there, Roddy. It will be well."
She hummed fragments of the tune she'd used to put me to sleep.

After a moment I glanced upward. My voice came shy. "I was helpless, when you rode from the cottage."

"I know."

"Why did you leave, then?"

"In hope that you'd follow." Her old eyes met mine. "Else all was
lost."

"All?"

"Your chance to grow to a decent man. The crown, that my lady
wanted—wants you to have. So." She cleared her throat. "We'll have no
more talk of renunciation."

I sighed. "I doubt I'm fit—"

"But you will be." The ghost of a smile. "Rustin will see to it, if not
I." She gestured. "And he awaits." It was a dismissal.

Shyly, I went to Rust.

He turned my shoulders, pointed me to Elryc. "He's next."

Sighing, I approached my brother, making the bow of courtesy, that any man might give another, regardless of rank. "If I've wronged you, brother, I'm sorry."

He looked away. "You've been yourself. Is that a wrong?"

"Apparently." I considered. "I swore to protect you, and let you ride off without—"

"I had them to defend me." His eyes were solemn, and a touch hard. "If you would redeem a promise, choose the more important."

"Which is?"

"The one you made when I was ill."

My tone was puzzled. "At the inn? All I said was . . . Oh!" I shifted from foot to foot. "Elryc, I'm sorry."

My young brother clenched my shirt in his chubby fists. "Don't offer a 'sorry'! Keep what promises you made!"

I thrust down my ire. He had cause to upbraid me, for a vow cast aside. I made the short bow of contrition. "Elryc, if I reign, you'll rule beside me at my right hand as the Duke of Stryx. Though I have to admit that at the moment it seems unlikely."

His eyes softened.

"And I'll rely on your wisdom, where mine fails." I dropped my hands, said simply, "Forgive me, brother."

"Oh, Roddy." He banged his head against my shoulder, as if annoyed, but his cheeks were damp. Then, a quick pat, and he was gone.

Satisfied, I returned to Rustin.

"Now the others." He flicked a thumb at Genard and Fostrow.

"Is this to humiliate me?" My voice held no protest; I was merely curious.

"No, Roddy. You've done them ill."

"What of it? They're servants!"

"Call Genard here, and repeat that."

"I see what you mean; he'd be miffed to hear it, but—"

"At once!" Rust's voice was hard.

I thought to rebel, quashed the impulse. My vow had been given, and I'd been inconstant enough. With a sigh, I did as he bade.

Genard but shrugged. "Is there anything else, m'lord?" He addressed Rustin rather than me.

"What would you say to Prince Rodrigo?"

"I won't rebuke my betters." His tone was sullen.

"You have our leave." Rustin eyed him coolly. "Go on, get it said."

"You hit me the last time I—all right." The boy glowered. "I'm just a servant, to him. Stableboy or prince's liegeman, it's all the same from his vantage. I'm as the straw in Ebon's stall: I'm there, but of no concern."

I nodded agreement. "Don't take it personally. Highborn can't worry themselves about the gripes of mere churls. What matter, if—"

His eyes flashed. "Why not?"

"Oh, Genard." I tried to control my exasperation. "You don't understand. We can't be bothered. In the great scheme of things, your kind doesn't count!"

His jaw quivered with suppressed emotion as he planted himself before me, hands on hips. "Why not?"

"Because—Rust, this is ridiculous—you just don't, Genard. You're peasants, churls. You're nothing."

He bared his teeth, stabbed a finger into my chest. "I am not nothing!" Amazed, I fell back. "I signify, to Lord of Nature, if not you!"

"Genard!"

"M'lord, was a time I worshiped the ground you trod. 'Fore I knew you, that is. You have a noble face, and walked so proud. Would I never learned what you were!"

"Can I help the way of things? Is it my fault you're of no consequ—"

"What if Genard's right?" From behind me, a quiet voice.

"Eh, Rust?" My brows knitted. "Where do you get such ideas? Should we beg their consent to govern, as well? What then the rights of kings?" I shook my head. "No, be sure that—"

Rust crossed to Genard, set his hand on the boy's shoulder. "He is not a 'nothing.' A true and loyal servant, and a boy of courage. So you'll apologize to him."

"To a churl? That's altogether uncalled for."

"Roddy." His voice was low, and I sensed menace.

My own fault; I'd let myself in for it, by my promise. I sighed. "Genard, I apologize for calling you nothing."

"And for treating him like dirt, these last weeks."

"And for treating you like dirt." My cheeks flamed.

"And you'll try to do better."

I scuffled the sod. "I'll try to do better. Enough, Rust."

"Leave us, Genard." The boy scurried off. "You will think on this conversation tonight, Roddy. Agreed?"

"How could I not?" My tone was hot with anger. "You made me grovel—" I swallowed. Lord of Nature, it was hard, keeping an oath rashly made. "All right, Rust."

"Good." We walked back to the cart. "Get your bed ready near mine." He fished in his belongings, tossed me a slab of soap. "You'll bathe."

"I'm really exhausted and—"

"Every day."

"Rust, that's—be reasonable!"

"Without fail. It's best if you stay on the bank, and dip the soap. The stream's quite cold." He glanced at the moon. "You'd best get started."

"But—"

Without warning he charged, slammed me against the cart, knocking my breath from me. "Can you not keep a vow for so much as an hour? Are you so untrue as that? Why then did you set yourself in my care? Would you I went back to Stryx, and left you to your schemes and evasions?"

"No!"

His face blazed. "Then for once in your young foolish life, do as you're told!"

"Yes, Rust!" I snatched up a flannel to use as a drying cloth, and fled.

After, I lay shivering under my blankets. "Is this a form of torture, until you're revenged?" My tone was forlorn.

"Hmm?" Rustin came awake. "Of course not."

Unseen in the dark, I grimaced. Freezing from my unwanted bath, flopping in Rust's overlarge borrowed clothes, I'd been sent to make humble apologies to Fostrow and Chela. The soldier was gracious enough, clapped me on the shoulder with what he imagined an encouraging gesture. The girl, in obvious pain from her ribs, nodded and asked me to send Rust to her.

My humiliation this night was almost as great—not quite, but nearly—as that visited by Danar. Yet, for reasons I understood not, I felt little the worse for it. I even realized a dim sense of pride, that I'd endured a grim and unpleasant task, and kept my vow besides.

What was Rustin to me, that I'd so put myself in his hands? Was he not son of a traitor, to be despised by all? With callous disregard, he'd abandoned me. Why then did I bask in his approval, fret over his impatience?

Rust scrunched his blanket closer to mine, raised himself up. "Roddy, though this time is hard for you . . ."

After a time I prompted, "Yes?"

"Know that I love your life more than mine." He turned on his side.

Warmed by I know not what, I slept.

Chapter 20

THE MORNING CAME COLD AND CLEAR. I HELPED HESTER
stow her gear. "How far to Cumber, Nurse?"

"In the cart, two days."

"How will the Earl receive us?"

"Who can say? He's a man of pride. We'll play on that, to ask his
beneficence."

I brooded. "Better the Prince of Caledon came as his equal, if not
his liege."

She sighed. "Don't start that again, Roddy."

While Fostrow made himself busy harnessing the team; I sat on a
rock, pondering. The more I mused, the more uneasy I was about our
course. How to convince them? Rust first, I decided. I'd have to tread
warily; he took offense at the merest trifles.

I approached cautiously. "Rust . . . we should—" I sighed, tried
again. "Even if I'm young and foolish, cannot I be right on occasion?"

"It's not beyond possibility." His smile vanished as he saw my
expression. "What troubles you, my prince?"

"Cumber." I twisted my fingers. "You haven't dined at Stryx as I
have, when he came to visit Mother. The Earl's . . . well, haughty. That
simpering valet accompanies him everywhere, and the two of them
turn up their noses at everyone. We can't go to him as beggars."

Rust waited patiently.

"He's allied with Mar, on the Council, and thinks little enough of me. If we stumble into his domain without even food to sustain us, he'll have no grounds to think I'll ever gain the crown."

"Roddy, we have no choice; we're destitute. Later, we can—"

"We have means. Excuse me for interrupting. There's coin that's rightfully ours. I want us—don't look at me that way, Rust, I beg you. Hear me out."

He sighed. "Go on."

I told him my plan.

After, he sat silent, his legs swinging from his perch. "Interesting. But why?"

"He owes us. And besides—" I broke off, looked to the ground. "Honor is involved."

"How?"

"Don't ask, I beseech you." My ears reddened. "It's something I want never to speak of. Rustin, trust me this once."

His eyes narrowed. "Did Danar hurt you?"

"I . . . not really." I scuffed my feet. "In a way. It's just—please, Rustin!"

Again he pondered, while I waited in an agony of impatience. Then, "All right."

My heart leaped.

"Your words convince me less than your manner. Not unless you were certain would you take such pains to persuade me. Not to Queen Elena herself did you show such courtesy as today."

"Thank you." My tone was humble.

He clasped me round the shoulder, hugged me as we walked. "At times I've hope for you. Hester, a change of plans. Fostrow, we must ride back. You, I, and Roddy."

"But, why?"

"A certain matter left unattended. Hester, would you tarry here, or drive on? Should Elryc ride with us, or remain underfoot?"

She scowled. "Do you lead this party, Rustin son of Llewelyn?"

"No, madam, but I must leave you, for some hours. What is your pleasure?"

Another frown. "Honeyed words of a transparent boy." Yet, sighing, she got down from the wagon. "Elryc, gather more kindling. I'll be wanting tea while we wait."

*　　*　　*

I was fortunate in wearing Rustin's loose clothes on the journey back to Fort, else my chafed thighs would have been in agony. As it was, I endured intense discomfort, made worse as the leagues mounted.

Still fatigued from my sleepless nights and wild ride to find the cart, I let Rustin set our pace. By day, the forest seemed harmless; imaginings add spice to a night passage.

Nonetheless, by midafternoon, when we paused on the ridge overlooking Fort, I was twisting sorely in the saddle, easing the pressure on my groin and buttocks at every opportunity.

"Not much farther, my prince."

"There's the ride back." My tone was gloomy.

"But we might have coin to cheer the journey." Rust held out his hand. "The half-sword, if you please."

Reluctantly, I unbuckled it. "I've a good lunge. Couldn't I—"

"No." He waited until I'd handed it over. "You'll carry the stick."

Disconsolate, I unlaced Fostrow's walking stick from my saddle. No fit weapon that, for a prince royal.

"You'll have your dagger as well." If he meant it as consolation, it failed. Little good my dagger had been, when Danar's man had felled me.

A half hour later we paced our mounts through the widened trail that served as Fort's only street, and turned off to the mill. Rust rode almost to the cabin before dismounting. In the clearing, at the mill's tie rail, two mules were tethered.

"Hold your temper, Fostrow, and watch for my lead."

"Aye, Lord Rustin."

"Prepare yourself, Rodrigo."

I retrieved the bundle from my saddlebag, clutched it tight.

"Now, then." Rust led us to the porch steps, and up to the mill floor. Hand on his sword, he swung open the door.

Danar was tending the spinning stone, and having words with two peasants who stood nearby, caps in hand. His man Jom was hard at work sweeping chaff from the floor.

Danar's glance lifted; his face tightened at the sight of us. "Jom, call Pern and Vassur. Run along, now." His words carried over the incessant rumble of the wheel.

"Aye, sir." Jom beat a hasty retreat, from a door to the rear.

"Why come you armed?" If afraid, Danar did a good job hiding it. "Do me harm, fellow, and the town will—"

"We've not come to do you injury."

"What then?"

The rear door burst wide; in scrambled two burly workmen, faces flushed. Jom followed, more slowly. Did I recognize the heavyset one, by his bulk? I tried to imagine him in dark garb, and hooded.

The two peasants retreated to the wall, edged toward the door.

Rustin paid them no heed. "Danar, you owe a debt to Dame Hester."

"That again? I told you: I've not a pence to give her, and owe her less. Say to her—why draw you a sword?" Quickly Danar stepped back among his henchmen.

"Fostrow, let's be about it." Rust took a step.

"Hold!" Danar's face had a glint of perspiration, whether from fear or labor I couldn't yet tell. "You men are witness, if he lays hand on me."

Rustin said, "We bring you to the King's justice."

"Hah; what King? Until one's chosen, there's—"

"Now, my lord." Rustin.

In nervous haste, I unwrapped the gleaming crown, placed it on my head.

Rust said, "You are in the presence of Rodrigo of Caledon, Prince and heir! Make you obeisance."

The miller's burly confederate would have bowed, but Danar stayed him with a gesture. "This boy? The one we . . ." For a moment his face paled, but he rallied. "Bah! Rue the day that such as he takes the throne. And uncrowned, he wields no authority. These are the domains of our Lord Cumber."

My voice was cold. "Seize him."

"You can't! Vassur, Pern, hold them back." The fat miller sweated freely now. "You're an outcast. Anyway, you can't drag me back to Stryx; Fort belongs to Cumber."

"Uncle Cumber embodies my crown's justice. We'll bring you before him, by force if we must. Or kill you if you flee."

Danar licked his lips. "What charge do you lodge? I knew not your rank when—"

"Your assault on me is of no consequence. We charge you with fraud on Dame Hester, while she was member of the Queen's Household, and therefore assault on good Queen Elena herself. With arson, to Hester's cottage."

"I was in Shar that day!"

"This man will say otherwise, I'll warrant." I gestured at his accomplice. "When the Earl puts him to question." I held Danar's eyes, and assayed a smile. My tension was such that it was surely a leer. It chilled even me.

Vassur spun and bolted from the room.

Rust held up a hand. "No matter, my prince. He'll be found, or be cried outlaw. His goods and land are confiscated, for the fleeing."

"Aye. And also the miller's, unless he comes with us of his own accord." I looked about, as if calculating the worth of the place.

"Let these townsmen go." The miller indicated the two farmers, who stood mesmerized by Fostrow's flicking sword. "I'll have your grain tomorrow. This can be resolved—please, have them go."

Rust nodded; Fostrow stepped aside.

The townsmen fled.

Danar wiped his brow. "A warm day. Surely, my lords, honest men can clear a misunderstanding. Let me review again—"

"He refuses." Rust turned to Fostrow. "Seize and bind him. I'll take stock of the goods and chattels."

"My lord, please! Let us settle this affair!"

"Too late. The matter's before the Earl."

For a moment, Danar found his bluster. "Have you warrant?"

My tone was lofty. "*I* am warrant; Cumber does the crown's justice in *my* name."

"It's not proper, not legal. I'm entitled—"

"Uncle Cumber doesn't fuss with niceties, when justice is at stake. Surely you knew that?" I doubted Great-uncle Cumber paid much mind to justice, or anything else, unless his flowerbeds were at issue.

"My lords, the town has need of me." Danar's eye sought a compassionate face. "It's harvest and the farmers' grain awaits. Let me settle to the good dame's satisfaction. She claims she's sent thirty-six silver pence, over the last nine years time. If I pay—"

Rustin said, "Treble that would make a hundred eight."

"Treble?" The man's voice shot into the upper registers, as my own was wont, at times of excitement. His face paled, then purpled. "A hundred eight silvers?"

"Of course not. A hundred twelve. Dame Hester's, plus one for each of us who served charges against you, and the last to feed the horses."

"I haven't that much in the whole world—" He broke off. "How could you demand three times her claim?"

"It's low, I'll admit. We'll ask Lord Cumber for five, but as we haven't yet been put to the trouble . . ."

"My lords, be reasonable!" Danar looked to Jom for support, then Pern.

"And then there's the arson." Rust was relentless. "We waste our time, Danar."

"How so?"

"As you've said, you haven't that much in the world. After all, how could an honest miller accumulate such a treasure? So, make yourself ready; we leave within the hour."

Danar licked his lips, turned his gaze from one to the other of us, and back. "Assuming I could—mind you, I had nothing to do with the firing of her cottage—if I could contribute some small measure . . ."

"Treble the cost of repair should amount to, let's see . . ."

Danar moaned, leaned against a pillar, clutched his chest as if a great force had squeezed his heart. I adjusted my crown, hoping he'd fall to the floor and die. Unfortunately, he rallied. "My lords, have mercy on a poor man."

Rust's tone rang contemptuous. "Mercy is for Lord Cumber to bestow. We but seek accounting."

"Treble." A groan.

Fostrow said mildly, "Only double, on the repairs to the cottage. It leaves you coin to give to the family of your accomplice who died."

"They're living with Vas—I had no accomplice! I mean, I wasn't involved—Pern, a chair, and be quick." The miller's face was ashen.

Rust said, "Roddy—my prince—bring him water, if you please."

Grumbling, I took a pitcher, went outside to the stream. Here I wore the crown itself, and Rust sent me on errands as if . . . I sighed.

Back in the mill, I handed Danar the pitcher. He grabbed it without seeing me, drank deep. His color began to return. "It's settled at a hundred, my lords? I'll want a writing that absolves me of any claim by Hester."

Rust's mouth was cruel. "How can it be settled, miller? You said you hadn't so much in all the world."

"And I don't. But I'll borrow, work my life away to free myself from the clutches of that vile witch."

I smashed the pitcher from his grip; it shattered on the hardwood floor. "Dame Hester was my nurse, and my brothers'! Speak of her with respect."

Rustin interposed himself. "Well said, my prince." Using his body as a shield from the miller's sight, he shoved me backward with force. "I pray you, sire, rest yourself on the porch, while we attend to the bothersome details." His glare made unmistakable his command.

Nonchalantly, but without delay, I retreated. "Call me when you're finished, Lord Rustin." I went outside to fume.

After a while the three of them came forth, crossed to the house. Rustin took station at the front door, Fostrow at the rear, while the miller disappeared within. A few moments later he emerged bearing a purse, which he handed Rust.

While Rustin counted, the miller glanced about cautiously, shifting from foot to foot with impatience. "Begone, I pray thee, my lords. If ruffians and brigands find I've kept silver in the premises, our very lives won't be safe."

"Surely you couldn't have more hidden?" Without waiting for answer Rust crossed to the mill, bowed to me low. "We're ready when it pleases you, my prince."

"Now isn't soon enough." Proudly, I stalked down the trail, wishing my breeches didn't chafe.

We untied our horses, clattered down the road toward the highlands. Once out of sight, we slowed our pace. Finally we reached the road to Shar's Cross. We stopped, to rest the animals.

"Let me see." I held out my palm. Rustin took the fingers of both my hands, made of them a cup, poured in the silver coins. Greedily, I let them tinkle from hand to hand. "A hundred silvers." Three years stipend; many times the sum Willem had given me that I'd lost to the wasps.

"Aye." Rust held open the purse.

Reluctantly, I poured them back in. "I'll warrant he had another fifty, hid well. You should have run him through, for the way he spoke of Hester. Why'd you silence me?"

"You've called her worse." He closed the purse, knotted it on his rope belt, twisted it inside his breeches. "Roddy, we went for coin, not revenge. Is it not so?"

"Yes, but—"

"It's a failing you have. You think more of the moment's concern than your prime purpose." His manner was stern.

I flushed at the rebuke. Who was he, to—I sighed. The vow. "I'm sorry, Rust."

"What if he'd gone hard, and let us take him to Cumber? We'd turned his archers and were sweeping the field. It wasn't time to send the horsemen on a wild new quest." He softened his words by a sudden and unexpected kiss, on my forehead. "You did well, when you donned the crown. I was proud of you."

When his back was turned I wiped the kiss, vaguely uneasy. It wasn't meet that I hunger so for his praise.

"Why can't I carry the purse?" I mounted Ebon.

Rustin grinned. "I can't trust you with it." I had no way to tell if he spoke seriously.

We trotted together, ahead of Fostrow. "All ends well," I mused. "Hester will have her recompense, enough to rebuild and furnish her cottage. Half the purse, I should say. And I lost about twenty silvers in the glade." I calculated. "That leaves thirty."

"Fifty." Rust stayed my protest. "The purse is for our mutual needs. What's that sullen look? Would you rather the purse, or me? You have the choice."

I gritted my teeth, kept my voice meek. "You."

"Thank you."

"It was a close decision." I allowed myself that, but no more.

It was near nightfall when we reached the turn to Cumber. Rust ignored it, swept on toward Shar.

"Do we stay in the inn?"

"No."

"Then why the town?"

"An errand." His lips were tight. Mystified, I glanced to Fostrow, who shrugged.

At the edge of Shar's Cross Rustin opened the purse, counted out a few coins, tied them in his shirt, concealed again the purse.

"Where go we?"

"The smith." Rust's eyes were hard. "He has my sword."

I paced alongside. "But the purse is for our mutual needs."

"We have need of a sword."

"Not so fine a one. For the five silvers he gave me, you can buy—"

"Roddy, shut thy mouth, as you value life." His tone brooked no defiance.

I fidgeted outside, with Fostrow, while Rust negotiated. At last he emerged, sword in scabbard. "It cost me eight."

"Outrageous! Think of the food and clothing such a sum would buy."

Rust's fist knotted, unclenched. "Have you ever been beaten? I must tell you, my prince, you're near to the event." He mounted, wheeled away.

"Fostrow, what's come over him?"

The soldier shrugged. "He's rather put out with you."

"Bah. I knew that much." I spurred, caught up with Rustin, rode in silence at his side.

Sometimes, there was no accounting for his moods.

Chapter 21

BY THE TIME WE REACHED CAMP IT WAS TOO LATE TO travel, so we made ready for night. Hester took her share of the purse, and walked with lighter step, her face actually dissolving from time to time into a smile. Twice she hugged Elryc, and spoke with less than her customary tartness to me.

Rust spent an hour with Chela. The girl seemed to be holding her own, despite days in a wagon. Hester had her bundled tight with blankets against the cool night air.

Over the campfire, we agreed on another trip to Shar's Cross, to purchase the best available in clothing and supplies, and perhaps a gift or two for Lord Cumber, even though the digression would cost us a day on the road.

I got ready for bed, after another miserable ordeal at the freezing stream. I'd have left it to the morrow, but Rustin gave me a scathing lecture about smell and dirt and promises, after which I thought it best to comply. After that, I was anxious to curl under my blanket.

Though I soon fell asleep, imps and demons came in the night to dance their cruel frolic in my mind. I woke in terror, crying, clutching the rolled shirt I used as a pillow. Before my fright subsided Rust was out of bed, blanket wrapped over his shoulders, to soothe me. For reasons I didn't fathom, I had more tears left in me, and expended them while Rust pillowed my head in his lap, gently stroking my face. It was thus I fell asleep once more.

Came morning, I felt ill at ease, especially in Rust's presence. I'd abdicated my manhood to his tutelage, and in the process, I'd revealed far more of myself than was proper.

After breakfast, Rust conferred with Hester on purchases, while Genard saddled Santree and Fostrow's mare. To please Rust, I didn't demand Genard take care of Ebon, but fetched his saddle myself.

Rust came up behind me, leading Santree. "Roddy, it's best you wait here while we go to town. They'll need a man to guard them, if Fostrow and I—"

"I won't wait behind with the children and an old woman. Besides, if not for my plan, you'd have no coin to spend."

He caught my arm, swung me round. "You'll remain." His eyes glinted with the first sparks of temper.

"No."

"By Lord of Nature, Llewelyn would beat me within an inch of my life for insolence such as yours!"

I grappled with my vow, but the provocation was too great. "You're not my father!"

"Father, elder brother, what does it matter? Did you put yourself under my care?"

I shouted, "Yes, and I beg you as once you begged me: Release me from my oath!"

He said instantly, "Done." I gaped, but he swung into the stirrups. "You and Fostrow do as you wish. I'm bound for Stryx. Fare thee well."

"Rustin!"

"Good-bye, my prince." His eyes glistened. "I tried, truly I did."

"Wait!"

"Why?"

"I just—I don't know. Wait a bit." I turned away, hugging myself, battling rage and fear. I didn't need him. If ever I were to be a man, I must throw aside his influence, stand on my own. I knew I could do it.

But not yet.

"Please, Rust." I struggled to meet his eyes. "Go with Fostrow. I'll wait here."

"And your oath?"

"I'll keep it. I didn't mean for you to release me."

He leaned over the pommel, stern. "I won't have your distrust, Roddy. Or your sullenness."

I nodded.

"I'm not your father, but you had none when needed. So for the moment, I'll do a father's task. Understand?"

"Yes, Rust."

He climbed down. "Put your hands at your sides." I complied. He slapped me hard. "At your sides!" Again. My head rocked. Once more he struck me, his palm echoing on my cheek like a clap of thunder. Mortified, I sagged against a tree, seeking to control my sobs.

He gave me time, spoke to my back. "From now on you'll behave decently. Yes?"

It was all I could do to nod. Without further word he rode off. After a moment I heard Fostrow's mare, in pursuit.

When they returned, it was with a pack mule loaded with treasures. For me, a fine new cloak lined with silk, and breeches that might have been used, but had the look of quality. For Hester, a wondrous robe that made her eyes widen. After she donned it, even her knobbed walking stick didn't look so rustic as before. She bussed Rustin on the cheek, which caused him to flush crimson.

We unpacked dried meats and vegetables, wine and fruit, and a jeweled dagger with which to gift Lord Cumber. And fresh bread, which we demolished with our dinner.

At least we'd go into Cumber fed, rested, and dressed. Contemplating the visit, I felt much more hopeful.

Yet, for what had passed between us that morning, I was shy as a maiden with Rustin. I blushed at his glance, felt myself flustered by his conversation. Was he my friend, or mentor? Was I boy to his man? Could we have changed so?

That night, lying abed, my lust arose. After struggling to ignore it, I let my mind drift to Chela and her wiles, and let my body have its way. Afterward, the pleasure of my repose was soured; by his utter stillness I realized Rust had been awake and aware of my doings.

I writhed in an agony of embarrassment. When desire came upon him, Rustin had Chela to share his bed; how could he fathom my needs? If at the morn he spoke of the matter I'd pretend he was mistaken, and if not, what was one more humiliation to those I'd already suffered? I lay drowsing, wishing with all my heart the Still of Caledon required not such a burden of me, hoping against hope he'd somehow been truly asleep.

Morning came, and my mood was such that it was all I could do not to get myself slapped anew. As soon as I could, I took myself aside, pondered how to wrest myself from the clutches of my vow to Rust. It was intolerable to endure, from my erstwhile companion, the rebukes and torments I'd fled Stryx to avoid from Uncle Mar.

"Let's go, Roddy. Get Ebon bridled."

I stuck my tongue at Rust's retreating back, but picked up the tack. At least I was a slave by my own choice, rather than Mar's imperious will. Should that make me feel better? It didn't, really.

For two days we followed the stream, heading upward into the hills. There were no more inns on the way to Cumber.

At the second night's camp, Genard, Elryc, and I blundered about searching for downed limbs for the fire, while Rustin set our beds. The wind blew cool. I glanced skyward, hoping it wouldn't rain; I didn't relish crawling under the wagon to escape a downpour. As usual, Hester and Elryc were to share a canopy tent, in the cart.

Rust tossed me his soap. "You'd best wash, before you get too comfortable by the fire. You haven't bathed in two days."

"There wasn't time; we—"

"I made time. You chose to wait. Go on, now."

My lip curled. "If I say no?"

"Would you say no, Roddy?" He gazed at me curiously.

Furious at the constraint he lay upon me, I grabbed a drying cloth, dipped a torch in the fire for light. At the edge of the circle I paused. "Rust . . . do you hate me?"

"Why, I—of course not!" His look held something odd.

I snarled, "Don't ask me the same."

The pitch might have been damp; for whatever reason, the torch sputtered and hissed all the way to the gurgling stream, and while I was looking for a way to prop it, promptly went out. I cursed it roundly while my eyes became accustomed to the moonlight.

I sat on the bank over a deep pool swirling with eddies, pulling off my boots. The stream was far too cold to stand in. I'd have to lean over the bank, splash myself with the icy water, scrub myself, and rinse. Why couldn't he use common sense? This could easily wait until morning, when I'd have no need for a torch that wouldn't stay lit.

Perhaps Rust's fetish with washing wasn't all bad—even Chela had made a vile remark about my cleanliness, the night I'd gotten carried away and touched her. But I could attend to such matters without his bullying interference. It was time I faced up to the error I'd made. Rust was little more than a boy himself, and certainly unable to teach me anything I didn't already know about manliness.

In the cold breeze I peeled off my stockings, hurled them into the dirt. "Two days you've lorded it over me, Rust. It's enough!"

"You gave your oath." He'd speak without passion.

"I was wrong!"

"Does that excuse you?" I could picture the reproach in his tone.

"Oh, be silent!" I grabbed a stone, slung it against the rock that jutted from the pool. My missile flew apart with a satisfying smash. "Take that! And that!" The rock became Rust's face, and I gathered an armful of stones.

I leaned closer. "Bully me now, you—"

My foot slipped on the mossy bank. Flailing, I toppled into the frigid pool. I sank to the bottom, turning head over heels.

The cold struck like a blow. My stomach and groin knotted in pain. Disoriented, I kicked and twisted, not sure in the dark which way was up. At last, gravity made itself felt. I clawed my way upward, broke the surface with a bound, sucked for air.

"Help!" My voice was little more than a croak. I spat water, tried again. "Someone!" My feet were almost numb. Water bubbled and frothed in wavelets around my ears. I couldn't touch bottom.

Nor could I see the rock on which I'd left my boots; it took me a moment to realize the current had carried me some paces downstream. Here, the embankments were rocky and steep. Even at the edge, the water was over my head.

Teeth chattering, I lunged onto the rock, my sodden clothes dragging me back. Moss or algae had left the bank as slippery as glass.

"Help! Rust!" Desperate, I heaved myself out of the eddy, clung to the bank with aching fingers. Again, the water sucked me back.

The cold was agony that coursed through my torso. Bubbling water splashed in my nose. I choked, gasping and wheezing, pulled myself as high as I could. With all my strength, I couldn't climb as high as before.

"No! You can't have me!" I managed to get head and shoulders over the bank, clawed at the slippery slope. Inch by inch, I slid back. "Lord of Nature, I beg you." A sudden sharp pain in my fingernail, and I lurched backward. "Oh, no. Not like this.." I wondered whose voice babbled so. My teeth chattered.

"Stop dawdling, Roddy!"

Sorry, Mother. I was just learning to be a man.

"Roddy? Where are you!"

Here. Drowning.

"Genard! Elryc, come here! Roddy, what's happened to you!"

Feet appeared, over my head.

"Lord of Nature!" Hands, gripping mine. "Hang on!" The voice was Rustin's.

I roused myself. "I'm sorry . . . about the clothes."

"Arghh!" His face, red with effort, glinted in the moonlight. "Help me get you out!"

I kicked manfully, doing no good. Inch by inch, he drew me out of the water, scraped me across the slimy rock.

All at once I was lying facedown on the stone. Most of my body was numb.

"Get up! We have to go to the fire!"

"I c-c-can't." My teeth chattered too hard to speak.

With an oath he hauled me to a sitting position, stooped, managed to get me over his shoulder. He lurched to his feet.

"Boots." My arms twitched when I tried to move them.

"Later." He staggered through the trees, back to camp.

He dumped me by the campfire, raced to the wagon, snatched my blankets, ran back. I sat jerking and twitching. Frightened by my dissolution, I made a whimpering sound. Every pore of my body smarted as if seared.

Hester said, "Lord, what's he done?" Slowly, she climbed down from the wagon.

"We've got to get those clothes off you!" Rustin.

"I'm too cold." I hugged myself, against the convulsions of my muscles.

He ignored me, worked with Fostrow at peeling off my shirt.

"The wind!" My teeth rattled. "Please, Rust!"

"Get everything wet off him," said Hester. "Be quick."

"I know." Rust rolled me over, worked to pull off my soaking breeks. "You'll die of cold with these on."

Even after they unclothed me and bundled me into my blanket on the edge of the fire, I shivered uncontrollably, my limbs twitching. "I'm freezing, Rust." I took another sip of the hot tea Hester had concocted.

"I know." He brought over his own bedroll, threw it atop of me.

Even that wasn't enough. The night wind seemed to pierce my blankets, rekindle the fiery frost in my veins. I ought to don fresh clothes, but nothing short of the demons of the lake would thrust me from my covers. I put my icy hands between my legs to thaw them. "See what trouble your damned bathing makes?"

"It wasn't the . . ." A sigh. "You'll soon feel better."

The excitement past, the others drifted off to bed, while I lay freezing and miserable under our two bedrolls. Rust donned his cloak, sat close by the fire.

I regarded his back, with mixed emotions. He'd caused my accident, sending me off on a ridiculous errand in the dark. But then, he'd saved me. It canceled out. Well, perhaps if I hadn't bent to throw that last stone . . .

I couldn't leave him to sit all night. "Crawl under the blanket, Rust; maybe you'll warm me."

Silent, he crept behind me, under the outer cover, behind the inner. I shivered. His arms came around, hugged me. "The stream comes down from the top of Fort, where the ice never melts."

"I wonder why not." My voice was sleepy.

"The Ritemaster says that in the worst heat of summer's memory, no man saw Fort without snow."

"Definitely a Power." I cuddled his warm arm as a pillow, listened to the throb of his pulse. "I'm glad it was you who saved me."

Another hour, and I began to feel myself warm. Deliciously drowsy, I dozed to sleep.

Strange dreams, in the night. Mother wagged her finger. *You won't listen, Roddy. You don't try hard enough.*

Is that why you didn't show me love?

That time is past. Her face rippled, dissolved into Chela's. "This is now, Roddy. You're clean and manly and brave. Come to me."

Elryc and Genard snickered behind my back at my chastity. Mother spoke sharply to gain my attention; Chela prevailed. "Come to me, Lord Prince. Come . . ."

Not with Elryc watching. I sought a private place. I dreamed I became aroused, and worried who might notice. With maddening insistence, Chela beckoned. I threw aside my unknown Power, went to her, entered her with savage thrusts. "Yes," she hissed. "Be mine, Prince."

Coupling, groping, the swift spurts of satiation. She gasped with pleasure, squeezed me tight. "Stay inside me, Roddy. Hold me." I stroked her breasts, ecstatic that I'd become a man at last. In bliss, I drowsed in her arms, until she faded, and there was nothing but the crackle of the blaze, the stars overhead.

Sticky and content, I wriggled in the aftermath of pleasure, and felt Rustin's hands resting where they had no right to be.

Taut with alarm, I barely breathed. What had I done? Bad enough he knew of my habits; had I relieved myself in his very embrace? Yet I lay on my side, my hands high, cuddling my pillow; if my flesh had felt caresses, they weren't my own.

Cautiously, I stirred, dislodged his fingers, inched to the far side of the bedroll, wedged a blanket firmly between us.

In the morning, I wore the blanket as a cloak while I fished through Rustin's clothes and mine for garments. After, I spread my wet clothing on the cart's many boxes; perhaps by the morrow they'd be dry. When my eyes caught Rust's I blushed scarlet, quickly turned away.

We mounted, resumed our interminable journey. I felt the prickle of perspiration each time Rust came near. It wouldn't do; better to flee back to Fort than continue so. When we paused for food and rest I drew deep breaths, steeled myself, took him to sit aside from the others.

"Last night." My voice was an accusation.

"It took you a long while to warm. Sorry I didn't tend to your clothes."

"That's not what I speak of." I waited.

He raised an eyebrow. "Yes, Roddy?"

I couldn't help blushing anew. "I'm not Chela."

"Certainly not." He sat against a tree.

"Don't play games! You know what you did!"

"Yes, my prince." His sudden smile that heartened one as the sun after a cloudburst.

"How dare you touch me so!"

"You're angry." He pondered, brushing his lips with a twig. "Roddy, you burn. Oh, don't roll your eyes; it's plain to see. You're desperate for relief and the comfort of sharing, and you can't have it with women."

I snarled, "What business is it of yours?"

"Would you rather be alone? Until your Power is spent?"

"Yes!" That said, I took breaths, to consider. A pang of remembered bliss washed across my senses. When I'd awakened in his arms I'd felt no shame, until I realized what had passed. Then, I'd gone rigid with fear and dismay. I said, lamely, "It's my body, not yours!"

"Would you rather I never touch you again?"

"Never like that." I stood, having endured as much of such conversation as I could.

"Once, long ago, we spoke of such matters. I asked if you couldn't take a lover into your bed. 'A cook's boy?' you jeered. 'A sniggering stablehand?' Roddy, am I no better than those?" It was almost a plea.

"You make me your plaything! You wash me, rebuke me, kiss my forehead. Say you that your advances are for my sake alone?"

He looked away.

Afraid of his response, I couldn't leave it. "Answer!"

"No, my prince." His eyes met mine. "Not alone for your sake." My lips fell agape, and I stood like a village dimwit. He said resolutely, "I take joy in giving you pleasure. You are precious to me."

"Speak plainly!" I felt every inch the Prince of Caledon. "I command it!"

In one smooth motion he arose, came close. "I enjoy your touch, and touching you. It's my nature." His eyes were riveted to mine. "I've felt your attraction ever since I was aware of such things."

"What of Chela? Is she nothing?"

"Chela too. Cannot a man feel for women and prize your beauty?"

I should have been aghast, but his very soul sat in my hands, to dash or preserve. Gently, I said, "Rust . . . it isn't meet. What would Uncle Cumber think if he saw us hand in hand?"

He snorted. "The Earl has eyes only for his valet!"

"He what?" My voice rose to a squeak.

Rust regarded me curiously. "You didn't know? How could you not?"

"How was I to—"

"It's hardly a secret. Once, when he was young, Earl Cumber took a wife, and had sons. Then he cast her away. All of Stryx knows."

"All except me." My tone was bitter. "And it's beside the point."

"Aye. Did you take pleasure, last night?"

"No!" I hated it when he forced me to lie; it built a wall between us, and risked the True. I sighed. "Some."

"That's all?"

"Don't." Not knowing what to do, I slumped back upon the grass. "It feels good to be held. I can't help that."

"Nor should you."

How could this be happening? "You would openly share my bed?"

"Is there shame in it?"

Not really; folk coupled with whom they pleased; all except Virgin Prince Rodrigo. Many of the guardsmen on our walls had companions. One heard snickers, as when a man took a notably ugly wife for her dowry, but no more. Still . . .

I glanced once more at Rustin son of Llewelyn. Reason enough had I to hate him: He'd struck me viciously, ignored me for his slut Chela, treated me like a very dog. Yet something there was, in his gaze, that I couldn't shatter. And, he'd saved me from the stream, guided me through castle politics, brought me safely out of Stryx.

And with him, I felt cherished.

Still, I couldn't destroy him later, by leading him falsely. "Rust, my thoughts are with women. I yearn to marry, to—" I found the coarse word hard to utter.

"I know, my prince."

"I wouldn't stay with you long, you see."

"Yes." His voice held a note of wonder.

"Of course, we have to put aside my vow. We can't be bedfriends if I have to do every little thing you—"

"No." He spoke with utter finality. "That comes first."

"You bastard's spawn, I—" All at once, I capitulated. "As you wish!" Had it not always been so?

Dazed and defeated, sad and joyous, I trudged back to the wagon.

Chapter 22

 ELRYC RODE THE NAG THAT ONCE HAD BEEN CHELA'S. "What delights you, Roddy?"

I wiped my idiotic smile. "Nothing. An old joke."

"Tell me."

"It's about little brothers who don't mind their own affairs."

"You're a toad." He shifted on the saddle. "Hester says we'll be at Cumber by night."

I nodded. Pretending he couldn't see I preferred to be alone, he chatted his way for a league or more.

As the sun beckoned to the horizon, Hester called a halt to confer with Rust and me. "If we goad the drays, we'll clatter into Cumber Town before midnight. But I'm thinking it's best to make a leisurely pace, arrive in full light of day."

I wanted an honest bed. "Let's hurry."

Rust said mildly, "Think as a prince, Roddy."

I spoke half to myself. "If we get there tonight, we'll have a proper place for Elryc, and your Chela too." I shot him a spiteful glance.

The castle gates would be closed, most likely, and the Earl in bed. Torches, servants calling to one another, the usual ruckus of a late arrival. Uncle Cumber cross, our party disheveled and tired after a long weary day of travel.

My tone was reluctant. "Let's push on, camp as close to town as we might. Best if we arrive at noon, or early after."

For a moment I basked in Rustin's nod of approval. He said, "How does that sit with you, Dame Hester?"

"For once the Princeling shows sense." She took up the reins with nary a glance my way.

I made my voice as injured as I might. "And you said you loved me still."

No response. I remounted, and we rode on. An hour later she muttered, "It's not the only time you've showed sense." I wiped my mouth to hide my grin.

We chose as our campsite an unused pasture, along the high winding road. Genard toiled with the horses, and after a stern glance from Rust I went to help. Rust gathered wood, then set up my bed, spread his own gear with mine. I acted as if I didn't notice.

At daybreak we arose, donned our best garb. I wore the new cloak Rust had found me, and my finer breeks. Impatient, I let Rust brush my hair, aware of the pleasure it gave him. At last, we set forth.

It was barely noon when we reached the plateau, and the outskirts of Cumber Town. Great-uncle's castle had always seemed huge in my memory, but I'd been only six the last time I'd seen it.

This day, Castle Cumber loomed over the surrounding plain. At first I thought it had been built on a great rock, but as we drew near I realized the sheer size of it made it preeminent.

Rustin drew close. "Roddy, when we meet the Earl, should you wear the crown?"

"He'd think it presumptuous." I spoke almost without thought, but was sure I was right.

"It would set a tone."

Tempting, yes. Reluctantly, I decided against it. "No, but announce me as Prince and heir. And for once, show me respect, at least in public."

He grinned. "I have nothing but respect for you, Roddy."

"Hah." My mood was mellow. During the night horsemen had passed our camp, awakening me. After, my dreams were uneasy. Rust had but held me close, comforted me when I stirred.

One hates to be alone.

Cumber was a substantial town, at least as large as Stryx itself. Shops overflowed into alleyways and side streets, from the avenue that led to the castle walls. We passed an inn. Impulsively, I sought Hester. "Let's stop to break fast."

"And leave the Earl to wait?"

"He doesn't know we're coming. Besides, it would seem less like we've fled into his arms."

"Rustin, what do you think?" How like Hester, to heed Rust's advice rather than my own.

"I think our Prince is hungry." His eye was mischievous. "No harm, I'd say. Perhaps the inn even has place for him to bathe."

Inwardly, I groaned, but a fresh hot meal overranked all drawbacks.

Rust looked into the cart. "Would you mind, Chela?" Whatever her answer, it seemed to satisfy him.

The Inn of the Seven Nations was grander than that of Stryx, far more busy than the one in Shar. The landlord came to us as soon as he could, found us a table to ourselves. "Welcome, all. You're from the Norland?"

Rustin said quickly, "From the coast." He hesitated. "What news of Stryx?"

"Of the siege, little word, though Tantroth's allowed riders to go forth from the castle, and Margenthar's pulled his troops back from the keep."

"What of Llewelyn?" Rustin's voice was taut.

"The keepholder? Who knows?" His eyes darted to the other tables, and his serving girls. "Except for the banning of Rodrigo, the former Prince, we've heard little. Well perhaps he's Prince still; who knows such intricacies. Excuse me, youngsire, I've guests to attend."

I pinned his arm. "What say you?"

The innkeeper's brow wrinkled. "Why, only that Rodrigo's been renounced, and was to be brought back to Stryx to receive a barony. His vagabond brother also. Margenthar spoke for the Council."

"He can't do that!"

Rust's hand fell on my arm, squeezed a warning. "Don't pester this good fellow. He needs to look to our meal."

I glared at the innkeeper's departing back. "Mother had the right to renounce me, but Council has no such power!"

Elryc muttered, "His vagabond brother. Hmpff."

"Never mind that; Uncle Mar takes my crown!"

Genard said brightly, "You never had it, m'lord. Unless you mean that dented circlet you carry in your saddle—"

"Shush!" I shot him a withering glare, which didn't seem to faze him. "You have a mouth like a magpie."

"If you're renounced, then Lord Elryc's next in—ow!" Genard rubbed his ribs, where my brother's elbow had jabbed.

"Anyway, Elryc's dethroned as well." Someone set sizzling ham before me, and hot bread. Mechanically, I began to eat. How would the news affect my great-uncle, the Earl? Would he seize me, send me back to Margenthar in chains? Fear soured my breakfast; under the table, my hand sought Rust's.

"Eat, my prince. The news does you no ill."

"How can you say—"

"Think."

What else was I to consider? Had I stayed in Stryx, I'd have been subject to Mar's every whim, and caught up in the siege as well. Perhaps Tantroth, if he'd caught word of my presence, would have demanded Mar hand me over, to put an end to our lineage.

I'd fled Stryx to help Elryc. Well, partly. Also because Mar betrayed his promise to present my claims to the Council, and set a date for my coronation. As Mother had warned me, he had sons, and his ambition burned bright. Yet Mar had merely done what we'd expected he'd attempt, soon or late, and I was fortunate indeed to be out of his grasp.

"What of Pytor?" My uncle would have no excuse to disinherit Pytor; he hadn't fled Mar's clutches. I answered my own question. "Mar's only hold on the regency now is Pytor. So our brother's safe for the moment."

Rust was somber. "Until Mar looks to his own line."

Hester said darkly, "And who knows when that may be. The sooner I get you boys installed with your grand-uncle, the sooner I can leave."

"You'd rush home to a burned out—"

"Home? Don't be daft. To Verein." She frowned. "Close your mouth, Roddy; flies are about. Think you I'd leave Pytor after swearing to my lady that I'd see my life blotted like a taper before harm came to her brood?"

Savagely, I attacked my ham. "Why, you old witch, you left me to die in a charred hut."

"Because you were beyond hope!" Her cloudy eyes found me, held my glare. "Perhaps you still are; you speak of contrition but call me names the moment you—"

"I'm sorry." My voice dropped. "Really. You aren't a witch." Under the table, Rust's hand patted my knee in approval.

After, we reassembled at the wagon. Rust fiddled with Santree's cinches while I waited, impatient to be off, hoping he wouldn't remember his threat of another bath.

"Rustin, come!" Hester, her tone urgent.

He flew to the wagon.

I thrust the reins into Genard's hands, hurried after.

Chela lay on her side, her face sallow. Her shift was stained with blood; droplets still oozed from her lips. "I tried . . . to sit. Something inside . . ."

"Is she dying?" All I could feel was curiosity.

Hester said, "She will be, if we move her far. The wagon jolts over every rut."

I said, "We have to go to the castle; we can't stay in Cumber Town under Uncle's nose."

"Chela could." Rust.

"Why waste the coin, when—"

"Roddy." His voice was flat, almost offhand, but it stopped me cold. After a moment he asked, "Where should Chela stay?"

My reply was swift. "Here at the inn, Rust." If he struck me in front of the others, it would be too much to bear.

"And I know you'd offer to pay, my prince, if you had coin."

The landlord had a girl who could tend to Chela's needs, and so it was arranged. With great care, three townsmen carried the injured girl up two steep flights of stairs, to a small chamber facing the street. Rustin gave the servant close instructions, and also had the innkeeper send for a physicker on the chance he might know some remedy.

At last, we set on our way. Elryc rode a horse, so our party would seem larger. Rustin galloped ahead, to announce us at the castle wall, as was custom, so the Earl and his minions weren't left scrambling to greet us. Really, we should have given Earl Cumber a full day's warning, by protocol. More than that, if I were visiting as King. I sighed. We'd done the best we could.

Cumber was a redstone fortress. Far above the keep swirled a fantasy of picturesque turrets that would fell any servant who had to climb to them daily. Below, high ramparts presided over thick brooding walls, surrounding a central donjon wherein the Earl lived and conducted his affairs.

"Stryx should look like this," I said.

Fostrow grunted. "Even the thickest walls fall in time to miners and sappers. Why isn't this place high on a hill, where an enemy can't march his whole force into position?"

"Look how the pennants fly."

"Pretty flags don't make—"

"Fostrow, you have the soul of a hedgehog."

We arrived at the gates without fanfare. Uneasy, I sat stiffly, waiting for the welcoming trumpets to sound.

Rust turned, paced Santree back to where Ebon stood snorting. "The Earl's been told."

"And?"

"I don't know," he said.

"Etiquette requires them to let us wait inside."

A voice from on high. "His Lordship the Earl of Cumber, Warden of the Great Forest, Councilman to Caledon, bids you go from whence you came!"

They hadn't even bothered to open the gates. I urged Ebon toward the throng of soldiers and townsmen crowding the wall.

"Go easy, Roddy, let me—"

"No. This is for me." I called out, "Rodrigo, heir to Caledon, awaits your master's greeting."

A long silence, while I wondered what we'd do if they gave no reply at all.

It began to look as if that would be the case.

Rust's face was a mask of patience. Only the beat of his fist on the pommel revealing his true state.

Elryc walked his sorry nag in stately dignity to where we sat. "Will he open, Roddy?"

"Yes." I spoke with assurance.

"How know you?"

"Because he must." I had no words to explain further.

A hand, on the stone high above our head. Then a wizened face, with a sour expression. "Go away, Roddy. I can't allow a visit."

From the saddle, I made the formal bow of greeting. "My lord Uncle."

His bow in response was automatic, but as he straightened he snapped, "Don't make a fool of yourself. Go set matters right with Margenthar."

"Sir, I would speak with you on matters of state." I glanced pointedly at the gate.

"You have a regent for that sort of thing." He peered. "Is Elryc with you? I thought he was still a baby. Young man, have your brother take you home where you belong. Lord Mar will raise you properly."

Rust breathed, "Whatever you do, don't alienate him."

Cumber made a shooing gesture. "Get thee hence, children. You seem a sorry lot; I don't want to set my troops to turn you around."

I tore open my saddlebag, groped for my bundle, scattering soiled clothing in the dirt. Setting the crown on my head I sang out so all could hear, "Earl of Cumber, now comes Rodrigo of Caledon to deliberate his coronation! I bid you, open!"

The old man blinked, shook his head. "I can't allow a disinherited whelp to dictate my course."

"Cumber, if thou wouldst have a future, consider well! Hast thou not children on whom to bestow thy holdings?"

"Don't try the formal speech with me, boy; I'm old enough to be your grandfather. Not that I'd care to be."

A moment's pause, while I waited all pins and needles.

He muttered, "Very well, come in and we'll talk."

I shot Rust a grin of triumph.

Rust hissed, "In safe-conduct, by his sworn honor."

"He has no honor." I raised my voice. "In safe-conduct, of course?"

A wave of assent. "Get that grotesque wagon inside, before I change my mind." The face disappeared.

Chapter 23

I REFUSED THE QUARTERS THE EARL'S CHAMBERLAIN offered, insisting on connecting rooms for me and Rust. Let them think what they would; I knew that only in bed could we whisper our thoughts so none of the Earl's minions could hear. That we'd be watched, I accepted as a matter of course.

I hurried to bathe and dress, and set again the crown of Caledon on my brow.

We joined the old Earl downstairs in his donjon. There, he introduced the highborn men and ladies of his retinue. He came to a tall graying fellow, dressed in good cloth, whom I recognized. "And this is Imbar, my valet and confidant."

"My lord." The man made too short a bow.

"Imbar." I gave him no more than a nod. When Cumber was done, I introduced Elryc, Rustin, Hester. Then, reluctantly, Genard and Fostrow. Rustin hadn't allowed me to insist they wait upstairs.

The keep was well appointed; it managed to look solid and light at the same time. The Earl led us to the blazing hearth, clapped his hands. Servants in matching livery brought wine and sweets. Imbar, the valet, sat with us as if such intimacy were common practice. I managed not to gape.

After polite small talk, Hester excused herself with dignity, taking with her the two boys, and asking Fostrow's help with the stairs. It was nicely done. In a moment Rust and I were alone with the Earl and his valet.

"Now that you've won the first round, what's your intention?" Uncle Cumber addressed me, ignoring Rust.

I stammered, "I think not of winning, my lord Cumber, but of seeking, ah, your advice." I tried to read Rust's face for direction.

"How charming. Isn't he a pleasant lad, Imbar? He threatens my inheritance as if he had an army, then sits smiling over my wine."

"Uncle Cumber, I ask your support—"

"The name's Raeth. If you must speak to me, stop using the demon-cursed title."

"Uncle—Raeth?"

"It's the name I was born with, the one I used for thirty years before I inherited. Why should I abandon it?"

"Uncle Raeth, I—"

"And I'm not your uncle; I was your father's. That makes me nothing to you."

I cast Rustin a glance of despair. The man was impossible. "Lord Raeth—no, by Lord of Nature! Mother always insisted I refer to you as Uncle, and that's how I know you."

His habitual look of disapproval softened, if only for a moment. "My nephew Josip married well. She was true nobility."

"Thank you. And also for rushing to her funeral."

"That wasn't for you; it's what Josip would ask. You know I favored him."

"I was but nine when he died, sir."

"Aye, he had no chance to make a proper man of you. See the consequences, Imbar?" A sigh. "No wonder Mar has his hands full."

Rust stood to warm his hands at the fire. "The mountain air is cooler than we're accustomed, my lord Prince."

The Earl nodded approvingly. "Well done. See, Imbar, how he reminds me of the boy's rank without so much as a gesture of rebuke?"

For the first time, Imbar spoke. "Who are you?" He addressed Rust.

"Rustin son of Llewelyn, Householder of Stryx. Prince Rodrigo's advisor and, ah, confidant." There was nothing in Rust's tone to which one might take offense. Nonetheless, Imbar flushed.

Uncle Cumber applauded quietly. "Again, nicely done. The boy has poten—"

I set down my goblet so hard it shattered. "Come, Rust. We've had our response." I stalked to the door. "On, to Soushire."

Rustin followed without a murmur.

"See how they take offense?" The old Earl's tone was light. "Hold a moment, youngsires. Shall we treat with them, Imbar? They come from Shar so destitute they must camp in the woods, yet they spurn our mockeries. What shall we make of this?"

Imbar said, "That they're not used to jests? Or, perhaps, that their hides are uncured and tender."

"Which is it, young Rodrigo? Come back to the fire; we'll talk of pleasant things."

I took off the crown, fingered the dent Genard had imparted to it. "This deserves your respect, Uncle, if as yet I've not earned it."

"Aye, it does, and you too, if you've the right to wear it. Come, let's discuss that."

I glanced to Rustin; he nodded slightly. We sat. I muttered, "Let us speak plainly, without derision."

"Plainly, yes. But derision is part of our nature, Imbar and me. Best you learn to live with it."

"Do you call yourself Earl and Councilor of Caledon, and protest not Margenthar's usurpation?"

"Look, Imbar, how he flies to the point. What usurpation, if you're but a child and unready for the crown?"

Rust spoke. "Judge him yourself, my lord. Is he that?"

I raised my eyebrow, at Rust. Had he not told me as much, at least a dozen times of late?

"He wears a noble mien today, I'll grant you, Lord Rustin. That's not what I recall a month past, at the Council meet."

I said hotly, "Mar's soldiers held me from entering."

"Make allowances, sir." Rust. "He'd just lost his mother."

"There's that. What shall I think, Imbar?" Uncle Raeth poured himself more wine, swirled it in his mouth before swallowing. "What would I say to Josip, if he admonished me?"

"He's dead, Rae, and doesn't know what you do."

"But I know." The Earl brooded. "He was my favorite, long before I knew you."

I blurted, "Tell me about him." Rust's jaw fell, but I didn't care.

"A lovely boy." The Earl of Cumber sighed. "I was married, my wife was of the Norlanders, and whatever dreams lay within me remained fettered. Still . . ." He looked long into his glass. "Lovely."

"And as a man?"

"His father sent the boy here for training. I taught him hawking, and we played at the bow. How fast he learned."

Imbar cleared his throat.

"Yes, I know, but it's an old man's privilege to mourn lost occasions. How fast Josip grew. As a man? What can I say; he met and wooed Elena. And won her. Best she'd kept her Power a few years and shackled Mar, but she could wait no longer."

I dared not breathe.

"Josip didn't mind her predominance. She took his advice, and perhaps that made it easier. Even while she had the Still, and they'd not yet bedded, he guided her." His eyes fixed mine, abruptly. "Are you virgin, still?"

I flushed.

"Answer!"

I said, "Yes. I am." I took a deep breath, for strength. "And I will wield the Still, to restore my kingdom."

He cackled. "Then don't throw aside your, ah, confidant. You'll have need of him."

His double entendre made me blush furiously, but my gaze never wavered. "Concern yourself not with my needs, my lord. I will suffice, until Caledon is wholly mine."

A long pause. "Imbar, I believe he means it. Well would it be to have a king with resolve, especially allied with us. No?"

"Perhaps." Imbar's face bore no hint of his thoughts.

"That's merely my view. Certainly not Mar's. And on this point, my opinion holds no water. Duke Tantroth devours Stryx even as we speak, and Mar is regent."

"Only through vote of Council." Rust.

"And I'm but one member. What could I do, even if I favored this lad?"

I growled, "Don't speak past me, Uncle."

"Don't 'Uncle' me, Prince Rodrigo."

The last strands of my temper snapped. "It was out of respect for my father Josip. I'll do as you said, and show him as little honor as do you. You're no uncle of mine, and curse him for a pretty boy, a sycophant who—"

"Stop!" Plea or command, it bore anguish I couldn't have foretold.

Imbar. "He taunts you, to turn aside your resolve."

"I know well what he does; also I know I ceded him the right. Rodrigo, forgive me. I honor Josip and wish that you do so. Call me Uncle if it pleases you."

I said nothing.

"And it pleases me." His tone was gruff. "Which is not to say that for Josip's sake I'll support your claim to the throne."

"Of course not. You'll do so for my sake, and Caledon." I wasn't ready to be mollified.

"You've more in you than I'd supposed. I'll think on it." He got slowly to his feet. "Come, let us dine. I'll have answer tomorrow."

It wasn't a formal meal, with full ritual, but the Earl set forth far more than the light refreshments guests might receive who had no special favor. We sat at long tables draped with soft linen and joined end to end in the center of the great hall. Candelabras gleamed, their tapers flickering with promise of a prolonged feast. I noticed more plank tables stacked neatly against the far wall, enough to fill the length of the hall should the Earl mount a true banquet.

Elryc was accorded a place two seats below mine, which was at Uncle Raeth's right hand. Rust sat across from me; Hester and Fostrow far below us. Genard I thought not even present, until I spotted him near the foot of the last table. Imbar was to Uncle's left.

No one seemed to take notice of the Earl's eccentricity. I tried to picture myself entertaining a visiting prince by seating him across from a servant. It was beyond my imagining.

They began with soup, and I tried hard not to slurp. To my right sat a comely young woman who would notice such things. Surreptitiously, I glanced at my fingernails, but thanks to Rust's obstinacy on bathing they weren't objectionable.

Great-uncle Cumber led us into small talk, steering us carefully from matters of state. Plied with wine, I felt myself begin to relax, and eventually to redden with the warmth of alcohol. Rust frowned, tapped pointedly on his water glass, and lest he make a scene, I diluted my drink until its color faded.

"Oh, I'm so glad; I'll do that too." The young woman followed suit with her own glass. "I feel such a child when I'm the only one to lighten my wine, and Uncle's remarks can make me blush."

The best I could think of was a polite smile, and I returned to my dish.

She added, "I met you once, in Stryx. I don't suppose you remember."

"Of course I do. You were . . ." I gave her time to supply the prompt.

Her face dissolved in pleasure. "How nice, my lord. A pity it was such a sad occasion."

"Yes." I tried to look solemn. "I'm sorry I didn't have more time to chat with you, but it was difficult."

"How could it not be?"

"Mother was a great lady."

"I remember how beautiful she was that day."

I frowned. "The coffin was closed."

"Oh." She put a hand to her mouth. "I know I ought not contradict you, sir, but it was open. Surely you remember."

"Perfectly." My voice was firm. "It was closed, for the public grieving."

"If you say so, my lord." Her manner took on a reserve it hadn't held.

I gulped my wine, attacked the broiled trout and scalloped potatoes they placed in front of me. The woman, whatever her name—someone had mumbled it but I couldn't remember—devoted her attention to her dinner.

I blurted, "Rust, was Mother's coffin open or closed for her funeral?"

"Closed, my prince."

I couldn't help myself. "You see?"

"I wouldn't know, my lord. I wasn't there."

I rolled my eyes. "Try to keep your story straight, my dear." Perhaps she was the castle fool, put at my side for Uncle's amusement.

We'd been left long enough to ourselves. "Tresa, what think you of our prince?" The Earl. "Will you take offense, Lord Rodrigo, if she speaks her mind?"

"No, Uncle Raeth." What else could I say?

"Must I?" Her tone was plaintive.

"But of course, when you sit at my table."

"The young Prince is . . . rude. He thinks I know not what I saw at the burial, and accuses me of lies."

I threw down my napkin. "Madam, it was barely a month ago, and I have all my wits. When Mother died—"

"Who speaks of the Queen?"

I shouted, "You do!" Heads turned, and I lowered my voice. "You said you met me at her funeral!"

"You dunce, I said no such thing!" She scrambled from her chair, cheeks red. "Forgive me, Lord Prince, I meant no disresp—oh, Lord of Nature." Eyes brimming, she scurried from the room.

Uncle Cumber sighed. "I'll have to coddle her for days, to restore her spirits." His tone mocked me. "Ah, boy, who can expect you to learn these skills, in your state?"

I gritted, "I'm sorry." I covered my wineglass, before the steward could pour more. Perhaps I had ought to stick to water. "But why did she say she'd been to Mother's burial, when clearly she hadn't?"

Raeth, Earl of Cumber, smiled with gentle malice. "Not your mother's burial, my lad. Your father's."

I reached for bread, knocked my glass into my lap. The remainder of the meal was lost in my indignity and self-recrimination.

Later, in the dark, Rustin curled alongside me like a spoon. "It wasn't so bad, Roddy. It entertained him."

"A fool of myself." I'd repeated the phrase some dozen times.

"It's all right. You've done it before." If it was intended as consolation, it failed.

I whispered, "What now? Certainly he won't support us after the fiasco I made."

His hand covered my mouth. I thought to bite him, contained myself. Instead, to annoy him, I licked his palm.

Refusing to let me goad him, he wiped his hand on my bare shoulder. "This afternoon is what counted, Roddy. When you wore the crown, you were magnificent."

"Hmpff."

He spoke softly, in my ear. "Both outside the walls, and within. I was so proud of you."

I lay listening, afraid to move.

"Often you're such a spoiled child, I—" A sigh. "Roddy, it's what you were today, whom I follow."

After a time, I asked, "Really?"

"Yes, my prince."

And I was comforted.

Chapter 24

RUSTIN HELPED ME CHOOSE THE BEST OF MY CLOTHING for the morn. It wouldn't do to be seen wearing the same garments as to dinner, but all I had was a scorched jerkin, soiled breeks, and his hand-me-downs. Somehow we put together a wardrobe that didn't leave me looking destitute.

He adjusted the ties on my jerkin, nodded with approval. "I'll buy you some finery, when I see Chela this morning."

"If you must." I'd forgotten her.

"Jealous, my prince? Are we to become Lord Raeth and Imbar, then?"

I cried, "How could you say such a thing!"

Taken aback, he shrugged helplessly. "A poor jest. I forget that you . . . sorry." He straightened. "I'll be back ere long."

Unwilling to go down to the donjon by myself, I found Elryc, sitting with Hester. They'd brought the old woman hot bread, and boiled eggs with her tea, and she was content to eat in her room. My brother and I strode down the marble staircase.

Elryc made sure no one overheard. "Aren't you afraid to go about, without Fostrow?" His voice was low.

"Think you I need a keeper?"

"Yes, but that wasn't what I meant. What if Uncle Cumber plays us false, seizes us for Mar?"

"I don't think he would."

"Yesterday you said he had no honor."

"He has something in its place, then." I waved it aside. "You worry too much."

"And you not enough." At the foot of the stairs Elryc gave solemn greeting to the first functionary he saw, asked where we could find to eat.

The man clapped his hands. Two servants appeared. He sent one to the kitchen, the other to the Earl. From the kitchen, footmen hurried to carry a table and chairs to the sunny side of the hall, and to set goblets and plates.

While we sat abashed, passing comments in hushed tones, a cook in preposterous dress emerged with bearers. Their trays disgorged fruits, rolls, eggs, puddings, steaming oat mash, exquisite pastries, and juices squeezed from oranges, apples, and exotic fruits. Into our mugs they placed small chunks of ice, as if it were winter, and the juice poured over.

I filled my plate and partook of the feast, but had barely swallowed a few mouthfuls when Lord Cumber descended the stairs, in a colorful houserobe embroidered with gold thread.

"I rise late." It might have been an accusation. He took the place across, and we resumed our seats.

"Forgive me, Uncle Raeth. At home I was accustomed to a simple meal, in the servants' kitchen."

"Eat plain food, if you wish, but never a plain meal." He waved vaguely at the fine-blown glass, the candles, the linen. "All this is what separates us."

"From whom, sir?" Elryc.

"The rabble. Imbar will be along in a while. No need to wait."

The day I'd wait my meal on a servant's pleasure was the day I'd . . . I sighed. It was Uncle Raeth's castle, to manage as he pleased.

"Is he a good brother?" The Earl, sharply, to Elryc.

"I—he—of course, sir."

"No, youngsire, the truth. It's a whimsy of mine; at table we speak of each other with candor."

"Only at table?"

"Isn't that enough? We spend the rest of the day repairing the damage. Is he a good brother?"

I leaned my head on my fist, curious as to how Elryc would placate both the Earl and myself.

"Lately he's learned better, sir. Before, he was—sorry, Roddy. He can be a bit arrogant."

"Is that all?"

"And a bully. He makes me cry, for the power of it. But he's changed, since Mother died."

"Is he clever?"

"Roddy, should I—" He eyed the valet, who was striding toward us.

"Ask me, youngsire; it's *my* table. Sit, Imbar, and we'll hear the truth about our young heir."

Elryc fell to toying with his food, but Uncle Raeth waited in merciless silence.

"He's, well . . . clever enough to lead me across the castle grounds dressed as a stableboy, so no one noticed. He even had us sniggering and mocking him, as churlish boys would. But he thinks himself more clever still. I mean—he's always had—I don't know what I mean." Elryc's face grew red.

"Ah, Imbar, I fear we've disconcerted him. Is he an astute observer, young Rodrigo?"

All at once I tired of the game, and could think of but one way to end it. "Yes."

"You're not so clever, then?"

I played with my fork. "I've learned that I'm not. I—made mistakes."

"And you're a bully also?"

I raised my eyes. "At times."

"By the imps' laughter, Imbar. He raises candor to new heights."

"And yourself, sir? Do you often bully your guests with these diversions?"

I'd gone too far, and knew it instantly. But the Earl, though his eyes flashed, was game. "Yes, youngsire. I do, for our amusement." He examined a dainty iced pastry, popped it into his mouth. "Imbar and I need sources of amusement, now that life shortens."

My tone was cool. "Would it amuse you to see me King?"

"That I don't know as yet. Come, finish your fruit, and I'll show you my garden."

When I rose, he took my arm, walked with me through a wondrous pair of doors whose panels were made of glass, like a window. They opened onto a huge veranda filled with a thousand flowerboxes bursting with color. "Here you see my zinnia." One by one, he introduced me to the nearby plants as if they were old companions.

I bore it as best I could, striving to conceal my impatience. Unaware, he chattered on. "I plant all my own bulbs, of course, and tend the seedlings. Imbar thinks I'm mad for not having the servants do it, though he helps design the pattern of colors. Last month was the peak; a pity you couldn't have been here."

"I was, once."

"With Josip, yes. I remember." For a moment his arm tightened on mine. "You were a tyke, and he carried you on his shoulder."

"I'd never seen such bright colors."

"Did it make a gardener of you? No? A shame." He shook his head. "When I die my Bouris will tear up the tract, I suppose. Make a kennel for his imp-cursed hounds."

I dived through memories of past lessons. Mother had deemed it important that I know the families of the realm, in all their generations, and the heralds had dutifully taught me. "Bouris is your first son."

"And my last. He has an elder sister who's too much like her mother; between them they drove me to other pursuits."

I examined a rose trellis to save a reply.

"She whelped well, though. Wouldn't you agree?"

I was hopelessly lost. "Sir?"

"Tresa. Know you not whom you snarled at, all evening?"

I puzzled it out. "Tresa is your daughter's daughter . . . your grand-daughter?"

"Who else? Are you set on undoing the impression you made last afternoon?"

"Uncle Raeth, *please!*" It caused him to stare intently. I blurted, "I'm not witty; I can't help it. I beg you, don't play on my clumsiness!"

"Don't ask me to pity weakness." After a moment he again took my arm. "Notice the bed of marigolds."

When at last he was done with me, I fled to my room with as much dignity as I could muster.

It was there Rustin found me, an hour later. "What, bathing on your own?"

I stirred, sending ripples across the tub. "Uncle Raeth made me sweat through my clothes."

"That never concerned you before." He untied a bundle, laid the contents on my bed with a flourish. "The latest Norlander styles."

I climbed out of my bath, snatched a cloth, dripped water across the floor. "Let me see."

"The best I could find. After yesterday, you deserve it."

"Don't mock me. I've had enough from—"

"I meant it." He helped me dry my back. "You set our cause forward by months."

"But today I set it back a year." I told him about breakfast, and Tresa.

"Sounds like the old ogre's testing you."

"Or softening me for the kill." I sighed, selected a jerkin. "Shall I wear this?"

"Only if you wish to appear handsome. And don't pout; the old man can hardly set much store by his granddaughter's opinion."

"Why not?"

"Because it is not his own." Rust selected gray breeks that set off the silver in my jerkin. "Still, it wouldn't do you harm to make amends. Seek her out."

"Must I?"

"It would be politic." He untied his own jerkin. "Where do you ring for a servant? I'll have a bath also." He grimaced. "Chela's in pain."

"She lives?" I was startled. She'd coughed much blood.

"A physicker bound her chest tight, with strips of cloth. He says she must cough, like Elryc, but not otherwise move. No bending or twisting."

"And she'll survive?"

"There's hope. She's angry I won't stay with her."

"Why don't you?"

He said carelessly, "Because I love you more." I'd have made less note of it had his neck not gone red. Seeing my stare he growled, "Find Tresa and make your apologies, in case she has her grandsire's ear."

A servant came in response to his ring, and I left.

I had no idea where Tresa's apartments were, or what the Earl's reaction would be if I sought them unchaperoned. I'd best ask his permission. Downstairs, I stopped a houseman. "Where may I find Lord Cumber?"

I followed the corridor he indicated, and came to a grandiose double door of worked bronze.

"Mind they pick the fresh ones! I want no wilting petals!" The door discharged a liveried servant, and slammed shut.

"Aye, sir." The houseman gave me the short bow of courtesy, in passing.

Tentatively, I approached. "Uncle?" I raised a hand to knock.

"—something of a young fool, but he *did* have that manner about him. What say you, Imbar?"

My hand froze, an inch from the bronze.

"I say you gain nothing. Why provoke Duke Mar?"

Uncle Raeth coughed. "Why not? He's a great boor, as well you know."

"But the boy's a lesser one, and will come to nothing. Mar might yet defeat Eiber. What then—"

"Then we'll send our congratulations, and a pretty present. We're too strong to besiege, unless he raised all of Caledon to war."

Imbar sighed. "Do as you wish. When have you not?"

"If I knew what I wished, we wouldn't be speaking of it." The old man's voice was testy.

"Why'd you let him in the gate? Did you see a shade of Josip in him?"

A pause. "As years pass you grow more spiteful, Imbar. Am I the same? Josip is long dead."

"And no longer a bone of contention, but the question remains."

"No, he's not another Josip, though he's pretty enough. Can I not respect him in a fashion, for—"

"You? Respect?"

"As I say, spiteful."

"You're my model, Rae."

A pause. I glanced to either side, ready to flee or knock if steps approached.

A creak, as if of a protesting chair. "Well, no matter. You're right about Mar. No need to alienate the regent; Lord Rodrigo hasn't the chance of a demon in a Ritehouse to push him aside."

I closed my eyes in despair.

"Still . . . he has that something. Definitely his father's son."

"Will you hold him for Mar, or send him away?"

A cackle. "You'd have him in my cells, for your pleasure?"

"Him? A whipping perhaps, to teach him manners, but no more. It's the other with whom I'd have words."

"Rustin? An odd one; from the look of him you'd never know his father gave up the keep without a murmur."

"I'd wipe that haughtiness from his face in a nonce." Imbar's voice held spite, or something more. "But the Prince, you won't risk Cumber for him?"

"You worry as if it were to be yours, not Bouris's. You know I've made provision for you."

"Rae, I wasn't for a moment—"

The old man's voice softened. "I know. Come, help me with these damned leggings. The Prince? Cumber comes first. Yet . . . a pity to disappoint him. We'll see. I doubt I'll hold him for Mar."

I crept away, disconsolate, to seek Rust's counsel.

At the stairs, the same servant who'd directed me to Raeth's quarters stopped me. "My lord, if it pleases you—" He glanced about. "The Lady Tresa would have a word."

I followed him, to an oaken door, knocked.

A token curtsy, and Tresa turned aside.

"I'm here. What did you want?" Inwardly I flinched; I hadn't meant to sound so gruff.

"To apologize, my lord. For last night's confusion." She blushed. "I thought you remembered me from the burial."

"I was but nine."

"And I barely eleven." Tresa smiled, and for a moment her face was one I could like.

"I don't recall any of the guests. It wasn't only you."

"That's nice." She frowned. "Why is that, do you think?"

"It's a private matter."

"I'm sorry." She shrugged, as if helpless.

I'd made it worse. Exasperated, I blurted, "Because my father was gone, and Mother was weeping, and she held my hand tight, and I needed to piss. Too many people crowded round, cooing their sympathy. I just shut them out, and pretended Father rode me on his back."

"Did you like to do that?"

"Shut people out?"

"Have your father ride you—"

"Of course. Is there anything else?"

"No, my lord, not if you're impatient to—"

"Who said that?"

"I assumed, from your manner—"

"Don't judge my manner, madam, until you know me well." I retreated to the door. "I accept your apology. Good day."

I took the stairs three at a time. Only when I was safely out of sight did I slow my pace.

It was midafternoon before Rustin returned to our room.

I demanded, "Where were you?"

"Out." His tone had an edge.

"With Chela?"

"For a time."

I decided to let Rust wallow in his ire, but before long a servant summoned us down to the donjon.

Earl Cumber's face was grave. "I think you'd better hear his words directly."

Standing before my uncle was a crier, in Mother's colors. He started when he saw us. "You have him here?"

"No. He has himself. Tell us again."

At this call to his profession, the crier drew himself up, closed his eyes as if in a trance, reopened them when his words flowed.

"Margenthar, Duke of Stryx, to the Earl and good people of Cumber, greetings. Know ye that the fugitive Rodrigo Prince of Caledon has taken Prince Elryc his brother from his lawful guardian, to roam we know not where. And that my words shall be cried in every town square, and posted, that they may receive them, for the brother of the princes, Lord Pytor of Caledon, lies gravely ill at Verein, and—"

"Rust, he's threatening—"

"Quiet!"

"—if the said princes are not returned to the guidance of the Regent Margenthar, their young brother may pass to his death with no parting words. And if any person shall come upon the fugitive princes, they must seize—"

"Demons take him!"

"Will you—"

"He's made us Pytor's ransom!" My fists were knotted so tight my palms ached. "If he harms one hair of Pytor's head . . ."

Uncle Raeth silenced the crier. "You have the gist of it. What think you?"

"That I'll spear him to the wall. Better, I'll cut out his liver."

"Roddy!" Rustin's voice was like ice.

"He threatens Pytor!"

The Earl watched us, unperturbed.

Rustin sighed. "I'm sorry, my lord Cumber. His wrath does have merit."

Uncle Raeth's hand fluttered in a wave of consent. "Of course. I find it fascinating."

I wheeled on him. "Don't mock me about Pytor's life!"

"Don't tell me what to do in my own donjon." He beckoned, and his valet rose from his unnoticed couch, across the room. "Shall we sympathize, Imbar? Mar has them in a vise: their lives for Pytor's, it would seem."

"They'll ignore the Duke, I wager. Regardless of the risk to the brother."

"What choice have they?" Raeth.

"To go back."

I said, "I can't!"

"Mar is a doting uncle; he'll raise them well, but how can our boy understand, Imbar? He's so full of loathing and contempt that he's blind to Mar's charms."

Words failed me. With a curse, I fled the hall, bolted up the stairs to our chamber. Inside, I threw myself on the bed, pounded the pillow over and again in rage.

Out of breath, Rust came upon me a moment after. "A brilliant leave-taking, my prince."

I hurled my pillow at him, wishing it were a rock.

He batted it aside. "Are you perchance irked? One would never know."

"*Stop that!*" I leaped from the bed, charged him with fists flailing. "Mock me again and I'll—"

He spun me around, dragged me to the washbasin. I struggled; he kicked my feet out from under me. "Control your temper, my prince." He emptied the wash pitcher on my head.

I sat stupefied, dripping, my shirt plastered to my chest. "You bast—" I stopped just in time; his open palm reared to chastise me. I wiped water from my eyes, with a soggy sleeve.

"You wish to be King, Roddy? Then set your feelings in check. Let no man know how to wound you. Be circumspect."

"Did you hear what the crier said?"

"Think you the Earl is awed by the working of your face, the knotted fists, the rage you cannot control? Think you he'd have you for his King?"

"Forget the throne." I turned away. Only a sniffle escaped me. "I want to go home."

"To Mar?"

"To Stryx." I fell on my bed.

"Out of that wet shirt."

I complied, to save the trouble of arguing. My eyes were damp; I rolled on my stomach, that he might not see.

"I'm sorry, Roddy." He sat, stroked my back. "Perhaps I spoke too harshly."

"Will you hit me if I say I hate you?"

"No."

For some reason, I couldn't say it. Instead, I gave out a muffled sob. Rustin sat at my side, stroked my flank.

For a long while my relief contested with rage, but by the time Fostrow knocked at the door, I was calmed.

"Dinner is soon," said the soldier. "And you're expected. Hester and Elryc will eat in their rooms. I'm uneasy, lads, if you don't mind my saying it. Lord Cumber has but to say the word, and you're a bird in a cage."

Rust asked, "Where would you have us go, that the danger is less?"

"I don't know." Fostrow sighed.

The Earl served us in the great hall as before. I had no chance to speak to Lady Tresa. I did, however, use Raeth's own greeting as an opening.

"My lord Earl, accept my apology for this afternoon." I spoke in an offhand manner, as if apologies came naturally. "I was upset for my brother, and spoke out of turn."

"Ah, Imbar, see how gracefully he makes matters right. Think nothing of it, my boy."

"But I do. A king must be above such rages." I walked with him to our seats. "How may I make amends?"

For a moment he pondered, then a roguish glint lit his eye. "Take our Tresa riding tomorrow, and let her show you our fair city. I hear you get along like a pair of twins."

I flushed, held my thoughts to myself. "Gladly, Uncle Raeth." The meal was sumptuous. We waded through course upon course, amid tedious small talk. With nothing better to do, I let myself be mesmerized by the flickering taper.

Uncle Raeth pointed to my glass. "You see, Imbar? He drinks as sparingly as his father."

"One night isn't proof of—"

"I'll wager I'm right. Lord Rustin, does your, ah, confidant overdrink?"

"No, my lord."

It was true. Perhaps I lacked some manly attribute; my cousin Bayard and his cronies had no hesitation at drinking themselves into stupor. More often than not, I was moderate in my wine.

"There you are, Imbar. I recall Josip diluting his glass 'til it were nearly clear. Once, I said . . ."

His tale went on and on. Resigned, I pretended to listen. The candle in front of my plate seemed to dim. I squinted, wondering if I was drunk after all.

"Josip was much annoyed, and warned me not to . . ."

Abruptly the flame went out.

I startled, almost dropped my goblet in my lap.

"A lovely boy, though sometimes his sense of humor was . . ."

Castles were drafty, and candles were always blowing out. But I'd felt no wind. I stole a glance to the window; it was locked.

A servant took light from another candle to relight the one that had guttered, but all at once several more died.

Uncle Raeth stopped in midword.

Not waiting for a servant, I reached for the nearest candle, to hold it to the next.

"Let it be, lad!" Something akin to fear was in Raeth's tone.

I hesitated. All at once, the candle I held throbbed as though it had a life of its own. With a yelp, I let it fall. It drowned in my sweet chestnut sauce.

As if suffocated by a demon's breath, the remaining candles blew out. But for the flicker from the hearth, we were in dark.

"Morovi, ignite the torches!" The Earl, his voice sharp.

"Aye, my lord."

From the hearth, a hiss, as of water. The blaze steamed, sent out sparks.

My neck hairs stood stiff. I stumbled to my feet, hand on my dagger.

The servant Morovi ran to the hearth with an unlit torch. The fire banked and died.

Lord Cumber snapped, "Everyone stay still! Morovi, to another room, and bring back fire. Hurry."

"Yes, my lord." A crash. "Sorry, sire. Someone put a chair . . ." More sounds of blundering and muttered curses.

"My guests, this happens from time to time. No need for alarm. The place has a Power, as I'm sure you've heard."

"Roddy, sing out! I can't find—"

"I'm in front of my chair, about—*arrkh!*" I stumbled against something sharp. Recoiling, I lost my balance, fell to my knees. My face struck a lap; hands shoved me away harshly. I toppled to my side.

Someone stepped on my hand. I gasped, yanked loose numb fingers. My head whacked the table. Half-dazed, I found a leg, slid myself under, curled tight.

Running footsteps.

"*Rodrigo!*" Rustin's tone held panic.

The door burst open. A torch flickered. "My lord?" Behind Morovi, other servants, and Fostrow, his sword drawn.

Earl Cumber said, "See if our candles stay lit! Be quick!"

I sucked at my aching fingers.

"Careful, man, you'll set the cloth ablaze!"

"Sorry, sire, I . . . there." A pause. "Now the next."

Dim shadows.

"They seem to be holding."

A muttered curse. A chair flung aside. "Roddy!"

"I'm all right." I uncurled, tried to crawl out from my haven. "I was afraid I'd be trampled. Help me up." Shakily, I got to my feet.

Rustin gaped.

"Someone stepped on my hand." I flexed my fingers. "I can't feel—"

"Fostrow, help me!" Rustin.

Lord Cumber stared at me with a fixed expression. "Give him a chair."

"Why do you make a fuss? I'm not—"

"Look at your jerkin."

"Did I dirty it? I'm—" My words dried.

The shirt was red with blood. "I must have cut—" I slipped into the chair.

The Earl clapped his hands. "Lords and ladies, clear the hall. Be quick, and don't think I jest. You too, Tresa."

"Please, Grandfather, let me stay a bit."

"No. He's—well, all right, but you'll have blood on your hands. Morovi, cloths and water."

With clumsy fingers I untied my jerkin, tried to peel it from my chest. I cried out.

"Easy, my prince."

"Is it deep?" The Earl.

"It's oozing. I can't tell." Rust poured water into a cloth, dabbed ineffectually at my chest.

Bare from the waist, I shivered at his cold touch. Incongruous with my fear of death was acute embarrassment, at being tended in view of Tresa. As if to make matters worse she took the cloth from Rust's hand, knelt beside me. "Are you faint, Rodrigo?"

"No. Yes." I wasn't sure. "May I drink?"

"Water." She wore a delicate scent of attar.

"Well? Is he dying?" The Earl, with a touch of asperity.

"Would that displease you?" Imbar.

I didn't want her so close.

"Yes; he hasn't yet tasted the raspberry torte. Well, Tresa?"

"It scraped across the ribs. A gash, no more."

"Hold still!" Tresa. "Grandfather, a stitch or two would help."

"No!" My cry echoed.

"If the tear reopens . . ."

"I don't care! Don't put a needle through me." My voice broke. "Please!"

"Calm yourself." Tresa, her voice soothing. "We'll bind you tight. You'll live."

I sought Rustin's hand. "I'm sorry; I saw a man sewn once, and . . ." I didn't finish, but squeezed for reassurance.

For an instant Tresa cradled my head in her bosom. Then, briskly, she tore cloths into long strips. "Whiskey, please, Grandfather."

"Will brandy do?" He handed across a bottle.

"Grit your teeth, this will sting." She splashed a glassful on my wound.

My eyes bulged. I squeezed Rustin's hand so tight my muscles ached.

Tresa set about wrapping my chest.

At last the fiery sting began to ease, and I could think of other things. "Why did the candles gutter?" Surreptitiously, I wiped my eyes.

Imbar's voice was as silk. "Yes, Rae. We'd all like to know."

The Earl shifted his weight. "The Power of Cumber. Not all of us are blessed with faculties like your Still."

I waited, but no more was forthcoming. "When the Power comes, you blow out candles?"

Raeth seemed discomfited. "When certain moods come upon me, candles gutter. I can't predict it, and have little control."

"What moods, Rae?" Imbar, again.

"It's nothing we need discuss." The Earl's tone was waspish. "I'm sorry, truly I am. But who did it?"

I stared at my binding. "Surely, it was an accident. Someone's utensil, held careless in the dark."

Rust and Fostrow exchanged glances. The soldier asked, "Who was closest, when the light was lost?"

"Someone pushed me aside," said Tresa.

I forced myself to think. "I was sitting next to the one with the buck teeth. Beyond him . . . I don't remember."

"But we do, Imbar. Crinan, was it not?" The Earl raised an eyebrow.

"And Crinan is late of Margenthar's court," said Imbar. "But any of us might wish to earn favor with Duke Margenthar."

"Or Tantroth." Uncle Raeth sounded gloomy. "Too many choices. Without question by torture, there's no way to tell."

Rust stood over me, dagger still drawn. "Apply it, then!"

"How admirable, that you'd protect our prince. But I'd lose too many dinner partners." Raeth's tone was dry.

I put my head in my hands. "I hurt, and I'm tired. Let's think on this of the morrow, before I leave." I waved away Tresa's supporting arm. "I'm well enough to walk." My tone was brusque. "Thank you for your attentions."

It was a dismissal. She colored. "As you wish, my lord."

"Is there a couch I can sleep on?" Fostrow looked about.

I reddened, not wanting him to see me bed with Rustin. "The door bolts."

"The door can be forced. Someone wants you dead."

"There's no need. Tell him, Rust."

Rustin looked at the soldier, made a helpless gesture. "Our rooms connect. I'll be near him tonight."

When Fostrow left, mercifully silent, Rustin unsheathed his sword.

I shuddered. "Lie close." I waited anxiously until he slid himself into bed. "Rust, why was I such a coward over the sewing?"

"You were afraid of the hurt."

"I lowered myself in Earl Cumber's eyes, when I needed his esteem." I was silent awhile. "I won't do it again."

"I know."

"No, hear me. I made a vow that I'd be coward no more. I meant it, as to large things. Death, and swords, and arrows."

"A noble aim."

"But isn't it as necessary to conquer small fears as large? If I can face a sword, I can face a tailor's needle."

He chuckled. "Shall I call Tresa to resume her work?"

"Don't mock me. I can't let fear turn me aside again."

"You ask much of yourself."

"I must, if I would be King. And, Rust . . . I would."

We lay silent a long while. At length, his hand crept to my loincloth. Stirring, I thought briefly of Tresa, of Chela. Their time would come. For now, I must have my Power.

Chapter 25

 IN THE MORN, TRESA KNOCKED WHILE RUST AND I WERE still abed. I hastily threw on a robe.

She asked, "Did you bleed in the night?"

"No."

"What troubles me," Rust said, "is who could have known the candles might gutter, and be prepared."

"Oh, anyone. It's a failing of Grandfather's, and well known." I waited, and she colored slightly. "I call it that, though he makes light of his Power. His, ah, moods are unpredictable."

My tone was cross. "Why are your words so opaque? Speak plainly!"

"I—well, all right. Grandfather is a passionate man. When his passions are . . . inflamed, the Power is likely to be present."

I tasted the words. " 'Passions inflamed'? I don't— Oh!" I felt myself blush furiously. "Lord of Nature!" With difficulty I met her eye. "You mean, he was . . . but for whom?"

She made no reply.

"He was staring at me, while speaking of my father."

"Yes."

Desperate to change the subject, I tried to stand too fast, and gasped as something pulled at my side.

"Move slowly! Here, let me adjust the bindings."

"Rust will do it."

"But I'm versed—"

I snapped, "It's not for you to help. You're only a woman."

Rust said swiftly, "I'll apologize on his behalf, since he hasn't the wit to know he's offensive."

"Rust!"

"You, be quiet. Accept my regrets, my lady." He bowed. "Prince Rodrigo is valiant and at times even kind, but he was raised in a stable, free of manners."

It brought a smile to her lips, though mine were set in a snarl. "Don't make him angry," she said. "His chest will throb. I take no offense, Rodrigo."

"None was meant." My words came grudgingly.

"May I see you this afternoon?" She stood.

"If you wish." I was carefully indifferent.

"Perhaps, then." A quick curtsy, and she was gone.

Rust dropped onto the bed, took my mouth in his hand, squeezed until I gawped like a fish and could say naught. His voice low but steady, he said many things, that after a time made me squirm in discomfort. Only when my eyes began to glisten did his tirade wind to a halt. He patted my cheek absently, went downstairs while I sorted myself out. In the hall, Fostrow said nothing. I hoped he hadn't heard.

At noon Rustin appeared, with the Earl and two servants.

"May we come in?" Uncle Raeth swept past, without waiting for an answer. "How do you feel, Rodrigo?"

"Sore. But we must leave, lest they make another attempt on my life."

"Sadly, I must agree. Oh, we can guard you, but for politics' sake I must have you gone. In the meanwhile . . ." His face brightened. "I brought a meal for the two of you." He gestured to the footmen. "And my own, if I might join you."

I had little choice. "As you wish, Uncle."

"Mushroom soup to start, trout almandine, and greens. Wine and bread, of course, and a few pastries for dessert. I thought it best you dine lightly. You'll forgive the omission of a few courses?"

In moments Uncle Raeth's portable meal was set up and ready. He and Rust gathered round the bed, and we set to.

For a while, as we ate, the Earl made small talk. At length, his eyes fixed on mine. "So, youngsire, what would you do, as King?"

A jest formed on my lips, died stillborn. "First, restore the realm. It's outrageous that Tantroth holds Stryx unchecked, even for a day."

"How would you dislodge him?"

"I'd raise a force."

"Paying them how?"

"Were Uncle Mar loyal, from the treasury."

"And if it's barred to you?"

"Taxes."

Uncle frowned. "And after you've driven out the invader?"

"I haven't thought that far." He raised an eyebrow, and even Rust rolled his eyes. "Well, would you have me lie? Mother died suddenly, and since then I've had to flee Stryx, find Hester, ride to a forsaken patch of weeds, fight fires, and argue myself into your castle. When was I to plan my realm?" My cheeks had color, from the force of my assertion.

"See, Rustin, how he protests. Well, young Prince, I'll give you time. Think, and tell me what you'd do, crowned and safe in Stryx."

I sought some grandiose plan that would please him, but could find none. "I don't know, my lord. Once, I thought the crown meant freedom to do as I wanted. Now I see it isn't so. And besides . . ." I bit it off, but was forced by his silence to continue. "I no longer trust my impulses. I've been wrong too often."

He raised an eyebrow.

An unexpected urgency hurried my words. "I know this costs me your support, but I value the True, and will not speak falsely. I've learned that in some things I'm ignorant, and"—I swallowed a lump— "I may never have wisdom. I have too strong a temper, too little control of my tongue. Mother failed to teach me better. Perhaps she should have sent me more often to the Chamberlain."

Silence permeated our chamber. My voice was husky. "I'll do my best, but I admit that so far, my best hasn't been much. At least I'll have Rustin to help, until I irk him beyond his bearing."

The Earl studied me without expression for a long while. Abruptly he rose. "Good day." He hurried to the door.

I buried my face in my hands. "What have I done?"

Rust sat beside me, stroked me gently. "I don't know, my prince. Whatever it brings, I fault you not."

For some hours Earl Cumber made himself unavailable. Rust went to see Chela.

Having little better to do, I gave myself over to fantasies that I'd achieved the crown, and set about my rule. Where before in my dreams I forced my cousins to heel, made them pay me exaggerated gestures of respect, I thought now of what I'd do, day to day, on the throne of Caledon.

My travel had taught me that the realm was not well knit. Our roads were atrocious, especially in the back country. I'd do well to repair them. I wasn't quite sure of the mechanism that governed their payment, and amused myself inventing new ones. Perhaps that was just as well; whatever system was in place seemed not to work.

The simplest way was to force the Lord who held the place under my liege to pay for the roads' upkeep, but it occurred to me that some, at least, might raise objection to a new and considerable expense. How much did it cost to repair a road? I made a note to ask Rust.

In midafternoon Tresa knocked at my room.

Unbidden, she threw open my windows. "It's stuffy in here. You'll get a headache, or worse."

"I had none." My voice was some smidgeon less than cold.

"Close them; it matters not." Her manner matched mine. "Grandfather wants me to examine your cut."

"No!" I couldn't let her handle me unclothed.

"As you wish, then." That small curtsy, a gesture more of dismissal than subservience. "If there's no other service . . ." She glanced at the door.

"Oh, stay awhile if you'd like. Rustin's gone."

"A charming invitation, my lord Prince." Her tone was cold. "Yet I fear I must go."

"How direct you've become, my lady."

She hesitated. "I would leave, as my lord seems blind to the need of courtesy."

It was what Rustin told me, oft enough. I sighed. "I've offended you."

"Not at—"

"I always do." It didn't seem sufficient. "It's a clumsiness I have."

"I've noticed." Her words struck like a glove on the face.

For a moment fury flamed, but, manfully, I swallowed it. "I've had my way a great deal, you see. Until recently." Carefully, I stood. "If I'm to be King, I'll have to learn better."

"I agree, my lord. If I may bid you farewell . . ."

"But I apologized! Didn't you hear?"

She paused at the door. "It was no apology, Prince Rodrigo. Merely an explanation. Good day." And she was gone.

"Foolish, ignorant woman!" I spoke to the empty doorway.

Fostrow looked in, came to pull up a chair. "It was no apology, sire. You might like to know."

"Keep your opinions to yourself!"

He scratched his head. "If you were my son," he said solemnly, "I'd thrash you. I thought you'd like to know that too." He set aside his chair, wandered to the window, looked out with hands folded behind him.

I fumed, knotting the covers in my hands. They all took advantage of me. Tresa vented her spleen; Fostrow took unwarranted liberties. His son? Bah. Were I King, I might hang him for such insolence.

After a time Rustin returned from town. "Chela looks to recover," he said. "How go things here?"

"No surprises," said Fostrow. "Rodrigo is his usual self."

When he left, I called for parchment, wrote out two notes, laboriously copied them over until I was satisfied. To please Rust, I showed him them before sending Genard with the first.

He folded the scroll, handed it back. "Flowery and pretty, but far better to have no need."

"I know." My tone was humble. "I'll really try, Rust." I glanced outside, at the advancing day. "Send Genard to gather the horses, and tell Hester. We must be gone. I'll say good-bye to Uncle Raeth."

"What of his support you seek?"

"It's lost, I assume. I've begged enough."

Holding my side, Rustin hovering, I negotiated the two flights to the walled veranda wherein my uncle tended his flowers.

Garden blooms attracted me not at all, but I was so glad to be in sunlight I examined each blossom as if it held significance for me.

"They droop, now that autumn is on us." The Earl, behind us, his hands and arms brown from the earth.

I turned, made the bow of courtesy.

"Ah, Rustin, he's healing. We're overjoyed, of course." His pinched face gave no support to his words. "Mar's courier made fast his journey home, I'm sure, with news of your presence."

I asked, "And you've sent along your own word?"

"Not yet. What would you advise?"

"That you help me. Can I have horses, and men-at-arms?"

"To go against our colleague Margenthar? To tackle Eiber's mighty army before the walls of Stryx?"

"To be a magnet, to which others might adhere, that I might have my throne."

"He flies to the heart of the matter, eh, Rustin? Tell me, Roddy of Caledon, why should I help you?"

"The throne is rightfully mine. Mother—"

"No, no. You're telling me why you want the crown. Tell me why I should want you to have it."

"Does justice not move you?"

"Not a whit, lad."

I looked for aid to Rustin, but he'd stepped back to let us have at it.

I took a deep breath. "What would move you, Uncle?"

"Mundane matters. Remission of taxes for ten years, for a start."

"Is there more?"

He threw up his hands. "Aiyee, how can I support you unless you act like a king? You're supposed to go choleric with rage at the very notion."

"Inwardly, I seethe. What else do you demand?"

"Nothing that would trouble you." His manner was offhand. "A few parcels of land in dispute with the Warthen. A barony for my friend Imbar, that sort of thing."

I tried not to let my lip curl. "Imbar is but a commoner, and a servant at that."

"That's why it wants the King to ennoble him," Raeth said agreeably. "Else, no need to ask."

Rustin cleared his throat. "The Prince will think on it."

I shook my head apologetically. "No need, Rust. May we sit, Uncle? I tire."

The Earl snapped his fingers, and servants materialized. "Chairs, at once, and hot chocolate. Pastries too, while you're at it."

In a few moments we were seated. I leaned forward. "As to the borderlands you covet from the Warthen, don't be too greedy in their choosing, and you may have them. I'll reimburse him somehow.

"The taxes I won't remit. It's not that I don't cherish your counsel and assistance"—I bowed, and he back—"but I can't very well tax the rest of the realm and exempt you. Folk would be outraged, and I'd end up collecting nothing. On the other hand, I could assist you in building the new roads we'll require, where others might have to provide for themselves."

"A pity, young Rodrigo. Were it not for such harsh edicts I might have supported your—"

"The barony flies against decency and convention, but you may have it, the day after I'm crowned. That's my concession, Lord Cumber. Were I you I'd prize it, for what other contender would consider such a thing? Lord Mar?"

The Earl's sardonic manner faltered. "He speaks like . . . a king, does he not, Rustin? How odd. I thought him a mere boy."

I blurted, "I *am* a boy, and want so to be a man. Will you not help me, instead of casting follies in my path?"

His face grew stiff. "I must go. Affairs bid our attention." He got swiftly to his feet, strode away.

Dismayed, I watched him depart, thinking I'd lost all. But at the entranceway he paused, bowed formally. "My lord Rodrigo. Until tonight."

"We must leave, Uncle."

"Tarry until morn. You'll be well protected." He disappeared.

Rustin bent over, kissed me once on each cheek. "How can you act such a fool, and be so magnificent scant hours after?" His eyes glistened. He walked away to examine vines hung artfully from a trellis.

I idled away the final hours of the afternoon, playing chess with Elryc, chatting with Fostrow as an added gesture of amends. He'd said nothing of the note I handed him.

Rustin was absent through the long evening. When the sky darkened I was concerned. When I got ready for bed, Fostrow sitting quietly in the corner, I was most anxious, lest some ill had befallen him.

Rust's knock came at last, as the candle dripped past the tenth hour. I threw open the door. "Why do you go off without telling us? Where have you—"

"Enough." He brushed past.

"We've been all day without word—"

He spun, his eyes blazing. "Will you be silent? I don't answer to you!"

I couldn't help a sneer. "Was she so good you had to run back to her?"

He took my shoulders, backed me to the wall. I winced as the jar pervaded my knitting wound. "Where I've been is my business. Ask not."

"Why do you anger so?"

"You're a stupid boy, and demanding. Why do I follow you, when I esteem you not?"

I framed a mean reply, but abruptly his eyes filled, and my harsh response died unuttered. He fled to his adjoining room.

"He's moody," I told Fostrow. "Pay no heed."

The soldier yawned. "Bar the door, my lord. I'll sleep on the bench." He departed.

I tried the door between our chambers. It was barred, from Rust's side.

The Earl of Cumber requested our company at his breakfast table. Rustin and I dressed with trepidation. This morning his mood was civil, but distant. I wore the fine new robe Rust had bought me, over my best clothes. We debated whether I should bear the crown, and decided not.

"My lords." The Earl rose. His table was set for an elegant repast, but for once his shadow Imbar was absent. He said, "Shall we have at it, Lord Rustin? Tresa tells me our prince believes in forthright discourse."

With a weak smile, I poured my tea. I'd heard nothing from Lady Tresa since my apology.

"I'll be frank: I believe the lad would be a decent king. Imbar was dubious, at first, but this morning he agrees. Of course, one must doubt what Rodrigo could accomplish without the Still of Caledon."

I said, "The Vessels haven't been swallowed in the earth."

"But you don't have them."

"I'll find them, if I have to rack Uncle Mar. But their loss isn't as bad as it might seem; they can't be used against me, if I'm crowned."

Raeth snorted. "I find that less than reassuring. Even if you're crowned, will you have the strength to hold your realm without the Still?"

My voice was heated. "Long enough to find my Power." I rested my arms on the breakfast table, leaned close to him. "Uncle Raeth, I will do what I must to become King. Your support will make it easier, but I'll go where I must. I'll raise armies, best my foes, even . . ." I faltered.

"Say on, lad." He was attentive.

"Even conquer myself." I hadn't meant to speak of what it cost to preserve myself for the Still, or admit I needed Rustin's help to become a man. But, speak I did, of these things, and more.

When I stumbled to a halt, Raeth raised an eyebrow, addressed Rustin. "As we agreed, Imbar and I. The boy would make a good king."

I said eagerly, "Then you'll support—"

"He's a bit too impetuous, of course. As you see."

I colored at the rebuke.

"Shall I support you, young Rodrigo? No."

My heart plunged.

"Not openly. I can't afford a rift with Mar while he's regent, and won't countenance one. But between us . . ." He toyed with his napkin.

I gritted my teeth, determined to wait him out.

"It would depend on certain assurances." His eyes met mine. "I would have to know, you see, that the promises you gave could never be treated lightly."

"You'd have surety for my word?" A repugnant concept. "You'd doubt a nobleman's—"

"Oh, don't take it personally. We who hold power lie routinely. Perhaps churls do as well. But lords of Caledon have an advantage in dealing with our sovereign; his lie costs him dear." A pause, for emphasis. "I'd have you swear on the True. An oath of my own devising, that assures me you'll have no reservations, play no tricks, that your intent and meaning is identical to mine."

I found it hard to keep my voice from trembling. "And the content?"

"Certain lands of Cumber, occupied these many years by the Warthen of the Sands." A scroll appeared from under the table, with a map drawn. "The barony of which we spoke, and at least partial remission of taxes, for five years. I'm firm on the point."

I waved assent to the scroll, wondering what I was giving away. "And I agree to the barony. All except the taxes. I won't begin my reign by fomenting civil war."

"Then we have no agreement."

I stood. "I'm sorry, Uncle." I moved toward the door. "We'll avail ourselves of the safe-conduct you offered, as soon as we're packed. I bid you—"

"Confound it, sit, and stop routing me at my own game. What would Imbar think if he saw me bested by a mere boy? Faugh!" A wave of disgust. "These pastries are specially made by a most talented baker. I taught him myself. I'll live with your demon-inspired taxation." He bit into a sweet.

I gaped. "You'll support me?"

"Try the ones with cherry filling; they're especially good. Not openly. You'll flee Cumber, with a few of my troops in somewhat lazy pursuit. I'll loan you funds, at a rewarding rate of interest, and a small complement of guards."

"How many?"

"Say, five hundred men-at-arms."

I sat stunned.

"I can't raise more without being too obvious. A few personal servants, to do your cooking and the like. Twenty goldens a month will pay their expenses, and leave enough for you to progress in style."

I managed, "We'll make do." Five hundred men were a force to be reckoned with. A glance at Rustin. His eyes showed triumph, but also pain. Puzzled, I set it aside for later. "I must have your vote in Council to put aside the regency and ratify my crown."

"Name three firm votes, and mine will be fourth. For less, I dare not risk war with Mar."

Rustin said, "He'll need the promise of your vote to convince the others."

"Then he won't be King. I like the lad, but I won't risk Cumber for him. How many votes have you?"

"I've one—"

"Two." Rustin, too late.

"One firm, and perhaps others. May I at least tell Soushire?"

"No one. Especially not her; the woman eats garlic cloves whole. How can I have faith in her judgment?" The Earl wiped his mouth. "Are you prepared to swear now?"

"Yes." I took a deep breath, and sat straighter. "Raeth, Lord of

Cumber, I do promise by the True of Caledon that I shall uphold fully and without deceit this vow: that as King I shall grant the petition you present me today—"

"Promptly grant."

"Promptly grant, to redress inequities in lands heretofore divided between Cumber and the Sands. Further, that I shall, the day after my coronation, ennoble and make Baron your counselor Imbar."

"That there is no trick or deceit, or hidden meaning, or attempt to cavil or avoid these commitments fully."

"All of that I swear, by the True." My hands shook; I steadied them over my tea.

"That you will keep secret every aspect of my support, until revealing it shall do me and Cumber no harm."

"By the True I so swear." My palms lay flat over the cup, as if it were the Chalice.

"And one other thing; you'll take my granddaughter to live at Stryx. Cumber's too small a place for her."

I frowned, before I considered the insult he'd see in it.

His lips turned upward. "She's a decent sort. A pity you don't like each other."

"It's not that . . ." I ran aground.

"Well." He pushed away his plate. "Now I've an investment in you, Tresa's to see your wound. I won't have you suppurate and die filled with pus." He wrinkled his nose. "Upstairs with you, as soon as we're finished."

I acknowledged his orders with a nod.

"Now, as to your brother." He raised an eyebrow. "He's welcome to our hospitality, while you go about seeking your crown."

"It's best if we're together."

"Best he have a clean bed and decent food, which you can't provide. We'll keep good eye on him."

"Thank you, but Dame Hester has the care of him. She'll want—"

"The boy stays here. Damn, Rodrigo, why do you force my fist from its velvet glove? Won't you allow me a touch of subtlety?"

My lip curled. "Oh, no, Uncle, too many candles will gutter if he stays."

It took him effort, but the Earl kept a firm check on his temper.

Eventually he said quietly, "It has nothing to do with passion, you twit. Lord Rustin, explain to our prince that I'm tending my self-interest."

"You'd control me through my brother? That's more vile yet." I was too angry to care what havoc my words caused, until Rust scraped back his chair, wandered around the table, rested a gentle hand on my shoulder, squeezed a warning. Slightly calmed, I added, "What control would you gain, Uncle? Is not Elryc my rival? Would it not be a service to find him no more?"

"Odd." Uncle Raeth stroked his chin, a sardonic smile playing about his lips. "You showed no disaffection while you played chess with him last afternoon."

"Perhaps I dissembled."

"Then leave him with me, and remember the favor you'll owe should you be rid of him. Ah, that displeases you? Then perhaps I gain power over you after all, by requiring his presence."

Again I stood. "Sir, your games are too subtle for my untutored mind. Elryc travels with our party, or there's no arrangement for me to honor."

"I but said—"

"If you seek hostage to my word, you err on three counts: to doubt my given pledge, to doubt that I treasure the True, and to doubt that I'd cast aside kingdom and life itself before allowing my brother harm. Come, Rustin." As best I could with side throbbing, I strode to the door.

From Uncle Raeth, a sigh. "How can a man negotiate, with you stalking off every time you're thwarted? After a time it grows stale. Sit, Rodrigo."

"Not this time, my lord. Know thee that I take offense at thy conduct. We'll pack, and be gone. *Now,* Rust." My voice snapped like a whip.

Together, Fostrow in tow, we mounted the stairs.

In our chamber Rust sealed the door, put his lips to my ears. "I hope you know what you're doing."

"He wants the barony."

"Not so loud. He told you openly you're watched." Rust glanced about, as if in search of the spyhole. "You may have thrown away—"

"Do you not listen? He wants the barony for Imbar above all things.

As I told him, Elryc makes a poor hostage because my interests aren't well served by keeping him alive. Don't give me that look; I speak impersonally, as others would see it. Think you I'd betray my own brother, and my oath?"

By way of answer, Rust dug into his purse, found a coin to flip. I put my hands around his throat, squeezed in sham fury. "About this, don't jest. I want the crown, but I'm not afraid to lose it. I'll certainly not have it by betraying my blood."

Rustin tickled me under my outstretched arms, and I leaped clear. "Roddy, I find it amazing that you're two distinct people. In matters of statecraft, you're mature. I hate to say it, but . . . wise too. In personal affairs, you're—"

"I know. A dunce. But I try to be less duncelike each day. Fostrow, did I do right apologizing to you?"

The soldier grunted. "The note was pretty enough."

"You mean I'm still in your bad graces. How do I get out?"

"A serious query?" Fostrow studied my face. At last, satisfied, he said, "You're Prince of the realm and I but a weary old guardsman. I accept that. But, laddie, I'm old enough to be your father twice over. Think you not every youngsire owes some courtesy to those who've aged before them? Is it not possible we ancients have yet some wisdom to impart?"

I sat on the bed, unlaced my boots. "Very well, I'll try to show your gray hairs more respect, since you have so many of them." I lay back. "Rust, I'm glad you're in better humor than last night. What was bothering you?"

It was as if Rust's mood were a delicate crystal I'd tapped too hard. His face clouded over, and he strode to the interconnecting door, passed through into his own room. "Leave me be, Roddy." The bolt slid closed.

I sighed. "What makes Rust so moody?"

"What makes any of us what we are?" With a grunt of effort Fostrow rose, took his place in the hall.

I sent for Hester and Elryc, to tell them of our debacle. We'd have to hurry our exit, before Uncle Raeth decided to deliver me to Mar. My faith in his promise of safe-conduct was less than I might like.

Our next aim would be Soushire, where I'd attempt to persuade the fat old Duchess to support my cause.

Hester, for once, listened without complaint of my behavior. "A difficult man. Always was."

"Even if he spoke in jest I couldn't—"

"Your mother never knew what to do with him. Glad she was he lived in the windswept hills of Cumber, and not under her nose. She was always polite to him, for Josip's sake."

I put finger to my lips, to indicate listeners.

Perverse, she raised her voice. "A difficult man, I said. He swore fealty to Elena, but toys with the ruin of her son." She glared at my discomfort. "There is a time for candor."

"Thank you, Milady Chancellor." My tone was dry.

A knock. I opened, to Imbar, in a flowing multicolored robe.

"Prince Rodrigo." A formal bow, with a flourish. "Lord Elryc. My lord Earl is indisposed, and bids me convey his regrets."

Rustin peered through our connecting door. Frowning, stiff, he took his place at my side. Imbar patted his shoulder indulgently. I waited for Rust to whirl, draw sword, and strike off the lowborn's hand, but he fastened his eyes on the far wall and said nothing.

"Rae's sent me to arrange details of your convoy."

"Convoy!" My heart pounded. "What about Elryc?"

"He assumes you'll want your brother along." Imbar's face was expressionless. "I'll show you the captain who'll have charge of our men."

"If they go with me, I'll have charge."

"He'll have charge of our troop, and carry out your orders."

I sighed. "Very well. Rust, let's go." I took a cloak against the still wind.

Elryc demanded, "Let me meet him."

"No, you stay—"

"Promises." Just one word.

I clenched my teeth, swallowed my ire. "Very well. Do we go outside, Imbar? Elryc, bring your cape."

Hester made a sound, almost a growl. Her rheumy eyes fixed Imbar, and held something sharp. "Tamper not with honor, or the lives of my boys, or I'll rot the skin off your bones while you scream in your bed." That odd gesture, she'd made once before. Involuntarily, I recoiled.

Imbar seemed unmoved, though he licked his lips. "My lord Earl gave his safe-conduct. Besides, I'm among you. Would I risk my own life for so little gain?"

A sentry came to arms as we neared. I wasn't sure if he gave honor to the valet, or me. Surely, even Uncle Raeth wouldn't have his men present arms to a valet. Yet Imbar comported himself as co-master of the house, which perhaps he was. He'd even laid hand on Rust's shoulder as if they were equals.

A grand stone edifice housed the Earl's officers. In Stryx, soldiers lived in outbuildings, in the castle warrens, or in tents. Even officers lived so; to provide them better was to suggest they were the equal of their masters, and how then could they be asked to die for us?

Imbar asked the sentry, "Is Tursel within?"

"At the common room, sir."

Indoors, I blinked, waiting for my eyes to accustom. Even the trappings were above the station we accorded to our officers; well-made hangings, sturdy tables with extra touches of grace, comfortable chairs. It would cost Lord Cumber a pretty penny to maintain a troop to this standard, and I wondered why he'd do it.

A door opened. A short man, hair close-cropped, a wide nose. "I'm Tursel. This way, my lords." I studied him as we passed his extended hand. Younger than Fostrow—what soldier wasn't?—but still old, at least twice my age.

Imbar said with proper formality, "My lord Prince, may I present Tursel, formerly captain of the second household troop of Cumber."

"Formerly?"

"He was dismissed as of last night, and his oath of loyalty dissolved. He seeks a new master. Tursel, this is Rodrigo of Caledon, Prince and heir."

From Tursel, a formal bow, with due acknowledgment of rank. "My lord."

Elryc tugged insistently on my arm, and I turned aside while he whispered. "He'll always be Uncle's man, no matter what he swears."

"I know, but—"

"If you put us into their hands, they'll guard us from escape as well as from enemies!"

I said gently, "We're already in their hands." Then, to Tursel, "How would you serve us?"

"I'd escort you whither you would go, sire."

"Why would you serve us?"

"For pay, and—"

My lip curled in disgust. "You're a mercenary?"

He drew himself up. "My life has been in allegiance to my lord Earl. I would be so today, but for his request I serve you."

"You'd give me loyalty?"

"I'd swear an oath so."

"And when my interests diverge from his, what then?"

"I—" His eyes flickered, and fell. "I know not, my lord."

All at once, I liked him. Honesty was a quality rarely found in the halls of nobility. As must be; it was too dangerous to be bandied about without constraint. "Tell me this much: If the Earl and I become enemies, would you leave me, or destroy me on his behalf?"

Tursel's manner seemed to relax. "Leave, my lord. It would be the honorable path."

"You concern yourself with honor? Good. Know then that to betray me to my enemies, to Margenthar of Stryx, would be to destroy me utterly."

"If I enter your service I won't do that, sire. Even at the Earl's bidding."

"Imbar, does your patron know he's unleashed a man of honor in our mutual service? Lord of Nature knows where it will lead." I smiled for an instant, then squared my shoulders. "Tursel, I offer you service to my person and in my domains, as captain of my troop, as my principal lieutenant in matters of arms, upon your vow of loyalty to me and mine, until the death of one of us. Accept you this commission?"

"I do."

Swiftly we went through the ritual of loyalty, in which he bound himself to me and I vowed to look after his material needs, as spelled out in the vows. A sordid bit of oath-taking, I'd always thought, but necessary, given man's lust for material goods.

When we were done, I asked, "Now, as to the men. Who picked them?"

"They're mostly from my old troop, sire. I know them well."

"Troublemakers?"

"A few, but they know me well, also. If I may have a free hand, you'll have no problems."

Should I involve myself, or leave all to him? "Elryc?"

He nodded.

"Done." I turned to Imbar. "What next?"

"Leave Cumber quickly. My lord Earl sends his regrets that it must be so, but we can't appear to be in collusion with you. And you can't depart openly; it would expose the pretense that you've evaded us. We'll first send Tursel and his troop on some mission, then you'll leave quietly, to meet them in the hills. A squad of our guardsmen will pursue you with full hue and cry. That should be theater enough."

"It's complicated."

"But necessary, if Mar is to be assuaged." His voice was smooth. "Don't concern yourself; I'll set up the details with Lord Rustin. Duke Margenthar will suspect, but he'll have no proof, so we'll be free to carry on relations. Diplomatic niceties will be observed."

I muttered, "They make me sick."

"Then don't seek to be King, my lord."

To that, I had no answer. We returned to the donjon.

We were packed, and waiting for servants to haul our gear down the winding stairs, when Tresa appeared once more. Her tone was businesslike. "Let me inspect your cut."

"I don't need—"

"Grandfather said I must."

Stifling my objections, I dropped my cloak on my bed, fumbled with the strings of the jerkin I'd managed to slide over my bandages. Tresa brushed my fingers aside, adroitly undid the crude knots while I stood uncomfortable, hoping yesterday's bath was still of benefit.

The bandages were wrapped tight about my incision, knotted on my good side. She untied them with cold fingers that made me flinch. The innermost cloth stuck to my side; she poured water on a fresh cloth, dabbed at the bandage until it came away.

"Raise your arm."

I was fully conscious how much more manly Rustin's chest was than mine. Never had the difference seemed greater than now. Where he was muscular, with fine strands of soft hair from neck to groin, I looked almost a baby, and was hairless but for tufts under my arms. I tensed my upper arms to show more muscle, but if she noticed she gave no sign.

"Does that hurt?" She prodded.

I recoiled. "Yes!"

She ran deft fingers across the well-formed scab. "No infection. That's good."

I longed for my jerkin. "I'm cold."

She finished reapplying the bandage. "Dress, then. Shall I help you?"

"No!" I turned away, to hide the flush of my cheeks. Gritting my teeth, I recalled kneeling by the stream at Hester's cottage. No humiliation could match what I'd already survived. I need not berate myself, for such a little thing as this.

When I looked back at Tresa, my tone was light, though the effort it cost was dear. "Thank you, my lady." I eased the jerkin over my wound. "I know it must have been unpleasant for you." Almost I'd added, "as well," but caught myself in time.

"Not really. I've grown used to it." Her mouth twitched with what might have been mischief. "And you're more handsome than most I've tended."

My tone went hard. "Don't mock me."

It was her turn to color. "I didn't, my lord." A curtsy. "I'll leave you now."

"No, stay." My words came before thought, and I was astounded. Whatever had made me say such a thing? Now I'd have to entertain her, and hadn't the slightest idea how it was done.

I sat, feeling an awkward child. Silence lengthened. Desperate for something to say, I blurted, "I don't know how to talk to a woman."

"A mere woman, you mean?"

I colored. "It was boorish, and I'm sorry. I haven't much practice at civility."

"Why not, my lord?"

"You might as well call me Roddy; everyone does. Perhaps because Mother made me show her courtesy, but didn't much care how I treated others."

"You're not the first arrogant Lord that lived." She sounded curious. "But how came you to be aware of it?"

I felt giddy, as from too much wine. "By making a fool of myself over and again, until even I couldn't ignore it."

"We all feel we've done that, at times." She looked to the window. "At the banquet."

"Don't remind me. I'm sor—"

"No, I meant myself. For supposing you recalled when we'd met." For a moment she blushed, but then it faded, and all that was left was an inexplicable lump in my throat. "I felt all the more foolish for knowing I made you feel the same."

Our eyes met.

Not knowing what else to do, I smiled. "Does it matter, in the great scheme of things?"

"Perhaps not." Tentative, her smile blossomed in answer.

I cleared my throat, searching for something to say. "Your grandfather wants you settled at Stryx, to find a husband."

Her face hardened. "He means well, of course."

"You find Stryx so distasteful?"

"I found it quite beautiful, when wind and tide raised the waves below."

"Yet you sounded displeased."

"At forced marriage."

"Arranged, for your benefit."

"Have I a choice?"

"Relatives could hardly arrange it properly if the woman could refuse—"

"The mere woman."

"I never said that."

"You had no need."

"How like your sex, to quibble."

"Good day, my lord." Her cheeks glowed color, but her face was stony.

"Wait, my lady."

I winced at the slam of the oaken door. After a while, I wandered to the window, stared down at the courtyard. "Women! Creatures of whim. Brainless hares, the lot of them."

"Does that include my lady Elena?" Hester, in a growl.

I jumped. "Who let you in?"

"Fostrow said you were alone." She glanced about, chose a stiff chair, eased herself into it, put her stick across her lap. "Will Elryc stay at Cumber?"

"It gives the Earl too much power over us." Even if his spies over-heard, I said nothing we didn't all know.

"Then he'll come with me, regardless of where you jaunt with your borrowed troops."

"But you'll travel with us."

"I go to Verein, for Pytor." Her tone was blunt. "Do you?"

"I need Soushire's vote, or the Warthen's, to undo Mar. After that . . ."

"Mar taunts us that Pytor's dying. We'll leave tonight, Elryc and I." She made ready to stand. "Cumber's stipend will buy servants, to make our travel easier."

"I can't let you haul my brother on a wild chase to Verein."

She struggled to her feet, approached me with a look I cared not for. "Let, Princeling?"

"Hester, be reasonable!" I backed away.

She waved her stick. "Let events be reasonable! Your mother entrusted your life to me, but you grow too willful for me to help. I can't protect Elryc by leaving him here; even you agree on that, and how can I leave him in the care of two brainless boys in the fever of a quest?"

"That's not fair."

"Pytor needs rescue. How can I choose twixt him and Elryc? The only way's to bring Elryc along."

"Verein lies past Uncle Mar's troops at Stryx, and past Tantroth's besieging army. To which of them would you give Elryc?"

"I'll find a way." Her face was troubled. "I know not what else to—"

"Verein and Soushire both lie to the south. Ride with us until our trails must diverge. By then, I'll decide."

"Pytor is eight!" For a moment her voice trembled. "And helpless. His succor cannot wait!"

I walked softly to the window, leaned on the sill, head in hands. Mother, pass me your wisdom. I beg you.

But there was only the cool wind.

Chapter 26

EBON'S HOOVES PITCHED CLODS OF MUDDY EARTH INTO the cattails alongside the trail as I clattered back through our slogging troops toward the cart. My brother perched behind the high seat, near Chela's bed. "Tursel's scouts found Tantroth's ahead," I told him. "We wait until the way is clear."

Chela grimaced. "They've bound me so tight I can barely breathe."

For Rustin's sake, I said peacefully, "You could have stayed behind."

She snorted. "I'll be on my feet soon enough. He needs care."

Hester set aside her reins, glowering. "Faster could I walk to Verein."

"Nurse, have patience."

"Your outriders dance with Tantroth's, valley to vale. Why wait? Soon or late, he'll learn your whereabouts. Had he force enough to hold every hill and dale in Caledon he'd long since—"

"Peace, woman!" My voice was sharper than I'd intended.

Hoofbeats, from behind. Rustin. His face was grim. "What now, my prince?"

"Another delay."

"Good. Come walk with me." He tied Santree to the wheel.

Dutifully, I followed, past the line of supply carts, to a secluded glade. "Not too far, Rust, or we'll be challenged by our own lookouts."

He nodded, his thoughts elsewhere. Abruptly, "What say you we leave our escort and ride alone to Soushire?"

I gaped. "Is that me talking, or cautious Rustin?"

Rust lowered his voice. "I like not Captain Tursel. He's altogether Lord Raeth's man. And while we dawdle on the trail, Mar has time to patch up his relations with Cumber."

"So?"

"What if the Earl sends word to seize us?"

"I'm the prize, Rust, and Cumber had me in his grasp. Why send me off with a royal guard, only to—"

Rustin said fiercely, "Cumber's but raised the cost of his loyalty. What if Duke Mar pays his price? Besides, your Raeth is a pawn in Imbar's hands."

"Why do you hate Imbar? He seemed pleasant enough."

"Fool! Simpleton!" Rustin's palm lashed out in a slap that echoed through the suddenly silent wood. Shocked beyond words, I rubbed my stinging cheek.

He spun on his heel, bolted back to the camp.

For some moments I sat stunned, my affront swelling to rage. I drew sword, slashed at branches and shoots in wild abandon.

When I was calm enough, I strode back to our wagon, caught Elryc's wrist. "Where's Rustin?" My face was a thundercloud.

Rust had led Santree to a clearing, where Tursel sat mounted with his officers, awaiting reports. Rust had one hand on the pommel, as if about to swing himself into the saddle, but he stood motionless, his forehead resting against his stallion's mane.

I stalked across the clearing, laid a firm hand on his shoulder.

"I'm sorry I struck you." His words were slurred.

"Come with me, or I'll have you dragged." I tugged at his arm, hoping he wouldn't put my threat to the test.

Rustin followed, leading Santree.

I led him off the trail, a few yards into the privacy of the wood, and backed him against a tree. "I could hate you," I said.

Eyes down, he nodded.

"But I don't. Oft enough you've slapped me when I deserved it. Today I didn't."

"Agreed."

"Why, Rust?"

"I lost my temper."

I shouted, "What passed between you and Imbar!" Santree snorted in alarm.

Rustin's eyes held something akin to fear. "Roddy . . ."

"Tell me." Almost, he tore free, but my grip was iron. "Did Imbar threaten you? Was it about your father?"

"Don't, I beg you. I'll make amends. Please!" He managed to break loose, and hoisted himself into the saddle. "It's nothing. You know how moody I get. Let it go!" He slashed through the brush, and was gone.

Alone once more, I walked slowly back to camp.

Captain Tursel rode to my left, Rustin on my right. Rust appeared to find our proximity as uncomfortable as I, though we both pretended it wasn't so.

Behind us, a procession of men and wagons struggled up a hastily widened deer path, through dense forest. I'd have liked to ride at the fore of the column, but Tursel's scouts fanned ahead, probing anew for ambuscade, and I knew better even than to suggest it.

We dragged our way east.

The valley beyond was free of Eiber's forces, at least for now. Once we descended the heights, we could ride south through the lush broad vale, and come closer to Soushire at last.

Behind us a horse snorted; two soldiers rode side by side.

I peered past Rustin, through the wood. Somewhere over the hill lurked troops of Tantroth, Duke of Eiber, whose force spread deadly tendrils through our land. I stirred in the saddle, hot with impatience to drive Tantroth into the sea. Imps and demons chew his entrails for his impudence in attacking Caledon.

Absently, my fingers strayed to my cheek. I tried to feel anger, discovered pity instead. "Rust . . ." My hand went to his arm. "Too long we've known each other to—"

A shriek. I whirled. A guardsman pitched to the ground, an arrow lodged in his temple. As I watched, a shaft shattered on his companion's shield, while another buried itself in his mount's throat. The soldier went down, flailing against the weight of his dying steed.

Screams. Calls to arms, shouts of confusion. Tursel cursed, wheeled his mount, galloped back down the trail screaming orders.

Rustin grabbed my bridle, spun us about, bent himself over Santree's neck. Sword flashing, he charged through our ranks.

Following his example, I bent low, hugged Ebon's mane. I gasped, "Where?"

"Our wagon!"

On our right flank, a horde of black-clad men poured from the wood onto our straggling and disorganized column. How strange to see men all dressed alike, fighting as one.

"Pikemen, here!" One of our guard, sounding a rally.

A withering volley of arrows dropped a score of Tursel's men in their tracks. Screams, moans. The clash of pikes and staves.

"Elryc!" I peered into the untended wagon, in the center of the melee. My brother and Hester were nowhere to be seen.

Two black-clad men darted from the brush, ducked under Rustin's steel. One seized Santree's bridle. The other raised sword to hack at his legs.

My sword leaped from its scabbard faster than thought. A wild slash. The first assailant was down, his arm near severed. Rust reared Santree. The bay's flailing hooves caught the second attacker's sword, knocked it from his hands.

Rust and I charged, blades raised high. Rust's may have descended first, by a fraction of an instant. I felt the snap of contact, a sudden give. Blood spurted; the man fell away, writhing.

"Stay together!" Rustin.

"I know!" Arrows whistled, too close.

Some of our guard gathered behind Hester's wagon, seeking shelter from the deadly salvo.

"Where's my brother?"

"Who knows? Flee!" Two of them dashed up the hill.

"No!" I jumped off Ebon, almost lost my footing. "Stay and fight!"

Rust shouted, "Ride to safety, Roddy!"

"I won't leave men to die!" Dismounting, I turned Ebon from the arrows, whacked his flank with the flat of my sword. He bolted into the wood. "Come on!" I ran toward the nearest guards.

"Get down, boy!"

Santree galloped past, riderless. Panting, Rustin caught up to me. "You idiot!"

I gasped to the nearest soldier, "Where's the enemy?"

"Their archers are formed along that hedgerow." I squinted. Some fifty bowmen knelt in rows, directed by a master of archers with his raised staff.

I turned to one who wore a corporal's feather. "Where's their guard? Have they set pikes?"

A strangled shriek; a young blond soldier fell, clawing the arrow in his chest.

The corporal blanched. "The archers need no guard. We haven't men to charge them."

"You've ten guardsmen right here."

"Into a hail of arrows? You're daft."

They loosed another volley. Up and down our line, more men fell.

"We've spears and pikes, and they've set no pikewall. We can wreak havoc, give our men time to rally."

"Do as you want, boy. I'm not risking my—"

Enraged, I clutched his jerkin, slammed him against the wagon. My voice rose to a shout. "You'd have your King charge alone? Well, then! Live with shame!" I whirled, raised my sword.

Rustin squawked, "Roddy, don't!"

Three arrows slammed into the wagon, inches from my head. My arm burned.

I ducked behind the wheel, cringing, until my resolve from the brook swirled to my consciousness.

Coward I might be, but coward I would not act.

"Imps and demons upon them! *For Caledon!*" I clawed my way atop the cart. At my feet, a tarpaulin moved. I snatched it aside, sword raised to plunge. Elryc, clutching a dagger, hugged Chela in protective embrace. I laughed, a strange wild sound, and let loose the canvas.

"Caledon! Cumber! Attack!" My voice was shrill. I vaulted from the wagon, snatched a shield from a corpse, charged down the hill toward the hedgerow. Someone screamed, a savage, exultant yell.

"Roddy, slow!"

The warning only sped me faster. My sword flashed overhead, as if eager for blood. I catapulted over a fallen log, had just time to raise my shield. Two arrows buried themselves in it, jarring my arm to the bone.

"Caledon!" Again my wild shout.

At the hedgerow, Eiber's master of archers raised his staff. In a moment it swooped down. I threw myself headfirst to the ground as a score of arrows whirred overhead. Behind me, shouts grew louder. I scrambled to my feet, charged on.

Sword in hand, Rustin raced down the hill, his long legs closing the gap. On his face was fear, anger, resolve.

I had just time to flash him a feral grin, and we were upon them. My sword slashed left, right, left. Bowmen scattered.

Screaming men. Swooping arrows. I parried a club with my shield, drove home the sword.

"Behind you!"

I whirled. A pike. I twisted my spine, just managed to evade the jab. I dropped my sword, grabbed the shaft, yanked as I turned it on my hip. The wielder stumbled, let go his pike. I snatched my sword, scrambled after.

Down the line, the master of archers wheeled a squad of his men. Coolly, he bade them nock, aim their deadly shafts at his own men we fought, and at us.

"No!" A plea of terror, as I cut down a boy hardly older than Genard. His eyes widened, and went dull forever.

The master hesitated an instant too long. A dozen of our spearmen crashed into his line. The bowmaster disappeared under the onslaught. I caught a glimpse of the corporal who'd cowered with me at Hester's wheel; he hacked at the enemy with savage blows.

In moments it was over, the archers smashed.

Panting for breath, I groped for the spear, used it as a leaning pole. Rustin, his mouth set, turned his back to mine, in guard.

The clatter of hooves: Tursel, with five of his men. "Are you hurt, sire?"

Too winded to speak, I shook my head.

"Stay with him!" Alone, he rode off. Two of his guardsmen dismounted; the other pair kept watch from their saddles.

"What news?" It was the first I could speak.

"They fall back!" The soldier chewed his cheek. "The captain had us abandon our supply carts, rally to the center of our column. He sent squadrons into the wood."

"How many attackers?" Rustin.

"Eiber? Who knows? Two hundred, perhaps."

"Our casualties?"

The man's face hardened. "Many."

"Have we lost our supplies?"

The man's teeth bared in a grin. "Not likely. If we hold the field, Eiber will be hard-pressed to—*down!*" His hand swept round to my shoulder, pulled me earthward. A spear whizzed past my cheek. Shouts, hoofbeats.

I hugged the ground, eyes shut, expecting to be skewered in the next moment. My knees were drawn up tight, as if protecting my belly. I tried not to gag from fear.

Moments passed; I forced open my eyes. Rustin stood over me, sword drawn, glancing this way and that.

My lips curled in loathing. I was but a coward, after all. Cursing, I stumbled to my feet.

"Stay down!"

"No. Where are the soldiers?"

"They chased three of Tantroth's men into the bush."

I took my place at Rustin's back, sword drawn, shield raised. Eiber's arrows still stuck from its padding.

"There you are! Imps and demons take you!"

I whirled at the new voice, tensed for death.

Fostrow rushed into the glade. "You're hurt! Let's see!" He snatched up my arm.

"Let go. I'm—" My voice died at the sight of my blood-soaked sleeve.

Anxiously, he tore at the cloth. "Thank Lord of Nature I found you. I've been looking all—"

"It's just a scratch. Brambles."

"An arrow, at the wagon." Rustin. "Didn't you know?"

"Really?" I giggled, frowned, pulled myself together. "It doesn't hurt."

"I should have been with you. Never again will I leave—"

My voice tightened. "I'm no infant. And if I'm so precious, why weren't you with us when they attacked?"

Fostrow's mouth was grim. "That's not a jest I like, sire."

"Answer!"

He sucked in his breath. "You don't know?" His brow furrowed. "When we set forth this morn, Tursel's aide bade me ride with the rear carts. I said I was sworn to protect you. Tursel himself intercepted me, said he'd confirmed his order with you, and you agreed."

Rustin and I exchanged a glance.

In the wood, a cry. My shield went up. As if trained for the maneuver, we took up our places, our backs to the center.

Nothing.

Lord of Nature knew how long we stood so, while my eyes darted from left to right, and I strained at every sound.

The fight petered out, to the moans of wounded, the clatter of horses bringing up the wagons.

At last, cautiously, we lowered our swords. I pushed aside brush, walked swiftly back up the hill with Rustin, Fostrow hovering.

Our battalion was reassembling along the trail. Squads of Tursel's men combed the bush for wounded. Ours, they carried with care, to emptied carts. Those of Eiber, they dragged by the heels.

"We need to wash that clean." Fostrow gestured to my arm.

"Aye, mother."

The guardsman snorted. "I'll find water. Don't leave the wagon."

A half-dozen soldiers passed, hauling three black-clad youths. One, his forehead bloody, had a dazed look. Another's tunic was soaked with blood, the third's arm hung as if broken. The last seemed quite young.

"Where are they taking them?" I followed the procession, and Rustin followed me.

The soldiers led the Eiberians to a glade where their dead companions lay. Tursel, clustered with his officers, looked up, nodded. A soldier ambled toward the new arrivals, lifted an injured youth by the hair. With one swift motion he drew his knife, sliced the young man's throat, let go the head.

I gasped.

The second boy's eyes widened in terror. As Tursel's soldier stalked him, he scrabbled backward, legs kicking for purchase on the blood-soaked turf.

Incredulous, I watched as if in a trance. The soldier caught the young fighter by the arm, his blade poised.

The boy's anguished cry broke my spell.

"Hold!" I strode forward. "Let him go!"

Tursel glanced up, raised his hand to stay the execution. "Lord Prince, go back to the wagons. A stray arrow might still—"

"Release them!" My words gritted through clenched teeth.

The boy's eyes swiveled between us as we spoke. His companion's gaze was locked on their mate's bloody throat.

Tursel said, "They're assassins. No flag of battle, they issued no challenge. Get on with it, Herut."

With an oath, I struck the knife from the soldier's hand. "What manner of man are you, to slaughter captives?"

Tursel was patient. "Sire, think. We have no base. You know we can't carry Tantroth's wounded where we roam; we've barely enough room in the carts for our own."

"Send them to Cumber!"

"Lord Cumber has naught to do with your quest. You fled his castle in the night!" His eyes caught mine, in warning.

"Then let them go."

"To limp back to Tantroth, and fight us again when they're fit? No. Herut, proceed." Tursel turned to go.

I took a deep breath. "I forbid it."

Tursel stood quite still, his back to me. Then, absently, he turned. His voice was yet calm. "My lord, time is short; I have to ready a camp before dark. I won't free enemy soldiers to attack again, and we can't carry them. Will you answer for them?"

I knelt by the cowering boy, whose forehead dripped blood. "Do you swear adherence to me as my bondsman, now and evermore? Be quick."

"Yes!" His young voice held a desperate note.

"And you?"

The second youth nodded.

With contempt, Herut planted a foot in the boy's back, shoved. The Eiberian toppled with a cry of pain.

Tursel said, "Leave these two. Tend to the others."

"Aye, sir." Herut plodded across the field.

It took me a moment to fathom their meaning. I raised my voice. "I forbid it, for all of them."

Tursel frowned. "All? May we speak in private, sire?"

Nodding, not trusting myself to answer, I followed him aside.

"My lord . . ." For a moment he looked abashed. "Do you know much of war?"

"I know to fight with honor!"

"Easily said, sire." He folded his arms, studied the ground. "Cumber's high reaches face the Norland passes, and oft bands of their raiders swoop down from the hills."

"So?"

"How many more would we contend with, if we let any flee home?"

"You kill them all? Are your own men never captured?"

"Occasionally, though the Norlanders prefer falling on fat farms to facing seasoned warriors. Our men are butchered, if caught. It gives every man incentive to fight without quarter. When we return the favor, the raiders fear us and hesitate to attack."

For a moment I considered it, before my sense took command. "I won't have it, Tursel. Obey me, or be dismissed."

"Aye, sire."

"Rodrigo!" At the interruption, we both turned. Fostrow's face was grim. "You were to wait by the wagon!"

"Am I your vassal, or you mine?"

"Ask rather how I'm to protect you, when you vanish?" He beckoned for my arm, emptied a flask of water upon it.

"Are we done, sire?" Tursel.

"For now. Tend to their wounds, and keep them alive."

Tursel nodded, left us, trailing an air of exasperation.

Fostrow muttered under his breath. I raised an eyebrow. He repeated, "Ask him why I was banished from your side."

Across the clearing Tursel heard, and bristled. "Ask what you will, sire, but in private. Not before Duke Margenthar's stray lout." He stalked off.

Fostrow's arm went to his sword. "Stray—"

My hand closed on his, held the sword in its scabbard. "Do you tend my scratches, or make war?"

He glared at the path along which Tursel had vanished. "While you're at it, Prince Rodrigo, ask how a gaggle of our scouts could miss so large an enemy force lying in the brush alongside the trail. This valley was supposed clear, I recall."

"A good point, that." Rustin tapped finger to teeth. "Yes, you might ask that, Roddy."

"Get on with it, Fostrow. I think I'm going to be sick."

"From the wound?"

"Not mine, his." I pointed to the lad with the slit throat. His two companions hunched in misery, among the greedy flies.

Rustin raised an eyebrow. "What will you do with them?"

"Let them go, I suppose."

At last, Fostrow finished binding my arm.

"They're wounded."

"Their misfortune."

"Aye, my prince. They're your bondsmen, so you owe them protection."

"That was just to stop Herut from—can't I get out of it?"

He cleared his throat. "A moment ago you spoke of honor."

"Damn honor!"

Rustin came close, raised a gentle hand to stroke my hair. "You asked me," he said softly, "to teach you manhood?"

My face red, I snapped, "Imps take the lot of you!" I pulled free of Fostrow, strode to the bleeding boy. "Your name!"

"Anavar, my lord." He had a thick Eiberian accent.

"Do you want me to free you?"

"Lord, no!"

It was what I least expected. "Why?"

"They'll kill us." He pointed to Herut.

"I'll give you safe-conduct from our camp."

"Then Lord Tantroth or our captain will hang us."

"Why?"

"How else would we gain safe-conduct, but by swearing you allegiance?"

I grunted my exasperation. "And you, with the bloody shoulder. Would you be free?"

"More than anything, sire." His accent was even stronger than Anavar's. "Yet I swore my bond. If I go back to my troop, it's my death."

"I'll remit—"

"Please, sire!" His eyes locked on mine. "Please!"

"May you burn in the demons'—" With an effort I controlled

myself. "All right, I'll do what I must. Fostrow, can you bind their wounds?"

The guardsman scowled. "Hester's skills are greater."

"Take these fools to her wagon, then. No, just a moment." I looked to the larger of the two. "How old are you?"

"Eighteen summers, sir."

"What are you called?"

"Garst, my lord."

"Are you highborn?"

He reddened. "No, sire."

I turned. "On your feet, Anavar. Are you of noble birth?"

The youngster struggled to his feet. "Aye, sire. I'm heir to the earldom of Kalb."

"Never heard of the place. What are you doing in Caledon? You're no more than a child."

Anavar flushed. "I'm full fourteen, sire. A page to my lord Treak, who is cousin to the Duke of Eiber himself." He straightened with pride, wiped an ooze of blood from his eyes. "My father said—"

"I don't want to hear it. Keep them out of mischief, Fostrow, lest someone cut their throats. Go with the soldier, both of you."

Anavar held his ground. "May we know whom we serve, sire? Are you a noble?"

I drew myself up. "I'm Prince Rodrigo, heir to the throne of Caledon."

His look of awe was worth the battle.

Chapter 27

 HESTER SCOWLED. "PERHAPS I TURNED INTO A BIRD."

I said, "I don't see why you won't tell me." I tried not to let my voice go sulky, but I was hungry, cold, and tired. The stewpot bubbled over the fire, but dinner wanted an hour or more.

Sitting against the wagon's muddy wheels, Anavar and Garst watched with wonder. Anavar's forehead was bound. Garst's shoulder was bandaged, his arm in a sling.

The old woman sighed. "I took myself to a safe place. Ask rather: why had I to flee, amid such an escort? We should have been—"

Tursel stepped into the firelight. "I might answer that."

Fostrow shot him a baleful look.

"Not here." I stood, shivered again. The stream where I'd bathed had been too cold. "Your tent."

Fostrow stirred anew. "Don't go in the dark with him, my lord. He might—"

"If he wanted me dead, it would be done."

The captain's tent was larger than all but mine, which Rustin shared. Within the canvas, dark green cloths hung as further protection from the wind. A row of candles sat on a low bench.

I closed the flap, took a seat on a trunk. "Well?"

He sighed, making himself comfortable on bed pillows. "Sallit and Teir, two of our scouts, are gone, their bodies not found."

"Betrayal?"

"So it seems. I'd posted them on the western heights, but it appears they traded places with Harg and Varian. Some tale about wishing to stay closer to camp."

"You allowed this?"

"Of course not!" For once, he seemed angry.

"Harg and Varian were assigned . . ."

"Our right flank, on the east."

"Where the invaders were hid." I was silent a moment. "How do you know it's not Harg and Varian, lying about switching posts?"

"The truth will out, before morn."

I shivered. "Torture?"

"Persuasion."

I stood to pace. "Tursel, you're too . . . bloodthirsty for my taste. Bring them here; let's question them together."

"We're at war, sire, not a game of rooks and kings. Traitors deserve no mercy."

"Nonetheless, do as I ask."

"Aye, my lord." He hesitated. "I assume you'll appoint another captain over me?"

"For disputing my orders?"

He seemed surprised. "Of course not; it's my duty to say when you're wrong. I meant for allowing Tantroth's men at you."

"It's not an auspicious start. You said you know your men."

"Yes. Not only were our scouts remiss, but Tantroth's host knew just where to find us. One way or another, treachery is at work. I can only assure you it's not mine."

"Imbar spoke well of you."

"Did he?" Tursel showed no interest. "It was my lord Raeth who trained me."

"Personally?"

"From a boy." Did he flush, in the dim light? I couldn't be sure. He asked, "Is there else, sire?"

"No. Um, yes. Fostrow."

Tursel sat. "What about him?"

I hadn't eaten, and diplomacy deserted me. "By the demons' own lake, you know well what I ask!"

"I apologize if I've offended—"

"You offend me at this moment! Speak!"

He faced me. "I sent him to the rear, away from you."

"Why?"

"I'm responsible for your safety. I don't know him."

My tone was scornful. "Think you he'd betray me?"

"He was Margenthar's man."

I said, "He could have killed me when first we met."

"Perhaps it didn't suit Mar's purpose, then." He shifted. "Politics is a high and bloody game, and I have no head for it. All I know is that while it's my task to protect you, I'll have men I know at your side."

I laughed, and the sound came harsh. "Why not banish Rustin too?"

"I've considered it." His tone was somber. "Sire, do you understand how grave a portent it is, that Tantroth's force lay in wait for us?"

At length, I said, "Tursel, answer me clearly. Am I your prisoner or no?"

"Of course not!"

"Am I free to leave your tent?"

"Yes, sire."

"Your camp?"

His eyes closed briefly, as if in pain. "Aye."

"Whom do you serve?"

"You, sire."

"In truth!"

He repeated, more slowly, "You, sire."

I pulled my seat closer. "Then heed me. All those of my original party may have free access to my person. That includes Fostrow."

"Aye, sire."

"Bring the scouts Harg and Varian, separately, for questioning."

"Here?"

"Or my own tent, if you prefer."

He wrinkled his nose. "Here, sire."

Harg was the first to appear, held between two burly soldiers. They sat him on the trunk.

Once released, he swayed back and forth, nursing a hand. When I went to take it he made a sound of protest, resisted.

"Let me see."

Reluctantly, he opened his fingers, to reveal red and oozing blisters.

"Persuasion." I spat the word. "You, soldier, bring ointment and a cloth." The man looked to Tursel for confirmation, and it enraged me. I snarled. "Who commands here?"

"Captain Tursel, sir."

Tursel said quietly, "The Prince commands overall. Go."

I studied Harg. His face drawn and sallow, he looked exhausted. "You've done wrong."

He nodded, but couldn't meet my eyes.

"Tell me."

The scout stammered in his eagerness to comply. "As I said, sir. They asked to switch places. I know I shouldn't have . . . we saw no harm, at the time."

"What reason did they give?"

"They always drew the lot farthest from camp, and we owed them a change."

Tursel shouted, "The truth!"

Harg cringed. "It's true."

I pondered. His story was too simple, and some sense told me to be wary.

Though we treated his burns, though I pleaded and Tursel blustered, we could get no more from him.

For a long while, Varian said likewise. I treated him kindly, even had him brought a bowl of soup. He left it untouched. Despite all our efforts, his story remained the same.

I thought to sit next to him, and took away the bowl that blocked my place. As I set it upon the trunk, my free hand passed over it, and a great weariness washed over me. For a moment I stood, hands outstretched, over the still liquid.

Behind me, Tursel snarled, "You try the Prince's patience. Confess, and be quick!"

"Varian, the authority is mine to pardon or condemn you. Tell the rest." Something pulled at my consciousness, and I tried to shake it away.

"I've told—"

My voice was low, insistent. "I would hear what's missing from your story." Why did I speak so? I felt a vague alarm.

He cried, "I did no treason!"

That was it. "I know." As if soothing an unreachable itch, I repeated, "I know." My eyes fastened on the unfortunate scout. "Tell me."

"Sallit—I'm sorry, Captain—he had bottles hid under the supply cart, and his platoon knew. He was afraid they'd steal his drink, unless he was posted near."

"Why did you care?"

Varian's eyes fell. "He shared with us."

Silence.

Tursel blinked.

I said, "Take him outside." When we were alone I added, "Now it's complete."

"You can't be sure."

"As sure as I need be. Pardon the scouts, but don't trust them again. Send them back to Cumber."

"If they're Tantroth's men they'll flee."

"And then we'll know. It's no matter; they've done their harm." I held his eyes until he assented.

Back at our campfire, I wolfed down my stew, but Fostrow assaulted me before I'd finished. "What of the two soldiers you brought into our fold? Do we bind them for the night?"

"Whatever for?" I looked across the fire, where the two wounded boys dozed under a blanket.

"Do you covet a knife in the ribs, my lord? Hours past, they were bent on killing you."

"What would you do?"

"Send them away, at the least."

I raised my voice. "Anavar, come here."

Obediently, the younger boy thrust off his blanket, circled the fire. As he came close, he stumbled. "Sorry, sire. I'm dizzy." He touched his bandage.

"Will you try to kill me in the night?"

He looked startled. "No, sire."

"Why should I trust you?"

"I swore to you, sire."

Rustin stirred. "Did you not likewise swear to Tantroth?"

Anavar's expression was bleak. "Yes."

"So, then?"

He shrugged. "I did all I could; my loyalty to him is paid. You'd have killed me had I not sworn fealty."

Rustin said, "It's that clear, in your mind?"

A pause. "No, but it's all I have."

My voice was gruff. "Have you weapons?"

"I lost my pike, and they took my knife after I fell."

"Go to your blanket. I'll trust your new loyalty, but don't go prowling in the night."

"Aye, my lord." He retreated.

I yawned. "See? He said he wouldn't kill me."

Rust snorted. "You risk Elryc as well."

I flared, "What, then? Cut his throat, as Herut would?"

"No. Not that." For a long while he was silent.

Later, in the warmth of our bed, Rustin whispered, "I'd not have taken them as bondsmen."

I stirred. "Was I wrong?"

"No." A time passed. "Such gestures suit a king."

"I'm weary." I settled my head on his shoulder, and slept.

We crossed endless hills, and never saw Tantroth's troops.

Two days dragged past. Soushire was near, and Hester was determined to turn to Verein when the road split.

Garst plodded alongside the cart. At first Anavar did the same, but within a day Genard had wangled a place for him on Hester's wagon, where he himself rode.

Elryc, after the attack, fastened himself to me and followed wherever Rustin and I roamed. He was full of questions, and brimmed with energy. I began to suspect his fear, but for his sake, made no mention of it.

Where the road was wide enough we rode four abreast: Fostrow, Elryc, Rustin, and I. Tursel cantered his mare up and down the line, closing gaps, urging the guards to greater vigilance.

At a pause, Anavar brought me water in a bucket. He set it down, offered me the scoop.

"Thank you." I drank, without dismounting. "Whose thought was this?"

He colored. "The old woman's."

"Dame Hester, to you."

"Aye, sire. Dame Hester. Sire, what will my duties be?"

"I haven't decided." I scowled. "You would work?"

His head came up proudly. "I ask no man's charity."

"You ask not mine? Would you rather I let you starve, while you heal?"

He flushed. "No, sire."

"Then hold your tongue. Back to the wagon."

When he was gone Rustin said mildly, "He only asked how he could serve you."

"Let him stay out of sight until I need him."

A sigh. "I'm glad the old Roddy hasn't vanished entirely. I'd feel useless."

Elryc hid a smile, but not before I saw.

I spurred Ebon, rode ahead.

I needed two young bondsmen like I needed . . . extra teeth. They were in the way. A nuisance. I brooded for much of the afternoon.

When at last we stopped for the night I sent Garst to get fodder, and took Anavar aside. He was to fetch and carry, I told him, to help light fires, stir our soup, set our tents. Make himself useful round the camp.

His manner was subdued but resentful. "My father is Duke of Kalb."

"And you're bound as page to Treak, Tantroth's cousin. So?"

"Can you not find more fit work—"

This, after saving his life? Where was the gratitude I deserved? "Do as I command, or flee and prove the worth of Eiber's oath. I won't chase you."

The boy sucked in breath, but his eyes never left mine. Perhaps I'd said enough. I let him be.

Late at night, in the tent, Rustin barely listened to my tale. "We've more to worry about, Roddy. By morrow's end we should reach Soushire's realm. Best you send envoys."

"To say what?"

"That you come peaceably, and would confer with her."

"If she refuses?"

"As I told you days ago, leave without a quarrel, and try Groenfil."

Outside, wind howled, and I shivered. "If Soushire knows Uncle Raeth's contempt for her, she won't join us for all the gold in the realm."

"She may not know. Send word we're arriving, and we'll decide how best to confront her when she's in our sight."

I grumbled, "Easy for you to say. It's not your crown we seek, or your Power that's stolen."

We made ready for our last day's ride. Genard raced up to me, stopped just short of knocking me down. "He's gone, m'lord! I've looked everywhere."

I snorted. "Anavar? I figured as much."

"Var is helping Hester load. It's Garst!"

"Tell Captain Tursel."

He ran off, and I mounted, pondering.

We rode in the middle of the column, guards at the ready, whether for Tantroth or Soushire, I couldn't tell.

When I caught sight of Hester's wagon I beckoned Anavar to approach. He trotted to Ebon's bridle, trotted between me and Rustin as we rode. "Did Garst tell you he was leaving?"

He hesitated. "No."

"If he had, would you have warned me?"

"My lord, I—no."

Rustin sucked in his breath at the boy's audacity, but I approved of his spirit. Nonetheless, I glowered. "What shall I do with you?"

Anavar panted from the exertion of keeping pace. "I did no wrong, sir."

"But you would have." Knowing I sounded childish, I let it be. After a time, when he was well winded, I sent him back to the wagon.

We wound our way from the hills onto a broad flat plain: the flats of Soushire. Only there, amid the well-tended fields did Tursel relax his guard, and join us on the wide dusty road to Castle Town.

I looked for a discreet way to mention Garst's disappearance, but Tursel saved me the trouble. "So your prisoner's on the loose, sire. An oath lightly given, to escape his fate."

I slapped my saddle with a flash of irritation. "Tursel, what would you have done, in his place?"

"Not let myself be taken."

"Say you were clubbed from behind, and woke in enemy hands."

"I'd expect death, and wouldn't beg mercy."

Rustin intervened. "Is it not done, in war?"

Tursel's words were clipped. "Perhaps by others."

"But not by one so honorable as yourself."

The captain snapped, "At least I know what honor is. It's not surprising the son of a traitor does not."

Rustin's hand flew to his sword. "You dare— Sir, accept my chall—"

"*Enough!*" Ebon startled at my raw scream. I soothed him. "Captain, leave us. Rust, be silent. No! I said to be still, *and I meant it!*" It was the first time ever I spoke to him so.

In the afternoon couriers approached from Soushire's Castle Town. To my surprise, the Duchess responded to our envoys with a note of welcome, bidding our escort to camp in her fields, and offering my personal party the hospitality of her citadel.

Reading the scroll, Tursel frowned. "We shouldn't be divided."

"She gives the usual assurances of safe passage."

"Words mean nothing."

I shrugged. "You can't expect her to invite us all into her keep; she hasn't the room."

"Then camp among us. Treat with her elsewhere."

Rustin. "She'd take it as insult."

"Roddy! Look!" Elryc rushed from the wagon, pointing down the road.

I peered. Soldiers, our own. Wagons. And Garst.

His walk was awkward, almost a limp, but purposeful. At last, travel-worn, his bandage awry, he came to a stop before me. From Hester's wagon, Anavar watched wide-eyed.

"Well." It was all I could think to say. It brought no response. "Explain yourself."

"I . . . came back."

"From?"

"I crept off before dawn, to find my people. It wasn't fair I should be your bondsman all my life, for answering my duke's call." His eyes darted about, as if seeking escape, then fastened reluctantly on mine. "But . . . I gave my oath. Imps and demons would pursue me evermore, if I failed it. So . . . I turned around, chased after you."

"After he reported our position to his regiment." Tursel's tone was cynical. "They set him to spy on us."

"I never found them. I gave up looking after a league, when I realized—"

I cleared my throat. "Captain, your scouts searched and found no foes. How could Garst wander from camp and make contact, not knowing even where to look? I believe him."

"He's not worth the risk."

"Garst, your return doesn't excuse your flight. In future, recall your oath before you violate it. Rust, take him to Fostrow, have him thrashed. Hurry back; we have to decide about Soushire."

Rustin grabbed the youth's arm.

Garst cried, "Sir, I beg thy grace. I returned on my own, and—"

With a sweeping blow, Rustin knocked him to the ground. "Now!" He hauled Garst to his feet, gave him a shove.

The boy went, protesting loudly. Tursel watched their retreating backs. "You'll be sorry."

"If so, it's my concern."

We pressed on, eager to reach Castle Town before dark.

Not long after, Anavar trotted over from our cart, summoning me to Hester.

The old woman favored me with a cross look. "There's a road a league hence, that will lead me west to Verein. No, don't argue; I must see to Pytor. The question is, what of Elryc, and where will the girl ride?" She glanced back at Chela, who, as usual, seemed sullen.

"Are you well enough for a horse?" It was the first time in days I'd addressed Chela directly.

"Have you spare, for one lowly as me?" Her sarcasm dripped.

"Answer!"

"Yes!"

I turned to Hester. "She'll ride with us. As for Elryc, it's not safe to take him to Margenthar's lair."

I expected fierce argument, but all she said was, "I know."

"It's not safe for you either."

Hester sighed. "I have no choice. I go, for my lady, and my boy."

My voice was strained. "Hester, my business is here."

For the first time in months, her voice was gentle. "You must seek the crown. My lady approves. With all her heart, she wished you to have it."

She leaned forward, gripped my wrist. "I leave Elryc in your charge. Swear by the True of Caledon that you will protect him and tend his needs."

"I've already sworn—"

"To him, perhaps, but not to me!" Her visage brooked no refusal.

I gave the oath, sitting on Ebon alongside the wagon.

"Elryc wants affection, as well as food and drink. Will you give him that?" Her tone was wistful.

I swallowed. "It's not much in my nature. I'll try."

"Be kind to Genard also. There's good in him."

My lips were dry. "Is this farewell?"

"For a time. I'll be back, with Pytor." She beckoned me close. "Take care to don clean clothes." Her fingers tidied my hair as if I were a child. "And listen to Rustin. He has sense, for a boy. Now, that Tursel . . ." Her glance flickered, to make sure we weren't overheard. "Trust his loyalty, but not his wit."

"Is he Raeth's man, or mine?"

"He doesn't know himself, I think. For now, it's the same."

Anavar was near, so I changed the subject. "Will you ride alone?"

"I've spoken to Tursel; he'll lend a few soldiers to help speed my way. When we near Verein they'll turn back."

I nodded.

"Take care for Elryc!" It was a plea from her heart.

Dismounting, I tied Ebon to the rail, swung aboard the cart. "Nurse . . ." For a moment, I yearned to put my head in her lap.

"Oh, Roddy." Her hand darted out, pulled back. She cleared her throat. "You're a babe no longer." She busied herself with bags and boxes. "Go. Make yourself King."

Chapter 28

THE CASTLE WAS SET ON A HILL, AS STRONG PLACES USUALLY are. Its walls were immensely thick and well fortified for so small a place. I'd never been to Soushire before, and had expected greater.

From the hill opposite, I scrutinized the fluttering banners, trying to remember from my heraldry whether the Lady of Soushire hinted, in her displays, of her alliances.

In Council she had acquiesced to Margenthar's regency once Uncle Mar proved he had the votes. I wasn't sure what Mar had given her for a sop, but, knowing Uncle, it was something she coveted.

On the other hand, Uncle Mar was on the verge of losing Stryx. Would she keep faith in his promises?

I sighed. Politics were too complex.

Rust and I—and Elryc, who kept tugging at my arm, demanding to take part—chose an honor guard large enough to put up a show of defense if need be.

As we rode down to Soushire, Garst crouched on the supply cart, his shuddering breaths still relapsing into occasional sobs. Whatever beating Fostrow had given him was less than he deserved. Why be merciful, if the beneficiary felt naught but resentment? At least Anavar seemed cool to Garst's distress.

Our approach to the castle was somewhat less than orderly; the stateliness of our column was marred by the carts overflowing with our wounded, and the few prisoners of Tantroth I'd prevented Tursel from murdering.

Rustin muttered, "Wave, Roddy. She's in front, in the green cloak." Obediently I waved to the plump Duchess, surrounded by her retinue.

Soushire's speech of welcome and my gracious reply were as short as ritual allowed. Her chamberlain indicated which fallow fields our military was to occupy, and our honored few trooped inside.

I presumed her invitation to the castle included my entire personal party, and brought Elryc, Rust, Chela, Genard, and Fostrow into the keep. For good measure I included my two new bondsmen, who'd at least be useful as message runners. If bedchambers were lacking, they could sleep on benches in the hall.

In our small and dingy chambers Rustin and I bathed, scrubbing each other's backs in an intimacy I was beginning to find agreeable. One needed to be touched, from time to time. To live otherwise was too lonely, too remote. After, we dressed in our better regalia, and awaited a summons to dinner.

Rust sat on the bed next to me, his lips at my ear. "Assume we are overheard in anything we say."

"Of course." I raised my voice. "If you can hear us, tell the Lady we're grateful for her hospitality."

Rustin frowned, shook his head. "Why reveal to them we're aware of being overheard?"

"So Soushire won't think me a fool." I gestured at the dank stone. "Too much is at stake for her not to spy. To think else would be to assume *her* a dunce, and I do her the compliment of believing otherwise."

Rustin was saved from further reply by a servant, calling us downstairs.

The meal was a formal banquet, in a great hall marred by insufficient light and a rather oppressive aroma of past cooking. During the introductions, we exchanged the intricate bows that acknowledged station, place, and subservience.

As heir to Caledon, I should outrank all but the Duchess, as she was in her own domain and was owed the elaborate courtesy due a host. Yet, her people tendered me the polite bow due any noble guest, instead of the deeper, more formal bow due royalty. I pretended not to notice. Lady Soushire, after all, risked Uncle Mar's wrath by allowing us within. Castle Town was much nearer to Stryx than was Cumber, and the fat old Duchess had to take care.

A bored minstrel played too familiar airs on a lute while dinner progressed. The Lady was a greedy eater, albeit a sloppy one; her robe was soon stained with soup and crumbs. She didn't seem to mind, and constantly fed morsels to a great mastiff hound that lay at her feet.

As time passed, wine flowed and the conversation grew louder. I was careful to water my wine.

The heavyset Lady was no match for Uncle Raeth in subtlety; as soon as the last course was cleared and the lesser guests dismissed, she charged into the fray with scant preliminary. "You may wonder why I took you in, given your uncertain status and your, ah, strained relations with Stryx."

"Your hospitality is known throughout the realm." I hoped my irony wasn't overdone.

She ignored my barb. "You're here because I have something you want, and you're in a position to reciprocate."

Rustin overrode my reply. "What have you that my lord Rodrigo desires, madam?"

I leaned back, content to let Rust joust on my behalf.

Again, Soushire drove straight to the point. "A vote in Council. What else?"

Even Rustin seemed a little taken back at her lack of delicacy. "And what would you desire, my lady?"

Soushire twirled her fork, her attention on her empty plate. "Groenfil."

I blurted, "Pardon?"

"Groenfil. All of it." She looked up, a gleam in her shrewd eye. "The lands, the title, the revenues. As your vassal, of course. The keep, too, and your assistance getting it."

"Good heavens. Why?"

Soushire looked perplexed. "What an odd question." Idly, she tapped her fork. "Which do you ask: why I want it, what justification I give, or why you should agree?"

I said, "They're all the same."

"Hardly. I covet Groenfil's lands because they're rich and adjoin mine. My justification is the Groenfil-Soushire marriage."

"That was thirty years ago."

"Forty-two, but the contract was valid and remains so. The lands were to be combined under their firstborn child."

"Who was born dead."

"Who died three days after birth, but not before a will was made leaving his goods to his father, that is, my grandfather."

"But the title hadn't been transferred to the child." The old quarrel was well known throughout Caledon.

Soushire slammed her fist on the table; my glass jumped. "It should have been!" Her dog jumped to its feet, growled ominously. "It's all right, Bakko." She took a deep breath, and the dog calmed.

Rustin said, "Pardon, madam, but that's preposterous. A generation has passed."

"It will serve, however, as my justification. Now, what was the third question?" The lady scowled. "Ah, yes: why you should agree. I'll trade my vote for your pledge of Groenfil. I assume you're close to four Council votes, but still lacking one. Cumber must be with you, since he sent his troops, and who else? The Warthen? He's Mar's oldest ally, and more avaricious even than I. The Speaker? He's old and conservative, and—"

Rustin and I exchanged glances. "I can't tell you," I said.

Soushire studied me closely; I tried not to blench at a whiff of garlic. "Do you know what you're up to? Do you grasp games of state?"

"I learn." I reached across to Rustin's undiluted wine, took a long swallow; I needed it.

"How many votes have you?" Soushire sat back, folded her hands across her belly, as I looked helplessly at Rustin.

"Our thanks for an excellent dinner, madam." Rust scraped back his chair. "Shall we walk in the cool night air, my prince? Perhaps it would help clear our heads." We stood.

"Oh, walk, by all means," said Soushire. "I'll want a response soon. How long did you string Cumber along, a week? Can't have that; you must be gone before Mar gets wind of your visit."

"He'll know we were here. News travels."

"But you'll be elsewhere, when he hears."

At the door, Fostrow came to his feet. "Where do we go?"

"You weren't invited," I told him.

"For a walk, is it? In the dark, even I won't be enough. I'll call our honor guard."

"You will *not*. Rust and I just want a few words."

Fostrow peered outside to where Tursel's guardsmen lounged, snapped his fingers.

I sighed. Servants.

I made the guardsmen—except Fostrow, who ignored me—walk behind us a score of paces, so we could converse in private. Their torches sent dancing shadows in our path.

I said, "She takes your breath away."

"She *is* direct."

"I can't possibly give her Groenfil."

"It's good you didn't consider it."

"I did." My blush was concealed by the night. "It's worse than Cumber's demand that I remit taxes. I'd have the kingdom in turmoil."

"Is that your only reason?"

"Need I others?"

"There's the matter of justice."

I grimaced. "Groenfil's the most corrupt earldom in Caledon. Mother always had to fight for her crown revenues."

"Is that reason to unseat him?"

"Of course not." How could an earl be thrown off his lands at a sovereign's whim? Who next: a duke? Perhaps then a king. No, the right of a noble house to its holdings and churls was paramount. I strode along the stone walk, between two high walls. "What does Soushire want? That we provide her a conquering army?"

"She hasn't made it clear yet."

"Demons take them all." Abruptly a shadow flitted across a parapet. I made a sign to propitiate imps and demons. What had come over me, casting curses in the dark of night? "Let's go inside." I glanced about the night, summoned a Rite of Banishing.

"What will you tell her?"

Something seized me from behind. I squawked.

"Quiet, you fool!" Fostrow, a hoarse whisper. "They're following you."

My heart thudded. "Make the five-sided square for protection, and recite—".

He shook me. "Two, perhaps three men, on the wall above. They're shod in something soft, not boots."

My voice was unsteady. "You're sure it's men?"

"What women would skulk in the night, overhead? Are you daft?"

I hadn't summoned imps, by my foolishness. I took deep breaths, subdued my panic. For some reason my legs were shaky. "Are they armed?"

"I can't see enough to tell. No, stay; the overhang gives protection."

"What's their purpose?"

"I'm not sure. Most likely, to spy, but . . ." He shrugged.

My skin prickled. "Take me inside!"

"Steady, my prince." Rustin.

"It's dark, and I want—" I made myself sound calm, by brute effort. "All right. What do we do?"

"Wait." Fostrow strode back toward the guardsmen. The buzz of voices, while he conferred. Rust quietly drew his sword, and I fervently wished I'd worn my own.

Our escort moved forward in a pack. Suddenly the overhang was bright with torchlight.

Fostrow. "Lord Rustin, sheath your blade. Best we not look like a war party."

"If Roddy's in danger—"

"You'll know in time to draw. You boys stay among us; we'll shield you as we walk. Together, now. Ready, all? Go!"

We surged out between the walls. Almost, I stumbled, but caught myself. Moving so fast it was almost laughable, we scurried to the gaping castle door. Only when I was safe inside did the prickling in my back begin to ease.

Fostrow beckoned the guardsmen; they rushed back outside to seek the stalkers. He turned to me. "I doubt they'll find anyone; our watchers knew well the lay of the place."

"Why that quickstep march?"

"We shielded you in case they meant to attack, but it's more likely they spied on your deliberations."

"Soushire?"

Rustin said, "It's her castle, but Mar's agents could be within. Or a myriad of others. Lord Cumber. Tantroth. Even Groenfil."

We returned to the banquet hall. Soushire was where we'd left her, at the head of her table.

"Ah, Rodrigo. A pleasant walk? You seem pale. Prince Elryc says you've brought an Eiberian noble to our house."

I gaped. "A what? Oh, you mean Anavar. He's pledged to me."

"Let me see him."

"No, that would . . . no."

Soushire raised an eyebrow. "Is that how you play at diplomacy? Know you not to please your adversary in the simple things, and withhold only the great?"

I flushed at the rebuke. "Are we adversaries, madam?"

"We may become so." She studied me, her eyes cold, and the dog stirred. "Unless you realize you need me more than I need you."

"How so?"

"If we fail to ally, all I lose is Groenfil, and I live well without it. You, on the other hand, will have nothing, and are finished."

My hand tightened on the edge of the table, but remained still. "Only if your vote is indispensable."

"It is."

I waited.

"You see, I know the other councilors, and can't imagine how you'd assemble four votes without mine. I also know, by your arrival on my doorstep, that you think the same." For a moment she frowned, then belched loudly. "Your pardon."

Her rudeness emboldened me. "If that's so, my lady, why ask for so little as Groenfil? Why not half of Caledon?"

"You'd balk at that, whereas Groenfil benefits me, yet costs you naught. I've thought the matter through. Where's your noble young prisoner?"

"Bondsman. Eating with the servants, I presume. If your support is essential, why wouldn't Margenthar pay you as well as I?"

"Perhaps he would. Will." A grim smile. "At the moment I hesitate to ask. With Tantroth loose, Mar's good humor is dwindled." The smile faded. "And were Margenthar to prevail, I'm too close to Stryx to invite his enmity. Unlike your patron Cumber, who tugs at the tiger's tail with impunity from his hills."

"Why say you Cumber is my patron?"

"Oh, nonsense, boy!" Her palm slapped the table. "I knew before you did. We could none of us survive without a close eye on the other."

I looked longingly at the wine, but held myself together. "If it's as you say, then Groenfil will know what we agree. How then could I seek"—Rustin stirred, made as if to speak—"his vote?"

Soushire's eyes narrowed. After a moment, she closed her eyes, mopped her forehead. "Excuse me, young prince. I feel not well." She heaved herself from her chair, hurried from the room.

Outside the window, dogs began to growl.

I turned to Rust. "What did I—"

"Later." It was a command. "To our rooms." His mouth tight, he led the way.

Candles fluttered when I flung open our door. Anavar, sitting cross-legged in a corner, started with alarm.

My voice was a snarl. "Out! I don't sleep with servants. Find where Genard and Chela stay, and bed there." I slammed the door the moment he was gone, and turned to Rustin. "Well?"

"We'll speak as we did in Cumber." He untied his jerkin, readied himself for bed.

Later, under the covers, he put his lips to my ear. "Roddy, you've imperiled us. You should have known better."

I replayed our conversation as best I could, but could find no error. "What did I do?"

His words were so soft I had to strain to hear. "Until you spoke of Groenfil, Soushire thought hers was the fourth vote. She had no idea you had only two others."

"Oh." I slapped my forehead. "I'm a dunce."

"Agreed." He put lips to my ear once more. "How do we undo the damage?"

For a long while I thought. Then, at last, I stirred, took breath, said a trifle more loudly, "Do you think it worked?"

Rustin tensed. My fingers went to his mouth, in a seal.

"I know, Rust, but you could see she guessed. We'll lose Speaker Vessa's pledge if anyone suspects we have it. Surely you know that." A pause. Rustin tensed, his eyes locked on mine. I said, "What choice did I have, but to confuse Soushire? She thinks we had but two others."

At last, Rustin nodded, and I removed my hand.

"But if Soushire refused to support you . . ." His voice too was audible.

"Then we make Groenfil the fourth, as we said." A creak. I strained to discern a movement, a hidden breath, but heard no more. "As long as Soushire thinks she's only the third vote, she won't price her support so dear. Wait 'til the morrow; you'll see. Now, let me sleep." I leaned back, heart pounding.

I had done what I might. Rustin nodded his approval, and nestled close.

I woke to a rainy morn. My head ached, and I snarled at whoever crossed my path. A castle servant brought water. I demanded my own bondsmen; they roused Anavar and Garst. The two tried to help with my ablutions, but had the clumsiness of untrained manservants. The throb of my forehead added to the vigor of my rebukes.

Lady Soushire called us to breakfast; I roused Elryc in the adjoining room, waited impatiently while he dressed.

Downstairs, Soushire greeted us with civility, as if nothing untoward had passed the night before. Pausing midway through a plate stuffed with viands she asked casually, "How long will you stay with us, Lord Rodrigo?"

My tone was dry. "Not long, it would seem."

"My apologies for last night. I was, ah, indisposed." She took a brimming forkful of egg bread.

I nodded, not sure what response was suitable.

"As to my vote in Council . . ."

I held my breath, waited for her to finish.

". . . I rather like your suggestion I negotiate with Margenthar." She downed her drink, signaled for more. "Unless you persuade me to bargain with you instead."

"Madam, don't play with us. On what terms may we have your vote?"

"You know my price. The lands and folk of Groenfil, and the title."

"Beyond reason." Still, relief washed over me; at least her proposition still stood.

Soushire snorted, refilled her plate. "But not beyond your ability to pay. And I wouldn't renew the offer but for other troubling questions."

"Such as?"

"Tantroth." She chewed moodily. "Why did Llewelyn abandon his keep? Why doesn't Mar bestir himself to throw out the invaders? Is a deal struck between them? If so, who among them would take the throne?"

"Crown me, and they'll be answered."

Mesmerized, Elryc watched our byplay.

"You're an unproven boy. I've risks either way. Further, my vote is pledged to Duke Margenthar."

"Yours isn't the only vote I could seek."

"You jest. Whom else would you pry loose? The Warthen?"

"Lord Groenfil, for one."

"Hah. Have you forgotten his sister is Mar's wife? I can think of nothing on earth that would separate—"

"I can." Rustin.

Soushire stopped short. "Oh?"

Rust said blandly, "If my lord Prince were to tell Groenfil you mean to negotiate with Mar for his title and lands . . ."

"Bah. Who would believe you?"

"Groenfil would." Rust spoke quietly. "When Rodrigo swore so by the True of Caledon."

I lifted a glass, to hide my exultation. Why hadn't I thought of such a maneuver?

"Clever." Soushire drummed her fingers on the tablecloth, considering. "But, no, I don't think he'd adhere to you even then. Though it might make him more wary of his brother-in-law." She looked up with a smile. "What you've done, lad, is make it more imperative that we strike a bargain. I don't want to risk the wrath of either Groenfil or Mar, and you can't afford to do without my vote."

I said, "Since when are a noble's lands subject to barter? It's outrageous."

Soushire's tone was curious. "Can one in your position afford principles?"

Elryc stirred. "Consider your own position, my lady." His voice was thin and reedy. "You alienate Uncle Mar, Groenfil, *and* the future King. Ask of Roddy something reasonable, that he can give."

Soushire mopped the last of her plate. "A good point, but I've long dreamed of Groenfil, and the moment is auspicious. I don't intend to vary one iota from the terms I've set."

She hoisted herself from her place. "Let us have your answer soon;

if we're not in agreement, be on your way by nightfall." Her napkin fell from her fingers. "Then, I'll put my terms to Mar." With that, she trudged from the room.

I nibbled at the remainder of my food, finally rose in disgust. "I need to walk."

Rustin said, "It's storming."

"Then I'll be wet." I crossed the outer hall.

"The spies . . ."

"It's day. At this hour they can't hide in shadows." Still, I was glad that Fostrow rose to follow.

The rain was chill. I stalked across the muddy courtyard, found a wall whose overhang offered shelter. I strode along its length.

Clearly, I had to refuse Soushire's demand. Groenfil might be untrustworthy, even corrupt, but Soushire was hardly better. Why favor one over the other? Besides, it wasn't for a king to redistribute his vassals' lands.

My shirt was soggy, and water dripped in my eyes. I wiped them, and stepped into a puddle. Cursing, I stomped my soaked foot, almost lost my boot in the mud.

Time for a deep breath. It seemed to help, so I took another. Rain wasn't so bad as long as one didn't mind getting soaked. Once, I'd stood under a small waterfall, and enjoyed it. I relaxed my shoulders, let the drenching rain pour over me.

At last I moved on, but this time I strolled, careless of the wet.

I could count on Willem and Cumber. Vessa's vote was unlikely; Groenfil's even more so. Therefore, I needed both Soushire and the Warthen of the Sands. Else I would not be crowned by Council, and couldn't wield the Still.

I climbed steps, brooding. Could I somehow swing the Warthen to my cause? A peculiar fellow, he, but . . .

I found myself on a low battlement, secured by a stone parapet. I braced myself on the embedded rock, leaned over the edge, stared blindly at Castle Town. Lord of Nature only knew what odious terms the Warthen would propose.

Water dripped from my nose. I watched it trickle down a groove of the stone, to the ground. Near my hand, a deep puddle had formed in a scoop of the rock. Shielded by my body, no droplets struck it. It seemed a lake in minuscule.

I moved; a drop of water struck, sent a ripple coursing. Reflexively, I covered the puddle, protecting it.

Ah, Mother. This puzzle is too deep for me. I'm close to my crown, but fuddled.

My palms spread low over the puddle.

When I must be brilliant, all I can do is stumble about in the rain. More proof I'm unfit to rule.

Mother's visage floated, stern, silent.

Madam, why didn't you renounce me when you could? Or else, live to see me through? My thoughts settled into a daze of regrets and yearnings.

Rain.

Time.

Was there a path through the thicket? Was it possible?

A hand grasped my arm. "Roddy!"

Rain.

"Roddy, come awake!" An insistent shake. I blinked.

Elryc peered up at me. "You were in a stupor. I couldn't wake you."

My eyes were wild, and I laughed.

"Don't! You scare me!"

Reluctantly, I closed my hands, let droplets splash into the puddle. "I'm all right, brother."

"Come inside."

"Yes, before you catch your death of cold. Hester would be furious." I rumpled Elryc's hair, laughed anew. "I know the way. Oh, it's not certain, but it's a chance!"

"What?"

"The way to Stryx!"

His eyes darted about. "Have imps stolen your soul? What way?"

I caught him by the shoulders, danced him madly about the parapet. "To the throne!"

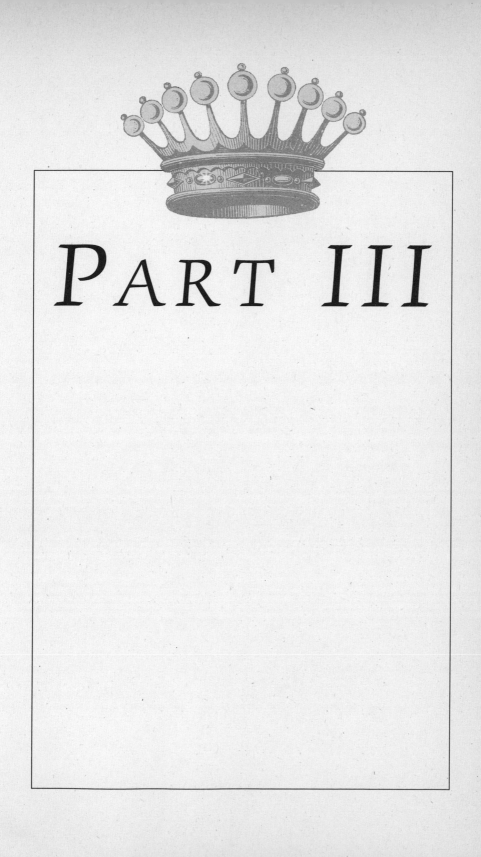

PART III

Chapter 29

 ELRYC IN TOW, I DASHED UP THE STAIRS TO MY ROOM, dripping and exultant. "Garst! Warm towels from the hearth, and call Anavar to help peel these sopping clothes!"

The Eiberian got to his feet readily enough. "I'll help you. Anavar's with the Lady Soushire."

"Impudence! I told you both—"

Rustin appeared in the doorway. "What irks you now?"

I scowled, but my jubilation was beyond quenching. "Anavar's gone downstairs without my leave, is all. Rust, this jerkin sticks like fresh sap. Help me pull."

Silent and glum, he did so. Eyes dancing, I pulled his face close to whisper my secret, but he jerked free his head, downed my hand with a sharp slap. "Don't act the fool, Roddy."

Like splintered glass my mood crashed. I tore the drying cloth from Garst's hand. "As you wish." I tried not to sound sullen, but gave it up. "Will you tell Soushire I would see her, or must I send Garst for that?"

"Oh, I'll go. Choose garb finer than you wore this morning, and if you eat again, try this time to keep the egg off your shirt." He left.

Garst helped dry my back. "He seems annoyed with you."

"Don't insert yourself in our affairs. Gather those wet towels." I waited until he was gone. "Elryc, what comes over people sometimes?"

"I've oft wondered." My brother finished drying himself. "You were in such high spirits, then . . ."

"Dress well, Elryc. I'll want you with me for the interview."

His meager chest swelled. "I won't be long. Wait for me." He trotted to his chamber to dress.

Outside, the downpour had finally eased to a drizzle. The sun made valiant effort to break through the swirling clouds, but in the keep the deserted and ill-lit banquet chamber was silent and gloomy. Elryc's hand crept into mine. Rustin, still cool, walked ahead.

"Ah, there you are." Lady Soushire, a torchbearer lighting her way. "Could we not wait 'til midday meal?" Her belly preceded her across the hall. "I had a chat with your Eiberian. Did you know his father is cousin to Tantroth himself? What a capture." She eased herself into her accustomed place. To the torchbearer, "Set it in the sconce and go."

Past the window, servants and boys called to their mates, but all I could hear was the thudding of my heart. Yearning for wine, anything, I licked my lips. "Your ambition for Groenfil," I said. "Can it be dissuaded?"

"No."

I paced, to calm my nerves. "Will you settle for any small concession, rather than the whole?"

"No."

"Well, then," I said. "What do you wish of me? Acquiescence?"

Rustin stiffened in his chair, his eyes radiating a bleak dismay.

"More than that, Rodrigo. The armed might of Caledon, to secure the Duchy of Groenfil for my House, and your authorization and recognition of my conquest." She folded her arms across her ample paunch.

"At the moment I have no force to lend, other than my paltry escort."

"Not so paltry that it didn't fend off ambush by Tantroth's regiment. But I understand your fulfillment must wait until the crown is secure on your head."

"Very well, I—"

"Roddy." Rustin's voice, subdued. "Please."

The interruption threatened my moment of triumph. My voice turned harsh. "No, it's decided, if Soushire meets my conditions."

The Duchess stirred. "I won't vary my terms."

"They're minor. I'll want funds, until the treasury is mine, and—"

"How much?"

I hadn't thought that far. "Negotiate with Lord Rustin," I said airily. "I'll ratify what he approves. My other condition is simple. For your conquest of Groenfil—as I assume the current Earl would object—I'll provide the same number of troops you send me to defend my realm against usurpation, and to repel Tantroth after I'm crowned."

"I need enough men-at-arms to hurl Groenfil off his land."

"Then raise half that number, to fight for me and Caledon when the time comes."

She made no objection, so I took a deep breath. "Now do I, Rodrigo, vow by the True of Caledon which I hold dear . . ." I swore, by my Power, to aid and ratify her conquest of Groenfil.

When I was done, she nibbled at a knuckle, her expression one of deep concentration. Then, "Rodrigo of Caledon, rightful Prince and heir, I swear that I shall, when called upon, vote in Council that you be crowned King, that thereafter I shall send men-at-arms to your standard."

Rustin put his head in his hands.

"Done." For lack of a staff, I rapped the table.

She held out her hand; I rose swiftly, gave the formal bow of completion, to avoid a touch of hands. "Good day, my lady Soushire. Be so kind as to send up my manservant Anavar; I have want of him."

I paced our bedchamber in near delirium. "Three votes! We need but one and I'll be King!" What if Soushire's spies heard me? It no longer mattered. "Now, on to the Warthen!" I ran to my bags, unwrapped the dented crown. "Remind me to find a smith to tap out the bumps. At coronation I can't very well wear—"

"Roddy." Rustin's voice was flat. "How could you?"

"It's not how it seems. My vow—" I bit off the rest, conscious of straining ears. Some things, at least, I must keep secret. "Groenfil's of no account," I said for benefit of the listeners. I beckoned Rustin close, to whisper.

"Isn't it?" With each emphasis of his words he thrust me closer to the wall. "I hoped you'd be a noble king, and find instead you'd be King at any cost." His eyes blazed. "You used Groenfil. As you'd use me, or anyone."

"Rust, that's not how—"

"You revealed your true character." He'd worked himself into a splendid rage. "Thank Lord of Nature I am but the son of a traitor, and not myself renegade to all that is decent!"

"Rustin!"

He took breath, and began an outpouring of my faults and foibles, that, for all its unfairness, left me flushed and discomfited. Never had I been censured so, by one whose opinion I cherished.

I waited him out with as good a grace as I could muster, aware of the one thought he'd overlooked. At last he ran down. "Rust, take a moment, hear what I have to—"

He flung a pillow; it knocked over a candlestand. "More lies, more evasions? Almost, I thought you were a man!" With that he left, and just in time; I'd snatched up a boot and hurled it at his head. It bounced off the door as it swung shut.

I sat fuming at my mentor's willful stupidity. Surely Rust must fathom that I wouldn't betray Groenfil without good reason. Why could he not trust my judgment?

A knock. Was he back to apologize, so soon?

"Pardon, Lord Prince." Anavar. "You called for me?"

With a howl I sprang from my bed, hurled myself at the startled boy, pitched him against the wall. "How dare you go from here without my leave!" My voice rose to a shriek. "Are you my bondsman, or no?" My fists beat a tattoo against his shoulders, his chest. "Think you I'll tolerate such insolence?"

"Stop!" The boy cowered against the wall.

"Good-for-naught! Lazebones! Ill-bred young jackanapes!" A blow, harder than the others, spun him about. He caught at the wall with one hand; reflexively, the other shoved me aside.

At that, I caught his jerkin, reared back with closed fist, caught him full on the jaw. Anavar dropped like a stone, but I wasn't done. "Lay hand on your master?" I pounded his ribs while he lay dazed. In fury I flipped him onto his back, took seat on his stomach. "Insolent! Peasant! Brat!" Each word was punctuated by a blow to the face. "Vile . . . scum . . . of Eiber!" His head rocked slack.

The door burst open. Hands seized me from behind, dragged me kicking and screaming off the senseless boy.

"Fostrow! Come! Be quick!" Rustin.

"Let go!" I struggled to break free. "I'll teach this lout—" I jabbed at Rustin's ribs.

The soldier rushed in. "What is— Oh, Lord."

"Carry the boy outside! Hurry, he has the strength of madness and I can't hold him long."

I screamed, "Take your hands off me!"

"Aye." Fostrow scooped up Anavar in his burly arms, heaved him over his shoulder, disappeared out the door.

"Are you satisfied? I'm not done—"

"Oh, yes, you are." Rust let go his bear hug. I launched myself at him, fists flailing.

He sidestepped, punched me hard in the stomach. I turned green, fell to my knees. "Oh, no." I gagged, tried not to vomit. Lord of Nature, it hurt.

With no show of sympathy, Rust dragged over a chair, sat. He gripped me firmly and painfully by the nape of the neck and held me in a kneeling position.

I could do little to resist. Arms folded across my belly, I gasped and moaned until the ache faded. I fumbled at his fingers on my neck. "Let go." No response. "Please." Despite myself, my voice was a whimper.

"You're to lie on the bed."

"I don't—"

He squeezed harder.

"All right!"

"Until I give you leave." His fingers dug like claws into my nape.

Weakly, I nodded.

He released me, hauled me to my feet, thrust me to the bed. When I was full on it, he stalked to the door, shut it firmly behind him as he left.

It was a full hour by the candle before he returned, and I'd time to work myself into high indignation. "What does Anavar matter? He's a mere—"

"Shut thy mouth." His tone was one I'd never heard.

My words died in my throat.

"He's not dead. Were he so, I'd be riding to Stryx, done with you forever."

There was a finality about his last word that chilled me. Silent, I waited.

His voice dripped scorn. "You were too cowardly to vent your rage on me?"

"No, I—"

"Yes." His eyes bored into mine, until I had to look away. "Roddy, I spoke harsh words to you, and came to regret them. Little did I know how soft they were compared to your conduct."

"That's not fair. A noble has every right to chastise a serv—"

"You call it that?" He stood. "Come."

"Where?"

For answer, he took my wrist, dragged me to the door and beyond to the servants' room. Within the dark and dingy chamber, Genard crouched by a bed, a wet and bloody cloth in his hand. When he glanced up, his eyes were full of reproach.

I leaned over for a look, and sucked in my breath.

Anavar lay on his back, his face swollen. Blood trickled from cut lips and from his nose. One eye was puffed. He was senseless.

My voice was small. "I didn't realize—"

"Contemptible." Rust snapped out the word, and I jerked like a goaded horse.

"Will he heal?"

"Out." He steered me from the room.

In my own chamber again, I sank to the bed. "I was beside myself . . ." I looked up. "Rustin, I'm truly sorry."

His mouth was tight. "Sorry isn't enough."

My stomach churned. "What, then?"

His eyes darted about the room, fell on the drapery. He lifted the hangings from the window, slipped free the supple rod that held them.

"What would you do?" My tone was wary.

"As my father did, when I merited it."

"But after, you couldn't sit for days!"

He said nothing.

I tried to keep the horror from my voice. "Rust, I can't. I'm to be King!"

Again, nothing.

"Even Chamberlain Willem never took wood to me! You haven't the right!"

"Innately, no. Only through your consent, by your oath to put yourself in my charge."

Had I really been so stupid as to make such a vow? My mind whirled to that day in the clearing, when first I'd caught up to Hester's cart.

Yes, I'd sworn. Now the True depended on it. Heart plummeting, I said, "Please, Rust. Don't hurt me."

"Kneel at the side of the bed, and lie across it."

My limbs trembled. Wildly, I thought to cast away all, even the True of Caledon, for my fear, but my mind fastened on another vow I'd carelessly made: that I might feel the coward but would not act it.

That vow, somehow, it was vital that I keep.

Forcing my courage, I steeled myself to do as I was told.

Rust took my hands, placed them on the bed above my head.

"No decent lord batters his servants. No decent man knocks a helpless boy unconscious. The next time you inflict pain, Roddy, recall the feel of it." To my consternation, he slipped loose the rope belt that held my breeches.

And then, with vigor, he beat me.

For two days there was no thought of our leaving Soushire; I passed most of them facedown on my bed, laden with misery.

I had been whipped like a cur, and, through a foolish promise, had been forced to permit it.

It went without saying that my friendship with Rustin was shattered. His indifference to my wails of anguish and the degradation he visited on me was ample cause. Yet, he seemed not to realize our association was ruined. When I healed, I would make my intentions clear. Until then, I needed his help, Garst's—anyone present—for the simplest tasks.

I had much time to think.

To myself I swore an oath that no matter how much he might beg, never would I reveal to Rust the plan I'd conceived, by which I'd made my promise to Soushire. Let him wait until its fruition, as would the rest of Caledon. On each visit I waited with spiteful glee for him to inquire, but always his mind was elsewhere.

Garst was angry with me, and his effort to conceal it failed.

Well, he had a right to his wrath; Anavar was his countryman, and I'd abused him. Despite my fury at Rust, I knew I'd erred. In Caledon, Anavar was my bondsman, but in his own land he had great rank, and I ought not to have treated him so meanly.

Anxious to clear my conscience, I asked Elryc to summon the Eiberian for me, but he said, "Don't be absurd," and changed the subject. When he'd gone, I struggled into my robe, walked with painful care down the long hall to the servants' quarters.

It was Chela who opened, and I saw she was much recovered from her injuries; she made an elaborate and derisive curtsy, which I ignored.

They were all inside: Genard, Garst, and the convalescent Anavar, who lay on the bed they shared. His face was bruised and puffy. Shame washed over me. I wouldn't allow Ebon to be treated as I'd done him.

For a moment I wished I hadn't come, then faced my task.

I faced Garst first. "For what I've done to you compatriot, I'm sorry." I studied his reaction, saw none. "I was wrong, and admit it." A generous concession, but he didn't seem impressed. I snapped. "That's all. Leave us." My true business was with Anavar.

When we were alone, I sat—knelt, rather—at the bedside. The boy's look was wary. I said, "I don't know whence came the rage that overtook me. I—well, I do, it was over Rustin, and politics, and had nothing to do with you. I apologize."

"Thank you, great Lord." His words came swift. His wary eyes watched mine.

"Don't be afraid," I said. "I won't hurt you again." My knees ached, and I shifted position. He said nothing. In the hot room my hair dampened and fell over my eye, and I raised my hand to brush it away.

Anavar flinched.

Could he not understand plain speech? "I told you to have no fear!"

"Aye, my lord!" His hand tightened on the bedcloth.

I ought to strike him for his obstinacy. It would serve him right, teach him—

Lord of Nature, what comes over me?

I hoisted myself to my feet, walked to the tiny window that was the room's only light. "I have a horrid temper," I said. "Rustin knows, and has tried to teach me better. Sometimes I forget. Sometime's I'm . . ." My voice dropped.

"Yes, my lord?"

I made myself finish. "Too witless to see what I'm doing." I swung to face him. "I don't intend to be evil, Anavar." My face was crimson. "Sometimes I can't help myself."

His voice was tentative. "I wasn't hurt so badly." He shifted. "I was dazed, and fell."

Lord of Nature; he thought to reassure me. Was it from fear or compassion? No matter; either was unbearable. "I'm very sorry." I hurried to the door, opened it to make my escape.

"—he'll give him a silver pence to make it all well, until the next time." Chela, her tone full of contempt. "Think you he'll change his ways? Sooner a cow lay eggs than—" Someone nudged her. Seeing me, she fell silent.

Scarlet, I retreated to the servants' room, slammed shut the door. Did all share such opinions of me? Was it for my bullying, or because I fled such moments as these? It must not remain so. I took a deep breath, faced Anavar once more.

He watched curiously, and I had nothing to say. Desperate to fill the silence, I blurted, "Have you ever been beaten?"

His swollen face showed surprise. "Of course, my lord. Who has not?"

I crossed again to the window. "I, until yesterday."

"Really?" He seemed astounded. "Had you no father?"

"I was nine when he died."

Anavar's brow wrinkled. "They say Margenthar of Stryx is your regent, and he is not among us. Who could beat you now?"

I hadn't foreseen such questions, but I'd opened the door to them. "My frie—Rustin. He acts as my guardian."

"You have a regent *and* a guardian? Who appointed Rustin to watch over you, sire?"

"I did."

The boy's bewilderment was almost laughable. "You set someone to chastise you? I've never heard such a thing."

Nor had I, until I'd done it, and look at the result. I bore welts that wouldn't fade for a week. I muttered, "It hurts."

"I can imagine, if he used leather. A switch is nothing to speak of, but leather, or worse, a rod . . ." His grin was shy. "What was your offense, sir?"

I started. "You don't know? My abusing you. He called it unforgivable."

"In your land I'm but a servant."

"But you were noble, in your House."

"That shouldn't matter." He spoke without thinking, then cringed in dismay. "I'm sorry, my lord! I mean no disrespect!"

"Go easy, Anavar. I won't hurt you." I walked with care to the bed, my rump smarting. "Why shouldn't your nobility matter?"

He studied me before risking my wrath. "In our land, sire, a noble must earn respect as any man. His station entitles him to land and wealth, but not to mishandle his servants."

I snorted. "I admit I acted wrongly with you, but not as a general principle. Your commoners don't fear your nobility, and as a result even the army you send must be hired, rather than drawn from loyalty and obedience."

"What nonsense!" His voice was hot. "Of course we pay our pikemen and archers; how else to keep poor folk in arms, when they could be home working their crops? But all the officers—oh!" His hand flew to his mouth. When he spoke again his voice was small. "Forgive my impertinence, sire."

"Bah. How many times must I say I won't hurt you? Must I remit your servitude to prove it? There, it's done. You're freed, as of this moment." I waved it away, a small thing. "Finish your thought."

Anavar's look was one of wonder. "You truly mean—yes, my lord. I was saying . . . Our officers serve from loyalty to their liege. We need no whips and chains to maintain order."

"It's unthinkable your servants have rights they may assert to their very lord."

"Well, they must use care in the manner they assert them." He flashed a grin, and for a moment his face was transfigured. Carefully, hugging his ribs, he sat. "Truly, Lord Prince, you allowed yourself to be whipped for beating me?"

"Yes." My voice was tight.

"A thing of wonder." He shook his head. "How strange a land is Caledon. Not at all what we were told."

"And that was?"

"That you're rustic boors, unwashed, uncouth, with no laws. That pigs and goats share your dwellings, even the castles."

"It's not so." We lapsed silent. Finally, I stood. "I apologize once more. I'll see you—no, I suppose you're free to go, now. There's naught to hold you."

He swallowed. "As I said, they'd never believe—I've no place to go. Might I stay with you, until war's end?"

"As what? Bondsman?"

"Not—" A sigh. "If need be."

By the imps and demons, I *liked* him. And he was a noble. "What say I make you my ward in Caledon? Until you're of age."

He hesitated. "Provided, I will not fight my own people. With that caveat, my lord, I would accept."

"That's fair." I allowed him to kiss my hand, make the bow that acknowledged his subservience. "Very well. I bid you leave, youngsire. I need to lie down."

"Thank you, sire—er, my lord. What should I call you? Will 'sir' show my courtesy?" I nodded. He got to his feet, showed me politely to the door. "Oh!" He blushed. "I shouldn't—yes, I must." He looked up at me. "On the trail, I said Garst hadn't told me he would flee. It was a lie."

I shrugged. "I understand. To protect him."

"No, sir." Anavar blushed. "So I wouldn't be beaten."

"Why confess it now, when it no longer matters?"

He looked down. "Your example shames me."

"Will you lie to me again?"

The boy took a deep breath. "Never, my lord. I so swear."

I rested my hand on his forehead, in a sort of benediction. Then I limped back to my room.

At last, we set forth from Soushire, to the obvious relief of the Duchess, who still hoped to conceal our visit from Uncle Mar. For most of the first day I walked with our infantry, too sore for the saddle and scorning to be seen hauled in a cart. The next morn, I gritted my teeth and swung myself onto Ebon.

We rode as a group: Fostrow, Elryc, Rustin and I, and now Anavar. From time to time Tursel joined us, to Fostrow's evident displeasure.

Soushire's domain stretched east to the foothills of the Warthen Peaks, the great mounts that barred the damp air of the sea from the desert. But the rise to the desert plateau was slow and steady, and the road wide and well kept. As we rode, I made note of the terrain. Tantroth's army—or any other—could sweep unchallenged across the high slopes, but at the High Pass, the way narrowed to a tiny gap between rugged cliffs. There, the Warthen's force stood guard. If we could pass, I would beg the Warthen, that his vote might free me of the need for Soushire's.

The first evening of our journey, deciding on a place for Anavar was a problem. As ward of the Prince of Caledon, he couldn't sleep with Chela and Genard. Garst was furious that Anavar had been remitted but not he, and his sullenness was such that I dismissed any thought of freeing him as well. Garst was eighteen, four years older than Anavar, yet his manner was by far the more childish.

I bade Anavar stay close to our band, and bed near Fostrow. Tursel might prove a danger to the boy. The captain had exploded with rage when he learned a freed Eiberian noble would travel at my side, and only my bluntest warnings held him in check.

Rustin had directed our tent be set up as usual. I noticed he'd even set our bedding together. He chatted to me with his usual good cheer, and I was hard put to limit my response to grunts and monosyllables. As we got ready for bed, he came at me when I didn't expect him, and enveloped me in a brief hug.

Cast loose, I muttered, "You take my willingness for granted." I busied myself with my bootstrings.

He dropped lazily upon our bed. "You'll get over your pique, won't you?"

"Not pique. Rage." I made my voice cold.

"Odd, that you don't sound the least enraged."

"I contain myself."

"Then you've learned something from your castigation." He smiled. "Stand still a moment. You grow ever more tall. Should I say, even handsome?"

"Say little, and infrequently."

He paused. "Because I lashed you?"

"Because you showed no forbearance. And I see now that you can't guide me and be my intimate, all in one."

He cupped his hands behind his head. "Which, then, would you have me be?"

"Neither."

"Would you have me leave?"

It took effort to say the word. "Yes."

"Your tent, or your camp?"

Why did he persist in goading me? "Both!"

Rustin's face was without expression. "Yours is to command." He uncoiled his lithe frame, swung to his feet. Within moments, his gear was packed. He thrust aside the tent flap. "Fare thee well."

Despite myself, I cried, "Wait!"

"Yes, my lord?" The dry tone, which maddened me.

I forced my words. "Stay."

"Where?"

"In camp."

He waited at the flap, saddlebags in hand. "In the tent?"

I floundered, cast about for succor, found none, struck my colors and surrendered. "Yes."

I felt relieved, when by all rights I should feel the opposite. Under the covers, I talked incessantly—babbled, even—and caught Rustin concealing a smile. That annoyed me enough to sulk, but his hands found me, and enticed me insistently until I had no choice but to respond.

Later, calm and drowsing, I brought up my offer of Groenfil to Lady Soushire, but Rust covered my mouth. "If you had not good cause, your folly will haunt you long, and I've no need to chide you. And if you understood that which I could not, time will prove you the wiser. Let it be."

"But, Rust, I—"

"For our sakes. For peace between us."

Outside, the wind snapped the loose cloth of the tent, and I curled against Rustin's warm shoulder. I wasn't quite ready for sleep. "I know little about the Warthen. His visits were rare."

"They said your mother held him in great respect."

A pause. "Rust, at the funeral, did you notice the Warthen's eyes?"

"I found myself wanting to look away, because of the pain."

"It's the Return, Rust. His Power has great cost."

The Rites were secret. They enabled the wielder—the Warthen, or his delegate—to return to an event he'd attended, no matter how far in the past. Not merely return, but, well, reenact. No, that wasn't quite it, either. Not like the acting of the mummers, where the same scenes were played in castle upon keep, and always the outcome was the same.

With the Return, one might change what had been.

There was a drawback, of course. Not only must the Return be bought by suffering, moment by precious moment. But the wielder of the Power could only return to one event in his life. He might Return as often as he could abide, so long as he paid the cost. But when the event was chosen, he could return to no other.

The next day, we chose a route more easterly than was necessary, to lessen chances of encounter with Tantroth. Though the land would not hide ambushers well, Captain Tursel took great precautions, sending pairs of scouts to recheck territory already scouted, and himself riding, with a few officers, to the top of each rise to survey the region we were about to cross.

Elryc rode sometimes with me, sometimes chatting amiably with Genard. Occasionally, they shared a horse, though I rebuked my brother for riding with a servant clinging to his back. Elryc shrugged, replied that Genard was vassal, not servant, and further, that I was hardly one to teach him genteel behavior.

For that I boxed his ears, but when he was done crying, he rode again with Genard, and I did not forbid it.

That evening, Fostrow was atop a wagon some distance from the cookfire, taking his evening meal. With him was Chela. The old soldier nodded placidly. "Have you rehearsed your speech to the Warthen, my lord?"

"What speech?"

"Why, the one that will rend him from the Duke's bosom."

I glanced to see if he had too much drink in him. "And what business is that of yours?" With a plate of stew, I perched on the tailboard, studiously ignoring Chela. I tore a piece of bread. "Ow. It's hot."

Chela's voice dripped venom. "Manly ruler. Rust savors entering you even more than he did me."

Thunderstruck, I leaped to my feet. Something hot stung my lap as the bowl overturned. I clawed for the dagger at my side.

"No, Roddy." Rustin's strong arms pinned me from behind. "Leave it. No!" He lifted me, turned me about despite my struggles.

"She said—"

"I know. Go to our tent. *Now, Roddy!*"

I broke loose, but he hounded me, keeping always between me and Chela, his face set. "Into the tent. Change your breeches; they're stained with stew. Fostrow, be a good fellow and get him another plate."

Weeping with rage and frustration, I stumbled into the tent, tugged shut the flap so savagely I heard cloth rend. I didn't care. I fell upon the bed, clung to my pillow. I knew not how I might emerge to show my face in camp. Better abstinence—better emasculation—than the scorn of servants. How could I have let one such as Rust touch me?

Outside, sharp voices; Chela's, Rustin's, others. I could make out few of Rust's words, but his tone had a harsh bite. From time to time he lowered his voice, but always it crept again into audibility.

Fostrow knocked at the brace pole, came in with a steaming bowl of stew, while I pretended I slept.

After a while, Rust pushed aside the flap, came to sit by my side. "I'm sorry. She won't do it again." His fingers soothed the small of my back.

With a curse I threw them off. "Is she dead?"

"No."

"A pity."

Rustin gathered me into his arms and after a vain effort to fight him, I clung to him as once I had to Mother, or my nurse.

When I felt myself recovered, I wiped my eyes. "See what I've made of myself? I'm undone, Rust. I might as well turn to the sea, take ship to some far place. You've made of me a figure of joke."

"You need have no shame."

"Speak of yourself!" My voice was savage. "I'll lie with one of the camp women, tonight. The True be damned; I'll relinquish the Power."

"You can't mean—"

I cried, "I won't be known as your concubine!" I'd spoken too loud; had they heard me through the canvas? I rushed outside, looked about. Chela sat weeping in the cart, but no others were close.

I stalked back to the tent. "Rustin, we have to end it. I can't stand the abasement."

"Do you feel abased, when I . . . touch you?"

"Yes. Well, not really. But imagine how others see it!"

"Chela is the only one who cares, and that because I abandoned her for you."

"Send her away."

He said simply, "I have. She leaves at dawn."

I said cautiously, "You won't miss her?"

"Her spirit is too bitter. And besides . . ." Idly, he examined the center pole. "I found better."

Chapter 30

THE WARTHEN'S EMISSARY AWAITED OUR COLUMN IN the rocky valley where snowy peaks gave way to the High Pass.

The Warthen of the Sands, he said, refused our visit. Oh, his address was cloaked in flowery words, but the meaning was unmistakable. And the Warthen was leagues distant, beyond my dubious charms and arguments.

I sat grimly, waiting for my tea to steam over the fire. "Tursel, can we force the pass?"

"Unlikely, and the attempt will cost us many men. The very geography conspires against us. Those cliffs, in the shadow, are stronger than walls. See how they swoop down toward the center, and how the rampart is anchored at either side in the rock? The land forces an attack to the middle, and the fortification is hardy."

"Well, you're my advisors. What do we do?"

"Vessa, I suppose." Rustin. Perhaps he hoped to avoid Groenfil, that I might not treat with one whom I betrayed.

Yes, Vessa, though his support was unlikely. His vote, like the Warthen's, might free me from my vow to Soushire.

"Shall I summon Vessa forth, or sneak into Stryx dressed as a mummer? Shall we ask Tantroth's leave?" My ill humor was noticeable, even to me. I reined in my temper. "We'll consult with our allies, then. Back to Cumber."

"Don't go back, sir." Anavar looked abashed. "My father is well thought of, in Duke Tantroth's counsel. He's led our men to sweet victory against the Norlanders and Cumber alike."

"So?" Tursel spat the word, perhaps annoyed at the reminder.

"His shield translates 'Press on.' He liked the phrase so, had it adopted as the family motto. When in doubt, press on. Never turn back, once you've committed; wolves will snap at your heels as you flee. If you in the first instance judged your cause worth the fight, why then, fight on."

"You've fought many campaigns, youngsire?" Tursel's tone was acid. "A natural wonder, Lord Prince: a beardless sage."

"Enough!" I got to my feet. "I would walk alone. When I return, my answer."

Men of my escort—Lord Raeth's men—stood about in easy idleness. I stalked past the first knot, barely noticed. Horses sweated in the sun, awaiting water.

I followed the rocky trail along the valley floor, under forbidding cliffs of white lime. Bending, I picked up a stone, hurled it. What now? Cumber? Soushire? War?

The crux of my problem was that I hadn't a plan. Events had propelled me, ever since I fled Castle Stryx and my uncle. Find Hester. Settle Elryc in the cottage. Rejoin my party on the way to Cumber. None of it planned, none designed to advance my cause. Other than Rustin, who of them had joined me whom I'd truly sought to enlist? Certainly not Fostrow. Genard was a child, Tursel a minion of Cumber.

"Pardon, my lord, may I help?" It was Anavar.

"I said I would walk alone."

"Aye, sir. Who would in truth want that?" He picked his way across the stony turf, hooked a thumb in the rope of his belt. "My father says, ask yourself questions, and find your way."

"What is that supposed to—"

"What do you seek?"

I sighed. His foolish game would do no good, but likewise, no harm. "My crown. I need a fourth vote in council." A fifth, to be safe, but that seemed impossible. I might have to rule without the Still.

"Who could vote for you?"

I snarled, "Whose pledge I hold is a secret of state! Think you I'd tell an enemy, when my friends know not?"

His mouth closed, and a light went from his eyes. "No, sir. Pardon me."

"Imps and demons roast you in the lake! Groenfil, Vessa the Speaker, and the Warthen are left."

"All the rest are pledged to you?"

"Except for Uncle Mar." His vote was beyond imagining.

"What would move Vessa?"

"Gold, perhaps; they say he's a venal man. But Mar can offer far more than I."

"Could your uncle himself be swayed?"

"By my head, on a pike."

"And Groenfil?"

"Mar took Groenfil's sister to wife. They are close bound."

"Which of them is least obliged to your uncle?"

"The Warthen, I'd think, but he's inaccessible. Of the rest, Vessa."

I bent for another stone, chucked it down the hillside.

After a time, the boy did likewise.

I said, "Vessa's in Stryx, if Tantroth hasn't deposed him." I headed back toward the waiting troops. "Vessa it is. I'll tell them."

The youngster matched my pace. "See, my lord? You had the answer within you."

"Not so I could find it. I'm grateful. If there's anything I can do for you . . ." I trailed off, knowing he would understand my thanks were enough.

We scrambled up the hill. Rustin would insist on coming along, but in Stryx we were known together. The two of us would be doubly conspicuous. I'd have to—

"Actually, sir, if I've done anything to warrant your favor . . ." Anavar's voice was hesitant.

Whatever he wanted, I'd refuse, but I had at least to hear him, after making the offer. "Get on with it."

"My father is a man of substance, and—that is—sir, I've never had to do without. For little things, I mean." He flushed. "Even under my lord Treak's command, I had coin enough, provided by my family. But after the battle, my purse was taken."

"You accuse me?"

His words came in a rush. "If your boundless generosity would permit a small stipend, that I might tip a servant, or buy a skin of wine . . . after the war, sire, I could make it good to you, and surely my father would be grateful."

Dumbfounded, I stopped dead. "You presumptuous urchin, we bested you in battle, took you prisoner! To save your life I let you swear adherence. Now you'd have me provide a stipend as if you were my—my child?" My voice rose to a squeak.

His face was quite red. "Only for a time, sir. Remember that I'm of noble blood, and utterly without means. If the request offends you—"

"Mightily."

"It is withdrawn. I pray your pardon."

We resumed our hike. Panting, I climbed the last of the way. I untied my waterskin from Ebon's saddle, gulped a long drink. "Tursel, we'll have to approach Stryx as closely as we may without battle. How long a ride?"

"One man could ride it in a day. With all our party as escort? Three, at least."

"We'd best get going."

"Aye, my lord. I'll want an hour to organize our march." He hurried off.

I retied the skin, swung up on the saddle, took the reins from Anavar. I growled, "Three coppers per week?"

He broke out into a grin, the first I'd seen from him, and proceeded to bargain away my patrimony.

We formed line, got under way once more. Our scouts fanned down the hillside, probing. Again, Elryc rode at my side with Rustin, but now, uninvited, Anavar attached himself to my inner circle.

Rust, in a philosophical bent, interrogated Anavar about Eiberian rites, while I was for the most part silent, pondering my approach to Vessa.

The Speaker of the City was, in theory, spokesman and intermediary for the masses of townsmen who lived below our walls. He was expected to intercede for them when necessary, in the councils of the kingdom. But the office was hereditary, as had been Llewelyn's, and over the years the Speaker's role as spokesman had become little more than a formality.

Vessa's prime concern was the port, and the open-air market that served the town, the keep, and Castle Stryx. From these he derived substantial revenues, though always he complained he was short of funds. Mother had said she tolerated him because he administered the town for her, more cheaply than she could do so herself.

Rustin broke into my musing. "Remember, Roddy, how the Ritemaster in Shar's Cross spoke of the tides of time? I think that's what the Eiberians mean when they talk of turnings."

"Gibberish."

"But what scope for imagining. Consider this place—all the world—in another turning, another tide. All the same, yet somehow different. Perhaps horses are green, or trees shatter like glass. Or perhaps there's no Power."

"You're daft."

The wild clatter of hooves cut off his reply. Cloak flying, a scout tore past our wagons, reined in his foaming bay in a cloud of dust. "Emissaries! Messengers!" He was as out of breath as if he'd run, not ridden. "A league ahead, three men in arms. They pray safe-conduct, and would speak with the Prince."

"Imps and demons!" I directed my ire at Tursel. "Tantroth might as well be among us; he knows always where we ride. How is this so?"

"Pardon, my lords. Not Tantroth. They're from Duke Margenthar of Stryx."

My jaw dropped, and as all eyes turned to me I sat there looking an idiot. At last, I managed, "Rust?"

"Hear them, to learn what they want."

"Obviously." I really had no other course; why then hadn't I known it myself?

Apparently there was an etiquette to the circumstance I hadn't yet mastered. It took a full hour, a hastily erected tent, pennants, pledges of our mutual safety, and the offer of wine, politely refused, before we sat across from each other.

In my faction, Rustin and Tursel; for Uncle Mar, two men I knew not, but led by Stire, Mar's trusted deputy, his favorite whom Rustin and I had disrobed in the wine cellar.

From his expression one would think he had no recall of his humiliation, but I knew if I was to fall into his hands without safe-conduct, I were dead.

I made a short bow of courtesy. "How may we attend you?"

He returned my bow. It was a civil nod, though not deep enough to be full acknowledgment of my rank. "From your uncle the Duke of Stryx, fond greetings." For a moment his eyes reflected the irony we both savored. "He asks after your health."

My tone was cool. "Surely you didn't ride all these leagues for that inquiry?"

"No." It was a bark, and Stire tried to soften it as he resumed. "He bids you confer with him for the preservation of the kingdom."

"I'd welcome his visit."

Stire shrugged aside my sarcasm. "Youngsire, you know he cannot leave Verein, as matters now stand. But he offers you most gracious welcome, safe-conduct within a league of his castle, and his oath that you may depart unhindered whenever you wish."

"On what issue would he confer?"

"I'm but a humble vassal, youngsire, and am not informed. It must surely be a matter of some urgency."

"Not urgent enough to call him here."

"Stryx is threatened, and Verein itself isn't far from Tantroth's troops. No commander can leave under such circumstances, youngsire."

"Stop calling me that! I'm Rodrigo, Prince. I have a man's station!"

Stire's flicker of delight made clear the gibe was intentional. "Please forgive me, youngsi—Lord Rodrigo. In your extended absence, your manhood escaped our notice. However"—his tone turned reasonable, almost wheedling—"is it not a mark of your station that my lord Duke begs to meet with you, rather than, as regent, summons you to his presence?"

Despite his animosity, I had to acknowledge the last was true. If real, it represented a distinct change in my uncle's approach. Yet Uncle had given me his assurances before. Regarding having the Council crown me, for instance. Not long after, I'd barely escaped his clutches.

No, I couldn't risk a journey to Verein. "Very well, tell Duke Margenthar—"

Loudly, Rustin cleared his throat.

I wished he had stayed silent, that I not look his puppet. Or Rust might have intervened sooner; now I had to reverse myself. I said smoothly, "You'll have your answer anon. Pray take refreshment, while I consult with my counselors." A series of bows, and we made our escape.

We huddled in the shade of the tall beeches, the three of us and Elryc, who shouldered past the sentries and inserted himself in our midst.

"Well?"

"Folly, to put yourself in his hands." Rustin. "You mustn't go."

How obvious; why would he interrupt me with Stire, for that? Out of stubbornness, I answered, "Mar himself has a vote in Council. Of course I must go."

"I agree with Rustin, my lord." Tursel. "As well put your head in a noose and draw it tight."

"Think," I said. "Uncle Mar must have some purpose in asking to confer. If I refuse—"

"His purpose is to get hold of you!"

"What if he has a plan concerning Tantroth? Or even, proposes to end the cursed regency?"

Elryc pawed at my arm. "Your wish doesn't make it so. You don't know enough to—"

Exasperated, I slapped his fingers. "Now you call me foolish?"

"No, Roddy. You don't know enough to decide." His childish voice had adult purpose, and I quieted. "Vessa is in the city. Seek him out; learn what he knows. Perhaps then your way will be clearer."

I blinked at the sense of it.

"In the meantime, don't refuse Mar."

I asked, "You mean, delay?"

"Or better, accept. Set a time for after you've met with Vessa. You can always change your mind."

I threw my arm across my brother's shoulder. "Truly, you serve well as counselor." He flushed with pleasure.

Rust held up a hand. "Just how will you meet with Vessa? Hurl our regiment through Tantroth's lines?"

"We could send an emissary, even if he had to circle the town to find entry."

"And then?"

"Ask Vessa to come out to us."

"If he refuses?"

I shouted, "No more questions!" Rust but raised an eyebrow. "How should I know? Think you the players move according to set rules?"

"That's my point, my prince. You can't set a time to meet Mar until you know when you'll see Vessa."

My head spun. "Tell him a week from today, at Verein. That gives us two days to ride to Stryx, a day to get through to Vessa, another to meet with him. We'd still have three days to reach Verein, and that's but one day's ride from Stryx."

"Assuming Tantroth stands aside to allow you passage." He sighed. "Very well. I'll tell Stire."

We waited in the shade of the beeches. "Tursel, if Uncle Mar and his men are barricaded in Verein, and we're still in Soushire's lands, how did Stire know where to find us?"

"The spies who watched us at Soushire's court. Or perhaps we're followed now."

"Wouldn't your outriders know of it?"

"It depends how skillful our pursuers are. It's easier to hide three riders from five hundred than the reverse."

I grunted, afraid he was right.

After much talk it was arranged. Shortly, Stire's party rode off in a storm of hooves and a miasma of dust.

That evening, a dull and dismal drizzle added to the chill of the night. Across the sputtering campfire, we debated searching for Lord Vessa, while Genard and Anavar set twigs ablaze and waved them in fiery circles.

Tursel proposed we send a few riders south through the ribbed range of mountains that paralleled the seacoast behind Stryx. Safely south, our men would veer west and travel back along the coast to the town.

I cared not what route the riders took; how would they manage to speak with Vessa? What if he were guarded, or a prisoner? What if he refused?

"You're heir," said Rust. "Certainly he'll listen to your plea."

"The Warthen didn't. Genard, put that stick down before you set yourself afire." I shivered, hunched closer to the coals.

Apologetically, Fostrow cleared his throat. "Roddy, the Warthen is safe behind his cliff barriers; he had no need to hear you. Vessa is menaced by Tantroth. You'd think he'd examine his options."

"Even if Vessa hears our messenger, it would be a great risk for him to leave Stryx to see us. If Tantroth learns of it, he would not be pleased. What would prompt him to—imps and demons!" I swatted sparks from my blanket. "Genard, I'll blister your—Elryc, govern your liegeman! Anavar, set that toy aside!"

Anavar tossed his twigs into the fire, settled on his knees at my right. "Your pardon, my lord." A pause. "It would seem . . ."

I waited, but he said no more. "Yes?"

"That *you* must go to Stryx." He added hurriedly, "If this Vessa must be convinced, is it not you who must persuade him?"

"Tantroth would seize me the moment I appeared."

"If he knew you."

Dare I enter the city in disguise? If but one soul recognized me and spoke, I were dead. On the other hand, I'd grown, and tanned in the sun. Lesser clothes, a tired horse . . . It might be done. But if I failed, my life was forfeit.

All waited, and I spoke with reluctance. "There's merit in what you say."

"No, it's absurd," growled Fostrow. "Seek Earl Groenfil, or some other lord. You can't ride into Stryx while it's held by Eiber."

Elryc intervened. "Roddy, if one of us is taken, the rest fight on for your cause. If you're killed or captured, your reign is ended before it's begun."

I snarled, "It's already finished. We sleep in borrowed tents, guarded by Cumber's loaned soldiers, eating only by his largesse, pretending I had any chance of becoming King even *with* a fourth vote in Council."

"Would you give it up?" Rustin.

"Yes. No." Angrily, I got to my feet. "How should I know these things?"

"Come back. We've yet to—"

I stalked to the edge of camp. After a time, I noticed a shadow behind. Staring through branches at the moon sailing above, I waited for Rust's calming hand.

"Pardon my lord." Anavar's alto, on its journey toward manhood.

I jumped. "I thought—why do you always follow me?"

"You're unhappy."

"Obviously."

"When I'm unsettled, I want someone to talk with."

"Talk, then."

"Why do you want to go to Stryx?"

"To settle the matter with Vessa, once and for all. I hate this business of intermediaries, messages I don't quite understand, promises that may not be meant. It's why I never paid much heed to Mother's statecraft."

"And why don't you want to go?"

"I just said . . ." I grinned wryly. "If you must know, I'm afraid."

"Of death?"

"Well, yes. But more of torture." I shivered. "At Stryx I saw a man who'd been tormented by the Norlanders. His hands . . ." The recall made me gag.

"Once I saw them put a man in the pit." Anavar grimaced.

"Still, Mar holds the castle, but not the town. Even if Vessa turned on me, he couldn't easily betray me to the Duke."

"Go on, sir."

"It's your Tantroth I fear. On bad nights, I dream of the black sails I saw from high on the hill. And his black-clad men who struck at us from the wood. Yet, I must see Vessa." I sighed. "Anavar, tell truth: What will happen if your master catches me?"

"I don't know, sir." He hesitated. "He won't let you go, I think. Not unless you make alliance with him, that he may gain Caledon. They say Lord Tantroth's thoughts never roam far from that purpose."

"If I refused?"

"I don't know him well. I'd guess he'd try to break your will. I mean, through your body." Anavar stumbled, caught my arm to save his balance. "Sorry. I don't see well in the dark. Father says . . . never mind."

My thoughts were elsewhere. "I might manage it. I know the streets, and I've supped at the tavern oft enough. The house of Vessa is near the harbor, on the promontory."

"Sir, I can't act against my lord Tantroth."

"I know, Anavar." My tone was gentle.

A long pause, while we negotiated rocks along the trail. Finally, Anavar said, "Guards roam everywhere. In the square, at the market. Through all the streets. Tantroth means not to be surprised should your uncle's troops sortie from the hill."

"Thank you." I glanced about; we'd strayed too far from the flickering fires. "Best we head back."

"Look how the moon rides through the clouds. Think you the demons get warmth from her as we do the sun?"

"So they say."

He shuddered. "I saw a demon once. He was perched on the windowsill." A time passed. "Of course, I was younger then. Lord Prince, what if I go with you?"

I gaped. "You mean to Stryx?"

His words darted as if to evade my objection. "In disguise, but wearing our black under my costume. If a guard stopped you, I could intervene."

"And hand me to your master."

"I'd give you my word."

"Against your lord?"

"Well . . . I wouldn't raise hand against him." He stopped, listened to a bird calling in the night. "You reminded me I'm your ward, tonight. Do I not owe you a measure of loyalty?"

"That's for you to say."

"I just said it. I would guide you in Stryx."

"And return to your people, if the chance arose?" I shifted irritably.

"I'd like that, if they'd believe my tale. But it wouldn't be just. If I go with you, I see you safely back." He drew himself up. "I give my oath on it."

I shrugged, forgetting he couldn't see. "No matter. It's idle talk. Let's go back; I'm freezing." A moment later, at the fire, I snapped my fingers to Garst, for hot tea. "Where's Fostrow?"

"Here, my lord." Breathing heavily, he stepped from the shadows.

"You followed?" I made no effort to hide my exasperation.

"After those stalkers flitted about in Soushire Castle, think you I'd let you walk unprotected?"

"I didn't see you."

"You weren't meant to." Sighing, he sat. "Don't look so surprised that I know my trade."

I set down my tea, shivering. "Refill it, Garst. Rust, I would speak with you in the tent." I glared at Fostrow. "Alone."

Inside, I braced myself, told Rust I intended to go to Stryx with Anavar.

He grimaced, but said nothing.

"You don't forbid it? Threaten to lash me if I try?"

"Keep a civil tongue, Roddy. I direct your behavior to make of you a man, as you asked. In matters of state I must let you have your way; who am I to steer your course?"

"I go without you, Rust. Untie your apron springs."

"Roddy I have . . . business in Stryx."

"What could you possibly—oh." Llewelyn, of course. "What would you do if you find him?"

"Ask." Rust's eyes were bleak.

"What possible answer could appease you?"

"None I could imagine. But he's my father."

"Rust . . ." Wearily, I sat. "How can I make you understand? I think no less of you for what he did. This is not the time for such inquiries."

"No time in war to explore treason? If not now, when?"

"When I'm crowned, and sit in Castle Stryx."

"It might be too late."

"How do you mean?"

"Roddy, I—" Unexpectedly, his voice caught. "Who knows what he'll do. Flee to Eiber, perhaps, or end himself with remorse. I can't live all my life without knowing!"

"If I go to Stryx, in whose hands could I leave Elryc, but yours? I'll have Tursel do your bidding while I'm gone. If I'm taken, I rely on you."

"You know what you ask?"

"I believe I do." My eyes met his.

Nothing, then a long sigh. "You'd trust that Eiberian, after beating him half to death?"

I was silent a long moment. "Yes. I think so." I looked up. "Rust, I have to trust somebody, do I not?"

A bleak smile, but it eased my heart. "You've learned that at last? We progress."

"Then it's settled."

We did our best to prepare. I entrusted my dented crown to Rust for safekeeping, packed my saddlebags with useful sundries. As usual when there was work to be done, Garst was nowhere to be found.

In principle, Rustin might have accepted my foray. But there was much advice to endure—most of it worth the hearing—before we were allowed to leave, and even then, my party had swelled to six.

Two picked soldiers were to escort us to the edge of Stryx, to ward off brigands and await our return. A third, a burly young fellow, was to dress in peasant garb, ride into town and keep us in sight.

Lastly, Rust prevailed upon me to let Genard ride with us. "He's clever, he's not noticeable, he runs like the wind."

"He babbles, he's full of unwanted advice, he pries into—"

"You may find him useful."

I waved assent. Possibly Rustin was right. One never knew.

Perhaps Rust shared my doubts. In the midst of the hullabaloo of our preparations, he caught Genard's arm, firmly led him behind the wagons, a switch under his arm. When they returned the stableboy was subdued and anxious to please.

Chapter 31

I CALLED A HALT TO REST THE HORSES, AND TOOK THE opportunity to dismount, wrapped in my old and dusty cloak. Despite the cold I went behind a shrub, pulled down my breeches, and rubbed ointment on my chafed thighs. Meanwhile two of the soldiers walked the horses; the third rode ahead as a scout, as he'd done since we left camp.

The day's ride had been long and weary. The route was muddy. We'd pushed south, on roadways, cart trails, and goat tracks, until by my reckoning from the rude map we carried, we were now southeast of Stryx, and would take the next trail west. No matter how far south we'd gone, if we turned west we'd run into the sea soon or late, and could make our way into the town.

"Best if you stand in the stirrups, m'lord." Genard walked me back to the horses. "That way you don't rub—"

I was in no mood for advice. "There won't be ointment enough for you, unless you hold your tongue."

He subsided, but as we remounted, thinking he was unseen, he made a rude gesture.

Anavar flicked his crop; Genard yelped. "Respect your prince," said the Eiberian. Without waiting for answer, he spurred to my side. "Rodrigo . . ." His brow furrowed. "Did you notice Garst this morning?"

"By his absence." I sniffed, wiped my nose.

"Yes." Anavar rode for a time in silence. "I looked for him."

"He's not your responsibility. Rust will chastise him."

"I fear . . ." Anavar seemed uncomfortable. "Lord Prince, he may have fled."

"Again? Doesn't he tire of it?"

"You jest, but consider the prospect. If he finds our camp—men of Eiber, I mean . . ."

"Will they put him to death?"

"It depends on the captain. And on the news he brings." He watched my face, saw no enlightenment. "Sir, he heard us talk of riding to Stryx."

"Imps and demons chew his liver!" I set my mouth tight. "We'd best hurry."

"To what point? I know not where our patrols ride, nor does Garst. If when he left our camp—"

"Anavar, you must choose a side, and call it 'ours.' Else you make my head spin."

"If when he left your—our—Lord of Nature, I know not!" He pounded his pommel, causing his gelding to start with alarm. "I—we—I am of Eiber!"

"That's true, and today you wear Eiber black. But you ride with Caledon."

"Because you showed me mercy. You saved me."

"Would you turn back? You have my leave."

"And be despised by both camps? To what infamy would you consign me?" It sounded an accusation.

To lighten his woe, I said, "You can always become my vassal, and settle your loyalty." He looked as if I'd struck him, and I added hastily, "In Caledon, I meant. Not for your lands and holdings in Eiber."

"Here I have no lands." He sounded sullen.

"Or holdings, other than your stipend. Have you spent it all?" For my perseverance, I was rewarded with a wan smile.

Genard trotted to my side. "M'lord, a trail." A narrow footpath, into the western hills.

"Good lad." I raised my voice. "Hold! We'll try this one. You, ride ahead and recall the scout." I waited while the soldier galloped off.

It wasn't long before the guard returned, with his companion. I said, "This footpath isn't on the map, but—what in the fiery lake are *you* doing here?"

Fostrow said, "Scouting, my lord. Someone had to ride ahead."

"You were to remain in camp! You were of Mar's guard, and your face is too well known—"

"And think you I'd trust that—that puppy they chose to watch you in town? He's a boy, and a Cumberan boy at that. He's never seen the close winding streets, never walked the harbor, never—"

"Never tried my patience like a stubborn old fool!"

He glared. "And who might that be?"

"Gah!" I drew sword, slashed at a nearby branch. "Lord of Nature, why?"

"We waste time, Roddy."

His look was unyielding, and I put aside my ire. "Too late now to send you back. We may need your guarding; Anavar thinks Garst bolted." Wearily, I urged Ebon onward. "Did Rust put you up to this?"

"Of course not, my lord."

I'd never know. "Anavar, do vassals act so in Eiber?"

"Only until they're hanged, sir."

Fostrow shot him a glance that boded ill. "One arrogant pup I can abide. Two . . ."

Anavar was silent, but for the next league or so, a smile played on his lips.

Uneasy, I patted the mane of my horse, urged the beast forward, wishing I were on Ebon. But even with my hair cropped short, and in my peasant garb, too many in Stryx might remember me, especially on my favorite steed. In any event, a peasant boy on so fine a stallion would cause remark. Ebon grazed in a copse on the edge of town, along with Genard's mare, tended by our two escorts. Behind, Genard clung to my waist.

Abruptly we came on a trio of black-garbed troops, Tantroth's outer guard. Two remained squatted, playing at dice. The third waited with drawn sword.

"Stay to the side of the road, m'lord." The stableboy's whisper was sharp in my ear.

My chest ached. "Nonsense. Act as if we've every right to be here."

Genard adjusted the thong of his sandal. "You sound too much like a prince. I've learned about not being noticed, and—"

I twisted round, peered through the drizzle past the huts that lined the narrow trail. Fostrow was nowhere in sight. I muttered, "Why the side of the path?"

"Here, I'll show you." With no warning, Genard hurled himself to the ground, scrabbled for a handful of pebbles. He swarmed back into the saddle, panting. "See?" As we neared the guards he tossed a pebble at a thatched roof, grinning idiotically.

"You're dim-witted. What else should I observe?"

"That's it, m'lord."

The sentry frowned at us. Genard jabbed my ribs; I jumped half out of the saddle, spluttering with fury. With a giggle, he tossed pebbles past the guard. "Go on, brother. Catch the stones." He scratched furiously at his leg.

I hissed, "Stop it!" Genard paid little heed. Instead, he pinched me so it hurt.

The sentry be damned. With an oath, I twisted, managed to get a hand on Genard, hauled him into position to cuff. For a time he endured the blows, then tore himself loose. "All right, m'lord, we're past them."

"—don't you ever dare touch—what?" I peered. "Oh."

"See, m'lord? You occupy yourself with little things. Give way the road, pay no attention, and they'll do the same."

Head low, Anavar brought up the rear. A whisper. "I think he's right."

"Must we ride to Vessa playing fools?"

"Sometimes, sir, when my father was angered, I'd go about humming and pretending to be immersed in childish things, until his temper soothed itself. Had you not the art of making yourself invisible in your keep?"

"Not really. Well . . . I watched the nobles at state dinners, sometimes, when I was thought to be abed. I curled in the corner with some houseboys, playing at jacks. Mother never noticed."

Our trail met the coast road at last. Thunder rolled over the squat stone houses; lightning flashed on the whitecaps lapping at the shore. Scudding gray clouds consumed the bell tower and the great castle on the hill above. I glanced south, couldn't see Tantroth's outpost along the sea road. He'd have one, though, perhaps half a league south. His main force, no doubt, would be manning Llewelyn's keep.

Genard seized the reins. "Turn here. Don't you know the way?"

"You distract me." We threaded through Potseller's Way, the narrowest of alleys, to the Shoemakers' Steps. A few shoppers dressed in Tantroth's black roamed the walkway.

Anavar prodded his mare, came abreast. "Buy something large, sir."

"Are you daft?"

"Best if we have some business, rather than riding to no purpose."

"We've no time for—"

"He's right, m'lord. Something not too heavy. Boots, perhaps, wrapped in cloth."

"Daft." Grumbling, I stopped at a stall, waited shivering in my saddle, while Anavar and Genard selected cheap boots I wouldn't wear at my own burial. Overhead, a flash, and a crack of thunder.

A hand squeezed my leg; I gasped, almost hurled myself from the saddle in terror.

"Move yourselves!" Fostrow, his voice hoarse. He'd acquired a large sack, slung over his shoulder. His helmet and sword were nowhere to be seen. "Why do you dawdle?"

I hissed, "They buy boots." It seemed too much to explain. "We won't be long. Where's your breastplate?"

He'd turned his back, and was drifting off. "Under this foul robe. Hurry."

Finally, the transaction complete, Genard hoisted himself and his sack into the saddle. "On, m'lord, but slowly. We're looking at wares."

"Half the stalls are closed," I growled. "What's to look at?"

Genard's brow wrinkled. "When Master Griswold let me wander the market, stalls were packed with goods and buyers, no matter the weather. Was it not so, in your recall?"

I took stock of the forlorn market. "Not many customers but for the soldiers," I admitted.

"They say a number of your townsmen fled, when our sails were seen." Anavar, hunched against the increasing rain. "Homes deserted, ours for the taking."

"Ours?"

He had the grace to blush. "Sorry, sir."

From around the corner, coarse oaths. A gang of rough-dressed youths appeared, their voices raucous. One carried a jug slopping dark wine.

Genard nudged my rib. "Trouble. Look down."

"Why?" I wasn't about to skulk about my own market to avoid such rabble.

"Don't catch their—"

Too late.

"You stare, churl?" The oldest, a stocky boy of eighteen, caught my reins. Water dripped from his matted hair. "Would you share our jug?"

My hand crept under my cloak to my dagger, but Genard's fingers caught my wrist.

"Answer us!"

"Leave him, Farath, you strike him dumb."

"A fine saddle, Bosat, and a good mount." Farath's eye roved. "Stolen, I'll wager, from our dead of the battle."

"Let go my rein." I'd have sounded more authoritative, had I not sneezed.

Farath sneered, "Hah. What if I shout, 'He has my horse'?"

A cold voice, behind me. "Then you'd lie." Anavar drew tight his black cloak, stared down at the intruder. "What business have you here?"

Farath's mouth turned ugly; his glance flicked to Bosat. "And if I ask the same?"

"I am Anavar of Kalb, page to Lord Treak who serves Lord Tantroth." He lashed his mount forward. "Take your hand from my servant's horse!"

Genard's grip tightened. "Head down," he whispered. Seething, I obeyed.

Farath took a step back, but his fingers kept hold of my bridle. "What if we dump you in a ditch, Eiberian?"

Anavar's sword whipped clear. "Were not enough boys of Stryx hanged in the square, a month past? Would you join them?"

"Come away, Farath." Bosat tugged at his companion.

"Together, we'd down him!"

"The Eiberians would post a reward, and some would claim it. Come *on*!" Grumbling, muttering curses, Farath allowed himself to be persuaded. With sneers, the youths retreated.

Anavar sheathed his sword. "Come along." Without a look back, he led the way from the square.

I contained myself until we turned the corner to safety. "Your servant? How dare you!"

"Thank me. I saved your life."

"Faugh. From the likes of them I need no protection. I was about to—"

"Make a scene, attract guards, be noticed. And get yourself taken." The boy's tone was sharp.

I frowned, but had no answer.

Anavar looked about uncertainly.

"I know the way, m'lord. Let me guide the reins." The downpour came harder as Genard led.

I sat shivering. After a time I asked, "What boys were hanged?"

Anavar shifted in his saddle. "They threw rocks."

"Tell on." My tone was curt.

"At our guards. Tantroth was angered. It happened too often, and when some were caught, he made an example."

"Tough louts like those you chased?"

Anavar's face was set at the stalls, so I couldn't see. "Younger. Urchins."

My fingers gripped the pommel, squeezed as if it were Tantroth's neck. "How many?"

"Five." At last Anavar turned to face me, his eyes bleak. "Their bodies hung a week, while birds had at them. Sir, I was appalled; many were, even within Tantroth's ranks. We wouldn't—"

"Hold your tongue." My voice was a rasp. I hated Tantroth, his folk, the Eiberian I'd befriended.

"It wasn't my doing," he said stubbornly. "Even Lord Treak was dismayed."

I withdrew into myself, brooding, until Genard nudged me from behind. "Is that not the dwelling, m'lord?" He pointed.

I peered. "Yes."

"Now what?"

I beckoned to Anavar. "What say that you knock at Vessa's door and demand audience?"

The boy looked dubious. "Has he guards?"

"Servants, no more. Unless your people put guards over him."

He studied the doorway. "If they're of Stryx, I'm safe; few know me. But if one of Lord Treak's troop sees me . . ."

For all Rust's warnings, we hadn't gone so far as to figure how I would gain entry. All depended on the situation we found. I said, "Genard, knock at the door. Say your master would have word with the Speaker."

"My master Elryc?" He gaped.

"Your master Anavar."

"But he's not . . . ahh, I understand. What if they're Eiberian and recognize his name?"

"Run, I suppose." I shrugged. "I can't think."

Fostrow trudged past, in his disreputable robe. "Don't loiter about," he growled, to the muddy earth. "Go to the door, or move on."

I grimaced. "Imps and demons gnaw him." I swung off my saddle. "I'll go myself. Anavar, stay near. If the Duke's men take me, intervene and do your best. If Eiberians pass by, lie low. From them I should be safe; they won't recognize me."

"This is madness." He licked his lips.

"Is it not?" I stalked across the road, rapped at the door.

It swung open, and a face peered at me. "Yes?"

"I seek Vessa."

His eyes probed my ill-fitting clothes, my ragged cloak. "Come three days hence, at the eleventh hour, when—"

"I bring word for his ears only."

"You?" In his tone, contempt.

"Aye, sir." I made my fingers twist at my cloak, as would a humble churl. "From a lord."

"Who?"

"Rustin son of Llewelyn."

It silenced him, as well it might. Then, "Wait."

I stood sweating in the hall, ruing my folly. In a few moments the doorkeeper reappeared. "Come."

Vessa, Speaker of the City, sat at a plain wooden table, an unfinished meal set aside. His wrinkled face bore distaste. "Yes?"

"Sire, he said for your ears only." I tried to look stubborn.

"Very well." To the servant, "Leave us."

In a moment we were alone, the thick chamber door closed. Vessa drummed the table. "Rustin is outlaw, vassal to the fugitive Prince."

"Rustin is loyal to his King, and no man's vassal." I threw off my cloak, spoke as to an equal.

"Lord of Nature!" He half rose, glanced to the window, lowered his voice. "What lunacy brings you here? Out, this instant!"

"I seek your vote in Council."

"Would you have me cast down for our converse? Mar spoke true; you *are* addled. Out!"

"Don't be swayed by my garb." I fingered my jerkin. "Our troop is in the hills. We've men, and horse. Arms."

"A gift from Raeth of Cumber; tell me something I *don't* know. No, don't bother. Guard! Help!"

His quavering voice didn't carry far. I lunged across the table, seized his throat. "Hush, old fool, lest you destroy yourself!"

He gaped. Oh, how proud Rustin would be, to see me assault the man whose favor I sought. I released him, awkwardly smoothed his shirt. "Think, Lord Vessa. How long will you keep your office, when Tantroth or Mar hold both city and castle? What need will they have of you?"

"Mar promised—" He bit it off. Again, he looked to the window. "To Margenthar, I could explain your visit. If Tantroth discovers I've had Rodrigo in my chamber, that's another matter. He's not known for kindness."

My smile was grim. "True, he's not. Would you give him Stryx, and Caledon?"

"The choice isn't mine."

"But it is." I drew myself up, all too conscious of my shabby apparel. "Mine is the Still of Caledon. I need but the crown to wield it."

"And the sense of a sheep." Unimpressed, he shook his head. "Mar is experienced in war, and diplomacy. Besides, you haven't the Vessels; Mar seized them. Without the Still, you can do nothing for the realm."

I studied him, fighting a hopeless despair. At last I threw caution to the winds. "Has Mar paid you?"

"Bah. Insults, again? If he had, would I tell you?"

"What if I paid more?"

His look was one of cold disdain. "You seek to buy my favor? I am Vessa, not a tradesman!"

For an endless time, I held his eyes.

He licked his lips. "How much?"

Outside, a commotion, "Run, boy of Stryx! Get thee hence!" It sounded like Anavar. Perhaps Genard had provoked him beyond bearing. Or perhaps it was a warning meant for me, but my goal was within my grasp.

"If I knew what my uncle—"

The door flew open. "Offer him all your treasure, false Prince!" Chain armor the guard wore, over black garb.

Instantly I lunged past Vessa, flung open the window, launched myself outward.

Hands grasped my waist, hauled me back.

Outside, no sign of Anavar or Fostrow. Across the road, Genard danced from foot to foot in a veritable frenzy.

I spun, broke loose from the restraining hands, whipped out my blade. "Die!"

The room was full of men. One bore a short club. He flung it at my head. A blaze of lights. Blinded, reeling, I lunged with my dagger. Strong hands seized my wrist, wrested the blade from my grasp.

In a moment my hands were bound.

"Thank you, thank you!" Vessa gabbled. "The rogue burst in, waved his knife at my throat, and I could do nothing. I cried for help; ask my servant!"

"You cried out, yet your man went about his work? Do you train your servants so?" The captain spat. "Guard this old buffoon, until my lord Tantroth speaks his fate."

"Let me go!" I twisted my wrists, to no avail.

"Take this boy to Tantroth. He's impatient to see the Princeling." The captain's lips curled in a sneer. "Can six of you guard a bound youngsire?"

"Aye, sir."

"Then bring up the horses."

Half a dozen of Tantroth's troops assembled in the road. Two helped me mount a russet mare, holding the reins beyond my reach.

A familiar voice. "You see? I told you he'd come!" Among the soldiers, my bondsman Garst pranced with excitement.

I made my look stony, beyond contempt.

"I told you!"

My captors urged their mounts into a slow trot, and I was borne with them. I debated leaping from the saddle, but I might only break a leg for my pains. I touched my tender scalp, winced from the pain it brought.

"Where are you taking me?"

The lieutenant disdained to answer, but the rider at my side said, "To the keep, to await Lord Tantroth's pleasure." We clattered over damp cobblestones toward the square of crossed roads, where sat most of the city's alehouses.

"Hold, sir!" A cloaked rider hurried to overtake us. "Hold!"

The lieutenant raised a hand, and our troop slowed.

The young courier said, "My lord Tantroth bids you ride by the shore road, that none may observe the former Prince. And send to the keep all who know of his capture."

"Who may you be?"

The rider drew himself up. "Anavar, first son of the Earl of Kalb, serving his lordship at the keep. Have any townsmen seen your captive, sir?"

The lieutenant looked about. "Not on this street."

"Could you cover his face? I suppose not. Hurry to the shore, sir, lest he be observed."

With an oath, the lieutenant grabbed the reins of my mount. "Back, lads." We cantered back the way we'd gone. I tried to catch Anavar's eye, but he rode in front, at the lieutenant's side. We turned onto the shore road, where it turned at the southern edge of town. Ahead, between us and the keep, Tantroth's black-sailed fleet lay moored.

A peasant boy played by the roadside, hopping over a fallen branch. As we passed he thrust the branch between the forelegs of the lieutenant's steed.

"Get away, you—" A guardsmen raised his whip, spurred at the boy.

As the lieutenant's horse stumbled, Anavar threw the Eiberian from his saddle. Letting go my reins, the man fell heavily, rolled over once, and was still.

Behind me, a shout. "Beware, it's an—aiyee!"

I whirled; Fostrow wrenched his blade from a guard's gut, whirled to slash at another. As the man fell in a spray of blood, Fostrow seized the reins of his mount, caught one foot in the stirrup, stood hopping as the horse skittered.

Genard ducked under a blow, raced to my side, swarmed up my

leg, mounted himself behind me. "The reins, the reins!" His voice was shrill in my ear.

I reached forward, but my bound wrists were too clumsy. Anavar sidestepped his mount, caught my dangling reins, handed them to Genard.

"Geeah!" Genard's heels galvanized my mare as he hauled her about. "Lie low, m'lord!" Together we leaned over the frightened mare's neck and swept through the confusion.

Helpless, I clutched the pommel and looked backward to the melee. Fostrow wasn't yet in his saddle. The last two guards bore down upon him, but one was in the way of the other. Anavar raced to their struggle.

Fostrow ducked one blow, unable either to mount or free his leg.

I gasped, "Wait, Genard." The boy slowed.

Behind us, the guard loomed over Fostrow. He raised his sword for a triumphant blow. From behind, Anavar's hand caught the man's jerkin. His steed reared, but the guard recovered his balance. With a cry of rage he turned, to receive Anavar's dagger full in the heart.

Fostrow threw himself on his captured horse with such vehemence he almost fell off the far side. Frantically, he righted himself. Anavar maneuvered to avoid the blows of the remaining guard. With a howl, Fostrow spurred toward him, sword raised.

The guard fled.

I hung dizzily to the pommel as we raced toward the hills.

"We can't slow, Roddy. Lord of Nature knows how many Tantroth sent after us." Fostrow ignored my glare. "You think we've eluded them, but would you gamble the crown on it?"

I looked back to our scout, who brought up the rear. "The way I feel, yes." We'd pressed onward ever since we'd rejoined our scouts at the edge of town, and it was all I could do not to fall out of the saddle.

Anavar sat dejected on his horse, staring at nothing.

I snarled, "Did you hear that scoundrel—what's the matter?"

Anavar rubbed his horse's mane. "I lost my dagger."

I snorted, "Is that all?"

The Eiberian said, "It's *how* I lost it."

"In battle? That's honorable."

"Not for me."

I stared.

"I warned you, sir, I would not raise a hand against my lord Tantroth." He pursed his lips. "I killed his man."

"But he would have—"

"It matters not. Surely even you can see that."

"*Even* I?" I reached across, grasped his jerkin. "How say you?"

With staggering insolence he slapped away my hand. "I would not be touched, sir."

My mouth worked in voiceless fury. If not for my dizziness, I'd have flung him to the ground. "I should beat you!"

Anavar's eyes met mine. "As you choose, my lord. Better I had accepted Tursel's death when I was felled."

"What's this?" Fostrow's tone was sharp. "At each other's throats, and for what?"

"For honor!" Anavar spoke before I was able.

"Faugh. For weariness, and relief from fear. And hunger. There's flat bread left, and a bit of the dried meat." He reached into his saddlebag. "Eat, before you—"

"Let Prince Rodrigo partake!" Anavar spurred ahead.

Not to be outdone, I snapped, "I'll starve first!"

Fostrow's voice was mild. "What was that about?"

"He stabbed a guard of Eiber, and has regrets."

"As well he should. You comforted him?"

"I would have." I rode in silence.

Fostrow sighed. "Go after him, Roddy."

"Is that a command?"

"If it were in my power, yes." Fostrow searched my expression. "He's your man, and in pain."

"*I'm* in pain!" I seized his arm. "This knot over my eyes, my wrists . . . where's your compassion for your lord?"

"His pain is greater. He's dishonored his oath."

"By his own choice. He could have remained in camp with Captain Tursel and Rust." And if so, I'd be screaming on the rack, or endungeoned. "Imps and demons take you!" I kicked, and dutifully, the horse responded.

I found Anavar not far ahead, resting on his mare, by a babbling rivulet. I knew not what to say.

"Will you beat me?"

"Have no fear."

"I have none. Will you?" It was a challenge.

"Punish yourself, if you did wrong to Tantroth. Don't demand it of me."

"I speak of my incivility to you."

"You speak of Tantroth!" I grasped his chin, turned it toward me, saw the tears I'd heard in his voice. "On the shore road you saved Fostrow, who was rescuing me."

"I know."

"It pleases you not?"

"That I betrayed my kinsmen?"

I lapsed silent, thought long. "Anavar . . . Stay my ward, or be released. Go home to your father, or serve Tantroth even against my cause. I give you leave to choose your life."

With a cry, he buried himself in his own arms.

I sat helpless. Rustin had the art of comfort. I did not.

After a time his voice came, strained. "Lord Prince, what should I do?"

I didn't want the burden of his choice. Yet his gallantry, his bravery, had saved me. I said, as if I knew truth, "You'll remain my ward. After, when Caledon is restored, I'll treat with your father, with Tantroth himself if need be, for your safe release. Until then . . ." I hesitated, grasping for something within reason. "You may harm your own people only to save me, or my brother, or Lord Rustin my guardian. For no other end. This, I command."

His voice was muffled. "Thank you, sir."

"As to tonight . . . your bruises haven't so faded that you would forget my foul temper. I don't know that I could restrain myself to beat you lightly as befits a boy; my cruelty is too great. Therefore do not taunt me, most especially when Rustin isn't near to stay my hand."

"I heed you."

"Anavar, it will be for your father, for your liege, to judge your loyalty to them, when time comes. For me, I deem you honorable and would so say to any man. Take that unto your conscience."

His hand crept out, found mine.

I shivered. "We've both scorned dinner, and I'll warrant we both starve."

He raised his face, with a shy smile. "I'll eat if you will."

"Done."

Chapter 32

As the soggy day waned, the banners of our encampment drifted into view. When we neared, my tent flap opened.

Like a small child to a mummers' wagon Rustin raced toward our party, bereft of dignity, legs pumping. "Roddy! Welcome, my prince! How did it go?" He seized my reins as I brought the mare to a halt.

"A fiasco." I practically fell into his arms. "Is there such a thing as a hot bath? Tea? A bed?"

With care, he raised the hair from my brow. "Who split your head? Where was Fostrow? What happened? What of Vessa?"

"Give the lad a moment's peace," Fostrow said. "I'll allow he's had a rough time of it."

I groaned as Rust helped me strip off my odious jerkin. "Vessa was Mar's man to the core. Tantroth caught me in his house, and I know not Vessa's fate."

"How did you—tell me all!"

"Later. Take care of me, Rustin." For a moment I thought I would weep. "Let me be a boy until I'm well."

That, he didn't do. But he clucked over me like a mother hen, brought me hot water to soak in, steaming tea to inhale, wrapped straw to lie on. I dozed in the crook of his arm and let him ply me with questions until he was satisfied.

"I told you to let me come along," he chided, but I barely heard. After a time, I slept.

By night I felt well enough to join my trusted few at the campfire. "Groenfil," I told Tursel. "I've no other prospect."

He frowned. "To avoid Tantroth's patrols, our best choice is to retrace our steps and cross Soushire's hills. I've no men who know those passes. We risk ambush, attack, betrayal."

Rustin said, "You forget, Roddy, we're expected in Verein."

"Where? Oh!" I'd managed to put Uncle Mar completely out of mind. "I escaped one snare by the fur of my tail. Why set myself another?"

Rust said, "We'd all be with you."

"Wonderful. We could swing together from the gibbet."

"Groenfil's citadel won't vanish in the night. Let's learn what wiles Margenthar would practice."

I scowled, stifling a cough. "Said you not once, that statecraft was my domain?"

"Yes. As advice is mine."

I sat shivering a while longer. "I'll go back to bed."

Anavar said, "Good night, sir. My father says thoughts during sleep are wiser than—"

"May imps gnaw your father!" I thrust aside the tent flap.

Later, Rustin and I lay talking, and before I knew it, he'd woven a ring through my nose: I agreed to visit Uncle Mar at Verein before riding as I wished to Groenfil. For spite, I made him rub the ache from my back, until the candle guttered.

Late at night, I went out of our tent to relieve myself, and heard a creak in the cart that carried our supplies. Wary of thieves and marauders, I crept close.

A groan from within startled me. Dagger drawn, I jumped into the cart, landed with a thud on Anavar, whose hands shot to his lowered breeches.

Under him lay a camp woman, her bare breasts gleaming in the moonlight.

Betrayal.

White rage seized me, such as seldom I'd felt. I'd have plunged my dagger into his back had not he gibbered in terror and brought me to my senses. I flung the Eiberian out of the cart. The woman screamed.

I leaped onto the frightened boy. "You'd rut with whores outside my very tent?" I aimed a kick, that barely missed. "Touch her again and I'll . . ."

"Please, my lord!"

Rustin charged out of the tent, sword drawn. Uncertainly, he lowered his blade. "Roddy?"

"Vile foreign scum! Stay away from our servants! Keep your parts sheathed, or I'll serve them to you for dinner!"

Rust strode across the clearing, interposed himself between me and the Eiberian. "Let go the dagger, Roddy."

"It's all right, I won't—"

"Now!" He caught my wrist.

Sullenly, I let it fall. "I won't go berserk."

"You already have." Rustin peered inside the cart, nodded. "So I thought."

"They were—"

"It happens." He turned, extended a hand to Anavar. "Up, boy." He swung the Eiberian to his feet. "Raise your breeches; the sight maddens our prince."

Half in tears, Anavar covered himself, thrust in his shirt. "We just— I didn't—it was only . . ."

"Easy, lad." Rust clapped his shoulder. I swallowed; I hadn't meant to harm the boy. Well, perhaps I had, but I'd mastered myself now, and—

"Roddy, run down the line, check all the campfires. Other soldiers may be lying with women."

"Don't mock me!"

"What else am I to do? Go to the tent."

It was a way out of my embarrassment. "I'm sorry, Anavar." I fled.

A few moments later Rustin slipped inside, tied the drawstring. "No doubt he'll remember the occasion."

I sat with head in my hands. "It's just . . . he's so young. He's free to frolic in the night, while I only . . ."

"Only have me. Tact, Roddy, is one of your lesser virtues." He sat by my side. "Is that a smile, hiding under the pout?"

"Oh, Rust." I was near tears. "Is the True worth it all?"

"Answer yourself."

"The kingdom's dissolving, and I've certainly not wit enough to hold it together without our family wisdom. I know that, but . . ."

"You want a woman."

"Desperately."

A long silence. When we returned to bed, we lay apart.

Verein was many leagues through the hills, far from the sea, well east of the tablelands of grain that fed Castle Stryx.

Recovered from my misadventures, I rode peaceably with Rustin and Elryc. The day was clear and cloudless, and Tantroth's black sails far from sight.

Under strict orders to refrain from pillage, our troop passed through the few hamlets that sprouted amid the rocky farms. Seeing we were in good order, folk came out from their rude houses to watch the procession. Almost, I donned the crown to show them splendor they'd not soon forget. But I knew it would be presumptuous, and might offend the True.

"Only one thing could ruin this day," I joked. "Coming upon Hester and her creaking cart."

"Think you she came this way?" Elryc studied the road, as if for ruts.

"How other?" By her years of service and her wild antics in departing Stryx, Hester had made herself too well known to pass again through the town; she'd make a wide detour. So our path might indeed be hers.

When Fostrow, Anavar, and I had circled the ravines behind the castle to slink into Stryx, we'd dared sneak close behind the stronghold, prepared to flee at the crack of a branch. Now, in paradox, though we were stronger by far, we must give the walls wider berth. It would not do to confront in force either Mar's loyal troops or those of Tantroth.

Hour after hour we trudged, and at night our campfires dimmed the blanket of stars. By day Tursel sent scouts ranging for provender. They were ordered to buy foodstuffs with Earl Cumber's stipend, rather than seize provisions, but I doubted all would. How were we to know the provenance of a lamb, or a brace of chickens? Such were the ways of war. Churls expected it.

As sun was fading, we found ourselves well past Stryx, entering the region of Verein. I asked Rustin, "Should I breathe easier when we're within a league from Mar's stronghold, in the province of his safe-conduct?"

Rust was half dozing in the last rays of afternoon. "Always breathe easy, my prince."

Elryc said, "Not so, brother." He shifted in his saddle. "Can you imagine Mar wishes us well?"

"Not really."

"Nor I." He patted his mount's flanks, guided her away from roadside brush. "Look." He lifted his cloak, showed me the small sharp dagger within.

"What of it?"

"If Uncle Mar plays us false . . ." He licked his lips.

I said lightly, "I'm sworn to protect you. If not, Hester will turn me into a toad."

"I won't be taken like Pytor, Roddy." His eyes lifted to mine, as his hand flitted to the blade. "It's for me, as much as them. I'll end myself first."

"Elryc!"

He shivered. "On the battlements of Stryx, hidden in that cursed barrel, I had little to distract my thoughts. Visions of a rope tightening around my throat, or an unseen knife in the night . . . no!"

"When we meet I'll keep you and Uncle Mar apart, in the tents. He won't even know you ride with us."

"Of course he'll know; did I cover my face when we cantered through the hamlets? Besides, I can't hide myself and take part in your counsels."

"You're too young to—" I sighed, biting off the rest. Someday, I'd learn not to make rash promises.

At last, late the next morn, we saw the pennant fluttering from the high tower. I bade Tursel call a halt. "Send an envoy, with the usual ornate greetings. We'll meet my uncle on the field."

Rustin stretched. "I have another thought. Invite him to our camp. With full safe-conduct, of course."

"Ha." My mouth twitched. "Neatly done, and he'd be livid."

"If he'd accept." He pondered. "We might squander days while envoys rode back and forth to bargain the conclave. Each day heightens our peril. And supplies will run low."

"Well, then." I smiled sweetly. "Tell him he's our host, and must feed us."

"Only if you come to the castle, he'll say."

"We refuse, and learn how much he desires a meeting."

"Ah, Roddy." He ruffled my hair. "You learn your craft."

Mar was furious. We'd agreed to meet at Verein, he responded, and that meant *in* Verein. Not in a damp tent perched in a plucked cornfield, not in a bivouac guarded by Earl Cumber's louts. Soft beds and refreshments awaited, and we'd do well to use them, or depart.

Elryc, Rust, and I huddled in conference. Very well, we replied. We would depart.

In that case, why had we traveled so far to see him, Mar inquired.

At his own invitation, we reminded him. But we were short of supplies, and unless he provendered my royal guard, we'd have no choice but to decamp. Not true, of course.

Duke Margenthar sent a wagonload of turnips.

We promptly struck our tents, and moved north a full league before Mar's envoy caught us. At my order, we heard his speech on horseback, riding ever north. The Duke would meet us in tent, field, or whatever place of my choosing, under my safe-conduct guaranteed him by the True.

"We won the first skirmish," said Rustin. "But try not to gloat."

And so, a full day after our arrival, we faced Margenthar, regent of Caledon, over a cook table borrowed from a supply wagon, in the shade of a hastily raised canopy.

"You summoned us, Uncle?" My tone was insufferably sweet, and Rustin frowned a warning.

"It's something less than a summons," Mar said dryly. "Nonetheless I'm glad you came."

I waited.

"Let's not spar," he said.

I made a gesture of assent.

He looked to Rustin, and past the tent pole to Fostrow and Tursel, who watched him as a pair of falcons would a mouse. "I'd speak with you alone."

"To what point? I'll reveal all to my counselors."

"Nonetheless."

I looked to Rustin, and shrugged.

Rust came to his feet in a graceful motion. "I'll withdraw, my lord Duke, when I'm satisfied you hide no blade."

Mar's affable smile vanished. "Dare you question my honor?" The back of his neck flushed red.

I said, "It's all right, Rust. Go."

"My prince, I will not obey you in this." Rustin stood his ground. "And don't glare so; I don't much care that you're incensed."

I made a helpless gesture. "I'm sorry, Uncle."

Holding his fury barely in check, Mar permitted Rustin to examine his person. In a moment Rust bowed low, and left us.

Mar's teeth were clenched. "You'd be King and can't control a vassal?"

"He's no vassal."

Mar breathed deep, restored his calm. "Let's walk a few paces." He led me on a random path across the field. "Roddy, our views differ strongly, as you know. I grant you've sustained yourself in opposition better than I foresaw."

"Thank you."

"But Raeth's largesse won't last forever; he's notoriously tightfisted. You look surprised; think you I don't know every step you've trod, and each word you exchanged with Cumber and Soushire?"

"What is it you want?" It was all I could think of that admitted nothing.

"To make common cause." He turned, started us back toward the canopy. "We've lost Llewelyn's keep, and that imperils Stryx Castle. Half our troops are bottled within; the others dare not leave Verein unguarded. You hope Tantroth will depart with the winter winds, but take my word he won't."

"How do you know?"

"How do I know Prince Elryc is concealed scarce twenty strides from our tent, and advises you? How do I know Vessa's office is now vacant?"

"Is what?" The meadow reeled.

"Tantroth is less informed than I, and couldn't take the risk you might acquire the fabled Still. As you may now deduce, your quest to obtain votes to end the regency is hopeless."

I said nothing, yearning for Rustin's guidance.

"By the way, Vessa wouldn't have joined you, whatever your offer. He only hoped to draw out your terms."

"So you say." Immediately I regretted it, but his darts had provoked me.

"Roddy, answer in truth: Do you wish Tantroth to take the hill of Stryx?"

"Of course not." That, he already knew.

"Submit—no, let me phrase it as I really mean. Cooperate with my regency. Together we can compel the aid of Cumber; Raeth might offend one of us but wouldn't dare wound us both. With his strength added to ours, Soushire's scheming is neutralized. You are aware, aren't you, that Soushire's been in touch with Tantroth on three occasions?"

I tried to let my face show nothing, and no doubt failed.

"It will be a regency in name only, Roddy. I'll consult with you on policy. I admit I spoke harshly to you, and treated you as a boy, but you've shown that's no longer suitable."

"In that case, crown me now."

"May I speak openly, assured that it will go no farther than your tent?"

I nodded.

"The Warthen has sons, and rests uneasily in the vassalage of Caledon. He's thought of the crown for his own line. And Lady Soushire entertains wild dreams of a strike at the castle."

"So?"

"They bear the situation, because it is fluid. Your coronation would dash their fantasies. It might provoke them to rash and desperate acts."

"If that's so, why didn't you tell me when we spoke of the regency?"

"While the Council sat, and you of a mind to blunder in and blurt everything you'd been told? I didn't want them aware how much I knew."

"But I'd have the Still."

"Yes. Unfortunately, it's a trifle overrated."

It stopped me dead in my tracks. I fastened on his face.

"Remember that Elena was my own sister. She always made of the Still more than it was, to impress the common folk."

"The Powers—"

"Oh, there's mild power of compulsion. You could probably use it to make Rustin scratch his privates at a state banquet, and be unaware of the offense. It doesn't operate at much of a distance."

"You lie!"

"You'll see, when the time comes."

Confusion welled, but I waved it away. "The true Power of the Still is the collective wisdom of Caledon's—"

"Would you know how Elena described it? A vague presence, a hint of awareness of the land. No crafty ancestors guiding her very thoughts. Just . . . a brooding presence."

I cried, "Great houses have great Power! Claim you that Caledon is a petty earldom, with Powers so paltry—"

"Varon of the Steppe, my grandfather and Elena's, seized Caledon and Eiber too. They were his fiefdoms."

"Our Power was diminished in that?"

"If ever it was greater."

I was near tears. "Why would Mother lie?"

"Don't you know, Rodrigo? Think."

"It's too much." My mind was a whirl, so much so that I even admitted it to him. I glanced to the tent fifty paces hence, and craved to rush to Rustin. "Tell me."

"Why, it's plain," he said. "So that others would fear the Still. By holding it as threat, she outwitted her adversaries, and made good her claim to Caledon."

If he spoke true, I'd been the fool these four years or more, ever since I'd become able. I blinked back tears. "And you told me not?"

"For the same reason Elena held her tongue. Even if you didn't cry the news from the battlements"—I flushed—"you'd have rutted through the keep like a stallion in a pen of brood mares, and all would have known you'd never claim your Power."

The sunlit field seemed to circle me gently. I forced my thoughts to what I knew. "Uncle, if this is so, show me good faith."

"How?"

"Give me Pytor."

"Lord of Nature, are you mad?" His eyebrow rose, hung quizzically. "You, Elryc, and Pytor, three noble brothers united? How long would you live? Hours? A week?"

"What say you?"

"Separated, you each have worth as players in the game of state. If Tantroth—or anyone whose interest is counter to yours—knew you three shared a camp, he'd lunge, and put to an end the House of Caledon."

"Then let me send Pytor—"

"No, Roddy, this goes beyond the crown. For what I owe your mother, I shall not cause your deaths. Trust my wisdom."

"Let me see him!"

"Of course. He's within the walls, guarded from harm. You'll recall I invited you—"

"Bring him hence!"

"No. Some spy might alert our enemies."

Stung, I cried, "If you know so much, why did Llewelyn betray our House?"

His face turned grave. "Ah, that I don't know." A twitch of a smile. "You see? I'm not all-powerful." Gently, he guided my arm, and again we walked. "He'll be made to pay, even if he's your Rustin's father."

"Of course." Casually, I wiped an eye, hoping Uncle Mar wouldn't know the cause. "Why has Tantroth attacked neither Stryx Castle nor Verein?"

It was his turn to stop, and for a brief moment his face betrayed his surprise. "You truly don't know?"

"I'm not clever enough to play such games," I said bitterly. "He seized the town, stole the keep, and halted. Why?"

"It's you, Roddy." He waited for my comprehension, saw none. "You escaped the castle, and ride hither and yon stirring up the nobility. Without Llewelyn's keep the castle is indefensible; Tantroth has no hurry. If Tantroth attacks Stryx forthwith, or Verein, he forces your hand. He waits to end his uncertainty before committing his troops to battle."

"But . . ."

"Even if he hadn't heard of your mad scheme to beard Vessa, he'd have guessed you'd try. He hoped to capture you himself. Failing that, he waits to see with whom you'll ally yourself."

I gaped. "What does he fear?"

"Why, the Still, what else? Remember, in the whole realm none but you and I know it is less than it seems."

"No more!" I turned toward the tent. "I'll speak with my advisors."

"Roddy, listen!" He caught my arm. "Forget for a moment that our aspirations disjoin. I took great risk telling you the truth of the Still. If you breathe of it to the others, all the realm will know within a fortnight. Let the Norlanders but learn of it, and Caledon will be lost. Eiber's might is a paltry shadow of theirs."

"How can I—" I thrust off his arm, strode to the tent. "I won't hear more, until I've time to think."

"Take heed."

"I won't tell them. Not yet. Rustin!" I beckoned. "See my lord Duke has refreshment."

Rust bowed in acknowledgment. "Of course." His tone was sardonic. "Perhaps a warm bowl of turnip stew."

I growled something unkind, fled to my tent, closed the flap.

By the time Elryc looked in, a few moments later, I was near frenzy. He asked what had been said. I told him what I could, pacing from pole to pole, sitting on the bed, jumping up to pace anew. Though I yearned to, I said nothing of the Still.

"I wonder," he said, "how Uncle knew about Vessa."

"Walls have ears." And so did tents. I threw open the flap, rushed outside, raced around the tent.

None lingered near.

I fell again on my bed. "A regency seems wise, if you look at it from his view." If the Still was nothing, why hasten to don the crown?

"Roddy, take a rake, and separate grain from chaff."

"It's a cornfield we're near, not a—"

"Don't be so literal. In what Uncle says, I meant. Let's divide lies from truth."

"He told me other things," I blurted, before I came to my senses and pressed my mouth shut. Had I been overheard? I ran outside, peered around the tent poles.

Elryc's look was intent. "What more?"

"Nothing you need know." I realized how surly I sounded, knew I didn't need another enemy. "I'm sorry. When I need counsel, it will be yours I seek."

He seemed mollified only in part. "Say what troubles you."

"No!" Unexpectedly, I blinked back tears, thought of Tresa's hand on my ribs, and my cool disdain. Mother had tricked me into tormenting myself for her statecraft. It would end, and soon, even if I had to pay a girl such as Chela.

The flap swirled open, and Rustin appeared. "Three times the tent opened, and twice you emerged, to dart inside a moment after. Have imps seized your wits?"

"Get out!"

"First tell me why you rush about the tent like a strangled chicken."

I bit back a sob. "This is no time for—"

"Elryc, leave." It was a command, and Elryc obeyed. The moment the flap closed Rust said, "My prince, what frets you so?"

"Nothing I would discuss. I'm ready."

"Ready to what?"

"Resume our parley." To concede the regency.

It seemed to decide him. "We'll take a walk."

"Not now."

"I insist."

"How dare you!"

"By your own oath, Roddy."

A vow by the True, else I'd lose the Still. My laugh was harsh. "I renounce it."

I'd thought it might enrage him. Instead, he came close, ran his finger softly across my cheek. "It's too warm for a cloak."

I thrust his hand from the chain at my neck. "Rust, please! I don't want to fight, but . . ."

"Take it off. Now!" His voice was like a whip.

Numbly, I complied.

"Outside." He held the flap.

It mattered not whether I allowed his domination. Caledon was all but in Tantroth's hands, I had not four votes in Council, and I knew I would submit to the regency ere the sun was set. Meekly, I followed.

He led me to a shady grove well within the perimeter of our guards. "Sit." I did, and to my surprise, he lay himself down, eased his head into my lap.

"Now . . ." He plucked a blade of grass with which to tease his lips. "Unless imps have stolen your sense, all that's occurred since this morn was your meet with the Duke. Since it's unhinged you, I'll learn why."

"I won't say."

"Of course you will. Rub behind my ear, will you? It itches. There's a good boy. You're desperate to tell me, we both know it."

"I'm not!"

After a moment he said, "Turn your head if you must cry. The tears drop on my nose."

"Imps take you!"

"Begin with the regency. The rest will follow."

Despite my stubborn resolve I spoke, and put the fate of Caledon in his hands, and felt the better for it.

"Rust?"

"Yes, my prince?" His hair was warm in my lap.

"How will I be a man, so I need not run to tell you all?"

"It will come." He sounded sure, and I ached to believe him.

"What shall we do?"

"Ask Elryc's counsel."

My tone was bitter. "Then it will be as Uncle said. If two know a secret, each knows who spoke it, but when three know . . ."

"Elryc trusts you with his life, and holds yours. It's as should be." He sat.

Sighing, I stood. "I wish you'd stop blathering about trust. Someday I have to rule."

"Yes, I've heard you speak of intrigue and the halls of kings. Very apt. But we can't live without trust, and without . . ." He glanced about. "I hope Elryc hasn't gone far."

"Without what?"

"Love. Ah, there he is." He beckoned, and Elryc came running. "Roddy has more to tell you. Is Genard handy? Have him bring us some dilute wine. Cold, if there's some been set in a stream."

I lay on my bed, drained of all emotion. We'd sent Mar home, saying we'd answer on the morrow. Rust, Elryc, and I had talked into the night, reviewing all possibilities.

If Mar's claim was true, there was no point fighting on. The Warthen was lost, by his refusal to parley. Groenfil was Mar's kin, and betrayed by my arrangement with Soushire; winning his support was doubtful. I could ride back to Cumber, but the longer I dithered, the more chance Tantroth would tire of waiting and strike, and learn in battle that the Still had no potency.

Elryc toyed with his empty cup. "Roddy, what if it's a lie?"

"Which part? The Warthen does have sons, and wouldn't see us. Cumber *is* stingy. What difference does it make if Soushire treated with Tantroth before we agreed—"

He said, "All of it."

Rust raised himself, listening intently.

"Every word. About Soushire and Groenfil. The Warthen's ambition, and Tantroth's intent."

"But why spin such a tale? Why go to the trouble?"

"Yes." Rustin. "That's it. Think, Roddy. You're yourself again."

"Don't set me a puzzle." I goaded my thoughts, found myself sinking in a marsh of possibilities. If Tantroth had other reason to stay his hand, that meant . . . If Soushire was true to our bargain, that meant . . .

Abruptly I looked up. It was so simple.

"I was on the brink of submitting."

"Yes."

"But . . ." There was more. I stood to pace; stirring my blood might help me to think. "His whole purpose in spinning his tale was to win my acceptance of his regency. That means he wants me in his control. My person has value. Why?"

Rustin lay back with a smile of contentment. "Think on it. If you haven't solved the riddle by morn I'll tell you."

I looked for dregs of wine to sprinkle on his face, but all was gone.

Whatever the answer was, it made Rustin happy.

What would give Rustin such pleasure, on this weary night? Ah. My heart leaped.

"He lied about the Still," I said. "The Power is more than a ruse."

Rust smiled, and I saw in him a stable cat that had just trapped a mouse.

In the morn, I proposed that we simply turn about and return to Cumber, but Elryc pointed out that would show Uncle Mar his tales were unbelieved. That was the case, I told him. But, he asked, why give that knowledge to Uncle?

So we summoned the Duke's envoy, to tell him I would have no answer for a week, that I would return to the hospitality of Cumber. Rust bade me act upset and angry when I spoke to the envoy, and I promised I would. But just before taking me within the envoy's sight he pinched me between the legs so hard my eyes bulged. Before I could draw breath to protest he hauled me to the canopy.

It was all I could do not to walk doubled over. Face red, aching, determined to revenge Rust's wanton brutality, I grated through my rehearsed speech, turned on my heel and strode out, or tried to.

As we broke camp Rust was nowhere to be found, though I sent Anavar, Genard, even Fostrow searching.

It wasn't until dark and the tents were set up anew that Rust ambled into view while we sat about the fire. "I suppose you're going to berate me?" He took a seat at my side.

"I know why you did it, but it *hurt*."

"Yes, otherwise it wouldn't suffice." He slung an arm over my shoulder. "Most humbly, I beg forgiveness."

"And you hadn't faith in my acting."

"Of course not. Your face mirrors your every humor."

"Bah. What does it reveal now?"

"That you wish you needn't pretend to be angry." A gentle squeeze.

How was it possible to stay piqued at him? "Genard, I'm sure Rustin is hungry. Fetch him a bowl of turnips."

As penance, Rust ate them.

The next morn, as we rode toward Cumber, I took Rustin aside. "I've been thinking."

"A dangerous habit. Overcome it, lest—"

"Be serious. What if all Mar said of the Still is true? What if I've denied myself for naught?"

"We decided last night—"

"And if we're wrong? His tale made sense. Of course Mother wouldn't tell me the Still had no value, as long as folk could see I prepared myself for it. Perhaps as I grew older she would have revealed the secret."

"If it were so, what would you do?"

"If the Power has no value . . . Rust, I'm older now, and wiser. No one need know who shares my bed."

He studied me long. "Is this about last night, my prince?"

I blushed. When finally we'd crept into our tent I'd shivered with cold, then found myself thinking of Uncle Raeth's granddaughter Tresa, and stirred with uncommon passion. I'd waited for Rust to notice, and when he seemed oblivious, I for the first time turned to him, instead of waiting for his touch.

"No," I snapped. "This is about Mar, and Mother."

He rode awhile. "You can't solve the riddle of your Power until you're crowned and have the Vessels. So, would you spend the Still like some exotic foreign coin, without first learning its worth?"

I opened my mouth, and closed it again. Surely there must be a solution that didn't leave me trapped in helpless chastity.

At that moment Anavar pulled up alongside. "May I speak with you, Lord Prince?" No others were in hearing, save Elryc, who dozed in his saddle.

At Rust, I rolled my eyes. "If you must."

"The other night—the girl . . . it would appear I owe you an apology. Forgive me. I didn't know the customs of your camp."

Gracefully put. Reluctantly, I nodded. "You startled me." After a moment I knew that wasn't enough to explain my bizarre behavior. I lowered my voice. "Know you anything of the Still of Caledon, or its requirements?"

"No, my lord."

I fell silent.

From Rustin, gently, "Go on, Roddy."

My voice was stiff. "Until I set down my Still forever, I must remain a virgin."

"Oh." A sound of wonder. His eyes darted to mine, in reappraisal. I reddened.

"It makes me . . . impatient. And, I suppose, jealous. You're but fourteen." I braced for the inevitable snigger.

"My lord, I'm so sorry!" His eyes were wide. "Please, I meant no harm, no disrespect. If only I'd known . . ." To my amazement, his voice was tremulous. "Truly, I would not hurt thee."

I snorted. "I've hurt *you* enough."

"It's nothing. I owe you my very life." He was silent awhile. Then, "Are there other ways?" His ears were red.

I shifted in the saddle, unhappy I'd brought up the matter. "None I'd care to discuss."

As solemnly as if he meant it, Rustin asked, "What would you suggest?"

For the next hour my Eiberian ward racked his brains to propose amorous possibilities, while I rode stiffly, eyes ahead, dreaming wistfully about Rust's funeral.

Chapter 33

RETRACING OUR STEPS WAS DISHEARTENING. NO MATTER how I recast it in my mind, returning to Cumber was defeat. But I dressed to parley with Groenfil, lest my plan bear fruition. Unless I plotted my course with meticulous care, I might find myself crowned, but without my Power. Perhaps Uncle Raeth could devise a way to interest the Warthen in our cause, and save me from an encounter with Groenfil.

We were riding disconsolately when, ahead, a trumpet sounded. Rust stiffened. "The call to arms!"

"Are you sure?"

"Yes." We spurred together. He drew his sword from its saddle sheath.

The trail was an anthill poked with a stick. Men and horses raced hither and yon.

"Rodrigo, here!" Fostrow waved, beckoning us. He'd collected a dozen of Tursel's troopers. We cantered to join them.

I called to Fostrow, "Why the alarm?"

"Foes lie ahead. The way is blocked."

"Who?"

"Their garb is black. Tantroth."

"Impossible. We're well behind Stryx Castle, far from the coast. Where's the attack?"

"Do you hear battle? No one's attacked."

Reluctantly, I sheathed my sword. "Let's look."

"Be safe with us, my lord. Tursel will report."

The captain cantered up, his mount lathered. "The trail is barred, sire. Tantroth's men are well dug in, and it's not sure how many we face."

"What is their aim?"

"Obviously, to stop our passage. No other force this way comes. I advise we turn our column, mount a rear guard, and retrace our steps. Just a moment." Tursel turned in the saddle, shouted orders to a nearby horseman. The guard galloped off.

I said, "Turn back to Verein? We'd hand ourselves to Mar."

"Two leagues toward Verein—well before the castle—we passed Seasand Cross. A tiny village, remember? A road runs from the Warthen's border down to the coast where—"

"I know my own realm!"

"Of course, sire. At the crossroads we'll be able to detour deeper into the hills, or even risk the coast road if you choose. It's better than camping here."

I looked to Elryc. He nodded.

I said, "Set it in motion, but first send envoy to ask passage."

"Very well, but they'll refuse. They won't have gone to such trouble for naught."

"Try, nonetheless."

"Wait here until I've rounded men to guard you." He went off.

"Come, Rustin, let's view their line." I selected a shield, just in case.

We met Tursel halfway. He summoned a dozen of our troop to ride guard. "Look, sire. Archers on the opposite slopes, pikemen in the center. We'd be annihilated if we attack." We were poised at the edge of the trail that descended into a shallow valley.

"Can the archers be driven off the hill?"

"Perhaps, but at great cost. They've but to lower their aim, while we charge uphill. And it leaves our center exposed for Tantroth's pikemen."

Rust said, "They chose well their place of battle."

Tursel said, "Yes. Interesting, given that they know not Caledon."

Who best knew this land? Soushire? Cumber? Mar? No matter. During Mother's reign Caledon was no secure camp. Any earl's man could have roamed it, and drawn plans.

"Our envoy?"

"In their camp, awaiting answer."

"I like not the look of this, Roddy." Rustin's tone was somber.

"Nor I."

An hour passed, while I swatted flies that buzzed about the horses. "Tursel, make ready our turn of march."

"I agree," the captain said. "You men, stay with the Lord Prince. Rodrigo, I bid you wait with the wagons in the center of our column. Here will be confusion."

"In a moment." I buttoned my cloak against a chill wind. Clouds raced across the peaks. I turned to Rust. "Will rain help us, or them?"

"I'm not sure. Come along, Roddy."

From the black lines of soldiery entrenched in the valley, a horseman galloped forth.

I tensed. "Do they charge?"

"One man at a time?"

The rider cantered across the open space, climbed the trail we'd sought to descend. "Hail, Caledon."

Our troops made way. It was the envoy I'd bid Tursel send.

He reached our height. A pause, while he drew breath, and summoned his speech.

"From Lord Treak, cousin to Tantroth, Lord of Eiber, Prince of the Inland Sea—"

"Yes, get on with it."

"—and heir to Caledon, greetings. Know ye that—"

"Heir to Caledon? *To Caledon?* Rust, did you hear?"

"Hush."

"Lord Tantroth graciously allows that Prince Rodrigo of the late House of the land may pass, together with guards and kinsmen numbering no more than twenty, through our lines and thence to the town of Stryx, that he may board ship thereat for exile in a land no nearer than three days sail—"

I rose in the saddle, my sword drawn. *"HOLD YOUR TONGUE!"*

"Sire, I am but an envoy, sent home with the words of—"

"Roddy, sheath thy blade." Rust's hand guided mine. "Wouldst thou smite the envoy for the tidings he bears?"

"Don't patronize me with high speech, Rust, not when . . ." I swallowed a sob. "Devils chew his innards! Damn him to the lake!"

"Lord Treak? Tantroth?"

"Every Eiberian born!" With an effort, I contained myself. "Tursel, strengthen our rear guard. Turn the column, and let us be off." I wheeled Ebon and galloped down the trail.

Smoldering, I hunched forward in my saddle, my cloak held tight against the driving rain.

I was surrounded by creaking wagons, cursing drovers, and my persistent guards, mired in the middle of the column. The trail was muddy and growing worse.

Rustin must have spoken to Fostrow; wherever I turned, one was at my left, the other at my right.

At last, able to stand it no longer, I pushed past Fostrow's mount. "Wait here."

The grizzled guardsman blinked reproach. "Where would you be going, lad?"

"It's 'prince,' or 'sire'!" I spurred Ebon, but abruptly the reins were swept from my grip, and it was all I could do to hang on to the pommel.

"Stay a bit, Roddy."

"Demons take you, Rust!" I snatched back my reins. "Don't treat me like—"

Atop the nearest wagon, a tarpaulin rose, and a damp head appeared. "Cork it, Roddy. Listen to reason." Elryc blinked, adjusted his cover, and disappeared.

I savored his betrayal as one of many to be revenged, until cold raindrops oozing down my neck doused my rage. Rust and Fostrow were right, and there was no shame in letting one's minions serve. To make amends I asked, "Rust, what if he follows?"

"Lord Treak?" He shrugged. "He'd lose choice of terrain."

"Would that stay him?" Tantroth's force had seemed daunting, enough so that I'd cast aside all thoughts of forcing the pass.

"We ride uphill."

I nodded. If Tantroth probed our rear guard, we'd again turn our column, and defend from height while his troops were forced to climb. For the moment we were safe.

The rain grew to a downpour. For three hours we slogged along a pathway turned into a bog. Guardsmen strained at the wagons; drovers lashed their horses; tempers grew foul.

Finally Tursel called a halt. "Sire, this isn't ideal resting ground, but if we go on we'll exhaust ourselves. We're guarded to the east by that fast-flowing stream, and to the west by the hills. I'll extend our camp along the trail, and double the outriders to the rear. We'll have ample warning should Tantroth stir. If you spread your tents there, and there, you'll be well surrounded."

"Very well." I eased myself from the saddle, dropped into an unseen puddle. "Demons' lake!" Inside my boot, my stockings squished. "Damn Lord Treak. Imps take Uncle Mar. Demons take you al—" Cheerfully, Rust reached down and clamped a wet hand across my mouth. It was all I could do not to bite him.

Chapter 34

ANAVAR OF EIBER GAVE A COURTEOUS NOD AS WE MOUNTED. "Good day to you, sir."

I tied my leather jerkin against the cool morning air, reveling in the sun that promised to warm the crisp autumn day. "Much better, yes. Genard!" I beckoned with my cup. "Have we more warm cider? Find me a beaker, would you?"

"I'm not your—"

"Please." I was feeling magnanimous, a legacy of the dissipated clouds and the news Tursel brought: Treak's troops remained camped across the gap, well to our rear. Genard trotted across the clearing with a steaming cup. I stretched, patted Ebon's flank.

Anavar asked, "May I ride with you?"

"Of course."

Proudly, he buckled on the sword I'd allowed him, while I watched Rustin direct the striking of our tent. I ought to help, if only to please Rust, but at some point he'd have to learn not to spoil the servants. I compromised by walking Ebon to the tent, and offering Rust a share of cider.

Absently he took the cup. "Which way will we turn at the crossroads? West to the Sands?"

"I suppose. As we move into the hills we'll find enough rutted cart trails toward Soushire, and from there it's an easy ride to Cumber."

"I'll be glad when we're gone from this region. That's enough smoothing, lads, lift it on the wagon. Here, Anavar, are you thirsty?" Rust handed the boy the remains of my drink.

I opened my mouth to protest, but thought better of it. We were all in decent spirits on this fine morning, and I would do nothing to spoil the mood.

Tursel sent his scouts to probe ahead, and we got under way. The ground was soft, but still we made good time.

Shortly our place in the line of march was crowded: at first Anavar, Rust, and I rode abreast, but after a time Elryc conjured a mount and joined us, which meant Genard was soon alongside, and Fostrow tagged near.

Tursel cantered up and down the line, vigilant. Eventually he paused to join us. "My lord, at this rate we'll be at the crossroads in— now what?"

Ahead, a clatter of hooves. Spotting us, a forward scout reined in. "Captain!" He ignored me entirely, and my fingers tightened on the pommel. "Outriders at the village cross! Cavalry moving fast."

I said, "There can't be."

"The road from Verein is clogged with Duke Mar's infantry, my lords! Their scouts set guide flags on our side of the cross. Perhaps fifty men have—"

I licked my lips. "Why would they—"

"Hie! Captain Tursel!" A soldier raced frantically along the trail, frantically waving his helmet.

"Now what?"

"Lord Treak's men assault our rear guard!"

A mutual attack? Fear stabbed so hard I reeled. "Tursel!"

He'd already wheeled off, discharging a stream of orders.

"Rustin!" It was a plea. "Help me think!"

His voice was calm. "Steady, my prince." His unwavering eyes met mine, until I managed a weak smile.

Tursel galloped back from his foray. "I've pulled in our rear guard; we'll make a better stand past those trees, where the road narrows."

I asked, "How long have we?"

"Two hours, perhaps, if Treak organizes his men to strike in force."

"Is the crossroads ahead a full league from Verein?"

"That, but not much more."

"Just outside dear Uncle Mar's safe-conduct, Rust. He's come to bottle us on this cursed trail. Tursel, send every man you can spare to the crossroads!"

"Sire, it's madness to split the column when—"

I reared in my saddle. "Gather your men. Attack before the enemy takes hold. If they deny us the crossroads we're trapped!"

Tursel said, "Better to ready an assault in strength than attack piecemeal and be destroyed. I'll need an hour, no more."

"*Now*, by the imps and demons!" I drew my sword. "Rustin, Anavar, we'll ride in the second rank. Stay close; we'll guard each other."

Elryc pawed at my arm. "Why attack Uncle Mar instead of Treak?"

I blinked, not sure how I knew my course. "Because . . . Mar's men were setting flags on *our* side of the crossroads, but they're not fully across; half their strength is hurrying to catch up. And men of Tantroth won't hesitate to slaughter us, royalty or no. In men of Caledon, there'll be some iota of doubt." I hoped fervently it was true.

"Mar's men are sworn to Verein."

"And to Caledon. Tursel, sound the horns. Mounted lancers at the lead; let foot soldiers race to follow."

"But, sire—"

"Every moment's a waste!" I raised my sword. *"Now, for Caledon!"*

"Take a moment for armor!" Rust jabbed at the wagon. "A careless spear thrust—"

Tursel said, "We can't abandon the wagons. If Treak overruns them . . ."

"Then so be it. I ride. Who goes at my side?"

"I do!" Anavar spurred to my flank.

"Stay, Roddy, a few moments won't matter."

"Now! I command it!" Without waiting for answer, I cantered Ebon to the arms wagon, snatched a javelin. "Tursel, sound the horns!"

With a curse, Tursel clattered down the trail, to the men making haste to evade Lord Treak. In a moment, trumpets blared.

Foolhardy I might be, but not suicidal. I led Fostrow, Anavar, Rust, and a squad of guardsmen through a maze of wagons and provender to the fore of our column, but not so quickly that we'd be alone when we reached the crossroads.

In a few moments, we were twenty. Then, fifty. Our wagons were but half a league from the village; Uncle Mar's forces couldn't be far beyond the next hill.

At the rise, one of our outriders flagged us down. "Stay, my lords. The enemy lies ahead."

"How many?" I made no effort to slow.

"A hundred fifty, perhaps more. They're cutting trees for barriers."

"Roddy, fall back. Don't ride the lead."

Ignoring Rust's caution, I searched for words to inspire my troop. Giving Ebon his head, I turned in the saddle. "We're few against many, but we have a cause, and our army panting after." Laughs. I grinned. "Verein's not expecting attack. When we clear the rise I'll charge at their weakest point. We have but to scatter them, and cause havoc until our troops gain the field."

"Hail, Prince!" Anavar, doing his best to help.

I spurred Ebon toward the rise. "Look to me." My voice gained strength. "If you'd see the first to join battle, look to me. If you ask why risk death for my crown, look to me!" We bounced along in a brisk canter. "If you'd know who'll ride through the knaves of Verein, *look to me!*"

I risked a glance at Rustin. His gaze bathed me.

I spurred Ebon to a welcome gallop, bellowed over my shoulder, "If you'd be led to victory, *look to me!*"

We thundered over the rise.

Ahead, the road widened as it crossed a flat pasture. A single felled trunk barred the way. Beyond it, in the grassy meadow, other fallen trees. A cluster of archers, horsemen milling in front of all. Behind them, Verein's troops trudged up the path from the crossroads. Not far behind, their supply wagons lumbered.

We were barely in time.

"Scatter the archers! Drive the foot soldiers past the cross!"

Fostrow grunted, closing his helmet. "Stay near, Roddy."

"Follow, if you'd guard me." No time; already Verein's outriders gave alarm.

"If you'd see Verein flee in terror, look to me!" My voice rose to a shout. *"IF YOU SEEK A KING, LOOK TO ME!"*

I dug at Ebon's flanks. He raced across the pasture at full bent. Wind tore at my jerkin. I set my javelin as our battlemaster had taught.

"For Rodrigo!" Rust sounded confident, even joyous. "For Caledon!"

No more time for words.

Driving Santree all out, Rust managed to close to my side. We sailed over the fallen trunk. A soldier reared; my javelin tore through his chest. I wrenched it free.

Fostrow whipped his chestnut mare, two paces behind. "Wait, Roddy! Form a line!"

I tugged gently at the reins, and Ebon slowed enough to let Fostrow close. In a mad gallop, others of our band raced to augment our line.

Behind the fallen trees the archers took aim. We couldn't charge head-on; the trees were too strong a barrier. But Verein hadn't finished boxing their archers with pikemen. To our right the way was open.

I waved my javelin. "Flank them!" It meant a dash the width of the field, across the massed archers. Death, for some.

Margenthar's cavalry spurred to block us. Head down, braced in the saddle, I aimed at their foremost rider. I'd use the javelin as a lance.

The foeman passed to my right, brandishing his sword. A thunk, and the javelin tore from my grasp. Cursing, I pulled loose my short sword. Behind, Rustin slashed at a helmeted trooper.

Anavar galloped to reach us. He hacked at men who barred his path. *"Ride for Caledon!"* My voice was lost in the melee.

A foeman swung at Rustin. Santree screamed and pitched forward. Rust flew headfirst over the saddle. Battle swept me onward. Anavar reined in, dismounted to stand over Rustin of the keep, legs planted wide, sword drawn.

I lay low. Ebon pounded across the turf. Nearing the archers, I whirled my sword, ducked a spear. I sliced at a passing horseman's wrist. A scream.

Two cavalrymen barred my way, bearing shields and swords. I had only the short sword. If I rode between them I could fend off but one. Scarce thinking, I rose high in the saddle, reared back my sword.

As we neared, I shrieked at the first rider. But, twisting in my stirrups, I let the sword fly instead at his companion's throat. Soldier and horse tumbled in a gout of blood. I galvanized Ebon into a mighty leap over the fallen horse and rider. We thundered on, leaving the surviving horseman in distant dust.

Verein's archers were paces distant, bows drawn, firing.

Maddened, I charged unarmed. Soldiers clawed their way clear as I raced closer. As Ebon plunged into the mass of foemen I tore a bow from an archer's hand. I hauled at the reins, whirling Ebon. We raised to strike. His hooves whistled down. From my perch I wielded the bow, slashing at faces and arms, screaming all the while.

One archer, braver than the rest, notched an arrow, raised his bow. Our eyes met. Suddenly his face contorted. He wheeled to flee, was caught in the back by a flung spear. Anavar and two of Tursel's troop burst into the throng, bloody swords thrusting.

Verein's horsemen spotted us, gathering to charge. But with each moment, more of our men reached the field. Meanwhile our few cavalry hacked at the enemy archers. Abruptly their line sagged. I rose in my saddle, gathering our troops with a wave and a cry.

Suddenly foemen sprinted toward the safety of the crossroads, casting aside their weapons. We gave jubilant chase, cleaving skulls, stabbing at leather shirts with savage abandon.

In moments our way to the cross was clear. I reined in. With a whoop, young Anavar spurred past to pursue the foe. I grabbed his tunic, and was nearly yanked from my saddle. "Hold, boy!"

His face was flushed. "After them, lest they rally!"

I shook his jerkin. "Where's Rustin?"

"On the field, sir. Guarded by four of Tursel's foot soldiers."

I glanced about. The battlefield was ours. I turned Ebon, spurred back the way we'd ridden across the archers' withering fire. More men than I cared to count lay unmoving. A few survivors paced the field, a somber group.

I pushed past his fallen mount. "Rust?"

Sitting, he looked up, his face pale. His breast was covered with blood. He clutched a crimson knife.

"Lord of Nature!" I hurled myself from my saddle, raced to drop at his side. "Sit still." I glanced about, my eyes wild. "You there, call a surgeon!" Gently, I swaddled his head in my arms.

Idly, he rested his hand on my boot. "The blood's not mine. Would that it were."

I pulled back an arm's length, gently touched his chest. "You're sure? I mean—" I took deep breath. "Whose, then?"

He gestured to the blood-drenched steed. "Santree." The horse lay unmoving, eyes vacant.

"His throat's been cut!" I looked about. "What villain did this?"

"I. To spare his agony."

My eyes strayed to the gaping wound in the stallion's side. "Oh, Rust."

"I've tended him . . . since I was seven." His bloody hand strayed to the foam-flecked muzzle, gave it a caress. "What will I do?"

"I don't know." The wind carried shouts, from the trail. I stood, looked about. The last of our wagons hurried down the road, past the tree-trunk barriers hastily pulled aside.

Ahead, Tursel's men had seized the crossroads. Mar's wagons had hastily turned, waiting for reinforcements from the Verein trail. I ought to help rally men, seize Uncle's supplies. But Rust sat staring at Santree. At length he said, "Help me stand."

Immediately half a dozen hands reached. He cast them aside, clutched at mine. I pulled him to his feet.

"Over there, by those trees." He pointed to a copse of elders.

I wrapped Ebon's reins round my arm. Obediently, I followed Rust to the seclusion of the grove. "Tursel can't hold the crossroads long. Mar's troops are coming."

"I know."

"What do you want, Rust?"

He stared at me a long moment. Slowly, he let his head fall to my shoulder, and began to weep.

Astounded, I stood dumb like a log. After a moment I patted his back. "It's all right, Rust. All will be well." I made soothing noises, as had Nurse Hester when I'd scraped a knee, eons past.

"I couldn't . . ." Rustin struggled for calm. "Not with the guards watching."

"Of course. Don't worry. I understand." With an effort, I quelled my babble.

After a while, when my jerkin was damp, Rust looked up shame-faced.

I essayed a light smile. "We'll get you another horse."

He blinked. His eyes sought mine as if perplexed.

"I mean, you can have any—the best we—" This was *Santree*.

Belatedly, I pictured Ebon lying in his own blood. My eyes stung with the horror of it. "I'm so sorry!" Again I'd acted the fool, when he'd turned to me—to Roddy the oaf—for comfort. Impulsively I wrapped myself round him in a fierce hug. "Rust, forgive me. Please!" I squeezed harder, biting back tears. "I know you'll miss him, really I do!"

And Rust was crying again, and we wept together, and for a bittersweet moment I worried not about being seen in his arms.

But even if we'd been of a mind to linger among the elders, Tursel wouldn't hear of it. He galloped at us as we mounted Ebon, Rust clinging from behind. "My lords, have your senses fled? Our rear guard's just topping the hill. Get yourself past the crossroads; we're still in peril!"

I nodded assent, and spurred Ebon gently. Rust clung to my waist. As we joined the column struggling uphill past the crossroads he asked, "So it's back to Cumber, another route?"

"No." My voice hardened. "To Groenfil." Imps take my fears about the Power; Still or no, I would be King.

"He's your uncle's man. He'll confirm your designs to the Duke."

I gestured at the dead and wounded of Verein. "Let Mar know what we seek. If our meet with Groenfil sows dissension among them, all the better. As to Mar, demons cast him in the lake."

It silenced him, as well it might. I thought of dour, sallow Groenfil, and the plan of which I dared not speak.

Under a blazing sun my brother sat horseback, outside the bare walls of Groenfil. No tree higher than a sapling could be seen. Outside the stronghold itself the buildings were all squat affairs, with heavy roofs.

Elryc waited patiently at my side. Others of our guard were near, but I'd insisted on leading the column.

The gates to town and castle were barred. After days of trodding dusty cowpaths and fording rivulets, I was bone-tired.

"Will he open?"

"I know not," I said again.

"If he does, it will be soon." At my raised eyebrow, Elryc added, "Why infuriate us, if he's to let us in?"

"I'm in no mood to riddle Lord Groenfil."

"Try. It's the craft of state."

I bit back a mean reply; my brother was right. If only I were King, safe in the comfort of Stryx. "Fetch Tursel."

In a moment the captain stood before me, wiping sweat from his helmet. "Yes, my lord?"

"Send another envoy. Have him say—" I hesitated, and threw caution to the winds. "We won't enter the town, invited or no. But Groenfil will meet his liege prince under safe-conduct before sunset, or all Duke Mar's might won't save his remains from the crows picking his eyes."

"My lord?"

"Have it said." I gestured dismissal.

For a moment I regretted my rash words, but decided I'd done no harm. Groenfil was either a committed enemy, or not. If so, best it be shown. If not, we still had a chance. Still, I knew his consent to a meeting wouldn't signify surrender, but merely prudence, in a noble seeking shelter from storm.

In an hour, my boldness was rewarded. Earl Groenfil rode from his holding with impressive retinue, banners flying.

We met under my canopy.

His servants bore welcome refreshment. Groenfil, a dark man with a pinched face, poured two goblets of dark wine. He offered me choice of glass. He took the other and drained it before I touched a drop, demonstrating his good faith.

I chose fruit and berries, and handed him a plate. We ate together. After amenities, we excused our servants and followers. Even Elryc I sent away, with a promise that I'd tell him all.

Rustin, ever vigilant, sat in the corner. His eyes never left Groenfil.

"So, Rodrigo. Why summon me with harsh speech? I was arranging suitable welcome for—"

"The demons' lake with such foolery!" I rode over his shock. "I've no soft words for you. Mar tried to kill us and failed. Are you his man?"

"Rodrigo—"

"Are you his?" My voice was ice.

"Margenthar wed Renna, my sister."

I waved it aside. It counted, but not for all.

"Times are troubled, Rodrigo. One seeks allies."

"Strange that you spurn *me*."

Groenfil took a cluster of grapes, set it aside, chose a larger. He said carefully, "I spurned you neither by word nor deed. Am I sheltered snug in my keep, my gates barred to you?"

"No." I forced myself to choose a fruit I was too agitated to swallow. "You know why I've come, my lord."

At least he didn't dissemble. "To seek my pledge, to make yourself King." A grim smile. "Almost, I believe you merit a throne. Yesterday I'd not have said as much." He was silent awhile. Then, "If you'd be our King, prove you know my cost."

"You'd lose alliance with Mar."

He nodded.

"And risk defeat with my House."

"True."

"What else?"

"Why, Roddy." His smile was mocking. "You were doing so well."

"Is this a game?"

"Isn't life itself?"

I bowed, acknowledging his thrust. "Very well. You'd lose . . . what? The power to bargain?"

He looked about, saw a bench. "By your leave?" His tone was courteous, but no more than as any guest to his host. "What could I possibly want to bargain?"

I hated riddling, and his manner raised my hackles. Still, much was at stake. I said, "Gold? Power?"

"Naught else?"

I turned my head so he could not see my flood of relief. "Land."

His smile returned. "Well, then. Offer me what Mar cannot."

"You have no thought for the realm?" I asked bitterly. "Or my rights as Elena's heir?"

"None," he said.

Good; it would make my task easier. I made my tone ingenuous. "Why, my lord Groenfil, what cannot Mar obtain for you?"

Our eyes met. "Soushire."

I turned away, waited until the tension was palpable. "Very well," I said.

Rustin shot to his feet. "My prince, speak with me alone."

"Not now, Rust."

"Roddy, I beg you!"

We strode through camp, while Tursel's guards followed. Earl Groenfil had retired to his keep; our meet would resume shortly.

"How could you show such daring and sense on the field, yet sell your soul to this—this greedy lordling? Can the Rodrigo who led us to the crossroads and this unscrupulous Roddy be one?"

Inwardly, I smiled. "Calm yourself, before you—"

"Can't you see how you debase yourself? What of the True? You risk your Powers!" Rust stumbled over a stone and, irked, kicked it so hard it clattered down the street. "I hate you!" Then he grimaced. "No, my Lord of Nature, that's not so. But I hate what you do!"

"All because I agreed with—"

"You allied yourself with Groenfil against Soushire, and Soushire against Groenfil! It's detestable. Contemptible. Despicable."

"Steady. You'll run out of epithets."

His eyes were dangerous. "You mock me?"

"You mock me all the time."

"Not in matters of . . . truth. Honor." His tone was anguished. "Roddy, how *could* you?"

"I've done nothing yet."

"You've all but agreed to help Groenfil wrest control of Soushire from the Lady."

I said gently, "Rust, come close. No, don't glare." I gripped his shoulders, waited until he calmed himself enough to hear. "Do you recall your fury when I bargained with Lady Soushire? I'd have explained, to ease your mind. You told me if I had not good cause, my folly would long haunt me, and you'd no need to chide me. Isn't it so?"

After a moment he nodded.

"Let it be, you said, for the peace between us. But, Rust, I'm in your charge. I'll explain, if you require it."

Briefly, his head rested against mine. "My prince, I want so to trust you." His words were barely audible.

I said carefully, "I think—really I do—that I've made no vow to break the True."

We ducked under the canopy. Earl Groenfil sat waiting. "So, my lord."

I waited. There was subtle advantage in his admitting the value of our treaty.

He seemed in no hurry. "Word's arrived of a skirmish near Verein." His tone was laconic.

"Men were lost, who were better spent fighting Tantroth of Eiber." He shrugged. "I'm sure my brother-in-law wanted only to parley."

"By blocking the—" *No.* I wouldn't be baited. "Perhaps another day it won't be my escort camped before your gates, but his."

"Yes." Abruptly he was serious. "That's why I won't cross him."

"Oh?" A pang stabbed at my ribs.

"I must have the autonomy of my lands, yet Caledon needs a strong monarch to repel Eiber." He paused. "But, you see, that man might be Mar."

"So, then?"

"I'll support the winner between you."

"Bah. Think you either he or I will let you straddle a pike fence while winter settles on the land?"

"Probably not." Groenfil's smile was cool. "I need only determine the likely victor."

Rust said harshly. "He stands before you."

"Naturally you'd say so, son of Llewelyn." Groenfil's tone was mild. "You're his vassal."

"I am not." Rust stood proud. "They said you were canny, my earl. I thought you'd see the obvious."

"Which is?" A cool wind stirred the flaps of the canopy.

"That Rodrigo's already won."

"Ahh, pardon." Groenfil leaned back, clasping his hands behind his neck. "I should have known a handful of men in ragged tents, who've no treasury, no lands to call their own, are the victors. Though they wander from castle to fief begging victuals . . . yes, it grows clearer."

Rust drew breath with a hiss, and for a moment his back arched like a cat. "Seek you the gilt paint, or the worthy metal beneath? Look what my prince has done!"

"You said you weren't his vassal."

"Yet Rodrigo is my prince." He crossed the tent, to set proud hand on my shoulder. I sat unflinching.

"What miracles has he wrought?"

"He escaped from Margenthar's restraint, and though penniless and nearly alone, secured the support of Cumber, among others."

I almost snorted. Elryc and Fostrow had abandoned me at Hester's cottage. Even Rust left without a glance behind. Now he made me sound the hero.

"Yes, I'm sure Raeth's candles sputtered in the night." Groenfil's tone was sardonic.

"While you cowered behind closed gates, Prince Rodrigo bearded Vessa in Tantroth's city."

Outside, the breeze grew stronger. Groenfil merely smiled. "To no avail."

"In yesterday's skirmish, he quelled Duke Mar's forces, while holding Lord Treak of Eiber at bay."

Groenfil raised an eyebrow. "Is your friend always so vehement, Rodrigo? He could alienate those he seeks to persuade."

"He doesn't like your toying with me," I said.

Groenfil regarded us both. After a time, he sighed. "When you came, I was of a mind to send you in chains to my sister's husband. He'd enjoy the gift."

"No doubt."

"Your summons brought me out. Oh, not from fear, I assure you. But a lad capable of such a challenge deserved scrutiny."

"And so?"

Groenfil paused. "I won't commit to you, though my mind could be changed. As you know, I have . . . requirements. First, Soushire's lands, to end our feud once and for all."

"And?"

"Mar's favor has value to me. Else I wouldn't have given him my sister Renna. I won't betray her. Should you prevail, Mar isn't to be killed or dispossessed."

"Ask for the Norlands, as well!" I gestured my disgust.

"We both know you've persuaded Cumber, and Soushire. Lord of Nature knows how much gold that took. Willem will follow the tide.

Perhaps you've his promise as well." He smiled. "But who else? Mar? The Warthen?"

"No," I said bitterly, "I need you to be crowned, you know it, and you mean to take full advantage."

Rust looked shocked, and gave a minute shake of his head.

I said, "Ease thyself, Lord Rustin. We but speak what is known to us both." Perhaps it was my high speech that soothed him. He quieted.

I turned to the Earl. "With the Warthen's realm closed to me and Vessa dead, I need your vote, but there are demands I won't countenance. Goad me not too far."

"I understand. And Vessa's not dead, by the way. Merely unseated and captive."

"What? Mar said—" I struggled to recall. Mar hadn't claimed outright that Vessa was killed, merely that his office was vacant. How clumsy of Groenfil to tell me.

Perhaps demons helped him and read my mind. "I told you what Mar would not, to demonstrate good faith. Because I ask more of you." He leaned forward. "Bring me proof you're fit to be King."

I gaped. "Do you jest?"

His hand slapped the table, overturning the bowl of fruit. "Roddy, you were a vile brat when we visited your mother. Yet you've changed. Mark me, if you gain your crown I'll pay no more taxes than before, and damn your soldiers who come to collect them. Still . . ." He stood to pace. "A king too strong is a tyrant, and one too weak leads to—" He swept his arms. "Chaos. A throne in contention, and enemies coursing the realm."

I swallowed, and forced myself to face him.

"Almost you persuade me, Rodrigo. But I would be sure. Mar has guile, but in perilous times that's not enough. Perhaps you could free Caledon."

"Join me." Hope swelled.

"I await a sign. Make one."

"Out of my tent!" I kicked aside a stool. "You play games of quest while a kingdom crumbles? May demons seize you!"

Groenfil paused at the flap. "Don't forget Soushire's lands. I must have those." And he was gone, into a whistling wind.

I raged the tent, throwing aside all that was in my way. Rustin disappeared, but in a moment he was back with a cool flask of water. "My prince, quench your fires."

"Bah. That son of a horned toad, that demon spawn, that—"

"Yes, Roddy. Drink."

Almost, I flung it in his face, but he had a look that made me not dare. Grumbling, I took a gulp. It *was* welcome. I drained the flask. "Are you satisfied?"

"Almost. Sit, and speak of what you gained today."

"His undying enmity." I threw myself on a couch. "Look how the tent flaps crack in the wind." It was the first I'd seen of the Power of Groenfil, and made me uneasy.

"He's also seen you won't abase yourself for a crown. That's of value."

"He'll follow Mar, if my uncle offers more."

"Yet he has concern for the realm. That surprises me."

"With Tantroth roaming the hills, Groenfil's no safer than any of us. 'I want a sign.' Have you ever heard such nonsense?" I brooded. "I survived, and am here. What more does he want?" I brushed away Rustin's caress. "Not now; I'm more of a mind to bite than be fondled."

I poured icy water in a bowl, washed my hands. "It's lunacy to seek Groenfil's help. Whatever I offer, he'll ask double." I dried my fingers on a wiping cloth, staring moodily at the basin.

"What were the limits of which you spoke? The demands you wouldn't countenance?"

"Eh? The honor of Caledon. Anything that would destroy my monarchy before it began. We went through that with Uncle Raeth." I rubbed my frozen fingers.

"Yet you pledged Groenfil's fief to the garlic-eating Lady."

"I had . . . no choice." Though I had a plan, that might yet come to fruition. Absently, I opened my hands over the bowl. The water was chill, yet it seemed to bring warmth.

"So. What sign will you bring my lord Earl?"

"He's heard too many cradle tales." For a long moment I was lost in revery. "Devils take him. Better I should . . ." Abruptly I withdrew my hands, stared at my palms.

After a moment Rusk asked, "Yes, my prince?"

I strode to the flap. "You, guard! Find your captain and bring him!

Make haste! Rust, pack your gear; we're leaving." Feverishly, I paced under the canopy.

"Roddy, what is your thought? You seem deranged."

"I won't speak of it. Not in sight of Groenfil's walls." I paced in growing agitation. Had we fodder? Enough food? Under the circumstances I couldn't ask Groenfil for provisions. "Ah, Tursel, there you are. We break camp within the hour."

"My lord? What's passed, that—"

"Within the hour, did you hear? Don't gawk, get thee hence. Haven't we tents to strike, men to rouse? Go!"

"Where do we head?"

"The way we came!"

Chapter 35

I REINED EBON AT TURSEL'S SIDE, NEAR THE HEAD OF THE column.

The captain's tone was reproving. "You're safer in the center of our force, my lord." I was silent. "Sire, when will we learn the purpose of this mad dash?"

"Tonight, in my tent. How far can we ride by dark? Can we reach Seasand Road?"

"No, only another league at best."

That night we stumbled about setting up camp, our men grumbling and dog-tired. At last we met in my tent: Elryc, Rustin, Tursel. I bade Genard and Anavar pace outside, lest anyone overhear. "Abide not so much as a crow," I told them. "Who knows what Powers be set upon us?"

Within, we gathered around the hour candle. First, I swore them to silence, by blood oaths that frightened even me. Then I said, "Margenthar let me think old Vessa, Speaker of the City, was dead. Lord Groenfil said nay, that Tantroth holds him captive. Can anyone think why he might lie of it?"

Elryc hesitated. "To fret you, for fear of what Vessa might say to Tantroth."

"That I sought his vote? All Caledon has heard by now."

"If it's a lie," Rustin said, "it serves no apparent purpose. But if truth, why would he tell us? How does he gain?"

I said, "He called it a morsel to show his good faith."

Tursel snorted. "What faith? He's allied to Mar by blood and interest."

"But he wants Soushire, and Uncle Mar won't agree."

"Why not, Roddy?" Elryc perched on my bed, wide-eyed.

"Combined, Soushire and Groenfil would outweigh Verein. Mar won't risk such a power in Caledon unless he wields the throne. Perhaps not then."

"But you will?" Rustin.

"I'll do what I must," I said carefully. "But Groenfil's demand confirms that he's venal. I'd not gain my throne by his hand." It risked the Still.

"Whose, then?"

I went to the flap, peered out. Anavar stalked past the flap, knife drawn. "No one, sir," he said. As he disappeared around the side, Genard appeared, going the opposite way.

I turned, faced my three confederates. "Vessa."

Tursel frowned. "Tantroth holds him."

"In Llewelyn's keep, I'll warrant. It's the strongest place outside the castle."

"You mean to sneak in, and take his proxy?"

I paced, my blood rising. "A small force. Forty men, say. No wagons, the freshest horses. We sweep down on Stryx, assail the keep, and take Vessa."

Stunned silence, from all.

"We've surprise, we know the terrain, we have just cause. We even have Tantroth's black garb that we stripped from their dead."

Rustin shook his head. "Why did you race from Groenfil's walls?"

"Caledon reeks of intrigue. The faster we move, the less chance word from Groenfil will outfly us."

"What could Groenfil reveal?"

"That he told us Vessa lives. And, if he overheard us tonight, who could say he wouldn't sell my plan to Tantroth?"

Rustin said quietly, "What good is Vessa to us?"

"We'll have the votes to ratify my crown."

"How so?"

"Are you fuddled? There's Willem, Cumber, Soushire—"

"And who else?"

"Vessa, you dolt!"

"Vessa is unseated. What worth has his vote?"

I said angrily, "A quibble. Who would object, were I to convene Council, with him as member?"

Rust regarded me gravely. "Man might recognize your ascension. But would the True?"

My breath caught. Either way, I risked the True, and my Powers. But Vessa, rescued and in my hands, was a sure vote.

Tursel looked between us; we spoke of matters beyond his ken.

"Vessa's all I have! His vote *must* be valid! Groenfil wants a miracle I can't provide; what choice have I? We'll seize the Speaker, and I'll take my chance with the True."

"Roddy, think it through. Tarry here a day, while—"

"I forbid it!" To soften my words I added, "Now the thought's spoken, we must fly to Stryx. We left in such haste Tantroth may not yet know. With surprise, we have a slim chance. Without it, none."

Rust looked exasperated. "We know not where Vessa is kept. Without that—"

I flung open the tent. Genard squawked in terror, retreating.

"Anavar! Come!"

My ward raced from behind the tent. "What? Who attacks?"

"Inside!" I thrust him through the flap. "Tell them, boy. I've beaten you, oft treated you ill. Now I'd send you into Stryx, to learn where Tantroth keeps Vessa the Speaker. Will you go, and not betray me?"

Anavar's head came up. "You've but to ask, Prince Rodrigo."

"There." I turned to Rust. "Now Vessa's found."

"And if he's truly in the keep?"

"We'll pry him loose. How can we fail, with you to guide—what's the matter?"

"Why nothing." Rust's voice was hoarse.

"The keep's but a stronghold. You'd fight Eiber in the hills, would you not? In the streets of Stryx town? Then why trouble yourself—oh!" My sense returned at last.

"You understand?" His tone was low.

"Llewelyn your father. He may abide in the keep."

"Shall I kill him for your crown, Roddy?"

"No, I—"

"Or rather for his treason?"

Tursel stirred uncomfortably.

"Out, Anavar. You too, Captain."

None were left but Elryc, Rustin, and I.

"Let it not trouble you," said Rust. He rubbed his brow, as if weary. "It were best long since done."

Elryc said uncertainly. "Roddy?"

"I know. Leave us. Tell Tursel to choose his best men. We ride before dawn. Have us awakened."

When we were alone, I went to Rust's bench, lifted his chin. "You'll kill me before you lift hand to your father. Swear to it."

"He's destroyed my honor. And his own. Mother's . . ."

"Your oath." Stern in gesture and voice, I made him give it. When we were done I urged, "Come to bed. We've little enough time 'til morn."

"I'll walk, I think." He rose.

"Help me with my thongs." I took his hands, put them to my jerkin. Mechanically, he did as I asked.

"I'm all right, Roddy. Let me go." He took his cloak.

If one thing was certain this night, it was that Rust must not walk alone.

I knew but one way to stop him. I quelled my distaste; he had done too much to redeem me. Quickly I shucked my clothes, padded across the tent, stood blushing before him.

We rode proudly, three abreast, Anavar, Rustin, and I. Tursel and Fostrow rode just behind. The promise of day lurked over the hills, and I felt every nerve tingle. Rust had kept me from sleep almost until Tursel's call. I leaned across, tweaked him in the ribs. "This is our moment, Rust. I feel it."

His smile was wan. "I'm glad, my prince." Since last night, his sadness had never vanished. Even in the throes of . . . hastily, I turned my thoughts.

We were some two score horsemen, on the strongest and best rested of our mounts. We all wore swords, and many bore javelins as well. Not for the first time, I wished some clever horseman had solved the problem of carrying a long sword while mounted. A saddle sheath rubbed one's leg incessantly, and an ordinary hip sheath could chafe a

steed's side with every step. And little was more laughable than a
sword-armed man trying to mount.

We clattered down the trail. We were nowhere near the Verein
crossroads, where the route widened to a respectable road. By carefully pacing our horses we might just reach Stryx before dusk. I dared not
spend the night between the cross and the city, lest Uncle Mar block my
retreat. No, we'd have to sweep into Stryx from the south, ride the coast
road through the market, past the wine shops to the keep.

At noon we left the road to water the horses, and stretch our aching
legs. By now we were mostly silent, each with visions of the grim work
ahead. My mouth went dry every time I thought of Vessa's dwelling,
and the thongs that had bound my wrists.

Yet my own mood seemed lighthearted compared to some of our
men. As we remounted, I called them near. "Some of you ride for me,
others from loyalty to Captain Tursel. Regardless, to each of you, a
month's pay doubled, for riding this day."

That, more than any noble words I could speak, brought a cheer.
And I suspected fantasies of gold would sustain them through the long
day's ride. These men had little enough to cheer them; far from home,
dependent on a rebel prince's meager purse. Were Uncle Mar to capture
them, or Tantroth or Eiber, they faced a bad end.

Afterward, I occupied my afternoon wondering how to pay them.
I'd sell my diadem, if I must, and judge cheap the cost.

As we neared, Tursel sent scouts to probe the crossroads, and as I'd
predicted it was unmanned. Its only value to Uncle Mar was when it
barred my way, with Treak the other jaw of the trap.

The cross safe behind us, we hurried on. Seasand Road crept out of
the hills toward the rocky shore, a longish canter south of Stryx.

At third hour, or thereabouts, I embraced Anavar, bid him race
ahead and prowl the city to learn what he could. "Take care," I said yet
again. "If the guards we fought recognize you—"

"I know." He put a hand on the pommel, to mount. "But there are
many young aides in Tantroth's troop. Some say we're all alike."

"I'd go myself, except I couldn't manage your barbarian accent."

"You mean our civilized manners." A quick smile. "Forgive me.
Father says offering a jest to one's elders is like proffering garlic stew to
a duchess. Even if she's hungry she won't thank you for it after."

"Anavar, our lives are in your hands."

"You honor me. And later, perhaps . . ." He spurred his mount. "You'll see your way to raise my stipend." And he was off before I could object.

I grumbled to Rust, "Is this what it's like to have a child?"

For a moment his eyes danced. "Oh, no. Much worse."

The closer to Stryx, the more chance we'd blunder across an Eiberian patrol. We no longer rode alone; we trotted past peasant carts and mule-driving merchants. If some gaped at our passing, we gave no notice. We wore our black cloaks now, to look as like men of Eiber as we could. We'd cantered past a guard post with an exchange of waves.

The afternoon was late, but still short of evening, when we trotted off the coast road to the ruins of a wharf and a warehouse that high seas had destroyed. Waiting among the broken walls was Anavar, just where I'd bidden.

"Hail, Prince." He stood straight in his saddle. His cheek bore a bruise, between eye and ear. "Vessa lives." He giggled. "We were at a tavern. I bought drinks, and had to join in downing them."

"Anavar!"

"Else I'd raise suspicion." He made himself serious. "What was I saying? Vessa faces execution, but no one knows when. Our lord Tantroth hasn't decided. Probably at a festival."

"Where is Vessa?"

He belched. "Who knows? Father says when you can't find your road, follow hill or dale until—"

Rustin gripped my knee before I could erupt. He slipped from the saddle, clapped his arm amiably around Anavar's shoulder, led him along the path behind a wall.

I fumed. See what came of setting a boy to a man's work? Strong liquor was a menace. Once, when we'd slipped out of the castle, Rust had to hold me while I heaved my innards into the sea. I was no younger than Anavar, not much younger than I was now—imps and demons! Was I boy or man?

Soon, though it seemed long, they reappeared. Rustin shrugged quizzically. "Anavar doesn't know because the soldiers weren't sure. He thinks the Speaker's in the keep. He's been at the keep, our Anavar has." His tone was brittle.

"And?"

"Full of Tantroth's men, but no special guard. The town is theirs, you'll recall."

"Rust, you'll wait here."

"And the gates at Castle Way are open. Though it takes no more than a moment to swing them shut. As they will if a band of horsemen charges down the coast road."

"You'll stay behind with Anavar and three others in case—"

"And miss my Rodrigo leading us in battle? No."

"Rustin, I won't have you contend with Llewelyn!"

"Why, my lord Prince!" His eyes were bright, almost feverish. "We're already adversaries. I'm loyal to Caledon, and he is not."

That decided me. "You'll remain."

"No." He drew himself up. "I'm not subject to your dominion."

I was desperate. "Fostrow, Tursel! Seize him. Bind his hands if you must!"

Rust's sword glinted in the late day's sun. "Who seizes me dies!" Behind him, Anavar gaped.

"Hold! Fostrow, back." I swung down from my saddle. Sword still in scabbard, I came close. "Strike me, if you will."

"You know I can't."

"Of course."

"Yet I'll break your arm if you move to disarm me."

"Come." I led him, protesting, away from the uneasy troop.

A few paces away, where foam crashed into the mossy remains of a jetty, I let go his arm. "Rustin . . ."

"I'll fight for you, Roddy." His tone had a manic gaiety. "Honor demands no less. Don't ask."

"Rust, I'm not man yet." My voice caught. "I need you. I need you sane."

He thrust me away, mouth set. I stared full into his face.

At length he approached, slipped sword in sheath. "Roddy?" Briefly, his fingers brushed my damp curls. Then, for the second time in our lives, his head stooped to my shoulder, and he wept.

Seven went ahead, Fostrow among them. Concealing their swords in packs and cloaks, they trudged wearily toward Llewelyn's keep, as if returning from patrol. One youth hid a bow, and a pitch-dipped arrow.

The dust of forty horsemen would raise alarm, especially if no patrol of that number had been sent our way. It was our forerunners' task to hold open the gates to the keep. A flaming arrow into the dusk was to be our signal.

We waited in the ruins with growing unease. Rust would ride with us; I could not prevent it. But he'd sworn on his very soul to turn away from Llewelyn, should they meet. As for Anavar, I bade him return to our force in the hills, to avoid war with his own.

"Sir, I'll raise my sword only to protect you, as we enjoined. Let me do that much."

"No, I won't have you consumed with guilt. And besides, you're drunk."

He flushed. "It passes."

"I won't—"

He shouted, "Let me choose my fate!"

My mouth opened, and shut. "Done," I grated. "But hope I'm taken, else in camp I'll take leather to you for insolence."

"Sir, I—"

"Be silent, youngsire."

Tursel's fingers nervously traced the hilt of his sword. "I don't know the town as well as you. How soon 'til our men are in place?"

"A few moments. When the arrow flies, ride as if demons pursue us."

"Aye. Our men can't hold the gate long."

I tried to quell my unease. What if Tantroth strengthened the evening guard? What if Mar divined my plan, sent word ahead to trap me? The worst fate I could imagine was to fall in my uncle's hands.

What if the arrow wouldn't light?

"Remember, men." Perhaps Tursel spoke also to me. "We seek only Vessa. No time for looting, or hunting those who'd run. No doubt the old man's in a saferoom."

"On the first floor, I'd wager," Rust added. "Behind the family quarters, west of the kitchen . . ."

Anavar tapped my shoulder. "I'm sorry, Lord Prince."

"You'll still be beaten."

"If . . . I fall, I wanted you to know."

I looked away, ashamed.

"Look!"

A fiery trail gleamed bright in the dusk.

"Together, for Caledon!" I lashed Ebon's flank.

We charged down the cobbled road, scattering townswomen with baskets, tradesmen closing their shops. Rustin drew sword, kept pace at my left.

The coast road wasn't all that wide. As we passed, a few folk pressed themselves into doorways, or jumped into reeking ditches to avoid our hooves. I glanced rightward. Behind the narrow streets of Stryx loomed our castle. Ahead, the massive keep. To the left, the sea crashed against the break.

We burst past Fullers' Inn, where Rust and I had oft taken drink. Then, along the shore, a familiar stone hut. "Look, Rust! Need another sword?" Months or days ago, when I was a foolish youth, Rust and I had visited the swordsmith. His burly young prentice gaped as we raced past.

The squared walls of the keep loomed. Over the thunder of hooves I caught shouts, cries of pain. I whirled my blade, "For Caledon!"

"For Rodrigo!"

A dozen guards struggled to swing shut the sturdy gates. Three barred their way. I dug my heels into Ebon. Behind me, riders leveled their spears. The cobbles flashed past.

A shield rose to obstruct me, a sword poised behind. I slashed down with all my might. The shield dropped, an arm with it. I closed my ears to an agonized scream.

Ebon snorted, rearing to strike.

Our column thundered past the gates. "To the villa!" Rustin's call penetrated the clamor.

Behind me, at the gate, Fostrow hacked at a desperate defender, sweat dripping from his brow. Blood drenched his jerkin. "Did you walk to join us, my lord? A pleasant stroll?"

I hauled on the reins. Ebon roared, crashed into the Eiberian's ribs. The man dropped without a sound.

"Are you hurt?"

"No," Fostrow panted. "But we've four dead."

"More, by now." I peered into the setting sun's haze. "Where's Rustin?"

"Stay with him, or with me!"

Shouts from above. A squad of Eiberians raced along the lower rampart. I cursed. As they hurtled down the stairs I cantered alongside, sword raised high. I caught one man in the chest, another in the leg. I slammed my sword hilt into a frantic face, watched the soldier topple. Then the rest of the squad was upon us. Fostrow and I fell back to the courtyard where our men formed a shield around the entry to the villa.

"Where's Rust?"

"Inside!"

I slipped off Ebon and raced to the door where once we'd greeted Lady Joenne. Within was carnage. Bowls of stew lay overturned on a table drenched with blood. A guard lay wailing, cradling his innards. Bodies lay about. Some still twitched.

I glanced outside. Our men braced as troops in black fell upon them from both sides.

In the next room, shouting.

A slim form hurtled past; Anavar planted himself in front of me, sword drawn. I thrust him aside, plunged into the chamber. Rustin was nowhere to be seen. Men of Eiber retreated through a far door. I glanced about. Where was the kitchen passage?

The last Eiberians retreated to the far doorway. A bearded face I thought I recognized. Eyes that met mine, turned away quickly. Was it Llewelyn?

From a hall, Rustin appeared. "This way! Move!"

I tore after him, Anavar at my heels.

In near dark I tripped, went sprawling. "Ow!" Something sharp jabbed my side.

As one, Rust and Anavar hauled me to my feet. I stepped across the body I'd stumbled over, peered into the room.

An Eiberian guard slumped on a stool, a knife in his chest. He stared dully as blood trickled. Behind him, a henchman lay unmoving. Vessa cowered against the far wall.

I stood straighter. "Come with us, Speaker."

"I couldn't support you—Tantroth had the city. I had no escape— please don't kill me!"

"Come quickly, if you want to live."

The old man tottered to his feet.

Hand pressed to my side, I ran through the passage, leaping over the Eiberian corpse. "Tursel, we have him! Sound the call!" Behind me, Rust and Anavar guided the Speaker. I raced to the front of the villa, plunged into the dusk. "Tursel!"

"He's rallying the guard." Fostrow limped slowly to the entry, breathing hard. His leg was bloody.

"Ebon!" I whistled shrilly. As I knew he would, he cantered to me. I swung into the saddle, wheeled to the courtyard.

Tursel loomed in the deepening dusk. "Everyone out! We'll charge the far gate, where they least expect it!" The north gate, from which Rust and I had escaped to the hills when Tantroth besieged the keep. Now, Eiber's ships lined the shore. We'd have to ride gauntlet. No matter.

We milled about the courtyard as arrows streaked from above, fired by Tantroth's folk on the ramparts. I shouted, "Caledon, ride!"

Fewer than twenty, we surged toward the north gate. "Rust! Anavar!" I searched our ranks. Both were among us. Old Vessa gripped a stallion's mane.

Anavar's sword was red, and his eyes wild. I snapped, "Stay with Fostrow, he'll guard you."

"I'm man enough—where is he?"

I stood in the stirrups. Ahead, our men clashed with the gatesmen. "Fostrow!" Cursing, I swung Ebon, cantered back toward the villa.

He sat on the entry stairs.

"Where's your horse? Move yourself!"

Around him, blood pooled. "I can't, Roddy." He had his helmet off. "Demons take me, it hurts." His face was pasty.

"No!" My cry echoed in the dusk. I slid from the saddle. "Where?"

"My leg. The tubes are cut."

"Bind it!"

"It's past that. Go."

"Not while you live." I wheeled. "RUST!"

"No!" He clutched me. "Damn you, lad, run!"

"Not without you." I sank to his side.

With a weary groan, Fostrow leaned his grizzled head against mine. "Don't you understand? That's what we're *for*."

"Roddy!" Rust galloped across the courtyard. "Out! *Right now!*"

"I'm . . . tired." With an effort, the old guardsman focused on my face. "That's what we do, we soldiers. We give lives for our lords. Doesn't seem fair, sometimes."

I could have wept, and hated that which stopped me. "I'll bind you. We'll find a horse."

"Need to lie down." It was a mumble. Fostrow let himself sink to the planks; I barely stopped his head from bumping. "Listen to . . . your mother, boy. She's a . . . good queen. Even Mar says so."

"Yes, Fostrow."

"Now, Roddy!" Forceful hands hauled me away.

I shook free. "Don't die! I'll take you—"

A clatter of hooves, as black horsemen swept across the courtyard.

"It's wars kill us, son."

My hand swept Fostrow's sweaty brow.

"Fight only . . ."

"What?"

Fostrow blinked, seemed to concentrate. ". . . *just* wars."

"NOW!" Rustin tore me from the huddled form, whose chest still rose and fell. He grasped my boot, raised it to the stirrup. "Move or die!"

Numbly, I swung into the saddle. Rust tore loose his empty scabbard and gave Ebon a mighty thwack. "Go!" Ebon shot toward the gate. I clung to the pommel. Rust galloped behind.

We raced through the gate onto the north road. Behind us, the cries of war faded.

The beach was rocky. The black fleet of Eiber lay offshore, riding on the swells. We were within bowshot of the ships, but who would keep archers aboard boats moored for the season? We were safe from that quarter.

What I hadn't expected was the rows of tents in the field to our right. The Eiberian camps had been roused by the clamor of battle in the keep. A few quick-witted officers had devised a roadblock, but they'd barely dragged wagons and brush into place.

Tursel waved shoreward. We scrambled through sand and stones. A horse went down; the rider screamed; a mate stopped long enough to hoist him behind. We raced on, and plunged into the hills.

Ebon pounded methodically along the trail. I rode dazed in the saddle, side aching. When the tents had faded from sight I spotted a familiar trail. "Tursel, hold!"

He swung his head, saw no one pursuing. Reluctantly, he slowed. "What, Lord Prince?"

"Call a halt."

"They'll be on us ere long."

"But not yet." I pulled Ebon to a standstill.

"What now?"

I fought to think through a haze. "That path. I think it leads to Besiegers' Pond."

"So?"

"Above is the castle."

"What of it?"

"I'll go. Rust, come along if you wish."

"Roddy, we've no time for nonsense!"

"Oh, there's sense to it." My teeth chattered, as if from cold. "Tursel, take your troop and cut west at the fork. Lead our pursuers to the hills."

"But why—"

"I'll meet you at Shar's Cross."

"No. Lord Rustin, take the Prince's reins. You, Thiel, guard his left."

I rose in my saddle. *"By the True and my crown, touch me not!"*

"Roddy—"

"Tursel of Cumber, lead our troop to the hills. Move! Anavar, come along."

"Me, sir?" His voice was a squeak.

"Yes, I'll need another." I lashed Ebon, and he leaped from the pack. "All you men, go to the hills. Your King commands it." I cantered into the thick wood.

Muttered curses, and Rustin emerged from the branches. Behind him, the crackle of hooves on downed wood. Anavar shot out of the brush. He reined in at my side.

If I'd not known the trail as a boy, I could never have followed it on this moonless eve. As before, I had to dismount and lead Ebon through the worst thickets. A stitch in my side made my task no easier. Finally, we emerged at the still pond.

"Roddy, I'm no use unless you explain what we do."

I patted Rust's shoulder. "The trail leads to Castle Way, at the turn."

"Don't teach me geography!" He was at the end of his patience. "Where do we ride?"

"Why, to the castle gates." I counted on the likelihood Tantroth would post no guards so close to the walls.

It was dark when we reached the turn. Below gleamed the torches of the keep. It looked like an anthill disturbed; men ran hither and about. Horns blared. As we watched, a great body of men gathered, and rode off to the north.

I turned Ebon up the hill. Anavar said nervously, "What are we about, sir?"

"We go within." As we reached the last bend I pulled off my sword, dropped it alongside the road. "Do likewise, both of you. We're boys caught out in the night."

Rustin growled, "Roddy, enough of this folly."

I said sharply, "Be still! I command it!" He drew in breath, but lay down his sword.

At the top of the hill, the great doors were shut. Above, soldiers patrolled.

A few steps from the gate I handed the reins to Anavar, jumped off. My side stabbed. Perhaps I'd broken a rib in the night's melee. Carefully, I stooped, found a stone. I trudged to the gate, hammered without cease.

Someone leaned over the parapet. "Stop that racket, lad!"

I tried to speak like Genard. "We been caught outside, Lor'! Soldiers runnin' round. Lemme back in!"

"Who are you?"

"Master Griswold's boys." I stole a glance to Anavar, who was doing his best to seem loutish. For emphasis he scratched his rump.

"Sleep under the wall. Lord Margenthar commands the gates be locked from sunset."

Lord of Nature help us if Mar were here. Yet surely he had too much cunning to trap himself far from Verein.

"If we're not tending horses by dawn, old Griswold will thrash us. Please, the small door at least!"

With much grumbling, the small door was unbarred. "I hope he beats you bloody, you fools. Why are you outside the walls when—"

I snatched a torch from a post, held it as close to my face as the heat allowed. My voice rang from cobbles to keep. "I am Rodrigo, son of Elena, Prince and heir to Caledon. Summon our chamberlain Willem."

Murmurs of disbelief. Someone called, "Seize them!"

I slapped my leg; the sound echoed in the night. "Where is my chamberlain?" A hand loomed. Contemptuously, I struck it away. "Willem!"

For a moment all hung in the balance, then my royal manner prevailed. As I stepped forward, men gave way. "You, there, go to Willem's chambers! Rouse him!" A man ran off.

Another asked hesitantly, "Does the Duke know you've come?"

I snarled, "You question me?" I snapped my fingers. "Lord Rustin, take his rank." Rust came forward, his manner imperious.

"Bring us wine." If I drank, I'd spew it into the dust; my nerves were that tight. Still, I had to maintain appearances.

Torches gathered. Men crowded round to marvel. I stood stiff, wishing I didn't feel faint.

It was years before Willem appeared on the steps from the donjon, a furred robe thrown over his shoulders. "Who goes in the night?"

He seemed to have grown in stature since Mother's death. For a moment, I recalled the charade Uncle Mar and I played out before the nobles, the day she left me.

"It is I. Rodrigo, Prince." Even in the dark, I could have sworn I saw him pale. "Come." I held out my hand. For a moment I thought he'd let my arm dangle, but he walked slowly down the steps, took my hand, bowed. The bow of courtesy, from host to guest, no more. I saw, and he knew I saw.

"Roddy, how did you—does Margenthar know?"

From the castle guards, rising murmurs. "Stire can't be far, find him. Hold them until—"

I said quietly, that no others might hear, "I call you to your pledge."

"What pledge?"

"Your vote in Council."

His eyes darted. "You said—you'd need three."

"I have them. Vessa, Cumber, Soushire."

Silence.

Rustin watched me by the torchlight. There was something in his eyes akin to reverence.

Willem chewed his lip. "Roddy, I can't leave. Mar would . . ."

I said, "You cherished Elena. Am I not her heir?"

Willem looked ready to weep. "Now? Right this moment?"

"Or never. A horse awaits." I gestured to the gate.

A soldier growled, "Where in the demons' lake is Stire?"

"He's coming."

"Now." Ignoring the bite in my side I strode toward the gate, my pace steady. "Do you join us, Chamberlain?"

As if rehearsed, Anavar and Rustin fell in alongside. At the gate, I turned. Deep breaths, for strength; never mind the hurt. "Look on me, Caledon! I am Rodrigo." I flung off my hated black cloak, the remnant of my disguise. "I will return as your King. Know me now, and then. Fight Tantroth, our enemy. But oppose me at your peril."

On the ramparts above, running boots. I clapped my hands. *"Anavar, Lord Rustin, Willem. Come."* I strode into the night.

I tried not to hurry as I made my way to Ebon. Anavar held my bridle as I struggled to mount. I gritted, "Fetch our swords. You'll ride with Rust." Seated, I glanced back. Rust followed.

Chamberlain Willem was a step behind.

I reached across, gathered the reins of Anavar's mare, presented them to Willem. "Welcome."

His face was grave. "I do this for Elena, and because you cajoled my promise. Not for you, youngsire."

I felt giddy. "No matter. You'll come to love me." I spurred down Castle Way.

Chapter 36

WE PLUNGED INTO THE WOODLANDS THAT CONCEALED the pond and picked our way toward the seacoast road. I dozed in the saddle, my shirt drenched with sweat. I sought Fostrow's face. I knew I'd oft abused him. I would learn remorse, if I lived long enough.

We made better time on the road. But Rust grew ever more restless. "Roddy, we're bound to meet Tantroth's patrol returning."

"I know. Take to the fields." I veered eastward, regretting the ease of the road. I stank of death, sweat, and blood, some of it Fostrow's. Even my hands were sticky.

"Will they chase Tursel all the way to Shar?"

I drowsed, until I realized Anavar's question was to me. "Unlikely." Ebon plodded, following Rust's mount. I let him have his head, hanging on to the pommel. Willem rode behind with Anavar. Neither spoke.

The night oozed past in an agony of torpor, as we climbed east into the hills. We passed a few miserable peasant huts, then more. Finally, as the sky ahead began to blot out stars with the promise of day, I felt the world reel. I clutched Ebon's mane just in time not to fall. "Rust . . . let me rest."

"Another league, my prince."

I bit back a sob. "I cannot."

Instantly, Rust jumped to the ground. "Anavar, keep guard." His hand gripped my knee. "Steady."

"Help me off." He did. "Is there anything I can wear save this foul jerkin?"

"I've a blanket, no more. You can wrap that over your shoulders."

"I stink in this." I pawed at my shirt. Rustin helped me. It stuck to my side, and I cried out.

"Anavar." Rust's tone was a lash. "Knock them awake in that hut. Willem, hide the horses."

I tugged at my jerkin. Something trickled.

I patted my side, and my hand came away red. Rust hissed. "You're covered with—"

I giggled, recalling Rust and Santree at the crossroads. "The blood's not mine."

Rust's tone was grave. "Yes, my love, it is."

I pitched into his arms.

"Hold him."

I clawed at Anavar's wrists. "Mother, save me! It hurts!"

"Let me sew, Roddy, else you'll bleed to death."

"I'm all right. Just a broken rib. Ow, no!"

"Imps and demons!" He reared back, thrust his face into mine. "Stop it!"

I howled.

"Bite the sheath."

"Rust, stop! I've no wound."

"I see your bone."

"No one stabbed me."

"You fell on a sword, I think."

Desperate, I pulled free from Anavar's grip. "No more!"

Rust grasped my hair, lifted my head, slapped me hard. "Lie still! I won't tell you again."

I wrenched free my arms to cover my eyes, ashamed that Anavar and Willem see me cry. Obediently, I forced myself to lie still, until Rust was done with his torture. Then he wrapped me, cradled my head, brought more water to my lips. "Drink, my prince."

I couldn't help but whimper. "You hate me."

"More water, Anavar." He waited while the boy filled the dipper. "Drink."

"Yes, Rust." I peered through the gloom. "What's that smell?"

"The hut. Sleep now."

I blinked away cobwebs. "Where are we?"

"Near Shar's Cross."

"What am I lying on, rocks?"

"A churl's bed. Be civil."

"Why?"

"He's by the wall, forming his opinion of his King."

Time passed. I woke again, ravenously thirsty. "Can I sit?"

"We'll raise you. Don't strain."

In a moment I sat propped in Rust's protective arm, drinking greedily. Across the dank, low-roofed hut huddled a man in rags. His arm rested on a woman, who crouched below. At his side a grimy boy of nine or so watched our every move.

"Where's Willem?"

"In the wood, helping Anavar water the horses. Tantroth's men passed twice in the night."

I flogged my mind; now was no time to laze. "They didn't search?"

He shook his head. "Who of royal blood would enter such a dwelling?"

I focused on the churl. "Your name?"

The man opened his mouth, closed it without speaking.

"Who are you?"

The boy piped, "Eol."

"Your name or his?"

"Fartha. He won't talk."

"Why?"

"He afraid."

"Aren't you?"

The boy said, "You g'a hurt us?"

"No."

"See?" He tugged at the silent man's fingers. Then to me, "Are you really King?"

"Prince. By new moon I'll be King."

His eyes grew wide. "Where crown?"

"It's . . ." I couldn't think. "Where, Rust?"

"In safekeeping with Elryc."

"If he doesn't steal—I'm sorry. Don't hit me. I didn't mean it."

"I won't Roddy." His lips brushed my scalp. "Now you're awake, take this." He handed me a warm bowl.

"What is it?"

"Broth, flavored with potato and rabbit."

"Ugh."

"You lost much blood."

I gulped the stew, as glad of the liquid as the nourishment. "Rust . . ." My voice was hesitant. "How is it that Fostrow bleeds and dies, yet I bleed and live?"

"His wound was worse."

"Am I favored?"

"By whom? Have you endowed Fortune's Well with silver?"

"I rode all night, and he bled in moments."

"His leg was half-severed. You had but a gash in the side." He roughed my hair, gently at first, then with anger. "You could have died, you dimwit! Why didn't you tell me?"

"I didn't know."

"You were soaked."

"Sweat, I thought. How oft have you told me I sweat too much?"

"Never. Only that you bathed too little." His eyes glistened. "My life is hard with you. But don't make me live without."

Across the room, the boy's wide eyes stared.

"You, child." I beckoned. "Would you serve a king?" He nodded. "Fetch more water." I handed him the bowl. "Don't spill it, and I'll let you touch my sword."

In a moment the lad returned, bearing the water with great care. Eagerly I downed it. Would my thirst never be sated? When I was done I groped for my sword, found it near my side. With an effort I pulled the haft a few inches from the scabbard, let the lad's fingers trace the jeweled design.

I asked, "When do we ride?"

"I'm not sure. I may send Anavar to find our troop. Tursel must be fuming."

"Or saying the Rites of our Passing." The captain would be beside himself. Our force was divided not in twain, but in three. Elryc waited with the wagons, Tursel and the survivors of our raid lurked near Shar, and Avatar, Rust, Willem, and I hid in a fetid hut. I stirred. "Help me sit. I have to piss."

"Use the pot."

"Are my ribs bound? Good. Let me walk outside."

"You're a dolt." Still, he didn't push me down.

"You there. Eol, is it? Take my arm." The swarthy man darted over, eyes down. He let me throw an arm over his shoulders. With Rust tending my injured side, we shuffled to the door. It was great labor, and I gritted my teeth against pain and waves of dizziness. Outside, I blinked. "When was morn?"

"It's long past noon."

"Then we'll ride. You'll help me up." I loosed my breeches.

"I'll decide that."

I was silent, until I'd wrung the last drop from my aching bladder. "No, I will. It's a matter of state."

"Not if—"

"Would you that Tursel took himself home to Cumber? We ride."

Very soon I regretted the decision. The churl and his silent wife watched as I swayed in my saddle, jaw clenched. Rust ran back through the trees, swung onto his mare. "The road's clear. Let's go." He took Ebon's reins, led us in a slow walk.

We passed under a leafy canopy that gave way to patches of afternoon haze, while I nursed my ribs. Willem paced to my right, looking very much as if he regretted his impulse.

"How fat is our treasury, Chamberlain?" Deliberately, I made my voice sharp.

"Eh? No more than—I've paid as Mar directed, Roddy. After all, he was regent."

"Are coins left for my stipend?"

He peered at my face. "You jape at me. I'm sorry if I seem . . . Know you my gamble, trailing you out the gate?"

I said, "Know you mine?"

A long pause. "There were tales, whispered where Stire wouldn't overhear. You charmed Raeth of Cumber, we heard. There were doings with Soushire. The Warthen wouldn't see you."

"I've been busy."

"Yes. Elena would be proud." He said it so simply, without guile, that I knew he'd spoken without thought.

"Would she?" I swallowed the hint of a lump.

"Yes. She wanted you fit to be King, and had no idea how to make you thus, except by my chastisement." He eyed me. "You've grown, within."

"Does it show?"

"Yes, Rodrigo. Though to hear you howl last night, one wouldn't know."

I flushed. "It hurt so."

"Apparently." Then, to the trees, "When you fled the castle, I'd not thought you capable of leading men to battle."

"I wasn't." I dropped my voice. "Rust taught me."

"Ahh, I'm appreciated." A familiar tone, from the horse ahead.

Suddenly I didn't feel it time for jest. "Yes. More than you know."

Willem returned to my abandoned query. "It's mostly gone, the gold. If I'd known, I could have brought what little remained, but the night guard sent for Stire, and . . ."

"We were well out of there."

I brooded, as we neared the outskirts of Shar's Cross. We paced slowly down the center of the rutted road. In a moment we passed the inn where we'd waited for Elryc to live or die. My side smarted, and I said little.

Rust sent Anavar inside, to ask if Tursel had been seen.

No sight of our force, the boy reported.

I roused myself. "What do you expect, sending a lad with the barbarian speech of Eiber? They won't speak of Tursel to him."

"I'll go, then."

"No, you might be remembered. You started a brawl, last visit."

Rust looked indignant, but I snapped my fingers. "That old Ritemaster, where you did the Cleansing. He'd recall us."

"Yes, your impatience, your vulgar—"

"Still, he might tell us."

We sought him out, leaving Anavar behind with Willem.

Rust gave him coin, as offering. "Ritemaster, we seek men of Cumber. They were to meet us near."

"I know of no such."

I said quietly, "Yes, you do." I held his gaze. "Should you demand it, we'll tell you who we are, and why we seek the captain of Cumber."

He hesitated. "You ride with Eiber."

"No. Eiber rides with us, as our ward."

"Our?" He looked from me to Rust.

I reddened, realizing I'd used the royal speech. "Our."

He was silent a long moment. "In the wood, along the road to Fort. Perhaps half a league."

"Aye."

"You'd best leave Shar, sir. Patrols buzz like angry wasps."

We thanked him. As we rode, I mused on the peasant, Eol. "How many in Mother's realm are of such station?"

"Enough. Why?"

"They lead a horrid life. Why would they choose it?"

Rust laughed. "Think you they do?"

"It's worse even than at Hester's cottage." I pondered. "What would it take to improve their lot?"

"Peace, for one."

"Easier said than granted."

Tursel's outguard spotted us an hour after, and raced back to the main camp. When we joined, I was weary enough, but afraid to dismount lest I tear my wound, so we pressed on.

Before leaving, though, I thought once more of the churl who'd sheltered us, and had Rust delve into our purse. "Tursel, send a rider back along our trail. It can't be far, what, Rust, a league? There's a cluster of huts to the left. Look for one with a split beech near the door."

Rust said mildly, "We don't have time . . ."

"He'll catch us in an hour; I must ride slow. Give these coins not to the man Eol, but the towheaded boy. Learn his name. Tell him to remember the King, and join our service when he's grown."

"That's more wealth than the family's ever seen."

"No doubt. Hurry, guard."

We wended our way through the hills.

I called Vessa near. He seemed old and shaken, a husk of his former self. "Well, Speaker. If I call Council, what say you of the regency?"

His eye met mine only for a moment. "I'll vote to end it."

"In favor of?"

He stared at the passing earth. "You, Prince Rodrigo."

"And Uncle Mar's protection?"

"Was less than he warranted."

"And his gold?" I was relentless.

"Sire, I meant no . . . I was sounding you out, to report to the regent. No more." His eyes beseeched me.

I knew the lie, but what point in proving it? I let him go.

It was two hours, not one, before the soldier returned, his mount lathered.

"You gave the coin?"

"No, sire."

I reined in.

"The hut—I found the tree, and what had been huts. All burned. The families were fired inside. I saw what might have been a boy."

"Lord of Nature!" I closed my eyes, tasted the bile of rabbit stew. "Did you search—"

"Horsemen in black were moving along the road. Banners. Archers and infantry behind. I gave warning to Shar. Wagons and townsmen were fleeing as I rode out."

I cried to Rust, "Why the churls?"

"Perhaps for hiding you."

"Oh." It was a moan, as if I'd been stabbed anew.

"It's not your doing, Roddy." His voice was gentle.

I kicked at Ebon; he trotted faster, jouncing me. "And I would be King. Rust, beat me tonight for what I've done to them."

"Easy, my prince."

"I killed them. We could as well have hid in the wood."

Willem cleared his throat. "Roddy . . . may I still call you that? Evil accrues to the man who looses it. You were but a candle that showed Tantroth where to strike. The sword was his."

"I'm not comforted." My tone was bitter.

Rust leaned close. "You wanted your throne. This comes of it." His eyes held mine, while I searched his reproach. Strangely, I found none. "War is man's folly," he said. "Good cannot come without pain, or hurt. Would you we ceased our quest, and rode back to Hester's cottage at Fort?"

"Yes. No, I . . . don't know."

"Here." He swung off his horse, climbed behind me. "Give me the reins. Lean back, it won't hurt as much." Gently, he tugged at my shoulders; I sagged against his weight. "Rest, my prince."

At last, as Ebon trod steadily, I wept, for Fostrow, for the peasant boy whose name I never knew, for my faded illusions.

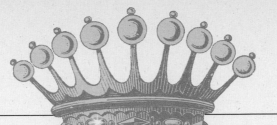

PART IV

Chapter 37

IT WAS A DAY AND A NIGHT BEFORE WE FOUND ELRYC and our wagons. Though we'd lost a score of men in the foray to the keep, our combined force was again strong enough, almost, to quell my nagging fears.

My skin was hot, and they made me ride in a wagon while my flesh knit. Rust hovered like a mother hen.

I bade Tursel lead us to Groenfil's realm. We had business unfinished. Chamberlain Willem was given a guard of honor, and made welcome in our camp. Vessa was treated with respect I doubted he deserved. Tursel posted extra rear guard, and seemed worried.

Elryc rode propped against the side of the wagon, chewing a piece of straw. He listened twice to my tale of Stryx Castle, asking whom I'd seen, what changes were apparent. After, he furrowed his brow while he thought.

Suddenly he blurted, "Roddy, don't leave me." His face puckered.

"I came back, brother. Just as I prom—"

"No, after. As King." He grabbed my hand. "You're changing, don't you feel it? Don't forget me."

"Changing how?"

"Becoming a man. The way you just spoke . . . it made me shiver. Don't shut me from your counsel."

I held out my hand. "I swore to seek your advice, and even setting that aside, you're my brother whom I love."

He collapsed into my chest.

After a time I said, "I was cruel to Pytor too, wasn't I?"

Elryc hesitated. "He only wants to be near you."

"I shunned him, complained to Mother, made him feel the baby."

"We taunted you too, Roddy."

"And I threw stones." I shrugged. "We all do that as children, but with Pytor, it was more. The whine in his voice . . . it drove me mad."

"He'll forgive you."

I was grateful for his certainty.

We stopped some hours at a stream outside Groenfil town, to refresh, mend, and elaborate what was left of our finery. I was weak, sometimes dizzy. Tursel argued strongly for pressing ahead, but only when we presented our best did I allow us to appear again before the Earl's walls.

Groenfil met us immediately, outside the city. We offered perfunctory greetings, and his bow was noticeably deeper, though still not offering the homage of noble to King. "So. What have you done to stir Tantroth? He's taken Shar's Cross, roams the hills, assembles a force to assail Stryx Castle itself."

Was it possible Groenfil didn't know? With quickening heart I beckoned Rust close, whispered, "Bring Vessa."

We of Caledon pride ourselves in our intrigue, but it gave immense pleasure to see Groenfil's jaw drop when the old Speaker pushed aside the flap. We took wine and chatted amiably until I suggested he might retire. When Vessa was gone, the Earl and I faced each other across a narrow plank table. My wound ached. The sides of the tent flapped in a sudden breeze.

"My congratulations, Prince; you've four votes. Now, how to proceed? I'm sure fat Lady Soushire will bring her garlic to any place you choose. But Margenthar won't permit a proxy vote on such an important matter as your crown. Do you think he'll give you leave to consult Chamberlain Willem in the castle?"

To Rust, I merely nodded. He left with a smile, and returned with the Chamberlain.

Groenfil rose to his feet. "We'll speak further, sir." A bow, short and perfunctory. Outside, the wind snapped angrily at our banners.

I called after him, "Certainly. By morn's light. In the meanwhile, I imagine you'll be pleased to lend us fodder and supplies for our troop?"

Though he gave no answer, apparently it pleased him. Two hours later, when the wind had died, wagons rumbled into our camp, filled with provender. The supplies were welcome, but I'd pressed Groenfil for more cause than that. Our parleys, his provisions, all coaxed him further from Margenthar. Uncle Mar would soon or late learn that Groenfil recognized my cause, and would assume the Earl was plotting to desert him. Their rift would leave Groenfil more pliant.

I spent the night dozing uneasily. In the morning, Tursel strode into my tent, with nary a gesture of leave. "Pardon, Prince. Word from the rear guard. Hundreds of armed men pour down the trail we followed."

Suddenly my knees were weak. "Tantroth's army, so soon? By extending his supply lines doesn't he risk—"

"Not Tantroth. Margenthar." Tursel's mouth was grim. "An excursion in force. He's heading here, as fast as his wagons allow."

Rust grunted. "With a supply train, he's committing to more than a raid."

I said, "He brought his wagons to trap us at the cross."

"Yes, but Tantroth was near. Mar was wary of being sucked into battle, lightly equipped."

"Rust, what shall we do?"

"Why, meet with Groenfil. He's waiting under the canopy."

"Does he know yet of Mar?"

Rust said, "He'll know soon enough. There are no secrets in Caledon."

I was amazed at my sudden confidence. "I'll see Groenfil now, while there's chance he hasn't heard. Wait here; I may need you."

As briskly as I could with bound ribs, I strode into our conclave. "Good morning, my lord."

"Good day, Prince." We bowed; he took his seat.

"Thank you for the provisions. My men—"

He said, "Shall we come to the point?"

An odd but refreshing approach to the dance of diplomacy. "Very well."

"I'll tell you what I know. And what I don't." He made a tent of his hands. "When Mar proposed a regency I approved, though I disliked seeing so much power gathered in his hands."

I nodded.

"Of course, in his view, that was the whole point. But you were clearly too young and too callow to be King."

I folded my arms.

"Not for the reasons you think. You'd never have kept us from each other's throats, you see. I want Soushire, and Cumber wants autonomy, and Mar wants to speak for the crown, and the Warthen trifles with selling his power of Return to the Norlanders. None of us can allow the others too great a success. Your late mother had her hands full."

I looked at him with dawning respect.

"The regency," he said, "can be dissolved by the Council that created it. We were seven, so one would think four votes can dismiss Margenthar." He made a show of counting. "Willem, Soushire, Cumber . . . but Vessa? Who controls the city to appoint a Speaker: Mar? Tantroth? Certainly not you."

"Ahh."

"That's what I know. As to the rest . . ." He leaned forward, intent. "What, exactly, is Caledon's Power, and how does it operate? They say you must speak True, before and while you wield it. Have you?"

"I believe so."

"And the other requirements, which make you blush so?"

"Kept." I spoke through gritted teeth.

"I've heard the third requisite of your Still is that you be lawful King. Is it thus?"

"Yes."

"I asked our Ritemaster and he knows not. Will you pledge to me by your True, that you're certain Vessa's clouded fourth vote will bestow on you the Still?"

I hesitated, and plunged into the chasm. "No."

"Will you swear it does not?"

"I think it shall. By all that's fair and just, it should. I cannot swear that I know." But with Vessa's vote I must give Groenfil's lands to Soushire, to keep True.

"What of the Rite by which you summon your Power? Does it require . . . accoutrements?"

"The Vessels." I'd thought it a family secret. "They're taken."

"By whom?"

"Uncle Mar."

"And without them?"

"I have no Power." I saw my crown fading into mist and added hopefully, "As King, I'll reclaim the Vessels." It sounded a forlorn boast.

"Mar will be delighted to hand them to you."

"Of course he won't. But neither Mar nor his Bayard can wield the True. They're . . . no longer eligible. So it's me or none."

Groenfil nodded. "Truth for truth. Well traded." For a moment he seemed uneasy. He stood, stretched, selected a fruit his own servants had brought the night past. "I asked for a sign, and you brought it. Your ragamuffin force secured not only Vessa, but Willem. I am persuaded: You are one to be King."

My heart leaped.

"My vote will assure your legitimacy. I believe I mentioned its price." He stood, as cold wind swirled about our legs. "Oh, a few other trifles. Ten crownweights of gold. I'll wait 'til you have your treasury; your oath on the True will suffice. My precedence over Lord Margenthar in affairs of state; arrange the protocol as you must, so long as it irks him. But most importantly, Soushire."

"No."

"Very well." He stood. "I bid you good day. Please leave my lands."

"Be seated!" My voice was a lash. "We did not give you leave."

His knees bent, but resolutely, he straightened. "You are not my liege lord, sir."

"Be seated, or our first crowned act will be to have you flogged!"

A sudden breeze stirred the canopy. "Without me, you risk your Power. Do you treasure it so little?"

"More than you imagine." My eyes blazed into his. "I will be King and crowned; with my other votes you cannot bar that. You may only cost me the Still, and make me blood enemy 'til death."

Outside, Ebon neighed, and someone soothed him. The tent walls flapped. It was all I could do to stop my voice from shaking. "You will sit, or I shall walk from the tent, and never shall we speak again."

Slowly, as if battling himself, he sank to his chair. The wind quieted.

"Now. The gold, I refuse. Absolutely, without quibble or haggle. No. We'll need our strength to rebuild Caledon." I stood to pace. "Precedence over Mar? Gladly. And I forget not your caveat regarding Renna, your sister. She will live safe, and so will Mar, unless he provokes me further after I am enthroned." I shook my head, shedding disgust. Gladly would I run Mar through with arrow or spear.

My side twinged; as casually as I could, I settled in my seat. "Now, as to Soushire. For such friendship as we may come to attain, for the benefit of Caledon, for your own sake, I beg you not to ask it." I held my breath. If he assented, I was undone, yet in decency I owed him the opportunity.

"No. I will have Soushire."

"You expect me to secure it for you?"

"Whatever arms I ask, in addition to my own."

I let him wait, so the prize would seem greater. "Very well. Provided you swear to end the regency and speedily crown me King, I swear by the True, and the Power I would wield."

That, of course, wasn't enough. He made me reword the oath to his satisfaction; when he was done I was well and truly bound.

Groenfil stood. Slowly, he bowed, the bow of respect, of vassal to liege. His tone was light. "Frankly, sire, I'm relieved."

"That you'll have Soushire?" I didn't much care. Now that it was done, I felt the throb in my side with each heartbeat.

"Why, that you're no better than I. For a time, you left doubt." Yet his face betrayed an odd disappointment. "Your oath is truly sworn: I am pledged to you, sire." He bowed, a proper bow, acknowledging duty of vassal to liege.

We agreed to set forth that very afternoon for Cumber, where Council would convene. I hoped to have Groenfil well away from his realm before word of Mar's army reached him.

I made note to invite the Warthen of the Sands and Uncle Mar to join in Council, but I knew neither would attend. After, I would be crowned.

The moment Groenfil was gone to his city, Rust rushed into the tent. "I heard shouts, and wind stirred the dust."

"We were annoyed."

"Both of you?"

"Yes," I said. "He pressed us."

"Ahh, my prince grows regal. Shall I be permitted to touch you, when you're King?"

"Perhaps," I said coolly, and was surprised at how his face fell. "Of course," I said. "As before." I eased myself onto a couch, gingerly patting my side. "Everyone says I'm becoming a man. But a crown won't make me one. You'll help me through the last of it?"

He knelt, and his eyes glistened. "I wish . . ."

"I know." I touched his hand. "It's not my nature. But for a time I must live by the True, and I need your comfort."

"I'll cherish each day." He rose, fled the tent.

Groenfil delayed several hours, preparing to ride forth. Word came from our scouts: Duke Margenthar watered his horses at the stream where we'd stopped to refresh, mere hours from the city.

I was frantic to keep Groenfil free of my uncle's snares, even if it cost the Earl his castle. "Set the column marching the very moment Groenfil appears," I told Tursel.

Nervous, not knowing what to do, I poured water, washed breakfast from my hands. After, I perched on a stool outside the tent they'd just folded, toying with the bowl of tepid washwater.

What was this Earl who'd joined his cause to mine? By Mother's account, he was among the most venal in Caledon. Certainly his lust for Soushire did him no credit. And yet . . . I shivered, idly rubbing the warmth of my palms. Was there something more to him? Did he adhere to our House only from self-interest? I spread my hands atop the bowl, looking into distance. Mother, could you have misjudged our Earl?

Would you were here to speak.

In a while I shook myself from my daze. I climbed onto Ebon, waiting with my household party for the Earl.

Genard raised himself in his saddle. "There he comes, m'lord!"

I reminded Tursel, "We're to ride faster than Mar, whatever the cost. Let our wagons catch us when they will."

"Your uncle's troop could fall on our supplies."

"But we'll be safe in Cumber with our Council."

Groenfil rode toward us. In addition to his guard, who fell in with our own, the Earl brought three noble retainers. He bowed from the saddle. "To your fortune, my liege."

I swallowed. Lord Groenfil was the first to grant me the honors of my title, and it affected me unexpectedly. I gazed at his face. "Why, sir, do you smile?"

He thrust out a hand, encompassing the crisp autumn sun, the waving banners, the scarlet shrubbery. "I've this day, your company, and Soushire. May not a man smile at such providence?"

Tursel beckoned an aide. "Sound the trumpet to advance."

"Not yet." I could scarce believe the voice was mine. With effort, I raised my eyes to Groenfil's. "I would not begin my reign in . . . falsehood." Resolutely, I thrust down my misgivings. "Sir, in all faith I must tell thee: Duke Margenthar of Verein pursues us in force, and is but hours distant."

Groenfil took the news with equanimity. "Where?"

"At a spring, where the trail turns toward—"

"I know the place. Runwald, Cheger, go." Two of his men wheeled, and galloped to the gates. To me, "How long have you known?"

My stomach churned; I'd cast away my crown. "Since the morn."

"Why tell me now?"

"To redeem honor."

"Ah." He studied me, his eyes shrewd. "Did you owe me these tidings?"

"No. Yes."

"When?"

Was he a tutor, to question me so? I forced a response through unwilling lips. "The moment you bowed before me, vassal to liege." My cheeks were hot. "I ask thy forgiveness."

"Very well. Consider your honor redeemed." He turned to his retainer. "Hermut, tell him."

The man's words were a snarl. "We had word of Lord Margenthar's march last eve, an hour past sunset. The keep is prepared for a month's siege."

I looked to the Earl with wonder. "Still, you'd ride with me?"

"The realm needs a king, not disarray." Groenfil's smile was bleak. "You're our best hope of union."

"And rightful heir." Elryc's voice was sharp.

"Why, that too." Groenfil nodded, as if to dismiss the irrelevance. "Truly, Prince Rodrigo, you surprise me."

"That I dabbled at betrayal?" I couldn't help my bitterness.

"That you'd risk your crown, to reclaim yourself." We waited while the Earl's two riders rejoined us.

"Shall we?" Groenfil gestured down the trail. Tursel gave the signal. Our column lurched into motion.

I looked back. "And your castle, sir?"

"Will stand without me. Mar can't afford a long siege; he can't leave Verein untended. It's too close to Stryx and Llewelyn's keep."

Rust's tone was courteous. "May I ask, sir, what orders you sent back?"

Groenfil's tone was equally polite. "I told my son, sir, that if I should fall, he was to be loyal to the House of Caledon."

I rode silent, chilled. Had I not spoken, who knew how fleeting the Earl's loyalty, or that of his kin?

With Groenfil committed, the march to Cumber became a regal procession, though in haste. Our regiment was augmented by soldiers of the Earl bearing burnished shields, under bright banners. Food was ample, and even coin flowed free, in loan from Groenfil. Only my wound troubled me. My side was red and hot, and at night, in the tent, Rust pursed his lips at the sight of it.

At Cumber, Uncle Raeth met us in full regalia, beneath the redstone towers. As he escorted us to the donjon he smiled gleefully to his valet. "So, Imbar, you were wrong. The prodigal nephew returns. Welcome, Roddy."

"Thank you, Uncle Raeth."

"And his companion." He almost purred. "Imbar, *do* escort young Lord Rustin to his quarters."

"I'll sleep near my prince." Rust's tone was a trifle too sharp. "I guard him."

"How valiant. Tresa, you'll entertain Rodrigo until the coronation?"

"Of course, Grandfather."

"So many guests, Imbar; we're hard-pressed to find places of honor. Do you imagine they've sent envoy to the Warthen and Mar?"

My mouth opened, and I closed it without speaking.

"Perhaps they overlooked that trifle?" Uncle Raeth beamed at Imbar. I nodded. There'd been so much to do.

"Imbar, send word as we did to Lady Soushire, there's a good fellow."

"Of course, Raeth." His valet left us, patting Rust's shoulder in passing. Rustin threw off his hand.

Raeth turned to Chamberlain Willem with a bow. Coolly, Tresa looked me over. "You've been in a fight."

"Does it show?"

"Your lip is swollen, and you keep your arm pressed to your side. What befell you?"

"We assailed the keep, at Stryx."

"Yes, I heard. How are you hurt?"

"A sword thrust." How could I tell her I fell over a blade gripped by a corpse? "It's been sewn."

"Let me see."

"Here?" My voice squeaked. I fought a furious blush. "Please, my lady."

"Not in the great hall, for Nature's sake. In your rooms. Let me show you." Without a glance back, she trotted up the stairs. I had little choice but to follow, Anavar and Rust trailing behind.

We clambered three flights. Tresa vanished into another stairwell. Cursing, I pursued her. "Where's he lodging us," I panted. "On the roof?"

Anavar offered a shoulder, but I pushed him away. I wasn't *that* enfeebled.

Two flights higher, the stairs gave onto a long narrow corridor. I hesitated. Could Raeth really be trusted, or might assassins lurk in these far reaches of the keep? "Rust, draw your sword." I did the same.

Tresa glanced back. "Whatever are you doing?" She threw open a door.

Cautiously, I peered in.

The room was the entry to a suite of chambers, all fitted with the most elaborate furnishings. A huge intricately carved bed of feathers stuffed in soft cloth dominated the largest bedroom. Fine chests, silk drapery, a washbowl of silver. And the room was delightfully cool.

Tresa threw open the windows. "Look, my lord."

Below loomed Raeth's crenelated towers, almost as far as the eye could see. Each flew the colors of Cumber. Directly below the window lay Raeth's magnificent garden, wherein I knew he labored each day. Beyond was Cumber Town.

"It's . . . breathtaking."

"And rarely used. You're this chamber's first guest in years."

"Who was the last?"

Tresa's face was grave. "Josip, of Stryx."

My father. I swallowed.

"Now, let's see your wound."

"Thank you, my lady, I'm—"

"You're shy, aren't you." It was more statement than question. "Come, off with your jerkin."

"I'm to be King!"

"Only if you live." She put hands on hips. "I have skill with healing. Grandfather says I'm to look. Please don't quarrel."

I appealed to Rust, but his eyes were elsewhere. Sighing, I took off my shirt. Her gentle hands helped unwind my bindings.

I sat gingerly on a stool. "Will this hurt?"

"Why should it?"

Across the room, Anavar grinned, and I recalled the beating I'd promised. Tresa's fingers caressed my wound. I flinched from the cold.

"Hotter than it ought be." Her lips tightened.

A chill stabbed. "Will I die of it?"

Again her fingers probed. "Your body tries to heal." Her foot tapped, as if impatient. "To be safe, you'll stay abed until the Council."

"Imps and demons, I will not. There's work of state to attend."

She frowned at my inflamed stitches. "What butcher did this?"

Rust was suddenly absorbed in the view.

"I've seen dishcloths better stitched. Who tied this ragged mess?" Her eyes fastened on the flush that slowly crept up Rust's neck. "You lout! He'll carry the scar for life!"

I said evenly, "I'll esteem it forever." Rust shot me a grateful glance.

"I'll visit every day, so you won't be too bored abed." She spoke as if it were a thing decided.

"Think you that you're my mother?" I filled my voice with affront.

"Why, no, else you'd be civilized." Two red spots graced her cheeks. "I suppose I ought to be sorry, Rodrigo. But truly, you bring out the worst in me."

"Pity any man who does." We locked eyes.

Abruptly she stalked to the door, gave a curtsy of scant respect. "Good day, Prince Rodrigo."

"Don't go!" My voice was too harsh; I tried again. "Please stay. I'm not . . . I've never known—Lord of Nature preserve us!" I looked for something to fling across the room. There was no help for it. To make it worse, Anavar and Rust watched. "Lady Tresa, I've no skill at discourse. Around you I feel a complete oaf. I want your company." I felt my face redden. "I just don't know how to ask."

She took two steps from the door. "Do I frighten you?"

"No, not at—yes."

"Why?"

My fists clenched. Rustin watched curiously. How often I'd humiliated myself before him. This Lady was nothing by comparison. I drew myself straight. "Because you're grown and I only want to be. You're a woman, and I've never—I've seldom spoken to one." I forced myself not to flinch as I met her eyes, though her ridicule might destroy me.

Instead, she asked, "You like me?"

"You've mettle. You don't fear your grandfather, nor me. It's . . . refreshing."

"Should I hear a yes, or no?"

How much could I bear? Was that a snicker Anavar hid behind his hand? "Yes, my lady."

"Well." She put hands on hips. "How old are you?"

"Sixteen." Lord of Nature, I felt young. Why was I standing before her without a jerkin?

"There's barely three years between us. And you've seen the world."

"Hardly."

"They say you must hold yourself chaste, to conserve your Power. Is it so?"

Nothing on earth could force me to meet her eyes. "Yes."

"How awful. Boys do it all the time, don't they? I mean—" She flushed. "I've heard . . ." Blessedly, she trailed off.

"This isn't seemly, my lady." Desperately I strove for dignity. How could I allow such discourse in front of Rust and my ward?

"Of course. I only meant you must yearn so."

I bared my teeth. If it was pity in her glance, I'd fling her from the window; the crown be damned.

It might have been pity, or some other sadness, that made her eyes glisten. My rage wavered.

"I'm sorry." Her words came in a rush. "At times I think as a healer, and forget the man behind the pain. Will you forgive me?"

I nodded, not trusting myself to do more.

"Do put your shirt on, before you take a chill. See that tower below, the one with the red streamer? That's where Grandfather sleeps. You're higher even than he; by his accounting that's great honor." Her finger crooked to Anavar. "Come, youngsire, I'll show you the spires of the town. You're from Eiber?"

I was glad to see my ward blush clear to the roots of his hair. Carefully, favoring my wound, I redonned my jerkin. Tresa chatted amiably, until my composure was renewed. At length, jovial, I was able to bid her farewell, and scarce realized I'd promised to spend the next days in bed.

"Lady Soushire is due this night, but it's two days to the Sands no matter how fast the rider." Rust spoke in soothing tones that only irked me the more.

"Every hour I lie here is time for ill to befall us." I threw aside the curtain. "What if Vessa dies of age, or someone poisons—"

"We only settled here this morn." He sighed. "Shall I call Anavar to amuse you?"

"Hah. He'd ask more silver." I brooded. "At least we won't wait long for answer from Mar." Our envoy had only to ride to Groenfil, not past it to Verein. Disconsolate, I lay back, wishing it were night. If days must pass, let them do so quickly.

Rust perched, elbows on the windowsill, gazing dreamily. "Your uncle is a true romantic."

"Mar?" I couldn't believe I'd heard aright.

"No, you dolt, Uncle Cumber. What a fabulous view he created. That laundry wench below looks like an ant with clothes. Come see."

"Lean any farther and you'll topple. Besides, who cares about your ants?"

A sharp knock at the door interrupted his reply. "Yes?"

"Imbar."

Rust's voice went lifeless. "Come in."

"Ah, our two young lords; how enchanting a sight. Pardon me if I take a seat." The old valet wiped his brow. "At my age five flights are an ordeal."

"What do you wish?" My tone was bland.

"My earl asks if you're well enough to join him in the garden at once. The Lady Tresa bids you take the stairs slowly."

I shot to my feet. "What's befallen us?"

"He'll speak of it himself."

I hurried out. Imbar's hand fell on Rust's arm. "A word with you, my lord."

He stiffened. "I go with Rodrigo."

"The Prince will come to no harm. I wish only a moment."

I couldn't wait, with news below. "Hear him, Rust. Join me after." I raced down the stairs.

Uncle Raeth waited in the garden, but so did Vessa, Chamberlain Willem, and Groenfil. Tresa knelt by a bed of chrysanthemums. I paused in the doorway. No servants were about, no refreshments on the table. Was I betrayed? My voice was harsh. "What say you?"

Cumber chewed at his lip. "He looks well, doesn't he, Willem? See what a few hours rest—"

"Imps take you, speak!"

Raeth looked shocked, but my ire spurred him. "We agreed you must be told at once. Mar has left Groenfil. He's headed here, at full gallop."

I gulped. "Can we withstand him?"

"Easily, were he alone." Cumber gestured past the low wall, and the groves beyond. "But Tantroth of Eiber races west through Fort. The scouts say he'll reach us by morn."

The clouds reeled, and I found myself in a chair, ashen.

Earl Groenfil frowned. "This is how you'd lead us? Perhaps we should reconsider."

"Let him be!" Tresa strode across the terrace. "He's hurt, and just rushed down the stairs. You bully him!"

At first I was grateful. Yet, how must I appear, swooning like a maid, while a lady brushed me protectively behind her skirts? Sweating, I made an effort to stand. "I'm well, Lady Tresa. No, be still, I beg you." I turned to Cumber. "What force does Tantroth bring?"

"Tursel's sending more scouts. We've only first reports, and they're grim enough." The old Earl's face softened. "Sit, Roddy. We won't hold it against you."

"I'm well. What word of Tantroth?"

"A huge force, perhaps a thousand horse, many thousands more on foot. There, sit. Tresa, put the bench behind him."

Someone fanned my face. Tresa patted my hand. "It's only his wound."

"No." I found my voice. "It's fear. I confess it."

All looked on me, astonished.

"But once, in a glade, I made a vow. Fear, I cannot elude. But I won't be coward. I shall not run from fear, if it cost my life." Once more, I struggled to my feet. "If you would not have me thus, I free you from your vows. But know you that I am Rodrigo, Prince, and shall fight to the death for my people, and Caledon." The solitude of the great hall wasn't far; only through the pair of stout doors. I could reach it.

At the entryway, I paused. "Bring me your decision."

Inside, a few more steps brought me to the bench where Cumber dined. I threw myself on it, lay my head in my arms. I'm sorry, Mother. Better they learn now that I'm unworthy. Perhaps Elryc . . .

Soft fingers brushed my neck. "You'll make a fine king." Tresa.

"Bah. By dissolving in tears?"

"By showing your true face. Think you that any on the terrace felt not what you expressed?"

"It's man's duty to cast aside terror."

"Why, Roddy, whoever told you that?" She pressed my head to her bosom. "If only Josip had lived."

Greedily, I embraced her comfort, more welcome even than Rust's. At length, footsteps neared. I raised my head, making no effort to hide my dampened cheeks. Willem watched gravely, Groenfil at his side. Vessa blinked in the gloom of the chamber, as did Cumber.

It was Groenfil who spoke. "There was naught to discuss. We'll crown you now."

Cumber shrugged. "Besides, it's too late to reason with Mar; he'd only double his offer—sorry, a bad jest." He struck flint, lit a candle. "Ah, you're so like Josip, boy. So earnest." The candle flickered.

"Now, Raeth." A dry voice, from the stairs. "You'll upset him."

"Too late for that, Imbar." Cumber sounded cross. "Where have you been?"

"I had word with my lord Rustin."

Rust's face was flushed. "You'll crown Roddy? Today?"

"There's urgent need." Willem.

I shook my head. "We'll wait for Lady Soushire." Was I *determined* to throw away my monarchy? I puzzled at my stubbornness.

"Are you—"

"And we'll allow Mar to attend. He'll be near enough." Beneath the walls raising engines of siege, no doubt. "Why look askance, Willem? Would you I risked the Still of Caledon, for a few hours pause? We'll await the Lady."

"What if Tantroth takes her? It's a near thing, her arrival."

I swung to Uncle Raeth. "Send Tursel with a hundred horse, to hurry Soushire before Tantroth blocks the road."

Raeth said mildly, "Tursel's returned to my service, now he's home again. I don't think it's wise—"

I slapped the plank table with open palm, tried not to flinch at the fiery blaze of pain. "Who commands Caledon, sir?"

Our eyes met. At length Cumber smiled uneasily. "What have we got ourselves into, eh, Imbar? Steel he has, and quickly unsheathed. Well, see that Tursel's told, and soon. If he must be off, I want him back before the noose draws tight."

Imbar grunted, and was gone.

Tresa put hands on hips. "Are you content? Give Rodrigo a few hours rest."

"Not up those stairs." Wanly, I smiled at my uncle. "It's a lovely room, but not today, I beg you. Someplace nearer."

I woke with a start. "What hour is it? Was I drugged?"

"Ninth hour by the candle," said Anavar, sitting by my bedside. "Genard reports that on the ramparts, they see torches nearing."

"From where?" I stumbled to my feet.

"The south, where Groenfil took his guard to delay Margenthar. But also north, and—"

"Where's Rust?"

"Out, and I know not where."

"What of Tantroth?"

"Either it's his torches that bob in the north, or Tursel's, escorting Lady Soushire. Sir, where go you?"

In the courtyard, Uncle Cumber stood grimly, a cloak flung over his shoulders, issuing orders to a handful of runners. Townspeople poured through the gates, pushing carts, lugging bundles, hauling wailing tykes. Horses snorted; dogs barked and snapped. Raeth saw me, nodded, but said naught. Elryc ran to my side.

We climbed to the battlements.

"Who goes? Oh, it's you." A burly guardsman stood firm in our path. "My lords, it's not safe. An arrow in the night—"

"Bah." I thrust him aside, succeeding only by the weight of my rank.

Anavar cautioned, "Slow, sir, or you'll tear your stitches."

On the battlement, I peered through an arrowport, while grizzled soldiers watched with amusement. I turned to the nearest. "Where are the riders with torches?"

He pointed. I could see nothing.

Carefully, clutching my side, I hoisted myself atop a keg of oil. "Ahhh." For a moment I watched the lights dance ever so slowly closer.

Anavar found himself a high place, and squinted. "That will be Tursel."

"How do you know?"

"There's only—what, a dozen?—torches. Tantroth would light the sky."

Suddenly I yearned for Rust. I forced a calm. "Unless he rode in stealth." I smiled down at Elryc. "See, all is well."

"Oh, Roddy, don't be an ass."

He sounded so disconsolate I almost forgot my dread. "What say you?"

"If not tonight, he'll be on us the morrow. What difference?"

"By morrow I'll be King."

"Will that provide an army? An escape from the castle?"

"Bah. If that were what I sought, we could ride now." I waved at the donjon, the thick, solid walls. "We're safe."

"For how long?" He turned away without answer, and trudged to the keep.

From the south, a clatter of horses. Two guardsmen cantered through the gate. "Make ready! Groenfil returns!"

Anavar and I peered over the wall, to the road below. At first, in the fading embers of dusk, we saw nothing. Then, in no great haste, Earl Groenfil's men appeared, in good order. A company of horse led the way, scouting for ambush. Behind them trod a long column of foot soldiers. They seemed weary but none the worse for wear.

The archers marched together, notable by their lack of arms; their bows and missiles would be hauled in a wagon. Groenfil's spearmen marched separately. A few horsemen galloped back and forth, carrying orders to tighten march, help free a mired wagon, or look sharp.

Behind the infantry rode the Earl, amid a troop of cavalry, distinguished by the plume of his helmet. I'd have to order him to dress circumspectly, so not to become a target.

I sought a torch, waited for Groenfil, gave formal words of thanks to him for all to hear. Then I climbed the battlements again. More torches, to the south. Margenthar's outriders advanced toward the gates, not far behind the last of Groenfil's guard.

My arm over Anavar's shoulder, I trudged to our chambers.

Chapter 38

ALONE WITH ANAVAR, I SAT, HEAD IN HANDS.

He knelt before me. "Father says demons breed fear in the night. By day, all will seem—"

"Is it so plain to see?" My voice was unsteady.

"I feel the same, my lord."

"Oh, Anavar." I drew him close.

The door crashed open. Rustin stopped short. Then he leered. "Enjoying yourselves? Don't mind me."

My hand darted from the boy's face, as if burned. What must Rust have thought, seeing him kneel before me?

Rust's voice was thick. "I see it's *my* touch you loathe, not his." He lurched to the window, thrust open the shutters. "Give us air."

I said softly, "Rustin's drunk. Pay no heed. Leave us."

Rust drew sword. I started in alarm, but he tossed it aside to unhitch his leather scabbard. "Yes, leave us." A mighty blow thwacked Anavar's calves. "Go!" Rust thrust him to the door, slammed it hard.

I sat quietly. "Will you use that on me?"

He stood weaving. "Which of us would it give more pleasure?" He turned to the window, sucked in breaths of night air.

With great effort, I put aside my own troubles, my wealth of grievances. "Rust, what troubles you?" Cautiously, I joined him at the shutters.

He thrust me away. "I won't be touched."

"Very well." We stared moodily into the night. "Look at the torches scurrying below. They're—"

"I hate this place," he said.

"Our rooms?"

"Cumber."

"Why?"

He gave no answer. I thought to put a hand on his shoulder, but didn't dare.

"An odious town," he said. "Greedy winesellers, a filthy market. Even the air is too chill." Angrily, he slammed the shutters closed. Then he turned to me, and I hated the malice in his eyes. "He's pretty, your Eiberian. A fine catch."

Lord of Nature knew what I'd have said, or done, had there not come a soft knock at the door.

Rust seized his sword. "Pray it's Imbar." He stalked to the door.

Tresa peered in, her face flushed.

"Oh, it's you." I realized how ungracious I sounded, and made a valiant effort to quell my displeasure. "What now, my lady?"

"Tursel's returned, just in time to scatter Mar's outguard and gain the gates. He's brought Lady Soushire!"

"Ahh." My black clouds lifted a trifle.

"Come see her," Tresa urged. "Are you well enough? Your face is flushed. I'll help you downstairs."

"I won't be touched," I said. Behind me, Rustin snickered.

Tresa sniffed. "Well, *do* pardon me. The King acclaimed, and all that."

"No, my lady, I didn't mean . . ." I gave it up. "I'll lean on you."

Rustin fell on the bed. "Snuff the candles." His eyes closed.

Tresa and I paused after the first flight. Her arm was warm on my flank, and inviting. To break the uneasy silence I said, "Rustin's in a foul mood. If you'd been Imbar . . ." I managed another flight. "I wonder why he hates the valet so."

Tresa stopped short, studied my gaze. "You truly don't know? I thought for your crown, you had . . ." Abruptly she sat on the stair. "Oh, dear."

"What is it?"

She brushed her skirt. "Not now. Your lords and ladies await." She guided me down the steps, ignoring my protest.

In the great hall, Groenfil, with studied politeness, handed Lady Soushire a flagon of mulled wine. "Ah, sire." He bowed to me. "You missed the telling of Captain Tursel's exploits at the gate."

The soldier looked pained. "The enemy hadn't arrived in force. Not quite."

Lady Soushire heaved her bulk out of an intricately carved chair alongside Vessa, who sat like one awaiting death. "Raeth, your captain is too modest. It's thanks to him I'm not caught between Duke Mar and Tantroth." She turned to me. "You've done all you said, Rodrigo. I'm here to carry out my part of the bargain."

Inwardly, I flinched, hoping Groenfil wouldn't perceive her meaning. "Thank you, my lady. My thanks for your journey." I looked to the Earl of Cumber. "Is there point in waiting for the Warthen? Mar would only deny him entry."

"And we've quorum without him." Uncle Raeth looked smug. "Do you know, Roddy, that Lady Soushire brought us four hundred men? Astonishing. Hardly any supplies, of course. Barely more than their full saddlebags, for speed. But Mar will be confounded by our reinforcements. Perhaps we'll even try a sally or two."

Lady Soushire grunted, eased herself back into her chair. "Safety, when I venture forth. Safety above all."

Uncle Raeth insisted on formalities. Trumpets blared in the courtyard to proclaim the Council, astonishing those peasants who hadn't yet been assigned shelter. The great hall was swept clean, huge quantities of refreshments laid out and the servants banished.

We took our places amid the blazing candles and burnished mirrors. Rust should be with us, I thought. He'd done so much on my behalf. But I recalled his hateful insinuation about Anavar, and set aside the thought. We'd reconcile, I knew, but now there was nothing I could give him, or cared to give.

Uncle Cumber headed the Council table. Fitting, as he was host, and I yet under regency. "The issue before us," he said, "is—blast it!" He glared at the door. "Who knocks? We're not to be disturbed!"

It was Tursel. For once, he seemed abashed. "Sorry, my lords. Margenthar has sent envoy, demanding truce to be seated at Council."

We stared at one another, astounded. A grudging respect seeped through my dismay. Uncle wasn't done yet; he would beard us in our very chamber. And I'd have to allow it. I couldn't risk the Still by false Council.

I stood, spoke with careful formality. "Tell our esteemed uncle, Duke Margenthar of Stryx, we bid him welcome at our meet. Make arrangements for his admission that satisfy our defense."

"Aye, my lord." He was gone.

"Well, now." I looked about. "Whose vote will he suborn?" At least, they all had the grace to look abashed.

Scarce an hour later, Uncle Mar came calling. They'd let him bring four retainers, though only he was allowed in the Council chamber.

He strode through the doors, his long gold-trimmed cloak trailing. His hair and graying beard were brushed; the silver buckles on his leathern boots gleamed. I'd have guessed his regalia came from a well-stocked wardrobe wagon, though I knew he'd dashed through the hills to pursue us.

"Good day, my lords. My lady." A deeper bow to Soushire. "Head of place belongs to the regent, though I won't insist on the protocol." Cheerily, he commandeered a chair near Groenfil. "I trust your wheat does well?"

"If you left it standing."

"Why, of course." He turned blandly to Willem. "Who summoned this Council?"

"I did." Uncle Raeth's tone was testy. "Shall we cut through the usual banter?"

"Why, no. I enjoy the civilities." Mar nodded in my direction. "Roddy. Are you well? You seem a bit . . . peaked."

"A slight injury. I recover."

"Ah, a pity." He let the ambiguity hang. "Well, now, shall we begin, if Roddy and Vessa will excuse us?"

I gaped.

"Oh, come now, boy. Surely you know Council is attended only by members. Did Elena fail to teach you *that*?"

I knew I mustn't let him goad me, but my face flushed. "I have business here."

"That's as may be. Raeth, would you show him the door, or shall I?"

Their eyes locked.

Once I was banished, my coronation would dissolve in bargains, pacts, and silken assurances. I gripped the arm of my seat, as if fearing someone would try to haul me from it.

Outside the keep, catcalls and whistles. Peasant voices rose.

Willem coughed discreetly. "He ought to be present, my lord Duke."

"We've rules and procedures, and reason to follow them."

"Yes, and one is that Council meets free of intimidation. Will you remove your besiegers?" A good sign, I thought. Willem no longer had common ground with Uncle Mar, and stood up to him.

"Verein's troops are here to protect you, and at great sacrifice, I might add."

Raeth's pewter wineglass slammed onto the table. It would leave a scar. "I'm too old, Mar. Too tired for a night of games. We've business, and let us to it."

Uncle Mar raised an eyebrow. "I take it we don't agree? Brother-in-law, how say you?"

Groenfil's tone was sardonic. "That Prince Rodrigo stays. Truly, I hope not to distress you."

"And you, my lady?"

Soushire stirred. "You've lost this round. Let it be."

"I wouldn't dream of doing other. Now, as to Vessa. What business has he here? Surely you don't claim he speaks for Stryx?"

Vessa, shrunken, examined his fingers.

I said, "He's Speaker."

"Of what? Did the city rise in indignation at his ouster? I think not."

Cumber snapped, "None has been appointed in his place."

"How foolish of me; I thought your spies were everywhere." Mar whipped out a scroll. "The city again has a Speaker, though not of our choosing. Tantroth's appointed—let's see, now . . . one Llewelyn, formerly of the keep."

I spluttered, "He can't—he has no authority to—"

Raeth said, "I don't recognize Tantroth or his appointments."

"Quite. But will the Still manifest itself, if tainted by Vessa's vote?"

So clever, Uncle Mar. Without Vessa, to be crowned I needed every single vote save Mar. He need cleave but one lord from my cause, to destroy me.

Willem looked shaken. Vessa stared at Mar with beady eyes, awaiting his fate.

It was Groenfil who came to my rescue. "The authority of Caledon rests in this room, my lord Duke. Council has merely to reappoint Vessa as Speaker."

"Even if the Still would recognize our act, Council cannot appoint. Only the Queen, and she's dead."

"But nonethe—"

"Or the regent. Yes, the regent, acting for crown, might appoint a Speaker." Idly, Mar played with the ruffles on his blouse. "Shall I appoint Vessa, or other?"

"We won't ratify anyone except Vessa."

"A stalemate, it seems."

For a moment all was silent. Groenfil took a deep breath, turned from Mar. "My lords, he seeks to divide us, and in this matter, I believe, our interests coincide." His eyes roved the table. "So, let's end Mar's regency, and if necessary, appoint a new."

I shouted, "I'll have no regent!" I stumbled to my feet. "What's come over you? He deceives you with one trick upon another! You'd quarrel over Vessa, divide yourselves over a new regency, and forget the very purpose of our meet?"

"Yes, *boy*, instruct us." Mar's words were a hiss. "You who lack the wit, the grace, the forbearance to govern yourself, teach us our duty."

"That's quite enough." Cumber too got to his feet. "Sit, Roddy, it's going to be a long night. Will you risk a vote, Mar? I'll wager the outcome."

Their eyes met. After a moment Mar's features lightened. "Raeth, I take it our business is the regency's end?" He waited for Cumber's nod. "Very well, gladly I surrender it to young Rodrigo. As you're so *old*, and *tired*"—on his lips, the words had a bite—"let me summarize. We need a king enthroned with the Power of Caledon to meet Tantroth's threat. The Still has such might that it warrants even so callow a king as our Roddy. That's it, more or less? I see you nodding. Good." His satisfaction brought a chill.

"Don't look so worried, my boy. I agree, you see. Despite what you misunderstood from our conversation in that wheat field, the Still is most powerful. It will light a way through our travail, free us from

Tantroth's boot, guide your reign. You have, of course, the Vessels to wield it?"

His challenge caught me unprepared. "I—no. You do."

"Another lie. How many does this make, so far? Seven, in matters of state, by my count. And you claim to live True?" He folded his arms.

I could barely contain myself. I'd kept the True. If now he invented lies . . .

Outside, angry screams that mirrored my mood, and the crack of a whip.

Uncle Raeth's eyes were cold. "Have you else to say, my lord Duke? You strain my vow to grant you truce."

"Hold yourself a moment longer, Raeth. Grant me—I ask all of you—a few moments, no more. Then I'll acquiesce in what you enact. Agreed?" He waited for grudging nods.

My jerkin was damp, despite the cool of the night. It must be the blaze of candles.

Uncle Mar stood to pace. "The Still of Caledon is our salvation. My sister maintained her Power in mystery, but we all know the tales of its use.

"Three attributes the bearer must enjoy." Mar raised a finger. "First, he must be crowned King, and that, you mean to do. Second"—another finger—"he must speak True, or his virtue is lost. Roddy, I ask you before Council, have you spoken True?"

"Yes." Not always, not in little things, but in all that must matter, especially of late. I prayed it was enough.

"Third"—again, a finger—"the King must be virgin, as was Elena when she wielded her Power. Roddy, I ask you by the True you claim, are you virgin still?"

"Yes!" I would kill him. By Lord of Nature, I would see him to his grave.

"That's eight." Uncle Mar looked disgusted. "The True must be cheesecloth, that his words drip through like water. My lords, I'll end this travesty. If you'll allow?" He stalked to the door, flung it open, clapped his hands, beckoned.

A beautifully dressed woman strode through the door. Gold glinted at her neck, above an ample bosom. It took me a moment to realize she was Chela, Rustin's paramour. For a time, I forgot to breathe. Had

Rust, in his rage, betrayed me? Why else flaunt her in my face? What tie bound him to Duke Mar?

"Is this he?" My uncle's words cut like a knife.

"Yes, my lord." Modestly, Chela looked to the marbled floor.

"Raeth, meet Chela, late of the keep of Llewelyn. My good woman, we're before the Council of Caledon, who must know the King's carnal relations. Have you, ah . . ." He paused, in apparent delicacy. "Have you and this boy had sexual union?"

Her placid face raised to mine. "Many times."

I shot to my feet. "You lie!"

"Go on, my dear."

"Five that I recall. It was while we rode, he and his brother and the old nurse." Chela blushed, and curtsied to the earls. "Pardon, my lords. Is a delicate matter."

Uncle Raeth snorted. "We know how horses, peasants, and lords are made."

"Though some might forget." Mar's tone was acid, and Raeth flushed. "Tell us, girl."

"What shall I say, Lord? We were alone on the trail, and he began fumbling . . ." She giggled. "I think it was his first time. He knew not where to put it."

"Chela!" Lacking sword, I clutched the hilt of my dagger.

"Soon he got the way of it. When he was spent, we rested, then did it again."

"Lies, all of it!"

Groenfil studied me thoughtfully.

Mar was inexorable. "And then what?"

"Well, you know. Whenever we could. When Rustin—his friend— wasn't looking." Her look was venomous. "Roddy said it made Rustin jealous."

"*Stop.*" I didn't know if it was command or plea.

"The harm wasn't in doing it, boy. Every lad sweats in the night, dreaming of his time. The harm was in the lie." Mar shook his head as if with compassion. "Almost we crowned you King, to gain the Still."

"But . . . I—"

"His parts are small, but . . ." She blushed. "He grew good at it, considering. But always he worried we be caught—"

"It isn't true," I cried. "Not a word of it."

Sorrowfully, Willem shook his head. I sat mortified, while Chela wove a skillful tapestry of falsehood. No one came to my defense.

". . . can prove it."

I roused myself. I was drenched with sweat.

"How, madam?"

"High on his leg, near his sac, is a mark. Not a scar. It's . . . brownish. Like a mole. It felt odd to my fingers."

Cumber turned to me, his eyes intent. "Roddy?"

My voice was hoarse. "I have such a mark. Perhaps she heard—"

"It looks like this." She reached to the Duke's wine, dipped her finger, drew on the table. All craned forward. "Roddy liked it when I played with him."

I tottered to my feet. "Lord of Nature!" I craned my head to the ceiling, blackened from the oil of a thousand lamps. "Take me if I say not True! Let me die forthwith, and cast me to the demons' lake! I swear before thee, all she says is lies."

"Am I a whore, to be mocked? Were we not in the woods, on the way to Cumber?"

"Yes, but—"

"Did you pull off my clothes?"

"That was—"

"Did you roll on me, hold my arms?" Her eyes flashed. "Say truth!"

"I didn't—Uncle Raeth!" I whirled, tears in my tone. "Let me speak to you in private!" I sank to my knees. "By Josip my beloved father I beg thee!"

Silence. Around the hall, candles began to gutter.

"We adjourn," said Raeth at last. "I'll speak with Roddy."

In his chamber I stood before him sweating, like a peasant boy confessing his misdeeds. I could scarce look up from the floor.

When I was done he asked gravely, "That's all that transpired?"

"I swear, Uncle Raeth!" Again, I studied my boots. "She kneed me so hard I couldn't walk. Ask Rustin."

From the Earl, an odd sound. I glanced up, spotted a twinkle in his eye.

"Please don't laugh, Uncle. I can't stand ridicule." I couldn't remember when last I felt so humble.

"Come here, boy." Dutifully, I did as I was told.

He brushed hair from my eyes, patted me absently. Then, to my infinite surprise, he leaned over, planted on my forehead a gentle kiss. I glanced at the candle, but it barely flickered.

"You'd best wait outside after all," he said.

"You'll—Mar will—"

"Trust in me."

"I'm so afraid of trust." I blurted it without thought.

"Naturally; we're a royal House. And thus, we're so alone. If it weren't for Imbar . . ." Uncle Raeth patted me again, sighed wearily. "Stay near the hall while I deal with Mar." He shuffled off with the weary steps of the elderly.

I paced the anteroom, recalling the debacle at Council in Stryx. Outside, peasants and guards shouted and cursed. I hadn't the spirit to look.

An hour, by the marked candle, I sat amid the stolid guards. Once, Tursel looked in, asked a guard, "All's well?"

I stirred. "What's the commotion, without?"

"Townsfolk are hungry. There's barely enough straw for beds, and a filthy old witch riles drunken louts with nonsense. And Mar's men surround the gate." He disappeared.

Another hour passed. Despite myself, I dozed on the stairs. My kingdom in the balance, all I could do was dream.

"Sir?" A foot prodded.

I came awake.

"I brought you this." Anavar crouched, with a bowl of hot broth. Wordlessly, I took it. He watched me spoon it down. Then, "Sir, may I ask a boon?" His tone was grave.

"Not another coin, youngsire. Not a copper. You'd—"

"If we come to war . . ." His face was troubled. "If we're besieged, and the castle falls to Tantroth . . ."

"Yes?" I looked impatiently to the Council door.

"If I'm taken, I'll be put to death, but not . . . I mean—not quickly." He swallowed. "If we're to die, sir, would you give me quick release?"

"What are you saying!"

"I've seen the torment of prisoners. Your captain meant only to cut my throat; when Tantroth learns I've aided you, he'll do worse. Behead me as a noble, if all fails." Resolutely, his eyes met mine. "Father says—no, you don't like hearing that. Please, sir."

The pressure in my throat was too great. I dropped the empty bowl and ran into the night.

The torchlit courtyard stank of ordure and rot. It seemed all of Cumber Town was camped within the walls. Making my way through the throng, I wondered if a knife would find me in the shadows. I wasn't sure I'd mind.

How I yearned to be King. But not as I was to be crowned. Not with indignity, in shame, by hasty act in the dark.

Behind the stable, a shriek of fury, the crack of a whip.

Tursel, on the battlements, spotted me and hurried down the steps. "Are the lords near done, my lord?"

"I don't know."

His wave encompassed the townsfolk who milled aimlessly, the carts scattered about, the haphazard piles of sacks. "They need the Earl's attention."

I had no care for his troubles. "Set things right."

"It's not for me to usurp my lord Cumber."

"You wouldn't for a moment let your camp stink so."

He frowned. "No, I wouldn't." A pause, while he rubbed his chin. "Do you think he'd take it amiss?"

"Demons plague Cumber and all in it!" At that, Tursel's eyes widened. Quickly I made the sign of contrition; only a fool summoned demons in the night. "Sorry. If I were Raeth, I'd expect you to keep order." Tursel nodded, and his expression firmed. He strode off.

Wearily, I pushed aside a bewildered woman, shouldered past her beetle-browed consort.

A gang of ill-dressed youths passed a wineskin from one to the other, giggling. "Stay a bit," one said to his fellows. "Any moment, they'll run her through."

"Imps and demons take the stench; I can't. And her whip near put out that guardsman's eye. They say she rode through Mar's army to reach the gate."

I eased past.

Another scream, and the crack of a whip. Dogs barked shrill.

"Quick, let's see!" A boy, his beard half-grown, elbowed me aside, raced toward the stable.

"Hey, you—" He was gone. For a moment I smoldered, then took off in chase. My sword was in chambers, but I had a dagger, and my rage.

Around the corner a filthy crone held a pair of Tursel's guards at bay with a bullwhip. Where was my prey? Hiding behind her cart?

"Plague on the lot of you! Death! Let the walls fall!" The hag's voice scratched like glass. "Touch my treasure and die!"

I skidded to a halt.

I recognized that cart.

"Hag, where'd you get your wagon?" If she'd hurt Hester, I'd—

She cackled, rubbing an oozing eye. "Wouldn't we like to know? A treasure cart have we, home to take!" The dozen bystanders began to swell to a crowd, at the prospect of new mischief.

Tursel's men edged close. "Sire, that wagon reeks and she drives us all mad. Keep her talking while we grab her from the rear."

"All right." I raised my voice. "Treasure, eh? Show me." I tensed, ready to duck the whip.

"Make way!" Half a dozen guardsmen, with torches. Ahh, reinforcements. Gladly I stepped aside, but they brushed past me to the stables, and flung open the doors. In a moment they emerged with snorting horses. "Make way for Lord Margenthar's horses!"

"Make way," echoed the crone. "Make way for the treasure of Caledon!" She capered. "You couldn't, the boy told me. Couldn't beard the lion of Verein, and steal his treasure!"

"What treasure? What boy?" A rock hurtled out of the night and struck her down.

For a moment I thought she was knocked senseless, but she surged to her feet. "The boy of Caledon who'd lead you, had you a brain among you! He too was my treasure!"

In a strangled voice I creaked, "Hester?" It couldn't be. Her hair streamed about her face; her robe was filthy. I peered into the stinking cart.

"I brought him home, I did, I did." She knelt, patted a foul blanket.

Trumpets sounded. At the gates, a blaze of torches.

"Who, Hester?"

"My lovely Pytor! Home to Fort, as I promised mil—" A volley of stones smashed her into the rail. A squeak of protest, from under the blanket, or from the springs below. She struggled. ". . . promised my lady."

I tore free my blade. "Who strikes her dies! Guards, seize those louts!" I spun back to the wagon. "Hester, you saved Pytor? Truly?"

"Yes, boy." She daubed her oozing eye. "Patience, it took. Mad old Hester skulked round the castle, 'til Mar no longer watched."

"He's . . ." I gestured to the blanket.

Hester bared her teeth. "Don't wake him. He's been a long time cold and wet."

"Oh, Pytor, we'll take care of you!" Heart pounding with joy, I bent over the wagon. "Let's have you inside!" Eagerly, I threw back the fetid cloth.

Chapter 39

 CLUTCHING MY ACHING STOMACH, GRITTING MY TEETH, I trudged toward the torches set in the donjon wall.

"There he is." Genard raced down the steps. "M'lord, we been search—" He skidded to a stop. "Anavar! Lord Elryc!"

Anavar flew to my side. "Sir, let me help you." Genard wheeled, bolted inside the keep.

"No." Gently, I set aside his hand.

Faces loomed out of the light, and despite my protests, guided me, shepherded me into the keep.

"My lord Prince." Raeth, Earl of Cumber, stood squarely under the candle wheel, flanked by the lords of Council. On the stairs was Rustin, bleary, with bloodshot eyes. He bore my dented crown on a velvet bolster. Above, a horde of moths challenged the shimmering lights.

Uncle Raeth bowed, and with him, Vessa, Willem, the Lady Soushire. Rustin. Even Elryc lowered his head to me, his eyes glistening. Groenfil asked, "Couldn't you hear our call?"

"He's hurt," said Anavar. Rust started.

"No," I said. "I was ill, but am no longer." The eons I'd spent spattering my innards on the donjon wall were past. All that remained was loathing, and resolve. I shuddered with the memory of tears.

Groenfil said, "Where were you, sire?"

"In thought." That, at least, was Truth.

Again, Raeth bowed. "Rodrigo, Council dissolved the regency. All so voted except Duke Margenthar, who left us under truce. It's done, lad. Congratulations."

"I would be seated." I glanced round, saw no bench. As if by cue, the throng parted, opening my way to the great hall. With slow steps, I trod to the table, eased myself into the chair at its head. Swiftly the lords crowded in, servants also, and Tresa, Imbar, Tursel, guards.

"Rodrigo . . ." Uncle Raeth gestured for the crown to be brought. "Will you be our King?"

I paused long. "No," I said, and sat stolid, as a storm of remonstrations rocked the stones of the citadel.

When the tumult abated, Uncle Raeth made himself heard. "Why, Roddy?"

"If I'm King, Uncle, must I carry out my vows?"

"Why, yes."

"I cannot."

Lady Soushire's beady eyes were suspicious. "What nonsense is this? You schemed and bargained to be crowned, and now . . ."

I looked to Groenfil. "I swore by the True I'd not harm Lord Mar. Now I tell thee, he shall die by my hand, if not first by another."

"Why?"

I beckoned to Elryc, and when he came close, took his hand. "In vengeance for my brother Pytor, whom he murdered."

"Oh, no!" Elryc's dismay echoed from the tapestries.

At once, Rustin thrust through the crowd, knelt at my side. "Roddy, how know you this?"

"Pytor lies in the cart behind the stable, rotted. Hester is gone mad."

"My prince—"

"I suppose it was prying him from the ground that unhinged her. Mar buried him by night in the very field where we met. The wire is still on his throat. Hester drove him here, seeking passage to Fort."

None spoke. Only Elryc's sobs broke the silence. Rustin stroked my hand. Tresa brought water, and set it before me. It sat untouched.

"So you see, I cannot be King."

Groenfil said, "How certain he did this?"

"Nurse Hester left us to seek Pytor in Verein. My brother was hostage in our beloved uncle's care."

Rustin's eyes rose, met Groenfil's.

The Earl nodded. "Sire, I release you from your pledge. My sister only I would see saved." He glanced right, and left. "A hard man I knew him. But Prince Pytor was an infant."

My voice was stony. "Hear me, all. I'm not a boy. The youngsire Rodrigo died kneeling on the cobbles, spattered with vomit. I discharge your vows of fealty. Crown me at your peril. I'll abide no grief, no compassion, no remorse 'til Caledon's free from Eiber, and Margenthar dead. The promises I've made, I'll heed to the letter; no more, no less."

I forced myself to my feet. "You feared a weakling as King? Be warned, my lords. Now am I strong, and without mercy."

Silence, that stretched forever.

Slowly did Raeth, Earl of Cumber, as if mesmerized, lift my crown and set it to my head.

The proper words were said. The trumpets rang, and my ascension was proclaimed from the steps of the keep. In the great hall, the lords one by one made their bows, as vassals to liege. The servants brought more wine. All drank to me. Through the uneasy festivity I sat motionless, savoring the ache of my belly.

Now would my careless promises come due.

I snapped my fingers, for Anavar's attention. "I will speak."

A noble's son was he, and knew the decorum of state. He sang out, "My lords, my ladies, hear the King!"

Silence.

I said, "In my quest to claim the throne, I promised what I ought not. My lord Cumber, bring Imbar hence." Quelling my distaste, I borrowed a sword, laid it to shoulder, granted him the nobility Raeth desired.

Vessa made no effort to hide his distaste. Nor did Groenfil.

"Uncle, provide us a chamber, wherein half a dozen may confer. Rustin, Groenfil, Lady Soushire, Tursel and you three guards, come." In moments, we stood outside a stone room, whose far wall was a huge hearth. Inside were benches, and a table spread with silk.

"Rustin, now you'll learn what first I conceived in Soushire's keep, what I've held privy." I took deep breath. "Now, my lady, my lord Groenfil: your weapons. Don't bother looking askance; I command it." Soushire surrendered a dagger; Groenfil dagger and sword.

"Tursel, you and your guards sit with them. Neither is to harm the other. They must stay an hour. Then, they're free to depart." I faced Groenfil. "Lady Soushire's price for her vote was your lands. I granted her petition."

"Demon's spawn!" But for Tursel, he'd have launched himself at my throat. "By the True you swore! I gave you fealty, put our fate in your—"

"Did I not beg you to forbear? Did I not?"

"Best kill me now, false Lord!" A moan, from the hearth, as wind stirred the ashes.

"Oh, have peace, sir. I begged you not to press your bargain, but you refused. Take comfort; I give you lands worth as much. My lady, your lands are sworn to Groenfil."

She growled. It was a sound I'd not choose to hear.

I grated, "I'll give arms and men to each of you, to secure what I granted. You're both fools; I abhor your greed. Stay awhile, and consider your course. Would you join in revolt against me? I give you leave. Would you trade estates? It's done. Would you negate what you require of me, and each keep your own? Merely say the word. Tursel, shut the door." I left.

Rustin gazed at me with wonder.

"For good or ill," I said, "it was the only way I could see."

"If Groenfil had not made his claim?"

"I'd not be King." I stalked to the hall. "I need air."

There was no guard. I flung open the door. A raging gale tore it from my hands. The candles guttered.

A slavering mongrel's red eyes blazed in the night. He lunged. Teeth fastened in my leg. I screamed. Rust's dagger sliced. The hound yelped and was still.

On the steps, a pack of frantic curs bayed. The wind shrieked. Together, Rust and I forced shut the door.

Shaken, I limped to the great hall. "Demons, Rust."

"Powers." His eyes flitted to the chamber we'd left. "You enraged both the Lord and Lady."

I swallowed, made my way to my seat.

Outside, a fierce storm battered the walls. The maddened howl of dogs stiffened the hair on my neck.

I glanced at the hour candle, burning long past midnight. It had been too long a day, too full.

"We will rest," I said.

The bedchamber was high above. I set my teeth against the weariness and the ache of the stairs.

Rustin and Anavar helped me disrobe, awkward and unsure as two fresh-trained body-servants. I rinsed my face, and in a daze, let my hands linger over the ewer. After a time, I let Anavar guide me across the chamber, and fell onto the down-stuffed bed. Rust dismissed Anavar, set the sturdy beam in the door's bolt.

He cast his gaze about, found pillows piled on a lounge. Quickly he threw them to the floor alongside my bed, drew his sword, placed it at his side, lay on the floor at my feet.

Fitting. Now I was King; the time for Rustin's touch was past. I need be strong, and cold of heart.

I blew out the bed candle, lay unhappy in the windswept night.

"What dreams the imps brought me, last night . . ." I yawned in the clear cold morn, and froze. Stretching, I'd felt pangs of protest from the stiff muscles of my stomach. "It was real?" Half question, half statement. "Lord of Nature." I rubbed away sleep, fearing my head would throb from drink. "Had I wine last night?"

"That was I." Rustin's voice was listless. "I'm ashamed."

"Pah." I padded across the floor, threw open the shutters. "A day we'd all soon forget. You were no worse . . . oh." I stared.

"What is it, my prince?"

Beyond Raeth's walls rippled a sea of black. Already sappers were at work, digging trenches from which they'd inch their way across disputed ground. Officers on horse directed the work, and cantered among an army of billowing tents. Black banners flew above fresh-planted center poles.

"Tantroth." Rust's reassuring hand crept to my shoulder.

"Duke of Eiber." For a time, I stared down at the labor.

"Look."

I followed his finger. To our north, Tantroth's force spread out of sight beyond the castle's east wall. And to our west, a narrow path, less than a spear-hurl, separated them from a second army, facing us for siege. "Uncle Mar."

"They've made common cause."

With sinking heart I reached for my clothes, and my coronet. "I'd best go down," I said. "And see who hasn't fled in the night."

Uncle Raeth's breakfast table was set with its customary riches. I found him presiding happily over so many lords and ladies as seldom gathered. "Ah, Rodrigo." He stood, made the bow of one intimate to another, of the royal family. "Do join us." Willem and Vessa stood politely.

Across the hall, Lady Soushire watched me with beady eyes. I nodded, choosing among a bowl of fruit. "Where's Groenfil?"

"Here," said a voice behind me, and I jumped. The Earl's eyes were cold. "My lord." He made a short bow, correct in every particular, cold as ice.

Inwardly, I sighed. It was no more than I deserved. I'd somehow have to undo my folly. To divert my thoughts I asked idly, "Has Tantroth sent envoy?"

"None," said Uncle Raeth.

"Odd, that he'd not seek to divide us." Or, perhaps he already had. Digesting the alarming thought, I kept my face impassive.

Soushire stumped to the table. "Why go to the trouble, when our King does that of his own?"

I chewed that over, with an unripe apple.

Elryc entered, saw me, ran to my side. "Roddy." He thrust my arm around his shoulder.

"What troubles you, brother?" My tone was gentle.

"I've been . . . Hester. She won't even . . . Oh, Roddy." He wept.

"She's no better?" We'd had her brought into the castle, and tended. He shook his head.

"Raeth, have you place in the courtyard to bury Pytor?" That detail couldn't wait. Idly, I listened to his proposal. A granite circle, upright stones, a marker of bronze. I waved assent. "Rust?" I craned my head. "Come talk."

Elryc stirred from my breath. "He's not here, Roddy."

"We came down togeth—very well." I brooded. "And, Anavar?" He too was missing. Abruptly, I stood. "Uncle, lend me your garden. I would be alone." Without waiting for answer, I crossed to the wide doors, slipped through, shut them behind.

Little was left of Uncle's pride and joy; the night's fierce gale had ravaged nearly all his blooms. Nervously, I glanced about, but saw no dogs.

I paced the ragged plantings until my legs grew tired. I sat at a marble bowl, in which the residue of the night's rain puddled. What would you say, Rust? That I deserved what I'd got? Of course; I'm not complaining.

Idly, I rubbed my palms.

And Rust, why are you so sullen? Is it that I'm King, and escape your counsel, your chastisement? No, you were foul two nights past, before it was decided. Oh, I've tried you, I admit. Not as before, in Nurse Hester's cottage, but surely enough. I'm impetuous, imperious, improvident. Imprudent, at times. But I love—that is, admire you, respect you. Can you not see? I'll tell you, when I find you. I'll speak True, so you must believe.

An autumn breeze rustled the torn leaves.

Well, Rust, pretend for a moment you're not annoyed with me. What shall I do about Groenfil and the Lady Soushire? I abused them, never mind their greed. I tricked them into voting lawfully for my coronation. That gave me the crown, but at the cost of their enmity. How can I make it right?

"Speak True."

I leaped to my feet, stifling a scream. That voice . . . "Mother?"

Silence, then a faint voice within. *"Do the unexpected."*

I sighed. I need not pretend it was Mother who gave such sensible advice. I'd duped my way to the throne; if I didn't learn honesty, my kingdom would melt away. As for avoiding the obvious . . . well, I'd learned *something* treading the halls of kings.

So, now. Shall I fight Tantroth with foes gathered under my very banner? What mischief will Uncle Mar stir among us now? Oh, I deserve it; I already know that. If only I had the Still. What wisdom it brought I sorely needed. But Mar had the Vessels, and we were blood enemies.

"To whom do you growl, my lord?"

I whirled, kneading my hands. "Tresa. My lady." I gave a short bow, barely polite. "I asked for solitude."

"I didn't know." A scant curtsy, and she was striding off.

"Wait!"

"You wanted to be alone."

"But now I don't." I stamped my foot. "Must I always be childish with you? Help me be other."

Something in my plea stayed her tart riposte. "All right, Roddy. I mean, Lord King."

"Roddy. It's how you'll always think of me." I made an effort to smile. "The name sounds sweet on your lips."

To my amazement, she blushed.

I paced amid the rows of earth. "I was wondering how to make amends."

"For what?"

"So much. I tried to be kinder, really I did. Rust helped. I even succeeded, after a fashion. But I've so much to learn, and no time." I cocked an ear to the clang and clatter of Eiber's troop, beyond the walls. "I would lead, but I'm thwarted by who I am."

"It was you they chose last night."

"But I—"

"Knowing your faults."

"Not all of them." I brooded on Groenfil and Soushire. Hadn't Rust warned me against deceit, ever more urgently? I turned to Tresa. "Even Rustin, I've driven away."

"No, my lord. He's your friend."

I studied her face, and at last recalled her words, cast aside in the heat of the day's events. "What said you that day when I spoke of Rustin? You thought for my crown we had . . . what?"

Her face was resolute. "It's for him to tell you, if he would."

"I won't have that!" I could bear no more. "Speak, my lady. As King I command it!"

A few moments later, she left. I stood ashen, staring at a rainbow of blossoms. Was it so lonely, to be King? Was this what must be?

I threw open the doors. Conversation in the great hall ceased. I crossed to the table. "Summon our Lord Rustin, and our ward Anavar." I took a seat. "By your leave, Uncle. This is your house, but we have business of state."

"Of course, Roddy. My lord."

"Very well. Outside, all of you, except my lord Groenfil and Larissa of Soushire. Await my call."

When we were alone the Lady glowered from across the table. Groenfil's face was cold and distant.

I hesitated, assailed by doubts. Still, I knew what must be done. "How have you decided?"

Neither wanted to speak. At last Groenfil said, "To keep our realms."

"It's wise. You see . . ." Abruptly I stood to pace; this would be harder than I thought. "Know you this: First, no matter what may come, I swear by the True, by Caledon, by all I hold dear, I shall not again use an oath to deceive you, to trick you by canny wording, or to let you believe that which is untrue. All I have attained by such oaths, I renounce."

"What say you?" Groenfil made no effort to hide his mistrust.

"This." I took the coronet from my brow, laid it amid the abandoned dishes of breakfast.

"What trick—"

I looked with longing at the coronet. "Yes. Renounce." A long pause. "Where was I? Oh, yes. I beg your forgiveness. If you grant it, I swear you'll have no truer friend, nor more grateful monarch, 'til I draw my last breath."

I had their attention, fully. I essayed a smile, but it didn't come out right. "Do I think you greedy and foolish, to covet each other's lands over some ancient quarrel? Yes. Do I think the less of you for it? Yes." I bore their searing gaze. "But I turned your greed against you, and sullied the crown I would honor. I can't have it so."

Groenfil snarled, "You've no right—"

"I've no right at all. Last night I bade you confer. Today I ask it again. When you're done, give the crown to Uncle Raeth for my successor. Or bring it to me in the garden, if truly you'd see me wear it."

"Roddy!" Groenfil's command caught me halfway to the door.

"Yes, my lord?"

"Don't expect the crown, after your treachery."

"Why, no, my lord."

"You don't want to be King?"

"More than I can bear!" I hesitated, looked past him to some dream of Caledon. "But there's a kind of King I'd be. I've started wrong, and must retrace my steps. I think of the honor you showed me, riding at my side from your keep, despite the secrets I withheld. Sir, I would deserve that honor."

His eyes bored into mine. Uncomfortable, I turned to the Lady. "Larissa, I cannot give you Groenfil. But I proffer my friendship, if you'll forgive my deceit."

She snorted. "What have you, to match what Mar and Tantroth would offer?"

"Myself. And that's little indeed." Hesitantly, I approached her stolid frame. "Have you never wished, my lady . . ."

"Yes?"

"For an end to the intrigues, the bargains, the schemes? I'm barely grown, and I choke on them."

Her lips bared in what might have been a smile. "You'd be King without them?"

I took deep breath. "Not entirely. But I must have those whose souls I trust. If I am betrayed, then so be it. I cannot live otherwise." I turned back to the garden.

Why was I not surprised, then, when the lords of Groenfil and Soushire brought my coronet to the garden, with civil words? I felt a player in a dream, afloat on a sea of indifference. I embraced them, wishing I could feel the gratitude I'd promised.

After, I bade the doors be thrown open, and my lords admitted. With them came Rustin, Anavar, Tresa. Even Genard, attending Elryc.

Uncle Raeth had been busy; he spoke of the orders he'd given for dispositions of troops, the relative strength of the various walls.

"Does Tantroth attack?" Of course not, else the alarums of trumpets would have overridden all other concerns. "Then send envoy."

"Why? What terms could you possibly—"

"Say that Rodrigo King of Caledon bids Tantroth welcome to our domain." I reveled in their consternation. "Invite him to dine. Safe-conduct, and all that."

"Roddy, have imps taken your wits? He's come to make war."

I chose not to hear insult. "See how Tantroth replies. Now, to other business. To each of you I humbly apologize for my late manners. And for toying with the True. I will speak honestly henceforth, and any noble is free to reprimand me should I not." I sat, drummed my fingers on the table. "The Council of State is disbanded."

"What?" Whoever said it spoke the dismay of all.

"I so decree. Who claims I cannot rule without Council?" I faced down their disapproval. "Now do I appoint privy councilors, to advise me in all things. I name Lord Groenfil and Lady Soushire, to remind me of humility. My uncle, Lord Cumber, who was first to support me, when my claim was weak. Elryc my brother, whose words are wise and honest. Lord Rustin. And Anavar, late of Eiber."

"Rodrigo!" Uncle Raeth's cheeks held spots of pink. "Myself, I appreciate the honor, but Anavar—that goes too far."

"How so?"

"If you'd reward a lover, give him gold, or—"

"He's not my bedmate. Rustin's been that." It brought stunned silence, as eyes across the hall flickered to Rust, and away. "Did I not tell you I'd speak True?"

The Earl rallied. "It's not fitting. The boy's an Eiberian."

"Easily remedied. Anavar of Eiber, come hence." I put a hand on his shoulder. "I declare you Baron of the southern reaches of Caledon. Will you be my vassal?"

He fell to his knees. "Don't toy with me, I beg thee."

"Will you?"

He gulped. "Sire, in all matters save war against Lord Tantroth . . ." He could say no more.

A borrowed sword, the ritual words, his palm to my chest, and it was done. "Lands will follow. Perhaps some part of Mar's estate in Verein, that doesn't go to Elryc." I stood. "This afternoon we'll confer regarding our attackers. Captain Tursel will join us. For now, I retire to my chambers. Lord Rustin, accompany me." I swept out, oblivious of the hasty bows in my wake.

In our rooms, Rust unbuckled his sword and stretched. "You were wonderful. Did you see—"

I spun him to face me, shoved him to the wall. "Vile creature!"

His eyes widened.

"Among the others, I was silent. But between us, let there be no—" I pummeled his chest.

He caught my arm. "Stay your blows. For what crime do you berate me?"

"Imbar!"

At first he held my eyes. I raised a fist to strike him, but he sank to a chair.

"How could you? I vomit at the thought!"

A whisper. "Stop."

"Only the son of a foul traitor . . ." My voice rose, and my invective soared. When I was done, I flung open the door. "Get out! Sleep with your new lover, or with Genard. Trouble me no more!"

In the corridor, his hand reached out, as if in supplication. "It was for you."

"I won't hear it!" I slammed the door with a mighty crash.

I'd no sooner begun pacing when a knock came. "My lord?" Anavar.

"What, boy?" I tried not to snarl.

His face was tear-streaked. "You do me too much honor."

"Bah. I'm protecting you from my rages."

"I have title, yet I'm still your ward."

"Well, of course. You're not grown."

"Father says—"

"Please!" I covered my ears.

"I'm sorry." Tremulously, he crossed to face me. "Sir . . . Lord King—"

"'Sir' will do, as before."

"I didn't know how to thank you, in the great hall. You raise me from servant to earl—"

"Not in one step." I had to smile.

"They speak of you in awe. They say Groenfil and Soushire converse, who've been foes for years. They say Earl Cumber . . ."

I sighed. "Anavar, already I'm lonely."

"I'll call Lord Rustin."

"No, he's the cause." I closed my eyes.

"What's come between you?"

"That's none of your—" I grimaced. Would I speak True, or no? "He allowed Imbar to debauch him, so the valet would urge Uncle Raeth to support me. Our friendship is done forever."

"Father says forever lies across steep hills; your steed may tire before reaching it." He hesitated. "Sir, I've no love for Rustin; he beat me with his scabbard. But don't lock him from your life."

"Who are you, to tell me what to do?"

"Baron, and Privy Councilor, sir." His gaze was defiant.

"Oh." I swallowed. "Yes. Well . . ." I sighed, suddenly finding it hard to speak. "I loved him. Not, of course, as I'd love a woman." My words seemed too hasty, and perhaps a touch false. No, I wouldn't think of that. "He was my true friend. And he betrayed me."

"As did his father."

My eyes burned. Smoke from the kitchens, no doubt. I forced my mind elsewhere. "Anavar, I have no proper court. The best service you can give is to attend me. Call those whom I seek; relay my words. When we're home in Stryx, protocol will sort itself out. Chamberlain Willem will help . . ." I made a vague gesture. "Let's find Raeth."

In the courtyard, Tursel had made great progress in settling the displaced townsfolk. His men had improvised rough shelters, in which villeins and merchants alike huddled. The pathways had been cleared of carts and barrows. Raeth's stables were full to overflowing with horses and mules.

I found my uncle outside the kitchens, glaring at sweating cooks who labored over bubbling cauldrons. "That we have a horde of guests doesn't mean you need oversalt the soup. By the demons' lake, you know better! Tresa, watch over them. We've a reputation to uphold. Hello, Roddy. Or shall I call you King?"

"You're too old to change your ways," I growled. "Tease me as you will. It's your nature."

"Isn't he a gracious sovereign, Anavar?" My uncle pursed his lips. "Perhaps I owe you an apology, my Lord of the Southern Reaches. Yet you were a foreigner at the time, perhaps I don't. What say you?"

Anavar gaped.

I said, "He'll delight in disconcerting you, boy, now you're landed nobility and worth the trouble. Pay him no heed, unless the candles flicker."

Uncle bowed to acknowledge a point scored. "No reply yet from our, um, guest outside the walls. Ah, Imbar, what have you, a scroll? Perhaps I spoke too soon."

Breathing heavily, the erstwhile valet read aloud his missive. Tantroth Duke of Eiber would partake of Cumber's hospitality, and meet under truce the boy pretender to the throne of Caledon.

I clenched my teeth, determined to make no outburst. After, I was proud of the effort.

So Tantroth would commit to our honor, knowing that one prick of a dagger could end him. He was no coward. I filed the knowledge.

For a warrior in siege, Tantroth made an imposing entrance. He'd been allowed only six retainers, but two dozen men-at-arms accompanied him as far as our torchlit walls. They bore banners enough for a legion. After the gates closed I would slip inside, and be waiting when Tantroth entered the great hall, but now I paced the battlements with agitation, disguised in a shabby cloak.

Was I wise to let Tantroth within our keep? He'd be well watched and amply guarded, but nothing would blunt his observations. Yet Caledon had never been an armed camp. His spies had entered Cumber's gates on many an occasion, and he no doubt had maps of the castle as fine as our own.

Tantroth's honor guard reined in well clear of the wall, so we need not fear treachery. Nonetheless, two scores of our guard stood ready to force shut the door.

Tantroth passed through without incident, and his six retainers behind. Black he wore, as did his men. Fine colors for autumn, I thought. But what of summer? Did his men, outlandishly forced to dress alike, suffer from heat in their garb? Perhaps someday I'd take that into account.

Tantroth's hair was gray, his face grizzled and lined. I was shocked; I'd not thought him old.

I stared down from the battlement, reminding myself it was his orders that had burned peasants in their huts, in search of me. Yet I'd invited him to my table. Was I any better than he?

The Earl of Cumber stood forth, to welcome Tantroth with due ceremony. It was a marvel we could all pretend the Duke of Eiber had no army waiting to breach our walls, and we weren't stocked for siege.

Reluctantly, I trotted to a side stairs, and disappeared into the throng of the courtyard. Moments after, I was at the head of Uncle Raeth's table, awaiting our guest. As I'd ordered, Elryc sat at my side. I'd promised he'd be my counsel, and today redeemed my pledge. Genard watched him from the servants' place by the wall, with eyes of pride.

As for Anavar, he was banished to my chamber with a plate of dinner, ordered to open for no voice save my own. I would not allow that he and his first liege meet. For a moment I wondered if I'd truly done the boy good service; how his head must spin in sorting out his loyalties.

Cumber's voice rang out from the entry. "My lord King Rodrigo: your vassal Tantroth, Norduke of Eiber, and his retinue." To me, Uncle Raeth made the formal bow, the deep bow of state.

Tantroth's lips played in a smile. He bowed politely to Raeth, and acknowledged me with barely more than a nod. Not the bow of vassal to lord, it wasn't even the notice of equals.

He'd left me no choice; I kept my seat. Better to ignore his bend entirely than to reply with similar discourtesy or, worse, bow to him as a superior. I glanced about, hoping for a moment to catch Rustin's eye, but of course he was absent. I said, "My lord Norduke, we bid thee welcome."

"Greetings, Roddy." He coughed. "A fine banquet, Lord Cumber." At that, Tresa caught my eye with a sympathetic smile. My fingers eased their grip on the armrest.

Uncle Raeth waved airily. "Simple fare, I regret."

I said, "Come, Lord Tantroth, sit at my right. Brother, meet our esteemed Norduke." Elryc stood, bowed with such respect that Tantroth was forced to bow in return or seem a churl. Perhaps I should have done the same, and set the Norduke in his place. I filed the lesson in the recesses of memory; I could learn much, if I watched.

Over the soup I turned to Tantroth and said pleasantly, "So, my lord. Will you presume on our hospitality this winter, when your men freeze in their tents?"

"I'll be long home—" He was stopped by a deep, hacking cough that seemed without end. Finally, he wiped his mouth, took a swallow of wine. "My seven thousand are ample to surmount your walls. I'll leave my barons here to rebuild our holdings."

"I think not." I smiled agreeably. I trusted Tursel's estimate of eleven thousand. Of course, Tantroth wouldn't want me to know his true strength, but it was a wily move to undervalue it.

He said sourly, "Boys your age know nothing of war."

Even Uncle Raeth drew sharp breath.

I said, "A pity you left me no choice. I really hoped not to cede Eiber."

"It's not yours to cede me."

"Not to you, my lord." I broke bread, dipped it in the remains of my soup. "To the Norlanders. They have the strength to evict you." While I seemed to watch my bowl, my whole being waited his reaction.

What I suggested was no idle threat. Eiber served as a buffer between us and the feared Norlanders. Their nation dwarfed Caledon, and moreover the Rood of the Norland was justly feared in battle.

"You haven't treated with the Norland. I'd know." His voice was confident. "And you wouldn't. Their sword is sharpened at both edges."

If he was certain I hadn't, he'd not want me to have the knowledge. My heart leaped. "You started so well, Lord Tantroth, taking us by surprise. And after, your intelligence was brilliant; how did you guess Mar sent plague victims to rest in Stryx Castle?" I barely paused. "I'd reckoned you'd enter and your armies be decimated by now."

His smile was crooked. "Say all of that by the True."

"Hardly. I won't ever speak to you by the True, not even in treaty. Else you'd know when I lie."

"As you do now."

"Perhaps you're right. Yet you're beaten, my lord, by your own miscalculation." I had to take care, and phrase my insinuations as questions. A false declaration might cost me the Still.

Again, the hacking cough, but only for a moment. "How say you?"

"Mother, fair Elena, would have died to keep Caledon whole. I'm a callow boy; I'll take what I can get. What if I ceded the Norlanders all Eiber, and half of Cumber with it, and gave Uncle Raeth Verein to compensate?"

I glanced to Lord Cumber for his accord, and luckily, he was up to it. He managed to look dour, and not surprised.

Tantroth was seized with a fit of coughing.

I said solicitously, "You're ill, my lord."

"Aye, it will carry me off, this wheeze." His face set in a death's-head grin. "But not yet. You were saying?"

"That you've erred. Do you think Hriskil of Norland will promise me your head? And should you try to withdraw, I'll harry you to the hills." I owed him no mercy.

Tantroth snarled, "You'd toy with me, youngsire? No wonder Mar wants to box your ears. Go with women, before you call yourself a man!"

A sharp rap, from several seats below. Willem raised his glass. "Your health, my lords. I salute you both." His face was earnest, and compelling. Seething, white of face, I raised my glass, spilling half my wine.

After the dinner, and Tantroth's ceremonial departure, Elryc and I walked to his room. "You confused him, Roddy. That's good. Even if he thinks you gull him, he sees you as a worthy opponent."

"Wonderful," I grumbled. "Now he'll respect me as he slays me."

"He won't." Elryc drew me into a hug. "You act the King. I'm proud."

I rustled his hair, speechless. What had come of our carping and enmity, in days so recent?

"Roddy . . ." He faced me, resolute. "We'll fight off Tantroth, or he'll leave. You'll rule well. But one thing you must do, and soon."

"What's that, brother?" After the night's tension, I felt magnanimous.

"Make your peace with Rustin."

"Devils and imps take—what's come over my court? You, Anavar—shall I have no reprieve? Rustin is my problem, not yours!"

Elryc was unfazed. "Am I your counselor? Do you keep your oath?"

"Yes!"

"Heed my advice. Else you'll be miserable."

"Because we shared a bed when I had need? I'm past that now. A man must—"

"Would I had a friend as close as he to you!" His eyes teared. "You throw away treasure!" He darted into his room.

Not knowing where else to go, I climbed the stairs, searched out Hester's chamber. Perhaps there was some remnant of sage advice in the ruin of her mind. A servant quietly let me in.

"Hello, Nurse."

She opened an eye, lifted her head from the table. She peered about, as if dazed. "Where are we?"

"In Cumber."

"Ah. They told me." She pried open her other eye. "I'm still half-blind." Pus oozed from under the eyelid.

I pulled up a stool, and sat. "It must hurt."

"I'm beyond hurt." A laugh, that became a cackle. "You've grown, Roddy. My lady will me amazed when I tell her."

My heart leaped. "You know me?"

"How could I not?" She sat rocking. "The boy who would be King." She shook her head. "Pytor was here, last hour."

"You mean Elryc," I said gently.

"Think you I don't know them apart? Pytor it was, after Elryc left. He cursed Mar." Her single eye glared balefully.

"I'll avenge him, Nurse." If I kept no other vow, I'd honor that.

"Of course." Her gaze flitted to the window. "Think you we'll go riding today, my lady and I?"

"Oh, Hester." I took her gnarled hand, laid it to my cheek.

"Go, you great overgrown—no, out!" She hobbled to her feet. "You've better to do than crumble my dreams!" She shooed me to the door. "Leave an old woman in peace!"

I beckoned the servant. "Tend her well," I advised. "As you value your life."

Chapter 40

IN THE GREAT HALL, SERVANTS CLEARED THE REMAINS OF our banquet. I waved away their bows, stared past the shutters into the night.

"The Norduke was rude, my lord." Tresa.

I nodded, turned, took her hand as if that were the most natural thing in the world. "Yes."

"Grandfather is chortling over your manner. None of us knew what you'd say next."

"Is that fitting?"

"It was necessary. We've little enough stores to last the winter, even if the walls hold. You sowed doubt." Did she squeeze my fingers, or was my imagination gone wild?

What could I say—how best to impress her? My mind spun, until I fell back on truth. "I don't know what to say, Tresa. I have little . . . experience." My face burned.

"Oh, Rodrigo. They say you hate pity, so—"

"Who told you that?"

"Rustin." Her voice was calm. "Days ago."

"Where is he?"

"About the castle, one place or another. He ate tonight in the kitchen."

"How do you know?"

"I asked, for your sake."

"For your own, rather!" I pulled my hand free. "I have no interest."

She glanced about, to the servants. "Walk me to my room, my lord. There's gossip enough."

The corridors were dim, the torches smoky. Her chambers were on the third floor.

"What will you do now, Rodrigo? About our siege."

"Who knows? Let them stew, until Mar and Tantroth set to quarreling." I shrugged. "It's a problem for the morn. I'll hear my advisors."

"Rustin among them."

"You too, my lady?" I couldn't hide my resentment. "Do you all conspire?"

"Why hate him?"

"You yourself told me why. Faugh!"

For a long moment she gazed at me, as if considering. "Come, Roddy. Sit." She waited until I complied. Then, "What is it you can't abide? That he lay with Imbar, or not with you?"

"My lady!" My cheeks were hot.

"Why can't we discuss it? You told the court he was your . . . companion. Think you it troubles me?"

My voice was strangled. "How could it not?"

"You must take solace, Roddy. That's no shame."

I realized I was kneading my jerkin, and made my hands be still. "My lady, I know you mean well, but . . ." I fought for calm. "Truly I must go."

As if I hadn't spoken she asked, "Are you jealous?"

"How dare you!" Almost I struck her.

She bit her lip, turned aside. "Grandfather adores Imbar, surely you know. It's not that Imbar has a hold over him, rather that to please him . . ."

I didn't want to hear.

"On your first visit, when you and Grandfather quarreled, the valet went to Rustin—explained he could sway Grandfather in your favor, that without him you had no hope—and told him the price." Her voice was pained. "Imbar loves Grandfather, truly he does, but he roves. There've been stableboys, and cooks . . . Grandfather shouldn't have . . ."

"Be silent, or say it all!"

"Twice Imbar took Rustin to his room." For a moment she seemed flustered. "Perhaps I should have told you before, but I thought you and Lord Rustin would speak . . . When first Imbar left, Rustin vomited on the stairs. The second time, a houseman saw his face. It was white as . . ." She said no more.

I whispered, "How could he?" My eyes sought hers. "I'm demeaned. He whored for my crown."

She dropped to her knees, took my face, raised it to meet her eyes. "Think you even now of yourself?"

"What say you?"

"What of him? What of your friend? He loved you so that even his manhood was not too great a gift."

The world wrenched into place, and I spun away, that she might not see me weep.

She gathered me to her breast. After a time my struggles weakened.

"I'm so sorry." Did I speak to her, or Rust?

Her soft fingers stroked the small of my back.

A long while passed. I kissed her gently on the nape.

She sighed. "I caused you such pain . . . my words were clumsy."

"No matter now." I kissed her again, and she raised her head. Our lips neared. Tremulously, I met them.

The candles flickered in the soft night breeze. After a time I undid my cloak. Tresa essayed a smile. We reclined on the bolster, half sitting. "Oh, Roddy. Never I thought I'd love you."

An electric thrill jolted my very senses. Could I have heard aright? I pulled back my head, looked into her eyes. They held no reproach. Her hand stroked my flank. Mine fumbled at her breast.

We lay entangled. For an instant my thoughts turned to Rustin. His touch, gentle as it was, held no compare. Joyfully, I sank into the bliss of love's embrace. Her curves were so soft, so appealing. We squirmed together, ever more urgently.

Suddenly her face twisted. "Don't!"

"Tresa . . ." I kissed her anew.

Her nails bit into my shoulder, "Roddy, the Still! *Your Power!*"

I thrust against her, eager fingers stroking her stiff nipples, my other hand sunk behind her. Her words reached me. Had I—did I—no, I still throbbed with desire.

Lord of Nature! I leaped from the couch, twisted my breeks in shame at the bulge beneath. "Imps and— Oh, what did—" I fumbled under my clothes at my tangled loincloth. Roddy, the Virgin King, exposed in the full drollery of his plight. I would be ever a boy. My face flamed beet red.

"Roddy, I'm sor—"

I bolted to the door, fled to the stairs.

An Eiberian envoy delivered the invitation, in the most flowery language of state. Ingeniously, Tantroth managed to avoid the matter of my station, addressing me most courteously, but only by name. A tourney of swordplay among his men. Dinner to follow. Safe-conduct and assurances identical to those we'd given.

Elryc, Lady Soushire, and Groenfil strenuously urged me not to go. Uncle Raeth was divided, and argued both sides. Anavar was silent and brooding. Rust was nowhere to be found.

As I saw it, I had no choice but to accept. Common folk noted the habits of their betters, and openly discussed their problems, honor, or cowardice. If I cringed in our keep after the example Tantroth set, who would follow me to war? And were the Norduke to betray his word, he'd be universally named villain.

I argued as much, but my councilors were adamant in their misgivings. I reminded them that theirs was to advise, mine to decide. For a moment I held my breath, but grudgingly, they accepted my judgment.

I yearned for Rustin, but hesitated to command his presence. To summon him against his will would only aggravate him further.

Yet I wanted not only his counsel, but his pardon. I might seek him out, demeaning as that was, but first I'd let his temper cool.

"Who will escort you, Roddy?" Uncle Raeth sounded impatient, and I forced my thoughts to the business at hand.

"Does it matter?"

"You need a train. Normally he'd expect me to do the honors, but my joints will swell tonight, and I'll have to send regrets. A pity, but together we'd be too great a temptation." He frowned. "I could send Imbar . . ."

"No." My voice was cold. "See that Baron Imbar avoids my presence."

In the end, we settled on Willem, Vessa, and a handful of servants, including Genard. Willem and Vessa were, to put it crudely, expendable; neither commanded a force at arms. On the other hand, they were at little risk, in that neither held an office of consequence.

Tantroth's troops stood back to allow us exit. It was their force that besieged the gate; Uncle Mar's troops were stationed somewhat south, near the turn of the wall.

We assembled near the stable. I wore my best cloak, and a ceremonial sword. As Rust had taught, I was fresh-bathed and scented with lavender water. My dented crown—reshaped by Uncle's goldsmith—gleamed from my brow. Cumber and the others of my Privy Council waited to see me off. I scanned the onlookers; Tresa was nowhere in sight. Thank Lord of Nature.

Ebon snorted in the brisk day's wind.

Vessa, on borrowed mount, did his best to look dignified. Chamberlain Willem seemed unhappy, but said little.

I was restless, eager to cast the die. "Are we ready?" I looked about. "Sound the trumpets. Open the gates." I spurred to the wall.

"King Rodrigo, hold!"

I reined so abruptly Ebon reared in protest. "Rustin!" Why had he engendered a public confrontation?

His tone was stiff. "Don't go."

"We'll speak privately, when I return."

"I beg you, trust him not."

I bit off a hasty reply; I would speak True. "Gladly would I have had your counsel, Rust. I even sought you. Now the time is past."

"Roddy, please. Your crown's at stake. Don't put yourself in Tantroth's hands."

I wavered. But even Rust should know not to upbraid me before my court. I took refuge in the high speech. "Lord Rustin, if thou wouldst reconcile with us, take rest in our chambers 'til our return." I turned to the guard. "Open the gate; we ride." I left Rustin in our dust.

A pity we left in day. Torches would have gilded the finery of our cortege. As it was, guards on the battlements who should have attended the enemy avidly watched our passage.

Tantroth himself rode forth to meet us. "Welcome, Rodrigo." All hint of his truculence the night before had vanished.

A proper bow from horseback is difficult. If your scabbard goads your mount as you bend, you may find yourself sitting in the dirt. We managed the amenities, and he escorted us to his tents.

He presented me to his retainers civilly enough, again avoiding my title. But I was truly taken aback when I found myself face-to-face with Lord Stire, Uncle Mar's trusted baron. His smile was that of a wolf confronting a rabbit. "Good day, my lord Rodrigo."

"And you." When last I'd seen him, he'd brought a flowery invitation from Uncle Mar, but neither of us forgot that Rust and I had once knocked him senseless in Mother's vault. I recalled his recurrent contempt, and turned to Tantroth. "Has this person been enjoined regarding our safe-conduct?"

As I'd hoped, Stire's neck flushed.

They'd marked off an arena with ropes and bunting. Tantroth showed me to a cushioned bench. Willem, Vessa, and the servants were shown lesser places.

Tantroth waved languidly. The first contestants took their places, wielding blunted epees. A red-haired fellow took on a tall, thin man whose concentration was so great he scarce saw us when he bowed our direction.

I was relieved to find the match scored by points, rather than blood. It would have been like a barbarian of Eiber to treat me to a lopping of hands and piercing of gizzards before dinner.

The swordfest was mildly interesting, but my temper had an edge. I pondered Tantroth's true motive in feting me. Was it to show the strength of his army? Each contestant was supposedly of a different corps, and adding them together, Tantroth's force far exceeded Tursel's appraisal. But pennants were cheap, and as he dressed his vassals all in black, one corps could resemble another.

The first match done, a second began. This time they used rapiers. At times the battle flowed close to our bench; I sat still and calm, though my heart raced.

The third match paired a mean-looking brute in stiff leather armor against an agile blond not more than Rustin's age. They wielded broadswords.

Falla of Toth, our swordmaster, had made me practice with the broad blade, while I was so young I could barely lift it. I loathed the task. One day Mother had watched us, and afterward, I'd not been forced to use broadsword again. A dangerous weapon, that.

Parry met thrust, over and again. The contestants grunted their effort.

Working with broadsword, the main trick is in the parry. By adroit maneuver, the fighters managed to avoid serious injury, though blood dripped from cuts and gashes. I tried not to grimace.

The heavier man, facing us, pressed the younger ever back, until he was barely a pace before us. Suddenly the youngster slipped, twisting as he fell. His sword flew down. The edge struck earth a thumbspan from my boot.

I leaped back, far too late, and fell over my bench.

Tantroth roared to his man, "Clumsy oaf!" He surged to his feet, red with rage. "Stop the match!" He hauled the unfortunate to his feet, struck him hard with gloved fist. "You there, guard him well 'til morn!" To me, "Are you hurt, Roddy?"

"No." How could my voice tremble with but one word? *I'll be coward no more,* I'd once sworn. Now, make it so. "I'm unhurt.He meant no harm." Perhaps. Perchance Tantroth meant it only as a warning. That it was an accident I didn't for an instant entertain.

"We'll see."

"I beg you, sir, not to be harsh—"

"Don't tell me how to run my camp!" Tantroth's eyes were dangerous, but a sudden smile doused his ire. "Come, let's to dinner. Enough games of war."

We trudged toward the tables set under bright canopies. If Tantroth wanted me unsettled, he'd succeeded. Willem managed to get close enough to murmur, "Steady, my lord." Genard babbled about amputations and injuries until I was at wits' end. Finally we began our meal.

Immediately the Norduke poured a full glass of wine. "Drink, Rodrigo. It was a close call."

I downed my glass, wished for another.

The dinner was adequate, and more. Cooked fruits, a delicate soup, game, a roast lamb. Taste the stewed beans, Rodrigo. Do you really think you can withhold a siege? How if I gave you free passage out of Caledon? Try the sprouts. Tantroth refilled my glass whenever I took a sip. I looked for water to dilute my drink, but found none.

All the while I searched for his purpose. Was it to fuddle my judgment, that I not understand him? To impress me with the bounty his army had bought, or looted from my people? To learn my abilities?

I untied the top laces of my jerkin. The candlelights were hot, and the tent took on a dreamlike glow.

An urgent hand, from behind. "Stop drinking, m'lord. You can't afford to be sotted!"

"Who set you my keeper, stableboy?"

"Lord Elryc said to speak as he might."

"Bah. Begone." Still, I put down my glass, contented myself with grapes to quench my thirst.

Tantroth alternated genial jests with shrewd probes he barely gave me time to fend, as if careless of my answer. I yearned for the moment I could mount Ebon and be away.

At last the banquet was done. Dusk was fast approaching. Pointedly, I stretched. I gave thanks for Tantroth's hospitality, urged him politely to return home before his cough was worse, or seek a healer's care in our stronghold. We sparred a few moments longer, and at last they brought Ebon.

"Genard, ride to the gates, bid Captain Tursel be ready."

"Aye, m'lord." He raced ahead.

A strange rendezvous. A peculiar host, but still a fine meal, if poison wasn't given. Yet Tantroth was careful to eat from every dish I'd taken. A common courtesy, that would be notable only by its absence.

Some paces from the camp, we said our words of parting.

I saw he'd withdrawn his troops a goodly distance from our walls. Not merely nearest the gates, I noticed, but for the length of the battlements. An extra courtesy, for which I was grateful.

As if fearing a well-placed arrow from our ramparts, Tantroth wheeled his horse and spurred back to his camp. I breathed deeply of the night. I was sluggish from overeating, and a glass too many of wine; I reined Ebon to a walk.

Ahead, Tursel appeared on the battlements, waving us on.

"So, Willem, what do you make of him?" A beautiful evening, save for distant thunder. Rain would refresh us, and keep full our cisterns.

"Tantroth's a deadly foe, sire. Be not deceived."

"Well, of course. But beyond that?"

The thunder grew louder. At the gate, Genard jumped up and down in his saddle, waving like a loon.

Willem said, "He's bent on—what's that noise?"

Genard bent over his mane and raced toward us.

"Is it hooves?" Alarmed, I glanced back, but in Tantroth's camp all was still. I whirled. "Lord of nature—to the gates!"

From their far camp along the wall Margenthar's cavalry roared past earthworks hastily abandoned by Tantroth for their benefit. My heels dug into Ebon's sides. Vessa bent over his pommel, whipping his mare.

Willem cried out as his horse stumbled. I reined in, clawed him to his feet. "Mount yourself!"

The stableboy tore past, circled, charged back at us. "Genard, help him!" Tugging at my sword, I galloped toward the wall. The gate was ajar, awaiting us.

The first of Mar's troops were paces away.

My cursed sword was nearly useless; resplendent with sapphires mounted in gold, it was a single-edged toy. I slashed at an outthrust arm, was rewarded with a scream.

Three horsemen barred my way. Behind them the gate swung closed. What treachery was this? With a shriek I launched myself, and barely avoided being skewered. Steady, boy. Remember your lessons. Thrust and parry. Feint. Defend.

Margenthar's troop thundered down on us. The gate swung open. Now, what madness? Were we ceding the keep to Uncle Mar?

Mounted and armored, Tursel raced onto the plain. He waved, urging on a mass of his riders mired behind our own infantry.

The two forces closed. Willem swung a short sword; he was no warrior. A foeman came up behind him. Genard leaped from his steed, clutched the attacker from behind, bit down on his neck. The soldier screamed. Genard wrestled the sword from his grasp, smashed the hilt to the rider's temple, threw down the slack body.

I swung Ebon about, avoiding pike thrusts. A dozen men barred my way to the gate. I saw Vessa canter to the safety of the walls.

"Demon's spawn!" Savagely, I hacked at an unyielding form. I needed a shield. "Begone!"

The man stumbled. I sliced at his helmet, was rewarded with a satisfying clang and a snarl of fury. I'd done no damage. I reared Ebon, let his hooves fight for me. The foeman went down. Again I reared, my right arm out for balance.

Someone seized my outflung wrist. Ebon plummeted, his deadly hooves striking, and restrained by the foeman's grip, I plunged from the saddle.

Flat on my back, I fought for wind. Whinnying, Ebon cantered off. Screams, shouts, the clang of steel.

I struggled to sit. A foot trod on my stomach. I rolled over, retching.

"There he is!" Soldiers helped me rise.

"Thanks," I gasped. Where had my sword gone? "Find me a—"

Men of Verein.

I broke free, to plunge into the melee. Someone grabbed my jerkin, hauled me back.

I spotted Tursel, frantic, his eyes upon me. I spun at my attacker, clawing at his face. He clubbed me with his shield.

The world reeled.

Mother, help me. Rust, you were right.

I'm sorry, Elryc. Do better than I.

Black.

Chapter 41

I WOKE, HEAD THROBBING, BOUND HAND AND FOOT IN A jouncing cart. The more I struggled, the worse the cords cut.

I bucked and heaved, trying to sit. I struck my temple against the side of the cart. My scalp blazed anew.

My hands were tied to my feet, on a rope with little slack. I tried to draw up my knees, to gnaw the ropes.

A shadow passed. Alongside the cart rode Baron Stire, his dagger drawn. His black eyes never left mine. Casually, I leaned back.

The wagon in which I rode was deep within a column of horse. The riders bristled with arms. Spearmen to the outside, swordsmen within, they trotted down the furrowed road. The wagoneer drove with reckless abandon, bouncing me from rut to rut.

I took stock. My dagger was gone, and of course my sword. I couldn't see my diadem; I must have lost it in the melee.

Stire leaned over, smiled, and spat in my face. I recoiled, unable to raise my hands to wipe off the spittle. Instead, I asked politely, "A trick you learned from your mother?"

He grasped my hair, slammed my head against the sideboard. I gritted my teeth, rode swirling waves of pain.

I lay too low in the cart to gain much sense of our destination, but I could guess: Verein.

Ah, Rustin, if only I'd listened.

I twisted my aching wrists.

At last the cart slowed. A clatter of hooves, shouted commands. For a moment I dreamed of rescue, but Stire paid no heed to the ruckus. Slowly, the craggy turrets of Verein drifted past the cart.

Through the gates. My cart stopped. Arms hauled me out, dragged me unceremoniously through the mud.

Moments after, I was in a stonewalled cell deep within the donjon. They'd freed my feet, but retied my hands behind my back. The door slammed shut. Bolts scraped.

In one corner, a pile of damp straw. High above, on the outer wall, a barred window; at least I'd know night from day. I licked my lips. There was no water, and with my wrists bound behind, no way to bring it to my mouth.

"Mother." I recoiled at my voice; I hadn't known I'd spoken aloud. Mother, what should I do? Wait? Scream? Sit?

What will Stire do with me? Is Mar here, or at Cumber? Is Raeth's castle breached? I sank on the straw. What of Rust? I'd spurned him before all my court; he could never pardon me.

It was all I could do to keep from gibbering. From Mother, no response, even in the recesses of my mind.

The day passed, and a night. My lips cracked from thirst. I could no longer feel my hands. To ease my terror I spoke to Anavar, to Elryc. I begged Rust's forgiveness. I curled under his blanket, rested my head in the crook of his arm.

The scrape of a bar. I staggered to my feet. The door opened. Stire, with guards. One bore a serving board. A shank of meat, an apple, a slab of bread. My mouth watered. Stire took the tray, dumped the contents into my straw bedding. "Root in that, youngsire."

"Untie me," I croaked, but I was barely audible.

Stire snorted his contempt, and the door slammed shut.

On my knees, weeping with frustration, I bobbed in the filthy straw for the apple. Behind me, pains tore at my wrists. At last I nuzzled the apple to the wall, got my teeth into it, carved out a bite. As I chewed, the remainder rolled into the bedding. I fell upon it, took a bite of apple and foul straw.

The juice teased my raging thirst. While I wrestled with the meat, many-legged creatures scuttled across my face. After, I lay exhausted. I needed to piss, but they'd provided no chamber pot. Not even a hole in the floor. Moreover, I had no way to loosen the rope of my belt. I wondered if I'd be spared the misery and humiliation of wetting myself.

As the distant light faded to night, the door scraped again.

"Get him up."

My eyes snapped open. Uncle Mar.

As hands dragged at my arms I cried out in torment. Nonetheless I found myself on my feet, held by each arm. I squinted past the torch. Mar, Stire, two guards. One of them carried another board of food, and a narrow-mouthed jug.

My uncle turned to Stire, his tone grim. "The pleasure of Roddy is to be mine, not yours."

Stire grunted.

Mar's eyes were coals. "Do you usurp me, sir?"

"No, my duke," Stire said quickly. He shot me a venomous look.

"Free his wrists. Don't slash him."

Stire spun me around. In a moment my hands dropped to my sides. I could feel nothing. I raised them to my face. My wrists were oozing and swollen.

"Stire dislikes you."

I croaked, "A pity."

Uncle Mar slapped me so hard I saw fire. "As do I." To the guard, "Leave him the board, but not water. Let him drink his fill while you wait, then take away the jug."

"Aye, my lord."

I stifled a sob. By all the demons of the lake, I wouldn't cry while they watched. I would not.

Mar strode out, Stire a step behind. The guard handed me the jug. I fumbled with numb fingers. No matter how hard I tried, I couldn't raise it to my lips.

One guard watched, impassive. The other frowned, pried the jug from my hand, held it to my mouth, tilted.

I drank of life.

After a time I had to stop for breath. Then greedily I sought again the stoneware teat. When the bottle was drained I nodded my thanks. They left me in dark.

I gnawed my dinner, pausing from time to time to lick the ooze from my wrists. My fingers began to sting; perhaps it was a hopeful sign.

After, I pounded on the door to attract a guard. None came. Unable to wait, I relieved myself in the farthest corner. Mother, Rustin . . . stay with me, take my hand. Tell me tales of yore.

I unhooked my bedraggled cloak, decided I needed it more as a blanket than an undersheet. The straw reeked almost beyond bearing.

Two days passed.

I no longer smelled the stench of the corner I used for a midden. Guards bearing meals were a welcome diversion. As always they left meat and bread, but waited while I drank from the jug.

I babbled incessantly. I told myself stories of Mother's grandfather Varon of the Steppe. Of the fabled Norland raids. Of a stunt horse I'd seen at a fair.

On the third day the guards reappeared, with Uncle Mar. He wrinkled his nose. "You always were a dirty boy."

I strove for dignity. "Why keep me here?"

"For amusement. You have no other worth."

"When you tire of your pastime, return the Vessels you stole from Stryx."

"Good heavens, you still think yourself King?"

I shrugged. No reason to reply.

"Shall I teach you manners, child?"

It stung me. "Could you?"

He punched me in the stomach, threw me to the stone floor, dropped atop me. He unsheathed his dagger. "Yes, nephew, I believe I could." He took my face in his hands and carved a long jagged slice, ear to chin.

My anguished shrieks echoed from the cell walls. I thrashed on the cobbles, blinded with blood. In my frenzy I rolled onto my bed, found my cloak, crushed it against my wound.

"Mother of Nature imps and demons *RUSTIN!!* No, oh, no!" I thrashed like a babe denied a sweet. "Make it stop!" Had he taken my eye? I didn't dare pull loose the cloak.

After a time I sensed I was alone. My throat was raw; how long had I been wailing? Each move brought agony; I forced myself to lie still. I would be no coward. I'd sworn not to let fear—I'd be no coward. A sob caught me, and the stretch of my mouth stirred the coals of pain. I howled. I was coward, and didn't care who knew.

In morn, I thought I'd had a frightful dream, until I tried to move.

When the guards came, I used half my water to soak my cloak so I could peel it from my face. After, I couldn't eat, from the hurt. That night—perhaps by chance—they brought mush in a bowl, and if I took great care I could swallow without greatly moving my mouth.

Days passed, and the pile of ordure in the corner grew. My face was hot to the touch. I was infested with mites, and some of my scratches bled.

Uncle Mar came to visit, with the usual guards.

"Well, boy, have you manners?"

I nodded, afraid to speak.

"Elryc is dead, by the way. From poison. No one knows his assassin."

I made an awful sound.

"I thought you'd like to know. Thank me for telling you."

I couldn't. Not for life itself.

"Hold him." Uncle Mar sauntered to where I stood, pulled out his blade. He cut the rope to my breeches, and they fell. I could do nothing. With one tug he split the seam of my loincloth. He reversed the dagger, prodded my shrinking testicles with the icy hilt.

I squealed, unable to loosen the guards' grip.

"Dear Roddy, in about a month I'm going to castrate you. I'll do it this moment unless you're exceedingly polite."

"Yes, Uncle. I'm sorry, sire. I'll be polite now. Thank you for telling me about Elryc!" Could I bite off my tongue, and end my gibbering surrender?

No. I was coward. "Thank you so much, sir!"

"Much better, Roddy." He ruffled my hair, as if with affection. "Let him go." He strolled out.

As days passed, Uncle's visits became more frequent. He had me agree I was a fool, a dolt, a stinking peasant, a lover of sheep. Once, when I failed to please him, he seized my left hand and, ignoring my screams, bent back two fingers until they snapped. That night, whimpering, I fashioned a makeshift bandage from my shirt, hoping they'd heal straight.

Next visit, Mar had me dance like a drunken vagabond around a campfire. At his urging, I thanked him for the instruction.

My face began to knit.

With the lessening of pain came the beginning of resolve. There was no hook from which to hang myself, but I began to seek to die.

One day, apparently, the stench of my cell was too much for Duke Mar. He sent guards with a barrow, a fresh bundle of straw, and instructions to have me washed. When afterward I was led back to my cell, the pile of filth was gone, and a chipped chamber pot sat in the corner. I was so grateful I almost wept. I sat rubbing the scab on my cheek, appalled at the station to which I'd sunk.

As before, they let me have no water, save what I could consume in their presence. Knowing I could only drink twice a day, I drained the jug, and as always, was beset an hour later with desperate need to piss.

Another day, another visit from Uncle. He asked nothing of me, but played with his dagger, a small smile flitting about his lips as his eyes roved my body. When he left I was drenched with sweat.

Yes, it was time to die.

Mumbling to myself, I measured the cell. Could I throw myself against the wall hard enough to snap my neck? I'd only get one chance.

I took off the belt I'd reknotted. Could I wrap it round my throat tight enough so my frantic efforts couldn't untie it?

In the end, I decided on the chamber pot. Smashed, it would yield jagged pieces. At least one would serve to slice my throat. With an imagined shard I practiced the motion. One firm slash, too quick to allow pain.

The day I'd chosen to be my last, after breakfast and my jug of water, I sat on the straw. "I was King," I told the dank cell. Only for a while, but the dream had been accomplished. "Sorry, Mother. I wasn't very good at it."

She made no answer.

"And I never used the Still." I giggled. "I held myself virgin for naught." I might as well have bedded Tresa. Or even Chela, that wicked day in the clearing.

No, not Chela. She was beneath me. But Tresa, now . . . I recalled our embraces. She was a good woman, and kind. And her breasts were inviting and warm. Despite myself, I grew hard, and didn't stop recalling her until my loincloth hung sticky about my waist. I looked down, ashamed. "Well, Mother, that's a virgin's way." I grimaced. Even Rust's attentions were preferable.

It was time. Resolutely I stood, hefted the chamber pot.

No, by Lord of Nature, it wasn't yet time. If I could play at Tresa, I could play at being King. With my good fingers I shook out my ragged cloak, pinned it about my shoulders. I paced the cell, adopting the stride of a monarch. I set a weave of straw on my head, for a diadem.

All I lacked was our Power.

Once, before I died, I would practice the Rite.

For that I needed the Vessels, but they were stolen. I wanted still-silver. I needed . . .

Was my diadem gold, or straw? It was make-believe, much as Elryc and Pytor and I had built toy kingdoms in happier days. I set my hands in front of me to summon the Still, recalling Mother's tutelage.

It didn't feel right. I needed the bejeweled Chalice. I needed the Ewer.

Well, there was the chamber pot, if I wanted to abase myself. I shrugged. Why not? No one would know, and after a short while even I would cease to care.

I opened the pot, wrinkled my nose at the reek of warm urine, placed my palms over the bowl. As solemnly as if I were in the vault with Mother, I whispered the words of encant.

Lord of Nature, what a fool I made. What if Mar appeared? He'd have great fun, making me reenact my play. "Yes, Uncle. Thank you for watching. I'm a good boy."

Faugh.

I closed my eyes, whispered the remembered words. Close to the pisspot, my hands grew warm.

The cell wavered.

The granite wall seemed to dim. Was it a cave I saw, beyond the stones? Who were those figures watching so intently? I squeezed shut my eyes and whispered over and again the words of encant.

Is this how you felt, Mother? Did this mummery bring you the strength to weld Caledon? Or was Mar speaking true, when he called it a pale deceit?

"Open your eyes!"

Mother, please, let me dream.

"Roddy, for the sake of—come to us!" Her tone was testy.

I peered into dark. "Where am I?"

A man's voice growled, "In a cell at Verein, you twit."

"Father, please!" Mother sounded exasperated.

"That is Josip's spawn? Pah!"

"He's confused."

"He's a dunce."

From the far corner, a deep rumble. "Let him be, Tryon."

Part of me knew of a frightened boy huddled over a bowl of urine, but the image faded. I blinked. "Mother? I can't see you in shadow."

"It's the piss. Use stillsilver. Even pure water, in a pinch. There's better bond."

"Are you alive?"

"Of course not, Roddy; have some sense. Grandfather Varon has no patience for fools."

"Or anyone else," remarked Tryon.

Mother said, "Don't goad Grandfather, we need his advice."

"Like a bride needs a wart." But Tryon's grumble subsided into silence.

"This is . . ." I hesitated. "The Still?"

"Aye, we are." A small waspish voice, from the dark. "Not impressed? You'd prefer a light show, like Raeth of Cumber? Or shall we stir the winds?"

Mother's tone had a bite, as when she was about to send me to Willem. "Enough. He's troubled. It's hard sorting us out at first." To me, "Why didn't you try water? You came so close in Cumber. I called to you. 'Do the unexpected . . .' "

"That *was* you!" I marveled. "I had no Vessels—you never told me any liquid would suffice."

"You could have tried." Her tone was acid.

"Oh, Mother." My voice was near breaking. "Would that I'd listened, paid you more respect. I'm so sorry for the son I've been!"

A shocked silence, and her tone was soothing. "Well, you *have* changed." She cleared her throat. "Don't berate yourself, Roddy."

"I've been a dolt. I quarreled with Rustin, with all my lords in turn. Tantroth fell upon us, and Uncle Mar. I lost—"

"Yes, you have a headstrong nature. If Tantroth attacked, no doubt you've been mired in Eiber's Cleave. That's excuse."

Absently, I rubbed my scar. "That's . . . I never pondered how it worked."

"No, you wouldn't think of it when it was on you. It's Eiber's Power. Tantroth cleaves his enemies with petty quarrels. None can ally effectively against him. Now you've found us, we'll help set it aside."

It was the Cleave, then. My foul words to Rustin, my constant offense to Anavar . . . all the times I belittled Elryc.

No, much of that was my doing. I lifted my head, proud in my humility. "I dug the pit. Tantroth but widened it."

From the rear of the cave, a grunt of approval. "I might learn to like him."

Mother said, "Time you were introduced. Roddy, meet your grandfather, Tryon King of Caledon."

"Grandsir?" Sitting with hands over still bowl, I stood, walked deeper into the cave. "So much I've heard of you." I gave the bow of deep respect, of lesser to better.

"You ofttimes vexed your mother."

"Yes, sire." I hesitated. "I was no more stupid than now. Yet I'd not do it again."

A grunt. "She said you had no manners, but you do. Elena, bring us to nexus, else he'll be dead and among us too soon."

My eyes widened. "When I'm dead, will I—"

Mother hushed me like a toddler. A wave of her hand, and a dull light glowed. They gathered around it: Mother, Tryon, Varon of the Steppe whom I recognized from a portrait, old and dozing. Younger men, a child, a form with great brooding potency and no clear shape, whose name I dared not ask.

Looking about I whispered eagerly, "Is Father here?"

"He never wore the crown."

"He lives not?" My tone was forlorn.

Varon opened one eye. "All men die," he rumbled. "Why be troubled?"

"I hoped . . . to say farewell." In his sleep he'd left me, with no premonition.

"That's why the Rites," said Tryon. He turned to the glowing light. "Be silent, young King."

I did as I was told.

I woke from deep sleep, near a fulsome bowl of urine. Groggily, I replaced the lid, sat and rubbed my eyes, careful of my broken fingers. Our conversation in the cave was an especially clear dream. But I recalled no end, no resolution.

I felt too lethargic to try again. Besides, what would it accomplish? And in any event, my stomach told me that the usual dinner hour was near.

In a while the guards came with meat and drink. They brought a fresh chamber pot, so I took especial care to drink well.

Later in the quiet of the evening, the bars grated again. From the doorway Uncle Mar waited, arms folded.

Hastily I stood.

"Amuse me," he said, setting a torch in the sconce.

I licked my lips. "How, sir?" Would I ever be free of his dread?

He brought in a stool, sat upon it. "Kneel."

Obediently, I dropped before him.

"As I promised, I'll geld you in a week or so. But I want you to enjoy the waiting." His eyes held mine, with no expression. "It was a merry chase you led me through the hills. Without Tantroth I'd not have caught you."

"What did you pay him?" For a moment, I forgot I was no longer a king.

"Lick the toe of my boot."

Abruptly my time had come. I measured the span to his throat.

"No, Roddy!" Mother's voice, sharp in my ear. I startled. "Obey him. *At once!*"

I'd never defied Mother, and couldn't now. Despising myself, I stretched out my tongue, stroked the muck from Uncle's boot.

"There's a good boy," said Margenthar, Duke of Stryx. He patted the grimy curls of my hair, raised me to my knees. "Actually, I paid him naught." He reflected. "I reminded him that he couldn't take Cumber without sitting out the winter, and perhaps not then. He decided you were better in my hands than in your own."

"So he withdrew his troops, leaving you free to charge along the wall, while his own safe-conduct was inviolate." My tone was courteous. "Thank you, sir."

"I brought you a present." He clapped his hands, and the guard at the door advanced, handed him a burnished silver plate. He held it as a mirror to reflect my face.

After a moment I realized the gasp I'd heard was mine.

The scar was far worse than I'd imagined. A clear blue eye stared past the ruins of my face: a hideous jagged line that blotched red from ear to chin. I turned; my right profile was undamaged, providing horrid contrast.

"As foul as your character, isn't it?"

My fists clenched.

To the guard, "Drop his breeches!"

"Yes, Uncle, it's foul. I'm foul. It's disgusting, sir, as I ought to look. Thank you for showing my face." Lord of Nature knew what else I babbled.

Uncle held up a hand. "Leave him." He stood. "You're turning into quite a pleasant young lad." Taking his mirror and stool, he left me cowering on my knees. The door slammed shut.

I paced the cell, prattled gibberish, threw myself on the straw, jumped up again. At last, knowing no other consolation, I turned to Tresa and the frenzy of my loins.

When I was done I took deep shuddering breaths, and sought resolve.

After a time I went to piss.

"I came to say good-bye."

They gathered in the mouth of the cave. I peered, wishing there were a torch, or sun.

"I don't know if I'll be with you after. I haven't been much of a king."

"Roddy—"

"And I won't ever be one, Mother, even if Mar freed me this moment. Could you see me cower? Can you smell the terror-sweat still on me?" My voice caught. "Look at my ruined face." I held up my damaged hand. "And this."

"He hurt you, yes."

"I swore once I wouldn't bow to fear. I was a dunce. I'll lick Uncle's boots, kiss his hand, crawl through manure, he has me terrified so. Any day now he'll—" My voice cracked. "He'll deball me like a meat calf. Only by dying will I be free."

"Now, Elena," Varon's deep rumble.

The light glowed, and they gathered near. A hand tugged at mine, and I found myself within the circle, sniffling. A chant throbbed, low and staccato as a drumbeat.

"Dear Roddy." Her voice was so gentle I wanted to bury myself in her bosom.

The chant boomed.

Time passed.

"Mother, why am I naked?" I cupped my hands to cover myself.

"Because you feel so." Her voice was soothing.

"Tantroth was right; I know not how to be a man."

"Nonsense." I recognized Tryon's gruff tone. "You showed your manhood in battle. Margenthar's torture would unnerve Lord of Nature himself. He's my child, as is Elena, but I'm not proud."

"Grandsir, I have no valor." I wiped my eyes.

"Young fool." I might have sworn his voice held no contempt. "Of course you'll cry and gibber when Mar threatens to unman you. What do you ask of yourself? He has a terror within him, that comes as a blast of icy wind. How could you face it alone?"

"Sir, I—"

"You have us, now."

"Only in my dreams!" I no longer cared if I wept. "The same fantasies that bring me Tresa, and soil my underclothes. Reality is my cell, and the cut of the Duke's knife."

From across the cave, a harsh sound, as if the night were clearing its throat. "Hear them, child." I waited, but the voice said no more.

I whispered, "Who was that?"

"One who lived before names."

Tryon said, "Father, are you awake?" A silence. "Varon?"

A rumble of annoyance. "What, whelp?"

"Show him what he's faced without aid."

A gnarled hand tapped at my skull and split it wide. Images drifted.

Mar's malevolence. The touch of Eiber, with its insistent disunity. Cumber's lust that unsettled us all. The distant, silky terror of the Norlanders. The hate of the uninhabited land. Groenfil's raging wind, Soushire's howling dogs . . . I clutched my ruined face, trying to block out the vision.

It was as if a portcullis crashed down, shielding me from the onslaught. I gaped.

"You have us, now," said Tryon again. It seemed a loincloth was about me, and a jerkin covered my breast. A cape settled about my shoulders. I wore trousers, strong leather boots.

I took a shuddering breath, and stood straight. "You'll be with me?"

Mother said, "All kings face danger, even when no Powers beset them. But we'll shield you from forces that pry at your mind. From the nameless terror, and the follies that follow."

"Are you stronger than they?"

"Often. Unequal, at times. On the whole we balance, so mettle decides."

"It's not that I'm ungrateful—" I hesitated. "Is *that* all there is to the Still? Speech with you in a cave?"

"We'll guide your thoughts. Give you ours. What more would you ask?"

"Can you get me out of the cell?"

Tryon stepped forward. His eyes were red coals. "Can *you*?"

Chapter 42

I AWOKE ON MY STRAW WITHOUT MY FINE CLOTHES. When I stirred, Mother's ephemeral hand flitted across my shoulder.

I yawned. Apparently the Still took something out of one. Absently I scratched my scar, and stretched. I hoped they'd let me wash again soon. The cell's odor and my own were one.

My eye roved about the dismal cell. No iron links hanging from the wall, no bars I could reach. Nothing to seize upon, no projections, except the sconce used for torches. A mere nub of iron, hammered into the joint of the stone wall.

I paced my narrow confines, working hard to nourish hope.

Breakfast came. I sat on the pot, and until it was emptied, I couldn't dream of using it to summon the Still. Agitated, I paced anew.

In midafternoon the door scraped, and two guards made way for Uncle Mar.

I jumped to my feet. "Good day, sir." Best that he see no difference in my outlook. I wasn't quite sure there was one.

He seemed preoccupied. "I may leave you for a few days." Then he smiled. "I'll have Stire take good care." Despite myself, I blanched.

"Look at me, Roddy."

I saw a burly, bearded man with a sullen mien, who studied me, watching my reaction. "Yes, Uncle?"

He slapped me hard, and smiled as I rubbed my cheek. "You have no idea what satisfaction that gives me."

"Thank you, sir!" He was right. It gave him great satisfaction. Abruptly all I felt was contempt. A petty man, full of paltry hate. Is that you, Mother, who makes me see him so? "I wish you wouldn't leave me," I said humbly.

"So do I," he answered, and I knew he'd spoken before thought. But he glanced at the sturdy cell and smiled anew. "Fear not, nephew, we'll have long to play." He stood.

"Uncle?" I stood respectfully. "Could you—if it please you, might you explain?"

"What say you?"

"About Pytor, and why I'm here. Oh, no, sir!" I jumped back, as his eyes narrowed. "I wasn't reproaching you. It's just . . . I don't understand the statecraft. Why did Pytor come to be of more value dead?"

He considered. Then, "No harm in discussing it." That didn't bode well. "As you grew in stature and power, you see, Pytor's worth dwindled. You were close to ending the regency; once you were crowned, he'd be but a puny rival. And Pytor was ailing; he wouldn't eat, and pined for that foul-tempered biddy who raised him. But most important, his presence turned greedy eyes at my lands. Whenever I rode from Verein I risked a lunge from Soushire, or Eiber, or the Warthen, who perhaps saw more value in him than did I. So I simplified the game, as it were."

I stood appalled, a mechanical smile frozen to my lips.

"Likewise, my boy, you diminish in value. Cumber's near worn down; we'll have at him any day. I might even hold off on your death and offer you in trade for their capitulation, letting them find they've ransomed a gelding. Who knows?" He shrugged. "I must be off."

"Thank you for visiting, sir."

When he left I pounded the wall until my fist was raw. Mother, you were supposed to help me stop gibbering. So what if I saw he was contemptible; why didn't it lessen my fear?

Again I paced, running my fingers across the stones. My soul was stuffed with impatience, as Rustin had once stuffed my mouth with grass. I would bear it no longer. All Grandsir and Mother offered was words. A touch of understanding, perhaps, but nonetheless only words. I wouldn't suffer Mar's knife, or Stire's blows. I would die this very day. I pulled at the slabs of the door until my fingers bled.

What if I kicked the door shut just as the guards opened it to bring dinner? I'd catch one man at least, perhaps even crush him. But there were always two, sometimes three, and always well armed.

Besides, I'd be in dark. If only they'd leave a torch in the sconce . . . I fingered the iron, stopped short. Did it move to my touch?

No more than a trifle, if that.

I worked the sconce back and forth.

Dinner came, and the guards went. In the dark, I worked endlessly at the sconce.

By early morn I was out of my straw, making sure the holder was replaced properly in its hole. Would they notice? Was it wedged tight enough to hold a torch?

I waited feverishly until the guards departed, and pulled my toy from its aperture. A rounded nub of iron, with a hole in the center in which to set a brand. My only implement, and what use was it? It might split a guard's skull, if I smashed him hard enough. If I got close. If he didn't first run me through.

Disgusted, I hurled it at the stone wall. A clang, as it fell. I stared, darted across the floor, snatched it up, hurled it again. Yes. Definitely a spark.

I fumbled at my straw. Was it too damp?

The afternoon passed with no visit from Mar. I nibbled at my dinner while the guards watched, knowing not what I ate, worried only that the sconce and its torch would tumble from the wall while they waited.

When night deepened I rapped the sconce repeatedly against the base of the wall, near the bits of dry straw I'd so carefully shredded. I had but one good hand, and the task was maddening.

The sconce cast off sparks one strike out of three, and invariably they flew wild.

Surely someone would hear my drumming.

Time after time I struck the stone; on occasion my spark flew home. Desperately I frayed more straw.

A glower, that died. After a sweaty eon, another. With fingers that trembled I fed straw to the flicker.

In nothing but loincloth and boots, I screamed my terror, over and over in the night. No one came. My shrieks grew louder, more desperate. I crouched by the far wall, head touching the floor.

At last, a muffled curse amid the crackle of my blazing pallet and clothes. The door swung open. "What's this?"

"I'm burning!" Smoke billowed. Howling, I scrambled to my knees.

The guard said, "Where are—"

I flung the chamber pot with all my might. It split the guard's face and shattered. He dropped like a stone. I seized his torch, darted to the door. The second guard drew sword and lunged. His blade came within a hair of skewering me. I thrust the torch in his face. His head snapped back as his sword whirled to chop off my arm. Dropping the torch, I lurched at his backswing. I caught his forearm, held clear the sword, slammed him into the corridor wall. The sword fell.

We grunted in sweaty struggle. I kneed him, bruised myself on his mail. He clawed my eyes. Suddenly he clutched me in a hug. His fists knotted behind me. My feet left the floor. My eyes bulged with the effort to draw breath. Mother, where's your demon-cursed Still when I need it? The guard's grizzled face was near. The world swam. I lunged, sank my teeth into his neck.

Instantly he let go, struck at my face. I wrapped my arms round him and gnawed.

A cry of horror. We were on the floor, rolling and thrashing. Weaponless, I pummeled him. I dared not take breath.

After a time all was still. I lay beneath an inert form, choking on blood. Footsteps pounded.

I heaved free, sucked in barrels of air. Somehow, I tottered to my feet, and seized the nearest torch. I whirled. The footsteps skidded to a halt.

A moan of terror. Guards fell over themselves in their retreat. "It's a demon!" Backing away, they made signs of propitiation.

Demons of the night! My heart seized. I lunged toward the stairs, and escape. The guards broke and fled. I risked a glance back, and saw no demon.

Leaning against the wall was the mirror Uncle Mar used to taunt me. I thrust it aside, not before catching a glimpse. I was bleeding half to death, but felt no pain. I wiped my mouth. My arm came away with blood.

I stumbled over the guard I'd fought. I turned him over, searching for a weapon. My back prickled. Some night beast had torn out his throat.

I backed away, unable to make a sound. *What monster had done thus?*

Again I wiped my mouth. I was quiet a moment, then doubled over to spew my dinner.

I was the demon.

I snatched up a sword, slippery with blood. Verein's guard would soon rally.

At the corridor's end, a long winding stairs. I took two steps upward, stopped short as shadows flickered. Another step and I could see them: a handful of guards at the landing, all with drawn swords.

Well, I'd chosen to die. I raised my sword high over my head, filled my lungs. With a bloodcurdling screech I charged the torchlight. Men clawed past each other to safety.

When I galloped to the top of the stairs the guards were gone. I raced on. From the width of the corridor, I guessed I must be at ground level.

A hue and cry echoed. Soon or late they'd rally, and take me down.

In younger days I'd visited Verein, but in my present state I had not the slightest idea where in the castle I was. But they'd expect me to head for the outdoors. Instead, I wheeled round the corner and charged up the second stairs.

I met men-at-arms rushing down from the sleeping floor, buckling on their gear. I slashed at one, tripped another and threw him to the ground.

I thudded down unfamiliar halls, flinging open doors. I needed a window, or a back stairs. I dared not risk going higher, to be trapped in the garrets of the keep.

I caught glimpse of a familiar face: Baron Stire, peering from a doorway. My teeth bared. Sword raised, I charged. He slammed shut the door. I pounded at the stout wood until I came to my senses. No time. Move.

I lunged past three doors, skidded past an open stairs. I plunged down, found myself in the kitchens. At this hour, no one toiled at the ovens.

I tore past guttering candles, found a likely door, heaved it open. The welcome breath of cold air. I rushed into the night, slammed into a barrel, rolled into thorny bushes.

My sword was gone. I slapped the ground, desperate to find it. A dull pain. I sucked a torn thumb, gripped the sword as best I could. Clutching a bleeding shin, I hobbled into the dark.

It was two hours since my escape.

The castle was in an uproar. Dogs howled. Guards pounded the battlements, sweating grooms led horses, soldiers raced to their posts. Torches flared.

Double watches manned the gates. Cries of alarm and shouted orders made clear I was the goal of their search.

I lay low, perched on the slate roof of the smokehouse. My thumb wasn't badly cut, but it smarted to distraction. I shivered. In my near month of captivity, winter had begun to settle on the land. It was too cold to lurk about in a torn loincloth.

I needed clothes. Warmth. And most urgent, a wash, or they wouldn't need the dogs to track my bouquet. I was sweat-soaked, blood-covered, and grimy from my ordeal in the cell.

The smokehouse, behind the kitchen, was far from the walls of the keep. I stole down from my aerie, padded to the well, hauled up a bucket, scrubbed my face. There was nothing to wash with. Cursing, I stripped off my loincloth, rinsed and wrung it, used it to scrub off the worst of my filth.

If I'd thought I was cold before, I'd been mistaken. My teeth chattered. I poured out the bucket.

"Who goes?"

"Just me." I turned, bucket in hand, and clubbed my interlocutor in the temple. He went down, moaned once, and was still.

I squinted in the pale moonlight. A groom, perhaps, or a houseman. No matter. I stripped off his clothes, donned them, tied and adjusted until I looked passable.

A sword gave the lie to my new garb, but I didn't dare go without. Nonchalantly, blade pressed to my side, I strolled to the stable, waited in the shadows until it was unwatched, climbed into a loft, and lay to rest.

Come morning, my bones were chilled and I hadn't slept a wink. I was girding myself for a foray to the kitchen when distant trumpets sounded the alert. The doors burst open, and soon the stable was cleared of mounts. I waited a few moments and jumped down to the floor.

Halfway to the door, the stall ahead opened, and a groom backed out with a barrow. I tensed, ready to strike.

He turned. We gaped.

"You!"

"Kerwyn?" Master Griswold's man, from our stables at Stryx.

He backed away, mouth open to scream. I cried, "Wait!" Dropping my sword, I wrestled him down, put my hand across his mouth.

He bit down on my wounded thumb, and I nearly passed out.

"Idiot!" I wrenched my hand free, shook him 'til he rattled. "Are you *trying* to be killed?"

Outside, trumpets sounded anew.

"Let me go! They turned the castle upside down searching. They say you transmuted to a demon, that you ate a guard's head. If I don't give the cry . . ."

"If I don't run you through . . ." Again I shook him. "What are you doing here?"

"Griswold sent me, when Duke Mar took most of the horses. Said he'd have no need of me. Prince, your face . . ."

"A gift from your new lord. Why the alarum? Are they sending horse to track me?" Cautiously I eased off him, gave him a hand to stand.

His eyes widened. "You don't know? Tantroth's racing home to Eiber. The siege of Cumber is lifted. Our men retreat to Verein, and Tursel harries their heels."

"We won!" I loosened my grip on his jerkin. "It's over." I could scarce contain my elation.

"No, my lord. It's the Norlanders."

Ice chilled my veins.

"They overran Eiber, sire. They descend in force on Caledon. Stire is off to garrison Llewelyn's keep, and Duke Mar goes to reinforce Stryx."

I sank onto a roll of hay. The Norlanders? Mother, look what calamity our disunity called down on us. No fools they; with Tantroth looting Caledon, the road through Eiber was open. Tantroth might have held them at the passes, if he'd had his full force to throw into the battle. But his army had been chasing me. Now he'd be hunted in his own land.

As I was in mine.

I raised my head. "Where do they strike?"

Casually, Kerwyn edged toward the door. "They say Earl Cumber leads his men to the northern reaches. Norland sail's seen south of Stryx, well clear of the Eiberian fleet harbored under the castle."

"South?" Then there was time yet to defend Stryx. I'd have to get word to Tursel, send for Groenfil and Soushire . . .

Kerwyn brought me to earth. "You'll have to hide, sire. Any guardsman will gut you on sight. Are you"—he hesitated—"really a demon?"

I sighed. "No, Kerwyn. Just a tired youngsire with a blade-split face. Don't fear me. Help me of your own will, if you would. I need food, and quiet."

He approached me with caution. "Truly? You're just Prince Roddy?"

"King, now. But, yes."

His relief was pathetic. "Aye, sire. I'll see what Cook has. Stay hidden."

After a meal—the first of my liberty—I thanked him fervently and bid him go about his business. But Kerwyn was no mummer, bringing oft-told tales to the castles. Soon or later, he'd betray me by word or look.

When he was gone I bundled my sword in a blanket, and trudged across the courtyard, eyes low. Somehow, I made it to the rampart unchallenged.

I curled up between two rain barrels stored behind an arrowport. From time to time I glanced about, and risked a sally from my rude base.

The bulk of Margenthar's troop was gone. The castle gates were barred. Peasants and soldiers passed through the small doors set in the gate, but I didn't dare present myself to the guards. My scar made me unmistakable.

No, I'd have to climb the wall. For that, I needed a rope, and night.

I crept about the least-guarded ramparts. In a store tower I found rope, and stuffed a coil under my clothes. When I thought it safe, I would tie it round the stone tooth of an arrowport, and lower myself to the ground. Somehow, I'd acquire a horse, no matter whom I had to kill in the doing.

Now that Mar was gone, the excitement of the castle subsided into routine. Haymen brought barrows of fodder, washerwomen took great baskets of clothes to the stream, boys played loudly while their elders cursed the bother. The rampart guard relaxed. On the opposite wall, a few played at dice, under the indulgent eye of a sergeant.

I dallied on the rampart. After a time I noticed a depression in the stone of the rampart deck. With cupped hands I spooned water from the rain barrel, until it filled the hollow. I waited patiently until it was Still.

I sat, back against the wall, staring at the tiny pool between my legs. Slowly I lowered my palms. I whispered words now familiar. The bright cold sun beat on my head. I closed my eyes, said again the encant.

"Now, lad, how say you?"

I opened my eyes. The cave was yet hazy, though much brighter than before. I could see my progenitors more clearly. "Grandsir." I bowed.

"Your mother is adrift. She'll be with us presently." Tryon studied me. "You've composed yourself."

I blushed. "I'm not squalling with panic, you mean."

"I say what I intend, living one."

"I'm sorry, Grandsir." I bowed. "I meant no offense." Now I sounded the terrified boy in Mar's cell.

He grunted. "Father Varon, would you speak with the young King?"

A rumble. "No."

I stammered. "Perhaps I shouldn't have come. I've escaped. I'm on the ramparts of Verein."

"What need have you?"

"Wisdom. Safety. A horse."

He chuckled. "In that order? Wake yourself, Varon. He's amusing, and now he's using water so we can see."

Other spirits drifted near. I said timidly, "You're all my ancestors?"

The waspish one who'd spoken at my cell said peevishly, "Think you I sired such a malformed outcast?"

"But I—Mother said . . ."

Tryon waved the creature silent. "They're kings of the land, as you are. Varon is the first of your ancestors. He overthrew the previous clan."

"Perfidy it was, and treason!"

"Give it rest, Cayil." Tryon rolled his eyes. "Some folk never abide their overthrow."

"Nor will my line, 'til time ends and—"

"Your line's mostly extinguished."

"That's true," Cayil admitted, glumly. "But I can bedevil your crimes through eternity."

"Not my crimes, Varon's. I wasn't born when—"

"Silence, whelp!" Varon's rumble quivered the floor. "I did no ill deeds."

Cayil's voice rose an octave. "My tribe did you strike, my house crumble, my—"

"Deserved!"

I covered my ears, but Varon spoke no more.

Tentatively, I said, "Grandsir, what is my station? Am I still King, as to the Still?"

"You're here." It seemed an answer.

"About the True . . . must I still keep it? Must I never deceive?"

He frowned. "Elena should have explained all that."

I flushed. "I didn't listen well."

"Deceive not your friends. Enemies . . ." He pondered. "If they demand you speak True, you must, else we'll lose you."

"It's a great strain."

A glint of a smile. "So I found it."

"Grandsir, what ought I do?"

Tryon frowned, and eased himself to sit, legs crossed, on the dirt floor. "Tell us your tale, boy. We've had but glimpses, when you've sat bemused."

Slowly at first, I spoke of what had befallen Caledon. Sometime during my recital, I felt Mother's arm drape gently across my shoulder. When I stumbled, she stroked my nape in reassurance, recalling dim memories of childhood.

". . . so the Norlanders are upon us," I said. "I'm free of the cell, but have no crown, no horse, no army. No escape."

Mother said, "Forget the coronet. The crown isn't a hat, it's acknowledgment of your lords that you're rightful heir."

"But the symbol is taken for—"

"Don't lecture me!" Her tone was sharp. "Was I not Queen?"

"Yes, ma'am." I bowed, as I would in life.

"Have you raised your standard?"

"Not formally. I was taken in Cumber."

"Do so."

"Yes, madam. But who'll answer the call? Since my crowning I've been boxed in Cumber Castle, done nothing except quarrel with my lords—look at me." I rubbed my scar. "I'm grotesque! Who would follow such a king?"

"Men see past a face. If it troubles you so, buy a Return from the Warthen, and undo the moment!"

"Could I?"

"Of course. Though the cost—worry later about a petty scar."

Tryon said gently, "He's new at this, Elena."

" 'Twas you who called him lame of brain, a nit—"

Tryon colored. "When he was acting the role. But still he's King." Tryon turned to me. "Raise your standard, yes. No matter your previous state. With the Norlanders upon us, the bones are recast. New alliances will follow. Even Mar will seek treaty, either with you or the Norland."

"You suggest I ally with him, after his perfidy?"

"He's greedy, but no fool. He'll know his best chance is to throw in with one of you."

"I can't, Grandsir. Forgive me."

Mother said, "Then gather Pytor and Elryc to safety, lest they be made pawns."

"Pytor's dead. And Elryc."

Mother raised her head, let out a shrill cry that made my bones throb. She drew fresh breath and keened.

Tryon watched without moving. In the dark corner, something stirred. A great form arose, drifted across the cave. Even in the heightened light, I couldn't make out more than a hint of features. It rumbled, "Death comes to men."

Mother's lips moved. "My boys . . ."

I felt rather than heard the response. "Comfort her, child."

I took Mother in my arms. She beat against my shoulder. She scratched. I stood stolidly. After a time, her mourning eased.

I prompted Mother to sit, and crouched alongside. "I'm sorry. I thought you knew."

"Who killed them?"

"Your brother, madam."

Elena closed her eyes.

Tryon said, as if in apology. "At times when you're not with us we sense your fears. But we haven't your knowledge."

I looked past him. "Varon? Sir? Would it be right—"

An angry blast knocked me flat. *"Who is he that dares?"*

Mother said quickly, "He didn't know." To me, "Don't speak directly to Grandfather. Let him attend you."

I sat cautiously. "Why?"

"He's gone far." It seemed an explanation.

Tryon said, "Save Caledon, while you've time. Look for new allies against the Norland."

"Who?"

"Tantroth of Eiber. The Warthen. Margenthar. Caledon's a small boat in a stormy sea. Seek shelter."

"But not with Mar." I appealed to Mother. "He killed my brothers. He'd have castrated me."

Mother said, "Tryon's right." She shook her head at my disbelief. "We can't hate, Roddy. We're practical. Not as in life."

"Have you no emotions?"

"I grieve." Her eyes teared. "Pytor was so small. Hester loved him so." She met my gaze. "But I'm in the cold ground. It's Caledon that counts. Ally with Mar."

"No, I won't have it!" With tremendous effort, I knotted my fists, tore my hands from the pool of rainwater. "I defy you!"

My palms were warm; I rubbed them in a gentle soothing motion, and stretched against the parapet wall.

I blinked. Much of the day had passed. Night was upon us.

Would they speak to me again, after my insolence?

I looked about, in moonlight and shadows. Interesting, that Mar valued Stryx more than his own domain. There were guards aplenty, but not enough to withstand determined assault. But the army he'd left at Cumber would swell his ranks at Verein, when they made their way home. Across the field four riders plodded. I wondered if they were the forerunners of his Cumber troop.

They rode for the wall, but not to a gate. In fact unless they veered, they'd be far from any portal.

Abruptly, as if reaching a decision, they spurred, cantered to the dark rampart. Their leader reined in, a long stone's throw from where I sat. He unwound a rope from his saddle, attached a hook, swung it upward until it caught in an arrowport. His companions stood back, scanning all quarters. I ducked low. I couldn't afford to be seen, no matter who breached the wall.

The agile young soldier swarmed up the rope. I risked another glance.

I stiffened.

Heedless of discovery I raced along the rampart, reached the climber just as his comrades hissed a warning. As I loomed above he snatched out his short sword.

"Take my hand, Rust." I reached to gather him over the wall.

A sound came from him, that was no word. He almost fell from the rope. I clung to him until he gained his balance. He swarmed over the parapet. "You're free!" His hand darted to my injured face. "Lord, no . . ."

Below, Genard held Rustin's mare. Alongside, Anavar sat his steed proudly, sword in hand. Captain Tursel beckoned us down.

On the far wall, a cry. A guardsman shouted orders. Horns blew. "We're seen!" I climbed the parapet, swarmed down the rope. Rust kicked my head in his eagerness to follow. Burning my palms, I slid to the ground. I clawed at the waiting horse's pommel.

"No, m'lord! I'm lightest!" Genard tore the reins from my fingers. "Ride here." He let loose his stirrups, squirmed to make room in his saddle. I climbed onto the black stallion. Genard wrapped his arms about me so tight I thought I couldn't breathe.

Rustin leaped atop his mare. A spear whizzed inches from my head. We dug in our heels, shot across the field. On the battlements, trumpets blared in frenzy.

We tore toward the distant hedgerow. I prayed there be no moles in the field; if my horse stumbled, I'd break my neck.

Squeezing my ribs, Genard bounced in the saddle. We neared the sanctuary of the trees. I craned over my shoulder, saw nothing but Genard. He yelled, "You ride, I'll look." Then, "Horsemen pouring out the gate, m'lord. A dozen. No, a score. They're wheeling off the road. They— Look where you're going!"

I swerved, barely avoiding a low branch that would have knocked us senseless. I waved to Rust. "Where's a road?"

"Right this—whoops!" He reined in, hard. The thicket sloped down to a wide trail, on which a hundred horse and riders trod their way home to the castle. Desperately, he hauled on his reins, forcing his horse to retreat or throw him. "This way!"

We plunged into the copse, brambles tearing at our legs. From the west came the cries of our pursuers.

After a time, we halted, knowing we had to rest our steeds or lose them. Genard gibbered in my ear. "We'll dodge them, have no worry. Can you see from that eye? Your face is torn like a—" I jabbed him with my elbow. "You were so pretty, before. Why is your hand crooked? Can you hold reins with—"

I hissed, "Get this toad away from me."

"Hush, the both of you!" Rust's tone brooked no argument.

Clouds passed across the moon. The weary horsemen trod on, those who didn't join our pursuers. We stole back and forth amid brambles and bush, never able to lunge across the road. We spoke in whispers, walked more often than rode.

At last a dull fury wrapped me like a cloak. I was no boar to be trapped by beaters. I peered down the slope. My voice was a hoarse whisper. "At the first chance, cross the road at that ravine. I'll join you on the far side."

Rust only shook his head. Anavar said, "Are you daft?"

I snarled, "Obey the King!" I hoisted Genard from my saddle, held him while his feet found the ground. "Ride with another." I wheeled my mount.

Rust cried, "Roddy, where go you?"

"Where you may not." I spurred my stallion toward the flickering lights of Verein.

In the pale moonlight I saw parties of seekers combing the fields. Many bore torches. Somehow, they beheld me not. My horse was black, and my raiment dark.

I trotted to the gate, straight as a bee to the hive. Fear roiled my mind, and a rage so fierce I'd never felt it prior.

Outside the gate, pikemen stood alert. Horsemen clattered in and out. I stood in the saddle, reached past the nearest sentry, pried a torch from the wall. The man gaped. I spat at his feet. He recoiled.

I turned, rode twenty paces, turned again to face Verein.

I took breath, and screamed.

My mount started, and I soothed him with my legs. I held my shout 'til I was bereft of air, and took new breath. Again I shrieked, a long wordless sound of nightmare.

Men appeared on the wall, jostling to see what phantom beset them.

Slowly, I rose in the saddle. I held the torch near my face. *"Look upon me, and rue your treason!"*

From the castle, utter silence. Behind me a rider spurred toward me. I spat, *"Come nigh at thy peril!"* He stopped short, as if he'd struck a wall.

An arrow thunked at my feet. I sat motionless. If this was my time, I would die. But I'd be hunted no more.

"King am I, of all Caledon." My voice echoed from cold stone. *"I ride to Cumber to raise my standard. You who would live, join me on the third day hence. Else guard your throat, for my bite is sharp!"*

Another arrow plucked my shirt.

I made a sign of warding. *"Think ye a barb can harm me? Shoot, and wither, and die!"*

Somewhere, a horse whinnied. I screamed again, until my throat was raw. From the wall a score of torches crackled and smoked, a hundred faces watched unmoving. Someone hissed an order. Arrows whipped past. First a few, then swarms.

"King Rodrigo am I. AND I WILL HAVE CALEDON!"

I wheeled, and galloped into the night.

Chapter 43

I PLUNGED ACROSS THE ROAD. BEHIND ME FOEMEN GAVE hesitant chase. When I stopped, they stopped. When I wheeled my mount, they scattered.

My horse trod on, at a pace he chose. I passed a grove.

A soft whistle. "Here, Roddy."

I tugged the reins, guided my mount. "Rust. Anavar." I let fall the reins. "We'll be all right now, if we ride the night. But one of you, pull the shaft from my leg."

Rustin spewed a string of foul oaths. His blade glinted, and ripped the cloth of my leggings. "You've bled."

"Not much."

"This will hurt."

"Hurt is an old friend."

He braced me, braced himself, pulled the arrow clear of my thigh.

In the distance, as if from a far mountain, I felt pain. I sat quiet, while he bound me with strips of his jerkin. "Can you ride?"

"If I sit still. Take my reins."

Weary hours passed, while I thought of Mother, and Grandsir, and Caledon.

We stopped to drink.

My leg was sore and stiff, but I could walk if need be. In the dawn's growing light, I took Rustin's arm and hobbled from our camp.

"Easy, my prince. Rest while you—"

Slowly, favoring my injured thigh, I sank to my knees. "Lord

Rustin, son of Llewelyn, Householder of Stryx, most humbly I beg thy pardon." I lowered my gaze, allowed my forehead to brush his fingers. He snatched them away as if burnt.

"I have wronged thee greatly." I swallowed, fearing his response.

"Roddy . . ."

"How oft have you called me a fool?" My voice cracked. "I know now what I am."

He bent, and stroked my face. "What is that, my love?"

"A boy who is near a man, and frightened. One who needs your guidance as before. Take me back, Rustin, if only you can forgive the filth that spewed from my mouth."

"It was truth."

I cast about for a stick, found none. "Cut a branch and beat me, I beg you."

Despite himself he smiled. "Why, such humility."

I cried, "Help me forgive myself!"

He dropped to his knees, brushed my face with soft fingers. "What have they done to you?"

I shuddered. "Never ask." I showed him my crooked hand. "This too, and worse within. I thought I was brave, but found I am not. I gibbered and begged, and did whatever Mar asked."

"Under threat of death?"

"No. Worse."

Anguished, he cried, "I came when I could!"

"Of course."

"We were besieged! Even a gnat couldn't—"

"I know, Rust."

"Tantroth decamped. Tursel led us against Mar's brigade. The instant the path was clear I took Anavar and—"

"Think thou I chide thy absence?"

"I left you, over petty words. My fault you went to Tantroth and were taken. My fault the ruin of your face—but it's a small scar, and time will heal—I didn't mean—"

I pressed his lips shut. "It's frightful to look upon, but I care not. As long as you don't blench." And so long as Tresa will have me, added a small voice within. But that was for later. Now, I must wield my Still. "Could you care for me without beauty?"

He kissed my scar.

Yet must I speak True. "I burn for Tresa. But I can't have her. Must I soil my bed alone?"

He drew sharp breath. "You'd yet have me . . . ?"

"As friend. And mentor. And more, as pleases you. Yet I will go to marriage."

He bowed his head. For a long time he was silent. Then, "Until that day."

We rode to Cumber, and arrived late in the night. Uncle Raeth, wan and peaked, was home from the hills he fought to hold against the Norlanders. He came forth to hold my horse as I tried to dismount. Anavar thrust his shoulder near, and bore my weight.

Uncle gazed at my cheek. "Oh, Roddy." His eyes teared.

"Love me, Uncle." I fell into his arms. Beside us, a torch guttered and went out.

"There, there." Raeth patted my shoulder blades. "Quick, lads, call Tresa for the healing." He hugged me tight. "You live, that's what counts." He drew back, brushed my hair from my eyes. With a smile, he glanced at the torch. "Let go, or we'll be groping in the dark."

With care, we walked to the keep. Within the doors I sank to a bench. "A long night, Rust? I'll sleep awhile, then—"

Tresa rushed down the stairs. "Are you—*oh!*" Her eyes widened in horror. She made a small sound, covered her mouth, rushed from the hall.

I groped for Rust's hand. "You'll have me long, it seems." I'd meant to sound merry, but something caught my voice. "Please, Rust. Help me to a bed."

Cumber was lost for words. "Roddy, she didn't mean . . . it isn't . . ."

"Of course." I sought to wave reassurance, as Rust helped me stand. "The nearest bed, or you'll need carry me."

From the doorway, a small voice. "Roddy?"

I spun, and my leg collapsed. Only Rust saved me from falling on my face. "Oh," I said, and opened my arms. "Oh."

Elryc ran into my embrace.

I said, "You were dead. They told me . . . I never dreamed . . ."

He hugged me as hard as I could bear. "I don't feel dead."

Was it simply for the pleasure of my pain that Mar told me of

Elryc's death? Had he perhaps thought it true? I knew not, but the joy he took in my grief was a sharp memory. I cursed Margenthar with every oath I'd ever heard. When at last I ran down, Elryc pulled away, looked at my cheek and made a face. "You look awful."

I giggled. "You're surely no ghost. Mother will be so pleased." My heart was too full to say more. Together, they lifted me to a bed.

Morn found me much improved, though my thigh and leg were so stiff I could scarce walk. Our room was far lower in the donjon than the aerie I'd occupied before, but it gave view of the devastation Tantroth had wreaked on Cumber Town. The keep had defied him, so he'd revenged himself against commoners. A foul barbarism, and thank Lord of Nature not customary, else whole realms would be devastated, merely because their nobles went to war.

Over breakfast I told Uncle Raeth, "The remission of taxes you once pleaded . . . I grant it, for the restoration of your lands." A necessary mercy; without my aid Earl Cumber would be hard-pressed. He thanked me profusely.

When he left to consult with his guardsmen I asked Anavar, "How is it Tursel rode to Verein with you?"

The boy grinned. "He said his earl would understand, or he wouldn't."

"That covers the possibilities." I pondered the fealty that led them to my rescue. Once, I'd have believed I deserved it. Now I knew better. Still, I was King, and had duty. "Rust, we'll need a spear, and a banner with Caledon's colors."

"When, my prince?"

"This afternoon, by fifth hour."

"I'll have it."

Anavar hesitated. "Pardon, Lord Rustin, but why do you not call him King?"

Rust said simply, "Rodrigo will ever be my prince."

Anavar looked between us. When he spoke to me his voice was grave. "My lord, I've had long to reflect, under siege."

"And?"

"Tantroth betrayed you. Safe passage means safe passage, and no other."

I shrugged. "Perhaps I'd have done the same."

"No. I know you, now." He bowed his head. "His act shames me. I renounce fealty to Eiber, so long as Tantroth holds that land. I am yours without reservation."

"Well, now." My eyes were too bright, my tone too gay. "Let us rejoice in Caledon's fortune." I struggled to my feet. "At the fifth hour, have the gates thrown open. Let the trumpets sound the call." I hobbled to the door. "I will be alone."

Rust found me in the garden, an hour later, weeping. I could not say why.

Toward end of day I planted my standard and said brave words about the deliverance of Caledon. Some who heard cheered. Of more matter, others pledged allegiance. A few days later, we made ready to depart. I took as many of Cumber's troops as I dared; most were needed in the north.

At the moment of riding Raeth's blue eyes found mine.

Disheartened, I asked, "Uncle, will we meet again?"

He looked north to the dark windswept hills. "Tantroth was a hazard," he said, "the Norlanders a cataclysm. But, Roddy, I won't let them have Cumber. Not while I live." He hesitated. "Many lands will see new lords ere they're quelled. Perhaps, in Nature's good time, we shall meet."

"Fare thee well, sir."

"And thou, my King."

Uncle Raeth stood watching until our long column plodded from sight.

We made our way to Groenfil, where I repeated my little play. I knew the Earl would join me; Mar had little to offer him, and my ranks had swelled with deserters from Verein. If rumors were afoot that I treated with demons, I paid no heed.

After receiving the Earl of Groenfil, we rode to Soushire. The Lady Larissa rode out on a white palfrey. I proclaimed my cause and set my standard in the earth. We bickered on how many defenders she'd leave behind, and, at length, turned west toward Stryx.

It was then that we had envoy from Tantroth, Norduke of Eiber. He asked my indulgence, and a parley. I took counsel of Rust, Elryc, and my ancestors, and only when I had their agreement did I give consent.

Tantroth rode alone into my camp under truce, to beg alliance. Now that he had no home, he would reaffirm the vassalage he'd mocked. I smiled at the irony, but only to myself.

I thought long, and agreed. I made him swear mighty oaths of fealty, that he would doubtless break when it suited him. In the meanwhile, he brought six thousand men to my standard.

So it was, that scarce twenty days after I'd cowered in Mar's cell, I sat on Ebon, my thigh still aching, at the head of a respectable column. Bright banners fluttered in the breeze. Behind us the horse troops waited patiently, baking and freezing in the winter sun. Farther back, infantry stood at march ready, ten abreast. Behind them, lost from view, were our wagons stuffed with the produce of Cumber, of Groenfil, of Soushire, surrounded by more horse, and a corps of infantry.

Only from the bastion of Stryx could the Norland be defeated. First I must drive the coastal invaders into the sea. Then I must turn to the usurper Mar, who sat in Mother's seat.

Night after night, when I woke in abject terror, thinking myself still in my cell, and clung to Rustin, weeping, I'd formed the resolve that guided me. I would wrest my castle from Duke Margenthar, or die in the attempt. I would not turn back, and I would not be taken.

Tresa was lost to me. At Cumber, she'd come, day after day, to beg pardon, but I would not heed. I couldn't bear pity, especially from her. Perhaps someday I'd know a woman. I still writhed in my virginity, and knew the shame of sideways glances, jests I could not be allowed to hear. I would bear it as long as I must.

I looked to my left: to the Baron Anavar, to Elryc, with his faithful Genard a row behind, to my lord Earl Groenfil at the last of the row. To my right sat Rustin of the keep, then fat Lady Soushire, and Tursel of Cumber. Just behind, with his three captains, Tantroth, late of Eiber.

I gave signal, and we rode at the walk, row by row, down the long winding road to Stryx.

About the Author

DAVID FEINTUCH is the author of the Seafort Saga beginning with *Midshipman's Hope*, for which he won science fiction's John W. Campbell Award as best new writer for 1996.

Before becoming a full-time writer, he worked as an antique dealer, photographer, real estate investor, and attorney.

A single custodial parent, Feintuch lives in a small Michigan town, "Where for better or worse, none of us are anonymous." His home is a stately Victorian mansion furnished entirely in antiques except for his writing room, which has every electronic toy he can find.

An inveterate traveler, he has had a lifelong interest in naval history, sociology, politics, and medieval European history.